Also by
New York Times bestselling author
Rachel Vincent

From MIRA Books

The Shifters
STRAY
ROGUE
PRIDE
PREY
SHIFT
ALPHA

Unbound
BLOOD BOUND

From Harlequin TEEN

Soul Screamers
Digital novellas
"My Soul to Lose"
"Reaper"
"Never to Sleep"

MY SOUL TO TAKE
MY SOUL TO SAVE
MY SOUL TO KEEP
MY SOUL TO STEAL
IF I DIE

Look for Rachel Vincent's next MIRA Books title,
OATH BOUND

RACHEL VINCENT

SHADOW BOUND

MIRA®

MIRA®

Recycling programs for this product may not exist in your area.

ISBN-13: 978-0-7783-1343-4

SHADOW BOUND

For questions and comments about the quality of this book please contact us at Customer_eCare@Harlequin.ca.

www.Harlequin.com

Printed in U.S.A.

This one is dedicated to my editor,
Mary-Theresa Hussey, who seems to see
what I envision for a story even before I'm able to
make that clear in the manuscript. This book was
tough. *Shadow Bound* is the most difficult book
I've ever written and there were days when living in
Kori's head put me in a very scary place. My editor
reminded me that shadows cannot exist without the
sun. Kori needed balance. She needed Ian.
And Mary-Theresa helped me find the man
Ian needed to be, both for Kori and for their story.

I learned a lot with this book. Thank you.

One

Kori

If you live in the dark long enough, you start to forget what light looks like. What it feels like. You may remember it in an academic sense. Illumination. A possible source of heat. But after a while those abstract memories are all you have left, and they're worth less than the memory of water to a man dying of thirst.

I didn't know how long I'd been in the dark. Long enough for most of the pain to fade into dull aches, though the latest batch of bruises would still have been visible, if anything had been visible. Long enough that I couldn't remember what shade of gray the walls were. Long enough that when the light came on without warning, it blinded me, even through my closed eyelids.

I'd lost all sense of time. I didn't know when I'd last showered, or eaten, or needed the toilet in the corner of my cell. I didn't know when I'd last heard a human voice, but I remembered the last voice I'd heard, and I knew what the sudden light meant.

Light meant a visitor.

And visitors meant pain.

The door creaked open, and my pulse leaped painfully—fear like a bolt of lightning straight to my heart. I clung to that one erratic heartbeat, riding the flow of adrenaline because I hadn't felt anything but the ache of my own wounds in days.

If not for the pain, I couldn't have sworn I was still alive.

"Kori Daniels, rise and shine." Milligan was on duty, which meant it was daytime—outside, anyway. In the basement, it was always night. There were no exterior windows, and no light until someone flipped a switch.

The dark and I used to be friends. No, lovers. When I was alone, I walked around naked just to feel it on my skin, cool and calm, and more intimate than any hand that had ever touched me. The dark was alive, and it was seductive. We used to slide in and out of one another, the shadows and I, always touching, caressing. Sometimes I couldn't tell where the dark ended and I began, and at some point I'd decided that division didn't really exist. I was the dark, and the dark was me.

But the darkness in the basement was different. It was false. Broken. Weakened by infrared lights I couldn't see, but I could feel blazing down on me. Caging me. Draining me. The shadows were dead, and touching them was like touching the stiff limbs of a lover's corpse.

"Kori," Milligan said again, and I struggled to focus on him. On my own name.

The guard shift change had become the ticking of my mental clock—the only method I had of measuring time. But my clock skipped beats. Hell, sometimes it skipped entire days. If there was a pattern to the granting of meals, and showers, and company, I hadn't figured it out. They came when they came. But mostly, they didn't.

I didn't sit up when Milligan came in. I didn't even open my eyes, because I didn't have to. I hadn't sworn an oath to him, and I hadn't been ordered to obey him, so participation was at my discretion. And I wasn't feeling very discretionary.

I rolled onto my stomach on my mattress, eyes still squeezed shut, trying not to imagine how I must look after all this time. Skinny, bruised, tangled and dirty. Clad only in the same underwear I'd been wearing for days, at least, because humiliation was a large part of my sentence and I hadn't been granted the privilege of real clothing. My period hadn't come, which meant I wasn't imagining not being fed regularly, and water came rarely enough that I'd decided I wasn't being kept alive, so much as I was being slowly killed.

I'd been a bad, bad girl.

"Kori, did you hear me?" Milligan asked.

I'd had no problem with him on the outside. He'd respected me. At least, he'd respected the fact that the boss valued me. Milligan had never gotten grabby and he'd only leered when he thought I wasn't looking. That was practically chivalry, on the west side of the city.

Now, I hated him. Milligan hadn't put me in the basement, in that rotten fucking cell of a room. But he'd kept me there, and that was enough. If I got the chance—if I ever got out and regained my strength—I'd put a bullet in him. I'd have to, just to show Jake Tower that I was down, but not out. Beaten, but not broken.

Milligan would be expecting it, just like I would, in his position.

The door creaked open wider and I buried my face in

the crook of my arm, nose pressed into the dirty mattress, braced for whatever would come. Prepared to turn myself off and make the world go away. That was the only way to survive in the basement. Convince yourself that whatever they do to you doesn't matter. And really, it doesn't. How can it, if you can't stop it and no one else wants to? So I dug down deep, to a place where there was no pain and no thought. Not my happy place. Thinking of a happy place—*any* happy place—only reminded me that I wasn't really there. That I never would be again.

I went to my empty place.

"Tower's on his way," Milligan said. "I think you're getting out."

My heart leaped into my throat, but I didn't move. Surely I'd only heard what I wanted to hear. If I wasn't careful, I sometimes imagined things, and there's nothing more dangerous in the dark than unwarranted hope.

"Kori?" he said, and that time my eyes opened. "You're getting out today."

I sat up slowly, blinking furiously in the light, wincing over the residual pain from the gunshot wound in my shoulder. I'd heard him, but it took forever for the words to sink in, and even once they had, I didn't let myself believe it. It could be a trick. Jonah Tower—Jake's brother—had told me I was getting out before, but he only said it so he could watch me suffer when I realized it wasn't true.

"If you're lying, I'll fucking kill you," I croaked, my mouth and throat so dry my tongue felt like it had corners.

"I'm not—" Milligan glanced down a hallway I couldn't see as a set of firm, even footsteps echoed toward us. "Here he comes."

I swallowed a sob. I'd expected to die alone in this false dark. In these dead shadows.

Milligan stepped back, and Jake Tower replaced him in the doorway, a steel-spined symbol of power and authority in his white button-up shirt and suit jacket, sans tie. I hated myself for how relieved I was to see him, when he was the one who'd locked me up. I hated his clean clothes, and combed hair, and tanned skin. I hated the apple wood smoke clinging to his clothes from the grill, making my stomach rumble and cramp. I hated the slight flush in his cheeks that told me he'd had two glasses of red wine with his steak—never more, never less, because Tower was in control. Of everything. Always.

Jake Tower was the heart of the Tower syndicate. We—the initiates—were the lifeblood of the organization, but Tower was the pump that kept us flowing through the veins and arteries of this living machine. He pushed the buttons and pulled the strings, and we belonged to him, all of us, bound into service, sealed in flesh, by blood and by name. We lived and died according to his will. And we obeyed because obedience was a physical mandate. Even when our minds resisted, our bodies complied, helpless in the face of a direct order.

But I'd found a loophole. I'd disobeyed the spirit of an order, if not the order itself, and as punishment, Tower had thrown open the gates of hell and shoved me inside. He'd locked me up and given Jonah free rein, and for all I knew, Jake had forgotten I even existed until…

Until what?

Until he needed me. Why else would he be here? Why else had he let me live, if my current state could even be called living?

Tower's nose wrinkled—I didn't smell good—then he closed the door at his back and sat on the edge of the bare foam mattress covering the raised concrete slab that was my bed. He grabbed my chin and tilted my face toward the light, studying me. I knew what he saw, though there was no mirror in my cell. Bruises. Dark circles and sharp cheek bones. Split lips. And the damage didn't end with my face. I looked like hell and I felt worse.

Tower looked...satisfied. "Does it hurt?"

"You fucking know it hurts." Everywhere. That was the whole point. With my existence reduced to fear, and pain, and dead shadows, surely I would never even consider another betrayal. "The lights?" I didn't want to ask, but I had to know. "Your idea?" Jonah wasn't smart enough to think of something like that.

Tower's lips curled up in a small smile, like he'd just remembered some distant childhood pleasure. "An irony I hope you fully appreciate. Absolute, inescapable darkness for the shadow-walker. Imprisoned by the source of your own abilities. How did that feel?"

I am a Traveler. A shadow-walker. I can step into a shadow in one room, then out of a shadow anywhere else I want to go, within my range. I can see better in the dark than most people. Sometimes I can look into one shadow and see through another one, somewhere else, like looking through a periscope, or one of those paper-towel-roll telescopes we used to play with as kids.

But the basement darkness was anemic, thanks to a grid of infrared lights, too high up for me to reach. So while my cell looked absolutely, claustrophobically dark to the naked eye, that darkness was too shallow for me to travel through. The shadows were dead. I was trapped in the element that had always been my ally. My escape.

How did that make me feel?

Like I'd been betrayed by my own body. Like I was lost to the rest of the world. Like I no longer existed at all, which would have been easy to believe, if not for the pain anchoring me to the reality of my own miserable existence. But I wasn't going to tell Tower that.

"It sucked, on ice. Happy?"

He said nothing. Whatever he wanted to tell me would come on his terms, and making me wait for it was just another way of making me suffer.

"Why?" I demanded, pissed off that my voice was as weak as the rest of me. "Why didn't you just kill me?" He'd killed others for far less than what I'd done.

"You needed to pay for your crimes, and others needed to know you were paying." He said it like he might explain that grass is green, as if it should have been obvious, and the emptiness in his voice was the scariest thing I'd ever heard.

"You told them?"

"You were an object lesson, Korinne. I showed them." He glanced at the slab of one-way glass in the top half of the interior wall, and my blood froze in my veins. I started to shake, and I couldn't stop.

"You let them watch?" He'd invited an audience to see me beaten, and broken, and humiliated, and… I closed my eyes against this new layer of humiliation.

"Only those who needed to see."

"Kenley?" No. *Please* no. I didn't want her touched by this. I didn't want her to know. If Tower was void of human emotion, Kenley was made of it, and she couldn't defend herself. That was my job.

Tower shook his head. "Your sister only knows that you're alive. She's anxious to see you."

I exhaled slowly and blinked back tears that would never fall, using them as fuel for the rage burning deep in my gut. Fury that would have no outlet for four more years. Anger that would fester and burn as I planned for the day when I'd be the one throwing punches and spilling blood. Jake Tower would *pay.* Jonah would pay. Milligan and the other guards would pay. Everyone who'd watched would fucking pay.

I would listen to them beg while they bled out on the floor.

But I'd have to survive to get revenge, and to survive, I'd have to play Jake's game. It was always his game, always his rules, and the only cards he dealt me were penitence and obedience. So I would play the shit out of penitence and obedience—anything to get out of the basement—and keep the cards I'd dealt myself up my sleeve. Until it was my turn to deal.

"I have an assignment for you, Korinne," Jake said. "A chance to redeem yourself."

I said nothing, because nothing was required, but my pulse raced so fast I had to lean against the wall to steady myself. Milligan was right. I was getting out of the basement.

"Ian Holt."

"Who?" I licked my lips, but my tongue was too dry to wet them, and now that I knew I was getting out, I found it hard to concentrate on the details, rather than the promise of regular meals, and showers, and relative freedom.

"He's a Blinder of extraordinary skill."

"You want him killed?" I'd never heard of him, which meant he wasn't ours. And if he could be used against us, he was a target.

"I want him whole. Preferably unharmed."

"Another acquisition?" In the weeks before I was locked up, I'd done quite a few of them, collecting whoever Tower wanted for his pet project.

"Only as a last resort. I want him on staff. Willingly." Because forced bindings were never as strong as those entered into freely. "Holt hasn't signed with anyone yet. In fact, he managed to stay completely off the radar until two days ago, when the JumboTron at an NHL hockey game caught him darkening the entire arena during a riot on the ice."

"How do you know it wasn't just a power outage?"

"Because he blinded the arena from the outside in, starting at the perimeter and moving toward the ice from all sides equally. The general public thinks he's just some idiot who saw the first lights go out before the camera did and pretended to be doing a magic trick. But I know what I saw, and I'm not the only one. Now that he's been exposed, everyone wants him. I've officially extended an invitation, and he's agreed to come to town as my guest and hear our pitch. You will be his liaison. You will show him the advantages of joining the Tower syndicate and make sure that he signs with us, or with no one."

"I'm not a fucking recruiter, Jake." I'd been part of Tower's personal security team. I'd killed for him. I'd kidnapped for him. I'd done other things I desperately wished I could forget, but recruiting was a specialized skill—one I didn't have. "I'm a soldier, and you need a salesman."

"You are whatever I say you are, and when Ian Holt gets here, you will be his recruiter. You will be his girlfriend, his best friend, his therapist, his mother, or his dog trainer, if need be. You will do whatever it takes to put a chain link on his arm." For emphasis, Tower glanced at the two black interlocking chain links tattooed on my own arm—the flesh-and-blood binding tying me to him until my term was up. "Whatever it takes, Korinne. Do you understand?"

I understood. "You want me to fuck him." And if I refused—if I refused *anything* Jake told me to do—resistance pain from violating my oath to him would shut my organs down one at a time until I died screaming.

"I want you to give him whatever he wants. And if he wants *you,* then yes, you will bed him, and you better be the best he's ever had, because if he refuses my mark, you will have to bring him in by force so I can drain him. And if that happens, I will kill you, and your sister will pay for your failure as you've paid for your latest mistake. She will serve out the years remaining on her contract in this room, under the same conditions."

My blood ran cold, and suddenly I couldn't breathe. "No one touches Kenley. You swore it when I signed on." My little sister would be untouchable, in exchange for my service.

"And *you* swore that you would guard my life and my interests with your own." Tower unbuttoned his shirt slowly, and I knew what he was going to do even before he pulled back the left half of the material to show me the fresh pink scar. "Your key card let the enemy into my house. Into my home, where my wife and children sleep. Your gun faltered where it should have fired, and I was shot in my own home, by my greatest enemy."

"I didn't mean—"

"You failed," Tower insisted. "You broke your word, and I have no reason to keep mine. If Ian Holt does not sign with me voluntarily by the end of his visit, I will have you executed, and your sister will pay the pound of flesh you still owe."

Nausea rolled over me, and if I'd had anything to vomit, it would have landed in his lap.

"You have two weeks to get back in shape and make yourself presentable. This is your last chance, Korinne. Save yourself. Protect your sister. Get me Ian Holt."

After Tower left, the lights stayed on, and I had several minutes to see the emaciated ruin my body had become. And to think. And to hate Jake Tower like I'd never hated anyone in my life. Then the door opened again, and my sister stepped into the room, a younger, softer reflection of the woman I'd been until Tower locked me up.

Kenley gasped. Her hand flew to her mouth, then she spoke from behind it. "What did you bastards do to her?"

Milligan stood behind her, staring at the floor. "I never touched her. I just work here."

"Where the hell are her clothes?"

Milligan shrugged. "This is how he sent her. You've got fifteen minutes to get her cleaned up." He backed out of the room and shut the door.

Kenley crossed the small space and set a canvas bag on the floor, then dropped onto her knees in front of me, brushing hair back from my forehead.

"How long?" I asked, staring at the mattress while she dug in her bag.

She pulled out a bottle of water and handed it to me. "Almost six weeks," she said, and I could hear the sob in her voice, though she tried to hold it back.

"I'm fine." I cracked the top on the bottle, scared by

how much effort that took, then unscrewed the lid. I'd gulped half of it before I remembered I should go slow.

"You're not fine. I thought you were dead. Jake kept saying you were alive, but he wouldn't let me see you. I was sure he was lying, just to keep me working." Tears formed in her eyes and when she blinked, they rolled down her cheeks.

"No. Don't cry, Kenni," I whispered, because they were listening. They were always listening, and they were probably watching through the one-way glass. I licked the moisture from my lips. "Don't ever let those steel-hearted sons of bitches see you cry. If they know you can be broken, they'll fuckin' break you just for sport."

Like they'd tried to break me.

She nodded, jaw clenched against sobs she was visibly choking back.

I opened my mouth to tell her it would be okay. I would *make* it okay. But then my stomach revolted, and I lurched for the toilet. I retched hard enough to wrench my injured shoulder, and the water came up. It was too much, too fast. I should have known better. I'd been sipping half handfuls of clean water from the back of the toilet tank since the bottles had stopped coming, but that was different from gulping half a bottle, ice-cold.

Kenley pulled my hair from my face and I sat up, wiping my mouth with the back of one bare arm. My stomach was still pitching, but there was nothing left to lose.

"No one knew where you were." She handed me the bottle again, and I rinsed my mouth, then spit into the toilet, thinking about how wrong she was. Some people knew where I was. Some of them had seen me, through the one-way glass. "Tower was shot, and you were shot, then he woke up and you disappeared. What happened, Kori? No one knows what really happened."

What happened? I'd been buried in the basement, at the mercy of the monsters. But that wasn't what she was asking.

"Liv said she needed my help, so I went. But it was a trap. They were waiting for me. They took my key and used it to break in." I was the breach in security that got one of our men killed, two more shot, and Tower's prize blood donor—my murdered friend Noelle's only daughter—taken. "Ruben Cavazos shot us both." I ran my fingers over the dirty bandage on my shoulder.

I should have run, regardless of the risk. I *would* have run, if not for Kenley. I couldn't leave her alone with Tower. Alone in the syndicate. My sister and I were a package deal, from start to finish.

"You're lucky he didn't have you killed," she said, but I shook my head.

"He can't. He still needs me." I had no clue why I had to be the one to recruit Ian Holt, but if Jake didn't need me, I would be dead.

"Let's get you cleaned up." She stood and headed for the canvas bag, but her shoulders were shaking and it took me a minute to realize why.

"Kenley, this isn't your fault." I used the edge of the toilet to push myself to my feet.

"Of course it's my fault." She dug in the bag and pulled out a bottle of shampoo, then crossed the room toward the narrow, curtainless shower stall in one corner. "I sealed the binding between you and Liv, so you have to do what she asks. Because of me."

Kenley was a Binder. A scary-good Binder. She was

so good Jake hid her from the world, to protect her and every contract she'd ever sealed for him. He kept her under twenty-four-hour guard, and he threatened me to control her, just like he threatened her to control me.

"It wasn't like that this time," I insisted, as she turned on the shower—it only worked when they wanted it to. "Liv didn't officially ask and I wasn't compelled. I went to help her on my own." Because it was the right thing to do. I was sure of that, even after everything that had come since.

"It's my fault you're here in the first place, Kori." Kenley aimed the shower spray at the opposite wall, then turned to look at me, arms crossed over her chest, and I sighed. I'd never been able to effectively argue with that one. But again, I had to try.

"I make my own decisions. We came into the syndicate together, and we'll leave together." Or not at all. "Four years," I whispered leaning with my forehead against her shoulder, while stray droplets of water sprayed us both. "We can do four more years, right?"

She nodded, but she looked far from sure. I'd been shot, starved, abused and locked in the dark for almost six weeks, but she was the one I worried about. Kenley was fragile, so I had to be strong enough for both of us. And Jake knew it. He knew what cards we held—what mattered to us—so he always won the game.

"Let me see your shoulder." Kenley blinked away more tears, and I leaned against the wall for balance while she peeled medical tape and gauze from my gunshot wound. I'd done my best to keep it clean, and I'd taken all the antibiotics Jonah had brought in the first couple of weeks, back when I was being fed and showered regularly, because *he* was the bulk of my punishment. But then Jake had figured out that his brother wasn't enough to break me, and that's when the darkness and isolation had dropped into place around me.

"It could be worse." Kenley wadded up the bandage and dropped it on the floor. "The stitches have dissolved and it's only a little red." Which kind of figured, because the rest of me was black and blue. "Get cleaned up. He's sending an escort for us in a few minutes," she said, while I stepped out of my underwear and dropped my grimy bra on the floor. Kenley kicked them into the opposite corner, then stuck one hand under the water and grimaced. "They could at least make it warm."

But they wouldn't. The basement cells weren't built for comfort. They were built for isolation and torture. They were built for hour after hour of darkness and silence, because when you can't see anything and you can't hear anything, you have no choice but to think about what you did, and how you would never, ever do it again.

But here's the thing. I would do it all over again, if I had the chance. I would take the gunshot wound, and the silence, and the darkness, and the worst Jonah could throw at me, if it meant sending Noelle's kid back home where she belonged.

I stepped into the shower and gasped as freezing water poured over my face and body. I let it soak my hair, then I opened my mouth and drank just a little, one hand propped on the tile wall for balance, because I hadn't eaten in days, and the room was starting to spin.

While I washed my hair slowly, shocked wide-awake by the cold water, my sister pounded on the one-way glass. "She's gonna need something clean to wear. Actual clothes, this time! And a towel!"

I lathered the cracked bar of soap while water and

shampoo suds ran down my body to swirl through the drain at my feet. It felt good to be clean on the outside, even if I might never be truly clean on the inside, ever again.

Five minutes later, clean and still damp, my hair dripping on clothes that weren't mine and didn't quite fit, I stepped out of the cell I'd spent almost six weeks in with one arm around my sister, as she half held me up. Milligan didn't look at me, and neither did either of the grunts Tower had sent to escort us to Kenley's apartment. But as the door swung shut behind me, literally closing on a chapter of my life I never wanted to reread, a man stepped out of the shadows in the hallway and crossed beefy arms over a barrel chest.

"Won't be the same around here without you, Kori," Jonah Tower said, cruel laughter echoing behind every syllable, and at the sound of his voice, my heart thumped painfully, pumping remembered pain and fear along with the blood in my veins. He stepped closer and whispered into my ear, too softly for Kenley to hear. "But I think you'll be back. And if you can't give Jake what he wants, I get to end you. Then the younger Miss Daniels and I are gonna get to know each other real well."

Kenley shied away from the hand he laid on her shoulder, and I stepped between them, close enough that I could smell the beer on his breath. "I'll be back all right, but you're not gonna see me coming. And if you've laid a finger on my sister, I'm going to tear them off one at a time and shove them down your throat until you choke on your own sins."

Two

Ian

"Have I told you you're an idiot?" Aaron asked, staring through the windshield at the tall iron gate and the even taller house behind it. If such a monstrosity could even be called a house. It was more like a modern fortress.

"About twenty times since my plane landed." I flipped down the driver's-side sunshade and checked my tie in the mirror.

"Has it sunk in yet?"

I glanced at him in the thick shadows of the car's interior, lit only by the green numbers scrolling across the radio's display in the dashboard. "Your puny verbal barbs are no match for my thick skull."

"You *do* have a freakishly thick skull," Aaron said, flipping through the stations on my rental car's radio. "But that won't stop a bullet. They may look civilized in tuxedos and sequins, but they're really monsters in men's clothing, every single one of them. They're going to eat you alive in there, Ian."

"Then may they choke on my corpse."

Aaron punched the button to turn off the radio, un-characteristically serious in concession to the job at hand. "Eight years since you left, and nothing's changed. You're still ready to charge in half-cocked and make the world bend to your will, consequences be damned."

"That's not true." The kid I'd been back then was idealistic but soft. Smart but naive. That kid had been burned by the real world—roasted alive—and I'd risen from his ashes, ready to breathe fire of my own. "Now I'm *fully* cocked, and well aware of the consequences. As are you."

He nodded at the somber reminder. "You sure you don't want me to go in with you? I could grab a monkey suit and be back in a second." Aaron was a Traveler, which meant he could step into the shadow of a tree outside my car and into his own bedroom in the space of a single breath, and be back just as fast. "You're gonna need someone you trust at your back."

Unfortunately for Aaron—or fortunately, depending on your perspective—traveling was one of the most common Skills in the world. Aaron's range was a little above average, but his accuracy was questionable at best, and unless his motivation was personal, no one would ever call him punctual. Which meant he had no value whatsoever to the Skilled syndicates.

That fact had kept him safe from their interest for years. So safe, in fact, I'd often wondered if he was faking his own incompetence for that very reason. He wouldn't be the first to try it. Hell, *I'd* tried it. But that wasn't why I couldn't use his help.

"Thanks, but no. If you show your face in Tower's house, within an hour they'll know you're an Independent."

They'd also know that Aaron was as good with a computer as he was bad with women, that he was late on the rent and quick with a punch line, and that he was addicted to those little melt-away mints people serve at weddings. His life was an open book, available to anyone who cared to read it. As were most people's lives. Which was why I was the only one who could do this job.

Because I had no life. No past. Officially, I didn't even exist, and if they ever figured that out, being seen with me could get Aaron killed.

"I need you to stay off their radar so you can be my emergency bailout, if this ends badly."

"Fair enough." Aaron sounded half relieved, half disappointed. He wanted to play badass assassin, but he didn't really want the risk that came with it. "Give me a call if you need a quick escape."

"I will," I said, as he pushed open the passenger-side door. But we both knew I wouldn't. There was nothing he could do to help me, if I couldn't get out of Tower's house on my own. The infrared lighting grid guaranteed that trespassers couldn't gain entrance through the shadows. His heavily guarded exits made sure no one got in the traditional way, either. Once inside, I would be on my own.

"If you survive this kamikaze mission, we should get dinner. And beer."

"Absolutely." But that was another lie. I had every intention of surviving, but wouldn't get the chance to hang out afterward, and I'd probably never be able to come back into the country at all, much less this particular city. If I accomplished what I'd set out to do, the price on my head would be high enough that preachers and Boy

Scouts would fight one another for the chance to profit from my death.

"Good luck, man." Aaron stuck his hand out and I shook it, then he stepped out of my rental car and closed the door. I watched as he walked into the patch of woods at the side of the road. One step. Two. Three. Then he was gone, not just hidden by the shadows, but transported by them. Through them.

I took a deep breath and checked my tie in the mirror again—I hadn't worn a tux in years, and my distaste for formal wear had not faded. Then I shifted the car into Drive and pulled onto the street at the end of a procession of cars all headed the same place I was.

The queue of vehicles moved quickly, greased by proper planning and a well-trained workforce. When I rolled to a stop in front of the house, feet from the curved, formal steps, a man was waiting to take my keys while another spoke into his handheld radio, his steady but unobtrusive gaze taking in every detail of my clothes and bearing. They knew my face.

Before I'd even rounded the front of the car, a brunette in a long, formfitting peach-colored dress came down the steps toward me. She smiled like a pageant contestant and moved like a waitress, quick and eager to please.

"Mr. Holt." She threaded her arm through mine and guided me smoothly up the steps, without ever faltering in either smile or stride. "We would have sent a car for you," she said, leading me through a door held open by a man in service dress. She was smooth, and polished, and poised—an experienced people handler and a beautiful woman.

But she was *not* what I'd requested.

"Unnecessary. I wanted to see the city a bit on my

own." I stopped in the foyer, and she had no choice but to stop with me, because I still held her arm. "I'm sorry, I didn't catch your name."

"I'm Nina. Mr. Tower's personal assistant."

"And you're my escort for the evening?"

Her smile faltered a bit over my implication, and the dissatisfaction echoing intentionally within the question. But then she rallied from the insult and her smile beamed brighter than ever, if a little brittle now. "No, I'm afraid Mr. Tower has chosen someone else to keep you company during your stay. I'm just here to make the introductions this evening."

Nina led me through the wide foyer, generically ostentatious with its soaring ceiling and gold-veined marble tile. Even in his absence, Jake Tower exhibited his own affluence and power like a peacock displaying plumage. Wealth was evident in the expensive furnishings and decor, while his power was even more obvious in the stream of well-dressed guests, several of whom I recognized from political pieces on the nightly news.

At the base of each curved staircase, dressed in black and carrying handheld radios, stood a member of Tower's security team, monitoring the party in general and me in particular. I was unbound—I'd taken no oath of loyalty or service to Jake Tower—thus untrusted. They would watch me, prepared to intercept or incapacitate, until the day I bore Tower's chain link on my arm, marking me as his to command.

And that wasn't going to happen.

Once those milling in the entry had their chance to see me, Nina guided me into the main event. Into the snake pit, where every hiss would feel like praise and every bite like a deep, hot kiss. The venom would flow like honey, too thick to swallow, but too sweet to entirely resist.

I knew how extravagant and generous the syndicates could seem when they wanted something. I also knew it was all a lie. The party was an illusion, from every plunging neckline to each glass of chilled champagne. It was a show. A seduction. I was being courted by the Tower syndicate because I had something they wanted. And I would play along because *they* had something *I* wanted.

Heads turned to look when we entered the party. Hands shook mine and voices called out greetings, but the faces all blurred together. The names were a jumble of syllables I didn't bother to untangle. These weren't the important names. Not the important faces. Remembering would be a waste of effort.

So I smiled and nodded in the right places, agreeing when it was convenient, changing the subject when it wasn't. I sipped from the glass placed in my hand and ate the hors d'oeuvres Nina insisted I try. But I tasted nothing and hardly heard the words that came out of my own mouth. I was too busy scanning the crowd for the faces I'd studied. The names I'd memorized. The important ones, not necessarily in power circles, but vital to my purpose.

And finally, nearly half an hour after I arrived, a soft buzz spread through the crowd and I looked up to find Jake Tower coming down the main staircase with his wife on his arm and two black-clothed bodyguards at his back. The host had arrived, late enough to demonstrate that he lived life on his own schedule, but not so tardy as to be truly rude to his guests.

"Let me introduce you to Mr. Tower," Nina said,

taking my arm again. She led me through the crowd toward the stairs as Tower and his small entourage descended into our midst.

At the base of the stairs, a glass of champagne was pressed into Tower's hand, but he handed it to his wife before accepting another for himself. A heartbeat later, his gaze landed on Nina, then slid to me, and I swallowed a lump of eager rage before it could shine through my eyes and give me away. Tower wasn't my target, but that didn't mean I'd cry at his funeral. When the time came, I'd be raising my glass to whoever finally put the vicious, arrogant bastard in the ground, as would everyone else he'd ever tried to put his mark on.

"Mr. Holt, may I introduce Jake Tower and his lovely wife, Lynne. Mr. Tower, this is Ian Holt, your guest of honor."

Tower offered me his empty right hand and I shook it, making eye contact for the first time. Trying not to show that I knew more than I should.

I shouldn't know that Tower's first name was actually Jacob and one of his middle names was David. His wife was really Gwendolyn, and before she married, she'd been a Pierce, a great beauty by all accounts, but not burdened with enough brains or initiative to ever get in her husband's way.

"Mr. Holt, so glad you could join us. I hope you're enjoying yourself so far?" Tower's brows rose, and I nodded in reply.

"Of course. You have a lovely home, and an even lovelier wife." I took Lynne Tower's hand briefly, and she smiled, then silently sipped from her glass.

Over their shoulders, the bodyguards watched me, and their surnames filtered through my memory, triggered by faces matching the photographs and notes Aaron had fed me for days. The taller, darker man was Clifton, and the shorter, paler, broader one was Garrett. Their Skills, like their first names, were unknown, but based on their size alone, either could break a man in half.

The group around me shifted to accept a new couple into our power circle, and I realized with one glance at the newcomers that they weren't a couple at all.

"Mr. Holt, this is my brother, Jonah, and our sister, Julia."

"My pleasure," I said, shaking their hands in turn, and Julia's left eyebrow quirked over one deep brown eye, like something in my reply amused her.

Jonah only scowled. He was dressed like one of the guests, but even if I hadn't known from my research, I would have known from his bearing alone that Jonah would have been more comfortable wearing all black like the rest of Tower's muscle. He didn't like dressing up, and he didn't like playing nice. And he didn't like me—that much was obvious in his first glance my way.

Almost as obvious was the fact that his dislike of me would be very much mutual.

"Mr. Holt, if I may say so, that was quite an impressive show you put on at the arena a couple of months ago." Julia—Lia—raised her glass just a little, offering her own personal toast to my Skill.

"Oh, thank you, but it wasn't intended as a show at all." *Lie.* "I was just trying to help out where I could." That part was true, but intentionally misleading. I was trying to help myself into Tower's power circle.

"Still, you made quite an impression," Tower insisted. "Lynne and I were impressed, anyway."

"Unfortunately you weren't the only ones. The news

clip got quite a bit of airtime, and it's been viewed on the internet ad nauseam. If I'd known there were cameras aimed at me, I might have done things a little differently."

Another lie, and a big one that time. I knew there were cameras. The arena was chosen for that very reason. For my Skilled coming-out party. For the exposure that would bring me to Jake Tower's notice, during his favorite sport.

"And you're uncomfortable in the spotlight?" Julia asked.

"Or maybe scared of it?" Jonah added. "Darkness is more your thing, right?"

"I'm most comfortable in the absence of both light and attention, but scared of neither." I faked a nervous laugh. "However, I will admit to being unnerved a bit at first by interest from organizations like this one."

"You've had offers from other syndicates?" Tower's frown was small, but telling.

"Let's just say I'm keeping my options open for now. Though no one else has gone to quite this much trouble to impress me before." I gestured one-armed at the entire party.

"Obviously we don't stand around drinking and talking every day, but I thought a party would be the best way to introduce you to the syndicate as a whole."

"And what an introduction it is," I said, as one waiter took my empty glass while another replaced it.

"This is only the beginning." Julia smiled, dark straight hair framing a pretty face I couldn't quite read. "By the end of the week, you'll understand that no one else can offer you the benefits, security and career advancement potential that the Tower syndicate can."

"And here is the woman for the job." Tower smiled coolly at someone over my shoulder and I turned as he waved two more women into our widening circle. The first was a small, delicate-looking woman in light blue, her platinum curls tumbling over pale, bare shoulders. She was smaller and fairer than my personal tastes ran, but I'd requested an escort of her exact description, and when her brown-eyed gaze met mine, some small bit of tension inside me eased.

"Mr. Holt, this is Kenley Daniels."

I took her hand to shake it and couldn't help smiling in relief. There she was, my target, hand delivered to me by one of the most dangerous and powerful men in the country, though he had no idea that he'd played the very card I wanted most. All I needed now was to get her away from Tower and his security team, and...

"And this," he continued, before my hand had more than grazed Kenley's, "is her sister, Korinne. Kori will be keeping you company this week."

I blinked, confused, and glanced from Kenley Daniels to her sister, whose coloring matched Kenley's exactly— same platinum hair, pale skin, and deep brown eyes. Korinne was only an inch or so taller. She was a virtual match to the description I'd given Tower when he asked what I'd desire most in a liaison—the description of her sister.

"A pleasure," I said on autopilot, as I released Kenley's hand in favor of Kori's, still reeling from the bait-and-switch. Only it couldn't be a bait-and-switch, because Tower didn't know I'd had anyone specific in mind as my liaison.

And I hadn't known his mistake was possible, because *Kori Daniels* wasn't possible. She was dead. Every single one of Aaron's sources had said the same thing. She'd been a fixture at Tower's side for years—a strategically visible threat—then she'd disappeared several weeks ago. Gone, with no trace and no explanation.

In the syndicate, that can only mean one thing.

Yet there she stood, clearly alive and breathing, and waiting for me to shake the hand she held out. So I did.

She let go of my hand almost the instant we touched.

"Kori will be your tour guide," Tower continued. "She will also be your assistant, your chauffeur and your personal security while you are here. Anything you want, Kori will provide."

But Kori looked like she'd rather perform CPR on a leper than ever touch me again, even if only to hand me a cup of coffee.

My thoughts raced while I struggled to recover from surprise and frustration, without showing either. "You have security experience?" I said as if I didn't already know the answer, grasping at the only reasonable excuse I might have to reject her services. There had to be a reason she was no longer guarding the boss, and if he didn't trust her, why should I?

"Six years on my personal security detail," Tower said, and I was starting to wonder if my new liaison even had a tongue. "I assure you, Kori is everything you requested, and more."

Something silent and angry passed between Tower and the taller, older Daniels sister as her jaw clenched visibly and his gaze went hard. Kenley Daniels stared at her feet in the awkward silence, and Jonah Tower smirked when Kori flinched first, and looked away from her boss.

"Well, then, Mr. Holt, I believe we're scheduled to discuss business later, but tonight is for drinking, and dancing, and mingling. I have some other guests to greet, so I'm going to leave you in Korinne's capable hands for the moment. Please make yourself at home in my home."

With that, Tower guided his wife toward a couple I vaguely recognized from the cover of some financial magazine, and the rest of his entourage followed. Leaving me alone with Korinne Daniels, who held an untouched flute of champagne but showed no sign of sipping from it. Or of acknowledging my presence.

How could she be alive? Where the hell had she been for the past few weeks? I'd made sure that none of the other women photographed with Tower recently had pale blond hair, specifically to avoid this kind of mistake.

Weeks of research and study, down the drain.

"So…" I said, watching Kori watch the rest of the room, trying not to let frustration leak into my voice. "You're one of Tower's bodyguards?"

"Was," she said, and her posture tensed almost imperceptibly as she stared at something over my shoulder. I twisted to see Jonah Tower guiding her sister through the crowd with one hand at her lower back, and when I turned back to Kori, I found her eyes narrowed, one fist clenched at her side.

Were Jonah and Kenley involved? If so, Kori clearly didn't approve. Neither did I. Jonah Tower didn't like me, which could make it very hard for me to get close to Kenley if they were together. Unless her sister trusted me…

I studied Kori as she watched them wind their way through the crowd, trying to assess her more clearly now that I was over my initial surprise at being saddled with the wrong Daniels sister.

Korinne was slightly taller than her sister, but much thinner. Too thin, really. Her hip bones showed through the material of her dress and the points of her collarbone looked like they might pierce her skin at the slightest pressure. Her makeup was expertly applied, but couldn't quite cover the dark circles under her eyes or skin that looked sickly pale, in contrast to her sister's naturally fair complexion.

Still, she was pretty, in a hard-edged, angry kind of way.

Kori glanced up and caught me staring, and I held her gaze. "What do you do now?" I asked, trying to pick up the thread of a conversation that already seemed destined to unravel.

"Now I babysit you," she snapped, and I blinked in the face of such candor. Then almost laughed out loud. I'd expected Tower's people to be overaccommodating and ingratiatingly polite. Perhaps even sycophantic. Unvarnished honesty was a surprise.

"I meant, what do you do for Tower? What's your role in his organization?" When my question produced only a blank, half-puzzled look, like she wasn't sure she even knew the answer, I tried again from another angle. "Would it be impolite of me to ask about your Skill, considering you already know mine?"

"Hell yes." She flinched and rubbed her temple with one hand. Then she rolled her eyes at nothing. "I'm a Traveler."

A shadow-walker, just like Aaron.

"I assume you're good with a gun, since you used to be a bodyguard. Any other special skills?" But I could tell with one look at her closed-off expression that I'd picked the wrong approach.

Kori Daniels didn't want to talk about herself. She didn't want to talk to me. And she certainly didn't want to relax. She looked a little like she wanted to rip my head off and spit down my throat. "A *special skill?*"

I nodded, and too late I realized she'd found innuendo where I hadn't intended it.

I shook my head and tried to rephrase the question, but then she stepped closer, until she was in my personal space, not quite touching me, but so close air couldn't have flowed between us. She went up on her toes, like she might nibble on my ear, or share some dirty little secret. Then she whispered, so softly no one else could have heard.

"I do have a special skill," she murmured, her breath warm on my neck, her voice soft and low-pitched, with that hot, gravelly quality some women get when they're really turned on, and my pulse raced a little in spite of my very clear objective. "I'm pretty good with knives. I'm so good, in fact, that I could sever your testicles with one hand and slice open your throat with the other, and you'd go into shock so fast you'd die without ever knowing you'd spilled a fucking drop of blood."

Korinne settled back onto her heels and smiled up at me like she'd just promised to fulfill my dirtiest, most secret desire, and I felt the blood drain from my face.

This was *not* the woman I'd ordered.

Three

Kori

I sipped from my glass and enjoyed Holt's shocked expression so much that I'd taken two more sips before I remembered I hate champagne. And for the first time since I'd woken up in the basement eight weeks before, I felt a little better. A little more like myself. Until I saw Jake watching me from across the room, fury dancing in his eyes. He couldn't have heard me, but he could see that I'd scared his guest of honor—disturbed him, at the very least—and he was pissed. Jake tossed his head toward an alcove mostly hidden by the curve in the staircase, and I had no choice but to obey the silent summons.

"Be right back…" I mumbled to Holt, and cursed myself silently all the way across the room. I'd known better. I'd fucking *known* better, and I gave in to temptation anyway. I couldn't afford to scare off Holt or piss off Tower—Kenley couldn't afford my mistakes—yet I'd managed to do both after less than five minutes alone with the man whose Skill Tower valued more than he valued my life.

"What the hell did you just do?" Jake growled, hauling me into the alcove by one arm. I tripped over the stupid stilettos Kenley had insisted I wear and would have gone down on my face if Tower wasn't holding me up.

"He asked if I have any 'special skills.' He said it just like that." Like *special* meant depraved or perverted.

"Was I not clear before?" Jake's eyes flashed with anger. "I only pulled you out of the basement two weeks ago for this job. For *him*. I don't care what he says, or what he does, or what he wants," he growled into my ear, squeezing my arm hard enough to bruise, though I'd die before I complained. "You will answer him with a smile, and the answer is always yes. Do you understand?"

"Yes," I snapped, and it felt good to throw the word back in his face, even if it tasted bitter on my tongue.

He let go of my arm, but didn't back down. "I'm not going to bother listing all the things you are not allowed to say or do, because I recognize that while unsophisticated and often crass, your mannerisms have a certain crude charm, and for all I know, Holt might actually want to play 'tame the beast.' That's up to you to determine. But however this plays out, I swear on every beat of my wife's heart that if you don't have Ian Holt eating out of your hand in forty-eight hours, you will pay for it with your life. And your sister will pay for it with the balance of hers. Do you understand what I'm saying, Korinne?" he demanded, and I nodded, but that evidently wasn't enough, because he repeated the question.

"Yes. I fucking understand," I said through clenched teeth.

"Good." He stepped back and eyed me from head to toe without a hint of desire. Tower, for all his faults, worshipped his wife like she shit gold and bled wine, and I'd never once seen him even glance at another woman with any real interest. "You look like a lady for once. Now go pretend to be one," he said. "And try to remember that though a sledgehammer may be the most prominent weapon in your verbal arsenal, it is seldom the most appropriate."

"Jake, please," I whispered, swallowing the lump of bitter pride in my throat. "I'm not the best woman for this job. If you really want him, you need a recruiter." Someone who was used to wining, and dining, and kissing arrogant ass. Someone who was *good* at it. "Don't you think Monica would be better suited to this? Or Erica?"

Tower's gaze went hard, and I knew I'd overstepped. Again. "Without a doubt. But he doesn't *want* Monica or Erica. The only other person in my employ who fits Holt's description of his ideal physical type is your sister, and even if you were willing to let her wander all over town alone with a man she just met, I am not. I need her here, doing her job, where I know no one else can get to her."

I wanted to protect my sister from the realities of life in the syndicate. He wanted to protect a very valuable asset from being poached or exterminated. Still, in the end, our goals were the same, so I couldn't argue.

"Now take the man a fresh drink and apologize like you mean it. And do *not* give me a reason to have to repeat this conversation. That's an order." With that, Tower stepped out of the alcove and back into his party, smiling at acquaintances like he'd never had a sour thought in his life.

I started to make my way back to Holt so I could publicly choke on the crow Jake had shoved down my throat, but when I scanned the crowd, checking on Kenley out of habit, I found her with Jonah Tower, who smirked at me silently while he rubbed her bare back with one hand, until she shrugged out from under his touch.

And suddenly I wanted to vomit.

I backed into the alcove again and stayed there for another minute, fighting the flashes of memory that played behind my eyelids—a montage of pain and humiliation, overlaid with the terrifying certainty that if I failed, it would all happen again, this time to my little sister.

I swallowed compulsively to keep my dinner down, breathing deeply, like Kenley had showed me. So far, when the basement resurfaced in my head, the only thing able to beat it back when I couldn't take out my rage on the nearest boxing dummy was steady, measured breathing. Balancing each inhalation with an exhalation.

Kenley said I was imposing calm on everything else by instituting order in the most basic of involuntary functions. Or some shit like that.

I didn't care how it worked. All I cared about was that it *did* work. Usually.

When I opened my eyes again, the buzz of conversation and laughter roared back into focus and the looming darkness of the basement was gone, at least for the moment.

Remember who you were before, Kori. I had to remember and become her again, or I might die without the chance to claim vengeance or reclaim the woman I'd been.

I straightened my dress—stupid fucking sequins— and squared my shoulders, then took one more deep breath and stepped back into the fray.

That was the only way I could think of this night and hope to succeed. The party was a battle to be fought, not with bullets, but with pointless social gestures and small talk. I could do this. Every polite smile would find its mark. Every swallowed curse would block a blow. And every bitter concession made to polite society would bring me one step closer to the goal. To signing Ian Holt and protecting my sister.

If the party was a brawl, then Holt was my enemy, but he couldn't be beaten with fists or knives. He could only be lulled into submission—into lowering his guard—with subterfuge. With careful answers and gestures of compliance.

I could play that part. I'd *have* to play that part. Starting now.

I watched him as I closed in on my target, dodging hits from other combatants—Jake would call them guests—even as I armed myself with two fresh glasses of champagne from a tray carried by a passing waiter, an unwitting accomplice in my campaign.

Holt wasn't *bad*-looking. In fact, he was actually kind of hot, blessed with broad shoulders, a strong chin, and the smooth, dark complexion only mixed parentage could give. Or maybe that was the champagne talking. I could toss back vodka all day long, but I'd never been able to think clearly on anything fancy. Probably from lack of practice.

While I was still several feet away, two familiar silhouettes stepped between me and my goal. They were both brunette and curvy, and less than two years bound, yet eager to make names for themselves. They were also on Jake's shit list for refusing to believe after one crack at him that he could not be tempted to stray from his wife, even for a double dose of sin served hot and ready.

Within seconds of their arrival, Holt looked ready

to flee the premises. I exhaled slowly and donned my mental armor, then stepped back onto the front lines, right between the two brash sluts, who gaped at me like I'd just insulted their strappy footwear.

"You'll have to excuse us," I said, handing Holt one of the glasses so I could link my arm through his. I couldn't come up with a believable reason *why* they'd have to excuse us, so I didn't bother. I just steered him away from the wild hyena women and through the crowd, half enjoying the angry looks they shot my way.

A victory is a victory. The venue is irrelevant.

"Not that I don't appreciate the rescue," Holt said. "But I'm forced to ask, in the interest of self-preservation… exactly how well armed are you right now?"

I laughed, and it wasn't even forced. Probably because even with the smile hovering on the edge of his expression, his joke wasn't really a joke—he was actually asking.

"Guns leave unsightly bulges in an evening gown." Which I was only wearing under direct orders. "Tonight, what you see is what you get." Jake had made it clear that I had not yet earned back the privilege of carrying weapons in his territory, after letting him get shot. "But don't worry, there's enough security in here to rival the U.S. Mint. No one could possibly get an unauthorized gun through the door."

"I wasn't worried about getting shot," Holt said, as we wound our way through the crowd. "Perhaps ritualistically castrated and dismembered…"

"Okay, I'm sorry about the threat," I said, though that wasn't really true. "But they say you can't underestimate the value of a good first impression."

He stopped walking to frown at me. "Your idea of a

good first impression is to threaten a man's groin and his life in one breath?"

I shrugged. "Why? Would taking a breath in between improve the delivery?"

"I suppose not." He drained the last inch of champagne from his glass, then set it on an empty tray as a waiter passed. Then he turned back to me, his expression caught somewhere between confusion and amusement. "You're not what I expected from Jake Tower's envoy."

"What did you expect?" I was honestly curious.

"Someone like her." Holt nodded at something over my shoulder, and I turned to find Nina, Jake's personal assistant, schmoozing with the lieutenant governor, one hand on his arm, her gaze locked with his as she laughed at whatever asinine story he'd just told. I'd heard every story he had. They were all asinine.

I started to ask Holt if he'd rather have Nina show him around—surely Jake wouldn't make me play recruiter if the recruit didn't want me around after all—but he was already speaking again, this time watching a group clustered near the windows on the west wall. "Or someone like your sister."

I glanced at him in surprise, then followed his line of sight again to where Kenley stood against the wall, Jonah hovering near her like a kid eager to show off his prom date, and I realized Jake had probably told his brother to stick close to her, to remind me of what was at stake with this job.

Everything. That's what was at stake.

Kenley and our brother, Kris, were all I had left, and Kris had his hands full with our grandmother. Kenley was my responsibility, and I couldn't let her down. Even if that meant conning some clueless asshole into service at Tower's whims.

"Kenley would make a terrible tour guide," I said, more to myself than to him, still watching my sister play the wallflower. She wouldn't give Jonah any excuse to touch her. "She doesn't get out much."

"Out of what?" Holt asked, and I forced my mind back to the conversation at hand.

"Outside. Jake keeps her close at hand. Because of the nature of her work." And too late I realized how that probably sounded.

"Your sister lives here? In Tower's house? Do they…? Um…?"

I scowled. "No, my sister isn't screwing the boss." Nothing could be further from the truth. "She's his top Binder—the only one he really uses anymore—so he keeps her close to keep her safe. She has a small apartment near here." And she was always under guard.

"Oh." Holt looked relieved, and briefly I wondered why he cared who Jake was screwing. Was he a prude or a perv?

"I used to live here, though," I said, picking at the seams of his reaction. "In this house."

"You used to…?" He glanced from me to Jake and back, and I could practically see the gears turning behind his eyes as he tried to puzzle out a polite way to ask a crude question.

I rarely bother with polite. Makes things much simpler.

"Were you and he…?" Holt let the question trail off to its obvious conclusion.

"Do you ever finish a sentence?" I asked, and his cheeks darkened slightly as his brows rose in challenge.

"Do you ever think before you speak?"

I blinked, surprised. Jake said impulse control was my biggest character flaw. I'd always assumed he meant my tendency to hit first, then survey the situation as an afterthought, but Holt was clearly caught off guard by the verbal version of that.

"That's your problem." I backed slowly toward the foyer, leaving him to follow. "You think too much."

"I don't consider caution and forethought a problem."

"It takes you forever to order at a restaurant, doesn't it? And to pick out a tie?" I stepped closer and flicked his obnoxious little bow tie, then turned and stepped into the foyer, desperately hoping Kenley's stupid stilettos didn't seize that moment to betray me on the slick marble. Why do women insist on crippling themselves with footwear obviously designed by sadists?

Holt caught up with me, his mouth open to reply, but I spoke over him. "I tell you what. If you can dig up enough nerve to ask what you really want to know, I'll answer the question."

"Nerve isn't the issue." He stared straight into my eyes, practically daring me to argue. "What makes you think I care, one way or another?"

"The fact that you think too much. You overanalyze everything, like life's one big puzzle you can solve, if you can just find the pattern, and now you're thinking that neurotic tendency will help you figure out where you stand with one of the most powerful men in the country. You asked for a blonde liaison, and he gave you a blonde, so you're thinking—correctly—that that means he really wants you."

"You're on track so far," he admitted, amusement peeking around the edges of his skepticism.

"I know."

His eyes narrowed. "You're a Reader now?"

I almost laughed. "Hell no, I'm still just a Traveler."
Readers, like Julia Tower, read the truth in a person's
words. I read *people.* Their posture. Their expressions.
The things their brains didn't even know their bodies
were saying. That was the one quality I had that might
actually come in handy for a recruiter.

Holt looked relieved, and I wasn't surprised. Readers
make people nervous. Everyone lies, and no one wants
to be called on it.

"So what else am I thinking?" he asked, and his grin
said this had become a game.

I was not a fan of games, but when I played, I liked to
win. So I swallowed my trepidation over the direction
the discussion was headed and pressed forward, wearing my game face.

"You know Jake wants you. But now it's a little more
complicated than that, right? If I'm Jake's sloppy seconds
and you take a big bite, it's gonna look like you're satisfied with his leftovers. And that's going to lower your
value. But on the other hand, he's given you what you
asked for, and turning your nose up at a gift from Jake
Tower could look like a massive insult. And you wanna
play hard-to-get, not difficult-to-stomach, right?"

Holt's green eyes were huge. "And you think *I* overanalyze things?"

But I was right. I could see that much in the irritated
way he crossed both arms over his chest, wrinkling his
expensive jacket. He'd expected to study Jake, and his
offer, and his people, but he hadn't expected a common
escort to study him back. Much less be good at it.

I shrugged and smiled, then turned away from him

and started across the foyer, calling softly over one shoulder, "Fine. Then don't ask."

His shoes squeaked after me on the marble, and I knew I had him. "Okay, I give up," he called, grabbing my arm from behind. I froze at his touch and had to remind myself that it meant nothing. *I* was flirting with *him*—albeit under orders to seduce him on behalf of the entire syndicate—so I couldn't justify freaking out over evidence that I was getting the job done.

But neither could I stop myself from pulling my arm from his grip, though I tried to disguise the movement by ducking into an alcove, drawing us both out of view from most of the rest of the party. "I admit it," he said, stepping close enough that I wanted to back up, but there was nowhere left to go. "I want to know."

With the wall at my back and Holt blocking my path, I felt like the world was closing in on me. My pulse raced with encroaching panic. But I'd brought us here, out of sight, and I was still in control of this little word game.

"Then grow some balls and ask," I said, staring straight up into his eyes, silently daring him.

One eyebrow arched in response to my challenge. "Were you sleeping with your boss?"

I shook my head solemnly. "I have never once fallen asleep in Jake Tower's company." In fact, it was tempting to try to blink one eye at a time when he was around, so I could keep the other one on him at all times.

Holt rolled his eyes. "You know what I mean."

"I know what you *asked*." I couldn't tell if he was adorably old-fashioned, hopelessly shy, or simply reluctant to offend a syndicate representative with a question about a very powerful man's personal life. "If that's not what you wanted to hear, then say what you mean."

"You're bossy."

I laughed. "And you're nosy, so get it over with. No more euphemisms. Bite the bullet, or I'm gonna have to tell Jake you don't have the balls for this job." That was a total bluff, of course. Jake would like him better with neither a mouth, nor the balls to use it.

That time when Holt frowned, I couldn't tell if he was pissed off or intrigued. Until he stepped closer, leaving no room between us at all, and I realized he was a little of both. "Did you fuck your boss?" he demanded, his voice lower and grittier than it'd been a moment before.

"Hell no." I slid along the wall, sidestepping him, and my heart didn't slow to normal speed until I'd regained personal space, and both flight and fight seemed possible again. Just in case. "Jake doesn't screw around on his wife." He wouldn't, even if he weren't contractually prohibited from touching another woman. At least, that was the rumor. "And FYI, he'll have you shot for looking at her for more than a few seconds at a time, unless she's talking directly to you."

"That's crazy."

I shrugged. "That's love."

That hint of a grin was back. "Isn't that what I said?"

"Ah, a cynic." I sank onto a gold-padded bench against one wall of the foyer. "You may fit in here after all."

Holt sat next to me. "So, why did you live here, if you weren't…with him?"

And, the euphemisms were back. "Jake used to keep a small staff on hand at all times. But he moved everyone out a few weeks ago." The day after I'd accidentally punched a hole in his home defense system and gotten him shot. "Now it's just his family, the nanny, and whichever guards are currently on duty."

"Smart." Holt nodded thoughtfully. "And he really doesn't cheat on his wife? At all?"

"Nope. Not once, that I know of. Why?"

"I want to know who I'll be working for. If I sign on." He glanced to his right, toward the party still going on in the main part of the house. "A man like that, with plenty of money, in a position of extreme power over dozens of beautiful women…" He glanced at me, as if to say I was one of those beautiful women. Or maybe he was pointing out that I was powerless. "It has to be tempting to sample the goods. It'd be easy to get away with. In certain circles, it's practically expected, right?" he said, and I could only nod. "But Tower's loyal to his wife. That says something, doesn't it? Something about him, as a man?" Holt watched me closely, studying my reaction, and an uneasy feeling churned deep in my stomach.

Most syndicate employees didn't have the luxury of caring what kind of man Tower was, or what kind of business he did. They signed on because they were desperate for something they couldn't get for themselves. Usually money, protection or services only a syndicate could provide. Why else would you sign over even part of your free will to someone who doesn't give a damn whether you live or die, so long as you do both in service to the syndicate?

But Holt was different. He actually gave a damn. Which could make him very hard to recruit.

"Doesn't that also say something about the way Tower runs his organization?" He waited for my answer, staring into my eyes like he wanted to see past them and into my thoughts, and suddenly I recognized the ploy, and my teeth ground together.

Ian Holt wasn't naive enough to believe that a man

with Jake's power and breadth of influence had climbed
to the top of the hill without stepping on a few heads. Or
that fidelity to his wife translated into any kind of integ-
rity in business. He knew what the Tower syndicate was
like—at least, he *thought* he knew—and this was a test
to see which I would choose: loyalty to my boss or honesty to the potential recruit.

Assuming I had any choice in the matter. And he had
no way of knowing whether or not I did.

He'd see through a lie—he seemed to be expecting
one anyway—but I couldn't exactly tell him the truth
about Jake and the syndicate, even if he already knew
most of it. Or even some of it. Which brought up an even
bigger problem.

If Holt already knew what kind of man Tower was and
what kind of business he ran, why did he accept Jake's
invitation in the first place? I could only think of two
possible reasons. First, Holt had no moral qualms about
syndicate business or lifestyle. Or, second, he couldn't
afford the luxury of indulging whatever moral qualms
he did have. Which meant he was either corrupt or desperate.

But then a third, even worse possibility occurred to
me and that uneasy feeling in my stomach swelled into
a roiling discomfort. What if Holt was neither of those?
What if he was just some curious, greedy asshole looking to get everything he could out of Jake before politely
turning down our offer and walking away with his free
will intact?

If that happened, I would have to harvest Holt's blood
instead. And if I handed over nothing but blood from a
venture this expensive, when what Tower really wanted
was Holt's service, Jake would kill me. But first he'd give

Kenley to Jonah, down in the basement, so that the last thing I ever heard would be my sister screaming.

Bile rose in my throat, and I swallowed a sip of warm champagne to keep it down. And when I looked up, I realized that Holt was still waiting for my answer to a question I'd almost forgotten.

"Does Jake's fidelity to his wife say something about how he runs the organization?" I said, rephrasing the original question, and Holt nodded. "Yeah, I guess it does. There's nothing Jake wouldn't do for his wife, and even less he wouldn't do for the syndicate."

Including kill me and torture my sister.

The thought of damning someone else to the hell I was living in made me want to light my own hair on fire and take a bath in gasoline. But I would do it. I'd do whatever it took to make Holt sign.

I had no other choice.

Four

Ian

"**W**hich is it you dislike, parties or champagne?" I asked, nodding pointedly at the virtually untouched flute in her right hand, as the party buzzed on without us.

Kori blinked, obviously struggling to refocus her attention, and twisted to face me on the ornate gold couch, both an expensive eyesore and an uncomfortable perch. "It's parties *with* champagne. And food served in bites too small to taste."

I laughed. "You'd rather drink from a trough and eat from a bucket?"

"I'd rather eat from a paper wrapper and drink from the fuckin' bottle."

"And your bottle of choice?" She had yet to say anything I'd expected to hear, and I couldn't help wondering what would come out of her mouth if we got a chance to talk about something more meaningful than appetizers.

"Vodka."

Any of the waiters could probably have gotten her whatever she wanted to drink, but I couldn't really talk to her surrounded by two hundred other partygoers, and if I couldn't talk to her, I couldn't make her trust me.

"And since you used to live here, you'd probably know where Tower might keep a bottle of vodka...?"

"I might."

"So maybe we could grab that and go for a walk on the grounds, free from the intrusion of pointless small talk as well as bite-size snacks."

Kori hesitated, and for a second, I was certain that she didn't want to be alone with me. Then she glanced at the guard stationed on either side of the front entrance. "They're never going to let you wander around the property without an escort from security."

"Aren't you an escort from security?"

She huffed, and I wondered what I was missing. "It's complicated. I protect you, but *they* protect Jake and his interests, which would not be served by giving an unbound man free access to the grounds. We could sneak out, but the patrol would probably find us."

"Then it sounds to me like we have two options. We can ditch the party entirely and forage for a bottle of vodka elsewhere—"

"Jake would be pissed if we leave without telling him..." she said, and I nodded, not surprised.

"Or we could go upstairs, which—I'm willing to bet—isn't being patrolled."

She gave me a conspiratorial grin. "That's because no one's allowed upstairs. Jake's kids are asleep in the family wing, so there's a guard at the foot of both staircases." She glanced over her shoulder, and I followed her gaze to the closer of two mirror-image staircases, where a huge man dressed all in black stood directly in front of the bottom step, arms clasped at his back. He was obviously armed, and if his expression was any indication, he suffered from a severe lack of personality.

"But you used to be a guard, so you could take one of them, couldn't you?" I teased. "If I were to snatch a butter knife from the kitchen, you could bisect him from neck to groin in a single stroke, right?"

Her smile spread slowly, and her brown eyes practically sparkled. "Hell yeah. But Kenley will kill me if I get arterial spray on her dress." She slid one hand over her own hip to where the dress ended above her crossed knees, and my gaze traced the path, before I realized what I was doing.

Oh, *hell* no.

Don't believe a word they say. Don't let your guard down. And do not *make friends.*

I'd heard it over and over, from Aaron. Hell, I'd said it over and over to myself. I couldn't get personally involved. I couldn't afford to see any of them as real people. They were a means to an end. Tools for me to use, like a wrench, or a hammer. Kori Daniels was the hammer I'd have to swing to smash through Jake Tower's defenses and gain access to his prized possession, and you couldn't be attracted to a hammer. Right?

But she'd have to *think* I liked her, or she'd never trust me. And if she didn't trust me, she'd never let me near her sister. Kenley Daniels. The woman whose blood had the power to ruin lives—or end them.

"Okay, blood splatter is a problem," I admitted. "But you're a Traveler, right? So, you could just walk us both through a shadow down here and out of one up there, couldn't you?" I glanced at what I could see of the second floor for emphasis.

Kori shook her head. "Infrared grid. There isn't a true

shadow in this entire house, except for the darkroom. None deep enough for me to step through, anyway."

"What if there was?" I glanced around to make sure no one was listening, then I stood and started to tug her into the alcove she'd led me to minutes earlier. But she stiffened before I could touch her, and I realized I hadn't imagined her pulling away from me before. But I didn't understand it.

She was just a hammer to me, and I was just a job to her. An assignment. Korinne was the bait sent to reel me in, and for all I knew, she did this on a weekly basis. She flirted and cajoled, in a teasing, I-dare-you kind of way, clearly gauging my interest, and she probably knew far better than I did how to stay detached. How to attract without being attracted. How to engage without engaging your emotions, or even your desires.

So why the physical distance?

Was that part of Tower's pitch? Show me the menu, but don't let me order until I'd officially signed on? Or was Kori defining her own boundaries between work and play?

I was almost jealous of how well she played the game. And I was more determined than ever to keep in mind the fact that this *was* a game. A charade, of sorts. The woman, the party, the champagne and fancy clothes— they were nothing but a pretty mask covering an ugly beast that, behind its beguiling smile, waited to devour me.

"What if there was what?" she asked, standing without my help, and I had to drag my thoughts back on topic. Again.

"What if there was a true shadow upstairs? What if I could *make* a shadow? A real one? There's no way we could both get past the guard, but if you distract him, I could sneak up and make a shadow for you to walk through. Then you could find that bottle, and we could both forget about the crowd for an hour or so."

Because that part was real. She hated the party and the champagne, and the more comfortable—and less sober—I could make her, the better my chances of conning classified information from her. Like how well guarded her sister was at various times of the day. Or better yet, how to get into and out of Kenley's apartment in the middle of the night.

Her pale brows rose in surprise. "You can black out infrared light?"

I leaned closer and put one finger over my lips. "Shh. I'm pretty sure that's most of why Tower wants me. So yes, if you can get me upstairs, I can open a hole in the infrared grid, through which you could then join me."

"A cynic *and* a rule breaker. I like it." Her smile widened just a bit, and too late I realized I was returning it with one of my own. "And if we get caught?"

I shrugged. "I'll say I was giving you a demonstration of my Skill, for recruiting purposes." But she looked uncertain, so I tried again. "Tower told you to keep me happy, right?" No one had actually come out and said that, but it was no stretch of the imagination. Kori nodded, her smile fading fast. "So he can't get mad at you for doing your job, can he?"

She frowned, like she wanted to argue, but wouldn't. Or couldn't.

I arched one brow at her. "Never mind. If you're too scared…"

"Motherfucker…" she mumbled, rolling her eyes over my dare, and I couldn't resist another smile. "Fine. But it'll have to be the far staircase, and you ll have to be quick. And make sure no one else is watching."

"No problem."

"You ready?" she asked, and I could tell from the curve at the edge of her mouth that she was getting into the spirit of the adventure.

"Almost." I took the champagne flute from her hand and drained it with one gulp, then set it on the floor next to the wall. "What's your plan?" I asked, glancing at the guard on the far side of the foyer. "Flirt? Take him a drink?"

She shook her head. "He wouldn't buy either of those, coming from me. Don't worry about it. Just wait until he steps away from the stairs, then haul ass. And be quiet." Then she turned and headed across the foyer without so much as a glance back.

I tried not to watch her walk away, but failed miserably, and by the time I realized I was staring, she was in position. She walked right past the guard without a word, and I thought she'd changed her mind about the whole thing until he called out to her, though I couldn't make out more than her name, from across the large foyer.

I started across the floor, my hands in my pockets, prepared to claim I was looking for the restroom if I were accosted. The guard in front of the near staircase eyed me as I passed him, but when I didn't try to race up the stairs at his back, he turned to stare into the party again, obviously disappointed that his post wasn't closer to the action.

There was a broad expanse of floor between the two sets of stairs, and in the center of that, opposite the double front doors, was a smaller set of doors leading to a courtyard in the middle of the house. Several couples milled outside, sitting on benches, drinking and nibbling from plates of those hors d'oeuvres Kori hated. I stood near the door, blocked from sight by the curve of stairs, listening to her conversation with the second guard. Which turned out to be less conversation than argument.

"Look who's playin' dress up…" the guard said, but his tone was neither friendly nor flirty. "I've never seen you in a dress before."

"And you never will again, if I have any say."

"You don't, though, do you?" he said, and when she tried to keep walking, he grabbed her arm, hauling her close, his back to me and the staircase. And in that moment, I understood why she'd pulled away from me when I'd held her arm. "You don't have a say in anything anymore, do you?"

"Fuck off, David," Kori snapped, and I started to step in, thinking that her plan had gone awry. Then she jerked free from his grip and walked off. When he took several steps after her, I realized this was how she'd planned to distract him. Not by flirting, but by pissing him off. She'd known he'd follow. Maybe they had some kind of history. A grudge, or a former fling.

"I caught the show, you know," the guard said softly, like he didn't want anyone else to hear. Which meant he had no idea I was there.

I started to slip up the stairs, but then I noticed through the railing that Kori had gone still again, this time staring at the floor, fists clenched at her sides. "Shut up," she whispered.

The guard stepped closer, so close his chest almost touched her back, and I could see her tense when he leaned down to whisper into her ear, words so soft I had to strain to hear them. "All this time, turning your nose up at everyone who wanted a taste, busting balls and splitting skulls with impunity because Tower liked you. But look at you now. My, how the mighty have fallen…"

"I'm pretty sure that's a misquote," she mumbled, as he circled her slowly, and I ducked behind the staircase again, out of sight, unless the guard on the other side of the foyer turned to look.

"Fits, though, doesn't it. The taller the pedestal, the harder the bitch on it crashes to the ground. Do you want to know what we saw?"

"I want you to back the fuck off before I decide you'd look better with your nose on one side of your face."

"That was some messed up shit, Kori," he continued, like she hadn't even spoken. "I mean, I wanted to see you taken down a peg or two, but that was hard to watch, even for me. How you doin' in the aftermath? Need a shoulder to—"

The guard's voice ended with the *thunk* of flesh against flesh, and I came forward until I could see him through the railing, lying flat on the floor, bleeding from his nose. Kori stood over him, feet spread in those stupid stilettos, bloodied fist still clenched from the blow.

She thought I was already upstairs—I could tell by the look of pure rage on her face, something she wouldn't have intentionally shown a recruit. She didn't know what I'd seen or what I'd heard. Hell, *I* didn't know what I'd heard. But it made my stomach churn.

Aaron was right—they were monsters in human masks, and those masks were less convincing with every second I spent staring at them.

The guard coughed at Kori's feet and started to sit up, but she planted one pointy heel in his crotch to stop him. I glanced across the foyer at the other guard to make sure he wasn't watching, and when I saw that he was staring at the party still going strong in the main part of the house, out of sight from my current position, I jogged silently up the stairs—hunched over so she wouldn't see me—and into the first open, dark room I saw.

Faintly, from below, I heard Kori's heels click on marble, fading with each step as she headed for the front door.

For one long moment, I stood frozen, listening for anything that would indicate the west wing—the employee wing, where Kori'd once lived—was currently populated. But I heard nothing. So I pressed my back against the wall with the door still open to the hall and closed my eyes, slowly drawing darkness toward me from every shadowed corner and shaded nook in the room. I called to it, from every darkened crack beneath every door in the hall. And the shadows began to coalesce around my feet, curling around my shins, wisps of pure darkness rolling over me.

I lifted my hands, and the shadows rose with them, roiling around me, an inky oblivion, deeper and more satisfying than the shallow dark rendered useless by the infrared lighting grid I could feel overhead, blazing beyond the visible spectrum.

The darkness was cool and quiet. It was peace given form and function. I could feel it with every cell in my body, deep into the marrow of my bones. Into my soul. The darkness was mine to command.

Until half a minute later, when Kori Daniels stepped out of it and onto my right foot.

"Ow!" I laughed as the pointed toe of her dress shoe ground into my foot, and she stepped back immediately.

"Sorry!" she whispered, and I felt rather than saw

her trip over her own shoes in the absolute darkness. I reached out for her instinctively, but let go as soon as she'd regained balance. "You did this?" she whispered again, from inches away, and I realized that if I couldn't see her, she couldn't see me.

"Yeah."

"Holy shit, that's incredible," she breathed. Something moved between us, and it took me a moment to realize she was spreading her arms in the shadow I'd made, like a child in the rain. "It's like finding a watering hole in the desert. A shadow on the sun."

"Yeah, except I didn't find it. I made it." Couldn't hurt to remind her how valuable I was.

I began to let the darkness go, a little at a time, and slowly light filtered in again from the hallway, feeling much brighter than it should have, after the absolute darkness. "That was impressive," she said, when she could see well enough that her gaze met mine in the shadows. "No wonder Jake wants you."

"He's not the only one," I said, and her brows rose in interest as she stepped back and glanced around at the unoccupied bedroom.

"Oh? Who else is courting you, Mr. Holt?"

"Ruben Cavazos, most notably," I whispered, following her toward the door. "Along with a couple of the smaller syndicates on the West Coast."

"Cavazos." She practically spit his name, stepping out of the first of her shoes. "You don't want anything to do with him."

I laughed softly and tried not to notice the shape of her calves as she took off the second shoe. "I'd hardly expect you to endorse the competition."

Kori straightened, holding both shoes by the straps in one hand. "He fucking shot me."

"Cavazos shot you?" I could hear the surprise in my own voice.

Instead of answering, she pulled the left shoulder strap of her dress down to expose a puckered scar on her shoulder, still pink and fresh. "Two months ago."

"What happened?"

"Clash of the titans." Barefoot, she peeked into the hall, then gestured for me to follow her. "Everyone fights for one side or the other."

"Are we sneaking?" I whispered, nodding at her shoes, wondering if I should take my own off.

"Nah. There's no one in this wing. I just hate heels."

I followed her down the hall and around the corner to the right. Three doors later, she turned left into a room with a billiard table in the center of the floor and a full-size bar along one wall. "Close the door," she said over one shoulder as she dropped her shoes on the floor and headed for the bar.

I pushed the door closed softly, then crossed the room and took a seat on the center bar stool while she took up the position of bartender.

"What'll it be?" She leaned forward with her elbows on the polished dark wood surface of the bar.

"Scotch?"

Kori rolled her eyes. "Of *course* you drink Scotch."

"Are you calling me a stereotype?"

"Not yet, but if you don't pull some surprises out of your hat soon, I suspect that moment is coming." She dug beneath the bar and came up with a single short glass while I tried to decide how to respond to such a challenge. She wasn't ready for any of my real surprises, and she never would be. Which was why I couldn't get emotionally involved. Why I had to keep telling myself that she was just a hammer. A hammer with really nice legs, and eyes the color of good caramel, and…

Focus.

"Creating darkness wasn't enough of a surprise?"

She laughed. "It was a start. Ice?"

"Four cubes."

Kori scooped ice into the glass and set a half-full bottle of very expensive Scotch in front of me. I held it up, examining the label, reluctantly impressed with Tower's taste. "How much trouble will we be in if we get caught?"

"We're not going to get caught. If we hear footsteps, you make it dark, and I'll make us disappear." She produced a bottle of Grey Goose from beneath the counter, then circled the bar to sit on the stool next to mine. "There's snack mix if you want, but you're gonna have to serve yourself."

"What are you going to do?"

"This." She twisted the lid off the bottle and gulped from it once, twice, three times, without flinching.

"Rough night?" I asked, thinking about what I'd overheard.

"Any night that sees me in three-inch heels and sequins is a rough night." She set the bottle on the bar, the cork stopper still clasped in one hand. "But I've certainly seen worse."

I watched her, and after nearly a minute of staring off into space, she turned to face me. "What?"

"You drink like a man."

She shrugged and glanced at the bottle I had yet to pour from. "One of us should."

I wanted to ask, but at the same time, I didn't want to know. Whatever the guard—David—had seen done to her was none of my business, and it wasn't relevant to the job at hand. I already knew Tower was the scum of the earth, without having to hear the specifics.

And for no reason I could have explained, I didn't want her to know I'd heard.

"So, what do you think so far?" She tilted her bottle up again as I poured from mine, then she wiped her mouth with the back of one hand. "Seen anything yet worth signing over your soul for?"

"Is that what I'd be signing away? My soul?" I happened to agree, but I was surprised to hear it from her.

Kori blinked, like she'd just realized she'd said too much—that pesky honesty getting in the way again. But she recovered quickly. "Nah. Just five years of your life. The standard term of service for most syndicates."

"How close are you to the five-year mark?" I picked up my glass and sipped from it, savoring a liquor I could never personally afford, trying not to think about the fact that if I were alone with the other Daniels sister, this whole thing could be over in a matter of seconds. My objective hadn't changed, but the strategy certainly had. Use one sister to get to the other. And to do that, I'd have to pretend to be recruitable.

"Five years came and went nearly a year and a half ago." She twisted to show me her left arm, and the two interlocking chain links tattooed there. Marks of service. "One for each term."

I'd already seen them, of course, and I already knew what they meant. She was six and a half years into a ten-year commitment to serve Jake Tower and his syndicate. Her oath had been sealed with two linking tattoos, each containing a tiny bit of his blood—a flesh binding. Until the day her commitment expired and her tattoos faded into the dull gray of dead marks, she would be compelled to follow his orders, or she would die fighting the compulsion.

Syndicate service was a miserable way to live. And often a miserable way to die. Only three kinds of people joined voluntarily: the ignorant, the ambitious and the desperate.

Which category did Kori fit into? Which would be most believable for me?

"You must like it here, then, if you signed on for another term," I said, trying to embrace the part I had to play.

Kori blinked, then took another swig of vodka, straight. Then she shoved the corked lid back into the bottle and pushed the Goose away, like it might be to blame for whatever she was about to say. "This is my home."

I frowned. It felt like she was starting a new conversation, rather than continuing the one already in progress. "No, this is your job."

"You really don't understand, do you?" she asked, and I let my frown deepen, so she would explain what I already knew, and I would listen and respond, and ask all the right questions, and with every minute that passed she would trust me a little more, because she would know I was no threat. She had all the power, because she had all the knowledge.

And because she thought she could cut my balls off with one hand while slicing my throat open with the other.

Kori exhaled slowly, and a brief glimpse of guilt flickered across her face, like she was already regretting the pitch she was about to throw at me. That told me she was neither ambitious nor ignorant—at least, not after more than six years of service, which came as no surprise, after what I'd overheard on the stairs.

And that only left desperate.

"When you sign on with a syndicate—any syndicate, not just this one—you're not just taking a job, you're becoming part of a community. Like an extended family. You're getting job security, medical care, personal protection and virtually limitless resources. The syndicate isn't just employment—it's a way of life. A very stable, secure way of life."

"Sounds awesome." It also sounded like a very well-rehearsed speech. "What's the catch? Is it all the following orders? Because honestly, that's what I balk at." To say the very, very least.

"There's some of that, of course. But that's not really so different from any other job, is it?" she asked, and I couldn't help noting that now that I'd pointed out a flaw in the system, she was referring to it as a mere job again. "Any workplace is a hierarchy, right? There's a CEO, management, and the rest of the employees. Everyone has a boss, except whoever's at the top. That's how we operate, too."

"Yes, but in any other job, you can quit if you don't like the orders."

"That's not true." She smiled, like she'd caught me in a lie. "You can't just quit military service if you don't like the orders."

"So, would you say service to the Tower syndicate is more like military service than like a civilian job?"

She had to think about that for a minute. "Yeah, I

guess, only without the patriotism and gratitude from your fellow citizens. Large community. Great benefits. They even get chevrons for time in service." She twisted to show me her arm again, to emphasize the parallel.

But I knew what she wasn't saying—in the military, you can take the chevrons off at the end of the day, but the syndicate owns you for the life of the mark, twenty-four hours a day, seven days a week. You're never off the clock. And the word *no* has no meaning. I couldn't understand why anyone would ever sign on for that.

"Okay, obviously following orders is what's bothering you, and I can understand that. So why don't we just lay the truth out on the table?"

"The truth?" I watched her in interest. The truth was a rarity in life in general and even more so in the syndicate. Only the fearless and the foolish wielded it so boldly, and I already knew Kori Daniels was no fool.

"Blinders are rare, and you're the best I've ever seen. That makes you very valuable, and I'd bet my best knife that we're not the only ones who've made you an offer?" Her sentence ended on a question, and I could only nod. "Right now, everyone's playing nice and pulling out the best china because you're being recruited. But if that doesn't work, you'll be hunted. And eventually you *will* be caught, and when that happens, you'll be all out of choices. It's a winner-takes-all kind of game."

"I'm assuming there's a silver lining to this cloud of doom?" The cloud that had been hanging over me since I was twelve years old, when my mother explained how the rarity and power of my Skill would shape the rest of my life. As a kid, I'd thought she was being paranoid. As an adult, I'd learned better.

"The silver lining is that at this stage in the game, you

can still decide what mark you want to bear. Who you want to serve. Because you *will* wind up serving someone." Kori shrugged and glanced longingly at the corked bottle of vodka. "Hell, I'm not sure how you went unnoticed as long as you did."

Flying below the syndicates' radar hadn't been easy, and dipping beneath it again once this was over would no doubt be even harder.

"That's a rather ominous bit of truth," I said, committing to nothing.

Kori shrugged again. "It can't be changed, so you might as well understand your options."

"And those would be…?"

"The Tower syndicate, or some other, inferior organization."

Or…door number three, the option she either didn't know existed or didn't believe possible: hide.

"And the others are inferior because…?"

"Because we have the best of everything." She leaned closer, and I expected to smell vodka on her breath, but I couldn't, and suddenly I wanted to kiss her, to see if I could taste it. Or maybe just to taste her.

I blinked in surprise at the thought, but Kori didn't seem to notice. She was still talking.

"Jake wants you," she said, staring straight into my eyes. "I mean he *really* fucking wants you, which gives you more power going into negotiations than most people have. You could get just about whatever you want out of him."

Was it my imagination, or did she seem a little pleased at the idea of me taking Tower for all he was worth? More than pleased. She looked…excited. Her lips parted and her eyes shone with eagerness. She looked *fierce,* like the chain links on her arm could restrain her, but never truly tame her.

And as she watched me, probably waiting to see the gleam of greed that would tell her I was interested, I had a sudden, dangerous, treacherous thought. What would Tower give me, if I asked? Would he give me *her?*

I hated the thought as soon as I'd had it. People can't be given as gifts. They shouldn't be, anyway. Especially people like Kori Daniels, whose nature obviously couldn't be suppressed, even by direct orders. Giving her to someone else would be like caging a wild bird, only to see the bright, beautiful feathers you loved fall out and fade at the bottom of the cage.

But with that one lecherous thought, and the momentary failure of my own moral compass, I suddenly understood why someone might join a syndicate. Someone who wanted or needed something badly. Something he had no chance of getting on his own.

Everyone has a price. Tower's advantage in life was that he knew that and had no problem exploiting it.

"What is it you think I should ask for?" I turned my glass up and drank until the ice cubes bumped my lip, Scotch scorching its way down my throat, where I wished it could purge that lascivious thought from me. I couldn't afford to want the bait dangled in front of me. "What could I possibly ask for that would make it easier to take orders?"

"An extra chain link." She poured more Scotch into my glass, and I watched her light up with excitement over an idea I obviously didn't understand. She was beautiful in that moment. Intense, and dangerous.

"If I don't want the orders that come with signing on for five years, why the hell would I sign on for ten?"

"You wouldn't." Kori smiled and pushed the glass toward me. "You'd ask—no, you'd *demand* a second mark for free. A five-year commitment, with the seniority of a second-tier initiate. With two chain links, there are fewer people who can boss you around, thus fewer orders to follow."

"Why stop there? Why not ask for three or four links?"

Kori's expression darkened, and that spark in her eyes died. She leaned over the bar to grope for something and when she sat down again, she had a plastic jar of snack mix in one hand. "Seniority comes with responsibility. The more you ask him for, the more he'll want from you in return."

Things I wasn't going to want to do, obviously.

"Two is the perfect number." She unscrewed the lid on the snack mix and offered me the jar. "You have enough rank to avoid static from the bottom two rungs, but not enough seniority to obligate you to do…things above your pay grade."

I took a handful of pretzels and peanuts. "Things like what?"

Kori just scrounged up a small smile and shook her head. "Even if I knew what my superiors' duties were, I couldn't tell you. Some things—many things—you can't know until you bear his mark."

I wanted to pursue the issue. I wanted to ask her if Tower had ever given her an order she didn't want to follow. If he'd ever made her do something that made her skin crawl or rotted a bit of her soul. But picking at her emotional scabs—making her talk about things she obviously didn't want to remember—seemed cruel. *Too* cruel, considering what else I had to do. I hadn't come into Tower's territory to be recruited by Kori Daniels.

I'd come to kill her sister.

Five

Kori

I'd said too much. I could tell from the way he was sipping his second glass of Scotch, looking at me like I was some code he'd already started to crack. Like he could rearrange the words I'd spoken until they said what he needed to hear.

Holt knew what to ask. He knew what *not* to ask. I wasn't sure whether I was playing him or being played *by* him, and that scared the shit out of me. I had to regain the upper hand, or Kenley would pay for my failure.

"You done with that?" he asked, and I followed his focus to the bottle of Goose.

"Almost." I uncorked the bottle and took another swig, then pushed the cork back in.

"Well, you might as well take it with you," Jake said, and I turned so fast the room spun around me. He stood in the doorway, leaning against the frame like he'd been there all night. "No one else is going to want any, after your mouth's been on the bottle."

I wondered how much he'd seen. How much he'd heard. But I got nothing from his expression, as usual.

"The alcohol will kill any germs," I said, but I took the bottle with me when I stood. Never let it be said that I turned down good vodka. The shit under my bed at Kenley's would take paint off a car.

"Are you ready to rejoin the party?" Jake said, as Holt finished his drink, still seated, and evidently unhurried.

Holt set his glass down, the remaining ice cubes small enough to swallow now. "Actually I'm kind of tired from my flight. I think I'm going to call it a night."

Jake nodded. "Kori will drive you to your hotel. But I'm sure Nina and Julia would like to say goodbye before you go." He stepped out of the doorway to let Holt pass, and when I started to follow, Tower blocked the doorway with his arm. "Korinne will meet you at the front door."

Holt glanced at me, then nodded and headed down the hall.

Jake closed the door behind him, and my hand clenched around the neck of the bottle I still held. "Explain," he ordered.

"You said to do whatever it takes."

"And recruiting Holt required Scotch from my personal liquor cabinet, in the off-limits portion of my home?"

I shrugged. "He has good taste."

"Shall I assume the privacy helped you get to know each other?" he asked, and I nodded. "And does he like you?"

"I don't know."

"Does he want you?"

"I don't—" I started, and Jake frowned. "Yeah, I think he does." There'd been this look in his eyes a few minutes ago… "But it's not personal. Anyone will do. We could send one of the girls to the hotel with him—"

Jake shook his head. "He rented a seventy-five-thousand-dollar car and drank my fifty-year-old Scotch. He's either putting on airs or living beyond his means, but either way, he doesn't want a common whore, Korinne. He wants something worth more. Someone with a little class. So dig deep and scrounge some up."

I didn't give a damn about the insult. I'd been called much worse than classless. But Holt had already seen me barefoot, drinking straight from the bottle. If classy was what he wanted, I wouldn't be able to fool him. But I couldn't tell Jake that, because if he thought I was worthless, I was as good as dead.

"Drive him to his hotel and walk him up to his room. Eat a breath mint, say please and thank you, and don't trip over the damn heels," he said, running one finger over the toes of the shoes I still held in my left hand. "Act like you're worth something, and he might just believe it. And Korinne?"

"Yeah?" My cheeks were flaming now. I could feel it.

"If you ever come upstairs in this house again without my permission, I'll put you back in the basement and let the guards draw straws. David's eager to pay you back for the broken nose."

It took every ounce of willpower I had to keep my hands from shaking. To pretend nothing he said could scare me. Jake didn't buy it, but that didn't matter.

What matters is the face you show the world, not the quaking mess behind it.

Twenty minutes later, I pulled up to the entrance of the Westmark Hotel and shifted into Park. The valet was waiting when I stepped out and handed the key to him, and the doorman had Holt's luggage out of the trunk before I'd even rounded the car. He followed us inside with the bags while I led Holt to the elevator. I'd checked him in and picked up his key cards that afternoon.

Tower had reserved a three-room suite for him. It was nice enough to tell Holt he was valued, but not nice enough to inflate his ego. The suite said "we want you, but not as much as you think we want you." And that might have worked, if I hadn't already told him that he could pretty much get whatever he wanted in exchange for his signature—my little fuck-you to the puppet master pulling my own strings. Jake would get Holt in the end, but he would pay out the ass for him, if I had anything to say about it.

On the twenty-third floor, I tipped the bellhop, then closed the door behind him and made a mental note of all the rugs likely to trip me in Kenley's stilettos. Then I began the tour.

"This is Jake's favorite hotel," I said, pulling back the curtains to show off the view. "They have twenty-four-hour room service. If you want something that's not on the menu, just use Jake's name. They'll get you anything you want. And there's a Jammer on duty 'round the clock, so you can't be tracked while you're here."

"Wow." Holt stared out the window at the city, and even I had to admit the view was amazing. You could see the river from his room, and all the boats were lit up, like a string of white Christmas lights. And if you squinted just right, you could see where the river split, dividing the city into three parts: the east side, the west side and the south fork, like the bottom third of a peace sign. I rarely ventured out of the west side—Jake's territory—

because the chain links on my arm could easily get me killed east of the river, on Ruben Cavazos's side of town.

"There's no place like home, I know, but you'll only be roughin' it for a few nights," I said, turning away from the window to take in the leather couches, thick rugs and huge flat-screen television. "Think you can manage?"

Holt pulled the curtains closed. "Only if the chocolate on my pillow is Swiss and the bottled water was flown in from France."

"Hand-collected by crippled orphans from the fountain of youth itself," I said, and he laughed, while I headed for the bedroom. I pushed open the double doors and sucked in a deep, shaky breath at the sight of the bed against the middle of the far wall. "King-size bed with pillow-top mattress," I said, crossing the room with quick, efficient steps.

The bathroom was next and I breathed a little easier just being out of the bedroom—until I remembered that the giant whirlpool tub was built for two. As was the walk-in shower with dual showerheads. I stared, frozen, desperately trying to summon words that wouldn't come, until his footsteps echoed behind me.

"You okay?"

"Yeah." I turned to see Holt in the doorway, blocking my path whether he meant to or not. "This is the bathroom, obviously." I brushed past him before he could step back and headed straight for the front room, where the exit called to me with singular purpose. But I stopped at the cabinet beneath the television instead. "And the best part is the minibar, fully stocked with overpriced snacks and alcohol." I pulled open the door to show off the selection. "I recommend…well, all of it. Help yourself. Take everything you can carry, and call down for more if you get the munchies in the middle of the night. It's all on Jake."

I looked up from the minibar to find Holt watching me, his expression caught somewhere between amusement and confusion, which I wished I could clear up for him. But I couldn't. I headed for the door and had one hand on the knob before I spoke. "Is there anything else I can do for you?"

The words burned my tongue, and I wanted a drink to put out the flames. Something strong enough to make the next part easier. Bearable. Maybe.

"No, I think I'm good," he said, and I blinked, sure I'd heard wrong. He didn't want…?

But I wasn't going to question my good fortune.

"Okay, then, I'll see you in the morning for breakfast. Around nine? Or did you want to sleep in?"

"Nine's fine," Holt said, and I dropped the key to his rental car on the small table next to the door.

"Good night." I was in the hall before he could respond. The door closed on whatever he was saying, and I took off down the hall, only pausing long enough to step out of my shoes, half convinced that if I didn't run, he'd change his mind and call me back.

My heart racing, I jogged past the elevator and into the stairwell, hoping for a shadow deep enough to walk through, but the stairs were lit up like a fucking runway, and I couldn't reach any of the bulbs to bust them. So I jogged down the first flight, then stopped on the twenty-second floor to use the elevator—no way I was going to walk down twenty-one flights of stairs.

On the first floor, I crossed the lobby like my bare feet were on fire and only breathed easy when I stepped outside, into the night, and spotted the entrance to an alley at the corner of the building.

Unlit alleys are the downfall of many an airheaded horror-movie bimbo, but they were my escape. My own personal transportation system, with free, unlimited rides.

I dashed past the doormen and valet attendants, still holding my sister's shoes, and ran into the alley, already picturing my room in Kenley's apartment, kept dark for situations exactly like this. My bare feet pounded from the grass onto the broken pavement, and a rock bruised my foot on my second step. With the third step, my foot landed on carpet, and a step after that, I collided with my own bedroom wall, and the rebound knocked me on my ass.

Dazed, I dropped the shoes and leaned back against the foot of the bed. A second later, my bedroom door flew open and the overhead light flared to life. "What the hell was that?" Kenley demanded, one hand still clutching the doorknob.

"Sorry. I forgot how small this room is."

"No more running starts, Kori," she said, letting go of the door to cross her arms over her chest. "You're gonna break your nose on the wall."

I half hoped she was right. A broken nose would make me ugly. And if I was ugly, Jake might pull me off the Holt job in favor of a prettier face.

Of course, knowing my luck, he'd kill me as punishment for messing it all up, then carry out his threat against Kenley, even though I wasn't there to see her abused. It would be just like him to try to make my afterlife miserable, too.

"How'd it go?" Kenley gave me her hand, and I let her pull me up. "Did you have to sleep with him?"

"No." *Not yet, anyway.*

She turned me by my shoulders and unzipped my dress. Which was really her dress, loose on me now, where it would have been tight two months earlier. I let the material slide to the floor, and she picked it up when I stepped out of it. "Is it just me, or does he look familiar?" Kenley said.

"It's you, and half the planet. The whole world saw that news clip."

"I kind of feel sorry for him," Kenley said. "They'll all be after him now." They, being the rival syndicates, of course.

"Don't." I grabbed the T-shirt slung over the end of my bed. The one I'd slept in the night before. "Don't you dare feel sorry for him. He's the idiot who revealed his Skill on national television. He's gonna have to sign with someone. It may as well be Jake." Holt's imprisonment may as well keep me alive and keep Kenley out of the basement.

"What's he like?" she asked.

"He's fine. Normal. Kinda funny. He doesn't deserve this." What I was doing to him. What I *had* to do to him, to save myself and my sister.

"No one deserves this." Kenley laid the dress across the bed and pulled a hanger from the closet, then stood staring at it, like she'd forgotten what to do with it. "I'm so sorry, Kori," she said, and I could hear the unshed tears in her voice.

"No." I pulled the T-shirt over my head, then lifted her chin, making her look at me. "You have nothing to be sorry for, so don't start this again. Please."

Kenley burst into tears and I pulled her into a hug, holding her until the wrenching sobs fractured into smaller cries, then broke down into teary hiccups I could handle. "This is all my fault," she said, wiping her cheeks when I let her go. "I'm so sorry for getting you into this."

"You didn't know. You couldn't have."

Six years earlier, at twenty years old, Kenley had still been sheltered and naive, because we'd made her that way. Kris, Gran and I had tried to protect the baby of the family, and instead we'd turned her into a victim, ready-made for a world full of predators. I shouldn't have been surprised when one found her. And I couldn't let her serve her time alone. "Besides, I signed on voluntarily. I make my own damn choices."

"Not anymore," she insisted. "And that's my fault."

"It's not your fault. But I can't argue with you about this anymore." I let go of her, and exhaustion washed over me, pulling me toward sleep with a force I couldn't resist. "Not tonight, okay, Kenni?"

She nodded and picked the hanger back up. "I'm sorry. You're not well yet. Two weeks isn't enough time for anyone to recover from…whatever they did to you. You still look half-starved."

"Some women do this to themselves on purpose, you know. Others pay to get this look." I spread my arms, trying not to see how thin I still looked in the mirror.

"Those women are crazy."

"No argument from me." I pulled a pair of fuzzy socks from my top drawer and stuffed my feet into them, trying to make up for the abuse they'd endured most of the night.

Kenley slid the straps of her dress into the notches on

top of the hanger. "So, do you know what you're going to do? How you're going to snag him?"

I followed her with the stilettos when she carried the dress into her own bedroom. "I'm going to snare him with my demure manner and natural charm, of course."

Kenley laughed.

"I don't think Jake realizes how much he's bitten off with this one, and I've tried to tell him I'm not a recruiter, but he won't listen to reason."

"It could be worse, though, right?" She hooked the hanger over the top of her closet door and knelt to dig through the junk on the floor. "I mean, he could be making you throw yourself at someone hideous, like the Tracker Monica had to reel in last month. He's truly—" She flinched when she realized what she'd said. I'd been locked up last month. All month. And I had yet to meet whatever ogre Monica had recruited to replace Cameron Caballero, when Cavazos bought out his contract. "Well, trust me, he's hairier than a gorilla and he smells even worse. At least Holt's clean. And he's nice-looking, right?"

I dropped the shoes into the box she held open for me. "He must be, if *you* noticed."

Kenley flushed and slid the box onto a stack of others in one corner of her closet. "Like you didn't."

I shrugged. We'd never actually talked about her taste in men. Or lack thereof. But I didn't give a damn whether she slept with men or women, or both at once, so long as it was her choice. So long as she wasn't being used for anything except the bindings she'd been recruited to seal.

"What the fucking hell is this?" She slid one hand behind the dress still hanging on her closet door and pulled the material closer to her face.

"You sound like a kid playing dress up when you cuss. Give it up. You lack the skill."

Instead of answering, she held the dress out to me. "How did you manage to get blood on my dress at a formal party, Kori?"

"Shit. Sorry." I sank onto her bed and folded my legs beneath me. "I thought I avoided the spray."

"Whose?"

"David's," I said, and she waited, obviously expecting more of an explanation, so I rolled my eyes and sighed. "He started it."

"What'd he do?"

"Doesn't matter. The point is that if I let the bastard get away with something small now, he'll try something bigger next time."

Kenley hung the dress in her closet. "It was about the basement, wasn't it?" she said, and when I didn't answer, my sister sighed. "The blood's dry now, but there may be enough for a decent binding, if I dampen it. I could make him leave you alone."

"No." I shook my head. "I fight my own battles." As well as most of hers.

"What happened in the basement, Kori?" She spoke with her back to me, like she didn't want to see my face when I answered. Like she already knew I'd lie.

"Nothing." Some lies between sisters are okay. Some are forgivable. Some are unavoidable.

Mine was all three.

Kenley sighed, but she let it go. "Come on. I'll make you a sandwich."

"I'm not hungry."

"You're skinny. You need to eat."

"Yes, Gran." I rolled my eyes again, but followed her

into the kitchen and sat at the bar while she made two grilled-cheese-and-tomato sandwiches, both for me. My mouth was watering before she'd finished buttering the bread.

"How bad is this, Kori?" she asked, as she set the first one in front of me on a paper plate.

"Looks good from here." I picked up the sandwich and Kenley frowned at me—she knew damn well that I knew what she really meant.

"What's gonna happen if you can't sign him?" she asked, and I set the sandwich down, my appetite suddenly gone.

"That won't happen. I'll get him."

"But if you can't? If he's only here to eat, drink and be merry on Jake's dime? What's Jake going to do, Kori? Tell me the truth. You owe it to me."

She was right about that, but I couldn't give her all of it.

I exhaled slowly and met her gaze across the counter. "He'll kill me." Slowly. Jake wouldn't want me to die without having time to truly suffer first.

But I couldn't tell her the rest of it. I couldn't tell my sister what would happen to *her* if I failed.

Because I wasn't going to let that happen.

Six

Ian

After Kori left, I sat on one of the couches in the front room and stared at the door for a solid five minutes, trying to figure out what I'd said to send her fleeing into the night. I couldn't remember a woman ever running away from me before, and I certainly hadn't expected that from Tower's liaison.

Whatever I'd done, I couldn't afford to do it again. This was my only shot. Tower trusted me—as much as he ever trusted anyone who wasn't bound to him— because he'd approached me, rather than the other way around. If I got caught, he wouldn't fall for the same trick again. But it wasn't just *his* trust I needed.

I lay in bed half the night, trying to figure out how to get Kori to trust me enough to reintroduce me to her sister. Maybe even take me to Kenley's house, or leave me alone with her somewhere else. Anywhere else. Because the alternative was too horrible to contemplate.

I didn't want to kill Kori's sister in front of her, but I would, if I had to. I'd do it for my brother, and for everyone else who'd ever been bound against his or her will by Kenley Daniels.

Few could have done what Kori's sister had done to my brother—most Binders weren't strong enough to make a nonconsensual binding stick. But Kenley wasn't most Binders. She had an *extraordinary* amount of power, and as long as she wielded it like a weapon—or let someone else wield her power like a weapon—she was a threat to the general population. As was anyone pulling her strings.

Which was why Kenley Daniels had to die.

Bringing down Jake Tower was a bonus. It was also the carrot I'd dangled in front of Aaron, a die-hard Independent activist, to get him to help with the research and intel.

The plan had been simple, at least in theory. Kill the Binder, and those she'd bound would go free. By Aaron's estimate, in the six years Kenley Daniels had been working for Tower, she'd sealed bindings not only for most of the new recruits, but for most of the existing employees who'd reenlisted during that time period.

Jake Tower was the king of a castle built around a single, crucial cornerstone—Kenley Daniels. With her death, he would lose the majority of his workforce—the legion of indentured servants blood bound to follow his every order—and with them, his power and influence.

The whole recruitment ruse was intended to put her within my reach. She was supposed to be my liaison to the Tower syndicate; I'd described her in perfect detail.

Kori wasn't supposed to happen. She'd never even met my brother, and she hadn't bound anyone to Jake Tower, which made her useless to both me and Aaron. But she was all I had, so I'd have to make it work.

When she knocked on the door the next morning, I was as ready as I was going to get.

"Nice boots," I said as she stepped past me into the living area. "They should make it even easier to run away."

"Meaning?" But I could see the truth in the tense line of her shoulders. She knew exactly what I meant.

"You ran out of here last night like the hotel was on fire." I headed into the bedroom and her quick, angry footsteps followed me.

"I wasn't running, I was…drunk. Too much vodka. I didn't want to puke all over your hotel room."

I glanced at her from the closet doorway. She'd gulped from the bottle like a pro, without even flinching. Kori Daniels might have been a lot of things, but she was not a novice drinker. Yet there was something new and vulnerable in her expression—something fragile and caged—and that surprised me so much I decided not to push the issue.

I selected a tie and stood in front of the mirror to knot it, watching her reflection fidget while she watched mine. She was uncomfortable in silence, and her hands needed something to do.

Interesting.

"So, what do you want for breakfast?" she asked, when the silence became too much for her. "There's a restaurant in the hotel, or we could try—"

"I ordered room service," I said, giving the knot a final tug to tighten it. "Should be here in—" A knock came from the suite door. "Right about now."

She followed me to the living area and stood with her arms crossed over her chest while I signed for the food and the waiter laid it out on the table. "I thought we were going out for breakfast."

"We were. Now we're not." I handed the bill back to the waiter and he left, while she continued to scowl at me. "I ordered a little of everything. Take your pick." She opened her mouth to complain—I could see it on her face—but I spoke over her. "And don't tell me you're not hungry. I hate it when women starve themselves to achieve some stupid physical ideal that only looks natural on a twelve-year-old. Men don't want women who look like children. Not real men, anyway."

Her eyes narrowed and I could almost hear her teeth grind together. I crossed my arms over my chest and watched her, waiting to see her head explode. She opened her mouth to start what would surely have been an award-worthy string of expletives. But then she saw my face.

"You're baiting me," she accused, hands propped on her bony hips.

"Yes." I started uncovering plates, stacking the domed covers on the coffee table. "You are the most interesting thing Tower has shown me so far. But I do think you're too thin. Will you eat with me?" I sat at the table and pushed another chair out for her with my foot.

She stood for a moment, watching me. Considering. Then she glanced at the plates steaming on the hotel table. "Fine. But I call the waffles."

"I'll split them with you."

After another moment of consideration, she nodded.

We rearranged food on the plates, splitting the eggs and bacon as well, unwrapping silverware and passing salt, pepper and tiny bottles of syrup back and forth. When I was full and her plate was empty—Kori ate an entire Belgian waffle in under three minutes—I set my remaining food in front of her and leaned back in my chair, watching her from across the table. Studying her.

Reminding myself that she was a means to an end. A tool. Nothing more. No matter how fast my pulse rushed when she looked up, and I realized I'd never seen eyes with such depth, like everything she'd ever seen was still in there staring back at me, daring me to take a closer look.

One moment she looked vulnerable and bruised, and I wanted to bandage wounds I couldn't even see. Then a second later, that woman was gone, and in her place stood a fierce hellcat, angry at the world and spitting flames with every word, and I wanted to poke her just to see the sparks fly.

I couldn't figure her out. But the more time I spent with her, the worse I wanted to, and that was dangerous. *Kori* was dangerous. Tower knew what he was doing when he sent her. How could anyone spend more than five minutes with her and not be fascinated by her? Not want her?

Focus, Ian. Play to win.

"Okay, this is your moment." I crossed my arms over my chest and leaned back in my chair. "I am rested, fed and as receptive as I'm going to be. Tell me why I should join the Tower syndicate."

Kori hesitated with her fork halfway to her mouth, egg yolk dripping into a puddle of leftover syrup on her plate. "Right now? Just like that?"

I nodded. "Wow me."

She lowered her fork slowly and stared at me from across the table. I'd thrown her off balance, and I was a little relieved to realize that was even possible. "Well, obviously there's a steady paycheck. A nice one, considering the strength and rarity of your Skill."

I shrugged. "Every job pays. What will I get from the syndicate that I'm not already getting as a systems analyst?"

Kori laughed out loud, and I almost joined her. Then I remembered to pretend that it was perfectly plausible for me to sit behind a desk all day weighing the pros and cons of various software options for a billion-dollar company, when the truth was that I lived more than an hour from the nearest internet connection, connected to my family only by satellite phone.

Too bad that part of my cover story was set in stone.

"What's so funny?" I demanded, though I could easily have answered that question myself.

"Can I answer in the form of a list?" she asked, and I nodded, curious now. "The fact that you think you're getting *anything* out of being a systems analyst is hilarious. The fact that I don't even know what a systems analyst *does* is even funnier. Then there's the fact that you *are* a systems analyst. I knew that, but now that I've met you, I just…can't see it."

"People are rarely what they seem to be at first glance," I said, trying to pretend I didn't agree with everything on her list. "It's my job to analyze systems. It's your job to tell me why I'd like answering to Jake Tower more."

Her smile faded, and I wanted to take it all back. But I had a part to play.

"The apartment." She set the fork down and pushed her plate away. "I know you haven't seen it yet, but it's really—"

I shook my head. "Dig deeper. You're still throwing money at me, but this isn't about money."

Kori frowned, and her eyes narrowed like they did when she got irritated—a pattern I was already starting to recognize. "Of course it's about money. You wouldn't be here if you didn't need cash."

"Is that why you joined? For the money?"

Her frown slipped a little. "I don't give a shit about the money." But I'd already known that. She hated champagne and hors d'oeuvres. She preferred boots to stilettos. This was not a woman interested in wealth or social visibility. "I had my reasons."

I wanted to hear her reasons. Badly. But if she'd wanted me to know, she would have told me. "I have my reasons, too." And that may have been the truest thing I'd said to her so far.

"Does that mean you're going to join? Or have I fucked this up already?"

There it was again, that vulnerability. That depth in her eyes, and the way she held her breath waiting for my answer.

"That means I'm going to give you another shot. Tomorrow. Maybe by then you'll have figured out what carrot to dangle in front of me."

"This isn't a fucking game, Ian," she snapped, and I smiled. I couldn't help it.

"That's the first time you've said my first name. And of course this is a game. Right now, you're losing."

She stood, hands flat on the table, eyes flashing in anger. "You can put on a suit and sit in front of a keyboard every day for the rest of your life if you want, but that's not going to change who and what you are. You're a Blinder, and a risk-taker. A thrill-seeker."

I shook my head, ready to deny what I already recognized as truth—words from my own head, falling out of her mouth. But she cut me off before I could speak.

"I saw your face when you let the shadows fade around us last night, and I know that look. Darkness is in you, Ian. It's part of you. You're not going to feel whole until you're free to live in the shadows of your own creation, and that's not going to happen for you as a fucking systems analyst. But it can happen for you in syndicate service. And if you're going to join one, you might as well join the best."

"And do you really think the Tower syndicate is the best?"

Kori blinked, and I glimpsed something she was about to dance around, without actually denying—a trick syndicate employees learned quickly. "You will never find a better financial opportunity than what Jake is offering you. You'll never find a syndicate with better security or fringe benefits. But if you go into this thinking you can work Jake Tower with a smile and a joke, he will roast you alive, feast on your flesh, then pick his teeth with your fucking bones."

"That may be the most honest thing you've said yet." But I felt my smile slipping. "Colorful, too."

Kori sank into her chair again, and I watched her face as understanding bled into fear for a moment before her defenses slammed into place and left me staring at a carefully blank expression. But she couldn't undo what I'd seen. She'd shown me a glimpse of the gritty reality beneath the shining surface of Tower's empire, and that wasn't supposed to happen. At least, not until I had a chain link tattooed on my arm.

"So now what?" She gripped the arms of her chair like it was all that was holding her up.

"Now you take me out on the town. Show me the syndicate in its natural habitat."

"Why?" she demanded. "Is there anything I can show you that'll make a damn bit of difference?"

"Why else would I be here?"

Kori sat straighter, eyes flashing again, this time with new understanding. Possibility. "You need something from him." I could practically see the bulb flare to light over her head, and I wanted to smile. "I'm a bad recruiter. I'm a *suck-ass* recruiter, but you haven't even flinched over anything I've said or done, and that means you need something bad enough that you don't care what you'd have to sign to get it."

I arched one brow at her. "I do care what I'd have to sign over. But I also know that nothing in life is free."

She frowned, like that cliché meant more than it should have for her, and I wondered what she'd paid for whatever she got out of signing with Tower. "So tell me what you need, and I'll get it for you."

I shook my head slowly. "That's not how the game is played." Because if she knew that what I needed was her sister's corpse, she'd try to kill me where I sat. So why was I more disturbed by the thought of being hated by her than of being killed by her?

"Fuck the game. I don't wanna play."

"You don't have any choice," I said, and fury rolled over her in waves almost thick enough for me to taste.

"Don't *ever* say that to me," she growled, her hands clenched around the chair arms so tightly I was afraid she might break them off.

I exhaled slowly, backing carefully away from whatever psychological land mine I'd nearly stepped on. "That's not what I meant. You have to play the game because *I* have to play the game. I want something Tower won't want to give. Which puts me in a pretty difficult position."

Kori actually rolled her eyes. "I don't think you fully appreciate how badly Jake wants to secure your services. There isn't anything he wouldn't give you, if you ask nicely and do a little ass kissing. Money. Car. Apartment. Women. Hell, men, if that's what you like."

"I don't—" I started, but she spoke over me.

"Recreational chemicals…" Drugs, of course. "Fine art. Exotic pets. A surrogate mother for your unborn child. He'd give you nearly anything, short of his own wife and kids." She stopped abruptly, forehead furrowed with a sudden unpleasant thought. "Please tell me you don't want his wife. Asking for Lynne would get us both killed."

I scowled, repulsed by the thought. "No, I don't want his wife."

"What, then? Tell me, and I'll get it."

I arched both brows, trying to hide a grin. "You should be careful what you offer a man you just met. What if I asked you to kill someone for me?"

"You wouldn't." She leaned back in her chair, obviously comfortable with her assessment of me.

"You don't know me, or what I want, or what I'm capable of. But I'm telling you that what I need, Tower's not going to want to give me. So if you want to make your boss happy you may have to go around him to get it. Are you willing to do whatever that takes?"

Kori watched me, her expression carefully blank, her gaze steady and colder than I'd seen since the moment we met. "Maybe you belong here after all."

Seven

Kori

"It all begins with the grunts. The foot soldiers, with just one chain link," I said, when we were far enough from the doormen that they wouldn't overhear me explaining the inner workings of the Tower syndicate to a man without marks.

"The bottom layer of the pyramid?" Holt said as we crossed the covered hotel entrance and stepped onto the sidewalk, greeted by honking horns, the bite of exhaust, and what little breeze reached downtown from the river.

"Exactly." I wasn't sure how much he already knew, so I started from the beginning. "This is the rank I highly suggest you skip, and I don't think Jake will balk at that, if you ask nicely."

"What's he like?"

"Jake? He's disciplined. Patient." In the same way a cat is willing to wait as long as it takes for the best shot at its prey. "Jake likes order. Rules. Straight lines and neat little boxes. I couldn't walk a straight line even stone-cold sober and neat boxes tremble in my presence. Which is probably why I'm constantly in trouble."

"You? Trouble? I am shocked and appalled."

I glanced up to see Holt watching me with no hint of a smile. "You may be the most sarcastic man I've ever met."

"It's a gift." We stopped at the corner, but only had to wait a second for the light to change so we could cross the street. "So, what is a grunt's primary duty?" Ian asked as soon as we stepped onto the opposite curb.

"Depends on the color of the mark. Rust is the most common. A rust-colored mark means unSkilled muscle. They're sentries, on the lookout for anything that doesn't belong. And they're everywhere, whether you see them or not. They do much more than the police to keep crime rates down on this side of town."

Unauthorized crime, anyway. No one intervened when Tower ordered someone found, punished or killed. But that was one of the things we didn't talk about. One of many.

Ian glanced at the people all around us, carrying shopping bags, having breakfast at the outdoor tables spilling onto the sidewalk from various restaurants, or just rushing to and from wherever they had to be on a Saturday morning. "What's green?" He nodded toward a woman stepping out of a coffee shop with a cardboard container of steaming paper cups. The two chain links on her arm were the color of tarnished copper.

"Green is for unSkilled service. She's a secretary, or accountant, or something like that. She's not muscle, but she's not Skilled, either."

"And there are red marks, too, I assume?"

"Yeah. Red for the skin trade, same as for most other

syndicates, but they don't work on the street. Private appointments only. Their clientele is established and wealthy, and unlike Cavazos, Tower marks them on their arm, same as all the other initiates. He doesn't see the point of either degrading or hiding them by putting the marks on their thighs."

Holt's brows rose. "Prostitutes are people, too?"

"It's just another way to serve." I couldn't spit the lie out fast enough. "Of course, whatever you want would be on the house—at least until he marks you."

Ian scowled, and I wasn't surprised. Jake was right; Holt didn't want a whore.

"And your mark?" he asked, glancing at the half sleeve covering the top quarter of my left arm.

"Iron-colored links are for Skilled initiates, no matter what the position. I'm security, obviously, though no longer on Tower's personal guard."

"Why not? Did Tower get a splinter on your watch?"

Yeah. A big metal splinter to the chest. "Something like that."

"So, after you recruit me—*assuming* you recruit me— what will your job be?"

"I don't know." I would never work as Jake's guard again, nor would I be trusted to protect his wife or kids. "General security, maybe. Like the guards stationed everywhere at the party."

Ian grimaced. "That sounds boring as hell."

But I'd take boring over the basement any day.

"What would I be doing?" he asked, as we turned another corner.

"Whatever Jake needs done. Blinding the opposition. Punching holes in a defensive infrared grid, so his men can get in."

"But we're talking about crime, right? Criminal enterprise?"

I hesitated, trying to decide what he wanted to hear, and how best to merge that with the truth. "That sounds a little…"

"True?"

"Yeah." I frowned. "That sounds a little true. Also, insufficient. Not all of the syndicate's business is illegal. Some of it's just highly discouraged by legal, spiritual and political authorities."

"Semantics." He brushed off my reply with an ironic grin. "What are we talking about? What's his bread and butter?"

I hesitated, weighing my options.

"What's wrong?" Holt glanced at me as we stepped onto another crosswalk. The light changed before we were halfway across the street, but no one bothered walking faster.

"I'm not sure I'm allowed to answer the kind of questions you're asking now, but I'm supposed to do whatever it takes to keep you interested. Which means I'm walking the line between a couple of conflicting orders." And if I actually got caught between them, my body would tear itself apart trying to obey both at once.

"I'd never intentionally put you in that position," Ian said. "So if I ask something you can't answer, just tell me and I'll withdraw the question."

I frowned up at him, trying to decide whether or not he was serious. Nice guys didn't usually last long in syndicate life. Neither did nice girls, which was why I'd signed on to protect Kenley.

"Have you ever been bound?" I asked, and his sudden,

startled look darkened quickly into something I couldn't interpret.

"No. So, no, I've never felt resistance pain, if that's what you're getting at. Nor have I been caught between conflicting orders. Have you?" he asked, watching me carefully, and I nodded. "What's it like?"

"It's like dying, in slow motion. One piece of you at a time…" But my words faded into silence when a pair of unfamiliar eyes caught my gaze from several feet ahead on the sidewalk. I pretended not to notice, but it took real effort to keep tension from showing in my step. The stranger had glanced at me, but his gaze lingered on Ian, and his casual stance was as false as my grandmother's teeth.

The would-be poacher was young, which hopefully meant he was inexperienced, but I was unarmed, which automatically put me at a disadvantage.

I prattled on for several more steps without really listening to myself. Waiting. Hoping Holt wouldn't freak out when the shit hit the fan. You never can tell with civilians. And finally, as we stepped even with a narrow alley, a hand grabbed my right arm from behind and something sharp poked me to the left of my spine, through the thin cotton of my blouse.

"Scream, and I'll cut you," a young voice whispered into my ear, and I rolled my eyes as he pulled me into the alley. Ian didn't even get a chance to look surprised before a second man—this one bald—shoved him after us.

"You okay?" Ian asked me, his voice soft and taut with caution as he backed away from the bald man, who carried a knife no one on the street would be able to see. If anyone noticed us at all. With any luck, no one would.

"I'm good," I said, stepping carefully as I was tugged steadily backward. "They don't want me. You feel like being abducted today?"

"Wasn't on the agenda, no." Ian stopped with his back to the brick wall, halfway between the bald man and the one holding his knife at my back.

"Plans change," Baldy said. "Come with us quietly, or he'll gut your girlfriend."

I rolled my eyes again. This was a farce of an abduction at best. "First of all, I'm not his girlfriend. Second, it's kind of hard to gut someone from behind, dumb ass."

The hand around my arm tightened, and the first fiery threads of anger blazed up my spine. "Anyone ever tell you your mouth is going to get you in trouble one day?"

"Only hourly," I said, and Ian laughed without taking his attention from the bald man's knife.

"Last chance," Baldy said.

Ian glanced at me, brows raised in question. "What do you think?"

I shrugged, in spite of the knife at my back. "Well, they're not *total* morons. Knives instead of guns, so no one will hear gunshots. And they've got balls, coming after you in broad daylight. That one's a Traveler," I said, nodding at the bald man. "I'd bet my last drop of vodka on it."

Ian frowned. "How do you know?"

"Because the other one can't drag you through the shadows while he's threatening my life."

Baldy scowled, and I gloated silently.

"So should I go with them?" Ian asked, and I could hear the amusement in his voice. He was neither scared nor rattled, and I was pleasantly surprised.

"Nah." I twisted away from the knife at my back and

pulled the man holding my arm off balance. He stumbled, and I jerked my arm from his grip, then faced off against him with my feet spread for balance. "I'd hold out for a better offer."

Knife guy reached for me, and I kicked his kneecap from the side. He crashed to the concrete on one hip and swung his blade at my leg. I kicked the knife from his grip, then stomped on his hand, satisfied by the crunch of several bones, and even more satisfied by his howl of pain.

Something scuffed against concrete behind me, and I twisted to see Baldy lunge for Ian.

Shit! I started toward them, but stopped, surprised when Ian simply stepped out of his path, then slammed Baldy's wrist into the corner of the Dumpster. The knife clattered to the concrete at his feet, and Ian kicked it beneath the Dumpster. His motions were smooth and fast, and he hadn't come close to breaking a sweat.

The man on the ground in front of me pushed himself up with his good hand, and I squatted to snatch his lost knife. When he stood, I stepped up behind him and held his own blade at his throat. He stiffened, good leg holding most of his weight, arms out at his sides, and I almost laughed. "I take it back. You *are* a complete moron."

"Who *are* you?" he asked, in spite of the blade I held.

"Kori Daniels. Why? Were you expecting Little Miss Muffet?"

"Daniels? No shit? That's just my fuckin' luck," he said, and his voice shook, in spite of false bravado. "I bet two hundred dollars they'd find you facedown in the river."

I shook my head, though I'd had similar thoughts, myself. "So now you're stupid *and* poor."

The bald man grunted, and I looked up to see Ian's left fist crash into his face. Again. His head slammed into the brick wall—hard—and a cut appeared on his right cheek. Then his eyes closed and he slid down the wall to slump on the ground, unconscious.

Ian stepped out of reach in case the bald man woke up. A hint of a grin rode one corner of his mouth when he saw me gaping at him. "Why do you look so surprised?"

"Because I'm so surprised." Jake didn't know Ian could fight; if he had, he would have told me.

I considered that new information for a second, trying to decide how long I could get away with silence on the matter, while the man in front of me breathed shallowly in concession to the knife at his throat. "What's your name?"

"John Smith," he spat. And that was exactly the alias I'd expected—a generic fuck-you to the question no one with half a brain would ever voluntarily answer.

I slid the knife beneath the short left sleeve of John's shirt and he flinched when I split the material with one upward stroke. The cotton flaps parted to reveal a single iron-colored ring. No surprise there. "How much is Cavazos offering for Holt?"

"Hundred grand, unharmed. Seventy-five, if he's bruised or bleeding."

I glanced at Ian over John's shoulder, brows raised in appreciation. "Not bad. But he'll go higher." I stepped back from John and shoved him hard enough that he fell to his knees in front of me, facing Ian.

"What are you doing, Kori?" Ian said.

"Showing you what it feels like to suffer conflicting orders." I squatted and slid the knife across the concrete, and Ian caught it beneath the sole of his boot. "And

John's going to help." I circled John slowly, and he turned with me to keep me in sight. "To break an oath, you have to first be sealed into one. You give your word, and a Binder like Kenley seals it, with ink, blood or spoken promise. Or some combination of those. A verbal promise is the weakest. A blood binding is the strongest, whether sealed on paper, flesh or any other surface. John, here, has a blood binding sealed in his flesh by Ruben Cavazos." I glanced pointedly at his exposed biceps. "He's unSkilled muscle. And I mean unSkilled in every sense of the word," I said, backing out of reach when John lunged for me.

"Bitch!" he snapped, as I started circling him again, and I could see his bad leg shake.

"Kori, I know what a binding is," Ian said. "I grew up in the suburbs, not on Mars."

"But your understanding is theoretical, right? Like how I understand that the better part of valor is discretion, but I can't truly know what that feels like, since I've never tried it."

"You've never tried valor?" Ian's brows rose.

"No, discretion," I said, and he looked like he wanted to laugh. "My point is that you can't truly understand what you've never felt. But sometimes a good visual helps." That, and I really needed to hit something and I wasn't sure when I'd get another chance. "So watch closely."

I turned back to John, who still favored his right leg and was edging toward the Dumpster, probably in search of something to use as a weapon.

"When you break your word, you send your body into self-destruct mode. And when you're given conflicting orders, there's no way to obey them both, thus there's no way to avoid pain. First comes a real bitch of a head-ache."

I feinted to the right, then slammed a left hook into John's temple. He grunted and stumbled backward, and I followed while he was still off balance. "Next comes un-controllable shaking and cramps. Then the loss of bowel and bladder control." I kicked John low in the gut for emphasis. He hunched over the pain in his stomach and I was already circling again before he stood.

"Then your body begins to shut itself down one organ at a time. Starting with the kidneys, and everything else housed in your gut." John lurched toward me, fists clenched, and I danced away from him on the balls of my feet. Before he could follow, I twisted into a midlevel kick, and my boot slammed into his right kidney.

John moaned, an inarticulate sound of pain, then fell to his knees.

"And in the case of conflicting orders, if one of them isn't withdrawn, the breakdown of your body continues until you die in a pool of your own evacuated fluids."

"Kori," Ian said, with a glance at the man curled up on the ground. "That's enough."

"Is it?" I grabbed a handful of John's hair and pulled his head back, one knee pressed into his spine. "What were you gonna do after you took me down?" I de-manded. "How were you going to stop me from coming after you? Knife to the chest?"

John shook his head, and several of his hairs popped loose in my hand. "Across the throat," he gasped. "Then I was gonna throw your corpse facedown in the river and cash in on my bet."

Ian scowled, but didn't press his position.

I shoved John facedown on the concrete and put one

foot on the back of his neck. "Tell Cavazos I consider this a personal insult. If he doesn't make a serious effort next time, I'm shipping his men back in a series of small boxes."

Then I stomped on John's good hand, and his screams followed us as I knelt to pick up the knife I'd taken from them, then followed Ian onto the sidewalk.

The first of the resistance pain hit me as I folded the knife closed and slid it into my pocket—a flash of agony behind my eyes, accompanied by the glare of white light in the center of my field of vision. An instant migraine. And that was only the beginning.

"You okay?" Ian asked, when I staggered on the sidewalk, one hand pressed to my forehead, as if that could stop the pain.

"No." I stopped to lean against the wall of a dry cleaner's storefront and Ian stood in front of me, blocking me from view without being asked. If I hadn't been in so much pain, I would have questioned that kind of instinct, coming from a systems analyst.

I slid my hand back into my pocket and felt the smooth edges of the pocketknife, amazed by how calm the feel of the weapon made me, even as pain threatened to split my skull in two.

I'd been forbidden to arm myself, a fact I'd forgotten in the afterglow of the scuffle in the alley—even that little bit of expended energy had helped release some of my bottled-up rage. Carrying John's knife was an ongoing breach of the oath of obedience I'd sworn to Jake Tower, and I would hurt for the length of the breach—until I got rid of the knife, or my body shut itself down in protest.

Yet even knowing my life could end right there on

the street, my undignified death witnessed by an endless parade of strangers—not to mention Ian Holt—I didn't want to give up the knife. I'd won it in a fair fight. The knife was mine, and so were the skills needed to use it better than its original owner could ever have managed. Weapons were freedom. Power. Autonomy. And by denying me the right to arm myself, Jake had denied me all of those things, too. Intentionally.

I was still being punished.

While my head threatened to crack open like a pistachio seed, my hands began to tremble and my stomach started to cramp, and the pain was too severe to be hidden.

"Kori? What's wrong?" Ian's voice was tense with concern, and he glanced back and forth between me and the people passing us on the sidewalk, to see if anyone had noticed my weakened state. And that was all I could take, not physically, but logically.

Resistance pain weakened me and made me vulnerable, which made him vulnerable by extension. There were people—even my fellow syndicate members—who wouldn't hesitate to take advantage of that weakness, for any of a dozen reasons. And if I let Holt get hurt, Jake would kill me.

"Here. Take this." I pulled the knife from my pocket, my grip shaky, and Ian only hesitated for a moment before taking it from me. The instant the metal left my hand, the shaking stopped. The stomach cramps eased, and slowly, the pain in my head began to recede.

Ian glanced at the knife, then slid it into his own pocket. Then he met my gaze, silently demanding an explanation. When that produced no results, he tried again, verbally. "What's going on, Kori? Why can't you hold the knife?"

I exhaled slowly, not surprised that he recognized resistance pain for what it was. Then I braced myself for more. "I'm not allowed to carry a weapon. At the moment."

Another bolt of pain shot through my skull and into my brain—I wasn't allowed to tell him that, either.

I squeezed my eyes shut as my hands curled into fists at my sides, like I could actually fight the agony. But I couldn't. This pain was much stronger than the previous bout—literally blinding, for a moment—but shorter in duration, because telling Ian something I wasn't supposed to tell him was a terminal breach of my oath to Jake. Over and done with quickly, as opposed to an ongoing breach, like carrying a weapon would have been.

Ian's frown deepened. "Why not? What moment? *This* moment? Saturday morning specifically?"

"It's less a Saturday-morning thing than an until-further-notice thing." That one came with no additional pain—the breach was in the admission, not the details.

"How are you supposed to defend yourself?" he demanded, and I noticed that he didn't ask how I was supposed to defend him, which underlined for me the fact that he didn't need to be defended.

"Like I just did. I'm not untrained in unarmed combat, and I can use any weapons I gain. But I can't carry them once the fight's over."

Ian scowled like he had more questions, but he wasn't going to ask them, and I knew why. He didn't want to force me to answer any more forbidden questions. I could see it in his eyes. In the way he watched me in pity and concern, and I had the sudden, irrational urge to punch him, just so I wouldn't have to see either of them anymore.

I didn't need his pity or his concern, and I didn't want either. So I pushed off against the wall and started walking, and Ian fell into step behind me.

"Are you okay?" he asked.

"Fine," I snapped. "I'm not some delicate flower that's going to dry up and blow away at the first sign of pain."

"I never thought you were. In fact, you almost seem to be looking for a fight. Was all that really necessary, back in the alley?"

"That was a mercy," I insisted. "If I'd reported the incident, Jake would have told me to kill them both. But then there would have been no one to deliver my message."

"Your message daring Cavazos to bring his A game next time?"

"That's the one."

"And you really think throwing down the gauntlet was a smart move?"

I shrugged. "Couldn't let him think those clowns were a challenge. What is a gauntlet, anyway?"

"It's like a glove—" Ian shook his head, like he could jar loose all unnecessary thoughts. "That doesn't matter. My point is—"

"*My* point is that Cavazos will do anything to get you, and he won't be the only one. Why should we wear ourselves out swatting flies all day, so that we're too tired to fight when the eagle finally lands? With any luck, that message will piss Cavazos off enough that he'll skip the preliminaries and bring on the main event."

"Does that mean you're not going to report this to

Tower? Aren't you under some kind of contractual obligation to?"

"Nope. Jake's doesn't do much micromanaging through direct orders. Sometimes that comes back to bite him on the ass—those are my favorite times—but usually that approach avoids much bigger messes."

"How's that?"

"Each command given is like a string that can't be broken. Give too many to one person, and you're eventually just going to tie that person in knots, and when that happens, nothing gets done. And sometimes people get hurt." Not that Jake gave a damn about hurting people. "Instead Jake saves direct orders for things he really, truly means, and everything else is guided by a set of standard expectations. For instance, I'm *expected* to report any trouble we run into. But I'm not obligated to. If I get caught, I'll be in trouble, but I won't suffer resistance pain from defying an expectation, whereas I would from defying a direct order. And if I don't get caught…" I shrugged. "No harm, no foul."

"And you're willing to take that risk?" Ian sounded surprised, no doubt thinking of the resistance pain I'd just suffered.

"What's life without risks?" But the truth was that defying Jake's expectations where and when I could was the only way I had of striking back. Of showing him that he might own my body, but he'd never own the rest of me.

"Long," Ian said. "Life without risks is long. And hopefully peaceful."

"And a long, peaceful life is what you're looking for, Mr. Systems Analyst?"

"Who says I'm looking for anything? You people

called me, remember? You're the ones who're looking for something, and we both know that gives me the advantage."

"Yeah. That'd be believable if I didn't already know you need something from Jake, too. If he finds that out, you've lost your advantage, and you may as well drop your pants and bend over for him."

Ian flinched. "That's a rather indelicate metaphor." His frown deepened. "It *is* a metaphor, right?"

"Yeah. And it's only as 'indelicate' as the point it makes. If you don't thoroughly understand that Jake will fuck you over eventually, you need to turn around right now and start running."

Not that I could let him get very far. If he refused to sign, I'd have to take him in to be harvested.

Ian blinked, his green eyes narrowing. "You're right. You're a horrible recruiter. If I didn't know any better, I'd swear you were working for the competition…."

"I'm working for myself." And for Kenley. "Ultimately we're all working for ourselves, no matter who we're bound to."

"That sounds a little…mercenary."

I shook my head. "Simple self-preservation. No one's going to look out for you the way you look out for yourself. That's no different than in corporate America. Right?"

Ian blinked, like my question had caught him off guard. "I don't think that's a fair comparison. No one in corporate America has tried to kidnap me at knifepoint."

"And no one in the Tower syndicate has tried to bore you to death with spreadsheets and casual Fridays. What's your point?"

He laughed, and I was startled to realize I liked the

sound. A lot. I hadn't heard real laughter—the nervous kind didn't count—in a long time.

And he had a *really* nice smile…

No! Don't look at his smile, Kori! I couldn't afford to like Ian Holt, because then I'd feel guilty for damning him to a life of crime and violence, and once I let myself feel guilty for one horrible thing I'd been forced to do, all the others would crash down and bury me in regret for a lifetime of necessary evils. Unrelenting guilt was a crippling blow to any assassin, and one I had no plans to suffer.

Ian blinked, and his eyes narrowed. He was studying me again, and I had to squelch the urge to flinch away from his assessment. "You know, Tower might think he's scary, with his gun-toting guards and over-the-top security system, but I know the truth."

"And what's that?" *Why* did my voice sound so…frail?

"You're the most dangerous weapon he has, armed with nothing but the tongue in your mouth. And what a nice mouth it is."

Eight

Ian

"I…" Kori sputtered, blinking at me like the day was suddenly glaringly bright, leaving her exposed, and I realized that the only thing I enjoyed more than making her spew expletives was leaving her speechless. "What the hell does that mean?" she finally demanded, and I frowned. In my experience, most women love to hear how pretty they are and I'd never once pissed one off by saying so.

"It means exactly what I said. And by the way, the proper response to a compliment is 'thank you.'"

Her scowl was unrelenting. "You're not supposed to be complimenting me!"

"I'm not supposed to…?" My frown deepened, and my confusion only grew.

Kori squeezed her eyes shut and shook her head, but when she met my gaze again, she still looked mad, for no reason I could understand. "I mean…you don't have to do that. It's not necessary."

"Necessary for what?" I felt like we were suddenly speaking different languages, and hers was nonsense.

Kori glared at me through narrowed eyes. "This is all a game to you, isn't it?" she demanded, then rushed on before I could answer. "You better start taking this seriously, Ian, because Jake never loses and I don't like games."

"That's unfortunate, because you play them well." I snatched a handful of napkins from a pretzel vendor as we passed on the sidewalk and handed one to her, then wiped the bald man's blood from my hands. One of my knuckles had split open, but I couldn't have left enough of my blood behind to be of any use to someone else.

"I'm not playing," she snapped, swiping at the blood on her own fingers without ever slowing her step. "I'm telling you one fucking truth after another, most of which I'll probably get in serious trouble for, and you're treating me like some bimbo who can't see past her own reflection."

I stared at her, almost as fascinated as I was confused. "How the hell did you manage to twist my compliment into an insult? I think that qualifies as some kind of special skill."

"We obviously disagree on what qualifies as skill."

I stopped, and she went several more steps before turning to frown at me. "I don't understand you."

"You don't have to understand me."

"I do, though." I wanted to understand her worse than I'd ever wanted to understand anyone in my life, and I couldn't quite convince myself that my motivation was purely professional. Yes, the better I understood her, the easier it would be to use her to get to her sister. But the more time I spent with Kori, the harder it was to remember that she even *had* a sister, much less what I'd come into Tower's territory to do. "We're going to be spending a lot of time together over the next few days, and I'd like to know where the land mines are buried *before* I step on the next one."

"I think your best bet is steel-toed boots."

I laughed out loud at the thought of boots—any boots—protecting someone from a land mine. Even a metaphorical land mine. Then I wondered again why her landscape was so riddled with them. "Why are you telling me things that could get you in trouble?"

"Because they're…true." She shrugged, and her frown deepened as she searched for more of an answer.

"And you like the truth?" Interesting, for a syndicate employee.

"I'd call it more admiration than true enjoyment, but yeah." Kori frowned and dropped her used tissue in a trash can on the corner. "I guess you could say I like the truth."

"Why?" Every time I thought I was close to figuring her out, she said something that threw me for another loop, and though I'd given up trying to anticipate the dips and twists in the conversations, I couldn't help loving the ride.

"Why do I like the truth?" she asked, and I nodded. "I don't know. Because it's the truth. Why does anyone like anything? Why do you like coffee?" she demanded, when I glanced into a coffee shop while we waited for the crosswalk light to change.

"Because it wakes me up, it's warm in my hands and it tastes good. Your turn. Why do you like the truth?"

"I don't know how to answer that." And from the stubborn set of her jaw, I could see she didn't even want to try.

"Yes, you do. You're smarter than you think you are, Kori."

"How the hell would you know that?"

"Because I'm smarter than you think I am, too." I glanced at the crowd gathered around us, waiting for the light, then nodded toward the coffee shop and was relieved when she actually followed me to a rectangle of shade beneath its awning. "Why do you like the truth? Dig deeper."

She crossed her arms over her chest and thought about it, and for a moment, I was sure she would refuse to answer. But then she met my gaze with a shrug, understating how carefully she'd obviously considered the question. "Because it's right there for the taking. A lie, you have to think about, but the truth is… The truth is easy."

"No, it isn't. In my experience the truth is usually the hardest thing in the world to say. Or to hear." Or to see, lying on a bed, unmoving, staring at the ceiling with no sign of life.

Her mouth thinned into an angry line. "You don't want an answer, you want a fight. You're going to come up with an argument for anything I say, aren't you? Why does it even matter why I like the truth?"

"It doesn't matter to me," I said, my lie as steady as her anger. And I should have left it at that, but I couldn't help myself. Her steel spine and the occasional glimpse of vulnerability reminded me of Steven, and the bitter truth surged through me, scorching a trail through my veins. The memories. The loss. The rage still burning inside me.

Remembering should have made it easier for me to do what had to be done. But it didn't. Kori's mouth and her fiery grit—so different from Steven's quiet determination—made her real. They made it harder to picture myself destroying Kenley Daniels, if that meant destroying Kori in the process.

"Why you like the truth doesn't matter to me, but it should matter to you," I insisted, still trying to sort through it all in my head. "You can't recruit a man you don't know, and how are you supposed to get to know me in a matter of days when you don't even know yourself, after a lifetime in your own skin?"

"I know myself," she snapped. "And I'm starting to get a pretty damn clear picture of you, too."

"That first part, maybe." But she didn't know me. She couldn't. And if I was wrong about that, I was as good as dead. "So tell me why you like the truth. The real answer." I looked right into her eyes, practically daring her.

Kori glared at me, and I watched her, obviously pissing her off with nothing more than the fact that *I* wasn't pissed off. "The truth is real, even when nothing else is," she said at last, whispering so no one else would hear, dragging the words out like she didn't want to let them go. "It's steady. It doesn't change depending on the circumstances. It *never* changes. The truth will look the same in the dark as it does in broad daylight, and it quacks like the duck it is. That's a relief—knowing what you're getting. I like it."

I smiled. I couldn't help it. She was fascinating, and she obviously had no idea. Not that it mattered. I couldn't let myself want her, and I certainly couldn't *have* her; she'd want to kill me once I'd killed her sister. And even if by some miracle she could forgive that—though she wouldn't—she liked the truth, and my entire existence was one big lie. The reasons she had to hate me were too numerous to count and too huge to see around.

"Syndicate life must be hard for someone like you," I said, trying to drag my thoughts back on target, which proved almost as difficult as dragging my gaze away from her eyes. From her lips, half open, like she'd forgotten what she wanted to say. I wanted to taste her, right there on the sidewalk. Just once. Just for a second. And for one terrifying moment I was suddenly certain I wouldn't be able to concentrate on anything else until I'd done exactly that.

Then her frown grew skeptical, like she thought I was baiting her again. "*Life* is hard, period. Dying when there's another option is easy, even when it hurts, but that's the coward's way out. Sometimes it takes guts to live, and that's the fucking truth."

"So it is." I dropped my soiled napkin into the trash can a few feet away, and her brown-eyed gaze followed me. "Show me something true, Kori. Show me something real about the syndicate, even if it hurts to see."

Something horrible. I needed to see or hear something so terrible it would drive all other thought from my head and purge the sudden need tugging on my fingers like strings on a puppet. The need to touch her.

"You sure? I could show you lots of pretty lies," she offered, her voice delicate. Brittle. "You'd know they were lies, but they'd make you smile." I just watched her, denying myself what I had no right to want, and finally she nodded. "The awful truth it is. Let's go."

I followed her into the coffee shop without a word, and Kori pulled me into the ladies' restroom, then flipped the light switch by the door. Darkness descended and I exhaled slowly, enjoying the sudden calm it brought, like the start of an evening, after a glass of good wine. Everything seemed a little easier in the dark. Even with a strip of light shining from under the door and an emergency light flashing in the far corner.

Something touched my chest, and the breath I sucked in was loud in the silence. Her hand slid along my stomach, slowly, lightly, and I held my breath, wishing for more. I hated myself for that, but denying it would be pointless. I wanted greater pressure from her fingers. Longer contact.

I wanted to pull my shirt off so her hand would trail over my skin and I would know, just once, what her touch felt like.

Her hand kept moving until it reached my arm, then it trailed lower and her fingers intertwined with mine. Her skin was warm and dry, her fingers soft but strong. I wondered if the rest of her could possibly feel so smooth.

"When I squeeze your hand, take three steps forward, then stop. That part's important, unless you want to walk into a wall."

I nodded, then realized she couldn't hear my brain rattle. "Okay."

"Aren't you going to ask where we're going?"

"No. I trust you." I had no other choice, because I was helpless in that moment, in spite of years spent fighting, training for the inevitable. I was more vulnerable to her touch than I'd ever been to a gun, or a knife, or a fist.

"Don't," she whispered, and the words sounded like they hurt. "Don't trust anyone, Ian. Least of all, me."

Before I could respond, she squeezed my hand and tugged me forward, farther into the dark restroom. As my foot hit the ground on my third step, the air around us changed. It felt colder and dryer, and more sterile. And everything was dark. Truly dark. There were no shadows, because there was no light to cast them. There was no infrared grid, nor any glow from any kind of power indicator or exit sign. This was real darkness. My kind of dark.

"Darkroom?" I whispered, and the echo of my own voice told me the room was small, the walls not far beyond our shoulders, with us standing side by side.

"Yeah. Hang on, it's about to get bright." Her fingers left mine, and my hand felt cold and empty in her absence. Kori took a small step forward, then something clicked and light blazed to life all around us, violent and jarring, like we'd stepped into the middle of a roaring bonfire. There was no actual pain, but after such peaceful darkness, my eyes ached beneath the glare, and the sudden sense of exposure—of vulnerability—was more than enough to set me on edge.

Static hummed in front of me and I squinted into the light to make out a small monitor next to a door with no knob or handle. A moment later, the static on the monitor gave way to a man's face, scowling at us. "State your name and business," he ordered, eyes narrowed in irritation, as if he resented having actual work to do at work.

"It's me, Harkins. Open the door."

"Kori?" The man's eyes widened as he studied her face. "Tower said you wouldn't be making any more deliveries, so just turn off the light and slink back into the shadows before we both get in trouble."

"I'm not delivering. I'm tour guiding. This is Ian Holt." She stepped back so Harkins could get a better look at me, and I nodded in greeting. "Jake told me to show him around, so open the fuckin' door so I can do my job."

"Tower sent you? Then you won't mind if I verify that." He picked up a telephone receiver and held it in front of the camera.

Kori shrugged and crossed her arms over her chest. "He should be sitting down to lunch right about now, so you can probably catch him at the house. With his family."

Harkins scowled again and lowered the phone. "If there's trouble to be had from this, I'm aiming it all your way."

"What else is new?" she mumbled, as he made a show of pressing a button somewhere on the desk in front of him. The door to the darkroom popped open into the hall with the soft *whoosh* of a seal being broken.

"Stop by the front desk for visitor's tags," Harkins ordered, and then the screen went blank again.

"Was that an air lock?" I asked, as she stepped into the hall.

"Yup. So they can gas you without killing anybody else." She leaned back into the darkroom and pointed up, where two vents were nestled flush with the ceiling, side by side.

"You're serious?" I said, trying not to imagine why Tower might want to gas someone in his darkroom.

"Serious as gasping your last breath in a pool of your own vomit."

I frowned and followed her into the hall. "You know, you really have a way with words."

"I have a way with guns, too," she said, pushing the door closed behind us. "Let's hope I don't need one, because I am drastically under-armed today."

"Are you expecting another ambush in one of Tower's own buildings?"

She hesitated, then met my gaze briefly. "I don't have permission for us to be here, technically."

"Then why are we here?"

Another shrug as she led the way down the hall. "You wanted to see something true."

"Should I have specified that I want to survive seeing it?" She wasn't the only one drastically under-armed. For authenticity in the role of a systems analyst, I'd foregone even my bare essentials for the second day in a row.

Kori twisted to grin at me over her shoulder. "If you wanted boring, you picked the wrong tour guide."

"I didn't—" I stopped before I could admit I hadn't picked her. "I didn't say I wanted boring. Just nonlethal." For me, for her, and for whomever I'd have to kill to get my hands on a decent weapon if it came to that.

"Don't worry. You're too valuable to shoot." With that she headed down the long white hallway, and I had no choice but to follow, wondering what Tower was protecting with restricted-access darkrooms and gas vents.

We turned a corner to the left and Kori stopped at a rounded reception desk, where a woman with two green chain links on her exposed left arm handed us a sign-in sheet and slid two visitor's passes into plastic cases attached to lanyards.

UnSkilled service, I thought, staring at her arm.

Kori handed me a badge and I slid the lanyard over my head, then held the badge up so I could read it.

Heartland Pharmaceuticals

"You wanted to show me a pharmaceutical company?"

Her teasing smile lit a fire low in my gut, where it continued to smolder as long as her gaze held mine. "You got something against pharmaceuticals? You know, they may have a system you could analyze."

Before I could reply, she turned and crossed the lobby, then led me down another hallway and past several offices to a door with a keypad above the handle. "Wouldn't they have changed the code, if you're not supposed to be in here anymore?" I asked, as she started punching buttons.

"Why bother, when I wouldn't be able to get past the darkroom anyway?" She grinned and when a green light appeared on the keypad, she pressed on the lever and pushed the door open. We stepped into another hallway, identical to the first, as far as I could tell. More white doors with no windows. More featureless white tile floor. Security cameras on both ends, near the ceiling.

"Where are we?" I asked, as our footsteps echoed down the hall. I felt like I should whisper, but she hadn't, so it seemed stupid for me to.

"I thought you trusted me."

"I thought you said not to."

She stopped in front of the last door on the left and turned to look at me. "I don't know if I can actually get us in here. This one takes an employee-specific security code, and chances are good that they've stripped my clearance. Either way, I'm taking a big risk bringing you here."

"Why?" I said, more worried by what I saw in her eyes than by anything she'd told me so far. "Why would you break into a building you no longer have clearance for, just to show me something Tower obviously doesn't want me to see?"

Kori glanced at her feet for a second before meeting my gaze again, and again I was astounded by how much

I saw in her eyes, and how little of it I understood. "Because I can't truly balance the scales."

"I don't understand." I felt like a broken record, spouting that same sentence over and over again, but I couldn't help it. I'd never felt so unsure of anything as I felt when I was with Kori. I didn't understand her thought process and I couldn't interpret her body language, because it seemed to constantly broadcast contradictory signals. Her silence seemed louder than her voice, and even when she did speak, I felt like the parts she left out were more important than the things she actually said.

"Now that the syndicates all know about you, you're going to have to sign with someone, and it's my job to make sure that someone is Jake Tower. But no matter how badly he wants—or even needs—your services, he'll still have the upper hand in negotiations. He'll still have all the power."

"And you don't think that's fair?"

"I think it's unacceptable. But it's also inevitable. I can't give you even footing. The best I can do is arm you with information I haven't been explicitly forbidden to give you. That way, at least you'll know what you're up against. And what you're in for."

I studied her, trying to see what lay behind her eyes and hear what hid between her words. "You don't think I should sign with him, do you?"

She blinked, and her armor slid into place, as easy as if she'd just lifted an actual shield. "I think you have to," Kori said. "When there are no good choices, you pick—"

"The lesser of all evils?" I said, and she shook her head slowly.

"The evil willing to pay the most for you. You look that evil in the face, and you take it for all it's worth."

Was that what she'd done? Had she sacrificed liberty for the almighty dollar? Or was the money merely compensation for work she would have been forced to do, no matter who she signed with?

"But you shouldn't sign anything until you know exactly what you're signing on for," she said, before I could voice my questions. "Even if you can't change the terms."

"And what's behind this door will tell me that? What I'm signing on for?"

Another nod. "This is his most promising new business venture. Top secret. It's still on the ground floor, but Jake believes it has penthouse potential."

But she made the word *penthouse* sound more like a deep, dark dungeon, which made me both tense and incredibly curious. Intel wasn't my primary mission, but I had no objection to being handed information that could damage Jake Tower even beyond the blow I'd be delivering by killing Kenley Daniels.

"How bad will it be if we get caught?"

"For you? He'll make you sign a sealed oath swearing you haven't yet and never will reveal what you learned here."

"And if I don't want to sign an oath?"

Her brows rose. "You *will* want to, because the alternative won't be as simple or as pleasant."

I didn't bother asking what the alternative was. "What about you? What will happen to you?"

Kori's jaw tightened for just a moment. "Nothing. Because we're not going to get caught, unless you don't shut up so I can get us out of this hallway."

And there it was again—that fear I'd glimpsed earlier. It wasn't there when she talked about people dying in their own blood and vomit, or when she bluffed her way into a secure building, or when she took down armed men with her bare hands. I couldn't find any pattern to the things that Kori feared, and I was almost as worried by that as I was fascinated by it.

Kori started punching buttons on the number pad, but I only caught the first five of them. When she was done, the light flashed red. She groaned and let her forehead thump against the door. "Well, that was a lot of buildup for nothing, huh?" Her smile looked forced, but her relief—just a fleeting glimpse of it—was real. But before I could decide what to say, something clicked behind the locked door and it swung open.

A man in a white lab coat glanced at me, then his gaze found Kori and his eyes narrowed. "Korinne. Didn't they ban you from the building?" I glimpsed an ID badge hanging just below chest level, but his arms covered most of it when he crossed them, and I could only see his last name. Abbot.

Kori shook her head and clucked her tongue. "There you go thinkin' small again. I've been banned from *several* buildings. I'm a regular pariah."

"And who is your partner in exile?" Abbot asked, blocking the doorway with his own body.

"This is Ian Holt, the man whose ass you're going to be kissing in a few short days. Better practice your pucker." She shoved him into the room and stalked past him, and I followed when he stomped after her.

"Get out now, or I'll call security."

Kori shrugged, half sitting on a table covered in forms and file folders. "Call 'em. And while you're at it, tell them how you broke security protocol by answering the damn door. Anyone with the clearance to actually be in this room would have his or her own functioning code."

She picked up a clipboard and flipped through the pages clipped to it, too fast to have actually read anything. Then she looked up with her head cocked to one side. "You ever been on Jake's bad side, Abbot?"

"We all know *you* have." He snatched the clipboard from her and tossed it onto another table, then propped his hands on his hips beneath the lab coat, revealing brown slacks and a very poorly chosen button-down shirt. "You fell from grace, and I heard the landing was pretty damn rough. I wasn't on the guest list, but I heard that you—"

Kori swung before I even saw her pick up a weapon. She grunted with the effort and something I couldn't focus on slammed into the lab geek's head. He went down without a sound, out cold, a huge lump already forming on his left temple. "How rough was *your* landing…?" she mumbled, already squatting next to his still form. And only then did I realize what she'd swung. What had left its manufacturer's icon imprinted in the skin just below his hairline.

"An ink drum?" I wasn't sure whether to laugh or back away from her slowly.

"A *big* ink drum. If Abbot had upgraded his printer when Jake suggested it, he could have saved himself from a concussion."

"Or maybe a coma."

Her brows rose in interest. "A coma? You think?" She stopped digging through his pockets long enough to glance critically at his face. "Nice." Kori stood with a key card in hand. "Bastard deserves that and more."

"What did he mean?" I asked as she turned toward another door, and Kori went so still I wasn't sure she was even still breathing. "What did he hear? Why are you *persona non grata?*"

She clutched the key card like it might disappear if her grip loosened. But she didn't answer.

"Why do they hate you, Kori?"

"They don't hate me. Well, *some* of them hate me. The rest of them..." She turned slowly and looked up at me in shadows too shallow to be useful, thanks to yet another infrared grid. "You know how in school, there's always one kid who's just a little better than you at everything? His art gets hung in the hall. He gets to be the line leader, or the door holder, or, if it's high school, he gets to score the winning touchdown and fuck the cheerleader. You know that kid?"

"Yeah."

The frown lines across her forehead deepened. "You weren't that kid, were you? 'Cause that would kinda ruin my metaphor."

"No. I knew him, though." I wanted to touch her. I wanted to hold her, or squeeze her hand, but I understood that touching her would make talking harder for her. Might even make her words stop altogether.

"You know how you watch that kid, and you want to be him, but you also kind of want to see him knocked down a peg or two?"

"Yeah." Why did I have the urge to hold my breath, like that might somehow change the ending to a story we all knew?

"Did you see him fall on his face?" Her voice was harder than I'd ever heard it, and I nodded, feeling guiltier than I had since junior high. "When he fell, did you give him a hand up? Or did you kick him when he was down, to make yourself feel bigger? Or maybe you just watched someone else do that."

"I…"

"You don't have to say it, Ian. We're all grown-ups now. This isn't high school. But if it was, I'd be that kid, and he'd be the one kicking me." She glanced at the unconscious lab geek. Abbot. "They all would."

"And Tower?" I dreaded the answer, even though it wouldn't tell me anything. She'd painted a vivid picture without giving a single detail. "Who's he in this metaphor?

"He's the kid who pushed me down. Hard." She looked away again and stepped toward a window covered with dusty horizontal blinds ending an inch above the table she'd leaned against earlier.

I didn't want to ask. Knowing wouldn't change what I had to do. What I *would* do. But I wanted to know what had happened to her, and who had done it. I wanted to know if there was anyone I should kill with a little more than the necessary force and pain, when the time came.

"What does that mean, Kori? How hard did he push you?"

She turned slowly, still clutching the key card, and looked right up into my eyes, her pale hair the only spot of light in an otherwise dim room. "There are some questions it's not okay to ask. You just found one."

I held her gaze so she could see the truth in mine. "Fine. I can respect that." She didn't trust me, and why should she? "But you left out part of the story. In my school, that kid who tripped and fell? Or maybe got pushed? He got back up and fought until there wasn't another kid left standing, and he didn't do it out of courage or a need for retribution. He did it because that's who he was. He was a fighter, and fighters never back down."

"Fighters die young, Ian." She sounded older—she *looked* older—when she said it.

I nodded, watching her, my blood boiling in fury at whoever had hurt her, in spite of the fact that what I'd come prepared to do would hurt her even worse. "Yeah, sometimes," I agreed. "But they die fighting." Yet even as the words tumbled from my lips—words I'd been saying to myself for years—I remembered what she'd said earlier.

Sometimes dying is the coward's way out. Sometimes living takes guts.

She blinked, but her gaze never wavered. "What the hell are you doing here, Ian? You don't belong here."

I could see what it cost her to say that—another difficult truth that probably skirted the very edge of what she was allowed to reveal to a potential recruit. "Neither do you."

Kori frowned and turned away from me, reaching for the chord hanging down one side of the blinds. "This is what you'll be helping him do," she said, her voice hard again, as if she'd turned off whatever I'd seen in her. Like flipping a switch. As if it was that easy.

She pulled the chord and the blinds rose, clattering, to reveal a long observation window looking out over row after row of beds. Gurneys, really. Narrow, thinly padded carts on wheels, each of which held a single body. Or patient, as the hospital gowns seemed to suggest.

"What the hell is this?" Why were they all asleep? Or unconscious? The chills running up my back were so cold and ruthless my spine could have been carved from ice. "Who are they?"

They were alive. I could see the closest of them breathing, chests barely rising and falling. And they were all—every single one of them—attached to an IV bag hanging from a stand to the left of each cart.

"They're donors," Kori said, and I glanced at her to find her jaw clenched as she stared out at the sea of bodies. "And that's all I can tell you." There were dozens of them. Easily one hundred or more cots, and at the far end of the room was a single nurse in green scrubs, checking the IV bags one by one, stopping occasionally to lift an eyelid and check for…something.

"Can he see us?" I asked, staring at the nurse, who didn't seem to know he was being watched.

"Nope. One-way glass. He can't hear us, either, unless you push that button." She pointed to an electronic panel on the right side of the window. "So, don't push that button. This is an observation room. I can't get us in there." Kori nodded at the glass. "I never had that kind of clearance, and without Abbot's password, this is useless." She dropped the key card on the table.

"Donors…" I couldn't seem to make sense of what I was seeing. "What are they donating?"

"Look back there. The last two rows." She pointed, instead of vocalizing what she was obviously forbidden to say. And I looked.

"Carts." They were no higher than the beds themselves, but the one on the end of the second to last row was unobstructed, because the person on the bed next to him was too small to block the view. I didn't want to think about what that meant.

I squinted a little more and made out something on the cart. A bag of something dark, with something connecting it to the donor's right arm. A wire or a tube.

Yes, a tube.

"Blood," I said softly, horrified by the thought. "They're donating blood." Blood was dangerous. Blood was power. Putting any of your blood in someone else's hands was like turning over the key to your home and inviting the monsters in.

"Not just blood. What comes with blood sometimes?" Kori said, and I had to struggle through a fog of confusion and horror in order to look beyond her words to their meaning.

"They're donating Skills? How is that even possible? Why the hell would anyone ever donate Skilled blood?"

She lifted both brows in surprise. "I never said they were volunteers."

Words deserted me. The entire concept was unthinkable. "They're not… They didn't…?"

"Wake up one morning and decide to open a vein for Jake Tower? No. They were delivered here, for this specific purpose. After being identified and screened by a staff of specialists."

The implications were revolutionary and terrifying. The methodology was inhumane and unconscionable. The fact that she was showing me this at all…it made no sense. "Jake will kill you if he finds out you brought me here." She started to argue, but I spoke over her, whispering, as if the chances of us being overheard had suddenly increased, now that I better understood the stakes of the game. "Don't bother. I know you're risking your life by bringing me to see something that would send most recruits fleeing. What made you think I wouldn't have the same reaction?"

Kori shrugged. "The fact that you kept your cool in the alley, which tells me you're not easily rattled. The fact that you held your own in that fight, which tells me you don't run from trouble. And the fact that you need something from Jake, which tells me that you're here because you *want* to be here, not because he wanted you here. Don't get me wrong—he would have gotten you here anyway, but you didn't even make him work for it."

She crossed her arms over her chest again and silently challenged me to argue with her. "All of that together tells me that you may be a systems analyst, but you are *not* a corporate automaton with clean fingernails and an even cleaner conscience. This might shock and disgust you—and I'd be worried if it didn't—but it won't scare you away."

How the hell was I supposed to argue with that? Insist that I *was* easy to scare? This was why I'd wanted Kenley assigned as my tour guide. Ten minutes alone with her, and the whole thing would have been over. Without the psychoanalysis and flight-risk assessment from her sister. Not to mention the dangerous, top-secret information I was now burdened with.

"You shouldn't have brought me here," I insisted.

"I *had* to bring you here. You had to see what he can do, and that he can get to anyone. You had to understand."

And suddenly I did. I wasn't just looking at a collection of human vegetables being milked for the source of their Skills. I was looking at my own future. Kori was trying to tell me without actually telling me that Tower would get what he wanted from me, one way or another. I could serve him, or I could bleed for him.

She wasn't trying to scare me away. She was trying to scare me into signing, to avoid the alternative.

My head spun. My stomach pitched. But I stood

straight and swallowed everything I couldn't say. "I appreciate what you're trying to do, but at least three people have seen us, and if any one of them talks, we're both screwed."

Though I hadn't known about Tower's pet project when I started this mission, I was fully aware of the risk to my own life. Personal risk I could handle, but I didn't want her death on my conscience.

Hell, I didn't want her death at all.

"They're not going to talk," Kori insisted. "The receptionist and the security guard don't even know about this—Jake has half a dozen other projects going on in this one building. There are no cameras in here—" she glanced around the perimeter of the ceiling for emphasis "—because Jake won't risk the footage being seen by the wrong pair of eyes. Which is also why the staff for this project is smaller than you'd expect. And Abbot can't report us without getting into serious trouble himself. So as long as we're gone before his replacement comes on duty, we're all good. Unless..." Kori frowned and picked up the clipboard Abbot had dropped onto the table. She glanced at it for a second, then set it down again and crossed her arms over her chest. "Nope. No deliveries scheduled for today."

"Deliveries?" I'd seen a lot of sick stuff both stateside and overseas, but nothing compared to this. To people kept comatose and harvested for their blood. This made me sick. "Are these the deliveries you're no longer making?" I could hear the anger in my voice, and I could tell from the narrowing of her eyes that she heard it, too.

"I can't answer that," she said. "But I can say that I was removed from Jake's personal security squad about half a dozen times to acquire a few of the more complicated things he required."

"Because you're a Traveler."

"And because I'm a petite woman, which makes me slightly less threatening than your average hulking male goon." I lifted one brow at her and she shrugged. "At first glance."

"Why would you do this?" I demanded, my voice lower and harder than I'd intended as I looked out at the neat rows of cots and identically dressed donors. Everything was designed to strip them of identity. To dehumanize them, so the employees wouldn't be bothered by that pesky sense of decency. Of human compassion.

"If you haven't figured that out for yourself by next week, you can ask me again, and I'll answer."

But the answer was obvious. She'd had no choice. And neither had any of the people she'd taken. Tower had found a new way to rob people of their most basic rights, and as important as my mission was to me, on a personal level, I couldn't overlook what I was seeing. I couldn't just walk away from all this when I'd done what I'd come to do.

"Who are they?" I whispered, my voice an echo of the horror roiling inside me.

"They're people," Kori said, staring through the glass. "They're from all over the country. None from this city, and few who would be missed by families or coworkers."

"Few? So some were missed?"

"That's inevitable. Some are presumed dead. Some are missed as runaways."

"And you put them here." It wasn't a question. It was a statement of fact I couldn't quite believe, and she couldn't outright confirm.

"That's how this works, Ian. This is what's under all the fucking sequins and champagne. Stuff like this, and people like me and you, making it all happen."

Her voice was sharp, but her expression was empty, and I'd learned that when she looked like that—closed off and unavailable—she wasn't feeling nothing. She was feeling too much. She was blocking it all out. That was a survival skill, and her still-beating heart was proof that it worked.

"It's not your fault," I insisted. "You can't hold yourself responsible for something someone else made you do. Which would you blame, the gun that fires the bullet, or the finger that squeezes the trigger?"

For a moment, she was quiet, staring through the one-way glass. Then she exhaled softly. "Doesn't really matter who you blame, Ian. Either way, I'm his gun, and guns are only good for one thing."

But even after less than a day spent with her, I knew Kori Daniels was good for much more than what Tower was using her for, even if neither of them could see it.

Nine

Kori

"**I** need a drink. A strong one," Ian said. We'd left Jake's pet project behind two blocks ago, and he was still looking at me like he was disappointed in me. Like he'd started looking at me in the observation room, the moment he'd found out that I'd kidnapped for Jake. That I'd killed for him.

But that was stupid, because he didn't know me well enough to be disappointed in me.

"Never let it be said that I stood between a man and his liquor. If you want food, too, there's a decent Italian restaurant around the corner to your left."

He shook his head firmly. "I don't think I could keep it down, after what I just saw."

"Okay. My favorite dive bar is half a mile up the street. Or we could head back to your hotel." Personally I favored the bar, for the lack of beds and availability of liquor.

"What are the chances Cavazos would send men to ambush us in this bar of yours?"

"Slim to none, unless he wants them returned in pieces too small to identify. Dusty's will be crawling with locals at one on a Saturday, half of them bound to Jake."

"The bar it is."

Ten minutes later, I pulled open the door to Dusty's and descended two steps into familiar, comfortable shadows accompanied by the buzz of conversation, the clink of ice on glass, and the practiced cadence of sports announcers from several small, outdated televisions mounted in the corners of the main room. The floor was sticky, but the glasses were clean. This was one of my favorite places in the world.

"Who's Dusty?" Ian asked, following me to a booth along the back wall.

"No idea. The owner's a woman in her sixties named Patience." I slid into the booth, and before Ian could pick up the greasy, laminated snack menu, a waitress stopped beside our table, notepad in hand. "What can I get 'cha?" she asked, making a decent attempt to hide the gum in her mouth. She was new.

"Stoli and Coke. And bring me another one in fifteen minutes."

"And for you?"

Ian slid the single-page menu between the grimy, glass salt and pepper shakers. "Crown and Coke."

"Another in fifteen minutes?" she asked, with a grin that went unreturned.

"We'll take it play by play."

"Be right back." Then the waitress was gone, and I couldn't pretend not to see the way Ian was still looking at me.

"What's Tower doing with the blood?" he asked softly, when the silence between us became too much.

"I can't answer that, but you're welcome to draw your own conclusions. What's usually done with blood donations?" I said, leading him to deductions I couldn't confirm.

"Transfusions. Shit." His eyes closed, and he inhaled deeply before opening them again. "He's making transfusions of Skilled blood. Presumably for profit."

"A logical assumption," I said, and for once, that was truly all I had to add. When I'd last been allowed in the building, the project was only in its testing phase.

The waitress set our glasses down on white napkins, and Ian gulped half of his drink at once, then clenched his glass so hard his dark hands went pale at the joints. I understood his anger. The Skilled are generally uncomfortable even thinking about blood spilled in large quantities, and the personal security risk that represents. Thinking of it stolen and redistributed was enough to make me sick to my stomach, even though I'd had plenty of time to get used to the idea.

"Is it permanent?" he asked, when he finally lowered his glass. "Is Tower getting ready to arm the entire population with Skills?"

"I wouldn't worry about that," I said, already tired of dancing around things I couldn't say outright. "After any transfusion, it only takes a few hours for the new blood cells to be absorbed by the body."

The key to communicating points you aren't allowed to make is speaking in generalities and implications. I'd had six years to polish my skills.

"So, the transfused Skills are temporary," Ian said, but I couldn't confirm that, so I lifted my glass for the first sip, wishing for the days when one drink was enough to relax me. Mostly because those were the days before Jake, and the syndicate, and the loss of my free will, and the start of my body count.

"Does it work on those who already have Skills? Can he strengthen someone's existing ability, or give people multiple Skills?" His voice got deeper and more intense with each question, but his volume never rose.

"I honestly don't know. I've been out of the loop for a couple of months, but I haven't heard about anything like that." I drained half my glass, then caught the waitress's eye and held my drink up, wordlessly calling for another, several minutes early.

"So, what other criminal enterprises will I be aiding and abetting, once I've sold my soul?"

I swirled the ice in my cup, thinking about all the possible answers. Things that would paint an accurate picture for him, but wouldn't scare him or piss him off any worse than I probably already had with the whole black-market Skills operation.

"Well, there're the classics, of course. He does huge trade in black-market blood samples and names. That's where he got his start." And those were the common-knowledge kind of things I was legitimately allowed to talk to Ian about.

"Whose names and blood?"

"Everyone's. Anyone's. Politicians are big business. Right before a big vote, we typically get an influx of requests from various lobbyists."

Ian shook his head slowly and set his empty glass at the edge of the table. "I'd heard rumors… So they, what? Bind a congressman to vote a certain way?"

"Or to speak to certain key individuals whose opinions carry sway. Or to mention or avoid certain topics in interviews. Or whatever. There are about a million different ways to wag the dog."

He started to ask another question, then waited while the waitress set down our fresh drinks and took the empty glasses.

"And Tower just sells these names and blood samples to whoever wants them?" Ian looked horrified. Again.

"Of course not. You can't even get in to see him unless you have significant cash to flash, or some other resource he values. Usually important names and blood samples, or partial names and locations of potential new recruits."

Ian sipped from his fresh glass, and I could smell the whiskey from across the table. "Don't any of them notice that they're being…compelled to do things? Or not to do things?"

I shrugged, swirling the ice cubes in my glass. "Anyone who knows what a binding is would recognize the symptoms, but if you don't know who's bound you and the Binder was strong enough to seal a nonconsensual binding, there isn't much you can do to fight it, especially considering that resistance pain of just about any kind would keep you out of the big vote, or off the radio, or out of whatever spotlight you need to be in. So, worst-case scenario, whoever's being bound won't be able to push their own agenda, even if they manage to resist pushing yours." I shrugged and finished my second glass. "And, of course, all transactions are nonrefundable, so Jake's been paid either way. Win-win."

"Unless you're the one being bound."

"Well, yeah."

"And your sister's the one who seals these bindings?"

"Most of them. She's the best."

"The best Tower has?" Ian said, looking up from his glass to meet my gaze in the shadows.

"The best I've ever seen. The best Tower's seen, too. That's why he keeps her so close."

"So no one else can steal her?"

"Yeah." But it was more than that. The seals Kenley had put in place were *kept* in place by her blood and her will. If those stopped flowing—if and when she died— any binding she'd sealed would be broken. Most of Jake's indentured employees would go free. His deals with local politicians and businessmen would be void. His entire kingdom might very well collapse.

That's why he kept Kenley close, and under twenty-four-hour armed guard.

But I couldn't tell Ian that. I couldn't tell anyone that. Unfortunately those with the most potential to hurt my sister already knew exactly what she was worth.

I shrugged, then motioned for the waitress to bring me a fresh drink.

"Is drunk the goal for the afternoon?" Ian asked.

I glanced at him in surprise. "Is three drinks enough to get you drunk?"

His brows rose. "Lush," he accused.

"Lightweight," I returned, and his eyes narrowed.

"I'll have one more, as well," he said to the waitress, when she picked up my empty glass. Then he met my gaze again as she left. "Your sister's not his only Binder, though, is she? Surely he has a fail-safe. A redundancy, in case of system failure?"

I laughed. "Spoken like a systems analyst. And yeah, of course there's another one." But the truth was that Jake rarely used him. Barker was in his mid-sixties and already having health issues when Jake started the search for a new Binder seven years ago. In fact, Barker's failing health was *why* Jake had started looking. He needed a new Binder in place to start sealing all service oaths—both new enlistments and reenlistment—long before the aging Binder died, and his seals died with him. It hadn't taken Jake long to realize how powerful Kenley really was, and she quickly became the primary Binder. The single, fragile brick the entire structure rested on.

That was one of the few tactical errors I could point out in Jake's quest to own the whole city—he depended too much on my sister. He got away with that by signing me—someone who wanted Kenley safe even more than Jake did. I would do anything to protect my sister—unfortunately protecting her also meant protecting Jake's interests. Which he'd counted on.

"How long has Kenley been working as a Binder?"

"That's a complicated question. She's been getting paid—" and locked away from the world "—for six and a half years. But she's been binding since she was ten."

"Ten?" Ian's eyes widened and his mouth opened a little in surprise.

"Yup. In fact, I was part of the very first binding she sealed. It was an accident."

"She *accidently* bound you to something?"

"To three of my friends. We were just messing around, like girls do, promising to always be there for one another, and Kenley said we should write it down. Looking back, it seems obvious that she was feeling the first manifestation of her Skill, but at the time, we didn't know we came from Skilled blood. So we went along with her suggestion that we prick our thumbs and stamp them under this promise she'd scribbled on a scrap of paper, and that was that."

"Wow. How long did the binding last?" Ian asked, and my laughter that time sounded bitter and tasted even worse.

"It's still intact." Sixteen years ago, my little sister had bound me to my three best friends—Olivia, Annika and Noelle—and I'd been tied to them ever since. That oath was the reason I'd had no choice but to help Liv and Anne when they'd called. That oath was the reason I'd gotten shot, the reason Jake got shot and the reason I'd spent six weeks being tortured in his basement.

"How is that even possible?" Ian frowned, and there was something new behind his eyes. It looked like…fear. But surely that was just the dim lighting playing tricks. He wasn't scared of signing with Jake, so why on earth would he be scared of my little sister?

"I don't know. She hadn't had any training. My best guess is that the purity of her intent was off the charts. She *really* wanted us to be friends forever." Another shrug. "She thought of them as her friends, too."

"And did that work? Are you still close to the other three?" Ian looked fascinated, but I couldn't miss the tight line of his jaw and the way his hand still clutched his glass.

"The binding worked flawlessly. The intent failed miserably." And all of us had suffered from both.

"So you don't talk to them anymore?"

I shrugged. "Noelle's dead. Olivia and Anne…well, it's not safe for us to see each other," I said, and Ian frowned, like he wanted to argue. Like he might want to convince me that nothing was more important than our human connections—a concept my grandmother had drilled into me from the day my parents died. But I didn't need to hear that from him. "Bindings never favor those being bound, Ian. Ever. Even most married couples who are totally, sloppily in love when they say the words will one day resent the binding that ties them together."

His brows rose. "You don't believe in love?"

"Of course I believe in love," I admitted, and his eyes widened in surprise. "But I also believe that binding yourself to someone is the quickest, most efficient way to kill that love. Love should stand on its own feet, with no force or obligation."

"So, you'd never sign a sealed marriage contract?"

"Hell no. Binding yourself to someone else is like literally tying yourself to them. Eventually the ropes start chafing and you can't move without pain and the constant reminder that even if you wanted to leave, you couldn't. When love has to be defined by an inability to leave, it isn't really love. Real love is staying with someone because you want to be there, not because you have no other choice. Anything else is just lust, or obsession, or something less innocent."

The waitress set our third drinks on the table, and I asked for the check and two glasses of water. But Ian was still frowning, still thinking through my discourse on love. "Is Tower bound to his wife?"

"Not in the way that you're thinking." He wasn't obligated to stay with her, and the opposite was also true. "And she's not bound to the syndicate, either. She's his wife, not his employee."

"And you like that about him?"

"No." There was nothing I liked about Jake Tower, except the fact that he'd kept Kenley safe, even if he had his own reasons for doing that. "But I respect it."

Ian nodded faster, like he understood. "But you don't

respect his business—the political influence that is his bread and butter?"

"Names and blood are his bread and butter. Which sounds kind of disgusting, when you put it that way. But he doesn't limit himself to politics. He works with casting directors, record labels, and all kinds of the rich and soulless who'll do and pay anything to slant the odds in their favor. He also has a growing reputation with patent holders and inventors in the technical sector. You wouldn't believe how much money there is to be made in new tech. And how reluctant the designers are to give up their rights to their own inventions."

"Bastards. Where's their team spirit?" Ian's eyes sparkled in good humor for the first time since he'd seen Jake's pet project.

"Always thinking of themselves," I said, grasping at an opportunity to lighten the mood, because anything was better than the way he'd been looking at me earlier. "There's no *I* in intellectual property."

"So, where does Tower get these names and blood samples? I assume he doesn't just go jabbing strangers with needles."

"Don't assume anything." I drained the last of my drink and thanked the waitress when she set two glasses of water on the table. When she was gone, he watched me, waiting for me to continue. "Let's just say there's a nurse's uniform hanging in my closet, and it's not for Halloween."

"Stealth phlebotomy. Illegal, immoral and incredibly dangerous. But also devilishly clever. I'm impressed."

"Don't be. It wasn't my idea, and I'm not proud of it. There are a million other ways to do it, though. Shadow-walk into one of the older courthouses, where they still keep physical copies of birth and marriage certificates. Steal someone's wallet. Break into the bloodmobile while everyone's gone to lunch."

"And you don't feel guilty about that? About taking blood meant to save someone's life?"

I shrugged, hoping he couldn't read the thoughts behind my next words. "Guilt is one of those concepts that has no practical application." And the truth was that the blood I took did save someone's life. It kept Jake— not to mention my own body—from killing me for disobeying orders.

"So, what would I be doing, specifically. What did the last Blinder do?"

"Not as much as you'll be able to do, that's for sure."

"Because I'm stronger?" He looked vaguely uncomfortable as he spoke, like he wasn't used to honking his own horn.

"That and because you're…um…" I made a vague gesture at his face, reluctant both to admit the truth and to understand that reluctance.

"I'm…um…left-handed?" Ian grinned. "A democrat? A nonsmoker?"

I huffed in irritation. He was going to make me say it. "Because you don't smell like cheese, jiggle when you walk, or snort with every other breath because you refuse to get your sinuses flushed out. Also, you're not… horribly offensive to the eyes." I mumbled the last part, hoping he wouldn't hear, yet wouldn't ask me to repeat.

"Ms. Daniels, unless I've misinterpreted that colorful description of everything I'm not, it sounds like you just paid me a compliment."

"I'm pretty sure that's not what I did." In fact, I'd gone out of my way to make *sure* that's not what I was doing.

"Oh, I think it is. I think you just said that I'd be better at the job than Tower's last Blinder was because I'm not unattractive. First of all, thank you. Compliment accepted." He bowed his head slightly, like I'd just offered to crown him king of the universe. Then, in the next second, he pasted on a frown. "Second of all, I am offended on behalf of pretty people everywhere. I'm not just a chiseled jaw and eyes you could get lost in. I am worth more than the sum of my defined biceps, sculpted pecs and a six-pack you could scrub laundry on."

I nearly choked on an ice cube. "You have a six-pack?"

"Okay, maybe a four-pack. At *least* a carton of hard lemonade. But my point is that you have no right to judge my potential as a crime lord's lackey by my looks alone."

I nodded solemnly. "Don't hate you because you're beautiful. Got it."

His brows rose and I knew what was coming before he even opened his mouth. "You just called me beautiful."

"My point was that you'll be able to blend in when you need to and stand out when you need to, and Ray Bailey couldn't do either of those. You'll be able to flirt your way into secure spaces, then open the door for a Traveler to bring in the rest of the crew."

"You're saying that Tower will exploit me for my looks?" Holt asked, and at first I thought that was another joke. It seemed too obvious a statement to be serious.

"He'll exploit everything you are and everything you have. Your job description will read something like, 'whatever the hell Jake Tower wants from you.'"

Someone cleared her throat next to our table, and I looked up to see the waitress standing there with nothing in her hands. "Is there anything else I can get you two?" she asked, and I realized she was hinting at the check, which meant her shift was probably over.

"No, I think we're fine." I set my credit card on top of the bill—the syndicate would reimburse me after I filed the receipt—and she slid both into the pocket of her black apron. Then she picked up my empty short glass and when she turned to say something to Ian, the glass she held slammed into Ian's full glass of water. Which then slammed into mine. The water from both glasses poured over the edge of the table and onto my lap like a miniature waterfall. An *ice-cold* waterfall that splashed all the way up to my chin and soaked through my jeans so fast I may as well have been sitting on a glacier.

The waitress stared, frozen. And for a moment, I was too stunned to move.

Then that moment was over.

"Son of a motherfucking, ass-reaming, shit-eating, hell-dodging soulless bitch!" I stood too fast and my head swam, and the water poured down my pants to form freezing puddles in my boots.

Ian burst into laughter, the waitress burst into tears, and more profanity exploded from my mouth so fast I couldn't even tell what I was saying. But the whole damn bar heard it.

"I'm so sorry!" the waitress blubbered. "Here, let me help." She pulled off her grease-stained black apron and started wiping at my crotch until a growl rumbled up from somewhere deep inside me.

"Get. The fuck. Off me," I said, so soft I barely heard the words. She backed away, clutching her apron in one shaking fist.

"I'm so sorry. Let me take care of the bill." She set my credit card back on the table.

"It's coming out of your check," the bartender called from across the bar, and the waitress flinched.

"That's not necessary." Ian dropped a fifty and a twenty on the table, then grabbed my credit card and reached for my arm. But he stopped just short of touching me and held one hand out toward the back of the bar instead, gesturing for me to go first.

I stomped stiffly toward the bathroom, acutely aware that everyone was watching me. There was no sound, other than our footsteps. No silverware clanged. No ice cubes clinked. There was just me and my walk of shame.

In the back hall, Ian held the door to the tiny, one-person women's room for me, then followed me in and bolted the door while I cursed under my breath. "It's just a little water," he said, pulling handfuls of brown paper towels from the dispenser next to the sink.

"It's fucking Niagara Falls in my pants. With ice."

"There is a backlog of crude jokes in here just begging to be cracked," he said, tapping his own temple for emphasis. "But I want you to know that I'm holding them all back out of respect for your pain. I, too, have been the victim of an ice-water crotch deluge. There's no way to bear it gracefully."

"You're fucking right about that." And frankly, I was surprised to hear that he knew any crude jokes.

He chuckled again while I snatched the first handful of towels from him and started blotting my pants. "You can't help it, can you?"

"Can't help what?" I was cold. And wet. And starting to shiver, which pissed me off.

"Profanity flows through your veins like blood,

doesn't it? I bet you can't go a single day without bursting into a string of expletives foul enough to set a nun's habit on fire."

"The hell I can't," I mumbled, and he laughed again. "I said I could. I didn't say I *would*."

Ian stared down at me, green eyes practically shining with amusement, and my pulse spiked when I realized how small the bathroom was, and how close together we stood. "I dare you." The words were soft, his voice intense, like he was challenging more than just my proclivity for profanity.

I had to reach around him to drop the first handful of wet paper towels into the trash, and for one dizzying second, the full length of his body was pressed against mine, because there was nowhere else to go. "What are we, twelve?" I asked, desperately hoping he didn't notice the tremor in my voice.

"No self-respecting twelve-year-old would balk over a simple dare."

"I'm not balking," I insisted, suddenly short of breath now that the shocking cold of spilled water had given way to the body heat building between us in the small space. "This is not what I look like when I balk."

"You're right." He tilted his head, pretending to study me from another angle. "This is definitely the face of cowardice. It's a subtle difference."

"Smart-ass." I took the next handful of tissues as he offered them. "Fine. But for the record, this is a stupid fucking dare. What are the terms?"

"It's a bet, not a contract negotiation." He shrugged. "Don't cuss. If you do, you lose."

I frowned up at him, trying not to see the flecks of brown in his green eyes, almost mesmerizing from such a close vantage point. "You're a piss-poor negotiator. Do yourself a favor. Take a lawyer with you when you meet with Jake."

"I kind of feel like I need one now."

"You and me both. State your terms." Was the air-conditioning even on? How could I be so warm now, when I was freezing a minute earlier?

"Twenty-four hours. No cussing. No exceptions."

"What about life-and-death situations? No one could keep from cussing with a knife in her back or a bullet lodged in her chest," I said, plucking at the wet material clinging to my legs—until my hand brushed his thigh, and I froze, half embarrassed, half…intrigued.

"Are you planning to be shot or stabbed in the next twenty-four hours?" he asked, like he hadn't even noticed, and I wasn't sure whether to be relieved by that or insulted.

"Were you *there* in the alley? If I get hurt, it'll be in the line of duty, keeping your ass from getting poached."

"No exceptions," Ian insisted. "But if that's too much for you…?"

I frowned up at him. "You are such a child. Fine. No cussing for twenty-four hours. Starting now." I pulled my phone from my pocket to glance at the time. "Two thirty-four p.m. What do I get when I win?"

He smiled and spread both arms, and for a moment, I thought he was offering himself as the prize, and I flushed at the thought. For just a second. "My undying respect."

I didn't even bother to hide my disappointment. "You'll have to do better than that."

His left eyebrow rose. "My respect has no value to you?"

"That's not what I…" In fact, for no reason I could explain, considering that we'd just met, I *did* want his respect. But I also wanted free will, a billion dollars and a bathtub full of Häagen-Dazs, and I wasn't going to get any of those, either. "How 'bout we assume the fair market value of your undying respect is…a bottle of Grey Goose. The big one. Because your respect means that much to me."

He laughed. "Oddly, I'm flattered."

"But are you ready to put your money where your mouth is? I dare you to go the rest of your visit without slacks."

His mouth actually dropped open a little in surprise. "You want me to take off my pants?" he said, and when I realized what my dare had sounded like, I could feel my cheeks flame. But I couldn't make my tongue work right.

"That's not what I… I mean, I dare you to wear jeans for the rest of your visit, instead of slacks. And no tie. I bet you can't go the next four and a half days without your stuffy, corporate zombie clothes."

His grin seemed to warm his face, like he might still be thinking about that first misinterpretation of my dare. "Why four and a half days? You're only on the hook for twenty-four hours."

"To make up for the difference in the degree of difficulty. Unless you don't think you can do it."

"You're on. And if I win?"

"What do you want?" I asked, and regretted the words as soon as they were out of my mouth.

Ian stared down at me again from inches away, so close I could feel the heat from his skin through both layers of clothes. I could see what he wanted—some hint of it, anyway—in his eyes. And again, my breath deserted me.

"A compliment."

"What?" His answer was so unexpected I couldn't even make sense of it.

"If I win, you have to tell me what you like best about me. With a straight face."

"That's it?" Was his ego that malnourished?

"That's it." His smile was a quiet challenge, and I couldn't help wondering if this was some kind of trick.

"Fine. Let's get out of here." I unbolted the door and turned off the light, and his hand slid into mine like he'd been planning that since the moment he'd closed the door behind us. I stepped forward—there was only room for a single step—and he walked with me. A second later, we were in the bathroom of his hotel room, left dark on purpose that morning.

He let go of my hand and pulled the door open, and light poured in from the bedroom, but I stayed put when he stepped into it. "I have to go change, and I need to report to Jake after that. Will you be okay for a couple of hours?"

"I've been staying home by myself since I was nine, Kori."

"So you've got it down by now, right? I'll see you back here at four."

Ian nodded and started to close the door, then stopped and looked at me, and there was something in his expression I couldn't quite identify. "Will we be working together?" he asked. "If I sign with Tower?"

"Maybe." I shrugged. "Probably. But you never can

tell with Jake. Why? Is that a deal-breaker?" I was joking. At least, I was trying to. But he didn't laugh.

"Quite the opposite. I think that may be the only thing that would make wearing his chain links bearable."

Ten

Ian

I don't know why I asked her that. It wasn't fair. And it didn't matter, because I wasn't going to sign with Tower. Kori and I would never work together.

The damn dare was a mistake, too. If she won, I'd have to present her with a bottle of vodka, right around the time I killed her sister, like some kind of morbid condolence for the crime I'd committed. I'd be lucky if she didn't beat me to death with it.

What the hell are you doing, Ian?

When Kori was gone, I glanced at my watch, then picked up my cell phone. Aaron answered on the second ring. "Hello?" he croaked into the phone, and springs creaked as he rolled over in bed.

"Get up. I need a lift."

"Night shift, man. I gotta get more sleep."

"This is the only chance I'm going to have, and I have to be back in two hours. Get dressed."

More springs creaked, and Aaron groaned. "Where are you?"

I gave him the hotel's address and the room number, then hung up. Five minutes later, the bathroom door creaked open and Aaron padded into the living room of my hotel suite in huge, dog-shaped slippers and a pair of navy boxer briefs.

"Where the hell are your pants?"

Aaron shrugged. "You said you were in a hurry, so I rushed right over."

"Did anyone see you?"

Aaron scowled on his way to the minibar. "Do I look like an idiot?" When I only glanced at his slippers, he rolled his eyes. "Do I *normally* look like an idiot?" Before I could answer, he knelt in front of the minibar and opened the fridge. "I need a drink."

I slammed the fridge closed. "You can make coffee when we get there. There's a robe hanging on the back of the bathroom door."

Aaron put the robe on, then stepped into the bathroom while I pulled my phone from my pocket and autodialed Meghan's number. "Ian? Why isn't it done?" she said into my ear, after only a ring and a half.

My eyes closed. *Of course* she knew it wasn't over. She'd be able to feel it when the binding was broken. "Turn off the light. We're coming over."

Meghan hung up without a reply, and Aaron turned the bathroom light off as I pushed the door closed. He took my arm, bared by the sleeve I'd rolled up, and a second later we stepped into another bathroom thirty miles away, in the suburbs.

This bathroom felt familiar, even with the lights off. It smelled like fruit-scented shampoo, bleach and the slightly scorched scent of every scrap of blood-soaked material that had ever been burned in the old-fashioned iron tub. When I stepped forward and reached for the light switch, my foot landed on ceramic tile, not as old as the tub, but older than I was, by several years. The tile was yellow, like the wallpaper exposed when I flipped the switch and let the light in.

The floors in the rest of the house were real wood, scarred from use and warped in places from the spills and drips of three generations. Aaron and Meghan had grown up here, as had their mother. This house was as safe a rendezvous point as any other, and a good deal safer than Aaron's apartment in the city.

Meghan stepped out of a bedroom and into the hall, pulling the door closed behind her. She waved us into the living room without a word, and she didn't even seem to notice that her brother wasn't wearing pants.

We followed her down the hall, through the living room, and into the small eat-in kitchen, where Meghan sank into a chair at the table and scrubbed her face with both hands. Long brown hair tumbled over her shoulders, and Aaron paused to set one hand on her head—a wordless, comforting gesture—on his way to the coffeepot.

"How is he?" I asked, and I regretted being the one to break the silence before the words had even fallen from my tongue.

"No better. A little worse, maybe," Meghan said, and for the first time in more than two weeks, the exhaustion in her voice outweighed the accusation. She couldn't do this for much longer. Not on her own. But it would be over soon, one way or another. If I couldn't kill Kenley Daniels and break the binding, he wouldn't last much longer anyway.

But no one wanted things to end like that, least of all me.

"Can I see him?"

"I don't want to wake him up. He doesn't sleep much anymore." Meghan sighed, and the weight of the world slipped a little on her shoulders. "What happened?" she said, as Aaron filled the pot and poured water into the reservoir. And the accusation that was absent from her voice found its way to her eyes, where it simmered quietly, waiting for the moment to flare into true flames and roast me alive.

I sank onto the chair opposite her and rubbed one hand over my head, trying to decide where to start. A minute later, the scent of coffee drew my thoughts into some semblance of focus. "Remember my brilliant plan to get Kenley Daniels assigned as my tour guide-slash-recruiter for the duration of my visit?"

"I take it that plan's proven less than brilliant in hindsight?" Aaron took a mug down from the cabinet and leaned against the countertop as the machine spit the first drops of coffee into the carafe.

"I stand by the simple brilliance of the plan. The flaw is in the execution. Kenley has an older sister who fits the same general physical description." Though the more I got to know Kori, the less she looked like her sister, at least to me.

Aaron turned with the pot in hand. "Korinne Daniels is Kenley's sister?"

"Who's Korinne Daniels?" Meghan said, glancing from her brother to me, then back.

"Tower's guard dog bitch. But she's dead." Aaron glanced at me with both brows raised. "Didn't we already determine that? Every source we spoke to said the same thing."

I shrugged. "She's a little less dead than the rumors indicated."

"You got the *wrong sister?*" Meghan demanded, and I nodded.

"The same thing happened to Jacob in the Old Testament," Aaron said. "He worked seven years to earn Rachel's hand in marriage and got her sister Leah instead. That poor fool then worked *another* seven years just to earn Rachel as his second wife. If you think about it like that, you got a bargain."

"This isn't the Old Testament, Aaron," Meghan snapped.

Aaron poked the pause button on the coffeepot and filled his mug without turning. "All that means is that Ian's not gonna get to bed both sisters."

Her fist clenched around the edge of the table. "This isn't funny!"

"Maybe not 'ha, ha' funny, but we're in some pretty deep shit here, sis, and if we lose our sense of humor, what do we have left?" Aaron said as he poured dried creamer into his cup.

"Nothing." Meghan folded her hands on the tabletop, but she couldn't keep them from twisting, as if her fingers were trying to tear each other apart. "I'll have nothing left, without Steven."

Aaron frowned over the implication that he meant nothing to his sister, but we both knew that wasn't what she'd intended. She was too tired to think clearly.

A moan echoed from behind the bedroom door Meghan had closed, and I stood, but her hand landed on my arm. Her fingers were cold, her skin was pale, and her eyes were damp, but she never hesitated. "Let me."

I started to argue, but Aaron shook his head at me

over her shoulder, and I sank back into my chair as she crossed the living room toward the hall again. "She needs to do this," he whispered, once his sister was out of sight.

"If Steven wakes up to find her dead of exhaustion, he'll kill us both," I said, and Aaron gave a bitter laugh, no doubt picturing Steven just as I was. Healthy, happy, in good humor, and willing to slay any dragon for Meghan.

"It's your job to make sure that doesn't happen," Aaron said, sinking into his sister's chair with one dog-slippered foot crossed over the opposite knee, the hotel robe gaping over his thin chest. "So what's this Leah like? Is she going to be a problem?"

"Her name is Kori. She's smart, but she doesn't know it. She's funny, but I don't think she knows that, either." I shrugged, trying not to see her in my mind, a little frightened to realize I could picture her with almost perfect recall, down to the freckle on her left cheek, about an inch in front of her ear. "She's a little thin, but she makes one hell of a temptation. Which is exactly what Tower's paying her to be." The carrot dangled in front of the ass, guiding him toward the farmer ready to put him to work.

Naturally I was the ass.

"Well, that's more than I asked for." Aaron's brows rose, like he'd heard more than what I'd actually said. "Can you use her?"

"Do I have any other choice? I'm almost twenty hours into this mission and the only time I've even been in the same room with the target is when I shook her hand at that damned party, in front of two hundred other people."

Aaron shrugged and sipped from his cup, then swore beneath his breath when he burned his mouth. "That's an easy fix. Just tell Leah—"

"It's Kori," I corrected again, leaning back in my chair.

"Fine. Tell *Kori* that you want to meet some of your future associates. Have her get a group together. If she's any kind of sister at all, she'll invite Kenley, and you can get her alone and put a bullet in her head. Problem solved." He leaned back in the chair, cradling his coffee and looking quite satisfied with himself.

An unexpected flash of anger licked the base of my spine. He wouldn't be so indifferent if we were discussing shooting *his* sister.

"Yeah, that might work," I snapped. "If not for the fact that Kenley is under twenty-four-hour guard, to prevent exactly the kind of idiotic plan you just rattled off. I might be able to put a bullet in her, but not without taking a few myself."

Dying for the cause was the worst-case scenario, and things hadn't gotten quite that bad yet.

"Oh, right. You wanted to survive." Aaron shrugged and blew over the top of his mug. "So what are you going to do?"

"The fastest, easiest solution I've come up with is to get Kori to bring her sister along on a tour of Jake's side of town. Surely Tower will let her come without her usual bodyguard, since Kori has security experience and more motivation than anyone to make sure Kenley is safe."

But when I thought about that for too long, I started feeling nauseated. This wasn't some armed, hostile insurgent or terrorist. We were talking about killing someone's little sister.

Kori's little sister.

That part shouldn't have bothered me any more than the rest, but it did. In fact, the more time I spent with her, the more the whole thing bothered me. But if I didn't kill Kenley, Steven would die, and if she refused to give up on him, Meghan would die with him.

"Wouldn't it be easier to shoot her in her sleep?"

"Yeah. If I knew where she slept. But that's the bit of classified information Kori is least likely to give up."

"Maybe so, but she's not going to let you near her sister—even in broad daylight—until she trusts you completely. Can you make that happen?"

"I think we're almost there." I glanced at my hands, suddenly wishing I'd poured some coffee, too, so I'd have something to do with them.

Aaron set his mug down and cleared his throat to catch my attention. When I glanced at him, he frowned, studying me. "No, Ian," he said, finally.

"No, what?"

"You know what. I know that look."

"What look?"

"That look that says you've found a wounded puppy and you want to nurse it back to health. And keep it, like that dog that got hit in front of your house when we were kids."

"That wasn't me, that was Steven."

"Bullshit. It was you," Aaron insisted, and I didn't bother arguing. "Korinne Daniels is no wounded puppy, Ian. She's a fucking Doberman, and she'll rip your throat out if she finds out what you're really doing here."

I forced a laugh. "I was in the marines, and you don't think I can take a one-hundred-pound woman in a fight?"

"I think you won't fight her, because you want to *keep* her, but she is not a fucking puppy, Ian. You can't have her, you can't keep her, and you sure as hell can't let her get in the way of what you're doing here."

"I know." But I also knew that Kori didn't deserve what was coming. Neither of them did. I scrubbed both hands over my face, yet couldn't scrub away the guilt.

Aaron set his coffee on the table. "Don't lose sight of the goal here, Ian."

"You don't think I should feel bad about shooting her little sister?"

Aaron eyed me sternly. "Don't do this to yourself. Don't overthink it, and do *not* get emotionally involved. You're here to save your brother's life, and keep my sister from killing herself by trying to save him. I'm as sorry as I can be for your girlfriend's impending loss—it's the same loss you and I are both facing right now—but let's not forget that this whole thing is Kenley Daniels's fault in the first place."

"I know."

"And it's not like Korinne is a Girl Scout, either. She's got blood on her hands."

"So do I."

Aaron growled in frustration. "You killed men with guns, to keep them from killing anyone else. She killed people who got into Tower's way. There's a big fucking difference, Ian."

Maybe.

Kori and I had fought in different wars, but I wasn't naive enough to believe that her life in the syndicate was any less a battle than what I'd seen overseas.

"Look, we can argue about this all day if you want, but that's not going to change the facts. Kenley Daniels has to die to keep your brother and my sister alive. Where does your loyalty lie, Ian? With your own flesh and blood, and friends you've known your whole life? Or with a woman you met yesterday?"

"Here. My loyalty is here. Why else would I be here?" Steven and I had had our problems over the years, but I couldn't let him die, and that would have been true even if it wasn't my use of his name that had gotten him into this mess in the first place. He was my brother.

Blood mattered.

"Good. It better stay that way, too," Aaron said. "I am *not* going to tell my sister that her fiancé's liberator fell not to a bullet, but to one of cupid's fucking arrows." When he caught me staring at his coffee, he stood and pulled another mug from the cabinet. "Please tell me you know you're being played."

"I know I'm being played." But so was she.

"You're being played like a fucking *harmonica,* Ian." Aaron dumped sugar into the mug and followed it with creamer he didn't bother to stir. "She's getting paid to do what you want done, show you what you want to see and say what you want to hear, but she'd kill you in a heartbeat if Tower told her to. Do whatever you need to do. Fuck her, kill her, stuff her into a crate bound for China, for all I care. Just don't let her get in the way of the mission."

Meghan cleared her throat from the doorway, and Aaron's mouth snapped shut. He set my mug in front of her when she sank into an empty chair at the table.

"Any change?" I asked, eyeing the circles beneath her eyes. Had they grown darker since she left the kitchen?

"His kidneys," she said, her voice a weak whisper. "He's better for the moment. Sleeping again."

Aaron's hand shot across the table so fast I barely saw him move. He grabbed his sister's left wrist, and she tried to pull away from him, but obviously lacked the strength. Aaron pushed her sleeve back, and we both groaned at the sight of her arm.

Her skin was pale, nearly translucent, and every vein and artery below her bunched sleeve showed through. But they weren't blue. They were black. Every single one of them, like they ran with tar, rather than blood.

"You're killing yourself," Aaron said through clenched teeth.

Meghan shook her head and pulled her sleeve back into place when he let her go. "I'm saving him." But she couldn't hold out much longer, which was exactly what Aaron's accusatory glare at me said.

He stood and started pulling food from the refrigerator. "You need to call Dad, Meghan. If you don't, I will."

"I'll never forgive you," she whispered, and he flinched as he piled meat onto a slice of bread. It was the same argument they'd been having for two weeks. Their father was a Healer, too, and he could help her save Steven. He could share the burden. But she wouldn't call him because of what he'd say, and what he'd do.

Meghan's father would tell her she was championing a lost cause—no Healer can save someone from death by broken binding, because as soon as she repaired one organ, another began to shut down.

And he would take her away, by force if he had to, to keep her from dying alongside her doomed love. My doomed brother.

"Eat." Aaron set the sandwich in front of her, then pulled a carton of milk from the fridge. "This is crazy, Meg."

She ignored him and turned to me as she lifted the

sandwich. "What about the binding? Have you at least figured out what that bitch bound him to?"

"I haven't had a chance to talk to Kenley alone," I said. "She's definitely strong enough to do it." I'd never heard of a Binder using her skill at ten years old, and Kori's story had scared the shit out of me. "But are you sure she's the one? I've never seen her before, and she didn't seem to recognize me or my name."

"It's her," Meghan insisted. "That Tracker cost nearly every dime we had saved up, and he swears it was Kenley Daniels. He's come across her work a lot, with people running from the syndicate. Her blood sealed the binding, and it's strong. But he can't tell what kind of binding it is."

In a way, that was the worst part. Steven was mostly conscious, but usually incoherent from the pain, and even during his rare lucid periods, he hadn't been able to tell us what binding he'd accepted, and from whom. And there were too many questions the Tracker couldn't answer.

All we really knew was that it was a name binding, and that meant that whatever had happened was my fault. Steven and I had switched names years ago—when we were still kids—to give ourselves an extra layer of protection. If anyone tried to track my name, they'd find Steven and assume they'd made a mistake.

But the plan we'd concocted in childhood had backfired on us as adults.

At some point—we had no idea when—Kenley Daniels had bound Steven to something using her blood and his real name. But I'd been answering to Steven's name since we were eighteen years old, which meant she'd actually meant to bind *me*.

Steven was inches from death's doorstep, and it was all my fault.

Mine, and Kenley Daniels's.

Eleven

Kori

That time when I shadow-walked into my bedroom, I stopped a foot short of smashing my nose on the wall. Two weeks, and I was finally getting the hang of the tight space, which Kenley had used as an office before I'd moved in. Well, before Tower's men had moved my stuff in, while I was still in the basement. Eventually I'd get my own place. Once I was sure I was going to live long enough to need one.

I felt my way along the wall to the light switch and flipped it up, then peeled my wet pants off, cursing in my head. I wasn't sure whether profanity in the privacy of my own room—away from Ian's ears—would violate the terms of our bet or not, but you can't police someone's thoughts. That was one of many, many truths I'd learned working for Jake—the only one that brought me any comfort.

Clad in fresh, dry clothes, I crossed the tiny hall— really just a square of floor with four rooms opening into it—and pushed open the bathroom door, where I blinked in surprise and nearly jumped out of my own skin.

A young woman—not my sister—stood in my bathroom, staring at herself in the mirror over the pedestal sink. Her first name was Vanessa, if memory served, but I didn't know her last name. I only knew she was one of Jake's unSkilled computer geeks, and that Cam Caballero had been forced to recruit her for Tower after he killed the Binder who'd sealed her in service to Ruben Cavazos a couple of years earlier.

"Hey." Van turned to smile at me. "I'm done, if you need in here."

"Why are you in there in the first place?" I demanded. Then I noticed that she was wearing Kenley's robe. And nothing else, if the lack of clothing lines beneath satin meant anything.

Kenley's bedroom door opened behind me, and I turned to find my little sister staring at me, legs bare beneath one of the long T-shirts she usually slept in. "I thought you'd be out all day," she said by way of explanation, and for a moment, neither of them moved. Obviously waiting for my reaction.

"So did I." I squeezed past Vanessa to get into the bathroom. "And I would have been if some clumsy—" I stopped just in time and turned to Kenley with a frown. "Hey, if I accepted a dare to stop cussing for the next twenty-four hours, does that mean I can't cuss at all, or just when I'm with the person who dared me?"

Kenley grinned for several seconds when she realized I wasn't going to make a big deal about catching her in postcoital glow with her new friend. Then what I'd said sank in. "You agreed to stop cursing?" Suddenly she looked concerned. "What were the terms?"

"No terms. It's not a contract…it's just a stupid dare." I ran water into the bathroom cup, then drained it in several gulps.

"Who dared you?" Van asked as they both followed me into the living room.

"It was Holt, wasn't it?" Kenley said on her way into the kitchen as I pulled open the front closet and squatted in search of a dry pair of boots. "Why would you take that dare? How many times do I have to tell you that 'Na na na boo-boo' is not proper motivation for engaging in self-destructive behavior?"

"Where was that voice of reason half an hour ago?" I turned with my second-favorite pair of boots in hand to find Van and Kenley both blushing furiously, which explained exactly where they'd been half an hour ago. "I withdraw the question."

"We were gonna make waffles. You want some?" Van asked, pulling a box of Bisquick from the cabinet over the toaster. And that's when I realized this wasn't her first visit. *I* didn't even know where we kept the Bisquick.

"Waffles at two in the afternoon?"

Van shrugged. "It's Saturday," she said, like that should be explanation enough.

"Thanks, but I have to go meet Jake."

"That should make this whole 'no cussing' thing interesting," Kenley said, pulling a carton of eggs from the fridge. "At least it's just a dare, and not a sealed oath."

I stepped into my first boot. "What, you don't think I can do it?"

My sister looked up at me from across the counter. "I think profanity is your native language. That makes it a hard habit to break."

I thought about that as I brushed my hair and teeth. And I decided she was right.

I started to tell Kenley and Van that I was leaving, but sudden suspicious silence from the kitchen made my pulse spike in warning and drew me forward before I remembered that I was unarmed. But instead of an intruder, I found only my sister and her girlfriend, leaning against the counter in front of the steaming, hissing waffle iron, holding hands and just staring at each other.

It was so sweet I couldn't stand to watch. So I backed up without drawing their attention and closed myself into my room again with the light off. A second later, I stepped into Jake's darkroom. I hadn't been there in two months, but I'd been hundreds of times in the past six years, and it still felt exactly the same. A little bigger than most of the darkrooms at his various other facilities, and a little colder. And as dark as a void, like space with no stars.

I started forward, my hand outstretched, and three steps later, my fingertips bumped the switch on the wall, next to the door. Light flared to life overhead and I squinted while my eyes adjusted. Then I pressed a button on the small full-color display set flush with the wall next to the door. Static appeared on the screen, and a moment later a familiar face replaced it.

"Kori?" Danny Larimore stared out at me from the screen. "What the hell are you doing? There's a big red sign next to the monitor in here that says your darkroom privileges have been revoked. It's laminated and everything."

Which was why I didn't have the key card that would have gotten me access to the rest of the house without having to deal with someone in the security room. "I know, but I have to talk to Jake. Buzz him if you need to. Tell him it's about Ian Holt. He'll tell you to let me in."

"If this backfires and he decides to shoot the messenger, I'm comin' in there to kick your ass."

"Whatever." I could take Larimore even unarmed. "Just buzz him."

The screen lapsed into static again, and I filled the silence by running through the list of reasons I wouldn't recruit Ian, if I had any choice. Then I started on the number of ways I could kill Jake Tower—if that wouldn't be the worst strategic mistake in history.

I was up to boiling him alive in the blood of his own murder victims when Larimore appeared on-screen again. "He's sending someone to escort you to his office."

"I know the way."

"And he knows *you*. Sit tight." Then the screen went blank again, and again I was alone with my thoughts— a situation I found increasingly less comfortable with every occurrence.

A couple of minutes later, the door swung open into the hall, and David scowled at me, a strip of medical tape over his broken nose, dark bruises circling both eyes.

Great.

I stepped into the hall and the door swung closed behind me. David crossed both thick arms over his chest. "Make one suspicious movement, and I have permission to drop you where you stand."

"I think we both know how well that worked out last time." I turned to the right and headed for the staircase. "How pissed was Jake about you lying down on the job?"

David growled, and when I reached the top step, his

footsteps stopped behind me. "You know, I could just kick you down the stairs and say you fell."

I shrugged and turned to face him, careful not to grip the railing, which would make me look scared. "You could. And even if I don't manage to take you down with me, I'd be dead at worst, hurt and pissed at the least. Either way, that leaves you to explain to Jake that with me out of the picture, he's lost all the headway I've made recruiting Ian Holt. And you know how Jake deals with bad news."

With that, I made myself walk down the stairs, trying not to look like I was worried about being shoved with every step. Because I knew from experience that logic doesn't always trump anger and humiliation, and I'd fed David heaping helpings of both.

In the foyer, he grabbed my arm and pulled me close. "You look like you might be about to run off," he said, and I realized this was a power play. He wanted to be seen hauling me through the house like he'd caught me making trouble. I wanted to laugh. His little show wouldn't make the damage to his face look any better.

Jake's office was just off the foyer, and when we got there, before David could knock on the double glass doors, I spun and pulled my arm from his grasp, then punched him in the nose. Again.

David howled, and blood poured from his face. Again. While a couple of housekeepers came running with disposable towels and bleach, I knocked on the door and waited for a response. When Jake called for me to come in, I pulled open both doors and stepped inside, while behind me, two women in simple black uniforms tried to staunch the flow of blood from David's nose.

"What happened to your escort?" Jake asked as I pushed the door closed behind me.

"Ran into something." I dropped into one of the chairs in front of his desk. "I bet he'd be a real hazard on white carpet."

"Would your fist happen to be what he ran into?"

"Could be." I pretended to examine the blood on my hand. "My knuckles are suddenly sore."

Jake chuckled, and I exhaled silently in relief. "I always could count on you to test the weak points in my security." He handed me a wet wipe from the carton on his desk and I scrubbed the blood from my knuckles, then tossed the tissue into the gas fireplace, where he incinerated it with one press of a remote control button.

There would be no consequence for busting David's nose. No consequence for me, anyway, because Jake was in a good mood. Or because he was already pissed at David. Or maybe because his horoscope said he'd find humor in unexpected places today.

As for David… He'd been taken down two days in a row by an unarmed women five inches shorter and eighty pounds lighter. That meant he wasn't pulling his weight. I wouldn't be surprised if he found himself on much lighter duty in the very near future.

Jake leaned back in his chair and crossed his arms over his chest. "I assume you're here to report that Holt is eating out of your hands?"

I shrugged. "Well, he hasn't bitten off my fingers yet, so it's looking pretty good."

"Does he like you?"

"Yeah, I think he does. But I'm actually here to report something else. Cavazos made a play for him this morning. Two low-level musclemen in broad daylight. It was insulting."

Jake frowned. "On the west side?"

I nodded. "Less than half a mile from the hotel."

"Casualties?"

"None. Like I said, they were in over their heads. It looks like they found out where he was staying and waited for him to show up on the street. They may even be recon guys who just saw an opportunity and grabbed it. Cavazos will try again, though, and the next team will be more competent. I need a weapon, Jake."

"No, you don't. Cavazos won't send anyone he can't afford to lose past the river, so just stay out of the east side." Jake's brows rose in challenge. "Or should I assign David to protect you?"

"I don't know, he's kind of delicate," I said. "I'd hate for him to get hurt again."

Jake chuckled, but his eyes weren't laughing. "So you can handle this on your own, then?" he said, and that question only had one acceptable answer.

"Of course."

Sure, I could walk all over downtown in possession of the second most valuable piece of human commodity in the city, armed with nothing but quick fists and a sharp tongue. No problem.

Jake watched me, and I was careful not to fidget or to look away, or to give him any nonverbal hint that I was less than sure of myself. Appearing confident is half the battle with Jake.

The other half is being willing to grab the man next to you and use him as a human shield.

"Good," he said at last. "Where did you take him today?"

"He wanted to see the city, so we walked around downtown and I explained the basics of syndicate structure."

"What's his disposition toward signing?"

I shrugged, and the leather upholstery creaked beneath me. "Understandably hesitant, but interested."

"Have you come across anything we can use to make him less hesitant?"

"Not yet." That was mostly true, because I didn't yet know what Ian wanted from Jake. And since Julia wasn't there to read the tiny kernel of a lie buried deep in that larger truth, I would get away with it.

"So you walked, talked and dined all day long, and you didn't come up with anything useful?"

"Um… He's left-handed, a democrat and a non-smoker," I said. Jake was not amused. "In my own defense, liquor was the main course at lunch, so it's not like we lingered over conversation and coffee."

"What about his things? What name is on his license? What numbers are in his phone? Are there pictures in his wallet? Credit cards?"

"I didn't realize I was supposed to be spying on him."

"You're supposed to be convincing him to join the syndicate. Whatever that takes. Too many credit cards could mean he has heavy debt. Pictures of kids in his wallet could mean he has someone we can threaten."

"But you already ran a credit check, and a background check, and every other kind of check there is." I'd seen the results. Ian's parents and only brother were dead, and he had no other close living family members. He lived alone, and well within his means. He had $17,000 in savings and no stock portfolio. He owned his car outright—a two-year-old midlevel sedan—and rented a two-bedroom house. He was an ordinary man with a good sense of humor and an extraordinary Skill.

"That won't tell me what bastards he fathered on the sly, or what debt he's racked up under someone else's name."

"He's not a thief, Jake." Or a deadbeat dad. He just wasn't.

Jake rolled his chair backward and pulled open a mini-fridge built into the credenza behind him. "You're a lot of things, Kori. A steady hand, a good shot, a beautiful face, a foul mouth, an abrasive bitch and, recently, a very big pain in my ass. But one thing you've never been is naive." He pulled a bottle of water from the fridge and pushed the door shut, then rolled his chair back to his desk and scowled at me over it, bottle in hand. "You don't know what he is, and the minute you start thinking you do is the minute you've failed this assignment. You only know what he lets you see, and the reverse damn well better be true."

I nodded—you can never go wrong with a noncommittal answer.

"Only two kinds of people join the syndicate. Those who have something to hide and those who have nothing to lose. It's your job to figure out which one of those descriptions fits Ian Holt."

"What if neither of them fits? He hasn't said he'll sign yet," I said, and immediately regretted reminding him of what I hadn't yet accomplished.

"He's here for a reason, Korinne. Find out what that is." Jake cracked open his water bottle and took a long drink, but his gaze never left me, disapproving stare intact. "Where are you taking him for dinner?"

I shrugged and, too late, I realized he probably wasn't going to like my answer. "I thought I'd let him choose."

Leather creaked as Jake sat straighter in his chair. He leaned forward, arms crossed over his desk blotter. "So, he ordered his own breakfast, you neglected to feed him lunch, and you've made no dinner reservations? The plan is to weaken him with hunger? Starve him until he signs?"

Making concrete plans for dinner honestly hadn't occurred to me. I never ate anywhere that required reservations unless I was with Jake—he took two bodyguards everywhere he went—and even then, his assistant always did the reserving.

"I can make some calls," I mumbled, digging my phone from my pocket.

"What, the fry cook at Denny's owes you a favor?"

I had no good response to his piercing sarcasm, so I bit my tongue. Until it bled.

"I'll make dinner arrangements. You go fetch my guest. I'm ready to discuss business." He reached for his desk phone and waved one hand at me in dismissal.

"Can I get a key card?" I said, standing.

Jake looked up at me, anger flashing in his eyes. "When and if I want you to have unlimited access to my home, I'll give you a key card. But don't expect that to happen anytime soon."

I nodded curtly, pretending that didn't sting. I didn't want it to. I didn't want to give a damn that he still didn't trust me, because I'd never trusted him a day in my life. But it did sting, and beyond that, it was a hell of an inconvenience, not being allowed into the syndicate's headquarters without being personally cleared by security every time I traveled into the darkroom.

I excused myself and made my way back upstairs alone and was not surprised to see that Jake had sent another guard to make sure I went no farther than the darkroom. This one didn't grab my arm. He didn't even speak to me.

He must have liked his face the way it was.

Twelve

Ian

I didn't know Kori was there until she stepped out of the bathroom without warning, and I nearly jumped out of my own skin. I'd met shadows that made more noise. "You know, you should give a guy some warning. What if I'd been naked?"

She shrugged and followed me into the living room. "I could use a good laugh."

"Ha ha." But unless I was mistaken, she didn't look horrified by the possibility.

"Your presence has been requested at syndicate headquarters," Kori said, perched on the arm of the nearest couch.

"Now?" I asked, and she nodded. "And headquarters would be where?"

"Jake's house. But don't let that lull you into a misplaced sense of comfort."

"Wouldn't dream of it." I opened the minifridge and pulled out two sodas, then tossed one to her. "What does he want?"

"To talk business. And probably to apologize for your mistreatment at my hands."

My brows rose in surprise and I spread my arms to take in the elegant suite around us. "If this is mistreatment, you can abuse me any day, Ms. Daniels."

She laughed, and I watched her. Making her smile felt like a victory.

"So, what if I don't want to report to Tower? What if I'd rather sit here and finish this soda with you?"

Her smile died a slow death. "Then I'd have to assume that you're not seriously considering our offer. And I'd be obligated to relay that to Jake."

"Obligated?" I said, and she shrugged.

"I can't lie to him."

I twisted the top from the plastic bottle and the soda inside fizzed briefly. "I take it he doesn't bear bad news gracefully?"

Kori blinked and seemed to consider the question. "Honestly, he doesn't get much bad news. Messengers tend to go out of their way to make sure they only bring him good news. Many a decision has been changed at the last minute by a messenger with a will to survive."

I watched her, waiting for a smile, or a laugh, or even one sharply arched brow to tell me she was joking.

She *had* to be joking. Right?

I wasn't going to take the chance, either way. I couldn't afford to piss off either Kori or Tower until I had a clear shot at Kenley Daniels.

Standing, I screwed the lid back on my bottle and set it on the coffee table. "So, anything I should know about this meeting?"

Kori shrugged and sipped from her own bottle. "Don't

promise him anything. Ask for more than you expect to get, so he can talk you down a little and save face."

"But I haven't agreed to sign yet."

"Exactly. This is his chance to try to buy you. Later, when you *do* agree to sign, the first draft of your contract will reflect whatever the two of you hash out in his office today. Nothing's official until the ink has dried, but you want a good starting place. You *need* a good starting place."

Except that I didn't want to start anything with Jake Tower and his organization. I'd come here to finish things.

An hour and a half later, after endless rounds of verbal posturing, thin pretense and precisely worded defensive blocks from us both, Tower leaned back, hands resting on the padded arms of his desk chair, evidently satisfied.

I'd been very careful to ask for more than he'd give the typical recruit, to show that I knew my own value, but I only pushed the issue on a couple of points, mostly because I had no real intention of signing and I didn't want to waste any more time making demands I would never see met.

In the end, Tower was satisfied that he was getting the better end of the deal, but not suspicious that his victory had come too easy. And by the time he pressed a button and asked his sister to bring in a round of drinks—signaling the end of our "business talk"—I was mentally exhausted. I'd had very little experience with negotiation, and overthinking everything I planned to say before I could say it had given me one hell of a headache.

When Julia Tower arrived with a tray of drinks, Kori

opened the door for her, then followed her in from the foyer, and I felt myself relax a little at the sight of her.

Then I realized that was *not* the reaction I should have to the woman who was trying to get me to sign over my free will. Tower wanted me to be comfortable with her. He wanted me to trust her. He wanted me to be blinded with need every time I glanced into those big brown eyes, so I wouldn't have the clarity and focus to understand what I'd be signing away when he put that pen in my hand.

But it wouldn't work.

Sure, I wanted her. But if I let my guard down even for a second in this den of lions, one of them would bite my head off.

Tower frowned up at Kori from his desk chair. "How much of the business side of things have you shown Mr. Holt?"

She froze, and I remembered what she'd said about being unable to lie to him. Fortunately there was nothing stopping *me* from lying to Tower. "Not much," I said. "Today I wanted to see downtown and get a feel for the syndicate's structure. Kori was kind enough to oblige me."

It wouldn't occur to me until later that night to wonder why I'd lied for her without a second thought.

Tower glanced at his sister, then his gaze slid to me, and I felt the weight of it. This was different from how he'd looked at me at the party. This look was skepticism and surprise, and for a moment, I thought he'd call me on my lie. But then he only turned back to Kori and nodded, and Kori turned toward the door. We'd obviously been dismissed.

"Mr. Holt," Julia Tower called, and Kori's hand froze on the doorknob. "How are you enjoying your stay?"

"Very well, thank you," I said, and Kori turned to face her slowly, dread written in every line on her face.

"I assume Korinne is treating you well?"

"Of course. She's gone to great lengths to accommodate my curiosity."

"Good." Tower stood and rounded his desk toward the door, brushing Kori aside as he gestured for me to walk with him. "I've made reservations for you both in my name at Philemon's. Best filet in the city."

"Thank you, but that really wasn't necessary," I said, and Tower frowned.

"I'm afraid it was. I'm confident that Kori is an excellent tour guide, and she has certain other gifts to share, I'm sure, but her perspective on the syndicate may be a bit…narrow." He stopped in the middle of the foyer and turned to look right into my eyes, ignoring Kori and his own sister like they weren't even there.

"Your Skill is formidable and your strength is very rare. That makes you much more valuable than any common Traveler, if I may be blunt, and the trajectory we foresee for your future soars far higher than hers, which, frankly, has already declined from its peak. So go out tonight and eat and avail yourself of any other amenities we have to offer. But please keep in mind that while Korinne is at your disposal, we have many other, more sophisticated treats for you to sample, should your appetite change."

He glanced at her on the last word, and Kori's fists clenched at her sides, but she stared at the floor.

Tower pulled her aside then, while his sister tried to distract me with pointless small talk, and I could barely hear the single sentence he growled at her, ius hand tight around her arm, though he flinched as if his grip hurt him, as well. "No. More. Bars."

Minutes later, after another trip through Tower's darkroom, we stepped into my hotel suite and Kori sank onto one of the couches, her expression carefully blank. She just sat there, staring at her hands, perpetuating the longest silence I'd endured since meeting her.

"He's full of shit, you know," I said when I couldn't stand to see her like that anymore. Kori was like a bonfire, blazing with bright light and sometimes harsh heat, and Tower had just kicked dirt all over her, smothering the flames. I didn't like seeing her light put out. In fact, sitting there watching her, I realized I hated it. "Ninety-five percent of sophistication is pretense. The other five percent is good wine, and I prefer the latter without the former."

"What does that even mean?" she asked, without looking up.

"It means that I don't want to trade you in for a more sophisticated model. I like the sharp edges and surprises."

I told myself it was okay to say that. To admit a truth of my own, after all the truths she'd already shown me. I even tried to convince myself that telling her was part of my job. I needed her to like and trust me. But I'd obviously managed to say the wrong thing.

"Yeah. You like sharp edges," she spat. "That's why you wanted me to stop cussing, right?"

Damn.

"That was just a game, Kori. A stupid game to push your buttons. To see how you'd react, because…" I took a deep breath and leaned forward, hoping to catch her gaze. "Because you never do what I expect. But you're right. It was a stupid game. Forget about it. The bet is off."

"Oh, no, the bet's still on," she snapped, and a flare of anger finally burned through the shield of ambivalence she'd erected. "I'm not going to break my word. But for the record—" She stopped suddenly and looked away, hands clenched around the edge of the cushion she sat on.

"What? For the record, what?" I could practically taste the gritty honesty of whatever she'd been about to say, and I wanted to hear it, because whatever it was, it came from her soul. It was a truth about her.

"Nothing."

"No, that was something. I want to hear it."

Her eyes flashed in anger again. "You can stop pretending we're on an even playing field, Mr. Holt," she snapped again, and I flinched over her cold, formal use of my surname. "Until your signature is dry on Jake's contract, you hold all the power here and I can't afford to say anything that will make you mad."

I blinked, surprised. "Why? You think I'm going to go tattle to Tower if you hurt my feelings? Is that really what you think of me, even after I lied about what you showed me today?" I demanded, and her anger faltered, just for a moment. "Tell me what you were going to say, Kori."

Let me in. Just a little.

"Fine." She sat back, arms crossed over her chest in a pose that was probably supposed to look unaffected, but really looked defensive. "For the record, I don't *care* whether you like sharp edges or sophistication. I don't care what you like in a woman, and I don't care what

Jake thinks about my social status. If you want to trade me in for a different 'model,' go ahead. You won't be hurting my feelings."

I shook my head slowly. "That's not it," I said, trying not to look disappointed. "That's not what you were going to say. I can see it in your face." I *would* be hurting her feelings if I traded her in. Which seemed to imply that she did, in fact, *have* feelings.

And finally she nodded. "This job—recruiting you— is my chance to get back into favor with Jake. I'm not cut out to be a recruiter, Ian. But I have to recruit you to get my life back."

That felt closer to the truth, but there was still something she didn't trust me enough to show me. But pushing would only drive her further away.

"Fine, then let the recruiting continue," I said. "I believe we have reservations tonight, on Tower's dime? Some fancy restaurant?"

"Philemon's. They *do* have really good lobster." And we'd missed lunch, as my growling stomach was quick to point out.

"Then we'll both get one. Maybe two. Let's go recruit me in style," I said, and finally she smiled, a glimpse of a rainbow after the storm. "What's the dress code at this fancy restaurant?"

Kori frowned. "You're gonna need a suit. And they'll probably make me wear a dress."

"I thought you hated dresses."

"I do."

"And I have a bet to win. So we'll both wear jeans?"

Her smile grew just a little. "Mr. Holt, I think we may make a rebel of you yet."

After a quick trip back to her sister's apartment, Kori

stepped out of my bathroom in a low-cut, drapey black silk blouse that bared a two-inch strip of skin down the center of her torso, all the way to the bottom of her sternum. I wasn't sure how the damn thing even stayed on, and I caught myself holding my breath when she turned, watching for accidental gaps in the material.

"Wow, you look beautiful," I whispered when she stepped into the light, trying not to stare. I hadn't meant to say it. The words fell from my mouth before I could call them back.

"Does this cover all my rough edges?" She held her arms out hesitantly, like she wasn't sure she wanted to be inspected. "'Cause I feel like it doesn't cover much of anything."

"Your rough edges are thoroughly hidden. But it's good to know they're still under there," I said, my voice deeper than I'd intended it to be, my gaze glued to hers. My stomach twisted with nerves like I hadn't felt since junior high. I clasped my hands at my back because that was the only way I could control them. I wanted to reach for Kori.

I was dying to touch her.

"I feel kinda stupid in the blouse," she admitted, plucking nervously at the material. "But Kenley insisted this would keep me from getting tossed out of the restaurant."

"Your sister has wonderful taste." I crossed my arms over a pressed button-up shirt, tucked into my spare pair of jeans. Then I made myself think about Steven and Meghan—the mental reminder I needed in order to focus on the job at hand, rather than the woman in front of me. "Do you think she'd like to join us? Your sister?" Kori frowned, and I slid my hands into my pockets. "I'm interested in her role in the syndicate. I haven't met many Binders."

"She's…with someone tonight."

I shrugged. "So ask her to bring him. I'd love to get multiple perspectives on life in the Tower syndicate."

Kori's frown deepened. "I don't think they're ready to be seen out together. In public. Yet." She reached for the bathroom doorknob. "Are you ready?"

"Yeah." I buried my frustration, along with a sizable amount of guilt over the fact that I was about to dine in a five-star restaurant, while my brother lay dying, hidden away in his girlfriend's childhood bedroom. "Let's go."

Kori took us through my darkened bathroom once again, this time into an alley behind the restaurant, deep with shadows in the setting sun. "Not the most glamorous way to travel, I know," she admitted, as we stepped out onto the sidewalk. "But it's definitely the fastest."

Inside, the hostess wore an ankle-length black dress and a too-tight bun, and looked down her nose at our jeans. "We have a reservation for two," Kori said.

"For what time?" She didn't even look at the reservation list, as if she'd already decided we were lying.

"Actually I'm not sure. I didn't make it," Kori said, and the hostess's gaze hardened even more.

"Mr. Holt? Ms. Daniels?" A man in an expensive suit plucked the list from the podium, brushing the hostess aside without even a glance. We both nodded, and the manager—who else could he be?—smiled like he was made of sunshine. "Mr. Tower reserved your table for the entire evening, so please take your time and enjoy your meal. Erin, if you don't mind?" he said, gesturing for the hostess to show us to our table.

She took us to a quiet corner of the restaurant, where

I somehow felt both sheltered and exposed, and before I could even glance at the menu, a waiter appeared to pour two glasses of red wine, explaining that Mr. Tower had selected it himself.

"Did he order our food, too?" Kori mumbled, and the waiter chuckled.

"No, but he did offer suggestions."

We ordered several courses, and while we waited for the first of them, I sipped from my glass, watching her. "Tell me something about yourself. Something I don't already know. Something about your family."

"Aren't we supposed to be talking about the syndicate?" she said, staring into her wine skeptically.

"Okay, then, tell me something about your family *and* the syndicate. Is this the family business, or is it just you and Kenley? Are your parents bound? Any other siblings?" I knew I was pushing my luck, but I had to find some way of bringing her sister back into the picture before too much time spent with Kori made me forget my purpose, or hell, even my own name. She was Calypso, and I was starting to worry that she'd caught me. And the scariest part was that in spite of the guilt, and the lies, and the ugly truth of my mission, I wasn't sure I wanted to be released.

Kori hesitated for one long moment, like she was trying to decide whether or not she could trust me. Then, finally, she spoke. "Kenley and I have an older brother, but he's not syndicate, thank goodness. He's his own brand of trouble, even without criminal ties."

I didn't ask her brother's name, and she didn't offer it. Either would have been a big faux pas among the Skilled, who know that names, like blood, carry power.

"What about your parents? Are they bound to Tower?"

"No, they died when I was a kid," she said, and I blinked in surprise.

"Mine died a few years ago," I said softly, and I recognized the echo of old pain in her eyes. "Who raised you?"

"My grandmother, and no, she's not syndicate, either. In fact..." Kori exhaled, like she couldn't believe what she was about to say. "In fact, she doesn't even know Kenley and I are bound. If my parents knew, they'd probably come back from the dead just to yell at us."

"So, how did you wind up bound to Tower?"

"I...um..." She stared at the stark-white tablecloth. "That's kind of a personal story, and it's not entirely mine to tell."

Not entirely hers? My curiosity doubled. "So just tell me your part," I said. "You have my word it will go no further. If that means anything."

I desperately wanted my word to mean something to her, but at the same time, I was fully aware that it shouldn't. I had been lying to her all along, and the lies would have to continue, but this part was true. I wouldn't betray this trust.

"I signed on to be with Kenley," she said after a moment of thinking it over. "I couldn't leave her here alone. She's not like me. She doesn't have any hard edges or any self-protective instinct. She's sweet. And nice. She would have been eaten alive."

But that didn't make any sense. The only thing I knew about Kenley Daniels—other than what I'd learned from Kori—was that she'd sealed my brother into a nonconsensual binding strong enough to kill him. And she must have done it by accident, because my brother didn't use his own name. She *had* to be aiming for me.

How could someone with enough power to seal the wrong person into a binding he hadn't consented to possibly be the sweet, innocent sister Kori had sold herself to Jake Tower to protect?

"You okay?" Kori asked, but I barely heard her, and I only distantly noticed the tray of one-bite salmon and rice appetizers the waiter set in the center of the table.

"You joined to protect your sister?"

She nodded. "I joined to try. But there's only so much I can do."

"What makes you think she needs protection?"

Kori frowned, like she may have heard me wrong. "The fact that she's here. Kenley got into some trouble when she was in college, and one of Jake's scouts swooped in promising to clean up her mess, in exchange for her services. She was terrified, and naive, and very young. She thought she had no other way out, so she signed up. Two days later, she showed up at my brother's New Year's Eve party in tears, begging for my help. But there was nothing I could do. She's a piss-poor negotiator and her binding had already been sealed. All I could do was negotiate protection for her in exchange for my own services."

"What kind of protection?"

Kori exhaled heavily and fiddled with the knife next to her plate. "I'm not allowed to discuss the specifics of my contract with Tower. But life in the syndicate can be really hard for a pretty twenty-year-old woman with only one chain link on her arm. Especially one who doesn't know how to shoot or fight. So I negotiated for a position with enough power to protect her. Then I defended that position by taking down everyone who got in my face, to make sure they all knew what would happen if they messed with either of us."

She shrugged to punctuate what felt like a confession, and I could only stare at her, trying in vain to reconcile the beautiful, almost dainty-looking woman with the warrior I—and the entire west half of the city—knew her to be.

Kori picked up one of four silver spoons on the platter and sniffed at the single bite it held, then set the spoon down again and made a face. "I think the salmon is underdone."

She was obviously trying to change the subject, and I decided not to push the issue. I didn't know what to do with what she'd already told me, and I wasn't sure how much more I could take with her sitting across from me, barely-but-elegantly draped in thin black silk.

There was nothing under that blouse. There couldn't be. Nothing but her.

"It's smoked," I said, picking up one of the spoons, just so I'd have something else to look at. And something to occupy my hands and my mouth, which seemed to be forming an alternate plan of their own, involving thin ribbons of black silk, bare skin and any room with a decent lock on the door.

"So it's raw?" Kori looked horrified. "People actually pay someone to not-cook their food? Even cavemen had fire."

I laughed. "Try it. You might like it." I ate one of the bite-size appetizers in demonstration, but she only frowned. "Am I going to have to dare you?"

"Low blow," she mumbled, choosing one of the three remaining spoons. "If I get sick from raw fish, I'm blaming you."

"If you get sick from a thirty-five-dollar smoked salmon appetizer at one of the best restaurants in the city, I'll nurse you back to health myself."

That time she smiled. And ate a spoonful of smoked salmon. But she obviously had to force herself to swallow.

"Not for you?" I asked, laughing at the face she made. In answer, she pushed the platter toward me and took a drink of wine, but that only twisted her expression into a stronger display of dislike.

"I'm two minutes away from ordering a burger and a beer," she threatened, pushing the wineglass away, too. "How can you drink this sh— Uh, this stuff?"

"It's an acquired taste," I said, lifting my own glass. "Much like the syndicate, I suppose."

"I guess." Kori shrugged and watched me from across the table. "The big difference between Jake and uncooked salmon is that eating what he serves *will* eventually kill you."

Thirteen

Kori

After the waiter came to refill his glass—mine was still full—Ian excused himself to go to the bathroom. I watched him make his way across the restaurant, pointedly ignoring my wine, wondering for the millionth time in the last twenty-four hours what Ian was looking for from Jake. And how I would be able to live with myself once he was bound, knowing I was the one who'd led the sheep to slaughter.

Halfway to the bathroom, Ian turned to speak to someone, and my heart nearly stopped when I saw Julia Tower stand from the table where she and Jonah had just been served their own appetizer. No doubt Jake had sent them to make sure I was getting the job done. Treating Ian right.

She and Ian spoke, and she laughed at whatever he'd said, and suddenly I desperately wished I could read lips. She would hear the truth—or lack of—in whatever he said. As a Reader, Julia was her brother's best and most trusted source of inside information. And one of my least favorite people in the world.

After another minute, she let him escape to the restroom, and if he'd come to hate her half as much as I had, the urinals in the men's room must have been a much more welcome sight than her face.

When he disappeared around the corner, she looked right at me, then started across the restaurant in my direction.

Fuck!

"I have to say, you've impressed me with this one," Julia said, sinking into Ian's empty chair uninvited.

"Because I'm still alive?"

"Because he actually likes you. And he thinks you like him." She picked up my wineglass and sipped from it, then held it as she crossed her legs and leaned closer, like she'd let me in on a secret. "I must admit, you're playing this one very smart. Jake will be pleased."

"Um…thanks?"

I never knew what to say to Julia, because I was never quite sure what she was talking about, but if I lied, she'd know it. So I usually treated her like I'd treat any snake in red satin—I avoided her like the plague. And when avoidance wasn't possible, I tried my best to dodge both fangs and venom.

She twisted the glass, swirling the red wine, and I found myself watching the way light shone through it. Anything to avoid eye contact with her. But I couldn't stop her from watching me.

"Uh-oh." She set the glass down and lifted my chin with one finger. I slapped her hand away, but it was too late. She'd already seen…something. Or maybe she'd pretended to see something. I never could tell with Julia. Her silence was as toxic as her words. "He's right, isn't he? You actually like him."

I didn't answer, because the answer didn't matter. If I told the truth, she'd know. If I lied, she'd know. Silence was my only defense.

"Don't do this to yourself, Kori," she whispered while my blood rushed fast enough to make me dizzy. "You know this isn't real. The reality is that he's champagne, and you're malt liquor." She spat the last phrase like it actually tasted bad, and my fingers twitched in my lap, itching to curl into fists. But if I punched her, that punch would be the last I ever threw. "His career path will take him soaring, and yours has already landed you in the basement."

"Shut up," I growled, itching to call her all the names running through my head.

"I'm trying to help you, Kori. I'm trying to keep you from hurting yourself."

That was a lie. It had to be. She would never help me, unless helping me somehow benefited her. But what could she possible gain from this?

"Just let him play his game. Let him fantasize until he's satisfied, then he'll sign with Jake and you'll be off the hook. There's no reason for you to get hurt by this."

I shouldn't have asked. I *knew* better than to ask. Just because she could read the truth didn't mean she would speak it. But after everything I'd already shown Ian—everything I'd told him—if I'd given him that much power over me and he was playing some kind of game, I was screwed.

"What game?" I hated myself for asking. For giving her that opening. But I had to know.

Her eyes widened and her jaw dropped open in a

staged display of surprise. She didn't even try to make
it believable. "Seduction, Kori. The game of seduction."
Fake surprise melted from her expression to expose her
natural look. Malice. The snake was about to strike.
"Don't tell me you haven't noticed."

I rolled my eyes. "He is *not* trying to seduce me."

"I think this has gone beyond 'trying.'"

"You are so full of…crap."

She lifted one brow over my uncharacteristically tame
language. "So, he hasn't told you you're beautiful? He
doesn't try to make you smile? He doesn't look right into
your eyes when he talks to you, so you feel important?"

"That doesn't mean anything, except that he's a nice
guy." Too nice for the syndicate. Too nice for me.

Julia leaned closer, looking deep into my eyes in
search of what every predator wants: fear. "Then why
did he lie about what you showed him this afternoon?"

Of *course* she knew he'd lied. She'd probably smelled
his intent before he even opened his mouth.

"Why do you think Jake let him get away with that?"
Julia demanded, her voice hard now, a little too angry to
be truly taunting. "Why do you think he let Holt cover
for you?"

"Because he didn't know?"

Julia's frown deepened, and I realized she hadn't
wanted Ian to get away with his lie. She'd wanted Jake
to punish me. "Jake knows everything. I make sure of
that. He let Holt lie for you because that's part of the
game. Holt was playing the hero, protecting the damsel
to win her over, and you fell for it."

"You're lying." But I couldn't even make myself believe that.

"Think about it, Kori." She leaned back in her chair,

arms crossed confidently over her chest. "Why would a man like Ian tolerate a woman like you? Why would he put up with brash and impulsive when he could have friendly and willing from any girl in Jake's stable?"

I couldn't answer. I *had* no answer.

"He's kept you around for the same reason a lion would rather kill its own dinner than eat from a dish. He wants the hunt. He wants to play the game. Even if the game is rigged." She shrugged, and her eyes flashed with cruelty. "After all, he *will* win. He gets to pretend to win you over with no chance of failure, because in the end, you're a sure thing. Right? The key is to never let him feel like he's hunting caged prey. The harder you feign disinterest, the more he will want you." Julia leaned even closer, staring into my eyes, enjoying whatever she saw there. "You can do that, right? You can make him feel like this is real? Like he's really working toward a prize?"

I couldn't speak. I couldn't think past the horrible ache in my chest. I didn't want to know what that pain meant, or how it could possibly hurt worse than what I'd lived through in the basement.

"I'm sorry, Kori," she said, her words sweet, her tone vicious. "I guess Jake just doesn't understand how badly a girl can be hurt by a game, if she doesn't know she's playing." Julia drained the wine from my glass, then set it down. "Or maybe he doesn't care." She smiled sweetly, then, and made her way back to her own table, where Jonah sat watching us both.

I sat at the table alone when she left, silently cursing Ian for accepting Jake's invitation, Jake for forcing me into this assignment and Jake's mother for giving birth to any of her three hell-spawn children in the first place. But by the time Ian got back to the table, just as the waiter brought out two bowls of soup, I'd moved on to cursing myself for ever believing a word any of them said. I could blame Jake, Julia and Ian until the day the sun devoured the entire planet, but that would never erase the fact that I'd broken my own number-one rule.

Trust no one.

Me, Kenley and Kris. It had been the three of us against the world since the day our parents died, leaving us with a grandmother who hadn't wanted kids of her own, much less grandchildren. They were the only ones I could trust. The only people I could lean on. Except that Kris was an hour away, and now Kenley had Vanessa. I was alone in a mess of my own making. And I had no idea how to get out of it.

"You okay?" Ian asked, lifting a spoonful of soup to his mouth.

"I saw you with Julia Tower," I said, stirring my own soup with my spoon. "What did she want?"

"She was asking about you," he said, and I watched him carefully, wishing for the first time in my life that I was a Reader rather than a Traveler. Shadow-walking had always made me feel safe and kind of stealthy, because I could get out of almost any situation armed with nothing more than a decent shadow. But whether or not Julia had been lying, she'd showed me one thing for sure—I could shadow-walk away from danger, but I couldn't walk away from the truth. Hell, lately I couldn't even identify it.

What if I'd been wrong about Ian from the start? What if it *was* all a game and everything I thought I knew about him was a lie? What else could I have been wrong about?

"What did you tell her?" I asked, when he studied my face, frowning.

"I told her you've been the consummate hostess. That you're beyond reproach, and that her brother couldn't have chosen anyone better to show off his empire and its many, varied offerings."

But Jake hadn't chosen me. He'd just given Ian what he asked for.

"So, you're enjoying yourself?" I heard the hollow note in my voice, but I couldn't fix it. I didn't know how to act like I was having fun when Julia had just pulled the rug out from under my feet and stuck around to watch me stumble off balance. I was angry, and confused, and more scared than I would ever admit, and it took every ounce of self-control I had to keep from spewing profanity into the heavens.

Unfortunately self-restraint was a poor substitute for gratitude and a love-struck gaze, or whatever Ian expected to see, if Julia was telling the truth. And suddenly I realized she'd known that. Had she set me up to fail, by telling me about Ian's game, knowing I couldn't play along if I knew I was playing at all?

Or was the whole thing a lie intended to make me paranoid and even more shrewish than usual?

"Well, this isn't exactly a vacation," Ian said, answering a question I'd forgotten I asked. "Why? What's wrong, Kori?"

"Is there something you want from me that you haven't gotten?" I demanded softly, holding his gaze. Silently daring him to tell me the truth, if there was anything to be told.

"Well, yes." He frowned. "Last I heard, you were still trying to figure that part out."

Right. Whatever it was that would make him sign. "And what you need from Jake, it's not some kind of game, is it? You're not just playing a game here?"

Ian pushed his soup bowl toward the middle of the table and leaned closer, his gaze holding mine captive. "No, Kori. I know I joke a lot, and the truth is that I like to see you smile. You don't do enough of that. But I'm not playing games with your boss. I came here with very serious intent. I swear on my own free will."

And that I believed. But whether he'd meant to or not, he'd misunderstood what game I was talking about.

"What brought this up?" he asked, handing his half-empty bowl to the waiter who already held mine. I hadn't taken a single bite. "Did Julia say something to you?"

"We don't get along," I admitted. "Which sucks, because Jake listens to her."

"Well, I gave her nothing negative to report, so try to forget about her." He smiled at something over my shoulder. "Your lobster is here."

I made it through the rest of the meal without losing either my mind or my temper, mostly because the food—the parts I recognized, anyway—was amazing and when I got back from my own restroom break, Ian had ordered something with vodka in it to replace the second glass of wine I'd turned down.

I tried to tell myself that he was being nice, not manipulative, but that was hard to believe because in my world the reverse was almost always true. Even a second drink and a huge slice of the most delicious chocolate cake I'd ever tasted weren't enough to completely settle my nerves. Julia's interference led me to look for hidden meaning in everything Ian said. She made me overanalyze every smile, every second of eye contact. And she wasn't finished.

After dinner, I ducked into the restroom one more time, and when I came out of the stall, she was standing at the row of sinks, watching me in the mirror. "It'll be tonight," she said, her mouth hardly moving as she dabbed gloss onto her lower lip. "He sounds like he's ready to move in for the kill. So to speak."

I squirted citrus-scented sanitizer on my hands. "What, you're psychic now, too?"

"You don't have to be psychic to see what's obvious. When you drop him off, he'll ask you to stay for drinks. Then he'll just ask you to stay…"

She turned to leave, then twisted to glance at me in the mirror one last time, her palm flat on the door. "Don't make it too easy for him, okay? Even a caged rabbit struggles a little before it's caught." Then she pushed the door open and left me staring at my own reflection, breathing too fast, my blood pumping fear and anger through my veins.

I tried to breathe, like Kenley had shown me. In and out, exhaling all the hate and pain. But this time it didn't work. This time memories weren't the problem, so burying them couldn't help. If Julia was telling the truth, I was trapped as thoroughly now by my own bindings as I'd ever been by the basement walls. And knowing what was coming didn't make it any easier to deal with.

You can do this. You have *to do this.*

I sucked in one last deep breath, then turned for the door, determined to cling to dignity until the last possible moment. But then the rage inside me crested and a wordless shout of fury erupted from my mouth. I whirled toward the sink and my fist slammed into the glass above it. The mirror shattered and slices of it fell everywhere, breaking into smaller shards in the sink basins and on the floor at my feet. And for about three seconds, I felt better.

Then I realized I'd just spilled my blood in a public restroom and had no good way to clean it up.

I snatched a cloth from the stack on the counter and tied it around my cut hand, then picked up the bottle of hand sanitizer and read the contents. Alcohol. I exhaled in relief, then upended the bottle and squirted a glob onto every single drop of blood I could find. I was still on my knees in the mess when the door opened behind me and the hostess came in.

She gaped at the destruction around me, her mouth open wide enough to catch a whole swarm of flies.

"The mirror fell right off the wall. Could have killed me," I said, dropping the nearly empty bottle of sanitizer in the nearest sink. "I might sue." Then I marched past her and out the front door to the sidewalk, where Ian was waiting for me.

He took one look at the cloth around my hand and lifted one brow. "Do I even want to know?"

"Probably not." I lead the way into the alley again without offering further explanation.

"Do you find trouble everywhere you go?"

"Sometimes it finds me."

I took him back to the hotel and he called downstairs for a first-aid kit, then refused help on my behalf from the man who brought it up. I cleaned and bandaged my cuts in the bathroom, then I stoppered the sink and dumped the bleach from Ian's travel kit—no Skilled person travels without bleach-solution in a spray bottle, even if it has to go in the checked luggage—over the cloth stained with my blood. Bleach would destroy the blood enough to keep it from being used against me.

"You want to tell me what happened?" Ian asked, glancing at my bandaged hand from the doorway.

"No." I didn't want to tell him anything until I knew whether or not Julia was lying.

"Kori, I can see that something's wrong."

"I'm fine." And maybe if I said it enough, we'd both eventually believe me.

In the front room, I glanced around at the view, and the couches, and the huge television, and the bottle of champagne sitting in a bucket of ice on a tall table against one wall—it had obviously been sent up moments before we'd arrived. This hotel suite probably cost more than I made in a month.

No one had ever wanted me as badly as Jake wanted Ian. But I knew better than anyone that the more Jake gave, the more he'd expect in return.

Angry, I marched across the room and plucked the small, embossed envelope from the tray the champagne sat on, trying to guess whether it had been sent by Jake or by Julia. But before I could take the card from the envelope, Ian gently pulled it from my hand. I looked up at him and immediately wished I hadn't. There was something there. Something in his eyes when he looked at me. Something important, but I didn't know how to interpret it. I'd lost all perspective.

Julia had *stolen* my perspective.

Ian looked worried—nervous—but I couldn't tell if that was because he genuinely cared that something was bothering me, or because his game wasn't working out the way he'd planned.

He stared into my eyes, and my palms started to

sweat. My head felt like it was floating above my body, not truly attached. I couldn't make sense of what I was feeling. Everything was all tangled up in a knot so complicated I couldn't follow the threads. And I had no hope of untangling them.

He wanted me. I could see that in his eyes. In the way he stood close, but not quite touching me. In the way he kept glancing at my lips, like he wanted to kiss me.

Some part of me wanted to kiss him, and that scared me so badly I couldn't breathe. I needed to back away. To put some space between us. But that same part of me remembered what things were like before the basement. Before every touch bruised and every mouth bit.

Ian didn't look angry. He didn't look nasty or cruel. He wasn't stalking or skulking. He just looked…interested.

If we'd met somewhere else.

If my life and Kenley's well-being weren't in Ian's hands.

If I were someone else, and *he* were someone else.

If the moment hadn't been manufactured by Jake Tower.

If any one of those things had been true, I might have wanted more than a kiss from Ian. I might have wanted to be with him. For a night. For a week. Maybe for more.

But this was… I couldn't do it. Not like this. Not when I had no choice. I couldn't breathe past the bitter lump in my throat or make my head stop spinning. I couldn't mute the voice in my head—*my* voice—shouting for me to run. Fight. Leave, before he said something neither of us could go back from.

"So, you all set?" I asked, and even to my own ears, my voice sounded brittle, like it might break any moment. Like I might break with it.

"Stay and have a drink with me." Ian waved one hand at a minibar. "No champagne, I swear."

I opened my mouth to say no thanks, and that's when the rest of me discovered what my brain had already known, at least in theory. I couldn't say no. Even *trying* to say it sent pain shooting through my temple, half blinding me. My hands started to shake. Jake had told me to do whatever Ian wanted me to do, and Ian wanted me to stay for a drink.

Just like Julia had said he would.

Ian was playing a game—*I* was his game. And I was going to lose.

With that realization, I knew what I had to do.

Turn it off. Turn everything off. Whatever happens, happens. But I didn't have to feel it. I didn't have to truly be there. No matter what Jake made me do or say, he couldn't shove his greedy fingers into my head. He couldn't control my mind, or where I sent it.

No one could.

"Fine. Just one," I said finally, and my hands stopped shaking. My voice felt empty, like the prerecorded message on my voice mail.

Ian pulled the bottle of champagne from the bucket and scooped ice out with a plastic cup. I flinched when the cubes clinked into two glasses. I sat on the edge of the leather couch with my hands clasped in my lap while he pulled tiny bottles from the minibar. A minute later, he turned around with two drinks and gave me one as he sank onto the couch next to me. "What should we toast to?" he asked, holding his glass up between us.

"Whatever you want." That was the game, right? The winner gets whatever he wants?

My glass smelled like vodka, a clean scent. Astringent. If I drank enough of it, could it make me clean on the inside? Could it wash the blood from my hands? Bleach the stains from my soul? If I started drinking right that moment and didn't stop until it was over, maybe I wouldn't remember anything in the morning. And if I didn't remember what had happened, I could tell myself nothing had happened.

A lie is always easier to believe if there's no evidence against it.

"Oh, come on. There must be something you want to toast. Dinner on someone else's dime? Low heels?" Ian glanced at my sandals. "Borrowed blouses?" He touched the short, flared sleeve of Kenley's shirt, and my hand clenched around the glass. He wasn't going to let me check out. Ian wanted to hear the wind-up doll speak.

"To free will," I said finally, looking right into his eyes.

He laughed, like I'd made a joke, and chills broke out on both my arms. "To free will," he repeated. "That most fabled of civil rights. May we all one day truly understand what we've lost." He bumped his glass against mine with a *clink,* and my stomach clenched around my lobster dinner.

"You don't know what real loss is," I said through clenched teeth, refusing to drink. He couldn't possibly.

Ian's smile died and he lowered his glass, frowning at me over it. "What the hell does that mean?"

"It means exactly what I said. You don't know a thing about loss. If you did, you wouldn't be sitting here in a suite paid for by a man who's just waiting to teach you what that word really means."

His gaze hardened and he set his drink on the coffee

table. "You're not the only one who's ever lost someone, you know."

"This isn't about dead parents," I snapped.

"Then what is it about? What did I say wrong this time?"

"Nothing. I wish you *would* say it. I wish you'd quit with the drinks, and the chitchat, and the deep eye contact. This doesn't have to be so much work. I'm a sure thing, Ian. No seduction required. Didn't you get the memo?" I turned my drink up and drained it in several long gulps, and when I finally set the glass down, he was frowning at me, his expression stuck somewhere between confusion and exasperation.

"What the hell are you talking about?"

I needed another drink. If he was playing the game Julia said he was playing, I'd just ruined the illusion of the hunt. And possibly tied a noose around my own neck.

"Nothing. I just… I'm sorry." I stood and headed for the minibar. "I just can't pretend anymore. Playing your game is one thing, but pretending it isn't a game is too much."

"What game, Kori?" The couch creaked at my back as he stood, but there were no footsteps.

"You. Me. Recruitment. Fringe benefits." I plucked another tiny bottle from the minibar and cracked the lid without even glancing at the label. Then I turned and met his gaze from across the room. "I'm what you asked for. I can't say no. So I wish you'd quit trying to make this feel like something it isn't and just tell me what you want me to do, so I can get it over with."

His eyes widened. Then his dark eyebrows sank low over green eyes and his hands curled into fists at his sides. I knew that look. Hell, I'd perfected that look. He was going to hit something.

Me? Was he going to hit me, because I'd ruined whatever fantasy he was playing out in his head? And if so, how many punches could I throw before the resistance pain kicked in again? Would this be like it was with Jonah, brutal and violent? Or would this be a civilized conquest, grown-ups playing pretend, polite until the last stroke?

In the basement, I'd been trapped by dead shadows and crippled by direct orders. Mentally fighting hands and teeth I couldn't see, crushed by weight I couldn't bear, pinned, humiliated, hurt. Wishing for death, but too scared to reach for it.

Would I have the guts to end it this time? To fight back until I couldn't move, drawing death closer with every punch I threw, in spite of the pain…

"Kori, what are you saying? Whatever I tell you to do, you have to do?"

I rolled my eyes and drained half the tiny bottle, wincing at the burn. "You knew that. You've known it all along."

"No, I… I hadn't thought about it like that. I hadn't realized…" He closed his eyes and sank onto the couch, his head in both hands. Then his hands fell away and his head snapped up. His gaze met mine and held it. And I realized I believed him.

Ian truly hadn't known. There was no game, except the one Julia was playing.

His forehead wrinkled, and each breath he released sounded angry. "Tower told you to…?"

My stomach tried to revolt, and I held down my dinner with nothing but willpower. If he hadn't known what I'd been ordered to do, then he hadn't thought of me as a whore. Until now.

"He told me to do whatever you want. He said if I wasn't the best you've ever had…" But I couldn't finish that sentence. I couldn't admit the consequences to him. Not with him looking at me like that. Not with disgust dripping from his words, revulsion written in every line on his face.

It was obvious what he thought of me now. I may as well have a red chain link tattooed on my arm.

"That soulless son of a bitch." He stared at the floor, fists opening and closing. Then he looked up at me with something new shining through the surface of his obvious anger. Was that…disappointment?

And suddenly I understood that I wasn't the only one hurt by this. If Ian's jokes, and obvious desire, and genuine conversation weren't part of some game he was playing, then…he'd meant them. He'd meant it all. And somehow that realization cut even deeper than the latest knife Jake had shoved into my back.

"So, this isn't real?" Ian demanded, anger edging out whatever pain I'd glimpsed from him. "Dinner? Telling me about your family? Was any of that true? Did any of that mean anything to you?"

I inhaled deeply. Slowly. I could admit that in spite of my orders and my own common sense, everything I'd said and done with him was real. That I liked him, and that's why I'd tried to paint an accurate picture of life in the syndicate, even as I roped him tighter with Jake's noose. But that wouldn't be fair to either of us. We couldn't be together, ever, even if Jake hadn't ruined anything we could have had by ordering me to sleep with Ian. Julia had been right about that much. Once Ian officially joined the syndicate, he would quickly outrank me. And even if my lower standing didn't put him off, association with me would do him no favors.

So I put on my work face. My stone-cold-bitch face. Because he was hurting just like I was hurting, and this time, the truth would only make that worse.

"This is a job. You are a job. Nothing more." It was the most difficult lie I'd ever had to tell. And it wasn't over. "After you, there will be another job. I don't know what that job will be, since I'm clearly the world's worst recruiter. But whatever that next job is, I'll do it. Just like I'm doing this one. So…" I swallowed and met his gaze, refusing to let mine falter. I could do this. I had no choice. "So just tell me what you want me to do—what it'll take to get you to sign with Jake—and I'll do it."

"I don't believe you." He said it softly, but his words were drenched in anger. I closed my eyes, desperately wishing I'd heard him wrong. Wishing I hadn't seen the pain in his eyes. The denial. "I don't believe you, Kori. The reason you're a horrible recruiter is that you're bad at selling something you don't believe in, and you don't believe in what you're saying right now."

"Yes, I do." I turned and reached for the tiny bottle again, but he was there in an instant, pulling it out of my grip.

"No, you don't. I can tell when you're lying, and you're doing it now."

"Don't pretend you know me," I snapped, reaching for the bottle, but he tucked it behind his back. "We just met. You don't know anything about me."

"The hell I don't. I know you love your sister more than you love yourself. I know you hate Jake Tower, even if you can't ever say that out loud. I know that you cuss

like a fish swims, but you haven't spoken a single profanity in the last seven hours, and as near as I can tell,
the only thing stopping you is the fact that you gave your
word. I know that he makes you do things that rot your
soul, and that you do them because you have to, but that
you'll never really forgive yourself."

I stared at him, stunned, knowing I should argue.
Knowing that for both of our sakes, I should have the
courage to lie and tell him he was wrong. That he didn't
know me and he never would. But words had deserted
me, for maybe the second time in my entire life.

"And I know they did horrible things to you. Things
you never talk about. I know they tried to break you,
but they failed, and that's why Jake talks about you like
you're trash, when we all three know that's not true. I
think he hates you because even though he tried his best,
he couldn't break you. Which means he won't ever really
own you, no matter what he tattoos on your arm or anywhere else."

His face blurred right in front of me, and it took me
several seconds to realize why. To realize there were
tears standing in my eyes and that I couldn't get rid of
them without letting them fall.

"You don't know what you're talking about. He does
own me." And he would, as long as he owned Kenley.

"No one owns you, Kori. People like you can't be
owned. Putting chain links on your arm is like putting a
lion in a cage. He may be locked up, but he'll always be
wild, and he'll eat his handler the first chance he gets.
You're that lion, Kori, and I see you watching. Waiting
for your moment. And it will come."

"No, it won't, because it's not just me in that cage, Ian.
Kenley's there with me, and she can't bite."

He blinked, and something passed over his expression too fast for me to understand. Something complicated and…conflicted. Then he shook that thought off, whatever it was, and captured my gaze again. "So you bite for her, too. You fight for the people you love, no matter what."

I shook my head, and to my horror, those tears fell. "I can't." I hadn't cried in the basement. I'd screamed. I'd even begged. But I'd never cried. Yet here I was in no danger whatsoever, and I couldn't stop the burning in my eyes, the hot trails down my cheeks. "I can't."

"So you're just going to give up? You're just going to do whatever he tells you to do? Let him pass you around to all his friends like a lit joint, until you're all used up and worthless?"

A sharp bolt of anger shot through me and I swiped tears from my face with both hands. "That's not… This is the first time. It's not a regular thing."

"And you really believe it won't be?"

I didn't have an answer for that. I hadn't thought beyond getting through this one job, because there was a significant chance that wouldn't actually happen, and if I was dead, I wouldn't have to worry about the next assignment.

Ian studied my face, looking for something, and when he didn't find it, he set the small bottle on top of the minibar. "So, if I'd asked you to stay the night, you would have done it? Not because you wanted to, but because he told you to?"

I sucked in a breath so deep my chest ached. "I wouldn't have had any choice."

"And last night, after the party? After knowing me

less than eight hours? Would you have slept with me then?"

I could only nod miserably.

"And if I was a real asshole who hurt you and called you names? Would you be allowed to stop me?"

"Stop it. You already know the answer."

"Yeah, I know it. I'm waiting for you to hear yourself say something awful enough to make you want to fight back."

"I do want to fight!" I shouted, fury buzzing beneath my skin like an army of wasps. "But it doesn't matter. That's the real problem here, Ian. After everything I've shown you and everything you've figured out on your own, you still think fighting back is an option. You still think that if I close my eyes and wish hard enough, I'll suddenly be able to break an oath sealed by one of the strongest—quite possibly *the* strongest—Binder in the world. But if there was a way out of this, you can bet your fancy rental car that I'd have found it myself. But there isn't. Kenley and I are stuck exactly where we are, doing exactly what we're doing, for the next four years."

Assuming I lived that long.

I exhaled and met his gaze again, digging deep for the anger that fueled my heart like gasoline in an engine, because I'd rather be mad than wallow in the pain my next words would bring. "Now unless you're actually planning to make me do what Jake told me to do, I'd like to leave. But as much as I hate to say it, I can't go without your permission."

He watched me, and emotions flickered over his face too fast for me to identify. But in the end, there was anger. Raw, pure anger of the highest quality. Rage. Ian wasn't just angry, he was enraged.

I knew exactly how that felt.

"Go home, Kori," he said through clenched teeth. "I think you should go home. Now."

I nodded in acknowledgment, because I couldn't bring myself to thank him for doing the only decent thing. Then I stepped into the hall and pulled the door shut behind me, and too late I realized I should have gone through the shadows in his bathroom. But I wasn't going back into that hotel room. I couldn't. Not after that.

For several seconds, I couldn't move. I could only lean against the wall outside his suite, sucking air in through my throat over and over, only to lose it an instant later. He hated me. Worse, he pitied me. I'd seen it in his eyes. He was disgusted by what Jake had turned me into, and even more disgusted that I'd let it happen.

And the worst part was that I couldn't argue with a damn thing he'd said. And if he told anyone—if Jake found out what I'd told him—Ian's recruitment would be reassigned and I would wind up in the basement again.

I couldn't survive it again. I *couldn't.*

You should have just let it happen. I should have just kept my mouth shut and stayed the night, and he'd never have known I was under orders. So what if he thought it meant more than it ever could? So what if letting Jake dictate what I did with my body made me sick to my stomach? So what if just thinking about that brought memories of the basement roaring to the front of my mind, so vivid and horrifying I could smell the sweat and taste my own blood?

I raced for the elevator, but my stomach lurched after less than a minute of staring at my own reflection in its mirrored wall, so I punched buttons until the elevator stopped, then ran down the last four flights of stairs. I burst into the alley behind the building, but I couldn't make it to the Dumpster. My dinner came back up in the middle of the alley, all over Kenley's sandals. I vomited until there was nothing left, trying to purge the memories along with the food, but they wouldn't go. I felt every blow. Relived every humiliation. I saw Jake closing the door on that very first night, leaving me alone with his brother, half-naked and still oozing blood from a gunshot wound.

When the retching finally stopped, I sank onto the concrete with my knees pressed against my chest, curled around the ache deep inside me. But finally I could breathe again. Finally the pain was gone, and in its place was a blessed numbness.

My stomach was as empty as the rest of me. That was the only way I knew how to be.

I closed my eyes and I heard Jake's words again, echoing from my memory. He'd pronounced my sentence in three words with one hand on the doorknob, a cruel smile on his face.

"Don't fight back."

That's how my hell had begun. And it had yet to end.

Fourteen

Ian

For almost a minute after she left, I stared at the door, willing her to come back, though I had no idea what I'd say if she actually did. How could she let him use her like that? How could she let him just *give* her to a man she barely knew? What fucking century were we living in?

And the worst part was that she'd thought I'd known. She'd thought I was party to forced prostitution and rape. That I was playing some kind of sadistic game with her, just waiting for the perfect moment to—

I couldn't think the words, but I couldn't purge them from my mind, either. I was caught between thinking it and not thinking it, an endless cycle of self-torture that built inside me until rage finally burst out of me like shrapnel from an explosion.

My hand closed around something I didn't even see and I hurled it without looking. Ceramic crashed into the door and rained shards of broken table lamp on the floor. The crystal shade shattered, reflecting tiny rainbows all over the room, but the cheerful colors only further infuriated me. So I stomped the shards into the floor until I couldn't see a single color.

Then I sank onto the couch with my head in my hands, trying to draw the chaos in my head into some semblance of order.

The mission was screwed. *Steven* was screwed. Kori would never trust me enough now to let me anywhere near her sister, and the more I learned about her and her reasons for serving Tower in the first place, the less likely it seemed that she ever would have anyway.

And just as suddenly as that thought occurred to me, I realized I didn't care. I couldn't let my brother die, but I couldn't hurt Kori to save him. She'd been through enough, and even if the grief from losing Kenley didn't destroy her, being left to bear the brunt of Tower's rage certainly would.

With sudden insight, I understood what I should have known all along. If I killed Tower's Binder and toppled his empire, he'd kill Kori for letting it happen. And I wasn't naive enough to think her death would be either quick or painless.

I dug my phone from my pocket and my fingers pressed buttons automatically. Aaron worked the night shift, but he answered on the third ring. "Is it done?"

"I can't do it, Aaron." I let my head fall against the back of the couch, one hand over my eyes to cut the glare from the light overhead. "I can't kill her."

"Fuck." For a moment, there was only silence, except for the distant sound of heavy machinery running in the background. Then Aaron groaned. "I'm coming over."

Several seconds later he walked out of the darkened bathroom in stained jeans and a T-shirt stamped with his company logo. He took a glance around, then headed straight for the open minibar, where Kori's half-empty bottle still sat. "So what's with all the drama?" He sniffed her minibottle, then drained it. "Go ahead and air your girly feelings so I can laugh at them, then kick your ass back into the game."

"This isn't a game. I can't do it."

"Which part?" He grabbed another tiny bottle, then dropped into an armchair and stared at me over the coffee table. "The part where you get wined and dined and put up in a fancy hotel room while Steven and Meghan are slowly dying in a great deal of pain? Or the part where you get to spend all week with a beautiful woman at your beck and call, while I work my ass off in a factory to keep all three of us fed and clothed while they can't work? Because in case you can't tell from the ripe scent of man-sweat I'm rubbing into your chair, in the real world, this doesn't qualify as a hardship." He spread both arms to indicate the luxury Tower had thrown at me.

"Tower is psychotic. He's fucked her up beyond what I can explain, and I can't kill her sister after everything she's already been through."

"So we're talking about the sister, not the target?" he said, and I nodded. "What's she been through?"

"She won't tell me. But it's bad. They talk about her like she's a piece of trash he just hasn't gotten around to throwing out yet. And he's using her like human currency."

"Meaning…?"

"He told her to sleep with me."

Aaron shrugged and cracked open the minibottle. "I'm still waiting for the psychotic part."

"Aaron, he fucking gave her to me, like she's some

thing he can use however he wants. Like she's part of the signing bonus. How would you like to see your sister treated like that?"

Aaron leaned forward in his chair and tossed the bottle cap onto the coffee table, where it slid across the surface and clattered to the floor. "*My sister* is in no danger of being treated like a slave or a whore because she wasn't stupid enough to sign away her free will in exchange for paycheck and a tattoo."

"Kori only joined to protect her sister, and she signed on as security. She never agreed to be used like this."

Aaron drained his minibottle and stretched to set it on the end table. "She had to know it was a possibility, and *you* knew what this would be like. You know he has whores as well as assassins and you know damn well that one's just as dangerous as the other. But you *swore* to my sister that you would save them both. Now you're backing out because you're too sensitive to call a whore a whore?"

"She's not a whore." Frustrated, I scrubbed my face with both hands, wishing I had something to shoot, or hit, or stab, so I could pretend I was killing Jake Tower with all the enthusiasm that task deserved. "You should have seen her. She couldn't even leave without my permission, and I think telling me that actually made her sick."

"Did you fuck her?"

"Hell no! I didn't touch her."

"Then you'll come out smelling like roses. You're the honorable man who didn't take the bait. So pull up your big-boy pants and apologize for the misunderstanding. Explain that you didn't realize this was supposed to be a full-service tour and you would never have made her do anything she didn't want to do. The facts will back you up on that, since you didn't touch her." Aaron shrugged. "*Voilà*. You're right back on schedule."

"On schedule to kill her sister."

"Well…yeah. That *is* what you came here to do."

"When exactly did you forget that Kori's a victim in this?" I demanded.

He rolled his eyes. "Around the time I started asking questions about her." Aaron sighed and stared at his hands for a moment, then made eye contact. "After I dropped you off this afternoon, I called a few of my local contacts and asked them what they knew about Korinne Daniels, other than the fact that she's evidently back from the dead."

"And…?" I said, certain I already knew at least part of what he had to say.

"The word from a couple of former syndicate members—guys willing to talk so long as their names never come up—is that she impressed Tower from the start. Not his most powerful Traveler, but she's a hell of a fighter and she's got nerves of steel. Word has it she disabled half of his household security team in a matter of minutes, just to get Tower's attention. That got her assigned to his personal security detail pretty quickly. One of the guys says he took a special interest in her. Nothing dirty, from what I can tell—"

"He doesn't screw around on his wife," I supplied.

Aaron nodded. "But he got a kick out of seeing her take down men twice her size. He treated her like a niece, and while she was in good standing, her sister was untouchable—a personal favor from Tower."

"Meaning?"

"Meaning hands-off. Completely. No one hit her, no

one screwed her. No one so much as breathed too close to Kenley Daniels, like she was made of glass. It was like that for years. But then something went wrong."

"She fell," I whispered, hearing Kori say the words in my head. Aaron frowned at me in question, but I just waved him on. "What happened?"

"None of my sources were still active in the syndicate recently enough to tell me that, so I had to go digging on the other side of the river." Aaron grinned. "You're welcome."

"Thanks. Now spill."

"I found a loose tongue—one of Cavazos's men—who claimed that a couple of months ago, Ruben Cavazos led a small team right into the heart of Tower's territory. They broke into his fucking house, in the middle of the night. I haven't been able to verify that with any secondary source—makes sense that Tower would have covered up an embarrassment that big—but the timing lines up."

"You think Kori had something to do with the break-in?"

Aaron shrugged. "She was still working security at the time, and within days of when Cavazos's man says this happened, she disappeared. I mean, gone. No one saw her. No one heard from her. I got ahold of her sister's cell record—I'd tell you how, but then I'd have to kill you—and it looks like she was panicking. She called their brother several times a week, and she also called this chick who works for Cavazos, of all people. So I looked her up. Turns out this other chick—Olivia Warren—went to high school with your girl Kori."

Olivia... Could this be the Olivia that Kenley bound Kori to when they were kids?

"Which gives Kori a connection to Tower's biggest enemy," I said, thinking aloud.

"Right. So what I'm thinking is that—intentional or not—Kori had something to do with Cavazos and his team getting into Tower's house. And if I'm right about that, it's a miracle she's still alive."

But I could still see her face when I closed my eyes. "I don't think she's feeling very miraculous."

Aaron shrugged. "Well, I'm sure she'd feel better if she was free from Tower. And she will be, if you do what you came here to do." Because killing Kenley would break Kori's binding to Tower. "We'll call that the bright side."

"You're an asshole."

"Yeah, but I'm also a fucking genius with a Wi-Fi connection and a keyboard."

I stood, pacing to burn off angry energy. "She's messed up. I mean, she's *really* messed up, and I think the only reason she's still alive is because her sister needs her. If I kill Kenley, what does Kori have to live for?" I stopped pacing to look at him. "I can't do that to her."

"So you're just going to let Steven and Meghan die?" he demanded. But I could see what he wasn't saying— that he couldn't let that happen. If I didn't kill Kenley, he would try. Which would get him killed. Then I'd have all three of their deaths on my head.

"Hell no, I'm not going to let them die. But there has to be another way."

"A way other than killing Kenley?" Aaron frowned. "If she's half as powerful as word on the street says she is, there's no other way, short of getting her to break her own bindings."

"Can she do that?" I frowned at him. Why hadn't anyone mentioned that possibility before?

"Is she physically capable?" Aaron shrugged, looking up at me from his chair. "In theory, yes. Is she allowed?" He shook his head firmly. "No way in hell. The first thing Tower would have prohibited her from doing is breaking her own bindings. That clause may only include the bindings she sealed for him specifically, but that depends on whether or not she insisted on tightening the language from the broad, basic phrasing." Which, according to Kori, she had not.

"Okay, so she's probably not allowed. What if she tried anyway? People breach sealed contracts all the time, right?"

"Yeah. There'd be resistance pain, but how strong that is depends on how strong the seal on her contract is, and whether or not she swore on her life not to breach it. If she just swore and signed, she'll be in pain—probably a lot of pain—but it'll eventually end. But if she swore on her life, then breaches the contract, she'll die."

Great. That was no better than shooting her myself.

"But, Ian, the consequences aren't the problem here. The real hurdle is convincing her to break her own seal. Seals are held intact by will of the Binder. You can't just hold a gun to her head and tell her to withdraw her will from the binding. She has to *want* to break the seal. And if you can't get within shooting distance of her, what makes you think you can get close enough to explain what you want and convince her to want it, too? Steven doesn't have forever, you know. Meghan can't hold out much longer."

I exhaled slowly, my brain racing. This should have been a no-brainer. My brother and his girlfriend—my

best friend's sister, whom I'd known her whole life—
or a woman I'd known less than thirty-two hours. I
couldn't let Steven die, but every time I thought about
killing to protect him, I saw Kori in my head. Pale hair,
petite build and pixieish features alternately reflecting fierce determination and haunted pain. I wanted to
touch her. I wanted to make her smile. I wanted to protect her.

I wanted her not to die a prolonged, agonized death,
screaming my name in fury, hating me until her last
breath.

I sank onto the couch again and met his gaze over the
coffee table. "One more day," I said. "Can Meghan hold
on for one more day?"

Aaron looked at me like I'd lost my mind. "What is it
about this girl? You've only known her for a day."

"You'd understand if you met her. She needs my help."

He leaned back in his chair, shaking his head slowly.
"She doesn't need you. She doesn't even *want* you—you
said that yourself. And even if she did, she's not worth
it. She's a killer!"

"If she's killed, Tower made her do it."

His frown deepened. "And you think being bound to
follow orders absolves her of any guilt?"

I exhaled slowly, trying to swallow a sudden surge of
guilt and anger when what I really wanted to do was un-
leash it on him. "*I've* killed under orders, Aaron."

"You were a soldier."

"That doesn't make it right. I'm no more innocent
than she is, so if you think hating Kori will make it
easier for you to kill her sister to save yours, you may
as well hate me, too. She had nothing to do with what

happened to Steven." But we both knew I had, even if inadvertently.

"You've lost perspective," Aaron said, and he sounded sad.

He was right. Being near Kori was like standing on an iron plate holding a compass. I couldn't tell which way was north. I couldn't tell what was right. I only knew that I couldn't kill her sister, and just knowing one plan was impossible made the other look more doable. "One more day, Aaron."

He frowned. "Ian, I'm not going to let my sister die."

"I know. Just ask her for one more day."

Aaron hesitated. He stared at me. And finally he sighed. "I'll ask her. But if you haven't broken the binding by this time tomorrow, I'll do it myself."

"It won't come to that," I insisted. But I couldn't tell if he believed me.

Hell, I couldn't tell if I believed myself.

Fifteen

Kori

I shadow-walked into my bedroom and didn't even have to stretch to reach the light switch, possibly the only advantage to living in very cramped quarters. I had Kenley's ruined sandals off before I even reached the door and I pulled her blouse over my head as I left the room.

The bathroom was two steps to the right of my room, but the door was closed and a line of light glowed beneath it, so I tossed the shirt through my sister's open bedroom doorway and ducked into my room for a T-shirt, then stomped through the living room as I pulled it over my head. In the kitchen, I opened the cabinet over the microwave and stared at a half-empty bottle of cheap vodka.

Another drink wouldn't fix anything. But it couldn't hurt, either, and I'd thrown up everything I drank at Ian's.

I was trying to decide whether to bother with a glass or gulp straight from the bottle when the bathroom door creaked open and Vanessa stepped into the living room, wearing her own robe this time.

She'd brought a robe.

"It's getting crowded around here." I set the bottle down and reached for a clean glass from the dish drainer.

"Sorry." Vanessa shrugged and sat on the arm of the couch. "I didn't think one extra toothbrush would make that much difference."

I pulled an ice tray from the freezer and dropped it on the counter to break up the cubes. Kenley always over-filled it, so they never came out easily. "I don't know if you've heard," I said, dropping the first cube into my glass, "but Kenley is off-limits. Untouchable." At least until Tower decided whether or not to kill me.

"I did hear that." She crossed the room and sank onto a bar stool across the counter from me, as if I didn't scare her. But that couldn't be right.

"Being a girl doesn't exempt you from that." I dropped in another cube, then poured an inch of vodka into the glass. Then I poured another inch.

"No, it doesn't. What exempts me is the fact that she wants me here."

I stared into Van's eyes, trying to see the truth, to believe that what I wanted for my sister was even possible in the syndicate. Trying to believe in human connection that wasn't based on a lie or born in pain. Could a new relationship possibly take root in Jake's world without being choked by the bitter weeds he'd planted?

What if Vanessa was one of those weeds? I knew nothing about her, and Kenley couldn't know much more. What if he'd sent her to get close to Kenley and earn her trust—maybe even her affection—so that after he'd killed me, he'd still have someone to threaten in order to control her.

"What are your intentions with my sister?" I said, twisting my glass on the counter when I couldn't read anything definite in her eyes. I thought she'd laugh. I wouldn't have taken that question seriously in her position. But her eye contact remained steady and she answered without so much as a smile.

"I intend to love her for as long as she'll let me. Then a little longer than that."

I blinked. Then I frowned. "You love her? You don't even know her."

"Love is supposed to *last* forever, Kori. Not take forever. But if it makes you feel any better, Kenley and I had been together almost a month before Jake locked you up."

I pushed aside the dark flash of memory her reminder dredged up—it hadn't been far from the surface anyway—and focused on the middle part of her statement. Three months. They'd been together for three months, and I hadn't known?

"Why didn't she tell me?"

Vanessa shrugged. "You'll have to ask her that. But here's why *I* didn't tell anyone. You know how when you're a kid and you get a shiny new toy, you don't want to share it for a while? You just want to keep it to yourself? It's like that."

I frowned. "Are you calling my sister your toy?"

"I'm calling our relationship shiny and new. And I'd really appreciate it if you could resist the urge to smudge it up for a while."

"Why would I smudge up your shiny new relationship with my sister?"

"Because you're worried about her. Or jealous. Or maybe both."

I wanted to tell Van she was full of shit, but that didn't feel true. I *was* worried about Kenley. Constantly. And as much as I loved her and as willing as I was to do anything to protect her, I'd never been more jealous of anyone in my life.

I hated myself for even thinking that, but it was true. I was jealous of the cocoon I'd wrapped around Kenley. Jealous of the decisions she'd never had to make. I was jealous of the fact that she could be with whomever she wanted, without wondering whether what she felt was real or was manufactured by a powerful man pushing her around a life-size chessboard like a pawn to be sacrificed at will.

I was jealous of how well Kenley slept at night, free from nightmares about a darkness she couldn't master and a sentence she couldn't escape.

Desperate to reclaim the numbness, I picked up my glass.

"That won't help," Vanessa said, before I could take the first sip. "In fact, drinking can make the flashbacks harder to fight. Anything that impairs your concentration will."

"You don't know what you're talking about," I snapped, then drained the glass, leaving only ice to clink in the bottom.

"Yes, I do." She exhaled slowly. "You're not the only one, Kori."

"Get out." I couldn't talk about it. I couldn't even think about it without feeling sick and wanting to break something. Some*one*. It was easier to drink until I didn't have to think about anything.

Vanessa didn't get out. She didn't even get off the bar stool. "You need to talk to someone, and you obviously don't want to talk to your sister."

"How do you know that?"

"Because you haven't told her." Van ducked to catch my gaze. "But that doesn't mean she doesn't know."

"Go away, Vanessa. This isn't social hour and I don't need your fu—" I'm not sure why I swallowed the word. I didn't give a damn about that stupid bet, and I'd consider us all lucky if Ian hadn't already called Jake and told him what I'd said. What I'd done. "I don't want to play group therapy."

"I understand. Just let me say one more thing, and I'll let it go."

"If you say it wasn't my fault, I'm going to punch you in the face." And I meant it. I wasn't in denial and I had no patience for stupid therapeutic clichés. Or for therapy at all, for that matter.

"That's true, but it's not what I was going to say." She leaned on the counter with both elbows and looked right into my eyes. "I was going to say that it will get better. Eventually, there will be days when you won't think about it. Days you won't see his face when you close your eyes."

"I don't see his face when I close my eyes," I insisted, pouring another inch of vodka over the melting ice cubes. My flashbacks were all pain and the stench of his sweat. His breath. The fact that I hadn't been able to see well enough to focus on his face was the only mercy. "But I do see him when they're open. I see him every day, and every day I want to kill him. And one day I will."

"Do you think that will fix it?" Van asked, and it took

me a second to realize she was honestly curious. "Will killing him make you feel better?"

"I don't know. And I doubt it matters. If I get the chance to kill him, it'll be the last thing I ever do." Because Jake would have me killed for killing his brother. "But at least he'll get to hell before I do."

After Vanessa went back to bed—Kenley slept through our entire conversation—I lay awake in my room, trying to assess the damage I'd done to both my life and my sister's. Based on the fact that no one had burst into the apartment to haul us out, I had to assume that Ian hadn't reported the night's events yet. But there was no guarantee that he wouldn't, and I had to be prepared for that very real possibility.

I needed a plan. Even worse than that, I needed a way out, if not for me, at least for Kenley.

The next morning, after a scant four hours of sleep, I waited until I heard Kenley get in the shower—I could tell it was her by the off-key singing—then I hurried into the kitchen, where Vanessa was starting a pot of coffee.

"How much do you love my sister?" I asked, sliding onto a bar stool in front of her.

She eyed me from across the counter. "As tempted as I am to demonstrate how incredibly none-of-your-business that is…" She set the bag of coffee grounds between us and met my gaze head-on. "I love her enough to be terrified that her feelings aren't as strong."

"And what if that's true? Do you love her enough to protect her even if she doesn't love you as much as you love her? Do you love her enough to fight for her?"

Vanessa tied her robe at her waist and planted both hands flat on the counter between us. "Kori, my dad sold me into the skin trade as a teenager," she said, and for a second, I couldn't think beyond the horror that thought brought with it. "Your sister is one of only two good things to happen to me since I was fifteen. The other was Cam Caballero. I lost my best friend when he left, and Kenley is the only thing I have left. I would do anything for her."

I smiled in relief. "That's exactly what I wanted to hear."

"Should I be worried?" she asked, pouring grounds into the filter.

"Terrified. We all should be." I took a deep breath, then launched into a quick summary of the trouble my sister and I were in. "If I can't get Ian Holt to sign with Jake in the next couple of days, I'm under orders to… make sure he can't sign with anyone else. And if that happens, Jake will have me executed." Though I doubt I'd be lucky enough to score a simple bullet to the brain. "But not before he puts Kenley in the basement. He's going to make her pay for my failure."

Vanessa dropped the bag and coffee grounds spilled out onto the counter. "I assume you have a plan?"

"Not much of one. I need you to stay with her today and text me if there's so much as a knock on the door. Text me if you guys go anywhere and let me know who he sends as security." Because Kenley wasn't allowed out alone. "And if her guard gets a text or phone call, let me know."

"Why?" Vanessa scooped most of the spilled grounds into her cupped palm, then dropped them into the trash. "Why today?"

"Because last night I messed up, and if Holt tells anyone, we're all screwed."

"Okay, so why don't we just run? Or hide, if we're not allowed to run," she said, and I had to remind myself that Vanessa was unSkilled, and even though she worked for and was bound to Jake, she wasn't as familiar with my world as she should have been. As she'd need to be, to help protect Kenley.

"Because if Jake tries to get in touch with Kenley and can't find her, he'll know something's wrong and he'll send them after us. Why set off an alarm when we may not have to? Holt obviously hasn't told anyone yet."

"Do you think he will?"

"I don't know. And it may be worse if he doesn't." After what I'd told him, I couldn't imagine Ian being willing to sign with Jake, no matter what he hoped to gain in the negotiations. And him refusing to sign would be much worse than just tattling on me. "But either way, if someone comes for Kenley, I need you to take her and run. Don't look back and don't stop for anything. Don't use public transportation or credit cards. And destroy your phones. Steal whatever you need, and get out of town, then call me from a pay phone. If I don't answer, call my brother. Kenley knows his number."

"What if he doesn't answer?"

If Kris didn't answer, that would mean Jake had already gotten to him, too. He wasn't syndicate, so he'd be harder for Jake to find than I would be, but Jake *would* find him, and he'd use Kris to get to Kenley.

He'd use anything and anyone to get to Kenley.

"If Kris doesn't answer, keep running and don't look back."

Vanessa nodded solemnly. She looked scared but determined, and I felt a little better knowing that I'd made the right call in enlisting her help. Other than me and Kris, no one would work harder to protect Kenley.

The shower stopped running in the bathroom, and I leaned closer to Van over the counter. "Don't tell her about this unless you have to run," I whispered. "She'll put herself in Jake's path if she thinks it'll help me."

Vanessa nodded again, and this time she wasn't just watching me, she was studying me. "I never had a sister…" she said, and I wondered how her life would have been different if she'd had someone to look out for growing up. Or someone to look out for her.

The bathroom door opened and Van blinked, then slid the filter into place above the coffeepot.

"Hey," Kenley said, and I turned to find my sister standing in the doorway wrapped in a towel, her hair dripping on the floor. "You staying for breakfast? I'm thinking omelets."

"Can't. I gotta grab a shower, then head out." I brushed past her into the hall, then stopped and tugged her into my tiny bedroom with me. "Why didn't you tell me about Vanessa?"

Kenley frowned. "That I'm gay, or that she's my girl-friend?"

"That you've been together for three months. How could you get so serious with someone without even telling your sister you're dating?"

"We're not really dating, exactly." She flushed and glanced at the ground, where her toes had curled into the carpet, a nervous habit she'd had since she was a kid. "And I didn't know if it would go anywhere at first. Then you disappeared, and I *couldn't* tell you."

"I've been out for two weeks, and you never mentioned it."

"Yeah, I don't have an excuse for that part." Kenley shrugged, holding her towel closed at the seam. "And I really don't know how serious this is. It still feels new."

I exhaled slowly, trying to decide how much I had a right to tell her. "She really likes you, Kenni," I finally said. "And she hasn't had it easy, so don't hurt her. If you're not serious, you owe it to her to tell her."

My sister eyed me skeptically. "This coming from a woman who loses interest in a fling before the sweat's even dry."

"We're not talking about me, we're talking about you," I said, but she wasn't listening. She was too busy trying to catch a glimpse of Vanessa around my door frame.

"Did she say that? She said she likes me?"

"Just trust me. And trust her, if something goes wrong."

"What does that mean?" Kenley frowned up at me.

"Nothing. I gotta get going." I stepped around her and into the bathroom before she could argue. Twenty minutes later, clean and dressed, I stepped through the shadows in my room and into the darkness in Ian's bathroom, my hair still damp from the shower.

Heart pounding, I stood there for nearly a minute, listening for voices, or snoring, or footsteps. Anything to tell me where Ian was and whether or not he was alone. But I heard nothing.

My pulse roaring in my ears, I pushed the door open and stepped into the suite. The bedroom and living room were empty. Had he left? Just completely bailed on Jake's offer? If so, I was dead.

I wiped my suddenly sweaty palms on my jeans, then walked silently down the hall and back into to the bedroom, intending to see if the sheets were still warm, and on the way, I glanced into the bathroom. I'd left the door open and the room was still empty, but his toothbrush lay on the counter.

When I got to the bed, I threw back the comforter— and nearly shrieked in surprise.

Ian was there, sound asleep, so motionless he could have been comatose. If not for the soft rise and fall of his chest, I might have thought he was dead.

Ian groaned and reached down for the covers in his sleep, and I backed silently away from the bed. When he couldn't find the covers, his eyes opened and he sat up slowly, one hand rubbing his forehead. He winced, then his eyes opened. He blinked. Then he turned and looked right at me.

I froze, but he managed a smile. "Hey," he said and flinched, like speaking hurt. Which made sense, considering the half-empty full-size bottle of whiskey on the nightstand. "You'll have to give me a minute here. Gravity's a real bitch this morning."

Sixteen

Ian

"You're hungover," Kori said, but there was no accusation in her voice. She sounded…relieved.

"Little bit, yeah." I ran one hand over my hair, then scrubbed my face, trying to wake up.

"We have to talk." She sank into a chair in the corner and sat with her hands in her lap, alternately staring at the floor and at me.

"I don't think I can manage more than single syllable words without some coffee. And maybe a shower." And definitely a toothbrush.

"I'll make coffee." She stood and looked at the open bathroom door, then headed for the hall.

The shower felt good—dual massage heads—but I did not. I hadn't been that drunk or that hungover in a long time.

Soaked, dizzy and nauseated, I stepped out of the shower and grabbed a towel, and only then realized that my suitcase and all my clothes were in the living room.

With Kori. Fortunately there was a fresh white terry-cloth robe hanging from the back of the bathroom door.

Wrapped in the robe, I followed the scent of coffee into the living room to find Kori leaning against the counter over the minibar. I reached for the suitcase against one wall. "Just let me get—"

"Did you tell him?" she interrupted, setting an empty coffee mug on the counter.

"Did I tell who what?"

"Jake. Did you tell him about last night? About what I told you?"

I set the suitcase down, resisting the urge to close my eyes and slide down the wall to sit on the floor. "Think about how hungover I am now and how drunk I must have been last night and see if you can follow that thread of logic to its natural conclusion."

Kori rolled her eyes, and just watching that made me dizzy. "Quit talking like an asshole and just tell me. Please. Did you report me to Jake?"

I crossed the room slowly, drawn as much by the thread of fear in her voice as by the promise of caffeine. "No. I haven't spoken to anyone in the syndicate since we left the restaurant last night." And frankly, I was a little insulted that she thought I would tattle on her, even though logically, I knew she had no reason to trust me.

Kori took a deep breath, then met my gaze. "What will it take to keep you from reporting me?"

I frowned and gripped the back of the couch for balance. "Are you trying to bribe me?"

"I'm negotiating." She opened the cabinet next to the minibar and pulled out a sugar dish full of packets of artificial sweetener. "And it'd be a lot easier if you'd give me a starting point."

"Why?" I sank into an armchair across from her, acutely aware that I was nude beneath the robe, and tried to catch her gaze again. "Why are you negotiating? Why do you live life like you're constantly volleying for position or looking for an advantage? Life isn't a contract to be negotiated, Kori."

"Mine is, and you're only making that harder."

"Okay, if you don't mind, I'm going to offer an amateur diagnosis." I'd come into the room for underwear and wound up playing shrink instead. "But please keep in mind that I'm extremely hungover at the moment. Either the room is spinning around me, or I'm actually tilting in this chair."

"You're tilting." Kori tore open a sugar packet and a million tiny crystals spilled onto the counter. "What is it you think you're diagnosing?"

"Your life. Your problems. Because frankly, I think those are one and the same."

"Well, you got that much right." She poured coffee into a second mug and dumped a packet of powdered creamer into it. "What's your diagnosis?"

I took a deep breath and closed my eyes until the room stopped spinning. Then I met her gaze. "I think the reason you value the truth so highly, even when it hurts, is that you don't experience much of it. Syndicate life seems to be lie after lie, strung together with cruel manipulation and brutal compulsion. So let me be completely honest with you for a moment." Well, as honest as I could be without getting us both killed. "I like you. I like you a lot."

Her eyes widened, and I couldn't tell if she was surprised by what I was saying, or by the fact that I was saying it at all.

She started to reply, but I cut her off. I wasn't done. "Yes, I wanted you to stay for a while last night, but not because I was playing some kind of sadistic game. I wanted you to stay because I like your company."

Kori stuck a stirrer in her coffee. "Now I *know* you're lying." But her grip on the mug was tense, like she didn't want to believe her own words.

"Why? Why is it so hard for you to believe that someone could want to be with you with no ulterior motive?"

"Because it's never happened." She set the full pot on the coffee table in front of me, along with an empty mug. "Everyone wants something. Even my sister needs me for protection."

"Okay, but I bet she'd do as much for you as you've done for her, if she had the chance. Every now and then, someone may just want to be near you, Kori. Or do you honestly think Kenley would kick you out if you were no use to her?"

"No. But she's my sister. You're…"

"A job. I know." And even hearing it from my own mouth stung a little. "But even if that's all you see in me, that's not all I see in you. I have no intention of reporting what happened last night to Tower. Nor will I report anything that happens today. I won't tell him anything you don't want me to. I swear on my life."

"You're serious?" She frowned, but I knew her skepticism ran much deeper than a cynical expression. "Why?"

"Because believe it or not, I'm not trying to hurt you, and I don't want someone else assigned as my recruiter. So nothing that was said here will leave this room." Except what I'd already told Aaron. "Think of this suite as our own personal Las Vegas. What happens here…"

"Stays here," she finished, and I nodded. Kori sank

onto the couch across from me and glanced at the coffee-pot. "I'm not going to serve you. Unless that'll get you to sign on. Or have I already ruined any chance of that?" She said it casually, but her eyes didn't match her tone. My answer mattered. A lot.

I picked up the coffeepot and filled my mug, glad my stomach was finally starting to settle. "What will happen if I don't?" I asked, but she only stared into her coffee. "The truth, Kori. You owe me that."

And finally she looked up, anger flashing in her bold, aggressive gaze, like she was daring me to disagree with something she hadn't even said yet. "If I can't get you to sign, he'll hurt Kenley to punish me. Then he'll execute me."

A bolt of anger burned through the center of my chest, and my jaw clenched. "Execute?"

She lifted her mug with shaking hands, and I felt like I was burning alive, consumed by my own rage. "Death by conflicting orders."

"That's sick. That's not death, it's torture."

"It's both. It's also an object lesson. Public executions tend to keep the masses in line."

I wanted to beat Jake Tower into the ground until the earth accepted him back.

"I'll sign," I said. My words were a lie, but my intent was true. I would do whatever it took to protect her from him, but that wouldn't involve signing with Jake Tower. I wanted to free her from him, not enslave myself along-side her.

"Are you sure?" She looked so suddenly hopeful, yet so skeptical. So…guilty. Because she thought she was condemning me to a life like her own.

"Yes," I said, and her obvious relief was like a ray

of sunshine parting dark clouds. "But not today. I want today off. My last day as a free man. And I want you to spend it with me. If you want to." I had to know that she wasn't just following orders.

"Now more than ever. But don't read too much into that." She was actually grinning. "It's a nice suite."

There was something in her eyes when she said it. Something I liked. I wanted to know what scared her and what made her smile. I wanted to know what she'd wanted out of life before she'd joined the syndicate, and if that was what she still wanted.

"Was any of it true, Kori? About your parents, and your grandmother? Or was that just part of the role he made you play?"

"I can't tell you everything," she said, meeting my gaze. "But nothing I said was a lie." She took another sip from her coffee, and the stiffness in her shoulders eased. She looked almost relaxed, and I realized she'd been tense since the moment I'd met her, and probably for years before that.

My lie had set her at ease and given her a borrowed sense of security. But I wanted her to have those both permanently. I wanted her to have a real life, free from compulsion, humiliation and pain. And I only knew of one way to make that happen.

I needed to talk to her sister alone—a chance to convince her to do the right thing, not just for Steven, but for Kori, too. Kenley Daniels was the source of so much trouble, but she might also be the solution.

But Kori couldn't know what we were planning, because she'd have to report me to Tower.

"So, what do you want to do today?" Kori asked, and I struggled to wipe my thoughts from my expression.

She couldn't know what I was thinking about until it was done.

"I don't know," I said, stirring my coffee. "How would you spend your last day as a free woman? What should I absolutely see before I sign?"

"The fork in the river," Kori said without hesitation. "My favorite place in the city. There's a park on the south side, right where the river splits, and you can see all three districts from there. And there's this vendor in the park that serves the best hot dogs in the city. The secret is the potato bread buns."

"Hot dogs?" I laughed.

Kori shrugged. "Jake said no more bars. He didn't say anything about hot dogs in the park."

"Do they have sauerkraut?"

"Of course."

"I'm in. Let me get dressed."

I threw on some clothes, and then Kori and I took a cab to the fork in the river, because she couldn't shadow-walk into a park in broad daylight. I don't know what I was expecting to see, but the carousel surprised me.

"My parents took us here once when I was a kid," she explained, leading me along the waist-high wrought-iron fence containing a crowd of children waiting their turn for a ride. "I was about five, so Kenley would have been three, and Kris was probably almost seven. I rode that black one, with the gold reins."

"Of course you did." The carousel horse she'd pointed out was one of only three not painted in some pastel shade with a white mane. Her horse was more dignified, and probably a little creepy from a child's perspective, its lips pulled back from its teeth like it was in midwhinny.

"I fell off and busted my knee on one of the bolts on

the floor," she said, watching the carousel turn. "My mom swooped in to pick me up while my dad sprayed all the blood with bleach solution." She stopped walking and crossed her arms over her chest. "I wonder if any of it's still there, in the cracks."

"If so, there's no way it's viable," I said, but I'd misunderstood her intent. She wasn't worried. She looked… interested.

"Isn't it weird, how we leave little bits of ourselves everywhere we go? Like, there's part of me in that carousel, and part of it in me. I still have the scar on my knee." She frowned then, and looked away from the carousel. "There's a part of Jake in me, too." She rubbed her left arm, where the tattooed chain links would be beneath her sleeve. "They're sealed with his blood. Not enough to use against him, unfortunately. Just enough to make it feel like you don't belong to yourself anymore."

And that was true. That was the whole problem.

"So, where are those hot dogs?" I asked, eager to change the subject. Smart-ass Kori was fun, and even angry Kori was usually entertaining. Scared Kori made me want to fight. To find a way to accomplish the impossible. But I didn't know what to do with melancholy Kori. She seemed directionless. Lost. Not like Kori at all.

"It's a little bit of a walk, but it's worth it," she said, altering our course toward a winding sidewalk.

"Does Kenley like these dogs, too?" I asked as we walked. "Think she'd like to join us for lunch?" Admittedly, my approach was less than subtle, but I was running out of time and options.

"Kenley's a vegetarian. Which is why I eat out so often."

"Oh. Well, maybe—" I started, but Kori grabbed my

arm and pulled us both to a stop, suspicion thick in the arch of her brows.

"What's with your interest in my sister? She's not into you, and Jake would never…"

"No, it's nothing like that," I insisted, but she didn't look like she believed me. So I told another lie, and I wasn't sure whether I should feel guilty or grateful that I'd had enough practice to carry it off. "I've never been bound to anything, and I feel like I'm diving right into the deep end with this. I just…I want to get to know the person who's going to be sealing the binding. I want to know I can trust her."

"You can't," Kori said, and I frowned. "You can't trust any of us," she continued, and that didn't make me feel any better. "Soon, you won't be able to trust yourself."

"That's comforting."

"Don't get me wrong. You'll like Kenley. Everyone does. But she has to do whatever Jake tells her to, just like the rest of us."

"What was she like before the syndicate?" I asked. If I couldn't talk to her directly, maybe I could at least get a feel for her personality in preparation.

"She was sweet, but gullible. Powerful, but naive."

"You said she got into some trouble?"

"Yeah. Kenley had trouble making friends as a kid, and that got worse in college, until her roommate found out about her Skill. Poor Kenni thought this little bi— um, this little monster was really her friend, so she gave her a little bit of her blood. The roommate said she needed it to get an aggressive ex out of her life. Kenley didn't realize she was being used until this Tracker tracked her down through one of the bindings and scared the shit out of her. Turns out the roommate had been using Kenni's blood for everything from revenge on a volleyball team rival to making sure her boyfriend stayed faithful."

"The boyfriend she was trying to get rid of?"

"That was a lie—she was actually trying to keep him. And he wasn't technically her boyfriend. But she used Kenni's blood to tie him into a particularly nasty Love Knot." A binding preventing him from committing to anyone else.

"Damn. So, how did Tower get involved?"

"The Tracker was working for Jake, looking for a new Binder. He hit the jackpot with Kenley."

I wasn't seeing the park anymore, in spite of the children racing past every now and then on their way from the playground to the riverbank. I could only see half-formed connections—threads that didn't quite meet.

Kenley had bound Steven to something unknown, at some time in the past, but he didn't recognize her name or her picture. But Kenley wasn't the only one who'd used her blood to seal a binding. Was it possible…?

"Wait, how would that even work? It's a Binder's will that actually seals a binding, right? If Kenley didn't know what her blood was being used for, how could her will be there?"

Kori shrugged. "Evidently by giving her roomie permission to use the blood, she was contributing her will to whatever the roommate decided to use it for."

"That's scary as hell," I said, and my voice sounded hollow.

"No sh—" Kori cleared her throat and started over, but I was too distracted to find humor in her near miss. "No kidding. Which is why she's not allowed to hand her blood out anymore."

We walked half a mile or so as we talked, following the sidewalk around the playground, a set of basketball courts and large patches of grass beneath sprawling trees. All around us, kids played and joggers jogged, enjoying their weekend in one of few green patches within the city limits. But I hardly noticed any of it. I was thinking about my brother and his girlfriend, and the invisible ties connecting them to Kori's sister, and me to her by extension. How long had those connections been there? How had Steven only breached this mysterious binding two weeks ago, if it had been in place for the past six years, if my hunch was right.

At the dock, a line had formed as people waited their turn for boat rides, and just past that, Kori led me to a quaint walking bridge spanning one branch of the river. My footsteps echoing on wood was what finally brought me out of my own head.

"Is this still the west side?" I asked as we reached the apex and she stopped to lean over the rail, staring out at the river flowing beneath us.

"Technically, this is nowhere. This is the space above the river, and no one owns the river."

"Like standing with one foot on either side of a state border?" I asked as she leaned so far over I was afraid she'd fall in.

"More like standing on neither side. I like it here. There's no ground beneath us, so it feels like this place doesn't really exist. And if it doesn't exist, then I don't exist when I'm here. And if I don't exist, no one can make me do…anything."

"Do you come here a lot?" I asked when she showed no sign of wanting to move on.

"No. If I did, it wouldn't be special." And she needed

this place to be special—this place, where she didn't exist—and I felt privileged to not-exist there with her.

"So, if that's the west side…" I said, pointing back the way we'd come. "Then that must be the east side. Is the hot dog stand on the east side? Are we allowed to go there?"

"Yes, because that's the south side. Neutral territory. The east side is over *there*." She pointed over the bridge and I saw the actual fork in the river, beyond where we stood, and the east side, on the opposite side of the thicker part of the river, before it branched.

Kori finally turned away from the water and we crossed the rest of the bridge slowly, side by side. "Neutral territory, huh? So it's safe for everyone?"

"No one is safe. No place is safe. The south fork is only neutral because no one's been able to take total control of it yet. Cavazos has a regular presence here, as does Jake. If either of them backed down, the other would claim the fork and have a larger territory. So really, it's land in flux. The heart of the struggle. Not coincidentally, the south fork has the highest crime rates of any area of the city."

"And the best hot dogs?"

She laughed. "And the best hot dogs. The stand is just over there." She pointed, and I followed her gesture to find a wheeled vendor's cart with a faded, striped awning and a line of customers stretching out beyond it.

We were almost to the cart when Kori stopped in the middle of the sidewalk. Her shoulders tensed and her fingers curled and uncurled at her sides. I started to ask what was wrong but before I could speak, a woman said her name.

"Hey, Kori."

I looked up to find a man and a woman on the sidewalk in front of us, carefully spaced to block our path. We could have gone around them, of course, but their positions were more statement than true barrier. A command to stop. As was their identical stance, feet spread wide, as if they were expecting a fight. Jackets unbuttoned, for easy access to whatever weapons they were carrying.

The woman was unfamiliar, but I knew the man from Aaron's research on the Tower syndicate. Cameron Caballero. The only man alive known to have gotten out of his contract with Tower before the term was up. Now he worked for Cavazos—a lateral move at best.

"Olivia," Kori said. "I wondered when you'd show up."

Seventeen

Kori

"I assume you know why we're here," Olivia said.

Cam flexed his fingers at his sides, like he wanted to be holding his gun, and I knew the only thing keeping his hands empty was his respect for me and the six years we'd both spent chained to Tower. Though we'd rarely actually worked together, Cam was the closest thing I'd had to a friend in the syndicate.

Until he'd left.

"You're here because Cavazos's first attempt was laughable." And because I'd dared him to send someone more worthy, hoping he'd choose at least half of the pair now facing us. This was my only opportunity to talk to them without disobeying a direct order from Jake, and I *needed* to talk to them. I needed to understand why Liv had used me and Cam had abandoned me.

Yes, they'd been under orders, but so had I, yet I'd done everything I could to help them. And I'd paid for that in the basement.

"Olivia Warren?" Ian asked, and I actually looked

away from the double threat of my former friends to glance at him in surprise. If Olivia and Cam hadn't also been caught off guard, my mistake might have cost me my life.

Jake would kill me if I lost Ian.

Liv frowned. "How did you…?"

"Your reputation precedes you," Ian said, and I did a quick mental inventory of every conversation we'd had since meeting at the party not quite forty hours earlier. I hadn't told him Olivia's last name. Names are power, and I wouldn't have given him that much power over a friend. Even a friend who'd ambushed me, tied me up, stolen my key, and ruined both my career and my life. "I'm guessing this isn't a friendly visit," Ian said, and Cam actually chuckled over the understatement.

"This is business. But we're free afterward if you want to get a drink."

"I'm sorry, Kori," Liv said. "This isn't how we want it."

"Any chance you could just claim you never found us?" Ian asked. "As a favor to an old friend?" He glanced at me for emphasis.

"That's not how it works." Olivia sighed, a sound heavy with reluctance, and directed her next words to Ian. "Ruben Cavazos extended an invitation, and it went unanswered. Come with us now and meet with him voluntarily. Pretty please."

"And if I decline?"

"If you decline, there will be weapons and threats. Inevitably Kori will say something she doesn't really mean and Cam will get his feelings hurt, and I don't think anyone wants that kind of drama in a public park."

"Is she serious?" Ian asked, and I nodded.

"Is she armed?"

I nodded again, my own fingers itching from lack of a weapon. "Gun on her right hip, blade on her right ankle. Unless something's changed in the last two months."

"A lot has changed," Olivia said. "But not that." She pulled her jacket back to reveal a pistol in a holster on her hip, then raised one brow at me in challenge. "As long as we're playing nice, what's your count? Three blades and a nine mil?"

"We're unarmed," I admitted, because she'd figure it out soon anyway, and Olivia laughed out loud.

"She means it," Cam said, studying my eyes, and I realized he knew me better than Olivia did. I'd gone to school with Liv, but I'd truly grown up in Tower's service, with Cam. "Jake won't use her as security anymore, after what happened."

"No thanks to you," I snapped, my temper wound so tight I was afraid that if I inhaled too deeply, something would pop, and I'd just explode. "I have yet to earn back the right to bear arms." No matter what the second amendment said. But I could use whatever I took from them until this little conflict was over.

"Sorry, Kori." Olivia pulled her gun, aiming at the grass between us, but I held my ground and directed my reply to Ian, who looked just as calm now as he had in the alley the day before.

"She's not going to shoot you, and she can't shoot me," I said softly, glad none of the other park-goers were close enough to see Liv's weapon. But if things escalated, we were in for some very public trouble.

"Because of the childhood binding?" Ian asked, and Olivia glanced at me in surprise.

"Have you been telling stories, Kori?"

"Only the ones that are true." My next words were for Ian, though I couldn't take my attention off Liv's gun. "She can't intentionally hurt me, and if I ask for her help, she has to give it. Which, I'm willing to bet, would put her smack in the middle of two conflicting compulsions. Right, Liv?"

Olivia's eyes narrowed, but both her gun and her voice held steady. "That sword cuts both ways, Kori. Don't make me ask you for help taking Holt to Cavazos," she said, and I groaned, mentally.

"I don't think it'll come to that," Cam said, pulling his own gun smoothly.

"You're not going to shoot me," I insisted, desperately hoping I was right.

Olivia shrugged. "He shot *me*."

"He was under orders."

Cam took aim at my leg. "That hasn't changed. Holt comes with us, or I shoot you. Don't make me shoot you, Kori." He didn't want to spill my blood in a public park—more blood than I could possibly clean up—but he would.

"You owe me. Both of you." I could hear the fury in my voice, and saying that was like popping the top on a shaken can of soda—the rest just came shooting out. "You used me. You got me shot, then you left me there to—" I bit my sentence off before the words could fall out into the daylight and leave me exposed by the truth. "You defected, without a word. Kenley heard it from one of the da—" Another pause, while I rerouted my sentence and I barely noticed Cam's surprise over the aborted expletive. "From one of Jake's secretaries."

I studied him, trying to understand what had happened two months earlier, and latent anger at Cam crashed over me with the weight of every wrong I'd suffered in the basement. Alone. Because when he'd switched sides, he'd left me to bear the brunt of Tower's fury.

Ian glanced from face to face, trying to make sense of a discussion he couldn't possibly understand. "What am I missing?" he said finally, but no one answered.

"I had no choice," Cam insisted, and I could read the guilt on his face. But I couldn't see any regret. "Cavazos was going to let Olivia die unless I signed, and I didn't have a chance to tell you. But I tracked you every day, to make sure you were alive."

"He put me in the basement." I shrugged and spoke through clenched jaws. "Obviously death is a mercy I haven't yet earned."

Cam looked like I'd just punched him. "I'm so sorry, Kor," he said. "Tracking you was the best I could do."

"Well, now you have a chance to make it up to me. Leave. Just tell Cavazos Ian is using a fake name and you couldn't track us."

"His name's real and Ruben already knows we found you." Liv's gaze shifted to Ian. "Ruben knows everything he needs to know about you, which means you're either stupid or naive for sticking with Tower when there's a better offer on the table." Liv frowned and her gaze slipped to me before centering on Ian again. "Or maybe it's not Tower you're sticking with…"

I ignored her inference and focused on the implied threat. "Whatever Cavazos knows, Jake knows, too," I insisted. "And Ian's made up his mind."

"Really? Is that what he told Meghan Hollister?"

Ian froze at my side, and I glanced at him quickly before turning my attention back to Olivia's words and

Cam's gun, trying to pretend I hadn't seen Holt's reaction. "Who's Meghan Hollister?"

When Ian didn't answer—I couldn't even tell if he was still breathing—Olivia took over once again.

"Meghan is Ian's girlfriend. They've been together for twelve years."

I tried not to react, not to let my disappointment and anger show through on my face. Ian groaned, but I could practically feel his posture relax, his arm brushing mine. He seemed relieved. What had he thought she'd say?

"That's not true," he said to me, without taking his gaze off the threat. "She's got her wires crossed. Meghan is my brother's girlfriend."

"Bullshit." Cam bit the last syllable off, leaving a sharp edge to the word. "Your brother died seven years ago. KIA overseas. What kind of a gutless loser pawns off his lies on a dead serviceman?" Cam demanded, and Ian's entire bearing changed, though he didn't move a muscle. He was just suddenly taut. Furious. Wound so tight the slightest vibration might set him off.

"They don't know what they're talking about," Ian said through clenched teeth. "I swear on my own name. Just please believe me, Kori. Trust me."

I didn't know what to believe. I didn't know who to trust. Nothing had made any sense since I got out of the basement.

Cam laughed, and again the sound was bitter. "Shows how well he knows you, huh?" Then he turned back to Ian. "Kori doesn't trust anyone. She just doesn't have it in her."

"I don't anymore," I spat. "The last person I trusted was you," I said, and Cam flinched.

"I'm sorry, Kori," Olivia said.

But I couldn't concentrate on yet another worthless apology, because I was busy trying to figure out something else. "Why are you still with Cavazos, anyway?" I asked Olivia, stalling for time to come up with a new plan, since the "you owe me" attempt had gone south. "I thought your mark died."

"It did." Olivia scowled. "Then this big dumb ass signed on for a fifteen-year term to pay for my medical care."

Cam transferred his gun to his left hand, which wasn't a handicap for him, unfortunately, and lifted his left sleeve. Above the three chain links that had connected him to Tower—now the pale gray of dead marks—were three freshly inked black rings, one and a half of which were already dead and gray, like the chain links beneath them.

"She died, Kori," Cam said. "I killed her, under orders from Tower, and Cavazos had doctors on hand, just standing there with a crash cart. He wouldn't let them touch her until I signed."

"So why are the marks half-dead?"

Olivia twisted to show her own bare arm, where there were two more rings, one half-dead. "Ruben said I could let Cam serve his fifteen years alone, or I could take half of it. Seven and a half years each, served together. A ring and a half for each of us."

"Liv…" I moaned, my anger at Cam momentarily swallowed by my ache for her. "You were free."

"And I will be again. But for now, Ruben's still calling the shots, and if Holt doesn't come with us peacefully, Cam has to put a bullet in your leg."

Cam strengthened his aim with a double-handed grip, and Ian exhaled.

"Fine, I'll go." He held his hands, palms out in the universal posture of surrender. "Just leave her alone."

"Ian…" I said, but he ignored me and stepped slowly toward Cam and Olivia. "Ian, stop." I reached for him, but he stepped around my arm.

"Can we at least keep this civil?" he asked when Cam pulled a plastic cinch lock from his pocket. "Most hosts don't tie up their guests."

Cam didn't even consider it. "Sorry, man. Turn around." He handed the strip of plastic to Olivia, who holstered her gun to accept it.

The moment her gun disappeared beneath her jacket, Ian leaned to the left and kicked her square in the chest. She flew backward, and I lost an instant to surprise, then I lurched into motion.

Cam aimed at me, but Ian stepped between us, and wouldn't move when I tried to shove him out of the way. "He can't shoot me, which means he can't shoot you *through* me," he insisted, and I'll admit it—I was impressed. He was both smart and evidently fearless. No matter what Jake paid for him, he'd be getting a bargain.

Olivia tried to get up, but I planted one foot on her chest, then squatted and snatched her nine millimeter from its holster while Ian danced the combat waltz with Cam, trying to stay between me and his gun. Then I stood and backed away from Olivia to aim at Cam.

My possession of a gun evened the odds. Their unwillingness to shoot Ian tipped the scales in our favor. Barely.

"How about we call it a draw, and retreat to neutral corners?" Ian suggested as we backed slowly away from them, while Olivia stood, fuming. "That way, everyone lives to die another day."

"Sorry, can't do it," Cam said.

"I *will* shoot you," I warned him, aiming at his thigh for emphasis.

Cam's aim rose. "Likewise."

"Okay, there has to be a way around this," Ian said, backing slowly, carefully toward a gathering of trees that would block us from the hot dog stand. No one had noticed us yet, but that wouldn't last. "You don't want to shoot each other."

Cam barked a bitter laugh and raised one brow at me. "Does he believe in Santa, too?"

"Kori, *please,*" Olivia said, and I could hear the stress in her voice. She loved us both and we were going to kill each other, if something didn't change soon. We had no choice.

"Don't say it, Liv," I warned when I realized just how bad this was about to get. If she asked me for help, I'd have to respond in kind, and the conflicting compulsions and resulting pain would complicate things beyond recovery.

"Okay, let's take this over there, out of sight of the general public." Ian tossed his head toward the small grove of trees.

Cam glanced at Olivia without altering his aim, then he nodded. "Run, and I'll shoot her." He was talking to Ian, but still aiming at me.

"No one's running." I backed slowly toward the trees with Ian, and Cam and Olivia followed. As we walked, I talked, my brain racing, desperate for a way out. "What are your orders, exactly? Maybe there's a loophole. A way we can all walk away from this."

"There is—so long as at least three of us are walking east," Cam insisted. "That's the only way we're all going to live through this."

Eighteen

Ian

Some measure of tension inside me eased as my left foot settled into the first patch of shaded grass, where I'd been subtly leading us since that first step off the sidewalk. I could feel the shadow against my skin, cool, like the first foot dipped into a swimming pool. Another step and I could feel it in my bones. Shadows always called to me, but that call was never stronger than when I actually needed the dark.

Unfortunately, the mottled shade cast by the trees was shallow and sparse. But it would have to be enough.

"Okay, then, why don't we all go?" I said, stepping farther into the shade with Kori at my side, still aiming her appropriated gun at Cam's leg. "We'll go see Cavazos together and discuss this like civilized adults. No weapons. No restraints."

"No," Kori said, and I bit my tongue to keep from groaning. I wasn't actually going to *go* with them. I was just trying to back us into deeper shadows to make for an easier escape. Then I realized I could let her argumentative tendencies serve as a distraction from what I was doing.

"Why not?" I glanced at her, careful not to let effort show on my face as I pulled the shadows toward us, letting them gather at our feet. If anyone had been looking at the ground, they would have seen the shade actually roll across the earth toward us from its natural placement, leaving spots of light where none should have fallen through tree branches and leaves.

But they didn't notice. They were watching and listening to Kori because she was armed with a weapon they could actually see.

"If you put one foot on Cavazos's property, you won't step back out unless you bear his mark," Kori said. "And I sure as hell can't take you there myself. Jake would kill me."

But it was her first statement that echoed in my head, momentarily distracting me from the stealthy gathering of shadows. "Cavazos would kill me if I don't sign?" I glanced at Cam and Olivia, trying to glean the truth from their reactions. But they didn't bother lying.

"Without even blinking," Olivia said. "He can't let you sign with someone else."

Cam nodded. "And Tower will do the same."

I glanced at Kori for confirmation, but she wouldn't look at me. Which had to mean that he was right.

I'd known Tower would go to any length to sign me— hell, Kori had warned me from the beginning that if I couldn't be recruited, I'd be hunted—and deep down, I'd probably known all along what would happen if the prey couldn't be caged. But I hadn't given serious thought to preserving my own life, because I was busy trying to save Steven's. And because I'd planned to disappear once I'd done that anyway.

But this revelation presented a new problem. If Tower would kill me to keep anyone else from signing me, he'd do the same to Steven, who would resume using my name once I'd disappeared.

And I wasn't going to disappear without Kori. I would not leave her alone in the syndicate. Not like Cam did.

"Isn't that a little extreme?" I said, faking ignorance to distract from the shadows I was gathering faster now.

Cam's aim never wavered, though his arms had to be getting tired. "It's common sense."

Olivia elaborated. "Mr. Holt, the strength of your Skill is unheard of, and it may never be matched. I don't know how you escaped notice as long as you did, but the display you made of yourself at that hockey game was idiotic, at best. The whole world knows what you can do now, and that's not ever going to go away."

"What does that mean?" The shadows were as thick as I could make them, but I let them simmer at our ankles for another minute, fascinated to hear Olivia saying the same things my mother had warned me and Steven about from the time we were old enough to listen.

"That means that even if you sign with Tower tomorrow, you're not going to be able to just walk away at the end of your commitment," Olivia continued. "He'll use everyone you love—hell, everyone you even *know*—to manipulate or just plain force you to stay. If you don't believe me, ask Kori why her sister's still with Tower."

But I didn't need to. As long as Kenley still had a brother, grandmother, or anyone else she cared about, Tower would have a way to control her.

"It'd be the same with Cavazos," Kori said as I pulled

the building shadows up to our shins. I couldn't go much farther than that without them being noticed. "That's how he got the two of you."

Olivia nodded. "And neither of us are anywhere near as powerful as you are," she added, looking straight at me. "You're going to wind up serving someone. Your only real choice is who that will be."

"Maybe," I said, and the shadows built higher, churning faster as my pulse began to race. I wrapped one arm around Kori's waist, sliding my hand beneath her shirt to make necessary skin contact without compromising her aim. "But last I checked, that was still my choice. Give my best to Cavazos." Then I pulled the shadows up around us like a cocoon, as fast as I could. Faster than I'd ever done it before.

"Hey!" Olivia shouted, as we disappeared behind the shield of darkness I'd built in broad daylight. But there was no gunfire. Cam couldn't risk hitting me.

Kori laughed out loud, a giddy release of tension and a celebration of the darkness that was a part of both of us. Then she tugged me forward. A single step later, everything changed.

We were inside—I could tell from the silence, and the absent scents of grass and trees. Those were replaced almost instantly with other familiar scents.

Dust. Wood. Wine.

I let the darkness around us melt into the ambient shadows, revealing a dimly lit wine cellar. A *huge* wine cellar. This wasn't someone's private collection. This was the real thing.

"Where are we?" I said, and I only realized my hand was still on her stomach when she turned to scold me with one finger pressed against her lips.

"Shh."

I let her go reluctantly, missing her warmth the minute it was gone. "I take it we're not supposed to be here?" I whispered.

"Not without an appointment and a traditional front-door entry. This is a local winery—the closest place I could think of that would be dark during the day. They have a vineyard outside the city, but this was closer and safer to travel into, since I've actually been here with Jake several times. They make his favorite wine."

"Wow." I pulled a bottle from the nearest rack and glanced at the label. I'd never heard of the brand, but that wasn't surprising, since it was local. "Are they any good?"

Kori shrugged. "You're asking the wrong person."

"You just haven't found your favorite yet. Or you're drinking it at the wrong temperature. Either of which can be remedied." I slid the pinot noir back into its slot and went in search of a good starter wine.

"Hold it down," she repeated, following me through the cellar, which was obviously used as more than storage. When I turned the corner around the next floor-to-ceiling rack, I found tables and chairs set up for a wine tasting, though nothing was set out at the moment.

"Can you point me to the whites? Maybe a pinot grigio…" I mumbled, rounding the nearest table toward another set of racks on the other side.

"No, I can't." Kori grabbed my arm with the hand not still gripping Olivia's gun. "Ian, we have to go. I have to tell Jake that Cavazos tried again."

I stopped and met her gaze, unable to quell the nerves churning in my stomach. "Are you under specific orders to report the very event that only *almost* took place? No one was hurt. No guns were fired. There was no public spectacle."

She thought about that for the moment and finally slid the safety switch into place on Olivia's nine millimeter and handed it to me—she couldn't carry it now that the fight was over. "I guess not. But if he finds out from someone else—"

I tucked the gun into my waistband for lack of a holster. "If he finds out, I'll take the blame. I'll tell him I wanted to explore his favorite winery." If we reported a second poaching attempt, Tower might assign extra security, which would render my plan completely useless. And that was the best-case scenario. "If we go make your report now, what are the chances that he'll ask me to sign on the spot?"

Kori shrugged. "Pretty good. But what does that matter, if you're going to sign anyway?" Which I'd told her I'd do. The lies were getting complicated.

"That would be robbing me of my last day of freedom, and I really want this last day, Kori. If I'm going to be stuck either bound to or running from the syndicate for the rest of my life, I'm damn sure going to have one last day of freedom. If you'd known what was coming before you signed, wouldn't you have wanted the same thing?"

"I still want that," she said, and the truth of the statement echoed in her words. And suddenly I had to know.

"Was Olivia right? If I refuse to sign, will Tower kill me?" I could hardly see her eyes in the dim light, but I saw enough to know there was something she hadn't wanted to say in front of Olivia and Cam.

"Yes. And if you were a normal potential recruit, he'd probably put a bullet in your brain. But because you're special and everyone wants you, if I can't recruit you I'm under orders to take you to Heartland Pharmaceuticals."

"You'd turn me into a vegetable?" The choice wasn't hers. I knew that. But it still hurt to hear her talk about my death.

"Not me. Jake. And no, not a vegetable. The whole world knows about you, Ian, and half the city knows Jake's trying to recruit you. If you disappear, people will try to track you, and if you're alive—even as a vegetable—they'll find you. If I can't recruit you, Jake won't be able to use you as a blood cow. So he'll have you completely drained."

Nineteen

Kori

Ian's eyes widened, but he looked more hurt than surprised. He'd known, at least on some level, that there were only two ways out of the mess we were both in: service or death.

And with the latest betrayal to slide off my tongue, most of my secrets were out. "I'm sorry. I should have told you that this morning, but then you said you'd sign, so I didn't see any reason to threaten you with death and the posthumous sale of your blood."

"You'd really do it? You'd turn me over to be drained just because Tower told you to?" The disappointment and betrayal in his gaze stung like little else I'd ever felt.

"I—" The answer was there, ready to go. It didn't require thought. So little did, with Jake pulling my strings. But the words wouldn't come out, and the new thoughts blocking them made me close my mouth. Then my eyes.

What good would it do to turn him over to Jake? Both Kenley and I were screwed anyway, if things went that far south.

"I honestly don't know," I said at last. "Physically, I'd have no choice. Resisting the compulsion would kill me unless Jake rescinded the order. And he won't. But if I turn you over to him, he'll kill me anyway, for failing to recruit you. So…"

And suddenly it all looked so clear.

"No, I wouldn't." Because I was going to die either way, and at least this way, I'd go out without having first killed an innocent man. Ever. And that might just be the only point of honor for me to look back on if my life really flashed before my eyes in those last few seconds.

I'd killed for Jake, of course. I'd had no choice. But he had never—up till now—ordered me to kill someone who wasn't at least as guilty as I was.

Ian's gaze never left mine. He was watching me think, and I wondered if he could read any of those thoughts on my face.

"You know none of that matters, though, right?" I said. "If I don't hand you over to Jake, someone else will."

"None of it matters, because I'm going to sign," he said, and again I wished for just a second that I was a Reader. He looked like he meant it, but he also looked like there was something he wasn't saying.

I thought about demanding the whole truth, right there on the spot, but then, in an unprecedented display of common sense, I held my tongue. Some secrets are kept for a reason and spilling them prematurely can mean spilling blood, as well. His silence was meant to protect someone. Probably himself, but maybe me. So I decided to wait.

Then I hoped I'd made the right decision.

"We should take Tower a bottle," Ian said when he

finally looked away, and some small bit of the tension inside me eased. "What does he like?"

"I don't know. Something dark red."

"You've eaten with him, right? What does he order most often?"

I'd spent years shadowing Jake. Protecting him. I'd seen him order dinner a thousand times.

He liked a thick cut of tenderloin, still cool in the middle. His baked potato came with salt and butter only, his mashed with a hint of garlic. And to drink, he ordered…

"Cabernet Sauvignon. Sometimes Bordeaux."

"Okay." Ian nodded. "Bordeaux is a blend, and I'm not familiar with this label, so the Cab may be a better bet." He started pulling bottles from the racks, reading the labels then sliding them back into place, working his way down one aisle and into the next until finally he read a label and smiled. "This should work." He held the bottle up for me to see, but other than the familiar icon on the label, I had no idea what I was looking at. "And maybe one for us…" He handed me the wine, then turned back to the rack.

I studied the bottle I held, surprised by how thick the glass was, especially at the bottom, where there was a pronounced dip in the base—a mountain of glass rising into the dark liquid. In the movies, I'd seen people whack bad guys with beer bottles, but holding my very first bottle of wine, I was convinced that it would make a much more effective weapon. Assuming I could compensate for the greater weight. Maybe an empty bottle…

I swung experimentally, and in one smooth motion, faster than I would have thought possible, Ian's hand shot out and the bottle *thunked* into his palm in the middle of my swing. "That is *not* a weapon."

"Everything's a weapon, if you know how to use it."

His brows rose. "You're holding a two-hundred-dollar bottle of wine, and all you want to do with it is bash someone's head in? I think that statement clearly illustrates the source of your problems. Everything doesn't have to be a fight, Kori."

"And *that* statement clearly illustrates the source of *your* problems." I enjoyed throwing his own words back at him. "You're chin-deep in the fight, and you don't even know it."

"I know it," he insisted, and suddenly that seemed possible. The rare somber look in his eyes hinted at some dark depth I hadn't truly seen yet. "My point is that some weapons are more suited to a delicate touch than to blunt-force trauma."

"I'm a blunt-force trauma kind of girl, in case you haven't noticed."

"I have. And so has Tower. Part of your problem is that he knows what to expect from you. So let's give him something new." Ian held the bottle up, like he was modeling it for a commercial. "Think of Jake Tower as the fly, and this bottle as the honey."

"Ooh, are we going to poison the honey?"

His brows rose higher. "No."

"Then how is it a weapon?"

"It's a distraction meant to outshine any report of trouble in the park. More a shield than a sword."

"Just as well." I sighed. "Killing Jake isn't an option." And it never would be. In fact, I dreaded the day of his death almost as much as I dreaded every breath he took.

When Jake died, something worse would rise from his ashes to claim his kingdom.

Ian was watching me again, like maybe he'd heard more than I'd actually said. Then he handed me the bottle with a warning frown and turned back to the racks.

"Why do you know so much about wine?" I asked as he read label after label.

"My father was an enthusiast. He tried to make his own several times when I was a kid, but by the time I was old enough to share his passion, he'd admitted defeat and committed to enjoying the fruits of someone else's labor."

"Oh. My dad drank tequila. The kind with the worm in the bottle." In fact, that was my clearest memory of him. "Your dad teach you about fighting, too?" I asked, and Ian chuckled.

"My dad was a pacifist. He marched in antiwar rallies before I was born."

"And your brother was a soldier? I bet Thanksgiving was interesting at your house."

"Yeah." Ian glanced at me, then pulled another bottle from the rack. "Where'd you learn to fight?" he asked, and I got the impression he was trying to change the subject.

"My grandmother said I needed a healthy way to burn energy and express my natural aggression, so she enrolled me in my brother's martial arts class when I was ten. I loved it."

"I'd say it loved you, too," he said, and before I could reply, something creaked from the other side of the cellar—a door swinging open—and light flooded the entire room. I froze, my heart racing. Footsteps clomped down a set of stairs I couldn't see from our position, and my hand clenched around the neck of the bottle, now slick with nervous sweat.

I backed toward the end of the aisle, my boots silent on the floor, and Ian followed, both of us peering through the open racks at what we could see of the rest of the cellar. High stools around high tables. The dark wood bar that had been lined in wineglasses and manned by two servers at every event I'd accompanied Jake on. And the open space in the middle of a cellar full of racks, where guests would mingle, and gossip, and examine the collection surrounding them.

Jake's wine-tasting parties were interminably dull, and I'd sometimes wished someone would try to kill him, just to bring a little excitement into the most boring room I'd ever stood in.

Now I had excitement, and I wanted nothing more than the dark, quiet cellar back.

"As you can see, there's plenty of room for the event, and we can set up more tables," a man said, and I recognized the slightly nasal voice of John Yard, the winery's events coordinator.

"How are you fixed for lighting?" Another man asked as their steps echoed closer. "This is nice for ambience, but my wife will fuss if the light isn't sufficient for people to admire her shoes."

"That's not a problem."

A switch flipped somewhere and another set of lights came on. I flinched, though the cellar was still much dimmer than the park in broad daylight. This was starting to feel too familiar. An underground room. No windows. Someone standing between me and the exit. Darkness that should have been a comfort to me, made terrifying by the light source caging me.

There were huge differences between Jake's prison cell and the wine cellar. But knowing that didn't stop my pulse from racing or my next breaths from sliding in and out of my mouth too fast to satisfy my need for air. Logic couldn't stop my feet from carrying me backward across the concrete, as quietly as I could move, my heart pounding, until my back hit something warm and solid, and I gasped.

A hand closed over my mouth before I could scream and another took the bottle of wine from me before I could drop it.

I clawed at the fingers over my lips and stomped on the foot between my own, and Ian sucked in a breath, so close his chin stubble caught in my hair. "Kori, relax," he whispered, so soft I understood more than heard the words. "Don't move, or they'll see us."

When I nodded, he let go of my mouth and stepped back to give me space, still holding the bottle he'd taken, and I concentrated on breathing slowly. Counting the breaths. This wasn't Jake's basement. Ian wasn't Jonah. I wasn't being punished.

But we both would be, if we got caught. Stealing a bottle of Jake's favorite wine as a gift to him was one thing, but getting caught looting his favorite winery was something else entirely.

I stood as still as I could, waiting for Ian to pull darkness around us again, so I could walk us out of trouble. The cellar was much darker than the park had been, so it shouldn't have been any problem. But no shadows gathered at our feet, cooling me from the toes up. No darkness built. And the voices only came closer.

I turned to glance at Ian and found him much closer than I'd expected. He was trapped between me and the wall, obviously trying to give me as much space as possible. I opened my mouth, but he pressed one finger against his own lips, still holding the bottle in his other hand.

I rolled my eyes and stepped closer until I was pressed against him, going up on my toes to whisper in his ear, acutely aware of how solid his chest felt against mine. "Make it dark, and I'll get us out of here."

"Can't," he whispered in return, so softly that it took me a minute to figure out what he'd said. Then he pointed at something behind me and I turned to find my cell phone lying on the floor across the main aisle from where we stood. It must have fallen out of my pocket, and thanks to the rubberized case, neither of us had heard it land.

We couldn't leave without it. I wasn't allowed to keep syndicate names or numbers programmed into my phone, but I hadn't cleared the call list since last night, and it would only take a cursory glance through the contents to figure out who the phone belonged to, and only a phone call after that to link my name with Jake's.

He was going to kill me.

My pulse raced again, so fast the room started to go dark around me, though the lights hadn't faded. John Yard and his customer came closer, still discussing whatever event they were planning, and I could see them now, through the single floor-to-ceiling rack of wine separating me and Ian from the main open area. Which meant they could see us, too, if they glanced our way. Or if any movement from us drew their attention.

"Shh…" Ian whispered into my ear, and I inhaled slowly, then exhaled slower still. His free hand slid down my right arm and I stiffened and would have pulled away if I weren't afraid to move. But then his hand brushed my palm and his fingers twined around mine, and I clung to his hand, not out of fear, but out of relief. I wasn't alone. I may have been feet from getting caught and minutes from facing Jake's wrath, but for the first time in years, I wasn't alone in either predicament.

Ian wouldn't let me take all the blame or bear the brunt of the punishment, even if Jake and I both tried to give it to me. He wouldn't desert me like Cam had. He'd said he'd sign—he'd promised to commit the next five years of his life to a monster—to keep Jake from killing me.

Ian wouldn't leave me.

I let myself lean against his chest, my heart pounding in some intoxicating combination of fear and indefinable need, and his hand tightened around mine. And for a minute, I couldn't breathe.

I'd never done this. I'd never felt anything as intimate as the feel of his hand in mine. His breath against my ear. His chest warm against my back.

I'd had sex. I'd even had sex multiple times with the same man, and until that moment, I would have considered that intimacy—the fact that I could tolerate one man enough to sleep with him more than once. But I was wrong. With Ian pressed against me, his heart beating in sync with my own, I understood that no connection I'd ever made had been more than physical gratification. Mutual back-scratching. I'd never *lingered* with anyone else. Never touched just to touch. Just to feel.

I'd never truly experienced or been experienced by anyone.

When Yard took his customer into another section of the cellar without noticing my cell phone, I breathed a little easier. They were still close enough that we could hear their voices, but far enough away that they wouldn't notice our movement if we were quiet. So I turned and looked up at Ian in the shadows, and his dark-eyed gaze searched mine. Waiting. Silently asking a question words couldn't have clarified.

I let go of his hand, and he looked disappointed— until I laid it on his chest. His breathing deepened, and his heart raced. I could feel it through his shirt. I slid my hand up slowly, over his sternum, then his collarbone. My fingers rounded the curve of his neck, scratchy with stubble, and I pulled his head down as I went up on my toes. Then I kissed him.

Twenty

Ian

Kori kissed me. I'd half expected her to rip my arm off for touching her hand, but instead she kissed me, and every bit of spark in her—every blaze of temper and passion she smothered just to survive in her world—it all burned bright in that kiss. She'd found an outlet for everything she felt but couldn't show, and I took it all. I swallowed her pain and her anger. I devoured her isolation and frustration. And I reveled in the hunger she was showing me, and in my own need, awakened by hers.

When she finally dropped onto her heels again, her hand trailing down my neck and lingering on my chest, I couldn't look away. I couldn't see anything but Kori, and the confusion and desire warring in her eyes. Flickering across her expression, one side of her face shadowed, the other illuminated by light shining through the racks from the lit section of the cellar.

Then the men's voices grew louder, accompanying their footsteps toward the cellar entrance. They'd have to pass by us again to get there, and if they got a sudden craving for an eight-year-old Cabernet—or even just glanced to their left—we were screwed.

Kori's breathing grew shallow and quick. She turned toward the sound of their steps and her gaze flitted back and forth as she tried to spot them through the racks all around us. I knew what she was thinking. What were the chances that they'd miss us twice? How could they not spot her phone?

I pulled her close, careful not to grab her arm and trigger automatic resistance, and with her pressed against my chest, her cheek on my shoulder, I wrapped the shadows around us. Not true darkness—an anomaly like that would be noticed in a semilit room—but just a thickening of the existing shadows, decreasing the chances that a casual glance our way would reveal us.

We both wore dark clothes, which blended easily into the shadows, leaving her face and hair the only pale spots in my darkness. So as the voices came closer, the footsteps echoing from mere feet away now, I wrapped my arms around her and turned us both carefully, putting my body—my own dark head and clothing—between her and the rest of the cellar.

She tensed, but didn't object, and I knew she wasn't used to being sheltered. Kori was the type to throw herself in front of a bullet to protect someone else, but I wanted her to know it didn't always have to be like that. That she didn't have to fight the world alone. That I wanted to fight with her. If she would let me.

The host and his customer passed our aisle, and I turned my head to watch their progress across the open area. And as I rotated us again, I couldn't resist touching her hair, where it trailed down her back. It was so impossibly soft, as if her hard edges couldn't quite tame that one feature, or disguise its beauty with function.

When the lights went out and the cellar door finally closed, we both exhaled in relief. But I held her a second longer, with no good excuse. And when I let her go, she stayed pressed against me for one more second, and my heart beat harder. I wanted to freeze that moment in time and live there for eternity. Alone in the dark with Kori. No immediate threats. No fear strong enough to push her away from me. No lies standing between us.

However, like all good things, that moment expired and real life descended again, bringing with it bitter obligations we couldn't ignore. But things were different now. Real life had been changed forever by that moment, at least for me, because Kori had let me in. She'd trusted me, and I didn't have to be told how rarely anyone saw past her shields to the woman beneath.

But with her trust came an obligation to prove myself worthy. If I let her down—if I betrayed her trust just once—I would lose her forever.

When I couldn't figure out how best to acknowledge what had passed between us without scaring her off, she finally gave me a tiny smile, then brushed past me to grab her phone from across the aisle. "You know, it's a minor miracle that we're not being drawn and quartered by Jake at this very moment," she whispered, shoving her phone into her pocket.

"That's a rather antiquated form of punishment," I said, handing her the bottle I'd picked out for Tower. "Please tell me you don't mean it literally."

"I've never actually seen anyone ripped limb from limb, no, but Jake's certainly pulled people apart figuratively, and that's bad enough."

"No argument from me…" I pulled another bottle of Cabernet from the rack to my right, then headed deeper into the cellar in search of something lighter and fruitier.

"Ian, we're not shopping, we're escaping. Let's go."

"One minute…"

"Thirty seconds," she conceded, following me past the blushes and into the whites. "Then I'm leaving you here." But she wouldn't, and we both knew it.

I pulled a bottle of pinot grigio from the nearest rack, crossing my fingers, since I was unfamiliar with the label, then I let her pull me into the shadows. A moment later, we emerged in the unlit bathroom of the hotel suite.

Kori followed me into the living room, where I set all three bottles on the occasional table against one wall. "I believe you still owe me lunch," I said, pulling open the minifridge. At which point I realized I was too hungry for snack food. "But I'm guessing going back to the park would be a bad idea."

"I think leaving the west side at all would be bad, with Cam and Liv after you. But if your stomach's set on nitrates, there's a decent street vendor a couple of blocks over."

"Or, we could order in." I held up the room service menu. "There's a vegetarian section, if you think your sister might like to join us."

Kori frowned. "Okay, I get that you want to get to know the person who's about to bind you to Jake Tower. But if I invite Kenley over, her bodyguard of the day will come, too, and I really don't want to spend the next hour with someone who'll report everything we do or say directly to Jake."

"Okay. No problem. What do you want from room service?"

"A burger. A big one."

Kori ducked into the bathroom and I placed an order, then texted Aaron for an update on Steven and Meghan. I'd just hit Send when I heard the bathroom door open, and when the message went through, I deleted it from my phone, just in case. I wanted to tell Kori the truth. I *would* tell her. But I couldn't, while the chain links on her arm were still live marks. And to fix that, I needed to talk to Kenley. Alone.

When Kori walked into the living room, she wasn't looking at me. She was looking at her phone. Staring at it. "What's wrong?" I asked.

Instead of answering, she dropped onto the couch across from me and handed me her phone.

On the screen was a picture of a framed photograph on an end table. It was a photograph of Meghan. And me.

"Okay, that's not what it looks like," I said, but she waved off my explanation.

"Don't bother. You don't owe me an explanation, and you never swore not to lie. But now I need the truth."

"About Meghan?"

She shook her head and gestured back and forth between us. "About this. About us. I'm not a Reader— though Jake does have Readers. I can't tell you who they are, so just…don't lie to him—but I know you were telling the truth last night. You didn't know I was under orders to do whatever you want. But today, you've been lying."

"It's not what you think," I insisted, setting her phone on the coffee table.

"Look, I don't care who you were screwing before two days ago. I don't care how long the two of you have been together, or how cute and sweet she looks, or what kind of jam she spreads on your fucking toast before she sends you off to analyze systems every morning," Kori said, and I had to glance at my watch to verify that it had indeed been more than twenty-four hours since she'd agreed not to cuss for a day. "What I want to know is whether or not what happened in the wine cellar means anything to you. If not, fine. No hard feelings." But now *she* was lying. I could see it in the line of her brow and hear it in the tone of her voice. "But if that meant something...I need to know."

"Yes, it meant something," I said, and she studied my expression so intently I felt exposed, like she was seeing more than I meant to be saying. "It meant a lot. And that's not me." I pointed to the image on her phone, and Kori rolled her eyes. "Seriously. That's my brother." I took a deep breath, then let it out slowly, preparing to say the part we never voluntarily told strangers. "My twin."

"You had a twin?" she asked, and I nodded, but I couldn't tell whether or not she believed me. "Seriously? Because now you sound like the subject of a made-for-television movie."

"I can't help what it sounds like. Twins are actually a pretty common natural phenomenon."

Kori laughed. "No wonder your ego's the size of Texas. You think you're a born phenomenon." She glanced at the picture again. "Identical?"

"Fraternal. But we always looked a lot alike."

"Okay..." She wanted to believe me. I could see it. "But your brother's been dead almost seven years, and Liv says this picture was taken an hour ago."

"Olivia sent you that?" It was from Meghan's apartment. It had to be. Thank goodness she and Steven were staying at her parents' house.

Kori nodded. "That, and an offer from Cavazos. He'll 'make every reasonable effort' to buy my contract from Jake if I take you to him."

For a second, I couldn't breathe. "Is that what you want?"

"Hell no. I'm not leaving Kenley. And Jake wouldn't sell my contract anyway—not if I take you across the river. Cavazos is getting desperate." She picked her phone up again and stared at the picture. Then she looked up at me, and this time she was studying me for a different reason. "He looks just like you. Like you look *now*. But this has to be at least seven years old. Right?"

I shrugged. "I've aged well," I said, and when she smiled, I exhaled in relief. "Kori, the wine cellar meant a lot to me. I understand if you don't believe me, but…I wish you could. I want more of you."

She stiffened, and I wanted to take the words back.

"I didn't mean that as any kind of order. I'm not asking for anything," I said. "But I am offering…whatever you want."

"Ian, I don't know where this is going." She looked like there was more she wanted to say, and there was definitely more I wanted to hear. "I don't know if it *can* go anywhere. So if that's really you in the picture, you should just—"

"That's not me. And this can go wherever you want it to go. Your marks won't always stand between us." I let her think that was because I'd soon have a mark of my own, but I'd never been more determined to find a way to rid her of hers, and her next words only underlined that fact.

"No matter what happens, Jake will be in the way," she said. "That's how he likes it—his hand in every pie, so that even couples who've been together for years know that's only because he lets them stay together."

Chills were building at the base of my spine, spreading icy fingers out from there. "How the hell does he justify dictating the terms of his employees' private lives?"

Kori shrugged. "Why would he bother justifying it?" she said, and my chills became a river of ice flowing up my back and down my legs. "If a match doesn't benefit him in some way, he'll dissolve it."

"If you want to be with me—even on a trial basis— I'm not going to let Jake Tower stand in the way of that." Since I was painting fantasies with a palette of lies, I might as well paint something nice for her. For us. "That'll be the first contractual demand I make—Tower and his people have to keep their fingers out of my personal life."

Kori met my gaze, her eyes swimming in guilt. "I never wanted this assignment. Not even for a single second. But I've never wanted it less than I do right now. I don't want to be the thing that ties you to Jake. I don't want to be the reason you sign away your free will. And I *really* don't want to be the person who makes you look like the sun just set and it'll never rise again."

My chest ached. "This isn't your fault, Kori." But I couldn't truly absolve her of her guilt without admitting my own, and I couldn't do that while she was still bound to Tower. "Besides, the dark is my natural habitat, remember? Who cares if the sun never rises again? We'll thrive in the dark together."

"No one thrives in the syndicate. No one worth knowing, anyway." Her eyes flashed with anger, and my pulse raced in response. I wanted to touch her. I wanted to kiss her again, and find out if anger made her as passionate as fear did. I wanted to snatch her away from the world and keep her for myself, so no one could ever put out the fire she breathed with every thought that sparked in her brain and every word that left her mouth. "He'll change you. He'll make you do things. Hurt people."

And finally I understood. "You're not responsible for what Tower makes you do. *He* is."

"You don't know—"

"Yes, I do," I insisted softly, wishing the coffee table wasn't between us. "I know he's used you as a weapon, but even when you're the gun, he's still the one pulling the trigger. The blood is on his hands."

"I've done horrible things, Ian. You may have heard, but you don't really know. You can't really understand. And I can't forget." Her voice cracked, but no tears came, and again I was floored by how incredibly strong she was. How determined to hold everything together, when her world was clearly falling apart beneath her feet.

I loved that she was so strong. But I hated that she had to be.

"What if we left?" I said. "What if we just go get Kenley and you take us as far as you can go? And farther still, from there? We could do it." I'd lived off the grid for the past seven years. "I could keep us safe."

She shook her head slowly, and that blaze of anger in her eyes evened into wistful frustration. "Even if defaulting on our contracts wouldn't kill me and Kenley—and it would—he'd find us. He knows our real names. Part of them, anyway. And if he couldn't find us, he'd go after my brother. My grandmother. Kenley's girlfriend."

My brow rose a little at that unexpected bit of information, but she was still talking, constructing verbal obstacles to every exit strategy I could possibly have come up with.

"Whoever you have, Jake'll find them, too. And they don't have to be bound to him to suffer at his hands. Or his surrogate hands."

I thought about Steven, and Meghan, and Aaron. I thought about everyone I wouldn't want to see hurt, any more than they already had been. But above all of them—above everyone I'd ever shared a cup of coffee or a kind word with—it all came down to one thing.

"You," I whispered, staring down at her. I hadn't realized how empty my life was, so far from everyone I'd ever loved—until I met her. "I care about you, Kori."

She blinked up at me, her eyes sad, and more scared than I'd ever seen them. "Then that's how he'll get you."

Twenty-One

Kori

Ian was up to something. I could tell from the way he kept glancing at me out of the corner of his eye as he stacked dirty plates beneath a silver room service tray cover.

"Don't tell me," I said from the couch. I was trying desperately to hang on to the rare, vague sense of contentment I got from watching him clean up, like we were some normal couple staying in a hotel on vacation. Like our lives weren't both at serious risk. But that look in his eyes was making me nervous.

"Don't tell you what?"

"Whatever you're planning. If you tell me, I'll have to tell Jake. So don't tell me. And stop plotting."

"Even if I'm plotting to whisk you away to some isolated homestead in the middle of the Australian outback, where we can forever live in peace and privacy, far from the meddling hands of both egomaniacal mob bosses and the IRS?"

He said it like it might actually be possible.

"*Especially* if that's the plan."

Ian rounded the couch toward me. I should have backed away, but I couldn't do it. I let him sit and wrap his arms around me and I cursed myself silently when my hands slid over his stomach and around his back, feeling hard planes and solid ridges. I couldn't help that, either. I wanted to touch him. I wanted to be touched by him.

And that thought terrified me.

He kissed me, and I kissed him back, and for that minute, with his arms around me, the taste of him on my lips, I forgot all the reasons this was a very bad idea.

I forgot that I was dooming him to serve a human monster. I forgot that my life and my sister's well-being depended on his compliance. I forgot about everything except how good he felt, and how much I liked the version of myself I saw reflected in his eyes.

Then he pulled away with a satisfied moan, his eyes still closed, and reality came crashing down around me again, the pain sharper, the aching hopelessness deeper than ever after the brief distraction.

"You know we can't do this," I whispered, clutching his shirt in both fists, my forehead resting on his collarbone. I wanted to hold him, but I needed to push him away, because the longer this went on, the harder it would be for both of us, when Jake ripped him from my grasp.

Jake might actually agree not to mess with Ian's personal life, but he could still do whatever he wanted with me. How would Ian react if Jake sent me to recruit someone else, under the same circumstances? Jake would do that—and worse—just to prove he could. To punish me. And maybe to punish Ian for trying to protect me.

"We can't do what?" Ian's hands slid up my back, touch demanding nothing. Offering everything. I'd never met anyone like him. I could step back, and he would give me space, but he'd still be there, ready to accept more whenever I was ready to give it.

"This. We can't do this. It won't last. It can't."

"I don't like how easily you toss that word around." He frowned, his green-eyed gaze narrowed on me. "Why is everything 'can't' with you?"

"I speak from experience."

"Not this time, you don't. If this had ever happened before, it couldn't be happening now. That's what they mean by 'once in a lifetime.'"

"I don't know what you're talking about." But that was only half-true. I might not have followed whatever convoluted logic his words mapped out, but I knew what he meant. I could feel it, too.

"I'm talking about you. Us. You can't possibly know how this is going to end, because this doesn't fit into the boxes you shove all your other issues into. This is bigger than that. This is bigger than you, and bigger than me, and it's sure as hell bigger than Jake Tower." He ducked, drawing my gaze back up with his, and the look in his eyes was so intense my pulse started *whooshing* in my ears almost loud enough to drown out his words. "Kori, I—"

"Don't." I stood and backed across the room in mounting panic, trying to hold myself together by pushing everything else out. "Don't tell me how you feel, and whatever you do, don't tell Jake. But don't lie about it, either, because he has Readers, and he'll know the moment you tell an outright lie. And he'll know you're hiding something even if you only *think* about lying. It's a trap. The whole thing is one great big trap and we're flies flapping our wings, trying to pull free from the sticky paper. But the harder we flap, the tighter we're caught."

Ian frowned and came closer, but I backed away again. "You're starting to sound paranoid, Kori."

"I *am* paranoid." The bitter laughter that bubbled up my throat actually burned. "But that doesn't mean he isn't out to get me."

"Okay, calm down."

I shook my head and backed around the glass coffee table, but he followed me slowly. Persistently. "You don't understand. You don't know what happened. I can't come back from what I did, and even if I could, I don't think I want to."

"I know what happened." Ian reached for me, but I backed away again. I couldn't help it. I wanted to let him hold me, and that's how I knew I should keep distance between us instead.

Wanting things is dangerous—it gives people power over you.

Wanting things you can't have is even worse.

But giving in to desire just because you want something is weakness. Inexcusable weakness of character and will. I didn't get many opportunities to exercise my own will, and I wasn't going to let any of it slip between my fingers just because his arms felt strong. Just because it felt good to let someone else stand guard for once. I wasn't that weak.

I couldn't be.

"How do you know?" I didn't want to believe him. If he knew what I'd done, he might also know how I'd paid for my crimes. And I desperately didn't want him to know that.

"People talk and I listen even when they're not talking to me."

That was the truth, and part of me was glad he respected me enough to give it to me without the sugarcoating. But the rest of me… The rest of me was…

I don't know what I was.

Something crawled beneath my skin, fighting to get out, and I wanted to scratch, but that would bring no relief. My throat ached from holding back words I couldn't say. My eyes burned from holding back tears I couldn't let fall. And in my head, one word played over and over, and I couldn't make it stop.

Nonononono…

"Kori…"

"No! Stay there." I backed toward the short hall, instinctively pulled toward the dark bedroom. Toward escape.

"Okay. I'll stay here." Ian stopped in the middle of the living room, reaching for me with his palms out. Unarmed. Unsure. "But you stay, too. Don't go, Kori. Please."

"I got him shot." The room blurred beneath my tears. "I was supposed to protect him with my own life, and I let Jake get shot instead. His kids could have been killed. He hates me now, and even though I'm out of the basement, I'm still being punished, and that's never going to stop. I'm poison, Ian." I looked right into his eyes, trying to make him understand how serious my predicament really was, because the words alone weren't enough. I wasn't overreacting. I wasn't unreasonably paranoid. My fear was justified, for us both. "I'm the most dangerous thing that could ever have happened to you."

"No. It wasn't your fault."

"Doesn't matter." I shook my head, and I couldn't stop. I couldn't make my hands stop shaking, and my breaths were coming too fast again. "If you try to stay with me after you sign, you'll piss him off, and you'll go down with me."

"You're not going down, and neither am I. No one can hold a grudge forever, and you were one of his favorites, right?" Ian asked, and I nodded, trying to see whatever possibility he was seeing for my future. I needed that light at the end of the tunnel. "When you bring me into the fold, all will be forgiven, and you'll get your place back. You'll get your job back. It'll be just like it was before."

I couldn't tell whether he meant that or was just trying to calm me down. I could feel panic building beneath me, a spiral of dread and alarm waiting for me to take that final step over the edge. And once I lost control, I wasn't sure I could ever regain it.

But that didn't really matter. None of it mattered anymore, because of the truth I hadn't been able to voice before. The truth I shouldn't have voiced, even then.

"I don't want it back, Ian. I *hate* him, and I'm scared that if he gives me my job back, the next time I have a chance to protect him, I just…won't. I'll just let the bullet fly right past me, or I'll pull him through the shadows a second too slow."

Pain exploded in my head, in reaction to thoughts I had no contractual right to speak, but I kept going because the pain in my head could never hurt worse than my memories. Than the gnawing deep in my gut as the nightmares and flashbacks ate at me slowly, devouring the me I'd been to make way for this new me—a whimpering coward I didn't want to face in the mirror.

"It'll hurt, but it's a terminal breach, so if I can ride out the initial pain, I'll survive, and that's too much temptation for me to resist. I want to kill him, but I can't. Letting him die is the best I can do."

"So let him die." Ian reached for me again, and again I backed away, and the walls of the narrow hallway closed in on me.

"I can't." I shook my head, trying to clear it. Trying to slow my breaths like Kenley had shown me. "I mean I *can,* but if Jake dies, everything'll be worse. So much worse. There are clauses in place. If he dies, every contract and piece of property not already in his wife's name automatically transfers to his heir, and we'll be so much worse off then."

"Who's the heir?" Ian asked, and I almost missed the note of quiet danger his voice held. He'd stopped advancing, so I'd stopped retreating, but I couldn't let him come any closer. This wasn't the kind of problem a little cuddling and some vodka could fix. "Do you know who it is?"

"I know, but I can't tell you. No one can. We're all sworn to silence."

"So, killing Jake Tower wouldn't free you?"

I shook my head slowly, watching him through narrowed eyes. I could see what he was thinking. Hell, he'd practically said it. "That wouldn't free me or anyone else. You can't kill Jake. And I can't let him die. And we can never, ever have this conversation again."

Ian

Kori sat in the hallway for almost an hour, one bare foot stretched into the unlit bedroom, like just the touch of darkness soothed her.

I wanted to touch her—to hold her—so badly my arms ached from emptiness. But I was afraid to get any closer for fear that she'd bolt into the bedroom and out of the shadows before I could even call her name.

I didn't know how to fix what was wrong with her, and it killed me to see her sitting in the corner—both literally and figuratively—when an hour before, she'd been ready to spit nails at anyone who crossed her path. I didn't know what had triggered this meltdown, and at first I thought it was me. I thought kissing her—or maybe touching her—had triggered some memory she couldn't conquer. And maybe that was part of it.

But when I replayed everything she'd said, I realized there was more than that. She wasn't afraid of me. She was afraid *for* me. Afraid that being with her would put me in danger. And because that wasn't a logical fear, she couldn't be reasoned out of it. So I didn't even try. Instead, I sat at the other end of the short hall, leaning with my back against the wall, my legs stretched out in front of me. And I talked to her.

"There are things I wish I could tell you," I said, and she glanced up, a cautious arch of curiosity in her eyebrows.

"There are things I wish I could hear. But it's probably better if we don't even start down that road."

I nodded reluctantly, and for several more minutes, we sat in silence. Then I tried again. "Do you remember much about your parents?" I didn't think she'd answer, so when she started to speak, it took every bit of self-control I possessed to keep from cheering over my minor success.

"Mostly my mom. My dad was gone a lot."

"Was your mom a Traveler like you?"

She exhaled in a small huff, like there was some humor in my question. "She was a Traveler, but not like me. She only walked the shadows in emergencies, and I only know that because my grandmother told me. My parents were totally paranoid about exposing us as Skilled. I didn't even know I could travel until after they died. One day I got in trouble for using the ground beef my grandmother thawed out for dinner as viscera for my brother's army men when I blew them up."

"You blew them up?" I wasn't sure whether to laugh or cringe.

Kori shrugged. "With Black Cats. They're more noise than anything, and Kris didn't care. My grandmother was pissed, though. She grounded me, and I stomped into my room, thinking about how I'd rather be with my mom and dad, and the next thing I knew, I was in the cemetery, three feet from their graves. Twelve miles from home."

"Wow."

"Yeah. But the real bitch was that I didn't know how I'd gotten there, so I didn't know how to get back. And that was way before I had a cell phone. I had to walk a mile and a half to a pay phone and call my grandmother collect. I thought she'd be pissed, but she looked kind of relieved. I guess because she didn't have to keep the secret anymore. And maybe because I didn't get my dad's Skill instead."

"What was his Skill?"

"He was a Silencer. I think she was afraid I'd suck all the sound out of a room when I got mad and nothing pissed my grandmother off worse than not being heard."

I laughed, and she relaxed a little more.

"What about your parents?" Kori asked. Then she frowned and seemed to reconsider. "Not their Skills.

Don't tell me anything Jake could use. Just...what were they like?"

I closed my eyes and leaned my head against the wall, remembering. "They were good parents. More in love with me and my brother than with each other, but they held it together. My dad died when I was in college, and my mom followed him five years ago."

"I'm sorry." Kori pulled her foot out of the bedroom and folded it beneath her, and I took that as a good sign. Like she was literally stepping out of the darkness. To be with me.

"I want to tell you something," I said, trying to hold her gaze in the shadows. Kori had trusted me with everything she had, and I owed her something in return. Something real and personal. Something that meant as much to me as the things she'd told me about herself.

"Maybe you shouldn't."

"You're probably right. But I'm going to say it anyway, and it would mean a lot to me if you'd listen."

"Okay." She turned to face me, giving me her full attention, though she still sat inches from the bedroom and the dark escape it represented.

"My brother's still alive."

"Steven?" Kori whispered, and I frowned. Then I realized his first and last names were public record, and of *course* Tower had done his research. "But he was killed in action. I saw the obituary. There was a funeral."

"It was a memorial," I said, trying not to outright lie to her, even as I let her believe her own misassumptions. Because this one truth was all I could give her at the moment, and I shouldn't even have done that. "Because there was no body. Because he didn't really die."

"He faked his death?" she said, and I was grateful that

she didn't really expect an answer to that. "Why would he do that?"

"To avoid this," I said, spreading my arms to indicate not the suite around us, but interest from the organization that had paid for it. "We knew from the time our Skills manifested that they'd attract the wrong kind of attention from the wrong kind of people. Our mom was paranoid, but she was right about that."

"So he thought it'd be easier to fake his own death than to avoid notice from the syndicates?"

I scooted closer, praying she wouldn't back away from me. "Faking death *was* to avoid notice from the syndicates."

"So, that picture of him with Meghan? That's not really seven years old?"

"Probably not," I admitted, and it felt good to voice even that little bit of truth.

"What's his skill?"

"I can't tell you that. I shouldn't have even told you he's alive—that wasn't really mine to tell—but you've told me so much…"

"You don't owe me anything, Ian. And I won't tell Jake about your brother. Even if he asks." I started to object, but she spoke over me. "If he wants me to suffer, I'll suffer. The question I refuse to answer is irrelevant."

I stared at her, awed by her strength and determination. She'd done time in a hell I could only imagine, and come out intact. "I feel sorry for all the people who will die without ever meeting you, Kori. But the selfish part of me is happy, because I don't even want to share you with the people you already know. Most of them don't deserve you."

Tears shone in her eyes, and my heart cracked within

my chest. "You okay?" I asked, aching to move close enough to touch her. "I didn't mean to make it worse."

"You didn't. I just… I need you to understand that whatever this is between us, it can't last once you're bound. I think we need to keep that in mind." The words came out slowly, like she wanted to pull them back in before they'd even fallen.

"Why can't it last?" I scooted closer across the floor, and she didn't back up. "Jake can't take this away, Kori," I said, scooting another foot closer to her, wishing I could explain that I wasn't going to be bound to Tower, and soon neither would she. He would have no power over us.

"He'll try. He'll renege on the apartment, and the car, and he'll take back any privileges he offers, unless you get them down in writing. I wouldn't blame you for bailing."

"I don't care about any of that. And I'm not bailing."

"He'll throw women at you. Beautiful women. Women who wear nice dresses, and drink champagne, and don't cuss."

"I don't want those women. I want you."

Kori shook her head slowly. "You don't even know me."

"I know enough to know I want to know more. I know I want to *kill* everyone who had anything to do with whatever happened in that fucking basement."

She sucked in a deep breath, and the next few came quicker, like she couldn't get enough air. "I don't need a knight, Ian. I can fight for myself."

I nodded. "And everyone else around you. I know. That doesn't mean I don't want to help."

Kori glanced at the floor and spoke while she picked

at the hem of her jeans. "I don't…I don't know how to do this. I've never really done the relationship thing, unless you count a few three- or four-night-stands."

"The only thing you learn from any relationship is how to be in that specific relationship. So even if you'd been married a dozen times, this would still be new. It's new for me, too. It's supposed to be."

She looked up then and met my gaze. "I'm kind of a wreck right now, and I can't promise that'll get any better."

"We're all messed up, Kori. We all have secrets. We all have problems. Part of the process is figuring those things out. One at a time."

"What if I scare you off?"

I scooted closer, and we were only two feet apart now. "You couldn't possibly. I know what I want." I leaned forward and hooked one hand behind each of her calves, where her legs were bent at the knee. When she didn't object, I pulled her closer, until our knees were touching. "I want you. I want *only* you. I want *all* of you. But I'll take whatever you're ready to give."

Twenty-Two

Kori

Ian kissed me, and I kissed him back. I couldn't get enough of him and how good he felt. How eager, but… safe.

Kissing was fine. Kissing was *good*. There was no kissing in the basement, and kissing Ian made me feel like I was fifteen all over again, and just discovering the art. Innocence and adventure. Power, because he wanted to kiss me, but I could pull away and he'd *still* want me, but he'd let me go.

Kissing Ian was like starting all over. Clean slate. No memories. No past. Just…us.

When I finally pulled back, desperate for both air and perspective, I couldn't hold back a groan. "You're playing dirty," I moaned, letting my forehead fall against his shoulder.

He laughed, his face pressed into my neck, and his words seemed to melt right into my skin. "Not yet. But I'm open to that."

"I mean you and your words. You always know exactly what to say." That he wanted me. That he'd take what I was willing to give. "Does that silver tongue work on most women?"

Ian leaned back so I could see his eyes. Or maybe so he could see mine. "I'm not feeding you lines, Kori. If I were I'd have told you how hot you are and how badly I want you. Both of which are true. But neither of which are how I want to start this."

This.

This is a mistake. Alarm bells were going off in my head. I knew better than this. This was going to get us both hurt, and not just emotionally. But for the first time in my life, the risk felt worth it.

"So, how *do* you want to start this?" I couldn't believe the words, even as they came from my own mouth.

"I want you, and not as a signing bonus. I want to *be* with you. I want to fall asleep touching you, and I want to see you first thing in the morning. I want you to answer the phone and smile when you hear my voice. I want to be the only one you ever look at like you're looking at me now. That's what I want. What do *you* want?"

"I want...I want to try it. No promises and no hard feelings if either of us changes our mind," I said, and though he nodded immediately, I couldn't help wondering if he would have agreed to anything right then, just to make me happy.

Then I realized it didn't matter. If he was that determined to make me happy, who was I to complain?

I kissed him again. Then I kissed him some more. And somehow, we made it from the floor to the leather couch, where he let my hands explore hard planes of muscle through the soft cotton of his shirt. My mouth trailed over the rough stubble on his chin and down his neck.

Ian groaned, and his hand glided over my hip. He felt so good. Sooo good. But then his fingers slid beneath the hem of my top, and—

"Wait…" I sat up, pushing him away, and after less than a second, the confusion in his eyes gave way to caution and understanding too raw for me to look at. I didn't want his sympathy. I didn't need to be coddled like a baby or seduced like a virgin.

I needed…time. Just a little more time.

"I'm hungry. Let's get some food."

"You okay? Is this too much?" That look—pity—lingered on the edge of his understanding smile, and I couldn't stand it.

"Don't look at me like that," I snapped, and I could hear the anger in my voice, but I couldn't control it. "I'm not fucking broken. I'm just hungry."

But that was a lie. I *was* broken, and there was no bandage in the world big enough to fix me.

"I'm sorry. I was just trying not to—"

"It's fine," I said, purging the anger from my voice with a staggering effort. "I really am hungry. I was going to take you to this awesome steak house in the south fork, but after what happened in the park this morning, we probably shouldn't leave the west side. There's a place a couple of miles away that's not too bad…?"

"Let's bring the food back. I don't feel like sharing you with a restaurant full of people."

I called in our order and gave the restaurant Jake's credit card number, and since our food wouldn't be ready for twenty minutes, we decided to walk. It was a beautiful night, cool for early summer, and the cloud cover had lifted, so if we'd been anywhere but the middle of the city, we could have seen the stars. Not that I knew what any of them were. But suddenly I missed the suburban sky view I'd grown up with, because as I walked next to Ian on the sidewalk, I realized I hated the city.

But that wasn't quite right. It wasn't the city itself I hated. It was how much of Jake Tower I found represented on the west side, everywhere I looked. His sentries stood on most corners of the main drag. He owned several apartment buildings and businesses. And everywhere I turned I found another arm bared to show tattooed chain links.

They all knew me, even the ones I couldn't have named for my life, because for years, I'd been at Jake's side, responsible for his safety and elevated by the job. And they all knew those days were over.

I could feel them staring. A few looked sympathetic—no one wanted to be on Jake's shit list—and that was almost worse than those who gloated, pleased by my fall.

Ian could tell I was tense, and he tried to distract me with small talk, but I couldn't relax, and being with him made that even harder. I wanted to touch him, but I was hyperaware that anything we were seen doing would be reported to Jake, who would either understand that we'd excised him from our relationship—which would piss him off—or misinterpret the reports as me seducing Ian on his behalf. Which would piss *me* off.

Finally the restaurant appeared in front of us. Inside, we had to wait for several minutes before the hostess handed me a receipt to sign, then exchanged it for a thick paper bag with twisted twine handles and an embossed logo. I resisted the urge to stick my head inside the bag and inhale the scent of beef grilled with onions.

Ian looked like he wanted to do the same thing.

Outside again, we headed for the alley behind the restaurant, intending to return to the apartment through the shadows so the food wouldn't get cold. But the minute I stepped into the alley I knew something was wrong.

I stopped, one hand clenching the bag handle, the other groping at my waist for a gun I wasn't yet allowed to carry. I reached for Ian's arm to warn him silently, but before I could, someone grabbed me from behind and hauled me away from him, nearly jerking me off my feet.

I grunted in surprise, and Ian spun toward us, but before he could reach for me, someone stepped between us, gun—plus silencer—pointed at the ground, but ready to take aim at either of us in an instant.

Cam.

I dropped the food bag and started to twist away from the hands holding me, but before I could, my right arm was released and something cold and sharp was pressed against my throat, just beneath my jaw.

Shit. Another alley and another knife fight. A blade at my throat could spill my blood and sever my vocal cords in one stroke—a silent death, in the middle of my own territory.

"Mr. Holt, no one needs to get hurt here, and if you come with us now, no one will," Cam said. "But you should know that if you refuse, my associate has instructions to kill Kori in an effort to motivate you. Should you *still* refuse, we have instructions to kill you, as well." Because like Jake, Ruben Cavazos didn't want someone as powerful as Ian working for his enemy. "I'm sorry, Kori," Cam said, and I could hear the strain in his voice.

I shrugged his apology off. He was the foot soldier, not

the commander, and I could certainly sympathize. And it's not like I'd never been threatened with death before.

"Liv...?" I called softly, moving my throat as little as possible, because of the blade pressed against it.

"Ruben rarely makes the same mistake twice. Unless it's a mistake he enjoys," said a female voice with a familiar Hispanic accent. Anger flared inside me when Michaela Cavazos stepped out of the shadows next to a large Dumpster, and I understood how they'd gotten into the west side without being spotted. Cam had tracked us, probably waiting for us to leave the hotel, and Meika was a Traveler. She was also Ruben Cavazos's wife.

Fuck. Without Olivia, who was obligated to help if I asked her to, we were screwed.

"I didn't know Ruben ever let you off your leash," I snapped, but Michaela only shrugged.

"It's a very long leash."

"Your husband still fucking every bitch with a gap between her thighs?"

Another shrug, like she didn't care, but I could see the truth in her eyes. In the perpetually angry line of her jaw. "He sets them up, I knock them down," she said, and my temper burned hotter. She wasn't kidding.

I owed Michaela Cavazos a knife to the gut, and the one currently pressed into my throat would do the job nicely.

"Holt?" Every muscle in Cam's body was tense and ready for action.

"I'm not leaving her," Ian said, looking straight at me, his hands open at his sides, his stance steady and confident.

Cam glanced at me in surprise, then back to Ian, and comprehension surfaced on his features, obvious even in the near darkness. "I understand," Cam said. "But if you don't go with Michaela right now, Stan will kill Kori, and I couldn't stop him even if I were allowed to. Please go. I can't do anything for Kori anymore, but you can."

My mind raced, looking for a way out. If I could get the knife away from my throat, I could take Stan—I was sure of that without even having seen him. I could take down most guys twice my size in a fair fight.

"If I leave her here, Tower will kill her," Ian said, and I flinched. That wasn't something I'd planned to broadcast.

Cam glanced at me again, brows raised in question, and I could only nod carefully to confirm the fact.

Michaela whistled, and what little light made it into the alley glinted off the knife she spun over and over on her open palm. "Sounds like you signed on with the wrong side."

"There is no right side," I said, and I'd never believed that more.

"What's it going to be, Holt?" Cam asked, and at my back, Silent Stan's grip on my arm tightened, his knife shaking almost imperceptibly at my neck. He was nervous. Or maybe eager.

"There's no good choice here," Ian said, and Cam nodded in acknowledgment. There was nothing he could do about that. "If I go with you, Tower will kill Kori. If I opt to stay here, you'll try to kill us both."

"*Try* isn't in my vocabulary," Michaela said, and Ian's brows rose.

"I suspect there are a great many words missing from your vocabulary," he said, and she bristled. "But my point is that in the absence of a good choice, a bold one will often suffice."

Meika scowled. "What the hell does that mean?"

Ian drew a gun from his waistband and aimed over my shoulder before I'd even realized he'd moved. Before Cam could even lift his own weapon. Ian fired, and the flash from his gun blinded me as gunfire echoed through the alley. I didn't have time to be scared or surprised, which was good, because if I'd realized what was coming, I'd have ducked, and that would have pulled Silent Stan out of Ian's aim.

The bullet *thunked* into flesh inches from my head, and for a moment, the knife pressed harder into my skin. Then Stan's hand fell from my arm and his blade slid lightly across my neck in a downward arc.

I shoved the knife away, but not before it sliced a long, shallow cut from the left corner of my jaw almost to the center of my throat. I hissed at the sudden pain, then cursed over my own spilled blood—the biggest security risk possible.

Turning, I glanced at the still form on the ground behind me, then another gun flashed in the dark, and I heard the muted *thunk* of a silencer as Cam returned fire. But Ian was already moving. Cam's bullet slammed into the brick wall just behind him. Ian fired again, and Cam shouted in pain. His gun clattered to the concrete and he slapped his left hand over his right arm.

"Leave, before they come for you," Ian said, both his gun and his gaze trained steadily on Cam, and I could already hear footsteps pounding our way from across the street.

I gaped at him, one hand pressed to the sticky, bloody wound on my neck. Ian was fast. And he was *good.*

Systems analyst, my ass. Ian Holt had serious training.

"I can't go back without you," Cam said, and movement on my right drew my attention to where Michaela stood with her back to the Dumpster, feet spread for balance, a knife in each hand, ready to be thrown.

Ian shrugged at Cam. "Stay and let Tower's men kill you. I don't give a damn." He turned to me then, his free hand open and waiting for mine though his aim at Cam never wavered. "Kori?"

I took one step toward him, then froze when gravel crunched behind me. I spun, one hand still pressed to my wound, and kicked the knife from Michaela's left hand as she lunged for me. She swiped at me with her other hand and I kicked her in the chest, afraid that any use of my hands would splatter my blood all over the alley.

Michaela stumbled back and I kicked again. Her knife arced toward my leg. The blade hit my boot and snagged in the leather, but didn't break through. I kicked one more time, and her knife clattered to the ground, then slid beneath the Dumpster. She howled in pain and clutched her arm, and as the first onlooker appeared in the mouth of the alley, I wasted one precious moment hoping her arm was broken. A lot.

"Stay back!" Ian shouted, waving his gun at the crowd starting to gather. Several ducked out of sight again, speaking into phones, but no one came closer. Not even Tower's men, and surely there were at least a couple already reporting the incident.

"Michaela, take Cam and get out of here!" I whispered, as anger at him battled with my sympathy for the position he was in.

"I'm bleeding," he protested as she tried to pull him into the darkest patch of night, on the other side of the Dumpster.

"Give me your bleach, and I'll clean it up," I said,

holding my free hand out as Ian retrained his gun on Cam. He wasn't taking any chances. And I couldn't afford to use my own pocket-size bleach solution on Cam's blood. But neither would I leave a viable sample of it in the alley to be used against him.

Cam hesitated, glancing from me, to Meika, to Ian, then back at me. Then he dug in his pocket with his good hand and tossed me a small clear plastic bottle, just like the one I carried at all times. Because you never know when you're going to be attacked in a dark alley by a psychotic bitch and a former friend and coworker.

"Thanks," he said, then he and Michaela stepped into the darkness and disappeared.

"Got a light?" I said to Ian as soon as they were gone. Then I realized I couldn't open Cam's bottle—not to mention my own—without the use of both hands.

"No." Ian flicked the safety switch on the gun and shoved it back into his waistband, then glanced at the mouth of the alley, where the crowd was reforming. "Anyone got a flashlight?"

After a moment of hesitant silence, three people produced key chain penlights and a fourth pulled a sizable LED flashlight from the pocket of his cargo pants. With their help—I recognized chain links on the arms of two of the men—we scanned the alley quickly but thoroughly for blood and poured bleach everywhere we spotted it.

Only once we'd destroyed both mine and Cam's blood did I realize that Ian was bleeding, too. Cam's bullet had grazed his upper arm before slamming into the concrete wall and his sleeve was dark and wet. None had dripped beyond the cloth, that I could tell, but that couldn't last forever.

"Let's go," I whispered, even as my phone began to

buzz in my pocket. I thanked the flashlight volunteers, then pulled Ian into the darkness with my good arm. A moment later, we stepped into his hotel bathroom, and I flipped on the light to see him holding the paper bag from the restaurant. Somehow, in spite of killing one man, shooting another, and being shot himself, he'd managed to salvage our dinner.

I laughed out loud. I couldn't help it.

"What?" Ian shrugged and set the bag on the marble bathroom counter. "You said you were hungry."

"Wow. What would you do if I said I was angry?"

"I would make fire rain from the heavens to smite your enemies with the flames of our shared rage."

My eyebrows arched halfway up my forehead. "That sounds like poetry and feels like war. I like it."

"I thought you might."

"You don't see that very often in the city. There isn't enough smiting with flames."

"No, but there's more than enough blood." He held up his arm, which was still dripping blood down his sleeve, and one glance in the mirror showed me what I'd already felt—that my neck and shirt were soaked in my own blood. "I'll call down for another first-aid kit," he said.

"I'm going to run home and clean up, but I'll be back as soon as I can, okay?" I said, and he nodded from the hall, already heading for the room phone.

I turned the bathroom light off, then stepped through the shadows and into my own room.

"Kenley!" I shouted, before I even had the light on, and she called back from the living room.

"In here."

"I need some help." I pulled my shirt off on the way to the bathroom and dropped it into the tub, then grabbed a clean rag from the rack over the toilet and pressed it to my neck.

Kenley stepped into the hall and her eyes widened with one look at the rag and the blood staining both my chest and my bra. "What the hell happened?" She took the rag from me and gasped at the sight of my wound.

"Looks worse than it feels."

"Good, because it looks like someone tried to slice your head off."

"Pretty much. And I think Jake's already heard about it," I said when my phone buzzed in my pocket again. A headache had already started—resistance pain from not answering his call immediately.

"Want me to talk to him?" She pushed me toward the toilet, where I closed the lid and sat while she dug beneath the sink for first-aid supplies.

"No, just patch me up and I'll call him myself." I didn't want her to have anything to do with Ian. Jake didn't need any more of an excuse to hold her responsible for my failures.

Kenley poured peroxide onto another clean rag, then pressed it against my neck. I hissed at the sharp sting, but I let her hold the rag in place while I reached back to unhook my bra then tossed it into the tub with my shirt.

Then I took the rag from her and returned Jake's call while my sister dumped bleach into the tub to destroy my blood.

"What the hell happened?" Jake barked into my ear, in lieu of a greeting.

"Cavazos moved on Holt," I said. "Ambush in the alley behind Sutherland's. One dead, two wounded, on their side." No need to mention that Cam was one of them… "We had to leave the body because we're both bleeding, but two of your men were there."

"They're already on it," Jake said, and some small measure of tension eased inside me. Even on the west side, where Jake's authority was almost absolute, gunfire could bring the police. "Witnesses say Holt fired two shots."

"Yeah. I'm unarmed, remember? Perhaps you'd care to revisit that issue now?"

"I'll take it under consideration. If Holt fired two shots and hit two people, that means he didn't miss."

"Yup." That's as much as I was willing to commit to.

"Any thoughts on why a pencil pusher from the suburbs knows how to shoot?" His voice was steady, and the silence that followed it was expectant. He knew something. Or he knew I knew something.

I closed my eyes and took a quick, quiet breath. "He's a man of many talents?"

"Obviously." But that wasn't the end of the issue. It couldn't be. "Where'd he get the gun, Korinne?"

I closed my eyes, bracing for what would follow. "I took it off Olivia Warren in the park this morning."

Silence.

Dangerous, tense silence, during which my stomach tried to devour the rest of me whole.

"What park?"

"The south side of Durham Park, at the fork in the river."

More silence, and I could almost picture Jake sitting behind his desk with his eyes closed, controlling his temper on the outside while it raged unchecked just beneath the surface.

"How badly was Holt hurt?"

I shrugged, though he couldn't see me. "He wasn't, this morning. From tonight, just a graze. He's fine. I am, too," I added, though he hadn't asked.

"I have a body to get rid of and witnesses to deal with. Get Holt patched up, get yourself patched up, and consider yourselves grounded for the night. Neither of you are to leave his suite before the sun rises. And I want you in my office alone at eight in the morning, or you'll be back in the basement five minutes after that."

Fuck!

"And, Kori, if I have to come looking for you, there won't be enough of you left to bury."

Shitshitshit! I hung up my phone and immediately set a timer for seven-thirty the next morning, because I knew from experience that Jake would be setting his for seven fifty-nine, and I couldn't afford to be late.

"Go on." Kenley took the bloody rag and handed me a thick gauze bandage to replace it. She looked sick, and I wondered how much of that she'd heard. "I'll take care of this." She dropped the rag into the tub with everything else I'd bled on and lit a match, then dropped it onto the pile. Flames flared behind me as I hurried into my room.

Holding the gauze in place with one hand, I plucked a hand wipe from a package on my dresser and carefully wiped all the blood from my neck and chest, then dropped the used wipe in the trash. The blood on it wouldn't be viable, thanks to the sanitizer. Then I left the gauze in place—it was stuck with drying blood anyway—while I put on a fresh bra and carefully shrugged into a clean shirt.

"Here. Wear this." Kenley stepped into my room with a gauzy blue scarf. She taped the bandage to my skin, then arranged the scarf around my neck to mostly cover it. Tower would still notice, and Ian knew what had happened, but with any luck, no one else would notice anything wrong.

"Thanks." I hardly recognized my own reflection with the scarf on. I looked like Kenley, only skinnier. "Where's Van?"

Kenley flushed. "She doesn't live here, you know."

But suddenly I kind of wished she did. I didn't want to leave my sister alone when Jake was pissed at me.

"Call her. See if she'll come hang out with you."

The blood drained from her face with one glance at mine, and she nodded without question. If I sounded worried, she knew she should be, too, and she rarely wasted time arguing. For which I was grateful.

"I have to stay with Ian, then report to Jake in the morning. But I'll check back in afterward, just in case."

"Okay. Be careful, Kori."

I hugged her, then she flipped the light switch for me and I tried to step back into Ian's apartment, only to find the opening blocked by blazing light in the visible spectrum, which could only mean one thing. He was in the bathroom.

Frustrated but not really surprised, I closed my eyes and reached out mentally until I found a patch of darkness in his suite big enough to step into. I walked forward and a moment later I slammed right into the inside of the closet door.

I opened the door and stepped into the bedroom, and was greeted with the sound of water running in the bathroom. "Hello?" I called, but there was no answer. "I had to come into the closet since you're—"

Half-naked and dripping wet...

Ian stood in bathroom doorway, hair dripping, wearing nothing but a towel he was just then tying loosely at his waist. His chest and stomach were bare, dark and defined against the thick white cotton, and beaded with clean water.

Carton of hard lemonade, my ass. That was a full-on six-pack.

I couldn't stop staring. He was beautiful.

Twenty-Three

Ian

I stepped out of the shower, still tucking the towel in at my waist, and looked up to find Kori standing in the bedroom in fresh clothes, a blue silk scarf only half hiding the bandage on her neck. Her conflicted gaze met mine, then traveled lower, and I let her look.

She took a few hesitant steps forward and her hand twitched, like she wanted to touch me, but also wanted to run from me. But she kept coming, slowly, and I stood still, afraid to spook her, because she kind of looked like a deer caught in oncoming headlights. Like she was mesmerized for the moment, but any small distraction could send her fleeing into the night.

"We're grounded," she said, her voice a whisper.

"Like a broken airplane?"

She shook her head. "Like a naughty child."

"What does that mean?" I asked when she stopped on the threshold, one hand clutching the bathroom door frame, like her grip was the only thing keeping her from fleeing. Or maybe from coming in.

"He knows about the park, and he knows about the alley," she said, still standing in the doorway, and I wondered if she was stuck there. Not in, but not out. Hovering in that liminal moment between realizing there's a choice to be made and actually making it. "So we're supposed to stay here all night."

I fought the urge to pull her closer. "Tower's punishment for not telling him about the park is to lock us up here together? All night? I'm not sure he understands how punishment is supposed to work."

"It's not punishment. It's a safety precaution."

Right. Normally I'd feel the need to remind Tower that I don't take orders from him yet. But I wasn't going to object to a night spent with Kori, even if we did nothing but play cards and watch TV all night long.

"How bad is it?" I asked, eyeing the scarf around her neck.

She shrugged. "It's just one night." Then I reached for the scarf, and she understood. "Oh, the cut. It's fine. It's hardly bleeding anymore." My fingers brushed the silk, feeling the rough texture of the bandage beneath. Then I pulled her hand away gently and tugged on the scarf. The filmy material fell through my fingers, and she sucked in a breath, like I was removing something more intimately located than the scarf around her neck. Her gaze locked with mine as I tucked her hair behind her shoulders and unwound the last layer of scarf.

The silk slipped over her arm as I pulled the material loose and let it fall to the floor between us. Her hands found my chest, but there was no clear intent in her eyes. She didn't have a goal, and for once she wasn't overthinking things. She was just…touching.

I closed my eyes as her hands skimmed my bare,

damp skin, skittering over my ribs toward my stomach. Her touch was light, just enough contact to make me desperate for more, and I wanted to lean into her. Offer her more. But she had to set the pace. That was the only way this would work.

Her fingers traced the edge of my towel, playing over the skin south of my navel, and my next breath was shaky. My fingers twitched at my sides, itching to touch her. To explore her like she was exploring me. It took every bit of willpower I had to let my hands hang empty, giving her free rein.

She bit one side of her bottom lip, and I wanted to taste it. Her hands shook at the tuck in my towel, and I wanted to steady them. Her gaze held mine, and I saw fear in her eyes, but I wasn't sure if she was more scared of giving in to the need gripping us both or resisting it. When she did neither, I grinned, my brows arched in challenge.

That did it.

Kori leaned into me, her hands on my sides for balance, and I didn't realize what she had in mind until she licked a drop of water from the left side of my chest. I groaned, and my hands clenched around air, aching to grip her hips instead.

She bent for another taste, and this time she moved from drop to drop, her tongue leaving a hot trail across my skin, higher and higher, weaving back and forth until finally she licked a drop beaded on my right nipple, and that was all I could take. I reached for her waist and pulled her closer.

Kori looked up at me and her hands stilled. Her mouth opened and I leaned in to kiss her, my heart beating so hard I could almost hear it. Then my phone buzzed from the counter and she jumped, startled by the sudden interruption.

Kori glanced at the screen. And froze.

I followed her gaze to see a text from Meghan.

Can't do this anymore, Ian. Tell her whatever it takes to get the job done. I'm counting on you.

I reached for the phone, but it was too late. She'd already seen the message. "What job?"

"It's not—"

"*What job,* Ian?" She shoved me away, and I stumbled backward, toward the mirror.

"Kori…" I said, but she was already backing away from me. She spun sharply in the bedroom, bypassing the dark closet in her haste and anger. I caught up with her halfway through the living room, and in my desperation to keep her from leaving, I forgot.

"Kori, *wait!*" I grabbed her arm, and she turned on me, already swinging. Her fist slammed into my jaw and my head rocked back sharply, pain spreading across my face.

"Damn it!" I dropped her arm to rub my chin, and when I reached for her again, she smacked my hand away and spun into a wide, high kick. Her boot slammed into my chest, and I stumbled backward, and had to grab the back of a chair to keep from falling.

"Don't fucking touch me, you lying, traitorous son of a bitch," she spat, and by the time I'd regained my balance, she was nearly to the front door.

I jogged to catch up with her, one hand clutching the towel at my hips, and I slid in front of the door just as she reached for the lever. "Wait. Please." I held both hands up, palms out, careful not to make my request sound like an order. "I won't touch you. Just please hear me out. It's not what you think."

"Fuck off." She backed up two steps, and rubbed her forehead so hard it looked like she was actually trying to shove her fingers through her skull. "Jake's going to kill me. You're some kind of a spy, or a…a *mercenary*."

"No. Kori, let me explain…"

"The fighting. The shooting. I *knew* you couldn't be a fucking systems analyst. You never had any *intention* of signing, did you? You don't give a shit about me or my sister." Then her eyes widened. "*Kenley*. Fuck!" She dropped into a squat, clutching the back of the couch with one hand and her stomach with the other, like all the pain from my betrayal had settled there, and my own chest tightened in response. "You're here for Kenley. You're a fucking poacher, aren't you? The whole thing was a setup, to get you through Jake's defenses."

"No! Well, yes." I exhaled slowly, trying to figure out how much of the truth I could tell her without spilling the beans she'd then have to feed to Jake Tower.

"The hockey game. I should have known. You're too smart to accidentally reveal yourself like that." She stood, angry tears building in her eyes. "You've fucking *screwed* us both!"

"No, Kori, I'm not going to let him hurt you or Kenley."

"Who do you work for?" she demanded.

"No one. I'm not a poacher. That's not what this is about, I swear on my life." I stepped closer, aching to hold her but she backed away. Her eyes lost focus. She wasn't hearing me. She wasn't even really seeing me.

She was seeing the consequences to come in what little future she thought she had left.

"I don't want to do it," she mumbled. "I don't want to let him drain you, but you *lied,* and I'm as good as dead, and the only chance Kenley and I have now is if I hand you over and beg for mercy in exchange for turning in a mole."

"Kori, please."

She woke up then, and focused on me with startling clarity. Resolve surfaced behind her eyes, hardening her gaze like a shield slipping into place between us, and my heart hurt like someone was squeezing it, milking the life from me drop by drop.

"Get the hell out of my way, or I will break your jaw," she growled through clenched teeth.

I crossed both arms over my bare chest and stood firm in front of the door. "Fine. Do it. I won't hit you back. I don't want to hurt you, Kori. I just want to explain." She came at me, fists clenched and ready, and I rushed ahead, words spilling from my mouth like blood from a gaping wound, and I wanted to take them back as soon as I heard them because they were true, but they weren't *the truth.* They were facts out of context, wielded like sword and shield. I said them to protect her, but I hated myself for it. For the foundation of lies supporting the most fragile and precious relationship I'd ever tried to build.

"The hockey game was a setup, yes, but I'm not here to poach your sister. I just needed to get Tower's attention. Quickly. I need something from him." Technically that was true. I needed his Binder. But I wasn't going to poach her for someone else.

"So you're not a systems analyst?" Her fists were still

clenched, but they hung at her sides now. Her eyes were still narrowed in suspicion, but she was listening.

"No. I only type thirty words a minute and can barely work a cell phone."

"But your name's real. What kind of spy uses a fake backstory, but his real name?"

I shrugged. "What kind of recruiter shows her recruit the dark side of the syndicate, instead of the advantages?"

"I'm not really a recruiter," she said.

"And I'm not a spy. Tower would have known inside a minute if I gave him a fake name."

"So what are you doing here? What do you need from Jake?"

I exhaled slowly, working up to the last part—the truest of these truths out of context. "Tower has the resources I need to break the seal on a binding."

Kori frowned. "Can't be done. The best you can do is destroy the binding itself. Burn the paper it was sealed on it. Assuming it was sealed on paper?"

"It's a name binding, so it probably was," I said. "But we have no idea where that paper is. If it even exists." For all I knew, Steven's binding could have been sealed in graffiti on some wall a thousand miles away. The binding itself was a dead end. We had no choice but to break the seal.

"And 'we' includes Meghan? Who is she, really?" Her gaze held mine, demanding truth while trying to hide how much my answer actually meant to her.

"She's really my brother's girlfriend. Well, technically his fiancée, now. He proposed a couple of weeks ago."

Kori frowned as the implications sank in. "Oh, shit, your brother's the one who's bound."

"Yeah."

"What's he bound to?"

"I don't know. He doesn't know, either. It's bizarre, and scary, and infuriating. I *have* to get him out of it. That's why I'm here."

"So, you need to break the seal on a binding you can't locate or identify…" she said, thinking out loud, and I nodded. "What makes you think Jake can help?"

"You said he did it for Kenley, when she got into trouble in college."

"*That's* why you keep asking about Kenley…" Kori looked so relieved I didn't have the heart to correct her. Not that I could have anyway. Not while she was still bound to Tower.

"Do you know how he did it?" I asked, but she only shook her head.

"She never told me and I never asked. A lot of things go unsaid around here."

"So, can I talk to her?" I was pushing my luck, and I knew it. But Steven didn't have much time left, and I couldn't tell Kori anything else until her binding was broken.

"We can't leave here tonight, and she can't come over without Jake's permission and an escort. And I doubt he'll let her, considering how much trouble I'm in right now. But I guess I can call her…"

I swallowed a moan. This wasn't a phone-call kind of conversation, and it certainly wasn't anything I could say in front of Kori, while Tower's marks were still live on her arm. "It can wait until tomorrow," I said at last, desperately hoping that was true. I was less than a day from losing both my brother and his fiancée, and I'd be lucky if my recruitment ruse with Jake Tower lasted that long.

The clock was ticking.

The noose was tightening.

And Kori was looking at me like I held her life in my hands. Because I did.

"You're still going to sign, right?" she said, and there was a thread of steel beneath the fragile surface of her voice. "Or was that part of the act, to get you in the door? Because you know that whatever Jake did for Kenley, he won't do that for your brother unless you sign."

"I know." But I had no intention of letting Tower anywhere near my brother. Or anywhere near Kori, if I had my way.

I took her right fist and uncurled her fingers until her hand lay flat in mine, and I placed my other hand over hers. "There are things I haven't told you. Things I *can't* tell you while your marks stand between us. But soon none of that will matter. What matters is that I am *not* going to leave you and your sister here. I would swear to that right now, if there was a Binder here. I'll do whatever it takes to be with you. To stay with you. If you want me." I stared into her eyes, trying to see past the anger she wore like a mask to cover fear and vulnerability. I tried to see past all of that, to the part she never showed anyone else.

"Do you want me, Kori?"

Kori

I couldn't make sense of the tangle of emotions balled up inside me. I was frustrated, and scared, and angry, and somewhere in there, I felt a tiny kernel of hope, struggling to survive in such harsh conditions. But every last thread in the jumble of conflicting emotions led back to Ian, through one twisted route or another.

He was hiding something, yes. He'd practically admitted that. But he'd shielded me in the wine cellar and refused to leave me in the alley. He'd talked me down from panic and he'd said I was a lion that could not be tamed. He knew what I'd had to do for Jake, and what Jake had done to me in return. And he wanted me anyway.

And I wanted him like I'd never wanted anything else in my life. So I pulled him down with one hand and kissed him.

Ian groaned against my lips. He tugged me closer, then his mouth opened beneath mine, pulling me in. My hands wandered on their own, slowly exploring the hard planes of his back until I realized his towel was loosening, and my fingers were damp with water from his shower, and we were pressed so tightly together I could hardly breathe. But his hands hadn't moved. One cradled my jaw, trailing beneath my ear. The other sat at my waist. Above my clothes. There, but demanding nothing.

Did that mean he didn't want to touch me?

No. I could feel how badly he wanted to touch me. But he had patience. Self-control. It almost felt like… manners.

"You okay?" he asked, when I pulled away and looked up at him.

In answer to a question I never wanted to hear again, I tugged him through the living room, hall and into the bedroom, where I let go and started to unbutton my shirt.

Ian's brows rose, but his gaze never left mine. "Are you sure?"

I nodded and pushed another button through its hole.

He watched me for another second, then he was there again, kissing me, and my hands fell away from my shirt so his could take over.

My pulse rushed too fast and the room spun, a blur of dark wood and rich fabrics, shadowed on the edges by the fear I pushed aside with every breath I took. I threw myself into that kiss, letting the taste and the feel of him chase everything else away.

When the buttons were undone, his hands slid beneath the cotton and gently pushed the material down my arms. He kissed my shoulder and unhooked my bra, and I let it slide to the floor. Then I reached for the towel at his hips and pulled it loose.

His towel fell off and he moaned, his lips pressed to the unbroken side of my neck. His arms slid around me, guiding me as he walked us backward, and I felt the mattress against the backs of my thighs.

I sat, then lay back, and for a moment, I couldn't breathe. Darkness closed in on the edges of my vision, and with it came flashes of memory I couldn't push back. Dead shadows trapping me. A weight on my chest. A cruel hand twisting, and pinching, and bruising, and invading.

Ian lay beside me, naked, reaching for me, and my throat tried to close.

"I can't," I whispered, and his hands fell away. I pulled the rumpled blanket over me, confused, and humiliated, and drowning in frustration. Pissed off by my own fear.

He propped himself up on one elbow and I made myself look at him. "It's okay. There's no rush," he said, brushing hair from my cheek.

But it wasn't. It wasn't fucking okay, and it never would be until I could push past the fear and anger devouring me from the inside out. Until I could touch and be touched and just live in the moment, without reliving other hands. Without feeling like the world was spiraling in on me, constricting around me, compressing me until I couldn't move. Couldn't fight. Couldn't breathe.

Why now? Why did I have to meet him *now,* when I couldn't tell from one minute to the next whether I wanted to touch or hit, kiss or bite?

This wasn't okay. And it wasn't *going* to be okay until I could do whatever the fuck I wanted with whoever the hell I wanted. Until I could take control back, not just of my body, but of my mind. If I gave up now—if I let fear chase me from what I wanted—the next time would only be harder.

Ian stroked my hair, spreading it over the rumpled comforter. Touching me without touching me. And suddenly I wanted to cry. He was so patient.

I looked up at him, and he was still watching me. Not smiling. Just watching.

"Make it dark," I whispered, and he frowned for a second. Then he sat up and reached for the bedside lamp.

"No." I laid one hand on his arm, and he turned back to me. "Make it dark. True dark." The kind I knew. The kind I loved. The kind I could escape into whenever I needed to.

The kind Ian carried in his soul and could gather at will.

He smiled, and the darkness rose around us, faster than ever before. Cool and calm. Quiet. Soothing. Like it had been there all along. Waiting.

I couldn't see a thing, but I'd never been more sure of where I was.

I reached for him and my hand found his stomach. I

trailed my fingers up the hard lines of his chest and over his collarbone, then around to the back of his neck. I pulled him down, and his mouth found mine. He couldn't see me, but he could feel me, and that was more than enough.

I kissed him. I couldn't taste enough of him. His hand found my side and threatened to linger there in chaste caution until I arched into his touch, and his fingers wandered up slowly. Gingerly.

The dark settled around me, touching me everywhere he didn't, and I reached for him, pulling him closer. His hand found my breast, his fingers brushing my nipple, and when I moaned into his mouth, his hand tightened, bolder now. I arched into him, fumbling with the button on my jeans, and his hand trailed down to brush mine aside. A second later, the button was free, my zipper down.

Ian sat up on his knees and his hands slid down from my waist, slipping beneath the material at my sides, sliding it over my hips so slowly I squirmed in anticipation, my eyes closed. He followed the material all the way to my feet, leaving a trail of kisses down my left leg. Then he kissed his way up the other leg, his hands blazing the same trail in advance.

When I couldn't wait anymore, I pulled him up, opening for him, reaching for another kiss. He settled between my thighs, and I could feel him, hot and hard, and ready.

"Are you sure?" he asked again, whispering in my ear this time. "I need to know that you want this."

I blinked in the dark, and hot tears trailed silently down both sides of my face. "Yes. I want you, Ian."

He exhaled, and I felt the tension in him ease. He slid one hand over my hip and down to my knee, then lifted my leg, guiding my ankle around his waist. My heart thumped almost painfully as I tucked my other leg behind him and pulled him down for another kiss.

He entered me slowly, and I gasped, sucking air from his mouth. Rising to meet him. When he was all the way in, he stayed for a moment, and I sucked his lip into my mouth, holding my breath. Reluctant to move.

Then he withdrew and slid inside me again, and we found our rhythm.

I clung to him, arching with him, holding him close. He buried his face in my hair, holding me with one arm, supporting his weight with the other. And everything else faded away, swallowed by the darkness he wrapped around us.

I remembered nothing but Ian. I felt nothing but him. I wanted nothing but him. And I never wanted that moment to end.

Then the rhythm changed, and I rode the waves, coasting toward an edge I could feel building, tighter and tighter. He moved inside me and I rose to meet him over and over, faster and faster, and the fire burning between us consumed all conscious thought for one precious moment. Then that fire crested to spill over the rest of me in a hot, desperate wave of pleasure and I clung to him again, riding it out to the finish.

Ian collapsed on the bed next to me and I rolled over to face him, unable to quell the languid smile I could feel forming. He leaned forward to kiss me, then I rolled onto my back again and put one hand on his chest, because I wasn't done touching him. I never wanted to be done.

Slowly he let the darkness fade, and as the light rose to replace it, I found him watching me. And for the first time in months, maybe even in years, I felt safe.

Twenty-Four

Ian

I couldn't stop watching her during dinner, after we'd heated up the meal that had almost gotten us killed. I loved the way she cut her steak into bites, then ate them two at a time and refused any sauce. The way she picked every single tiny sliver of carrot from her salad, then offered to trade them for my cucumber. I loved the way she laughed when I dribbled wine from the lip of the bottle because I was too busy watching her to pour with anything resembling competence.

She made a face over the red wine, but she liked the white enough to have a second glass after dinner. She was different now. More comfortable. More confident. Still brash, but less angry. She was funny and quick-witted, and on the rare occasions that night when her smile slipped, I suffered a renewed, intensified hatred for everyone who'd ever so much as bruised her, body or soul.

After dinner, I asked her if she wanted to stay the night—Tower's order wasn't good enough for me—

careful to phrase my question so that she had an out, just in case.

She stayed, and we made love again, and afterward, with her head on my shoulder, my dark hand splayed against her pale stomach, I saw a snapshot of our life and what it could have been, if not for Tower. What it might *still* be, if I pulled off the impossible and freed us both, after I freed Steven.

After I freed all *three* of us, because she wouldn't leave without her sister.

Kori fell asleep in my arms, in the dark, but rolled away from me in her sleep, so I curled around her, treasuring her warmth, wondering how so much woman could possibly fit into such a small, beautiful body.

Something woke me in the middle of the night, and I lay still, trying to figure out what I'd heard. Then I heard it again. Kori. I rolled over to find her mumbling in her sleep, half word, half moan of pain.

She was dreaming.

"No," she murmured, and when she started twisting, the covers tangled around her legs, which seemed to upset her even more. "No, *please*..." Her eyes were closed, but her head rolled back and forth, a vague outline in the dark room.

"Please," she begged in her sleep, and a tear rolled down her face, glittering in the moonlight shining between the cracks in the blinds. And that was all I could stand.

"Kori." I touched her arm, and she froze. Her eyes flew open and her hand slid beneath her pillow. "Are you—" Before I could finish the question, she'd shoved me down on my back and I felt the cold steel of a knife at my throat. My pulse roared in my ears, my heart thumping painfully.

She was awake, but unaware, still caught in the nightmare. Still trapped in the basement. Only this time she was armed with a knife from the room service tray.

"Kori, it's me," I whispered, afraid to move my throat much because there was actual pressure behind the blade. It was a miracle she hadn't yet broken skin. "It's Ian. Remember? We're in my hotel room."

She blinked, and some of the confusion cleared.

"See the window? Can you see the moonlight? Do you know where you are?"

Kori gasped and let go of my shoulder, then retreated across the bed with the knife still in hand. "I'm sorry. Fuck! I'm so sorry. I could have killed you."

"It's okay. We're both fine." I probably could have subdued her, but not without making her nightmare worse. "But maybe you could put the knife down?"

She lifted her hand and seemed surprised to see the knife still in it, the serrated edge shining in a thin beam of moonlight. "Shit." She dropped it onto the marble-topped nightstand, where it bounced and clattered, then went still. "I'm so sorry."

"It's okay. Do you mind if I put the knife away?"

"Get rid of it, please. I don't even remember bringing it in here."

"Do you sleep with one at home?" I stepped into my underwear, then rounded the bed toward the nightstand on her side.

"Yeah. Sorry. I guess I should have warned you."

I took the knife into the front room, and when I got back into bed, she was in the bathroom. A minute later, the toilet flushed, then water ran in the sink. When she came out, she left the door open and the light on, without even seeming to notice. And that's when I realized she was afraid of the dark. Or at least afraid of sleeping in it—surely a complicated problem for a shadow-walker.

She climbed back into bed next to me, wearing only plain black cotton underwear, and sat with her legs crossed beneath the covers, her hands over her face, visibly trying to collect herself. I reached out, aching to comfort her but hesitant to touch. Finally I laid my hand between her shoulder blades, and when she didn't flinch, I started to rub her back.

But my hand froze after a couple of inches, when my fingers skimmed over a smooth, thick line of skin. A scar.

An inch later, I found another.

I scooted toward the headboard for a better view of her back, and in the light from the bathroom, I saw more than I wanted to see. I saw it all.

Bruises, still healing two weeks after she was let out. Burn scars, small and round, like the tip of a cigarette. Long thin strips of scar tissue I couldn't identify. Teeth marks—an entire set of them—in three different places.

I don't know what I'd expected, but this wasn't it. She hadn't been punished. She'd been tortured.

Rage burned so hot in my gut I felt like I was roasting alive. I wanted to kill something. Someone. Everyone who'd had a hand in what happened to her. But I swallowed that rage. I held it inside, because my anger could trigger hers, and justice for Kori couldn't be had in that moment, in the middle of the night, with her still shaking from the latest bad dream.

But she *would* have justice. I would make sure of that.

"Do you have a lot of nightmares?"

She shrugged. "Sleep is overrated."

"You can tell me about it," I said, and her hands fell away from her face. She shook her head without looking at me. "It's not going to scare me or make me want you any less."

"I don't want to talk about it, Ian. That'll make *me* want me less."

"I don't understand."

"I know." She sounded so alone. So convinced that she had to be.

"I don't understand, but I *want* to. If you want to tell me, I want to hear."

For a long time, she didn't say anything. She didn't lie down. She didn't even move. She just wrapped her arms around her knees and stared at the end of the bed, breathing slowly. Deeply. Then she took one more deep breath, and her mouth opened.

"I don't know where to start."

"Can you tell me who did this?" I rubbed her back again, and I felt kind of guilty for my own ulterior motive in asking that question. I wanted to know who had done it so I could kill him. Even if killing the bastard who had hurt her didn't make her feel better, it would make *me* feel better.

"Doesn't matter who it was. Jake gave the orders. Jake told him he could do whatever he wanted with me, so long as I survived intact. Then he told me not to fight back."

"What?" My blood ran cold.

"That was my sentence. Before he left the day they locked me up, Jake looked right into my eyes and said, 'You like to fight, don't you, Kori? Then let's let the sentence fit the criminal. Don't fight back.'" She sucked in a choked breath and swallowed thickly. "Then he just left. I spent nearly every day at his side for the past six years, and he looked at me like I was worth less to him than the lint in his pocket. He just left me there, alone with—"

"With who?" She obviously didn't want to say the name. She probably didn't even want to think it. But she was seeing him in her head. I could tell that much. "Who did he tell you not to fight?" The very idea of which horrified me to no end.

"His brother. He told me not to fight Jonah. Six weeks, and I never lifted a fist, because the first time I tried, the resistance pain nearly killed me, and if I'd died, there'd be no one to protect Kenley. That, on top of the rest of it…it was just too much."

"Sadistic *bastard*," I hissed. Just thinking about it made me feel sick and useless. The fierce ache in my chest rivaled the vicious twisting in my gut, and if hearing about it was that painful, I couldn't imagine how she'd held it together. How she'd come out of that cell traumatized, but mentally intact.

"I hate myself," she whispered, and I blinked, sure I'd heard her wrong. I wanted to hold her, to comfort her, but I didn't know how she'd react to being touched in the middle of remembered trauma.

"No, you don't. You don't hate yourself." How could she? None of it was her fault.

"Don't fucking tell me what I feel!" she snapped, her pale hair practically glowing in the light from the bathroom. "Do you want to hear this or not?"

"I want to hear whatever you want to say."

"I hate myself," she repeated, and if anything, she seemed to believe it more this time.

"You hate *him,*" I insisted, because I couldn't help it. I hated hearing her say that.

"Yeah. I hate him more than anything else in the world. Except Jake. I hate Jake more. But that's normal."

"Normal?" How could any of this be normal?

Kori shook her head, confused, like she could feel what she was trying to say, but the words wouldn't come out right. "They're heartless. Cruel. Jake and Jonah are sadistic, and I knew that from the beginning. Sadistic people do sadistic things, so they were just being who and what they are."

My jaws ached from being clenched in anger. "That doesn't excuse anything they—"

"No, it doesn't," she agreed. "Nothing can excuse what they did to me, or to anyone else, and I'll hate them until the day I blow their heads into a million shards of bone and splashes of gray matter. And that day *will* come. But they aren't the ones who betrayed me. I betrayed myself."

"You didn't—"

"Yes, I did." She stared straight into my eyes, trying to make me understand. "Bad men do bad things. That's what they do and who they are. I fight. That's what *I* do, and who *I* am. But in the basement, I didn't fight. I couldn't."

"That's not your fault, Kori." She was killing me. She was carving out a piece of my soul with every word she spoke, and pain flowed in to fill the void.

"Don't…" She shook her head in frustration. "I can't explain what I mean. You can tell me it wasn't my fault until the earth cracks into a billion pieces of space dust, and in my head, I know that's true. But that doesn't change anything. I fight for Kenley. I fight for myself. I even fight for Jake, but that's really just another way of fighting for me and Kenley. But in the dark, I couldn't fight. I couldn't do what I do, and that means I failed. I wasn't strong."

"Kori, they took away your strength," I insisted, and she flinched, like my words actually hurt.

"Yeah. And if someone can take away your strength, you weren't strong enough in the first place. I wasn't strong enough to fight, and if I'm not a fighter, I don't know who I am. I don't know how to be me now. I don't know how to be *anything*. I lost myself in there, Ian." Her fists clenched around a handful of comforter, and her eyes watered. "The Kori who went into that cell isn't the Kori who came out. I can't find the old me, and I don't know how to be this new one." Her gaze held mine. I was captivated and devastated by the pain she was showing me. "I'm not the Kori Daniels you would have met if you'd come here two months ago."

"Good." I reached for her hand and she let me take it. "I'm so very sorry and angry about what happened to you, but I like this Kori. I might even love her." How could I not? She was a force of nature—a sudden fierce storm that had blown into my life, overturning everything I thought I knew about myself and exposing new truths. She was stronger than anyone I'd ever met, whether she could see that or not. "You may not know who you are, but I do. I know you, and I know you can be anything you want. What do you want to be? *Who* do you want to be?"

"I don't know!" She pulled her hand from mine and shoved blond tangles back from her face. "All I know is that I don't want to be her anymore. I don't want to be the woman I hear screaming and begging whenever there's nothing else loud enough to drown it out. I *hate* her. I hate what she said and what she let happen. I hate her so much that it actually makes me sick. She's there, in the pit of my stomach, rotting me from the inside out, and every time I think about it, I need to vomit. But no matter how many times I throw up, I can't purge her. She's in there, and she's scared and hurt, and I hate her."

"No." I shook my head and took her hands, and finally she looked at me again. "You may not be the woman who went into that cell, but you're not the woman who lived there for six weeks, either. That Kori died so you can live, and that's what you have to do. You have to live. And I want to be a part of that life. When the time comes for Jake and Jonah to die, I want to help you hunt them down, and slice them open, and watch their insides fall out."

"Again with the poetry." She managed a small smile. "That sounds so much prettier than blowing their brains out."

"I doubt Jonah would agree with you," I said returning her smile with a small one of my own. "But I think it's worth dreaming about. Why don't you try that? Try dreaming about what we're going to do to them, instead of what they did to you? I'll do it with you. We'll share the dream. Then we'll share the reality. I promise."

She blinked at me for several seconds, like she was trying to decide if I was serious. Then she nodded and kissed me, and we slid beneath the covers together. A few minutes later, she fell asleep in my arms again, and this time there were no nightmares. For her. I lay awake for three more hours, trying to figure out how to make my promise a reality. How to help her kill Jake and Jonah, without getting both of us killed in the process.

Her binding had to be broken. All roads led to that one conclusion. And there was only one person in the world who could make that happen.

Kenley Daniels. It all came back to her.

The next morning, I woke up to find Kori watching me, her fingers curled around mine on the comforter. There was something new in her eyes. Something fragile, but full of promise. After a moment, I realized what I was seeing.

Trust. She was trusting me. She *had* trusted me, and that couldn't have been easy, considering what she'd been through. And what I'd come to do. But she didn't know I'd come to kill her sister, and she *wouldn't* know, because I wasn't going to do it. If I'd had any doubts about that before, they were gone now. I could not betray this fragile new trust.

"Breakfast?" I asked.

She smiled, and my heart beat so hard it bruised the inside of my chest. How could she do that? How could one smile make me ache deep inside, in places I hadn't even known existed? How could she mean so much to me, in so little time?

"Yeah, but first—" Her sentence ended abruptly as her phone started beeping from somewhere on the floor. Kori popped upright like a jack-in-the-box, fear suddenly as clear in her features as satisfaction had been a moment before. "Shit!" She glanced at the bedside clock, which said it was seven-thirty in the morning, then scrambled off the bed and snatched her jeans from the floor, digging in one pocket in search of her phone. "I have to be in Tower's office in thirty minutes, or he'll lock me back up."

"What?" I rolled onto the floor and flipped up the lid on my suitcase, then snatched a pair of pants from the top of the pile.

"I'm in trouble for not reporting what happened at the park," she said, stepping into her jeans as I stepped into mine.

"Why didn't you tell me?"

"Because there was fighting, then there was sex, then I told you a whole bunch of other things, and this one just kind of slipped my mind. It's messy in there, you know."

"I'm coming with you." I pulled on my shirt, then sat on the end of the bed to shove my feet into a pair of socks.

"No, I have to go alone." She buttoned her pants, then took the bra I handed her and I fastened the hooks at her back while she dialed on her phone. "Kenley?" she said, when her sister answered. Kenley said something I couldn't make out, and Kori nodded. "I know. Twenty-five minutes." She shoved one arm into her sleeve, then transferred the phone to her other hand and slid the opposite arm in, too. "Is Van with you?" she said, and I buttoned her shirt, so she could hold the phone.

"I don't want to leave you alone," Kori said, in response to something else I couldn't hear, and I saw my opportunity.

"I'll stay with her," I said, and Kori looked up at me. And that trust faltered. I could see it. "She can come here, or I'll go there. Whichever's easier."

"I don't know…" Kori said, and I realized that her devotion to Kenley might be the only thing in the world strong enough to threaten the connection we'd just made.

Good thing I wasn't planning to kill her sister anymore.

"I swear on my life that I won't let anything happen to her," I said.

Kori closed her eyes and took a deep breath. "Okay." She wanted to threaten me. I could almost hear the words she was holding back, and I understood them. She was trusting me with the only thing she had left in the world, other than her heart, and I was hoping she'd trust me with that, too, if I kept Kenley safe from…whatever was threatening her at the moment.

"Kenni, I'm going to drop Ian off on my way to Jake's." Another pause, and Kori frowned. "He's not a babysitter. He's a friend, and I trust him. Just humor me, okay? We'll be there in a minute."

Thanks to the miracle of shadow-walking, she meant that literally.

Kori threw on the rest of her clothes, then we brushed our teeth and I helped wind the scarf around her neck again. Then we stepped from my bathroom into her sister's apartment.

Kori let go of my hand and a second later, light flared to life overhead, illuminating a cramped room stuffed with a twin bed, desk and dresser. A pile of free weights stood in one corner and a collection of handguns and knives were laid out on a towel stretched over her dresser, next to a squeeze bottle of gun oil sitting on an aluminum case that could only be a gun kit.

"Kenni!" Kori called, and an instant later Kenley Daniels appeared in the tiny hall. The three of us would hardly have fit in the bedroom together. "I have to go. I need you to stay here with Ian. He'll protect you."

"From what?" Kenley crossed her arms over her chest and glared openly at me. "There's a guard right outside the front door."

"We can't trust Jake's men. This is just in case."

"No way. We can't trust *him,* Kori! He's not bound. You hardly even know him."

"I know enough," Kori said, and I realized she was using my words. And that I loved hearing them in her voice. "Just stay with him until I get back." Then she turned to me, her hand already on the light switch, ready to step into the darkness once again. "If I'm not back in an hour, get her out of here. Same thing goes if anyone comes for her. Kill the bastard and get her as far away as you can."

I nodded, but she shook her head, like that wasn't enough. "Fucking promise me, Ian."

"What's going on?" Kenley demanded, but Kori didn't even glance at her.

"I swear, I won't let anything happen to her," I said, but Kenley's scowl didn't soften.

Kori watched me for a second, then went up on her toes and kissed me. "Thank you." Then she reached back and flipped the switch to kill the light, and as soon as she was gone, I realized that I could feel her absence, even though I couldn't see it.

Twenty-Five

Kori

I stepped out of my bedroom and into Jake's darkroom in an instant, my heartbeat measuring the seconds, burning through them faster than should have been possible. I had minutes to get out of the darkroom, down the stairs, and into Jake's office, and if I wasn't there when his timer went off, I might never see either the light of day or true darkness again.

I flipped the light switch up and pressed the button beneath the monitor mounted flush with the wall next to the door. Static buzzed on the screen for several seconds, while impatience buzzed beneath my skin. Then a familiar face appeared in its place, his broken nose and black eyes rendered in full color from the closed-circuit camera in the security room.

David. Shit. He'd been demoted to hall monitor because I'd taken him down twice in twenty-four hours.

"Kori Daniels, what an unpleasant surprise."

"Let me out. Jake's expecting me."

David leaned back in his chair, arms crossed over

his chest, and I realized that—at least from my vantage point—the security room was empty behind him. His supervisor was gone—cigarette? Bathroom?—and it was just the two of us, for the time being. "Apologize for rebreaking my nose with a fucking sucker punch, and I'll let you out."

"Sucker punch my ass." I crossed my arms over my shirt. "You fight like a twelve-year-old girl with menstrual cramps."

"Bitch!" he growled, leaning closer to the camera. "You know Jake won't let them set my nose? He wants me to see it every day as a reminder of my arrogance. Or some shit like that." His eyes narrowed in fury. "If I ever get another shot at you, I'm going to break every bone in your face. Then there'll be no jobs left for you, except as a freak in the haunted house on Halloween."

"Don't listen to the rest of them, David. Your threats are sounding more credible every day. Someday I might even tremble." I pulled my phone from my pocket and dialed Jake's number. "Hey, it's Kori," I said, when he answered. "I'm in the darkroom."

On the monitor, David scowled and pressed a button, and the darkroom door swung open into the hall.

"Be there in just a sec," I said, then hung up without waiting for a response from Jake. I had a minute and a half. I shoved the door open, and David's shout chased me halfway down the hall.

"You'll never see me coming, Daniels!"

Maybe not. But his angry bellow seemed to suggest that I'd hear him coming from a mile away.

I raced down the curved staircase, across the foyer, and into Jake's office with thirty seconds to spare, and his timer started beeping before I'd even caught my breath.

"Slow start this morning?" he said from behind his desk, one brow raised in amusement over my huffing and puffing.

"Nah. Traffic was a bitch, though."

"Well, *you* seem to have regained some of your former spunk." Julia crossed one leg over the other from her perch on the credenza to the left of Jake's desk. "It almost sounds like recruiting agrees with you, Kori." I spared one moment to visualize exactly how far through her face I'd like to shove my fist, then I dismissed her in favor of her brother, almost proud that I'd resisted rising to her bait.

"Tell me about the park," Jake said, and Julia scowled. She hated being ignored by anyone, and by her brother most of all.

I shrugged and dropped into a chair in front of his desk. "There's a swing set, and a slide, and on Thursdays, if you bring two dollars, you can get a cherry-pineapple snow cone from a clown with a red nose."

"Korinne…" Jake's angry voice was all the warning I'd get, but if I didn't at least try to push his buttons, he'd suspect something was up.

"Oh, fine. Cam and Olivia showed up with guns and tried to take Ian to the east side."

Jake's brows shot up again. "Cameron was there?"

"Yeah. Is it true you let Cavazos buy his contract?" I'd never heard of anyone else getting out of a contract with Tower early.

Jake folded his hands on his desk, and suddenly I felt like a kid called before the principal. "Korinne, it doesn't benefit you to remind me of the part you played in letting Cavazos into my home. In fact, it makes me want to lock you up again until I manage to forget just how badly behaved you've been."

My jaw clenched, and I fought to unlock it. "I'm more use to you here. On the outside."

Julia huffed and leaned forward, gripping the edge of the credenza on either side of her knees. "That remains to be seen."

"Well, it's not like I can compete with all that useful sitting around *you* do," I snapped, relishing the glower she aimed my way.

"I was well compensated for the loss of Mr. Caballero," Jake said, as if neither of us had spoken. "But please understand that no one will pay for you like Cavazos paid for him. Your Skill is common, your strength and range mediocre. You are worth more to me for your influence over your sister than as a Traveler, and you've never been worth less to me as a bodyguard." He leaned forward, eyeing me closely. "And to elaborate on the recent decline of your value, reports from the guards who protect your sister tell me she's had frequent company recently—a certain pretty former prostitute who seems quite taken with Kenley. You know what that means, don't you, Korinne?"

Yeah. I knew.

"That means that you're about to become obsolete," Julia supplied, and Jake nodded.

"So if you have any worth to claim, I suggest you start demonstrating it now. What happened with Caballero and Olivia Warren at the park?"

I sighed and swallowed the rest of the sarcasm burning in my throat. "They pulled guns on us, so Ian called up darkness, and I stepped us through it and into the wine cellar. We picked up a bottle of Cabernet for you, but I seem to have forgotten it in my rush to be threatened and insulted here today."

Okay, I swallowed *most* of the sarcasm. But neither Tower sibling seemed to notice.

"He made it dark in the middle of the day? Outside?" Julia said, and for once there was nothing in her voice but genuine surprise.

"Well, in the shade from some oak trees, but yeah."

"Amazing." Jake nodded, pleased. "Tell me about his fighting. He's good?"

"Yeah. He's fast, and strong, and accurate with a gun." I didn't want to increase Ian's value, but I wouldn't get away with lying. "We actually make a good team—he creates darkness and I use it. We could do good work for you." I flinched as soon as I heard the words falling from my own tongue. They reeked of desperation. But it's not like I was giving away my hand; we all knew what I stood to lose.

Jake leaned back in his chair, eyeing me in ruthless interest now. "Did you fuck him yet?"

I stared at the floor, silently refusing to answer. Hating how dirty the question made me feel. "He's going to sign. That's what you really want to know."

"Don't tell me what I want to know. This assignment is equal parts recruitment of Holt and punishment for you—an extension of your sentence in the basement."

I bristled, my temper flaring like heartburn. "I thought this was a chance for me to prove myself." To save my life and secure Kenley's future.

"It's all of that at once. Efficient, isn't it?" Jake smiled, and I wanted to break every tooth in his mouth. "Now, did you fuck him?"

I'd never hated Jake more.

"Yes," I said, fists clenched at my sides. I despised him for asking, and Julia for listening, and myself for answering. "But it wasn't like that."

"What was it like? Were there roses, and chocolates, and soft music?" Julia said, her words oozing saccharine venom. "Was it beautiful, Kori?"

"Fuck off."

Julia laughed. "You know, it's those clever, articulate retorts that tell me you're exactly where you belong in this organization, Korinne. On the bottom."

Jake rounded the corner of his desk to sit on the edge, less than a foot away from me now. So close he could kick me, if he wanted. Or I could kick him, if I went bat-shit insane in the next few minutes. "I don't give a damn what it was like, so long as it made him happy. Did you make him happy?"

"Yes." My stomach lurched over the truth of it. I *had* made him happy, and he'd made me happy, and Jake was soiling that. Defiling the memory. He was leaving his mark on a moment he'd had no part in, just by making me discuss it.

"Good. You may yet prove useful."

"I didn't do it for you," I spat, rage bubbling inside me, threatening to boil over. "I did it in *spite* of you."

He laughed out loud, not just a chuckle, but a great, full-bodied laugh. "Everything you do is for me. You're not privileged anymore, Kori, and those in the general population do what I tell them to do. And you'll fuck Holt again if I tell you to. Or *never* again, if I tell you not to."

"Oh, now, Jake, that would make the poor girl miserable!" Julia said, her voice dripping with fake sympathy. "She was telling the truth. I think she really likes him."

Jake's left brow rose. "Is that true? Do you like him?" When I didn't answer, he nudged my thigh with his foot. "Speak, Kori."

"Yes. I like him," I said through clenched teeth.

Julia closed her eyes and inhaled, like she was scenting the air. What she was really scenting was the truth of my statement. "It's more than that," she announced, glee dancing in every syllable. She loved seeing me suffer.

Jake frowned. "Is there more? Do you *love* him?"

"I don't know. Maybe." I swallowed the rest of what I'd almost said—the rest of how I felt—because it couldn't be captured in mere words. But that one word was enough for Jake.

"And he's going to sign?"

"Yes." *That* word, I wanted to take back. I wanted to chew it up and swallow it just so he couldn't have it. I didn't want Ian bound into the same hell I'd served in for the past six years.

Jake nodded, pleased. "Once he signs, you are done with him. You'll never touch him again, and you won't let him touch you. Understood?"

Tears formed in my eyes and rage burned in my chest. "Why?" I demanded, whispering to keep from shouting. "Just to make me miserable? To make him miserable? You're getting what you want. He's going to sign. What we do after that is none of your business."

Julia leaned forward in anticipation, and I could feel her watching me. Watching her brother. Waiting for him to snap. But that wasn't Jake's style.

"You're an investment, Kori. If you love him, you'll put him ahead of me in your heart, and that would be bad for business. So once he signs, you will stay away from him, and he from you. I'll send someone else to him.

Someone prettier. Someone nicer. Someone better in bed. He'll be with her and he'll forget about you, because none of this was ever real anyway. I created this little love connection, and I can take it apart just as easily."

"But you didn't," I said, when understanding surfaced with sudden brilliant clarity. "Ian and I clicked in spite of your involvement, not because of it, and you hate that. You're threatened by it, and that's why you're trying to tear us apart."

Jake stood and pulled me up by one arm, then leaned in to growl directly into my ear, and if I hadn't known he wasn't allowed to touch me, I might have missed the flare of pain behind his eyes. "If you don't watch your mouth, you might find yourself in another bed, performing a similar function for someone else who needs to be reminded that nothing and no one comes before the syndicate."

"Do it," Julia said, and the eager cruelty in her voice made me flinch. "Give her to someone else. She needs to be reminded who's the boss around here."

I held my breath, waiting for his decision, fighting the need to punch something.

Some*one*.

Julia.

Jake let me go and turned to her with a scowl, and I'd never seen him so close to losing his temper. "That *was* her reminder," he snapped. "She knows who the boss is, and she knows that's not *you*."

Julia flushed, but kept her mouth shut. A lesson I probably should have noted.

"Bring him in," Jake said. "I have a statement of intent already drafted and I want Holt here within the hour."

"An hour?" My heart thudded in my ears, racing in

panic. "I can't. I don't even know if he's out of bed yet. I need more time."

"Lies…" Julia hissed.

Jake glanced at me in surprise, and I cursed silently. Nothing in my contract actually forbade me from lying to him, but with Julia there, I wouldn't get away with it. I'd known better, but panic made me foolish and rash. I'd never been more afraid of anything than of signing Ian and losing him. Of seeing him every day, but not being allowed to touch him.

In that moment, facing monumental loss, I realized that I could love him. I might already. Either way I could no more lose him than I could lose Kenley.

I couldn't let this happen.

"One hour," Jake repeated, angry now. "He will sign, then you're done with him."

"You can throw women at him, but he won't touch them and he won't forget about me," I said, rage burning deep inside me, fueled by my terror at the thought of losing Ian. "And you can send me to whoever you want, but I won't fucking do it. I won't bring Ian in, either. If he wants to sign on his own, fine, but I won't be the one who hands him the damn pen. I want no part of it. I'll kill myself first."

Everyone had a limit, and Jake had just found mine.

"She means it," Julia said, her eyes flashing in anticipation.

"Well, she's wrong." Jake slid off his desk and onto his feet again, and he stepped so close I could smell the coffee on his breath. But I held my ground. "You won't kill yourself and you will bring Ian Holt in for the same reason you do everything else I tell you to. To keep your sister safe."

I glared back at him, my fists clenching and unclenching at my sides. Viewed through the red-tinted lenses of my own rage, everything suddenly seemed so clear. So simple.

"That threat won't work anymore. You already said I'm expendable." Kenley would be fine without me. Jake still needed her.

"You aren't afraid to die?" His gaze searched mine from a couple of inches away, and I stared back, letting him see the truth.

"There are days I fucking *wish* for death, Jake. Whether it comes from your hand or mine matters less every second, and your threat to kill me is starting to sound more like a promise."

His brows rose in interest, and he glanced at Julia, who nodded to confirm the truth in my statements, and her cruel smile was reflected on her brother's face. "Lia, go get Kenley Daniels and find a cell in the basement for her."

My pulse spiked painfully, but I refused to let my fear show. "That won't work." Why hadn't I seen it before? "If you're going to have her tortured anyway, what's her motivation to keep sealing bindings for you? Resistance pain doesn't seem so bad, when your whole world is pain."

Jake's smile gave me chills. "I'm not going to have her tortured. I'm going to have *you* tortured, and she's going to watch. How do you think your sweet little sister will react to seeing you beaten and humiliated, knowing there's nothing she can do to stop it? Do you think she'll still be psychologically stable after several days of hearing her only sister scream? Do you think she'll ever forgive herself for not being able to protect you like you protected her?"

I closed my eyes, horror rolling through me, deeper with every word he spoke. In six years, I'd never seen Jake Tower bluff. He would do it, just because I'd pissed him off. And he was right—even if I survived another stint in the basement, Kenley couldn't, even if no one laid a hand on her.

And he wouldn't let me die. There would be no out for me, and there would be no recovery for her. There was only one way to stop Tower from signing Ian, caging Kenley, and putting me back where I'd sworn I'd never go again.

We had to run. Even if we got caught. Even if we didn't get very far in the first place. Even if we spent the rest of our lives traipsing from one shadow to the next in search of peace.

"Stop," I said, when Jake waved Julia toward the door, on her way to send for Kenley. "I'll bring Ian in. Leave my sister out of this."

"She's lying," Julia warned, and Jake nodded perfunctorily, like that's what he'd expected from me all along. "Which is why she won't be going alone. Lia, ask Harris and Milligan to come in here please."

Julia stuck her head out of the office and gestured to someone I couldn't see. A minute later, she held the office door open and Milligan—one of my basement jailers—and Harris stepped into the office. Both were members of Jake's security team—men I'd worked with for years.

"You will escort Kori to pick up Ian Holt, then bring them back here. If she so much as hiccups without permission, haul her straight back to the basement, then bring me Holt and Kenley Daniels. Understood?"

Both men nodded. Neither looked at me.

Jake stepped close to me again, and every hair on my body stood on end. It was his calm that scared me. I knew people who'd killed in self-defense and many more who'd killed out of rage. But Jake was the only person I'd ever met who could order someone brutally tortured or slowly, viciously murdered without blinking an eye. Even someone he'd known for years and shared meals, and drinks, and conversations with. The suffering of others truly didn't touch him. That knowledge terrified me because it told me he wasn't human. Not in any way that counted.

And that meant there would be no mercy from him. No hope.

"This is your very last chance, Korinne," he said, so close to me his breath brushed my ear. "If you mess this up, I will bury you in the basement and forget I even have a key. Your binding will expire and your mark will die, but you'll stay buried, alone in the dark with the voices in your head, and no one will ask about you, because they'll all think you're dead. I will keep you there forever, Kori. Alive in body, but dead in every other sense of the word. If you want anything at all from the rest of your life—anything other than pain and dead shadows— think very carefully before you try to screw me over. Do you understand?"

"Yes." There was nothing more to say.

Jake nodded and stepped back, dismissing me without a word as he rounded his desk and sank into his chair. When I left the room, escorts in tow, Jake was already speaking into the phone, demanding that an Intent to Sign document be sent over for Ian Holt.

Milligan and Harris followed me silently across the foyer, up the stairs, and into the darkroom while I did my best to ignore the buzz of impatience and fury tingling beneath my skin. Jake meant what he said, but I'd meant what I said, too. I wasn't taking them to Ian, and they would never get their hands on my sister, either.

"Kori...?" Milligan said softly, as I pulled the door to the darkroom shut, closing us in with absolute darkness. "Whatever you're thinking about doing—"

"Shut the fuck up and give me your hand," I snapped, and a hand found each of mine in the dark, one thick and rough, the other smooth and strong. "When I tug, take two steps forward, then stop."

Without waiting for their acknowledgment, I pulled them forward as hard as I could and they stumbled alongside me, out of the darkroom and into Ian's bathroom, where I let them go and fumbled for the doorknob.

"Where are we?" Milligan asked, as I shoved the door open and stepped into the bedroom without them. Light flooded the bathroom, illuminating marble countertops, a hot tub and a dual-head shower.

"Holt's suite. Stay here. I'll go get him."

"Hell, no." Harris grabbed my arm and pulled me back into the bathroom. "I know what a Traveler can do."

I turned on him slowly, jaw clenched, eyes narrowed in fury. "You have no fucking idea what I can do. Let go of me."

"Not till we see Holt."

"Let her go, Harris," Milligan said, but I didn't need his help, and I knew better than to trust his words or even glance at him.

Focus. Power. Speed. Those were the tools of survival.

"She's not going anywhere without us," Harris insisted. "Start walking." He shoved me by the arm he still held, his fingers tight enough to bruise. I turned like I'd lead them into the living room, but instead I grabbed the hair dryer hanging from the wall by the door. Spinning, I jerked my arm from his grip, and swung the dryer at his head as hard as I could.

Harris reached for his gun instead of blocking my arm. The dryer slammed into his temple before he could draw his weapon, and he crumpled to the floor, unconscious, without even a whimper. Blood dribbled from the gash in his head, and pain ripped through mine— the beginnings of resistance pain for violating my oath of loyalty.

"*Damn* it, Kori," Milligan swore as his partner fell at our feet, one arm draped over my shoe. Milligan already had his gun aimed at my thigh. "Are you *trying* to make Tower kill you?"

"Yeah. But that won't do it." Trying to ignore the steady waves of pain deep inside my head, I bent and pulled the pistol from Harris's holster, and Milligan tensed, but didn't shoot. "Was he there? In the basement?" I asked, but Milligan only frowned in confusion. "Did he *fucking watch?*" I demanded, and Milligan nodded.

I flipped the safety switch off and shot Harris in the thigh with his own gun. I wanted to kill him. The only thing stopping me was the knowledge that the more I violated my oath, the worse I'd hurt.

"Motherfucker!" Milligan shouted, as the echo of violence thundered around us. He raised his aim to my chest. "Are you *insane?*"

"I might just be." I stepped over Harris's prone form and into the bedroom, and Milligan still didn't fire. Because unlike his partner, he wasn't an idiot. "I'm guessing we have about five minutes before building security gets here. I can tie you up or shoot you. Your call."

"Kori, stop!" he shouted as I bent over the nightstand and ripped the phone cord from the wall. "Don't make me shoot you!"

"Holt isn't here, and if you shoot me, you'll never find him." I glanced at him over my shoulder and shoved the nightstand back into place. "Tower's already gonna be pissed at me, but if you go back without Holt, you'll be on his shit list, too." I held up the cord in one hand, Harris's gun in the other, as Milligan considered, his aim steady. "But if you give me your gun, I'll take you someplace safe and you can start running. That's the only shot you have now."

"Where's Holt?"

I leaned against the glass-topped desk and glanced at the alarm clock next to the bed. "Tick tock, Milligan."

"What the hell is *wrong* with you?" he demanded, sweat beading on his forehead. He exhaled slowly and held my gaze. "Just give Tower what he wants, and we'll all walk away from this intact."

"Intact?" I grabbed the desk lamp and hurled it past his head and he flinched when it smashed against the wall at his back. "Do I sound intact to you? Did you miss the part where Jake tried to drive me insane with solitude and torture? Or maybe you missed the part where it fuckin' worked! Shoot me!" I shouted, advancing on him with my arms spread, gun held loosely in my right hand, my head throbbing so badly my vision was starting to blur.

Milligan lifted the gun again, aiming at my chest, but his finger wasn't even on the trigger. He knew what would happen if he killed me without finding out where Ian was.

"Shoot me, you fucking coward!"

"Take me to him," Milligan said, like we were bargaining. "Just take me to him, and you can go. I won't try to stop you."

I rolled my eyes and reached for his gun, and his finger finally found the trigger. "If you're going to shoot me do it. Otherwise, hand the damn thing over."

Milligan frowned, and I read determination in his eyes an instant before he lowered his gun, aiming for my leg. I threw a fist up and out, knocking his arm to the side. His shot went wild. The bullet tore a chunk of wood from the headboard to my left.

I slammed his gun arm into the edge of the desk as hard as I could. Bone crunched, and Milligan howled. He dropped his gun and I picked it up while he clutched his fractured arm to his chest.

"Kori…" he mumbled, as footsteps thundered toward us from the hall outside the front door.

"Did you watch?" I aimed both guns at his chest, but he only shook his head, not in answer, but in refusal to respond. "Did you fucking watch!" I demanded as the first fist pounded on the door to Ian's suite.

"Mr. Holt? Are you okay in there?" some hotel employee called from the hall. "We heard gunfire! The police are on their way!"

"Not for sport, Kori, I swear," Milligan said. "I was working. It made me sick, I swear on my life!"

"Good." I shot him in the left shoulder with Harris's

gun and in the right with his own. "That's why you're still alive."

Milligan stumbled back into the desk, sucking in deep breaths, face already pale from shock. I staggered on my feet as the pain in my head echoed deep in my stomach, and my hands started to shake. Then I pulled in a deep breath and stepped past him and into the bathroom, as something slammed into the front door. Security was trying to break it down.

Harris's feet were blocking the bathroom door, so I had to shove him over to make it close. Armed and surrounded by true darkness, I sucked in one deep, calming breath, trying to get a handle on the agony my body had become. Then, as wood splintered and the front door gave way, I stepped over Harris's body and out through the darkness.

Twenty-Six

Ian

When Kori was gone, her sister glared into the dark bedroom at me, though I was pretty sure she couldn't actually see me. And for just a moment, the opportunity I was passing up made my head hurt and my fingers itch for action. I was alone with Kenley Daniels. I could kill her in seconds, and my brother's body would stop shutting itself down and finally start to heal.

As a bonus, I'd be permanently crippling Tower's empire. He'd never find another Binder as strong as Kenley, and with her blood no longer flowing, actively reinforcing the bindings she'd sealed for him, most of them would break. Flesh marks would die. People would go free.

That was the very least he deserved, for what he'd done to Kori.

But if I killed Kenley, I wouldn't just be crippling one monster—Tower—I'd be creating another one. Myself. And Kori would never forgive me.

Before I could master my thoughts enough to speak,

Kenley stomped out of sight and I followed her through
the tiny square of hallway, across a small living area and
into the kitchen, where she waved one hand at a bar stool
across the counter. I sat, and she watched me, assessing
me, like I was an obstacle to be overcome. Though she
probably had no idea how close to right she was.

"Coffee?" she said at last, and I nodded. Kenley
opened a drawer and pulled out both a bag of coffee
grounds and the cutest little .22 pistol, then set them side
by side on the counter. "I don't trust you."

It took most of my self-control to keep from laughing.
Her gun was a peashooter, and if she'd been any good
with it, she never would have set it within my reach. But
I respected her intent.

"Good. You shouldn't trust anyone."

"I trust Kori," she said, running water in the coffee
carafe.

"And Kori trusts me," I pointed out, voicing the part
of the equation that was obviously troubling her.

She turned off the water and set the full carafe on the
counter, eyeing me skeptically. Then she pulled a push-
pin from the corkboard hanging on one side of the fridge,
and before I realized what she was doing, she'd grabbed
my left palm and shoved the pin into it.

"Whoa!" I tried to snatch my hand back, but she
wouldn't let go, and I couldn't get loose without hurting
her. Which was sorely tempting, considering she'd just
breached my skin and spilled my blood—the greatest af-
front possible against anyone who understood the power
inherent in blood. "What the *hell* are you doing?"

"Shh." Kenley held her left index finger to her lips,
smiling behind it with a glance at the front door, beyond
which—I gathered—one of Tower's men stood guard.

Then she swiped that same finger across the drop of blood welling from the hole in my palm.

"Whatever you're about to do, don't," I growled as she let go of my wrist and tossed me a paper tower for my bleeding hand. Instead of answering, she grabbed a notepad from the front of the fridge and a pen from the countertop and jotted three words on the paper.

"Speak only truth," she mumbled as she scribbled, and my blood chilled in my veins.

"No!" I whispered fiercely, but before I could grab the paper, she pressed her bloody index finger onto it, leaving a smear of my blood beneath the words. Binding me to them.

"Son of a bitch!" I hissed. My heart beat against the inside of my chest like a captive beast demanding freedom. I'd never been bound to anyone or anything, and the sudden caged feeling pissed me off and made me want to strike out just to prove I still could. I lunged across the counter, grabbing for the impromptu binding, but she snatched the paper out of reach before my fingers had more than brushed the edge.

Kenley folded the paper and stuffed it into her back pocket, and I realized two things at once. First, I'd have to hurt her to take the binding and destroy it, and I'd sworn to Kori I wouldn't let anyone hurt her sister. Second, Kenley Daniels was not the sweet, naive young woman her sister had described. Not entirely, anyway. She was fast, and she was smart. And she had guts.

Just like her sister.

"It won't hold," I said, though I was virtually certain I was wrong about that. An involuntary binding—especially one sealed without the Binder's blood—wouldn't hold for most Binders, but Kenley wasn't most Binders.

If she had been, neither of us would have been in Tower's territory in the first place.

Kenley flipped open the top of the coffeepot and poured the water in without spilling a drop, though she watched me the whole time. "Based on your reaction, Mr. Holt, one might think you have something to hide."

"Everyone has something to hide," I growled, angry, but not sure what to do about it, a dilemma I'd only previously experienced with Kori, who was enough to drive a man mad and make him love the journey.

She set a coffee filter into its cup. "True. But some secrets can get you killed. Are you sleeping with my sister?"

"I don't have to answer that," I said when I realized she'd left me a loophole. Had she done that on purpose? If I spoke, I could only tell the truth. But I could choose not to speak at all.

"No, you don't. But a refusal to answer is as revealing as the answer itself. So, have you had sex with my sister?"

"Yes." She was right. Silence was as good as an admission. "But for the record, you're invading her privacy as well as mine with questions like that."

Kenley's brows shot up in surprise, then she nodded again. "Fair enough. One more question, and we'll leave that issue alone. Did she want it? Did she have the chance to say no?"

"That's two questions. And yes to both." I leaned closer to catch her gaze. I wanted her to understand that I was answering not because I had to, but because I wanted her to know. "I'm not one of your heartless syndicate thugs, Kenley. I would never hurt her. Never. In fact, that's the only reason I haven't already taken your juvenile little oath and burned it."

Her gaze held mine, and I felt like we were facing off at high noon, in some long-abandoned Western town. "We all use the weapons at our disposal, Mr. Holt. This is the only way I have to look out for her, and I'm damn well going to do it."

"Fine." I could respect that. "Ask what you want to know."

"Are you going to sign with Jake?" Kenley said, and I blinked in frustration. I'd expected more questions about me and Kori. Stuff I could answer without getting anyone hurt.

"No." She'd know the truth whether I answered or not, and I didn't like being forced into things any better than Kori did.

"Does Kori know that?"

"No. I had to tell her I would sign, to protect…her." I'd almost said "you both." *To protect you both.* But I couldn't be sure Kenley knew she was in real danger, especially considering she didn't know why Kori had brought me over in the first place. "I lied to keep her from having to tell Tower something he wouldn't want to hear."

"If you're not going to sign, why did you come here?"

I exhaled, suddenly eager for some of the coffee she hadn't yet started brewing. "I won't answer that, and for the record, you're putting all three of us at risk with this line of questioning." She now knew I was in Tower's territory under false pretenses, and if and when he asked her, she'd have to tell him what she knew.

"Something's wrong," Kenley said. "More wrong than usual. How am I supposed to know how much danger any of us are in if I don't ask questions?" She pressed the brew button and coffee began to drip into the pot. Kenley stared at it, her forehead furrowed, her lips pressed together as she thought, obviously trying to decide which verbal land mines to avoid and which to hit head-on. "Does you being here have something to do with my sister?"

"She's not the reason I came to the city. But she's the reason for nearly everything I've done since I met her."

"Why does Kori think I need to be protected, today in particular?" she asked, and I picked at the edge of the Formica where it was starting to lift from the countertop, trying to decide whether or not to answer that. "Please. If it involves me, I have a right to know."

"Because Tower threatens you to keep Kori in line."

Kenley rolled her eyes. "I've known that from the beginning. What's different about today? What does any of it have to do with you?"

I exhaled slowly, hoping Kori wouldn't hate me for what I was about to say. Because Kenley was right—she did have a right to know. "If I don't sign on, Tower's going to kill Kori and put you in the basement in her place."

Her face paled so fast I thought for a minute that she'd pass out. "I don't… I can't…" She didn't seem to know how to finish either sentence.

I carried my stool into the kitchen and set it on the floor behind her, then started opening cabinets in search of coffee mugs.

"Kill Kori?" she said, sinking onto the stool, and I could only nod. "And put me…?"

"In the basement. But we're not going to let that happen." I pulled two mugs from the third cabinet I'd tried and pressed the pause button on the coffeepot, then filled them both.

"You can't stop it," she whispered, accepting the mug I pushed toward her. "You can't stop Jake."

"No. Not on my own, anyway. At first I thought I could just kill Tower, but—"

"No, you can't!"

"Because of his successor. I know."

"You know who it is?" She reached absently for a container of powdered creamer, and her hand shook as she lifted it.

"No. Do you?"

Kenley nodded. "I can't tell you who it is, but I can tell you that things will be worse for us both—maybe for all three of us—if Jake dies."

Jonah. It had to be. Who else would both Kori and her sister be so terrified of?

"We don't have to kill Jake." Though, personally, I was on board with killing both him *and* Jonah. "I can stop him from hurting Kori—with your help." And if she could break the seal binding Kori, she could break the seal binding Steven, too.

She poured the creamer but forgot to stir it. "How?"

But she wasn't ready to hear that just yet. I'd have to work up to it. "Kori loves you more than anything, you know," I said, and Kenley nodded, still dazed with shock, sipping from her mug, and when she lowered it, a clump of powdered creamer stuck to her upper lip. "She's given up her whole life to protect you, and because of that, she's been through things I can't imagine."

"There was nothing I could do." Her voice shook. "Jake wouldn't tell me where she was. I couldn't help her."

"She's melting down, Kenley. They fucked her up in that cell. She's out now, but it's not over for her. One minute, she's spitting nails and throwing punches, and the next, she's cowering in the corner, fighting flash-backs and panic attacks."

Kenley nodded miserably. "I know. She screams in the middle of the night, and the first time I tried to wake her up, she punched me before she even had her eyes open. I've done everything I can think of to help her, but she won't talk about what happened, and therapy isn't cov-ered under Tower's medical plan. Not that she'd go if it was. Not that he'd let her. He wants her to suffer."

"We can help her. You and I." I held her gaze, trying to emphasize the importance of what I was saying. "She's given up everything for you. It's time to give something back."

"How?" Her mug shook in her hands.

"Let her go, Kenley. Break the binding keeping her here."

Her head swiveled back and forth, her eyes wide with terror. "I can't."

"Yes, you can. You're the *only* one who can. It's time to set her free."

She shook her head, and I could see her thoughts flicker over her face before they fell from her tongue. "I can't. I can't be here alone. I'm not strong like she is."

"Bullshit." My hand slammed into the counter. "You pulled a gun on me, then stole my blood. You are as strong as you need to be, and you *can* survive this place. I couldn't say it if I didn't believe it was true, right?" I said, holding up my palm to remind her of the binding she'd sealed without my consent. "You can even sur-vive the basement. But if you free Kori, she and I will do everything within our power to make sure you never wind up there. You know she'd never abandon you, and she'll be even better able to help you when she isn't bound to obey Tower. Do this for her. Do this for all three of us."

Kenley studied whatever she saw in my eyes for one long moment, then she closed her own in thought. Or maybe in prayer. "Yes," she said finally, and when her gaze met mine again, I recognized the determination shining in her eyes. I'd seen that same look on Kori at least a dozen times since we'd met. "What do I have to do?"

"I've heard that a Binder can break her own seal if she remembers enough specifics about the particular contract." Which was what worried me about Steven's binding—if my hunch was correct, she'd never even seen the binding her blood had sealed.

But Kenley shook her head. "I've tried. I tried for years to break the seal binding Kori to three of her friends, and I can't do it. And I remember every word of that oath. I wrote it."

"Try it," I insisted. "Just think about Kori's contract, as specifically as you can, and remove your will from the seal."

"Okay." She set her coffee down and took a deep breath, then closed her eyes and laid her hands flat on the counter. Her forehead furrowed and her lips pressed together. And she sat like that for nearly a minute, her eyes rolling behind closed lids as she thought.

Then, finally, she looked at me again, and I could read the outcome in her slumped shoulders and the disheartened way she rubbed her forehead, fighting resistance pain, because what we were attempting was no doubt a violation of her oath of loyalty to Tower. "Try it again," I said, before she could tell me she'd failed. "You have to do it. You have to set her free, or she's going to die."

"I tried!" Kenley's eyes watered, and though she and Kori were only two years apart, she suddenly looked much younger than her twenty-six years. "I don't know how to remove my will. I don't even know what that means."

"It means you have to want to break the seal." And as soon as the words left my mouth, I realized what was wrong. "You don't want to, do you? Deep down, you don't want to break the seal because you're scared of being alone here."

She blinked and those tears rolled down her cheeks. "What they did to her in the basement—they broke her. And if they can break Kori—the strongest person I've ever known—they can break me. I want her to be free. But I'm terrified of being here without her."

"Okay." *Patience, Ian.* I'd been a soldier when I was younger than Kenley, and Kori had obviously been fighting all her life. But we were the exceptions, right? Kenley's fears were rational; who wouldn't be scared of what Kori had been through? She just needed the proper motivation—a dose of the raw truth.

"If you don't set her free, you're going to be alone anyway, because they'll kill her. They'll fucking kill her, Kenley, and then you *will* be sent to the basement. And there's nothing she can do for you from beyond the grave."

More tears fell, and her chin started to quiver.

"Try it again," I insisted, and she closed her eyes as the first tear rolled down her cheek and fell onto the countertop. "This is what she needs," I whispered, as she breathed slowly in and out. "This is what *you* need. You *have* to want this."

"I'm trying…"

"Try harder," I demanded. "If you don't free her, they will lock Kori in a basement cell and they'll put you in the one next to her. They'll shoot her, or stab her, but somewhere not immediately fatal, because they want her to suffer awhile. They want you to hear her scream."

"Stop," Kenley whispered, clutching the edge of the counter.

"That's good. Get used to saying that, because it'll be the last thing Kori hears. You, screaming for it to stop. Because whoever Tower sends into that cell with you will beat you to within an inch of your life. He'll strip you and humiliate you. He will fuck you while you scream, and Kori will hear it all while she bleeds out on the floor in the room next door, and she'll know exactly what's happening to you, because that's what happened to her."

"Stop it!" Kenley cried, tears pouring down her face, the guard outside forgotten.

"You stop it!" I hated myself for what I was saying almost as much as I hated her in that moment. I hated us both for our inability to help Kori, not to mention Steven and Meghan. For our weakness, where they had nothing but strength and sheer determination to live. But their own strength wasn't enough to save them. They needed help. *"You* make it stop, Kenley. Only you can do it. Free her so she can fight, and we can help her. Break the binding, for both of your sakes. Save your sister. You owe it to her."

Kenley gasped, and her eyes flew open. She turned to me, eyes wide, jaw slack, tears still running down her face. "I think I did it. Something…snapped. Inside. I think I broke the seal."

A rustling noise drew my gaze up, and I found Kori staring at us from across the room, a gun clutched in each fist, the back of one hand pressed to the chain marks tattooed on her upper arm. "What the *fuck* did you just do?"

Twenty-Seven

Kori

Flames licked my upper left arm, a brief burst of pain that died almost as soon as it had flared to life. I tried to touch it, to feel the heat, but I still held Harris's gun, and that was just as well, because the burning had already stopped. But I could still feel the shape of it, like an echo on my skin, in the form of two chain links.

My headache was gone, in spite of the guns I still held. My stomach felt fine, though I'd disobeyed Jake on purpose this time.

My marks were dead.

"Kenley? What happened?" I demanded, trying to process her tears, and Ian's look of shocked relief, and the newly dead marks on my arm, all while the clock ticked in my head, counting down the minutes until either Jake or the police came looking for me.

"Where'd you get those?" Ian rounded the end of the counter and crossed the room toward me, eyeing my new double handfuls of death. "Whose are they?"

"Jake sent a couple of men back with me. I ditched them at your hotel. What just happened to my arm?"

"Kenley broke the seal on your oath."

I blinked, stunned, though I could feel the truth of his statement.

"You're serious?" I hadn't expected to see my marks die. Ever. I'd been sure *I* would die first.

"Of course I'm serious. Are Tower's men alive?" Ian took Milligan's gun from my left hand, checked the safety, then tucked it into the waistband of his pants.

"They were when I left. Hope you didn't need anything from the suite. Pretty sure it's all being logged into police evidence as we speak." Ian's eyes widened. "Don't worry." I stepped past him on my way to the kitchen, where my sister was bent over the counter clutching her head in both hands, eyes squeezed shut in pain. "They know you had nothing to do with it. I left a conscious witness."

"Kori, what the hell happened?" Ian demanded, staring after me.

I set Harris's gun on the counter, then pulled a clean rag from the drawer to the left of the sink and ran cold water on it. "Jake told me to bring you in. Immediately." I helped Kenley onto the bar stool and pressed the cold rag to her forehead, offering what little comfort I could for what was obviously severe resistance pain from breaking her oath of loyalty to Jake.

I could hardly even process what she'd done, but I knew exactly how badly she must be hurting. "You okay? I need you to breathe through it, Kenni. We're leaving in five minutes and you have to pack."

"I'm trying." Kenley took the rag from me, and her hand shook. "Are we running? There's nowhere to go."

She moaned and clutched her stomach, and her rag fell to the floor. Then her hand slid into her back pocket and pulled out a folded scrap of paper, which she set on the counter, then pushed toward Ian. "Burn it."

Ian grabbed a match from the box on the counter, then lit it and set the paper on fire. When the flames reached his finger and thumb, he dropped the charred scrap into the sink and exhaled slowly.

"What was that?" I asked, bending to pick up the rag.

"Nothing. How long will this last?" Ian asked, watching Kenley.

"I don't know. I've never seen her disobey before, and she picked a hell of a way to start. Fortunately, it's a terminal breach of her oath, so if she can ride this out, she'll be fine." Unlike an ongoing breach—such as refusing to obey an order—for which she'd suffer until she either gave in or died.

I contorted my shoulder for a good look at my left arm, where the two interlocking chain link tattoos had faded from iron-gray into a dull, muted gray. "How'd she do it? Did she burn my contract?" How the hell had she even gotten hold of it?

Kenley shook her head, one fist pressed against her gut, as if she could physically stop the pain. "I unsealed the binding." Her voice was strained and her legs were shaking on the stool. "You're free, Kori."

I blinked at her. Then I glanced at Ian, brows raised in question. He nodded. I burst into tears. "How? Why?" Sniffling, I wiped my cheeks, but the girly fuckin' tears just kept coming.

Kenley was crying now, too, but obviously trying to hold it back. "He said if I didn't break your binding, Tower would kill you and put me..." Her words faded into unspoken thought and her mouth twisted into a grimace beneath another wave of agony. "So I just... I stopped wanting you to be bound to him."

"What?" When had she ever wanted me bound to Jake?

"She removed her will from the seal," Ian said as I rewet her rag and blotted her face. "The only way I could explain that to her was to tell her she had to stop wanting you to be bound to Tower." He shrugged, hands shoved into the pockets of his jeans, claiming no credit for an event he'd obviously set into motion. "So, now you're free."

I smiled—I couldn't help it—and for one short moment, I enjoyed the most wonderful words I'd ever heard.

Then I realized that in securing my freedom, Ian and Kenley had just screwed things up for his brother.

"Jake will never help you now." I rubbed the dead marks on my arm, horrified by what my freedom had cost him.

Ian glanced at the ground, and guilt left deep lines in his forehead when he met my gaze again. "I don't need him," he said, his voice soft and low, like he was making a confession. "I never did. I need her." He glanced at Kenley again, and I frowned as her grip on the countertop began to ease, the resistance pain finally ebbing.

Kenley's mouth opened, and I could almost see the question hanging on her lips, but before she could ask what we both wanted to know, her front door opened and the guard-of-the-day stepped into the living room, gun drawn, but aimed at the floor.

"I'm supposed to take you all to Tower. Now."

Shit. I was hoping to be gone before Jake got his ducks in a row.

"And if we won't go?" I stepped in front of Harris's gun on the counter, so he wouldn't see it. If I used it, others would hear and come running. Ian had Milligan's gun—also absent silencer—tucked into the back of his pants, out of view unless he turned.

"I shoot you and take them," Kenley's guard said. "You're acceptable collateral damage."

"Always good to hear." I turned toward the hall. "Just let me grab my phone."

"Stop." He raised his gun, aiming for my chest, and I tried not to look like my breath had frozen in my throat. "One more step and I'll shoot you."

"I need my fucking phone. I want to talk to Jake on the way."

"Let her get it." He nodded at Kenley, his aim never wavering from my chest. "Jake said not to let you two out of my sight," he added, glancing from me to Ian, who looked alert, but seemingly unarmed with his hands at his sides.

"Fine." I turned to Kenley, so that the guard couldn't see my face. She sat up straight, carefully hiding the last of her resistance pain. "The phone's on my dresser. It's on silent." I didn't dare emphasize that last word—even a stupid guard might pick up on what I was really asking for—so I lifted both brows instead, hoping she understood.

Kenley nodded solemnly, eyes wide with fear, hands still shaking as she stepped into my bedroom. The light went on, and I turned back to the guard, ready to capture and hold his attention.

"I can't believe they let you carry a gun. I mean, how can you see where you're aiming, with your head stuck so far up Jake's ass?"

The guard glared at me and started to speak, then something over my shoulder caught his attention. He raised his gun, but before he could squeeze the trigger, a *thwup* echoed behind me and he stumbled backward into the door, one hand over the new hole in his gun arm, blood pouring between his fingers.

He started to raise his gun again, in spite of the pain. I turned and took the silenced nine millimeter from my sister and squeezed the trigger twice more. Two new holes appeared in the guard's chest, and he slid down the door to sit on the tiled entry, his eyes sightless, his mouth hanging open. His fingers relaxed, and the gun fell to the tile between his thighs.

Something thumped behind me, and I turned to see my sister on the floor, leaning against the living room wall. "Kenley?" I crouched next to her as I flicked the safety on my gun, and Ian was there with us in an instant.

"I shot him," she mumbled.

"Your aim's definitely improving."

"Kori, I *shot* the man who was here to protect me." Her hands were shaking harder now, and I couldn't tell how much of that was from resisting standing orders from Jake and how much was shock.

"You didn't kill him," Ian pointed out. "You just kept him from shooting Kori."

"Anyway, he wasn't here to protect you. He was here to do whatever Jake told him to do, and Jake told him to bring you in. That's the opposite of protecting you." I reached down for her arm and hauled her up. "Hold it together, Kenley. We have to get out of here."

She tried to pull her arm free, but I held on to it, looking right into her eyes to emphasize the importance of what I was going to say. "Call Van, if you want to bring her with us. It's her choice, but if you can break my binding, you can break hers, too, right? And your own? We'll all run, and when we're safe, we'll see what we can do for Ian's brother."

My range wouldn't be great with three other people in tow, but I could take them, even if we had to make several layovers to get where we were going.

"What's wrong with his brother?" Kenley asked, already digging her phone from her pocket. But before I could answer, Ian shook his head.

"She can free…Van?"

He glanced at my sister, and she nodded. "Assuming she sealed Van's contract and remembers enough specifics about it. But I'm guessing Kenley didn't seal her own binding." He turned to her again for confirmation, and Kenley nodded again.

"Barker did it." He'd been Jake's top Binder until Kenley was recruited as a naive, twenty-year-old prodigy.

"Then only Barker can break the seal." Ian frowned at her. "How do you not know any of this?"

"Jake wouldn't teach her anything she could use against him," I said as the ramifications of what Ian had just explained sluggishly came together in my head. "So wait. I'm free, and Van can be free. But Kenley can't?"

"Not right this minute, no." Ian sighed and met my gaze with a somber one of his own, and the clock in my head kept ticking, driving me as surely as my own pulse did. "There are three ways to free Kenley. We can find her contract and burn it. We can kill the Binder who sealed the contract. Or—and this is a long shot—we can convince him to break the seal himself, just like Kenley did for you."

"Okay, we don't know where the contract is, and I don't want to kill anyone," Kenley said.

"Do you know where Barker is?" Ian asked, and we both nodded.

"Tower keeps him protected, but he's not as hard to get at as Kenley is." Especially for me.

"Do you think you can convince him to break the seal?"

I held up my silenced nine millimeter. "I can be pretty damn convincing." But I was running out of places to stick guns. I needed a holster. A double.

Ian shook his head. "You can't scare him into it. He can't remove his will as long as he wants her to be bound to Jake, and scaring him won't change that."

"So we explain that he only lives if she goes free. He'll want to break her binding to save his own life, right?"

Ian shrugged. "I guess it's worth a try."

I turned back to Kenley. "Throw some clothes and essentials into a bag and call Van while you pack. Don't tell her what's going on, though, or she'll have to rat us out. Just tell her you want to see her. You can break her binding once we're on our way." I was afraid if she tried to break it without telling Vanessa what she was doing, Vanessa would feel the burn on her arm and accidentally give us away before she understood what was going on.

Kenley nodded sluggishly, and I laid one hand on her arm. "You okay? Resistance pain?" I asked. The pain from unsealing my oath had passed, but as long as we were actively working against Jake, she would be hurting, and if we couldn't break her bindings soon, that hurt would quickly become unbearable.

"Just a headache so far." Kenley dialed as she crossed

the living room, then stopped cold less than a foot from the hall, phone pressed to her ear.

"Kenley? What's wrong?" I asked, and she turned slowly, eyes wide in terror, index finger pressed to her lips in the universal sign for "shh." She pressed a button on her phone, and Jake Tower's voice greeted the entire room, on speakerphone.

"I heard her, Kenley. I know your sister's there. Is Holt there with you?"

Kenley glanced at me, the phone shaking in her hand, and I shook my head.

"No," she said, phone held near her mouth.

"I know you're lying, but I'm not angry," Jake said, and Kenley swallowed nervously. "I understand why you'd want to protect them both. I also understand that you're not responsible for the massive clusterfuck your sister has just laid on my doorstep. Did she tell you what she did in Holt's hotel suite?"

Kenley nodded, then when she realized he couldn't see that, she whispered, "Yes."

"Avoiding police interference cost me quite a bit of money. More than your sister's service is worth to me. More than her life is worth. Do you understand?"

"Yes," Kenley said, her voice no stronger now.

"Good. Then you'll understand how very generous I'm being with the offer I'm about to extend to her. Korinne, can you hear me?"

"Fuck off, Jake," I snapped, picking up the gun on the counter, just for the comforting feel and weight of it.

"Kori, I'm willing to let you live if you bring your sister and Ian Holt to me right now. Walk them right into my darkroom, and you will all three live. You have my word."

"No way in hell," I said, more than loud enough to be heard.

Jake chuckled, but there was no true amusement in the sound. "That must hurt. Why don't you be a good girl and do as you're told, and that nasty headache will go away."

I glanced from Kenley to Ian in surprise, and we all seemed to come to the same conclusion—Tower didn't know my marks were dead. And I saw no need to tell him.

"I'd rather die from resistance pain than bring either of them to you," I said, careful that every word I said was true, in case Julia was listening.

"Okay, we tried this the civilized way," Tower said, evidently speaking to all three of us. "Now I'm going to give you one guess where I'm standing, and who's with me. I'll even give you a hint."

There was a moment of quiet over the line, then a scream cut through the silence like a scalpel through flesh. I knew that voice.

"Vanessa!" Kenley screeched, and Tower laughed again.

"Good guess. Vanessa and I are in the basement, and she's just had her first taste of my displeasure. Tell them what happened, Vanessa," Tower said, and Van's ragged, uneven breathing grew louder as the phone was moved closer to her.

"Cut," she gasped, and the word was bitten off, like she'd swallowed back sobs. "Fucker cut me."

"And I'll let him do it again," Tower said as Vanessa's shocked pants faded. "Once every fifteen minutes until you show up. If the three of you aren't here in ninety minutes, the last cut will be across her throat."

"Kenley, don't—" Vanessa shouted, but her words were swallowed by another scream of pain, and tears rolled down Kenley's face.

"Ninety minutes," Tower repeated. Then the phone went dead.

"Oh, shit. Shitshitshit." Kenley sank onto the couch in shock, her phone still cradled in her hands. She was pale from ongoing resistance pain, and her hands were starting to shake again. "What are we going to do?"

"Surely he won't kill her," Ian said. "If she's dead, what's our motivation to turn ourselves in?"

If Jake said he'd kill her, he'd kill her. Then he'd find new motivation. But I couldn't say that with my sister listening.

"But he'll cut her!" Kenley shrieked.

"There's nothing we can do about that," I said, brushing past her and into my bedroom. "But we're going to get her back, and then we're out of here. All four of us. You can break her binding, and we'll figure out how to break yours, even if it means killing Barker."

"The minute someone sees your dead marks and reports them, Tower will know Kenley broke your binding," Ian said, following me into my room. "And he'll know you're going after Barker to free Kenley. Beyond that, if we get caught and Vanessa's binding is already broken, he'll have no reason to keep her alive."

I settled my double holster onto my shoulders and adjusted the straps, watching him in the mirror. "So Kenley won't break Van's binding yet, and he won't know she broke mine." I turned to my sister as I slid the silenced nine millimeter into the custom left hip holster. "Kenni, get a black permanent marker."

While she rooted through kitchen drawers, I handed

Ian a spare double holster and he chose one of my extras to go along with Milligan's gun, which he obviously meant to keep.

When Kenley came back with the marker, I exchanged it for a slim folding knife. I would have given her a gun, except that she was still bound to Jake, and the gun would be easier for him to make her use against us.

Then I turned to Ian with my left sleeve pulled up over my shoulder and handed him the marker. "Try to stay inside the lines."

Twenty-Eight

Ian

"How does it look?" Kori asked as I put the cap back on the marker.

"Not bad. Unless he carries a magnifying glass, he'll never know the difference. How did you know that would work?"

She stood and examined her arm in the bathroom mirror. "I used a wig and a black permanent marker to sneak around the east side a couple of times when I first came to the city, before anyone really knew who I was."

"So, what's the plan?" Kenley asked from the doorway, twisting her fingers together. She hadn't stopped fidgeting since Tower hung up on her, and she kept ducking into the living room to check the clock hanging over the door.

I'd been checking the time, too. Eight minutes until her girlfriend would get cut again. No wonder she was melting down.

"Well, even if Jake doesn't know my marks are dead,

I'll never make it to the basement like this," Kori said, patting her guns in their holsters.

"What if we go in from the basement?" I said, from my seat on the edge of the tub. "If I could get down there on my own and call up true darkness, you could come through it, right? We could grab Vanessa and go."

"Can you do that?" Surprise shone through the shock still lingering in Kenley's eyes. "Can you make darkness deep enough to blind the infrared lights?"

Kori's brows rose. "Kenni, he can block out the fuckin' *sun*."

"Not the *whole* sun," I amended. "Just a little of its light."

"Daylight?" Kenley gaped at me. "You can kill daylight?" she said, and I nodded. "No wonder Jake wants you."

"Well, he's not going to get me. He's not going to get any of us."

Kori nodded, obviously thinking. "Okay, we'll drop Kenley somewhere safe, then you'll turn yourself in to Jake. Once you're in the house, find some excuse to go to the basement. Say you won't sign until you know Van's okay, and if that doesn't work, do whatever it takes to get down there, and I'll come get you both. But take this gun and leave that one here." She pulled the pistol from my right holster and replaced it with one from her dresser.

"Why this one?"

"Because they'll confiscate your weapons, but if you don't try to bring some in, you'll look weak. And I don't mind losing that one."

I gave her a grim nod, trying not to show how much this plan was growing on me. If Van was in the basement, Jonah would be, too. I would get a shot at him, and that would make the whole thing worth it. But...

"But my brother comes first."

Both Daniels sisters looked at me like I'd lost my mind. "Ian, Van's being tortured," Kori said.

"So is Steven. He's been on the verge of death for two weeks. His organs are failing. He can't talk. He can't sleep. He's so pale you can almost see through his skin. He's dying, and I've made him suffer two days longer than he had to because I didn't want to hurt either of you. But now that I know Kenley can break his binding, we have to go help him. Now."

"Wait, he's in *breach*?" Kori's eyes were so big the rest of her features looked smaller in comparison. "You said he was bound, but you never said he was in breach of his binding. How could he survive that for two weeks?"

"Meghan's a Healer."

"Who's Meghan?" Kenley asked, and Kori answered with only a brief glance at her.

"Steven's girlfriend." She turned back to me. "Meghan's been healing him for two weeks?"

I nodded. "Almost two and a half, now. They're both hanging on by a thread, and I came here to break the binding. And for that I need Kenley."

"What the hell are you talking about?" Kenley said, crossing her arms over her chest so I couldn't see them shake—a clear sign of the resistance pain she was fighting.

Kori's hard gaze flicked from me to the clock over the microwave—we were all counting the minutes. "But you said she can only break bindings she actually sealed..."

"Yeah. She's the one who bound Steven. We don't know what or who she bound him to, but we know it was her. The Tracker recognized her psychic signature—he evidently sees it a lot in this area." Because Kenley had bound nearly three quarters of Tower's current employees, according to Aaron's sources.

"Whoa." Kori stepped away from me, eyes narrowed on me in suspicion. "You never said Kenley was the one who bound your brother."

"I couldn't. I couldn't tell you any of this while you were still bound to Tower." And now Kenley was suffering the resistance pain I'd tried so hard to spare Kori.

"He works for Jake?" Kenley frowned in both confusion and pain. She hadn't caught on yet to the truth already surfacing through her sister's ambient anger. "Because I haven't bound anyone to anything except service to Jake in six and a half years."

"This would have been sometime before that," I said, watching Kori even as I answered her sister.

"Why are you here, Ian?" Kori demanded, her voice as soft and dangerous as I'd ever heard it. "Why are you *really* here?" Her hand hovered at her hip, ready to draw on me like a Wild West outlaw. A tiny, scary, blonde outlaw.

"Kori, wait…"

"At least have the balls to admit it. You didn't come for her help. You came here to kill her," Kori said, and Kenley stared at us both, pain and confusion warring for control of her expression. "That description you gave Jake—that wasn't me, it was Kenley. You requested her so you could get close enough to kill her."

"That doesn't make any sense," Kenley said, hunched over now from the pain in her stomach. "I didn't bind your brother. I've never even heard of him."

Kori drew her gun. "Kenni, go to your room." Tears

filled her eyes, but her aim didn't waver. And I didn't draw against her. I couldn't.

"I'm not going to hurt her." I held my hands up, palms out, demonstrating how harmless I was. "I gave you my word."

"What good is your word, if you've been lying the whole time?" Kori demanded, rage flashing behind her eyes, fueled by something even stronger. Something she didn't want to admit to.

"I had no choice!" Anger rose through me slowly, winding its way up my spine. "You'd do anything to protect Kenley. So how can you blame me for being willing to do the same for my brother? I didn't know her." I spared a glance at Kenley, who still watched us in shock. "I didn't know you. All I knew was that killing her would save Steven, and he's my *brother.* We shared the same fucking *womb!* But then I met you, and you were horrible, in the most wonderful way."

"Don't…" Her aim held steady, but her eyes were watering again.

"You were tactless, and scary, and funny, and easy to provoke, but I knew from the start that you were *so strong.* You're a fighter, and I loved that about you from the beginning, and I knew I couldn't hurt you, even to save my brother. So I found another way, and I had to do it without telling you. To protect you. I did what had to be done, and if you'll just put the damn gun down and think about this for a second, you'll realize that you would have done the same thing."

"No, I wouldn't." She lowered the gun. "I would have gone through with it. I wouldn't have hesitated to kill your brother to save my sister."

For a moment, we stared at one another, a silent brutal

understanding passing between us. Then she blinked, and one more tear rolled down her face. "And I would do the same for you."

My chest ached like someone had tried to pry my ribs open and pull my heart out through the gap.

"I don't know what's going on here." Kenley sank onto the couch, drawing both her sister's attention and mine. "I don't remember binding anyone named Steven Holt, but if this doesn't stop, I'm going to ask you to reconsider shooting me." Her face was twisted with pain, her arms clutching her stomach in obvious agony.

"Come with me." I dropped into a squat in front of Kenley, to catch her gaze. "If you can break Steven's binding while Meghan has anything left in her, she can help you, at least long enough for us to work on your binding." I glanced up at Kori, appealing to her mercenary logic. "We can't stay here anyway. Tower's probably already sent men after us."

"What about Van?" Kenley demanded, and I recognized the angry flush in her cheeks—she looked just like her sister in that moment.

"I'm not going to let the princess die in the dungeon. Kori and I will go after her as soon as Steven's unbound."

"But…" Her foot began to jiggle—a very bad sign. And every minute she didn't turn herself in to Jake, it would get a little worse.

"No more arguments. We're going. Ian, get the lights." Kori wrapped one arm around her sister and carefully pulled her up from the couch while I crossed the room to flip switches in the kitchen and by the front door, where I had to step over the dead guard's body. When the room was dark enough to travel through, I took Kori's free hand and gave her the address. She spared a moment to visualize the general location and search for a pocket of darkness. Then she stepped forward and Kenley and I went with her.

Two steps later, I banged my shin on the toilet in the house Meghan grew up in. They'd kept the house when they moved out a few years earlier, but it was currently unrented, which made it a decent hideout. Though Tower's Trackers would find us, if we stayed too long.

Kori's foot hit something and she cursed, while I felt around on the wall for the light switch.

Something clicked behind us just as I found the light, and I was still half-blind when I turned to find Aaron aiming a gun at me from the hall. He exhaled in relief when he recognized me, and his aim shifted to Kori.

"We haven't met." Kori half held her sister up with one arm, leaving her left hand free to go for her gun. "I'm Kori Daniels. If you don't get that gun out of my face, I'm gonna take it, then I'm gonna break your jaw so I can unhinge it and shove your own pistol down your throat. That way the bullet goes through the long way."

I groaned and gestured for Aaron to holster his gun, but he looked distinctly disinclined. "She believes in making a strong first impression. But she's here to help. They both are."

Aaron held his position for another second, then reluctantly lowered his gun and stepped aside, so we could enter. I took Kenley from her sister and carried the Binder in both arms down the hall and into Steven's room, where he lay on the bed, a skeleton wrapped in skin so thin it looked like it might tear at the slightest pressure.

"Oh, hell," Kori whispered. "He should be dead."

"Don't ever say that again," Meghan said from her recliner next to the bed. The circles beneath her eyes had darkened and swollen. Her arms were thin and pale, and the veins stood out like dark tree branches, stretching beneath her skin.

Kenley gasped when I set her in a chair on the opposite side of the bed and she got her first look at my brother. "Twins?" she asked, and I nodded, surprised she could see the resemblance in what little was left of him.

"He's nine minutes my junior." I knelt next to the bed, searching for something familiar in the living skeleton that used to be my brother. I wanted to take his hand so he'd know I was there, but I was afraid to touch him.

Steven's eyes rolled beneath his lids, and he groaned in his sleep. Only he wasn't really sleeping—he was barely clinging to consciousness.

"I don't know him." Kenley's eyes filled with tears and she sounded half-choked by them. "I thought when I saw him I'd remember, but I've never seen him before. I didn't bind him."

I pulled up a folding chair and sat next to her, while Aaron and Kori hovered near the doorway. "You may not have personally bound him, but your blood and your will sealed the binding."

Kenley blinked in confusion, but then comprehension surfaced so hard and fast her body actually jerked, like someone had slapped her. She turned to her sister, anger and guilt warring behind her eyes, pain evident in every movement she made. "Nadia? You told him about Nadia?"

Kori shrugged. "I was explaining how we got involved with Jake in the first place."

"Who's Nadia?" Aaron asked.

"Her college roommate," Kori said. "Years ago Kenley

gave a sample of her blood to some bitch she had a crush on, who abused the fuckin' privilege."

"But Jake fixed all that. None of those bindings are still intact."

"I don't care who made the mess and who cleaned it up," Aaron said from the edge of the room. "His bindings are obviously still intact, and your blood is keeping it that way. So break the fucking seal now, or I'll end this once and for all." He drew his gun and pointed it at Kenley's head, and she gasped.

Kori burst into motion so fast I hardly saw her move. She shoved his gun arm up, startling Aaron, who accidently fired into the ceiling, and the rest of us ducked. Kori threw her knee up and into his groin, and when Aaron fell to his knees, too shocked to make a sound, she took his gun hand in both of hers and twisted viciously. I heard his bone crack from across the room, and I flinched when Aaron howled in pain.

Kori plucked the pistol from his grip, then kicked him in the stomach for good measure.

"You ever point a gun at my sister again, and I'll strangle you with your own intestines. Got it?"

Aaron moaned from the floor, and Kori must have accepted that as a reply, because she checked the safety on his gun, then kept it, and suddenly I understood where most of her weapons collection had come from.

"Carry on," she said, waving her empty hand at both Kenley and Steven, but when Meghan stood to help her brother, Kori shook her head and raised the gun again. "Sit. Save your healing juice for my sister. He'll be fine," she added, with a contemptuous glance at Aaron, who was still curled up on the floor.

Meghan sank back into her chair reluctantly, and I turned back to Kenley.

"I don't even know how to start," she said. "Breaking Kori's seal was hard, but at least I knew what I was doing. I don't know what Steven was bound to, so I don't know what to remove my will from."

"Okay..." Kori came close, obviously thinking, and I didn't miss the glance she threw at the alarm clock next to the bed. Vanessa's time was slipping away, along with Steven's. "Whatever this binding is, he only breached it a couple of weeks ago, right?" she said, and I deferred to Meghan. I wasn't even in the country when the whole thing started. I'd been gone for nearly seven years.

"Um, yeah." Meghan sniffled. "I'll never forget because it was the night he proposed. We had a wonderful dinner, then there was the question, and the ring..." She held her hand out and studied the diamond on her left ring finger. "Half an hour later, he got a migraine, and we had to leave in the middle of dessert."

"Oh, hell," Kori said, turning to see if I'd come to the same conclusion. And I had. Only I knew more than she did. More than any of them could possibly know. "Love Knot," she said, and I nodded. But the name was a misnomer—you can't control someone's emotions, no matter what you bind them to. But that didn't stop the occasional love-sick adolescent—or desperate college student—from preventing the object of her affection from marrying—or proposing marriage—to anyone else.

Kenley watched us, obviously trying to think through her own pain to follow the conversation. "You're saying the Love Knot my college roommate used my blood for six years ago was targeting your boyfriend's twin brother? What are the chances?"

Kori shrugged and shook her head slowly. "I stopped asking that years ago. How did Jake break the seal?"

"He didn't. He said he *couldn't,*" Kenley said, and my temper flared.

"He only said that because he didn't want you to know you could break your own bindings."

"So, what, he just lied and said the binding was broken, when it wasn't?" Kori asked.

Kenley shook her head. "He helped me transfer it."

I frowned. "You can't transfer a binding."

Kenley shrugged. "Evidently you can, under certain circumstances. In this case, he said the target had a dead brother, close in age. And Nadia didn't have a sample of Steven's blood, so she used a name binding. Jake's man showed me how to transfer the binding to the dead brother, where it couldn't hurt anyone." She gave another little shrug, brow furrowed from the headache. "Dead people don't fall in love, you know." Then she turned to me, frowning. "Except that you're not dead."

"He's not bound, either," Meghan pointed out. "If you transferred the binding, why is Steven still bound?"

I exhaled heavily and rubbed my own forehead, leaning back in my chair. "Because she transferred the binding *to* Steven, not *from* him."

"I don't understand," Kori said.

"Oh, shit. Your names," Aaron said, and I looked up to see him still sitting on the floor, his fractured arm clutched to his chest. He wouldn't take care of his own injuries until he knew his sister was safe.

"What about your names?" Kori asked. "The quick version," she added, with another glance at the clock.

"My mom raised us to be paranoid," I said. "She told us from the time our Skills manifested that people would want to use them. She said we'd have to hide our Skills, and possibly hide ourselves. Turns out she was right. When we left home for college—we picked schools on opposite sides of the country—we switched names, to help protect our true identities. That way, if someone tried to track me by my name, they'd actually be tracking him, and he was so far away even the best Tracker in the world couldn't pick up his signal."

Fortunately, Steven's skill as a Reader was more common and less powerful than mine, which was why he'd felt safe enough just hiding his name, whereas I'd had to hide my entire existence.

"So, you're not really Ian?" Kori said.

"No, I'm Ian. But in college, I called myself Steven, and I registered with his records and ID. So when Nadia bound Steven, she was actually binding me—Ian— because he was using my name. He got his degree as Ian—my brother really *is* a systems analyst—got his first job as Ian, and applied for his mortgage as Ian Holt. He still uses my name to this day," I said, glancing at Meghan for confirmation, and she nodded. "And I joined the Marines as Steven Holt."

"*You're* the dead serviceman?" Kori's eyes were narrow, her voice unsure. She was trying to untie a knot of identification my brother and I had worked for years to tangle. To keep each other safe. But that had obviously backfired. "You faked your own death?"

I shrugged. "I just took advantage of the opportunity when the Corps thought I died, along with most of the rest of my unit. Steven chose to hide in plain sight. I chose to hide in Australia. In Steven's name, which now belonged to a dead U.S. serviceman."

Kori sat on the end of the bed, eyes closed, thinking

out loud. "So, Nadia bound Steven, but she used your name—Ian—so she was actually binding you. Then, when Kenley transferred the binding to you—in Steven's name—she was actually transferring it back to the intended target. Is that right?"

"Yeah. I think so." I turned back to Kenley. "Does that give you enough information to break the seal?"

"I sure hope so."

"Please, do it," Meghan begged as Kenley closed her eyes. Her hands shook in her lap as she concentrated, and I wondered how much harder this would be, with so much resistance pain already crippling her. Her eyes moved behind her eyelids, and her hands clenched around the arms of her chair

The rest of us waited, hardly breathing. I watched my brother—my twin—trying to find some change in him to indicate her success. Or her failure. His breaths were shallow, his chest hardly moving. He'd grown way too thin, especially in the past week, when food became too hard to keep down, even when Meghan managed to get it in him. He'd stopped letting me help. In fact, he'd kicked me out of his room eight days earlier—that was the last time he'd had the strength to shout—and it took me a while to understand that seeing me was hard for him, because I looked like he remembered himself, even as he wasted away a little more every day.

Finally Kenley gasped and her eyes flew open. "I think I did it."

Meghan burst into tears and pushed herself out of her recliner to sit on the edge of Steven's bed. I couldn't see a change, but she looked happy. Relieved. She laid one hand on his cheek, then touched his arm. Then she turned the sheets back to touch his bare, gaunt stomach. And when she finally looked up, silent tears poured down her cheeks.

"They're working. They're all working again." She turned to Kenley, wiping her face with both hands. "Thank you."

"I'm so sorry," Kenley said, clutching her own stomach. "I didn't mean to hurt anyone."

"He's going to be fine soon," Meg said, and I stood, already turning to Kori.

"Ready?" We had twenty-five minutes to get to Vanessa.

Kori turned to Meghan, who was fussing over Steven, trying to make him more comfortable, obviously eager for him to wake up. "Swear you'll take care of her." The gun in her right hand made it kind of hard to hear her request as anything less than an order, complete with implicit threat.

"What's wrong with her?" Meghan turned to look critically at Kenley for the first time.

"She's in breach of her oath to Jake Tower just by being here."

"If she dies, three-quarters of Jake Tower's private army will go free. His empire will collapse," Aaron said from the floor near the door, injured arm still cradled at his chest, and I started to reconsider my original assessment of his IQ.

Kori turned to him slowly, pistol aimed at his head. "If she dies, you die, even if I have to chase you across the fuckin' planet. And you should know that one of the best Trackers in the country owes me a favor." She lowered her gun, and Aaron looked up at me, anger smoldering in his eyes.

"You're with her on this? You're gonna pick some

bitch you just met over a friend you've known all your life?"

"I'm hoping I won't have to. Don't be stupid, Aaron. Kenley just saved your sister's life."

"She's the one who put it in danger!"

"No, I put my own life in danger," Meghan said, rounding the bed for a closer look at Kenley. "I chose to heal Steven. And now I choose to heal the woman who saved him." She turned to Kori, as she knelt next to Kenley. "She'll be fine as long as I am. But I don't know how long that'll be. I've been doing this too long as it is."

"It won't be long," Kori said, and I could see the solution in her eyes. In the set line of her jaw. She was going after Barker. In killing one of Tower's Binders, she'd be freeing the other. The king's castle would come crumbling down on top of him. "Let's go."

Twenty-Nine

Kori

I walked us out of Meghan's bathroom and back into Kenley's living room, and neither of us bothered with the light. "I need to be gone before Jake's men get here, and it'll look better if you go in voluntarily."

"Where will you be?" Ian asked.

"Recruiting backup."

"You know, if you hadn't broken Aaron's arm, we could have used him as backup."

I huffed. "If he was that easy to disarm, he wouldn't have done us any good."

"So who are you calling?" Ian asked as I dug my phone from my pocket.

"My brother. And Olivia. I trust them both at my back."

"Olivia Warren?" I could hardly see his frown in the deep shadows. "*Cavazos's* Olivia?"

"She was *my* Olivia before she was his, and I know how to avoid his claim to her." I glanced at the microwave clock. It had been seventy-five minutes since Jake called Kenley's phone. In the basement, Vanessa was being cut again. I couldn't hear her scream, but I could almost feel it.

I dialed Liv's number from memory, then pressed the speaker button and my phone rang out into the room. After four electronic bleats, Olivia answered, her voice thick with suspicion. "Hello?"

"Will you help me?" I said, in lieu of a greeting.

"Kori?" Liv was pissed. I could hear it in her voice, in the way she bit my name off at the edges. But she was also worried; she knew I wouldn't call unless I was in trouble. "What's wrong?"

"I need sanctuary. Are you at your office?"

"Yeah."

"Turn off the light. I'm coming over."

Olivia sighed. "Fine."

I hung up and turned to Ian. "I'll see you in the basement."

"Be careful." He pulled me close for a kiss, and I didn't want to let him go. Ever. But this wouldn't be over until Van and Kenley were free. Hell, it might never be over. And Van was running out of time.

I took a deep breath, then made myself let him go and step into the shadows.

The moment I stepped into the darkened bathroom in Olivia's tiny two-room office, I could see her. And hear her. She sat on the couch opposite her desk, fully visible in the well-lit main room.

"Kori's here," she said into her phone as I rounded the desk toward her. "Yeah, I'll let you know when—"

"You still bound to Cavazos?" I asked, and she nodded, scowling at the interruption.

I snatched the phone before she could finish the

aborted sentence and threw it at the ground as hard as I could, where it broke into several large plastic pieces.

"Damn it, Kori! Do you have any idea how many phones I go through in a good year?"

"Sorry," I lied, shoving her stapler over so I could sit on her desk. "I can't chance Cavazos calling you while I'm here." He'd use her against me.

"That was Cam, not Ruben."

"He'll understand. Text him from my phone." I tossed my cell to her and she started typing with both thumbs, pausing frequently to glare at me.

"What's this about?" she said as she handed my phone back.

"As of about an hour ago, I am a free woman, and the best part is that Jake doesn't know yet."

Olivia reached over and pushed up my left sleeve. "Your marks aren't dead."

"Black permanent marker." I sat next to her on the couch. "Take a closer look."

She leaned down, squinting at my arm from two inches away. "Wow. How'd it happen?"

"Ian taught Kenley how to break her seal. It's no piece of cake, but she pulled it off."

"Is she still bound?"

"Yes, and she's in a lot of pain, but a friend of Ian's is a Healer, so she's in good hands, at least until I can kill the Binder that sealed her to Jake."

"If you're killing Tower's men, I'm in."

I grinned without bothering to hide my relief. "I was hoping you'd say that. But first I have to bust Kenley's girlfriend out of Jake's basement."

"Her girlfriend?"

"Yeah." I stood and shoved my phone into my pocket. "She was a friend of Cam's. You two might have met."

"Van?" Olivia sounded horrified, and I nodded from the bathroom doorway. "Why would Tower torture her?" Cam had obviously told her what goes on down in Jake's basement.

"To get to Kenley. And by extension, me and Ian."

"How are you going to get her out?"

"I sent Ian in to bust a hole in Jake's infrared grid. Once he has, I'm gonna walk in alone, and walk out with Vanessa. Then we're going after Barker, Tower's secondary Binder."

"Want some help in the basement?"

"Thanks, but I'll have Ian and Van on the way out." And if she got too close to Ian, she'd be obligated to try to take him from me. "I do need another favor, though. Are you under any standing orders to give Kenley to Cavazos?"

"Nope." She smiled, and I welcomed the sight. "Obviously he knows Tower has a Binder, but he doesn't know who that is, to my knowledge. Or that I have any connection to her."

"Good. If you can do it, I need you to call Kris, so he can get both Van and Kenley somewhere safe, as soon as we're done with Barker." Because Jake was probably already tracking Kenley, and the farther away she was, the harder that would be for him. And she couldn't stay with Liv, because if Cavazos got his hands on my sister, the mess we were already in would be infinitely worse. And bloodier.

"No problem," Olivia said.

I thanked her, then closed my eyes and mentally reached out toward Jake's house, ignoring all the other pockets of darkness between. As usual, his house was an inferno of infrared light burning beyond the visible spectrum, except for the cool, dark sanctuary of the darkroom. But I reached deeper, lower, hoping against all hope that Ian had already found his way to the basement, and that I wasn't too late to take advantage of it. Because once he'd created darkness, they'd realize what he was doing and they'd try to stop him.

So when I actually found that spot of true dark in the basement, I nearly choked on my own surprise. We'd caught another break.

"Hopefully this won't take long," I said, backing into the bathroom. Then I took another step backward, and this time my shoe landed not on cheap, faded linoleum, but on gritty concrete.

The basement.

"Ian?" I whispered, because I'd need him to let go of the dark long enough for us to find Vanessa and take care of whoever was with her. I was close. My bindings were dead and I'd broken into the impenetrable Tower fortress. I was minutes from true freedom.

I might just survive the day after all.

A footstep whispered on the concrete behind me and I started to turn, my heart thumping. Then something slammed into the side of my head and the world spun around me, unseen in the dark. The floor crashed into my back and the lights came on overhead. Stunned and out of breath, I could only blink as a foot pressed into my neck and someone pulled my guns from their holsters.

I blinked again, and a face came into focus against the glare of the lights overhead. Jonah.

"Welcome home, Kori. We've missed you."

Thirty

Ian

After Kori left Kenley's apartment, I double-checked the clips in both of the guns she'd lent me—not that I'd have a chance to use them—then took the jacket off the dead guard still slumped against the front door. The jacket was a size too large and had an uneven spot of blood near the hem on the right side and a blood-soaked bullet hole in the right sleeve, but neither would be easily visible in the dark material, which would hide the fully loaded double holster.

Satisfied with the functionality of the jacket, I hauled the guard into the kitchen, then went downstairs to catch a cab, intending to report to Tower's fortress for Trojan horse duty. But as I stepped onto the sidewalk, a sleek black car pulled to a stop at the curb in front of me. The window rolled down to reveal Julia Tower. Alone, except for her faceless driver.

"Mr. Holt, may I offer you a ride?" Her head was tilted slightly to the left, but her cool smile was on straight.

I crossed my arms over my chest. "You say that like I have some choice in the matter."

"In fact, you have three choices. You may ride in here with me, up front with the driver, or in the trunk."

"And if I decline all three options?"

"My brother Jonah is in a basement cell right now, hoping that's exactly what you'll do. The young woman with him is no doubt praying you'll show better sense."

"Vanessa?" I asked, and Julia nodded. "What makes you think I care what happens to a woman I've never even met?"

"I know you care, because I know the *real* Ian Holt— the man who doesn't own a personal computer and doesn't even know what kind of systems he supposedly analyzes." She paused a moment to let me truly experience the shock of her words. "I know Ian Holt, the soldier who defied a direct order to pull an injured friend out of the line of fire. The brother who rose from the grave— feigned though that grave was—and stepped back into his own identity to save his twin from certain agonizing death. That Ian Holt can't help himself—he's at the mercy of a ruthless hero complex."

"How…?" I started to ask how she knew. Then I realized that didn't matter. What mattered was, "How long have you known?"

"Mr. Holt, we would never have asked you to become one of us if we didn't already know how many fillings are in your teeth and how you broke your arm in the third grade."

I *had* broken my arm in the third grade… "Lila Sobresky—"

"Pushed you off the slide. I know." She folded her hands in her lap, and I couldn't take my gaze from her face. From eyes that saw more than they should and ears that seemed to hear my very thoughts. "I also know that your mother is first-generation Irish-American, which is where you get those striking green eyes, and your father is fifth-generation African-American, the source of your lovely dark skin. You and your brother are fraternal twins, but you looked virtually identical until he began wasting away in excruciating pain two weeks ago. Steven was named for your paternal grandfather, who spelled his name with a *ph* instead of a *v.* Your mother named *you* after her older brother. Sweet, but stupid. Almost as stupid as it was for you and your brother to keep the names. But switching them…?" Julia laughed, and the sound bounced around inside my head like nuts and bolts clanging in the dryer. "That was clever. We might never have figured that part out, if you and your brother hadn't already pinged our radar years ago, thanks to the younger Miss Daniels."

Her gaze trailed over my face and down the front of my shirt, like she could see the flesh beneath, and my teeth ground together so hard my jaw ached. "You are quite a prize, Mr. Holt. A soldier with a philosophy degree under a stolen identity. A thinker and a fighter, with a strong, thick—" her gaze traveled lower "—protective streak. No wonder Korinne fell for you."

My anger built with every word she spoke, like my secrets were worth less than the lipstick staining the mouth that spilled them. I'd rarely wanted to punch a woman, but I wanted to drive Julia Tower's straight, white teeth through the back of her skull, just so I wouldn't have to hear another word come out of her mouth.

"Get in the car, or Vanessa loses a finger."

I hesitated, gripping the car door where the window

had receded into it, letting my anger swell a little more. Grow a little more useful. Then I opened the door, not because Julia had told me to, but because she represented the most direct path through Tower's heavily guarded headquarters to the basement, where Vanessa and Kori needed me to be. But before I could sit, Julia held up a hand to stop me. "Place your weapons in the front seat." Where they would be beyond my reach, thanks to the panel separating driver from passengers.

But that was not unexpected.

I opened the front door and dropped both guns on the seat, then slid onto the backseat next to Julia Tower. Before I'd even closed the door, I wondered if I'd made a tactical error. If bending to her will, even for my own purpose, was the first of many steps in the devouring of my soul by the beast that was her brother's organization.

"Kori didn't know any of that, did she?" I asked, twisting to face Julia on the bench seat. Why would they keep their recruiter in the dark about her own recruit?

"Korinne knew only what she needed to know," Julia said as the car pulled away from the curb. "But Jake and I knew why you really accepted our invitation from the beginning. And we knew you would never go through with your cold-blooded mission because at your core, pulsing where your heart should be, is a stubborn kernel of chivalry, rotting you alive like a cancer. You didn't kill Kenley Daniels when you had the chance because you couldn't. And you fell for Kori like a schoolboy in love the moment you got that first glimpse of her poor, abused, damaged heart. Just like Jake knew you would."

My fist clenched around the door handle. "If Tower knew I had no intention of joining, why send Kori to recruit me?"

Julia laughed, like she'd never heard anything truly amusing until that very moment. "Korinne wasn't recruiting you. She was living out her sentence. Jake got bored with her in the basement." Julia frowned in thought. "That's what he says, anyway, but he's lying."

And suddenly, studying her expression—the first raw, unfiltered look I could remember seeing from Julia Tower—I understood what Kori hadn't been free to tell me. Julia was a Reader. She'd heard—and no doubt reported—every lie she'd heard me tell. But now that I knew what she was, she'd lost her advantage. The key to fooling a Reader is to tell two lies at once, and make one of them obvious. That way the Reader doesn't know there's a bigger untruth buried beneath the surface lie. I'd learned that, if nothing else, from growing up with Steven.

"The truth is that he started to hate her, because Jonah couldn't break her and Jake couldn't do it himself. That's in his vows, you know." Julia's eyes sparkled with bitter amusement. "The only thing he promised his wife—that he would never touch another woman. Not ever. So when you came along, he saw a possibility involving you both. For Kori, the impossible task. Recruit the man who cannot be recruited. The immovable object."

My blood burned in my veins like liquid fire. "He set her up to fail."

Julia nodded. "And to hate every single debasing, humiliating moment of it."

"And me?"

Her smile grew smaller, tighter. "For you, the irresistible force. Korinne, our own shattered doll, pretty, yet fierce. Delicate, yet dangerous. The damaged woman who cannot be fixed—Kryptonite to any man with a hero complex."

"He played us." The truth of it echoed inside me, ringing over and over, resonating in every bone in my body.

She nodded again. "He did. And he watched you both struggle and flail for two days, butting heads and bruising egos for his entertainment, knowing that in the end, you would sign with him for the same reason you came out of hiding—to protect those you care about. My brother is cruel and smart, and he is without mercy. Which is why I can tell you without a doubt in my mind that if you don't sign whatever contract he offers you, he will cut poor Vanessa in places that should never feel pain. And if that fails to motivate you, he will move on to your brother, and your brother's fiancée, and—"

Before she could finish threatening everyone I'd ever met, Julia's phone started ringing and she frowned, then reached into a slim purse and pulled out her cell. Her frown deepened when she glanced at the display, then she pressed a button and held the phone to her ear. "Hello?"

She listened in silence for several seconds while a voice I didn't recognize said words I couldn't understand. Then Julia's brows rose in sudden interest. "Yes, I'll show him. We're on the way."

She ended the call, then started pressing more buttons on her phone. "You're a very lucky man, Mr. Holt. As it turns out, Jake won't have to target what remains of your family after all," she said, and a cold ball of dread formed in my stomach, growing with every second of silence from Julia Tower. But I wasn't going to beg for information.

Finally she looked up and her usual smug smile was

absent. She looked almost somber. Instead of offering
me an explanation, Julia simply handed me her phone.

I took it, dread churning in my stomach. But when I
glanced at the screen, my rage swallowed all other emotions like the ocean swallows a single raindrop. Kori
stared out at me from the display on Julia Tower's phone.
She was shouting, but I couldn't hear her, because there
was no sound. But I could see her gesturing in fury, her
mouth open wide with each enraged shout. Behind her
were a toilet, a curtainless shower stall, and a rollout
mattress on a raised concrete block.

"That's a live feed. From Jake's basement," Julia said.
And as badly as I wanted to believe this was old footage, even on the tiny black-and-white screen I could see
that Kori was wearing what she'd put on that morning,
including the double holster, though the guns—and no
doubt the knives—were gone.

"Let her out." I could hear the rage roiling in my voice.

"That's beyond my authority. The only way for you
to help Kori is to sign the contract."

I pulled the phone out of reach when she tried to take
it. "Can you honestly tell me that if I sign, he'll let Kori
out?"

Julia watched me closely for a second, like she was
sizing me up. Trying to decide whether or not to gift me
with the truth. Or maybe to curse me with it. "No," she
said at last. "We both know Korinne will never set foot
outside that cell again. There's nothing I can do about
that."

"Get her out, or I won't sign."

"Sign, or she'll suffer before she dies," Julia
countered. "And if you do it quickly, I might be able to
arrange a visit with her."

"That's not good enough." I dropped the phone on the leather between us and grabbed her by the throat, pinning her to the opposite door, letting my fury echo in my growl. "Get. Her. Out."

Something hard pressed into my stomach and I looked down to find her holding a gun, the barrel digging into my navel.

"You're not going to shoot me. Your brother needs me."

"And you're not going kill me, because you need *me*," she insisted hoarsely, using the fingers of her empty hand to pry at mine, trying to free her neck.

"You just said there's nothing you can do for Kori."

"There isn't—as long as Jake's in charge."

I blinked in surprise. Then I frowned. Then I frowned harder and loosened my grip on her neck. It almost sounded like… "Are you asking me to kill your brother?"

"I'm not asking anything of the sort." Because she couldn't. She was no doubt contractually prohibited, just like the rest of Jake's employees.

"But you can speak in hypotheticals, right?"

"As can you," she said, and I let her go.

"If Jake were out of power, you could help Kori?"

"I could." She rubbed her neck with her free hand, but her gun remained pointed at me.

"Why should I believe you care one way or another about what happens to her?"

"I don't." Julia shrugged, like that should have been obvious. "I care about what happens to me." Her brows rose in question, silently asking if I was understanding the things she wasn't allowed to say.

"You're not happy under your brother's reign?"

"You mean under his thumb? I'm chained to him just

like Korinne is, only I've been serving since I was six-teen. Since before service came with a time limit." She lifted her left sleeve to show me her binding marks, which seemed to ring her entire arm. "As long as these marks are live, I'll never have a family or a home of my own. I can't leave the city without authorization, which never comes. I can't even leave the *room* without per-mission. All because of one stupid oath I took as a kid, in exchange for my older brother's protection."

"Protection from what?"

Her lips pressed together for a second before she an-swered. "There's a skeleton in every closet, Mr. Holt."

"Fair enough. What about his heir? Do you honestly think it'll be better with Jonah pulling your strings?"

Her brows rose again, and her smile was back, small and reticent this time, like she was about to tell me a secret. "I can handle Jonah, Mr. Holt. His bark and his bite are both fierce, but I know how to leash him."

I thought about that for a moment, weighing my op-tions and her sincerity. "If I were to give you that oppor-tunity, you'd make sure Kori goes free? Immediately?"

"You have my word that if Jake is removed from power, Kori Daniels will go free immediately." I wasn't sure I believed her, but since I planned to kill both Jake *and* Jonah anyway, Kori would go free whether or not Julia kept her word. What I really needed to know was…

"Can you get me a second alone with Jake?"

She nodded without hesitation. "My contract predates time-in-service limits, but it also predates the stricter obedience clauses. I have more leeway than most em-ployees. But I'm going to need some reassurance from you, Mr. Holt. A handshake won't do."

"What do you want?"

"Protection. When people find out that I helped rid the world of Jake Tower, those loyal to him—or to his wife—will be out for my head. I want your word—signed and sealed—that you'll protect me until that threat is gone."

"No bindings," I insisted. Kori's bindings had gotten her tortured. Kenley's had gotten her caged. Steven's had nearly gotten him killed.

"Then no deal," Julia countered. "It's a simple promise, Mr. Holt. Not a service agreement. Jake's secondary Binder is bitter about being replaced by Kenley Daniels and he's loyal to me."

Secondary Binder? A glimmer of an idea surfaced on the horizon of this new complication. "Is his name Barker?"

Julia frowned. "Yes. And I assure you, he's heavily guarded. Especially with Kenley currently on the run. Though that won't last long."

"I have no plans to harm your Binder." Big lie—if Kori couldn't take him out, I damn well would. "In fact, I'm looking forward to working with you both." Smaller, obvious lie, to cover the larger fib.

Julia rolled her eyes, and I knew I had her. "I know you don't want to be bound, Mr. Holt. But I assure you this is the least painful solution for all involved. I've already drafted the binding, and we can strike through and initial minor points of compromise before we sign. Then when we get to Jake's house, you will play your part. After that, you and Kori can walk off into the sunset, if that's the kind of cheesy, happy ending you sentimental types like."

"Just like that?" I studied her face, searching for the catch. "It sounds too good to be true."

"I assure you it's not. Jake knows how to defend himself, and even if you're successful, you'll have to fight your way out. I'll do my best to rein Jonah in immediately, but in moments of passion and fury, men are often uncontrollable."

A fact I was personally familiar with. But if Jonah was so uncontrollable, what made her think she could control him? Especially once he'd inherited her binding from Jake?

There was something she wasn't saying, and I wouldn't trust Julia Tower even if my *own* marks had been tattooed on her arm.

"This Binder? How far away is he?" I asked as that idea on the horizon came into even clearer focus.

"Less than a mile." She pressed a button on the glass separating us from the driver, then gave him an address. "I'm pleased we could come to an agreement."

Barker turned out to be a grizzly looking man in his mid-sixties who subsisted on nothing but pizza and beer, if the garbage covering his kitchen counters was any evidence.

I was sorely tempted to kill him where he stood, to free Kenley, which would cut Kori's last tie to Tower. But if I killed Barker, Vanessa was as good as dead, and Kenley would never forgive me. Which meant Kori might never forgive me. So I watched in silence as the Binder read aloud from the document Julia had produced from a briefcase taken from the trunk of her car.

The document was short and to the point. It said that I would protect Julia Tower from any threat rising from the demise of her brother until such threat was over. I insisted that Barker add an expiration date—Julia wanted five years, but I whittled her down to two, max—as well as a statement that both Vanessa and Kori would be released from the basement the moment Jake Tower died.

I tried to end their terms of service, too, along with Kenley's—why not shoot for the moon?—but Julia insisted she didn't have the authority to do that. And we both knew she wouldn't have freed them even if she could have.

The phrasing was all very careful, because Julia could not actually ask me to kill her brother or offer to reward me directly for that service.

Julia signed. I signed. Barker stamped the agreement with a bloody thumbprint, symbolizing his own will to seal the deal. And after several tense moments, we agreed to leave the document with him, because neither of us was willing to trust the other with it. Then we got back in the car and rolled steadily toward Jake Tower's fortress of a home, while I tried to think about exactly how I wanted to end his life instead of how dirty I felt, like I'd just signed over a piece of my own soul.

Thirty-One

Kori

"**L**et me the hell out of here or I'm going to rip your head off and finger paint with your fucking gray matter!" I shouted, roughly the twentieth variation of the same threat. Plausibility and creativity had expired about six versions earlier.

"That's gonna be kinda hard to pull off, with you in there and me out here," Jonah called back over the intercom, and I pounded on the glass again.

"Then come face me like a man!" My demands were useless—the glass pounding even more so—but I was alive with rage that had no outlet. My fists *itched* for Jonah's face. I was finally free to fight, but couldn't reach the target.

"Honey, if I go in there, only one of us is coming back out," Jonah said.

"That's the general idea!"

Silence answered me, and my rage burned on, unspent. I whirled around and scanned the cell for something to throw. Something to break. But there was nothing. I couldn't even tell if this was the same room I'd occupied before, or just a neighboring look-alike.

Either way, there was nothing that wasn't bolted to the floor, except for the worthless two-inch-thick mattress and… My gaze hovered over the toilet, one of the few differences between Jake's homemade prison and a real one. This toilet was commercial, not detentional. The tank had a lid. A heavy, porcelain lid.

Someone was going to get his ass reamed for overlooking that security risk.

I picked up the tank lid and hefted it, getting used to the weight. If it would kill a Hollywood zombie, it would kill an actual asshole.

"You're scared, aren't you?" I demanded, stalking closer to the glass, my porcelain weapon hanging at my right side. "You're scared to face me, now that I'm armed and free—" I bit off my own words in a sudden belated spasm of common sense. They didn't know I was unbound, and telling Jonah would mean giving up my only advantage.

"Now that I'm free to fight back," I finished instead. Because Jake hadn't ordered me not to, this time. "Does your brother know what a sniveling coward you are?" I pounded the glass with one fist. "Is there anyone else out there? Can you guys actually *see* Jonah's balls shrivel up and retreat indoors, or are they so small to begin with that you can't tell any difference?"

"Keep talking, Kori," Jonah said over the intercom, fury riding his voice like light rides a bolt of lightning. "Every word you say buys you a little more pain." But beneath his worthless threats, I heard what I really wanted to hear. Laughter. He wasn't alone, and the other men were laughing at him. Helping me taunt him into disobeying orders, at least long enough to open the door to my cell.

I glared at the one-way glass, pissed off that my reflection was all I could see. "A *little* pain, huh? If memory serves, a little's about all you have to offer."

I couldn't hear the laughter that followed from the peanut gallery, but I could practically feel it.

"You know you're in there because of your own stupidity, right?" Jonah said over the staticky intercom, obviously trying to claim the verbal upper hand. "You walked right into a trap."

Unfortunately I couldn't argue with that. But...

"It wasn't your trap, though, was it? Leaving me in the dark last time wasn't your idea, either, right? Was it Jake? No, it was Julia, wasn't it? The ideas come from Julia. The orders come from Jake. But what good are *you,* Jonah? What do you contribute to the Tower team effort?" I paused to give him time to answer, but I wasn't the least bit surprised when he didn't.

"Nothing. That's what you contribute," I shouted. "They could give your job to a fucking monkey and the result would be the same. How does it feel to know you contribute *nothing?*"

The intercom buzzed with static for a moment before he spoke. "It's not going to work. I'm not coming in there."

"Because you're a fucking coward!" My vision started to darken with fury and I swung the tank lid without thinking, smashing it against the glass. The glass cracked but held. The porcelain shattered into several large chunks and a zillion tiny slivers of white glass.

Shit! My fearsome bludgeoning weapon had been reduced to half a dozen mediocre stabbing weapons. Still, any one of them was sharp enough to open a vein if wielded with enough enthusiasm. But to even have a shot at Jonah, I'd have to get him in the room.

"Are you gonna cower and quake out there with your guns and knives because you're scared of one unarmed woman? Did Jake actually *say* you couldn't come in, or are you using your binding as an excuse to cower out there in the hall? We all know you bend the rules when you want to. You thread the loopholes like a seamstress threads a fucking needle. Don't tell me you don't!"

In another fit of fury, I reared back and kicked the glass, but it didn't budge. The crack didn't even widen. So I kicked it again. And again. And finally the crack started to spread, and a jolt of triumph burned the length of my spine.

Then the door opened.

Jonah stood in the doorway, one hand on the butt of his gun, like the idiot deputy from any old spaghetti Western. His jaw was clenched in fury and his eyes were narrowed in rage. "Are you trying to make me kill you? Because you know death is the only way out of here."

I squatted without taking my focus from him and felt around on the ground for a large chunk of broken toilet tank lid, desperately wishing I had something to wrap it with, to keep it from cutting my hand. The last thing I wanted was to leave a sample of my blood behind— Jonah had taken my pocket-size bleach bottle along with my weapons.

"You're bigger and better armed," I said, hoping the men in the hall could hear. "But I'd lay money on me to win, any day of the week."

"Arrogant little *bitch!*" But he didn't move. And that's

when I realized he actually *did* have orders not to touch me. Or at least not to shoot me.

Jake still needed me, no matter what he'd said about me being obsolete. He needed me to draw Ian and Kenley back into the fold.

I couldn't let that happen.

I clutched the three-inch splinter of porcelain and curled my other hand into a fist. I could kill Jonah caveman style, but I'd need his gun—and a lot of luck—to take out whoever was watching from the hall.

But before I could rush him, Jonah pulled the handheld radio from his belt clip and pressed a button. "Go ahead," he said, and I froze when Jake's voice invaded the cell, staticky, but perfectly audible.

"Why do you do this to yourself, Korinne?" he asked. But he didn't wait for my answer, and Jonah didn't let go of the button, which would have let him hear me. "You know the drill. Don't fight back. And don't touch the damn glass."

For a moment, the old terror washed over me, and it actually took me a moment to remember that I didn't have to obey Jake. His orders were worth less than the breath it took to say them, forgotten before the last syllable even faded from my ears.

Jake held no power over me. But my initial thoughtless fear probably saved my life. If I hadn't looked scared, Jonah would have realized something was wrong, and my advantage would have faded into nothing, like Jake's worthless order.

"Thanks," Jonah said into the radio, teeth clenched in resentment. He hated needing his brother's help.

"Move her to another cell and this time don't leave the fucking toilet tank lid. Mess this up again, and you'll be in the cell next to her, where you'll have plenty of time to think about the fact that you can't control one small woman without needing her muzzled first."

Jonah seethed and clipped the radio to his belt again without answering. I waited. Watching him. Trying to remember how I'd looked and acted when I was actually scared of him. The memories were there, but they were disjointed and clouded by fear.

"Let's go." Jonah stalked toward me, even angrier than usual because of what I'd just overheard.

"Don't touch me." I backed up until my spine hit the wall, then slid the hand clutching the shard of porcelain behind my thigh, even as I scooted to the left, avoiding his reach like I had no better options.

Jonah grabbed my arm and a slimy smile appeared at the corner of his mouth—an instant mood-lift in response to my fake fear. He hauled me across the cell and I let him, biding my time.

When he got close to the door, I began to drag my feet, resisting, but not truly fighting back. Jonah jerked me forward and pulled the door open with his free hand.

I sucked in a deep breath and swung my right arm as a primal screech of rage erupted from my throat. His eyes widened, but I buried the three-inch chunk of white porcelain in his jugular before he could make a single sound. "There's a reason I was his bodyguard and you were his lapdog," I said as his mouth opened and closed, gasping uselessly.

Blood dribbled between my fingers, most of it his. He gurgled and grasped at my fingers, but he was already weak from massive blood loss.

"Don't fight back," I whispered, throwing Jake's words at him as I pulled the glass free and stabbed him again, and when he slid to the floor, propping the door open with his weight, I knelt with him. "Beg me to stop." I didn't realize I was crying until the first tears dripped onto his shirt. "Does it hurt? Tell me how much it hurts."

He blinked up at me, his eyelids sluggish, and then he stopped breathing. He just *stopped,* and my tears fell faster.

Finally, it was over.

Distantly, I heard men shouting my name, rounds being chambered, safety switches clicking off.

I hunched over Jonah's body, my back to the other men, crying tears of joy and relief they no doubt mistook for some weaker, more primal emotion. And while they watched me sob, waiting for me to stand and face the inevitable consequences of my actions, I pulled Jonah's gun from his holster and checked the chamber, then flicked off the safety. Then I stood, the pistol hidden by my own body. I turned slowly, sliding the weapon behind my thigh, and counted the men aiming guns at me while I sniffled, displaying my trauma.

There were only three.

"Kori, we need you to turn around and put your hands behind your head," the guy in the middle said. Roscher. I'd known him since he signed on two years ago, but now he was talking to me like I was a child. Or insane. They thought I'd lost it.

I could work with that.

"He was right," I said, letting my voice go light and shaky as I stepped forward. "Death was the only way out."

"Stay there," Roscher said, as they all three aimed at my chest. "Turn around and show us your hands."

"My hands?" I stepped into the hall and took a moment to be grateful they were all on my right. As was the exit. No one could sneak up behind me. "You want to see my hands?" I held up my left hand, red and slick with Jonah's blood. "See?"

When they all glanced at my bloodstained hand, I dropped into a squat and swung Jonah's gun up, firing twice in rapid succession. Roscher and the man to his left stumbled back, hit, their bullets whizzing over my head.

"Drop it!" The third man called, aiming at my head, no doubt picturing how grateful Jake would be when he'd caged me where his coworkers failed.

His mistake.

I fired again, and a hole appeared in his shirt, right over his heart. He was dead before he hit the ground, and his bullet shattered the glass I'd already cracked.

I felt bad about killing them. But not too bad. They would have locked me back up. They would have helped Jake use me to get to Ian and Kenley. They would have let more bad things happen to Vanessa. And if our positions had been reversed, they would have killed me in a heartbeat.

Pulse racing, I snatched the key ring from Jonah's belt and checked the other basement cells one by one until I found Vanessa, huddled in the corner on her bed in her underwear, holding one arm out from her body, because of the series of bright red cuts marching up her forearm in neat, bloody rows. She had a black eye and bruises on both legs. But she looked intact.

Van burst into tears the moment she saw me.

"Are you okay?" I asked as she crawled to the edge of the bloodstained mattress.

She nodded, in spite of obvious pain. "Are you alone?"

"Not anymore. Cover your ears." She put both hands

over her ears and I shot into the ceiling, using bullets four through six from Jonah's full clip to shatter at least three of the infrared bulbs. Then I helped her off the bed and leaned outside the door to flip the switch controlling the regular lights. Her cell fell into shallow darkness, and I felt my way into the only patch of true dark, beneath the hole in the infrared grid. There was only room for a single step.

I closed my eyes, took a deep breath, and squeezed her hand. Vanessa stepped into the deeper darkness with me and out into the bathroom in Olivia's office.

Someone yelped, startled, and I opened my eyes to find myself staring at my brother, Kris, who'd been about to step into the bathroom. I hadn't seen him in nearly two years, but nothing had changed except for his hair, which he now wore in short, dark blond waves. "Kris!" I dropped Vanessa's hand and threw my arms around my brother.

He hugged me back, so tight I could hardly breathe. Then he let go and held me at arm's length. "Why are you covered in blood every time I see you?"

"Be fuckin' grateful it's someone else's," I said, smiling in spite of the grim circumstances of our reunion.

"Still got that dirty mouth," a gruff, shaky voice said, and I looked over Kris's shoulder to find my grandmother frowning at me in gray slacks and a cardigan over a white blouse.

"I learned every four-letter word I know from you, Gran," I said, and couldn't resist a smile, even as I leaned closer to whisper into Kris's ear. "Why the hell did you bring her here?"

"She thinks it's 2004. Where was I supposed to leave

her?" he asked, and I shrugged, conceding the point, then tugged him away from our grandmother.

"Have you talked to Kenley?" I asked, sinking onto Olivia's office couch as Van followed my grandmother into the office.

"Yeah." Kris sat next to me while Olivia handed Van a spare set of clothes. "She's in a lot of pain, and that Meghan woman's about out of juice."

"Okay, Ian wasn't in the basement when I was there, so I'm going back for him—"

"Who's Ian?" Kris asked before I could finish my sentence.

"He's...complicated. But he saved Kenley's life and he helped her break my binding to Jake, so I'm not going to leave him there."

"Okay. What can I do?"

"Um...get me George Barker, Tower's other Binder. He's the one who sealed Kenley's oath. We'll give him a chance to unseal it voluntarily and save his own life. If he won't...there's always plan B."

"The B stands for bullet?" Kris said, grinning.

"What else. I'm going to take Gran and Vanessa to Kenley, then I'm heading back to Jake's, through the hole I punched in his infrared grid in the basement."

"How much security does Barker have?" Liv asked, perching on the edge of her own desk while across the room my grandmother was interrogating Vanessa under the misguided assumption that she was Kris's new girlfriend.

"Probably more than usual, now that Kenley's MIA. Kris could use another gun if you're interested." But I wouldn't ask her. I wouldn't force her to help me, when I could very well be leading us both to our deaths.

Olivia shrugged and grabbed a loaded extra clip from her top desk drawer. "I have nothing better to do at the moment, and since I have yet to replace my phone, I don't anticipate any orders getting in the way."

"Thanks, Liv."

Kris glanced back and forth between us. "Aren't you two on opposite sides of the turf war?"

Olivia shrugged. "With friends like Kori, who needs enemies?"

"Ain't that the fuckin' truth!" Gran called from across the room, and Vanessa burst into teary laughter.

"Okay, I have my phone. Let me know how it goes with Barker," I said to Liv and my brother as I ushered Gran and Vanessa into the darkened bathroom.

Kris nodded and closed the door behind us as I took one of their hands in each of mine. Two steps later, we emerged in Meghan's bathroom. "Nobody shoot, we come in peace!" I shouted, and Aaron stepped into sight in the hall, still clutching the broken arm he obviously hadn't yet sought treatment for.

"Well, you can just step right back into that shadow and take your sister with you. If Tower tracks her here, we're all as good as dead."

"I'll be back for her as soon as I can. For now, I need you to watch a couple of valuables for me while I go storm the castle."

"No. No more women with prices on their heads…" Aaron started, shaking his head firmly, but his sister shouted over him from the bedroom.

"Bring them in here!"

I led Vanessa and Gran toward Meghan's voice. Kenley struggled up from her chair in spite of obvious pain the moment she saw Van.

"This isn't Europe," Gran said as Kenni and Vanessa embraced. "You don't have to kiss everyone you meet on the mouth, Kenley."

I would have laughed, if I weren't so close to tears.

"This is *not* a home for wayward women!" Aaron insisted.

"They'll be out of your hair soon," I said as Meghan gently began to examine Vanessa's butchered arm. She obviously didn't have the strength to heal three people at once—which explained Aaron's persistent fracture—but most Healers knew more than a little about first aid, to supplement their natural Skills.

I took a deep breath, double-checked the gun I'd taken from Jonah, then marched back into Meghan's bathroom, then into Jake's basement through the hole I'd blown in the infrared grid. Vanessa's cell was still dark, so I peeked into the hall cautiously. The bodies were all still there. Nothing had changed. I'd been gone less than ten minutes.

I spared a moment to grab extra guns from the downed men. Two went into my holsters and a third stayed in my hand, while I shoved their extra clips into my pockets. I'd never actually made an action-movie-style assault on a heavily guarded modern fortress, but I was pretty sure Hollywood was dead-on with at least two of the typical clichés: bullets would fly and blood would flow.

Properly armed, I walked right by the elevator—installed for easy transport of prisoners—and took the stairs instead. I didn't want to be surprised by a room full of men aiming guns at me as soon as the doors slid open.

At the top of the stairs, I opened the door just wide

enough to peek out. The foyer was empty, except for the usual guards, one at the foot of either staircase. No one in the basement had lived long enough to sound the alarm, but they'd be found as soon as Jake discovered he couldn't raise Jonah on his radio. If not sooner.

I pushed the door open and stepped into an alcove off the foyer, my heart thumping painfully with each step. I glanced toward Jake's office just as Julia pushed the door open and stepped out. A second later, movement from across the foyer caught my eye. Two armed men were getting on the elevator.

Shit. The elevator only went to the basement, and they would sound the alarm the minute they saw the bodies.

I turned back to Julia as she rounded the corner into the back hall, without noticing me—a blessing that would die with the first screech of the security siren. Then I stepped into the foyer.

"Hey!" the guard at the closest staircase shouted, drawing his gun, and I shot a hole through his left shoulder. He stumbled back onto the stairs as I shot his counterpart from across the room. But my silencer turned out to be pointless, because no sooner had the second guard fallen than the brain-skewering screech of the security alarm started wailing from everywhere.

Time was up.

Thirty-Two

Ian

"**W**on't this look suspicious?" I whispered as Julia led me up the steps and into Jake Tower's house, and I couldn't help remembering the first time I'd walked that very path, only two days earlier. How could everything have fallen apart in such a short time?

"No, it'll look like I've done my job," Julia said, her steps bold and confident. "Jake sent me to pick you up, and that's what I've done."

"I don't suppose you can sneak me in with a gun?"

She glanced at me in disdain, and I bristled even before she spoke. "You're going to have to contribute *something* to this effort on your own."

"You mean, other than pulling the trigger?"

"I mean finding a trigger to pull." She opened the front door and marched inside like she owned the place. Like we hadn't just been plotting the assassination of her brother, leash holder and the man who signed her paychecks. "I'll take you into the office," she whispered as we crossed the foyer, accompanied by the click of her heels on the marble. "But then I'll have to go. If I'm there when you make your move, I'll be obligated to stop you."

I nodded, my hands steady, my spine steeled. With one shot, the man who'd sentenced Kori to six weeks of a living hell would be dead. Then I'd make my way to the basement and kill the man who'd delivered that hell, and both Kori and her sister would be free for good.

No doubt easier said than done, but never had a challenge promised a better reward.

"Wait here for a minute," Julia said, and while she crossed the foyer for a private word with the guards at the stairs, I pulled my phone from my pocket and texted like a madman. I hit Send as she turned back to me and motioned for me to follow her.

Julia threw open the door to Jake's office and marched inside, then held the door for me. "Out," she said to the two extra men in the room, one standing guard at Jake's back, the other seated in a chair in front of his desk. "Mr. Holt has come to negotiate his contract."

Tower didn't even stand. "My men are sworn to secrecy on private matters," he said. "Anything you say will stay in this room."

"But they won't," I insisted. "Or this negotiation is over."

Jake's left brow rose. "You'd walk out over a little compromised privacy?"

"I'd walk out over too little ice in my whiskey." I turned to Julia. "Four cubes."

She scowled, but made no complaint. I'd given her the excuse she needed to leave the room.

Tower looked more amused than truly threatened, but he waved the men out of the room. "Go check on Kori Daniels. She was giving Jonah fits a few minutes ago."

I tried not to laugh, hoping whatever fits she'd given Jonah hadn't resulted in any more bruises for her.

"Can I get you anything?" Julia asked her brother, one hand on the door as the men crossed the foyer toward the elevator behind her.

"Call Barker and find out where that Intent to Sign document is. I want Mr. Holt bound by Kenley Daniels, but Barker will do for the preliminary document."

Julia nodded and stepped out of the room.

"Oh, and, Lia, pay a visit to Kori and explain exactly what will happen to her if she doesn't give up her sister. Quickly."

Julia nodded again and disappeared into the foyer.

"Nothing will happen to her," I said, sinking into one of two chairs in front of Tower's desk.

"What?"

"Nothing will happen to Kori," I repeated. "I want that written into the contract. You will release her and swear that she will have no further contact with you or anyone in your organization. Ever. When I have that written and sealed, I will sign."

"No deal." Jake stood and rounded his desk to sit on one corner of it, and his jacket parted to reveal the gun at his hip. If I could get it, this would all be over.

"You don't need her," I said, waiting for opportunity to knock. Negotiation was pointless, since I wasn't going to sign. "You've already got me here, and your Trackers can find her sister without Kori's help. Assuming Kenley can stand the resistance pain long enough to get out of the city. Kori's useless to you."

"Korinne is a living object lesson, Mr. Holt. My people know what she did, and if I don't make sure she lives and breathes pain until the instant she dies, someone else will think they can get away with what she did. And I can't let that happen."

I shrugged. "So tell them she's dead."

Tower folded his arms over his chest. "They need to see her die."

"I think *you* need to see her die. But I swear on my own life that if you kill her, you will never have my service."

Tower watched me carefully. Thinking. Hopefully weighing his options. While I bided my time. My moment hadn't yet come.

"Why Kori?" he asked at last, studying my face like he couldn't quite make sense of it. "I'm afraid I don't see the attraction."

"That's because you are threatened by her strength, while I am bolstered by it. But you don't have to understand that," I said, pleased to hear that my voice sounded much calmer than the rest of me felt. "You just have to let one of us go. Which do you want more, my service or her death?"

Tower's eyes narrowed, and his jaw clenched in anger—a first from him, at least that I'd seen. But before he could answer, a screeching siren echoed from all over, visibly startling us both.

Tower stood, eyes wide. "Security breach!" he shouted into the radio he'd grabbed from his desktop. And suddenly I realized what had happened. Kori was free. Everyone would be gunning for her.

My time had come.

"Lock the door," Tower said, reaching for the phone on his desk—no doubt an internal, secure line.

I lunged for his gun instead. Tower fought me and the gun went off in its holster.

He screamed and blood ran down his leg. Tower slapped one hand over the wound and I took the gun.

I backed up, aiming at him, and Tower leaned over his desk, fumbling for the top drawer. I fired before he could get it open, and blood poured from the new hole in his chest.

"No!" Kori shouted behind me, and I spun to see her standing in the doorway, gun drawn. Kori raced around me and pressed her free hand to the wound in Tower's chest. Blood ran between her fingers, but she was already covered in blood anyway, though I couldn't find any wounds, at a glance. "No, don't die!"

She turned to me, still trying to stop the bleeding, and the siren stopped screeching as suddenly as it had begun. But it rang on in my head. "I told you not to kill him!" Kori shouted, like she could still hear the ringing, too, as footsteps pounded toward us from the foyer. "He has an heir clause!"

"Yes, he does," a new voice said, and I turned to find Julia in the doorway, two large men at her back. "Or rather, he *did*." She glanced pointedly at her brother and I followed her gaze to find Jake's eyes open and staring blankly at some point near the top of the wall. "Call the police and report a break-in," she ordered, and the men stepped past her. "Speak to our man in Homicide. He'll take care of the details."

The first guard brushed Kori aside, and she sank onto her knees next to the wall, defeat dulling her eyes as one man picked up Tower's desk phone and began dialing.

"Don't fret, Korinne," Julia said. "The evil king is dead, thanks to your loyal lover." She spread her arms and gave me a broad smile. "Long live the queen." She stepped closer and ran one hand up my arm, practically purring. "Jonah was never Jake's heir." She trailed her fingers over my shoulder and across my chest, and the movement became bold as she watched my face for shock, or anger, or whatever she'd expected me to feel in the face of her betrayal.

"I know," I said, and her hand fell away. Her eyes narrowed, then her jaw clenched as she read the truth in my statement. "Jonah's a sadistic monster, but not overburdened by brains. Jake wasn't stupid enough to leave his kingdom in reckless hands, and *you're* not stupid enough to think you could control Jonah—unless he was bound to you."

"None of that matters now," Kori said, standing, still stunned by Jake's death, and still holding her gun. "Jonah died voiceless, in a pool of his own blood. In the basement. I'd call that irony, except it seems so fucking fitting."

Julia's eyes narrowed further, and her fists clenched at her sides.

"What do you want us to do with her?" The remaining guard asked, aiming at Kori even as Kori took careful aim at Julia. And behind her, I caught a blur of motion and a brief glimpse of a welcome, familiar face in the foyer.

"Nothing. You are free," Julia said to Kori. "I suggest you go out the way you came in, now, before the police arrive and start to draw the inaccurate conclusions I have every intention of fostering."

"Sure." She chambered a round in her gun and shifted her aim up to Julia's head. "Right after I send you after your brothers."

The sudden bolt of pain in my head was almost enough to paralyze me, but I'd been expecting it. "I can't let you shoot her." I stepped between Kori and Julia, whom I'd sworn to defend.

"Ian?" Kori stared at me, confused. Heartbroken.

"Ian is my new bodyguard." Julia ran one hand lightly over my shoulder from behind, and I hated her touch almost as much as I hated the pain and betrayal shining in Kori's eyes. "My own personal bringer of the night. You'll have to kill him to get to me. And I don't think you want to do that, do you, Korinne? In fact, I don't think you want anyone else to do that, either, do you?"

Kori lowered her gun, but didn't holster it. "What did you *do?*" she whispered, her eyes alive with pain.

"I did what I had to do. I can't let you hurt her. But you're more than welcome to hurt *him*."

"What?" Julia demanded as I turned, and she spun to follow my gaze. Olivia Warren and a tall blond man stepped into sight in the foyer, with Barker between them, still wearing the grease-stained shirt he'd worn an hour earlier.

"Ian?" Kris said, and I nodded. "Kenley gave me your message. Here's what you asked for." He pushed Barker forward a single step, without letting go of the Binder.

Julia's men raised their guns, but Kris and Olivia were faster, even with each holding one of Barker's arms. Their silencers *thwupped,* and Julia's men fell, their guns unfired.

Julia gasped, then she opened her mouth to shout for more help.

"Don't." Olivia aimed at her head. I pulled Julia out of reach of both Kori and Olivia—I had no other choice.

"Break Kenley's and Ian's bindings, and I'll let you live," Kori said, aiming her gun at Barker now.

"If you even think about it, I'll have your tongue cut

out and shoved down your throat so that you drown in your own blood," Julia spat.

Barker stared at her, terrified and confused.

Kori shrugged. "At least my way's quicker and less painful. I'm sorry." She aimed, and her gun *thwupped* once. A neat hole appeared in Barker's head, and he fell over backward in the middle of the foyer.

Kris and Olivia both stepped away from him as Kori took aim at Julia. And this time, I let her. Because I could.

"I'm unarmed," Julia said, her tone reasonable, her fear almost hidden by steady hands and a firm jaw.

"You'll never be unarmed as long as there's a tongue in your mouth and a brain in your head," Kori spat. "It was your idea to turn the lights off wasn't it? In the basement. It was your idea to let me rot in the dark."

"Jake wanted to kill you," she said, arms held out, displaying her defenselessness. "I saved your life."

"Because you wanted me to suffer."

Julia couldn't argue with that.

"Don't worry," Kori said as the first police sirens wailed in the distance. "I want you to suffer, too. Everyone's gonna know you betrayed the king of the castle. And Kenley's going to take away your loyal subjects, one at a time."

Across the foyer, a door opened, and armed men came running toward us. Kris and Olivia ducked into Jake's office, but Kori didn't seem to notice. She moved closer to Julia with every word, threatening the new queen with her very presence. "And when you fall from the throne, and the castle comes crumbling down on you, I want you to remember who pulled down the first stone."

Kori holstered her gun as I began to gather shadows

from the corners of Jake's office. Julia backed slowly away. Kori smiled. Then she kicked Julia square in the chest.

Julia flew backward into the foyer with an *oof* of stolen breath. She landed hard on her ass, her mouth open, her legs sprawled in front of her.

Kori slammed the office door shut as the first bullets whizzed toward us, over Julia's head. Glass shattered, and we all ducked. Kori grabbed my hand while Kris took Olivia's. I pulled the shadows up and around us, and Kori exhaled, her hand warm in mine. I could feel her smile, even if I couldn't see it.

Then she pulled me forward, and we stepped out of Tower's hell and into the rest of our lives. Which looked suspiciously like Meghan's bathroom.

Kris and Liv tripped over one another in their haste to check on the others, but I pulled Kori back before she could go. Then I kicked the door closed and pulled her closer, wrapping the shadows around us again. "You're free," I whispered, running my hands over her back, while hers slid beneath my shirt. "So what do you want to do now?"

She kissed me, then her lips trailed over my chin toward my ear. "Now?" she whispered, and chills shot up my spine. "Nothing. Everything. Isn't that the whole point? From now on, we can do whatever the hell we want."

* * * * *

Acknowledgments

Thanks, as always, to my critique partner, Rinda Elliott, the first to read everything I write. Thanks most of all for your willingness to tell me when I suck. The truth is greatly appreciated.

Thanks to #1, my husband, for endless patience. This book and the subsequent revisions took up a crazy three and a half months of our lives and I may not have been the most pleasant person during that time.

A huge thank-you to the MIRA Art department for the *SHADOW BOUND* cover art. The models are perfect. The colors are beautiful. The tone is dead-on. I love it.

And, of course, thanks to all the readers willing to give this dark and twisted world a chance. I promise, there is a light at the end of the tunnel....

Jennifer d
Das Leben

atb aufbau taschenbuch

Jennifer duBois, 1983 in Northampton, Massachusetts, geboren, hat Politik und Philosophie studiert und ihren Abschluss als Stipendiatin am Iowa Writers' Workshop erworben. Die Stanford University, wo sie heute unterrichtet, hat sie mit dem Stegner Fellowship ausgezeichnet. »Das Leben ist groß« ist ihr erster Roman. 2012 wurde sie von der National Book Award Foundation als eine der fünf besten Nachwuchsautorinnen geehrt.

Leningrad in den frühen 80er Jahren: Das Schachwunderkind Alexander Besetow gibt seine Ideale zugunsten des Luxus auf, den die Kommunisten ihm bieten. Cambridge, Massachusetts im Jahr 2006: Bei der jungen Dozentin Irina Ellison wird Chorea Huntington diagnostiziert – eine Krankheit, die schon ihrem Vater den Verstand geraubt hat. Vor seinem Tod hat er dem Schachweltmeister Alexander Besetow eine alles entscheidende Frage gestellt: Wie kann man weitermachen, wenn die Niederlage nicht abwendbar ist? Um die Antwort zu erhalten, reist Irina zu Alexander. Dieser hat sich ebenfalls einer aussichtslosen Sache verschrieben: Er tritt bei den Wahlen gegen den russischen Präsidenten an. Irina unterstützt ihn dabei und sucht mit ihm die lebenswichtige Antwort auf die Frage: Wie weiterleben, wenn die Niederlage unausweichlich ist?

Jennifer duBois

DAS LEBEN IST GROSS

Roman

Aus dem Amerikanischen
von Gesine Schröder

atb aufbau taschenbuch

Die Originalausgabe unter dem Titel
A Partial History of Lost Causes
erschien 2012 bei The Dial Press, New York.

ISBN 978-3-7466-3058-8

Aufbau Taschenbuch ist eine Marke der Aufbau Verlag GmbH & Co. KG

1. Auflage 2014
© Aufbau Verlag GmbH & Co. KG, Berlin 2014
Copyright © 2012 by Jennifer duBois
Die deutsche Erstausgabe erschien 2013 bei Aufbau,
einer Marke der Aufbau Verlag GmbH & Co. KG
Umschlaggestaltung Originalcover hißmann, heilmann, hamburg
unter Verwendung eines Motives von Millennium images/LOOK-foto
graphische Adaption capa Design, Anke Fesel
Satz LVD GmbH, Berlin
Druck und Binden CPI – Clausen & Bosse, Leck
Printed in Germany

www.aufbau-verlag.de

Für Richard duBois, der sein Leben zu lieben wusste,
und für Carolyn duBois, die ihres zu leben weiß.

»Wir alle sind verdammt, aber einige sind verdammter als andere.«

Vladimir Nabokov, *Ada oder Das Verlangen*

»Und wenn ich in dieser weiten Welt einst sterbe, dann sterbe ich vor Freude, am Leben zu sein.«

Jewgeni Jewtuschenko

TEIL EINS

KAPITEL 1

Alexander
Leningrad, Sowjetunion, 1979

Als Alexander endlich in Leningrad ankam, beeindruckte ihn am meisten die große graue Masse der Newa. Der Fluss war ein pulsierendes Organ der Stadt – nicht ihr Herz, dachte er, sondern etwas Zweckmäßigeres, weniger Sensibles und doch Lebenswichtiges. Der Mandelkern vielleicht oder die Nieren. Seit der Abreise aus Ocha war er sechs Tage unterwegs, zu Wasser und dann mit dem Zug, und hatte vor den Fenstern das ganze Land vorüberziehen sehen: erst die schwankenden Fördertürme auf Sachalin, die er kannte wie seine eigenen Träume, dann, am Hafen, den verlassenen grünen Zug, der seit dem Krieg gegen Japan allmählich im Sand versank, dann die zehntausend Lachse, die an der Ostküste in der Sonne faulten und auf das Telegramm mit der Verladegenehmigung aus Moskau warteten, und die gekräuselten Rauchsäulen über den unglaublich weit auseinanderliegenden Dörfern (er hatte nicht einmal geahnt, in was für einem unfassbar großen Land er aufgewachsen war). Er hatte umgewidmete Kathedralen gesehen, Bergleute, deren Gesichter schwarz und hart wie Kohle waren, endlose Ebenen aus verkümmertem Gras unter einem ausgebleichten Himmel. Als der Zug in den Moskowski Woksal einfuhr, hatte er mehr als genug gesehen, fand er. Dabei hätte er dankbar sein sollen. Die Reise nach Leningrad hatte monatelange bürokratische Taktiererei erfordert – beantragte, unterschriebene, verlorengegangene Dokumente, erste und zweite Anläufe und Bestechungsversuche von Andronow, der Alexander an der Akademie unterrichten sollte. Eines Tages war sein Einreisevisum plötzlich da gewesen, so unerwartet wie ein Schneesturm im Juni, wie Frösche, die vom Himmel regnen – und das, dachte er oft, war das Entscheidende: nicht, dass nichts funktionierte, sondern dass man nie, nie wissen konnte, was funktionieren würde und was nicht.

Und auf dem Bahnsteig, beim Kreischen der Bremsen, inmitten der scheidenden Paare, im Dunst von Talg und Zigaretten, Bratfett und stechendem Parfüm, hätte er fast die Nerven verloren. Fast hätte er sein Gepäck auf die Schienen fallenlassen, wäre wieder eingestiegen und den ganzen Weg zur Pazifikküste zurückgefahren, obwohl sein einziges Schachbrett im Rucksack war und sein Bestechungsgeld fast aufgebraucht. Kurz bevor der Zug hielt, hatte sein Sitznachbar dem ganzen Waggon mitgeteilt, dass heute Stalins hundertster Geburtstag war. Alle hatten rasch den Blick abgewandt. Doch hier war der Beweis: Die Sinopskaja Nabereschnaja war voller Polizisten, deren Uniformen in der grauenhaft weißen Sonne rot und golden glänzten. Sie waren da, um sicherzustellen, dass niemand vorlaut oder übermütig wurde.

»Papiere?« Hinter ihm stand ein Polizist, dem anzuhören war, dass Alexander ihm schon jetzt den Tag verdorben hatte. Als Alexander die Hand hob, um die Sonne abzuschirmen, rieselten ihm Rußkörnchen aus den Augenbrauen. Über eine der gewaltigen Schultern des Polizisten erhaschte er Blicke auf die grüngraue Newa. Ihr starker Arm, dachte er, hielt die Stadt im Schwitzkasten oder stützte sie wie eine osteoporotische Wirbelsäule.

»Papiere!«, sagte der Polizist noch einmal. Der Kinnriemen grub sich in seinen fetten Hals, und seine goldene Kokarde blitzte. Alexander durchwühlte seinen Rucksack. Als er seine Reisepapiere fand, begutachtete der Polizist sie verdrießlich und klopfte sich mit dem Schlagstock an den Oberschenkel.

»Sachalin?«, sagte er. »Wohl in den falschen Zug gestiegen?«

Und Alexander dachte: Ja, das könnte schon sein.

»Und? Auf den Mund gefallen, was? Na, egal. Weitergehen. Sie wissen ja wohl, welcher Tag heute ist.«

Ja, das wusste Alexander. Und auch was die Newa anging, kam

er jetzt zu einer Entscheidung: Sie war das Gehirn. Nicht der Teil des Gehirns, der sich Sonette oder eindrucksvolle Schachzüge ausdenkt; nicht der Teil, der schmachtende Seufzer ausstößt, Solschenizyn liest und nach der tieferen Bedeutung fragt. Sie war der Teil, der fickt, der flieht, der überlebt, auch wenn das Gewissen dagegen spricht.

Jahre später, als Alexander das Schachbrett gegen die politische Bühne eingetauscht hatte, sollte die Stadt sich vollkommen verändern. Gelangweilte Frauen ohne Augenbrauen standen, in türkische Seide gehüllt, vor den Nachtklubs Schlange und kippten lachend wahnwitzig teuren Wodka in den Schnee. Gewaltige Werbetafeln und Neonreklamen stempelten den Abendhimmel mit mehr oder weniger erreichbaren Träumen, Meinungen und Lebensentwürfen. Aus Leningrad wurde Sankt Petersburg, und aus Sankt Petersburg wurde ein Umschlagplatz für große Mengen Geld – Frauen und Geschäfte warteten an jeder Ecke darauf, erobert zu werden. Irgendwann wurde auch Schach zu etwas anderem, als Alexander Weltmeister war und man so oft sein Genie in den Himmel lobte, dass es ihn zu ermüden begann. So musste es jemandem mit einem ungewöhnlichen körperlichen Merkmal gehen, mit bezaubernd verschiedenfarbigen Augen oder unglaublich roten Haaren: Irgendwann sind die ständigen Komplimente für etwas derart Zufälliges nur noch eine Last. Das Schachspiel gehörte zu Alexander wie seine schlechte Körperhaltung oder sein unauffälliges Gesicht. Und irgendwann wurde es zu einer Demütigung, zu einer Anklage – als er den Titel verloren hatte und seine besseren Momente in Vergessenheit gerieten, während nur der beste, nur die eine Schachpartie im Gedächtnis blieb und ihm überallhin vorauseilte wie das Warnglöckchen eines Aussätzigen. Eine Zeitlang war er sehr gut, und dann war etwas anderes besser.

Doch als er jung war, hatte er sich sein ganzes Leben noch ausmalen können.

Der Weg durch den Bahnhof in den Tag hinaus fühlte sich an,

als hätte man Alexander aus einer Zelle befreit, nur um ihn vor ein Erschießungskommando zu stellen. Er schob sich durch dichte Trauben finster dreinblickender Menschen, um in seine Kommunalka zu kommen, und mehrere Kinder versuchten ihn zu bestehlen, noch bevor er aus dem Gebäude war. Er folgte seiner sorgfältig auswendig gelernten Wegbeschreibung und konzentrierte sich stupide auf seine Ausweispapiere. Es gab atemberaubend viele Menschen hier, und mehr von ihnen, als in ganz Ocha lebten, waren ihm auf die Füße getreten, bis er seine neue Unterkunft erreichte.

Das Gebäude war drei Stockwerke hoch und sah aus der Entfernung aschgrau aus. Im Vorgarten stand ein sehr junger Mann neben einem umgekippten Schrankkoffer im braunen, festgetretenen Schnee. Der Deckel des Koffers klaffte auf wie ein ausgerenkter Kiefer, und sein Inhalt war über den Vorgarten verstreut; offenbar hatte jemand ihn die Treppen hinuntergeworfen. In der Haustür stand eine alte Frau mit grauen Locken in einem roten Hauskleid. So wie sie drohend die Faust schüttelte, musste sie wohl die Verwalterin sein. Aus der Nähe sah Alexander, dass die ehemals vermutlich rote Haustür Risse hatte. Die Fenster darüber waren vernagelt.

»Entschuldigen Sie«, sagte Alexander. »Ich soll heute hier einziehen.«

Die Verwalterin würdigte ihn keines Blickes. »Verschwinde!«, rief sie dem jungen Mann mit dem Koffer zu. »Verschwinde, und komm bloß nie wieder!«

Und Alexander dachte: Vielleicht ist es nicht zu spät.

Die Verwalterin gab Alexander die Schlüssel. In der Küche gab es ein rostiges Waschbecken, das nach Urin stank. Eine ältere Frau im Bademantel, das Haar in einem unwahrscheinlich hohen Handtuchturban, röstete unter den freiliegenden Rohren Brot. Hinter ihr hingen Damenstrumpfhosen in Strähnen von der Decke herab. Auf dem Duschvorhang im Badezimmer hüpften leuchtend grüne Frösche durch einen Morast aus schwarzen Schimmelflecken. Ein Schild im Flur verbot es den Mietern, ihre Unterwäsche aus dem Fenster zu hängen.

In Alexanders Zimmer gab es ein am Boden festgeschraubtes Bett, einen wurmstichigen Schreibtisch und einen urnenförmigen Samowar, den vermutlich sein Vormieter zurückgelassen hatte. An der Decke waren durch den bröckelnden Putz die Holzbalken zu sehen. Durch ein winziges Fenster fielen schmale Lichtstreifen auf das Bett, und Alexander legte sich hinein. Die nackte Matratze berührte klamm seine Haut. Alexander streckte die Beine aus. In Ocha hatte er mit seinen zappelnden kleinen Schwestern im selben Bett geschlafen, die sich nachts hin und her warfen wie Fische auf dem Trockenen.

Er starrte auf den halbmondförmigen Schimmelfleck an der Wand; er spähte durch die Eisblumen auf der Fensterscheibe. Er versuchte einzuschlafen. Am Ende seiner tagelangen Reise hatte er sich so verzweifelt nach Schlaf gesehnt, dass er versucht hatte, in der Zugtoilette einzudösen – windschief über das Loch zu den Schienen gelehnt –, bis jemand schrie, er solle seinen Arsch da raus bewegen, verdammt. Doch hier im Bett fehlte ihm das ozeanische Rumpeln des Zugs. Ihn trieb das ruhelose Gefühl, an einem neuen Ort zu sein, nach einem ganzen Leben an alten Orten. Er hatte noch keine Lust, die Schuhe auszuziehen.

Alexander dachte an die Polizisten am Bahnhof. Er fragte sich, ob irgendwo da draußen wirklich jemand so dumm war zu feiern.

Er kramte den Stadtplan aus seiner Tasche, setzte den Rucksack wieder auf und ging. In der Küche begegnete er einer Frau, die mit einem schmutzigen Spatel Eireste aus einer Pfanne kratzte. Sie blickte Alexander finster an und sagte kein Wort. Draußen hatte sich die Kälte breitgemacht – hatte ihr Revier abgesteckt wie ein Schmerz nach der ersten Schrecksekunde –, und von dieser Kälte und der Erschöpfung nach sechs Tagen Zugreise (davon zwei im Stehen) wurde Alexander schwindelig. Die Gebäude um ihn herum waren nur bis auf Kopfhöhe blau gestrichen, als liefe er durch das Gemälde eines Kindes, das plötzlich die Lust verloren und sich davongemacht hatte. Der Wind nahm zu.

Auf dem Newski-Prospekt war es schön: Die Friese und Säulen

sahen aus wie im Alten Rom, und die Kellerläden, die leuchtend orangefarbenen Schilder, die Lichtspielhäuser wirkten wie der Mittelpunkt eines sehr modernen Universums. Dann entdeckte Alexander die Kundgebung: Ein strahlenbekränztes Bildnis Stalins schwebte über den Köpfen einer Menschenmenge wie ein großväterlicher, schnurrbarttragender Gott. Es waren nicht viele, die dort fröstelnd und verstreut in einem Ring nervös aussehender Polizisten standen. Im Näherkommen entdeckte Alexander Stalins Bild überall: Aus einem Foto starrte Stalin dem Betrachter drohend entgegen; auf einem anderen sah er mit einem wohlwollend strengen Ausdruck in die Ferne. Am Mikrophon leierte ein Mann die Geschichte der Schlacht von Stalingrad herunter. Am Rand der Menge drückten sich ein paar Männer mit schwarz-weiß gestreiften Irokesenkämmen und karierten Hemden herum. Alexander lehnte sich an einen Telefonmast und versuchte zuzuhören. Er war erschöpft, und er hatte das Gefühl, genau hier – in dem letzten blassen Sonnenfleck, im Windschatten der Gebäude, im monotonen Dröhnen militärischer Heldentaten aus den Lautsprechern – könnte er im Stehen einschlafen. Er zog sich die Mütze tief in die Stirn. Die Augen fielen ihm zu. Sein Kopf nickte nach vorn.

»Na, mächtig beeindruckt?« Ein Mann hatte ihn angesprochen. Alexander hob seine Ohrenklappen und blickte auf. Der Mann war lang und dürr; wenn er sich bewegte, sah es aus, als würden seine Gelenke sich aus- und einrenken und schmerzhaft neu zusammenfügen. Er hatte eine Pepsi-Flasche in der Hand und keine Handschuhe an. Neben ihm standen noch zwei Männer. Einer war selbst für Leningrad auffällig blass und hatte kopekenfarbene Augen. Der andere, klein und vernarbt, kritzelte in ein Notizbuch. Sein Mund bewegte sich, als kaute er etwas, doch Alexander glaubte irgendwie nicht daran. Alle drei hatten gestreifte Matrosenhemden an, wattierte Jacken und durchweichte Ohrenklappenmützen. Der Lange trug ein kleines silbernes Medaillon um den Hals.

»Allerdings«, sagte Alexander. »Es ist sehr eindrucksvoll.«

»Dass Koba schon hundert geworden wäre«, sagte der Lange.

Sein Tonfall war trockener als trocken. »Wie schade, dass er nicht mitfeiern kann.«

»Sehr wahr«, sagte Alexander. »Unbestreitbar wahr.«

»Seine Reformmaßnahmen waren den Herausforderungen der Modernisierung wahrhaft angemessen, habe ich recht?«

»Sehr angemessen. Mehr als angemessen.«

»Und dann der Schnurrbart«, sagte der Blasse. »Dieser Schnurrbart war eine ehrfurchtgebietende Leistung, nicht? Koba hatte mehr Haare auf der Oberlippe als andere auf dem ganzen Kopf.«

Alexander drehte sich nach ihm um. Der Mann hatte etwas an sich, dass Alexander ihm nicht gerade ins Gesicht sehen mochte: etwas Verhärmtes unterhalb der Augen, das unangenehme Fragen über das Leben in Leningrad aufwarf. »Ja«, sagte Alexander und starrte unglücklich zu Boden. »Eine eindrucksvolle Errungenschaft.«

Der Lange sah Alexander amüsiert an. Er beugte sich vor und senkte die Stimme. »Wusstest du, dass er eins dreiundsechzig groß war?«, sagte er. »Wirklich. Eins dreiundsechzig, und er hatte einen schlimmen Arm. Auf Fotos wurde das nie gezeigt. Sie haben ihn nie neben jemanden gestellt. Auf Bildern mit anderen Politikern sitzt er immer.«

»Das wusste ich nicht«, sagte Alexander zögernd. »Ich habe immer gedacht, er sei ein Mann von Format gewesen.«

Alexander fragte sich, wie alles so schnell so schiefgegangen war. Er wandte sich dem Kleinen zu, dessen Narben Kampfspuren oder Überbleibsel einer entstellenden Hautkrankheit sein mochten, und streckte ihm die Hand hin. »Guten Tag«, sagte er. »Alexander Kimowitsch Besetow. Bin gerade hierhergezogen.« Er lächelte breit, weil das bei den alten Weibern in Ocha immer gut angekommen war. Die Männer sahen einander an und schienen eine Art kollektive Gesichtsmuskelzuckung zu erleiden. Es war nicht gerade ein Augenverdrehen, doch Alexander hatte das verstörende Gefühl, dass es in etwa dasselbe bedeutete. Er sah die Männer aus zusammengekniffenen Augen an und suchte nach Anzeichen der Gefahr, doch sie wirkten wie alle anderen, die er seit seiner Ankunft getroffen hatte – unausgeschlafen und latent feindselig. Der Lange war dürr, und die anderen beiden wirkten trotz ihrer dicklichen Statur schwächlich und ausgezehrt, als hätten sie zu viel von immer demselben gegessen. Der Kleine hockte sich auf den Boden, so dass seine wieselartig gerundeten Hüften sichtbar wurden.

»Iwan Dimitrijewitsch Bobrikow«, sagte der Lange. »Das hier ist Nikolai Sergejewitsch Tschernow.«

»Angenehm«, sagte Nikolai vom Boden aus.

»Und der Sowok hier ist Michail Andrejewitsch Solowjow«, sagte Iwan. »Woher kommst du?«

»Aus Ocha«, sagte Alexander. »Aus dem Osten.«

»Wir wissen, wo Ocha liegt«, sagte Nikolai. »Wir studieren nämlich Geographie.«

»Geographie?«, fragte Alexander höflich.

»Na ja, Geschichte«, sagte Iwan. Er ließ seine Knöchel knacken.

»Wirkliche Geschichte«, sagte Michail.

»Sei still, Mischa«, sagte Iwan. Er zwinkerte Alexander zu wie ein Erwachsener über den Kopf eines Kindes hinweg. Alexander wusste nicht, was er auslösen würde, wenn er zurückzwinkerte, also ließ er es bleiben. »Und was willst du hier, Towarischtsch?«, fragte Iwan.

In der Menschenmenge hob ein Sprecher zu einer zärtlichen Lobeshymne auf Stalin an. Seine Stimme bebte, und seine Nase wurde vor Ergriffenheit knallrot.

»Schach spielen«, sagte Alexander. »Ich habe einen Platz an der Akademie. Bei Andronow.«

»Ach ja? Und was soll ein Junge aus Ocha bei Andronow an der Akademie?«

Alexander kratzte sich an der Nase. »Ich war vorher in seinem Fernkurs.«

»So, so«, sagte Iwan. »Hast du dann einen Lieblingsspieler? Spasski vielleicht?«

»Er ist nicht schlecht. Aber er hat sich von Fischer 72 psychologisch fertigmachen lassen. Mit dem Geld und dem Zuspätkommen und so.«

»Aber die Partie wurde von den Amerikanern manipuliert, oder?

Sie haben Spasski durch chemische und elektronische Vorrichtungen ferngesteuert, nicht?«

Alexander starrte ihn an. Er wusste wirklich nicht, was er zu so etwas sagen sollte. »Nein«, sagte er schließlich. »Nein, das glaube ich nicht.«

»Und Russajew? Du bewunderst doch sicher Russajew?«

»Er ist langweilig.«

»Langweilig!«

»Er hätte genauso gegen Fischer verloren, wenn Fischer nicht verrückt geworden wäre.«

»Willst du damit sagen, die Amerikaner sollten immer noch Weltmeister sein?«

»Ob sie sollten, weiß ich nicht. Aber sie wären es.«

»So, so«, sagte Iwan. »Das sind ja interessante Ansichten. Was bringst du sonst noch mit?« Er besah sich Alexanders Rucksack. »Leichtes Gepäck. Ein Zeichen großer Parteitreue.«

Alexander gefiel es nicht, dass Nikolai noch immer am Boden hockte; es sah aus, als setzte er zum Sprung an.

»In meinem Zimmer habe ich noch mehr Sachen«, sagte Alexander. »Aber ich bin ein treuer Anhänger der Partei.« Es tat gut, in der fremden Stadt einen vertrauten Satz auszusprechen.

»Natürlich«, sagte Iwan und zog irgendwo aus seinem riesigen schwarzen Mantel Papier und Stift hervor. Er hielt die Stiftkappe mit den Zähnen und schrieb etwas auf. »Hier.« Er reichte Alexander den Zettel, und Alexander sah darauf herab. »Café Saigon«, sagte Iwan. »Schon davon gehört?«

»Nein«, sagte Alexander entschuldigend. Dauernd musste er zugeben, von irgendetwas noch nicht gehört, etwas nicht gekannt oder nicht getan zu haben, und wurde es allmählich leid.

»Es liegt an der Ecke Newski und Wladimirski. Das Haus, das aussieht, als wäre es noch im Bau. Wir sind fast immer da, weil zu Hause die Heizung nicht funktioniert. Komm vorbei, wenn du magst. Alle anderen in dem Laden reden über Musik, aber wir könnten uns über Geographie unterhalten.«

Alexander starrte ihn an. »Ist das nicht ein ziemlich abgeschlossenes Gebiet?«

»Weniger, als man denkt.«

»Na dann«, sagte Alexander. »Also gut.« Unschlüssig hielt er den Zettel in der einen und den Rucksack in der anderen Hand. Aus den Lautsprechern auf dem Platz drangen die ersten blechernen Takte der Nationalhymne herüber. Alexander wollte sich danach umdrehen, doch Iwan packte ihn an der Schulter.

»Übrigens«, sagte Iwan, »taugst du auch was? Im Schach, meine ich.«

»Oh. Ja. Vielleicht bald.«

»Also bist du hergekommen, um das herauszufinden?«, fragte Nikolai.

»Ja.« Es war peinlich: Dass er den ganzen Kontinent durchquert hatte, nur um seine Spielstärke zu ermitteln, kam Alexander unfassbar kindisch vor. Genauso gut hätte er sagen können, er sei auf der Suche nach etwas, das er im Traum gesehen hatte.

»Gut«, sagte Nikolai. Sein Gesicht sah im schwindenden Licht aus wie ein Katastrophengebiet. »Das ist gut. Leningrad ist genau der Ort, um herauszufinden, was in einem steckt, nicht? Wie viel man verträgt.«

Die andern lachten. »Sehr wahr«, sagte Mischa. »Und, was meinst du, Towarischtsch, wie viel verträgst du?«

Alexander wendete den Zettel in seiner Hand hin und her. »Das weiß ich nicht.« Die Hymne näherte sich ihrem pompösen Ende, und Textfetzen segelten über das scharlachrote Banner und die unsterblichen Ideale über Alexanders Kopf hinweg.

»Keine Sorge«, sagte Iwan und steckte seinen Stift weg. »Das findest du schon noch raus.«

Und Alexander fand es wirklich heraus. Es war nicht wenig, was er vertrug, stellte er fest: Das Gemeinschaftsbad, die dünnen Wände, der Mangel an Privatsphäre kümmerten ihn nicht besonders. Er hatte nichts zu verbergen, keine Geliebten, keine Geheimnisse, keine Abweichungen vom politisch Erlaubten. In Ocha hatte er mit seiner Mutter und den kleinen Schwestern gelebt, die ihn nicht weiter beachteten, und hier wünschte er sich manchmal, sein Leben würde um ein dunkles Geheimnis kreisen. Die Kommunalkas waren darauf ausgelegt, Familien zu zerstören, Intimitäten einzuebnen, jeden zum Mitwisser des anderen zu machen, bis jedes Geheimnis verharmloste und verflachte. Auch Alexander wusste bald mehr über seine Mitbewohner, als ihm lieb war – wenn bei einem der Türgriff nach unten zeigte, war dieser Mann ausgegangen, und er war wieder da, wenn seine Hausschuhe fehlten; wenn ein anderer nach längerer Abwesenheit zu seiner Frau zurückkehrte, wurde erwartet, dass die Nachbarn die Kinder zu sich nahmen. Alle liefen spärlich bekleidet herum – die Frauen, deren blasse Beine aus ihren Bademänteln hervorglitten, wie die Männer, die in fleckigen Unterhemden Kartoffeln kochten. Jeder stahl dem anderen Lebensmittel – kalt gewordene Reste auf dem Herd verschwanden schnell und spurlos –, und als einen Monat lang das warme Wasser ausfiel, setzten die Frauen große Töpfe auf und wuschen sich in der Küche, ohne die Tür zu schließen. Alexander hörte noch mehr, als er sah – das Geschrei von Kindern und Betrunkenen und Liebenden und Witwen –, und manchmal spürte er den Drang, selbst Lärm zu machen, damit die anderen einen Moment lang innehielten und darauf horchten, was bei *ihm* los war. Doch seine Abende vergingen in aller Stille. Er trank Tee, las seine Schachbücher und zerlegte die Zeit in erträgliche Abschnitte, bis er darauf hoffen konnte, einzuschlafen.

Tagsüber war es nicht viel besser. Er schrieb sich an der Schachakademie ein und begann sein Studium bei Andronow, dem Lehrer, der über seine Kontaktleute im Osten von Alexander erfahren, ihn zu sich bestellt und mit Verbindungen, Bestechungen und verhüllten Drohungen seinen Umzug möglich gemacht hatte. In den Monaten vor der Abreise hatten Alexander und seine Familie begonnen, Andronow als eine Art Engel des Verderbens zu sehen, der Alexander willkürlich auserwählt hatte, eine Ehrfurcht gebietende, erhebende, alles verzehrende Prüfung zu bestehen. Jetzt kam es ihm beinahe ketzerisch vor, zuzugeben, dass Andronow eine Enttäuschung war: Er stellte sich als kleiner Mann mit Stiernacken heraus, der beim Sprechen spuckte. Beim Einschreiben warf er einen raschen Blick auf Alexander, einen etwas längeren auf dessen Papiere und sagte: »Du kannst gehen. Du spielst gegen Nummer elf.« Alexander nahm seine feuchten Dokumente wieder an sich und ging in die Richtung, in die Andronow zeigte. Nummer elf war ein mürrischer, pickliger Junge aus Irkutsk. Angesichts seiner Pickel nahm Alexander an, Nummer elf bräuchte ebenfalls einen Freund, doch da irrte er sich. Seinen Fragen nach dem ersten Spiel begegnete der Junge mit langen, vernichtenden Schweigepausen und einsilbigen Repliken. Ganz so dringend brauchte Alexander vielleicht doch keine Gesellschaft.

Einige Wochen nach Semesterbeginn sah Andronow Alexander bei einem Spiel zu. Alexander besiegte seinen Gegner – wie er jeden bisherigen Gegner besiegt hatte und in seiner gesamten Zeit an der Akademie weiterhin jeden besiegen würde, zuletzt Andronow selbst –, doch Andronow schniefte nur und sagte: »Nicht schlecht für deine Verhältnisse.«

Seine Tage verbrachte Alexander also in zugigen, hohen Räumen am Tisch, mit wechselnden Jungen und Männern, die es offensichtlich furchtbar fanden, dort zu sein. Zuerst verhielten sie sich ihm gegenüber gleichgültig; dann, als seine Siegesserie allmählich auffiel, straften sie ihn mit glühender Verachtung, so unterschwellig, dass sie von der ursprünglichen Gleichgültigkeit durch nichts zu unterscheiden war. Andronow begann ihn nach einer Weile ein wenig anders zu behandeln – nicht freundlicher, doch er sah ihm interessiert beim Spielen zu und bedachte ihn häufiger mit unwirschen Anweisungen. Offenbar sah er in Alexander ein teures Rennpferd, das man gleichwohl wie alle anderen erschießen würde, wenn es lahmte.

Trotz allem waren Alexanders Tage erträglich. Die Pausen waren endlos und unangenehm, doch die Schachpartien schienen jenseits der Zeit stattzufinden – er fiel in sie hinein wie in eine Ohnmacht und gewöhnte sich nie an das Gefühl, beim Erwachen festzustellen, wie viel Zeit ohne ihn vergangen war.

Schlimmer waren die Abende. Manchmal rief seine Mutter an, und dann schlurfte er, möglichst ohne auf die grauen Flecken zu treten, in Hausschuhen den Flur entlang zum Telefon. Seine Mutter jammerte ihm von seinen Schwestern und den Kosten ihrer Schulbildung vor und fragte, ob er Geld schicken könne. Andere Bewohner brauchten das Telefon für dringendere Angelegenheiten: Krankheiten, Geldtransfers, halbgeheime Verabredungen und Verhandlungsgespräche. Sie verdrängten Alexander mit ihren forschenden Blicken, ihrer absichtsvollen Nähe. »Nein, Mamotschka«, sagte er jedes Mal. »Ich kann noch kein Geld schicken.« Dann schlurfte er in sein Zimmer zurück, zündete eine Kerze an, kochte Tee im Samowar und schloss die Augen, bis er durch das Fenster fast das Rauschen des Pazifiks von früher zu hören meinte.

Richtige Freunde hatte er in der Kommunalka nicht, doch er lernte die Bewohner so intim kennen wie kaum jemanden sonst. Neben ihm lebte eine Familie, ein Pärchen mit einem sehr schmutzigen Kind im Krabbelalter, und Alexander begriff mit der Zeit, dass der Mann die Frau schlug, dass die Frau das Kind kniff, und dass das Kind in verschiedenen Tonlagen schrie, je nachdem, wer gerade geschlagen oder gekniffen wurde. Auf der anderen Seite wohnte eine alte Frau, die sich tagaus, tagein mit jemandem unterhielt, den es, soweit Alexander wusste, gar nicht gab. Dann war da ein langhaariger, zartgliedriger Mann, der Männer mit aufs Zimmer nahm. Er arbeitete an der Universität, und zwischen zwei Semestern wurde er ertappt und hinausgeworfen und musste die Stadt verlassen. Alle sahen zu, wie er vor dem Auszug sorgfältig seine verfilzten, ausgefransten Hausschuhe am Türrahmen ausklopfte, während die Verwalterin mit den Schlüsseln in der Hand daneben stand. Es gab einen Säufer, der einem das Haarwasser oder das Parfüm wegtrank, wenn man es im Badezimmer stehenließ. Es gab zwei junge Frauen, die tagsüber schliefen, abends Anrufe entgegennahmen und die Nacht über ausblieben. All die Geräusche und die Geschäftigkeit um ihn herum gaben Alexander das Gefühl, im Inneren eines keuchenden Körpers zu leben, eines Organismus ohne inneren Monolog, der in unbewussten, abgehackten Suchbewegungen durch einen Wald hastete.

Bei Anbruch der Nacht legte Alexander sich ins Bett, kniff die Augen so fest zu, dass er grelle Muster vor sich tanzen sah, und stellte sich das Leben seiner Mitbewohner vor. Er sah die Nachtmädchen, Elisabeta und Sonja, auf ihrem Bett liegen, die Beine mit jener widernatürlichen Selbstverständlichkeit ineinander verschlungen, wie sie Frauen im Umgang miteinander haben. Ihr Zimmer roch ein wenig nach Flieder – mild und kühl. Sie hatten einen Wellensittich, stellte er sich vor, um den sie sich viel zu viel kümmerten. Winters stellten sie nach der Heimkehr ihren Samowar an, schminkten sich ab und lachten über die Körper, die Macken und die Vorlieben ihrer Männer. Ganz unglücklich, stellte Alexander sich vor, waren sie nicht.

Die Alte nebenan, beschloss er, sprach mit ihrem verstorbenen Ehemann. Anfangs hatte er sich für die beiden eine so ergreifende Liebesgeschichte ausgedacht, dass er manchmal aufhören musste, an sie zu denken – wenn der Wind dem Gebäude in die Flanken schnitt wie eine Klinge in ein Leintuch und die überwältigende Kälte seiner Einsamkeit ihm Angst einzuflößen begann, als hätte es ihn ins All hinausgeschleudert – und sich an seine Schachbücher setzen musste, um sich zu erholen. Die Alte und ihr Mann hatten zu den seltenen Menschen gehört, die nichts weiter wollten, als jemanden zu lieben, und die das Glück gehabt hatten, einander zu finden, und von dem Augenblick an miteinander glücklich waren – nicht widerstrebend, nicht aus resignativer, verbitterter Zufriedenheit, sondern wirklich und wahrhaftig glücklich. Dann wurde der Mann wegen antisowjetischer Umtriebe verhaftet und zu zehn Jahren Lagerhaft verurteilt, und als die Amnestie kam, wartete und wartete die alte Frau und versuchte vergeblich, ihn zu finden. Seither starrte sie Abend für Abend aus dem Nordfenster ihres Zimmers, sprach mit ihrem Mann, versuchte ihm den Weg zurück zu weisen und flüsterte ihm ihre Geheimnisse, ihre Erlebnisse, ihre Liebesbekenntnisse zu.

Irgendwann kam Alexander diese erste Version zu rührselig vor – als sich der Oktoberfrost zu der dicken Eisschicht des Novembers härtete, als Ocha und der Sommer in immer weitere Ferne rückten und die Schachakademie ihm Fortschritte und gute Noten, aber keine Freundschaften bescherte –, also dachte er sich eine zweite aus: Die Alte hatte ihren Ehemann gehasst, der ein fettleibiger Funktionär mit weichen Händen, verzärtelten Begehrlichkeiten und ohne jede Loyalität gewesen war. Er hatte für Nichtigkeiten Freunde verraten; nicht das ehrliche Streben nach vollkommener sozialer Gerechtigkeit trieb ihn an, sondern der seichte Wunsch nach den Schmeicheleien und Belohnungen seiner Vorgesetzten. Die Frau war vor ihm davongelaufen, weil die bittere Gleichgültigkeit der einsamen Großstadt sie weniger schreckte als seine kleinlichen Zuwendungen und Grausamkeiten. Seither verfluchte sie ihn Tag für Tag, von morgens bis abends, und hielt ihn mit ihrem brodelnden, unauslöschlichen Hass von sich fern. Der Hass strömte wie Dampf aus dem Gebäude und verhärtete sich zu einem Zauber, der sie beschützte – und sie durfte nie aufhören, Flüche vor sich hin zu murmeln, egal, wie verrückt sie dabei wirkte und ob die jungen Leute ihr im Hausflur aus dem Weg gingen.

Im Nachhinein waren es, so ungern Alexander es sich eingestand, nicht die Demütigungen, die moralischen Kompromisse und die allgemeine Erosion menschlicher Werte gewesen, die ihm am meisten zu schaffen machten. Er befasste sich nur mit den Nachrichten des Tages, wenn die Nachrichten sich mit Schach befassten, was oft genug vorkam, dass ihn die Lücken bei anderen Themen nicht weiter störten – auch wenn ihn die Inkompetenz der Stadtverwaltung weit härter traf als früher die Inkompetenz der Verwaltung seines Dorfes. Wie schon in Ocha türmte sich in Leningrad der Abfall in den Straßen, nur dass Leningrad viel mehr davon produzierte. In Ocha hatten sich die Fahrbahnen Jahr für Jahr in Schlammpfade verwandelt, in denen Lastwagen stecken blieben und erst freikamen, wenn der Juli alles wieder trocknete, und einen Winterdienst gab es ohnehin nirgendwo – doch in Leningrad bildeten sich so dicke Eisschichten, dass die Straßen selbst zum Gehen nicht zu gebrauchen waren, geschweige denn zum Fahren, und Alexander verstauchte sich einen Knöchel, der dunkelblau anlief, bevor er allmählich wieder heilte. Aber unerträglich war es nicht. Er hatte zumindest ein Dach über dem Kopf, und auf dem Markt gab es immer etwas zu essen, wenn auch selten das, was man essen wollte. Alexander machte sich nichts aus den Propagandaplakaten und glaubte nicht an die Parolen, aber das tat ohnehin niemand. Der Kommunismus war für ihn so etwas wie eine kollektive Notlüge, wie das stillschweigende Abkommen aller Menschen, nicht über die Tatsache zu sprechen, dass jeder einmal sterben muss.

Was Alexander wirklich zu schaffen machte, war die Kälte. Die Kälte nistete sich im Oktober in seinen Knochen ein und blieb. Seine Finger und Zehen nahmen eine reptilienhaft bläuliche Färbung an, die sich durch noch so viel Kneifen und noch so viel Zeit unter der lauwarmen Dusche in der Kommunalka nicht vertreiben ließ. In Ocha musste es fast genauso kalt gewesen sein, dachte er, aber wenn man allein war, fühlte sich Kälte anders an. Die Arme und Schultern schmerzten ihm vom ständigen unmerklichen Zittern; nachts wachte er immer wieder auf, rollte sich zusammen und atmete in sein Kissen, um ein wenig Wärme zu erhaschen, die gleich wieder verging. Im Januar wusste er kaum mehr, wie es war, Nacken und Kiefer zu entspannen und einen tiefen Atemzug zu tun, an dem man nicht beinahe erstickte. Das, dachte er, das konnte einen um den Verstand bringen – wie ständiger Hunger oder wie Schlafentzug oder was man noch in Sibirien den Gefangenen antat. Hätte er Geheimnisse gehabt, er hätte sie alle gestanden, für nur eine Stunde in der Sonne, für eine Stunde Schlaf am sommerlichen Meer. Er träumte von Wärme, wurde ihm später bewusst, wie Häftlinge von Frauen träumen.

Also ging er nicht aus Idealismus in das Café an der Ecke Newski und Wladimirski. Später interessierten sich Journalisten dafür, was ihn dazu gebracht hatte, sich in Leningrad mit den anderen Unzufriedenen einzulassen, welche Erniedrigung das Fass zum Überlaufen gebracht und ihn in die Arme der Dissidentenbewegung getrieben hatte. Und zuerst tischte er ihnen Lügen auf – über die Einschränkungen seiner freiheitlichen, weitreichenden Vorstellungen, seiner Neigung zur Literatur, seines Stolzes –, und sie nickten anerkennend und bewunderten ihn nur umso mehr. Dann, eines Tages, lange nach dem Höhepunkt seiner Karriere – er wusste noch genau, dass es in dem Jahr seiner Niederlage gegen den Computer gewesen war, die damals weltweit Spekulationen über den Triumph der Technik und den Niedergang der Menschheit im Allgemeinen auslöste – beugte er sich zu dem Reporter einer kleinen aserbaidschanischen Zeitschrift vor und sagte die Wahrheit: dass er begonnen hatte, das Café aufzusuchen, weil es in jenem gnadenlosen Winter der einzige Ort gewesen war, wo ihm für Momente warm geworden war. Deshalb war er das erste Mal dort hingegangen.

Und aus anderen Gründen war er wiedergekommen.

KAPITEL 2

Irina
Cambridge, Massachusetts, 2006

Ich war zwölf, als ich zum ersten Mal meinen Vater im Schach besiegte, und zuerst dachte ich, es läge an meiner überragenden Intelligenz. Ich schlitterte und tanzte auf Socken durch die Küche, wedelte ihm triumphierend mit seinem geschlagenen König vor der Nase herum und wunderte mich, dass er nicht mitlachte. Als meine Mutter nachsehen kam, was los war, krähte ich: »Ich habe Dad schachmatt gesetzt!«

Meine Mutter sah meinen Vater an, der mit eingezogenen Wangen und gerunzelten Brauen auf sein Schachbrett starrte.

»Hast du sie gewinnen lassen, Frank?«

»Hast du das, Dad?«, fragte ich beleidigt. Ich setzte mich an den Tisch und begann mit den Springern herumzuspielen. Sie waren meine Lieblingsfiguren, weil man mit ihnen die schönsten Überraschungsangriffe starten konnte. »Hast du nicht, oder?«

»Nein«, sagte mein Vater und begann die Figuren in die gepolsterte Schatulle zurückzulegen, aus der er sie nie wieder hervorholen sollte. »Nein, das würde ich nie tun.«

Aber wer würde wollen, dass jemand posthum seine Vergangenheit nach dem ersten Aussetzer durchforstet? Im Nachhinein kann man die Spleens, Besonderheiten und Fehler jedes Menschen als düstere Vorzeichen werten. Alles, was ich sicher weiß, ist, dass mein Vater mit vierzig keinen Funken Verstand mehr besaß. Also dürften meine Prognosen in Bezug auf mich selbst nicht übertrieben pessimistisch sein.

Wenn man sich dafür interessiert, was jemand in einer kurzen Lebensspanne erreichen kann, ist die Geschichte des Schachs eine Fundgrube. Sie handelt fast ausschließlich von Menschen, die kurz nach der Pubertät den Höhepunkt ihrer Karriere erreichten. Bobby Fischer natürlich, wobei seine Geschichte leider traurig ausging (mit Paranoia, Exil in Island und Antisemitismus), und Alexander Alexandrowitsch Aljechin, dessen Geschichte allerdings genauso böse endete (mit Alkoholismus, Ausfällen und noch mehr Antisemitismus). Und dann ist da noch Alexander Kimowitsch Besetow, der mit neunzehn Schachmeister der UdSSR und mit zweiundzwanzig Schachweltmeister war. Auch seine Geschichte hat ihre tragischen Seiten, aber das wusste ich nicht, als ich nach Russland floh, um ihn zu suchen.

Bis Chorea Huntington meinen Vater erwischte, interessierte er sich nicht nur für Schach, sondern auch für die Sowjetunion. Ich bin aufgewachsen, als der Kalte Krieg in den letzten Zügen lag. Haltlose geopolitische Spekulationen waren damals ein beliebter Zeitvertreib. Doch für meinen Vater bedeuteten sie mehr – er pflegte sie wie ein Hobby, wenn er abends vom College zurückkam, wo er Musikunterricht gab. Er zerbrach sich den Kopf über die grundlegende Ironie eines Regimes, das die Zensur zensierte. Auf Partys konnte er ganze Abende lang darüber diskutieren, ob Breschnews Sowjetunion totalitär war oder nur autoritär. Einmal, als ich ungefähr sieben war, fand ich ihn auf dem Boden seines Arbeitszimmers, wo er Fotos einer sowjetischen Militärparade betrachtete. »Was machst du da?«, fragte ich.

Es kam öfter vor, dass er ungewöhnliche Dinge tat. Mein Vater hatte eine gesunde Abneigung gegen soziale Konventionen: Einmal erlaubte er es mir zum Entsetzen meiner Mutter, die Fenster unseres Hauses mit Wasserfarben regenbogenbunt anzumalen, und im Herbst applaudierte er manchmal Bäumen, die sich besonders eindrucksvoll rot verfärbten. Wenn ich nicht schlafen konnte, ließ er mich Johnny Carsons Tonight Show ansehen und Ginger Ale trinken. Als ich lilafarbene Tusche auf dem neuen weißen Sofa vergoss, half er mir, die Polster so hinzudrehen, dass meine Mutter es nicht bemerkte. Einmal ging er mitten in der Woche um Mitternacht mit mir nach draußen, um einen Meteoritenschauer anzusehen – ich erinnere mich noch an den kalten Wind und die subversive Erkenntnis, dass das Universum nachts weiterexistierte, auch wenn man es nicht sah oder zumindest nicht hätte sehen sollen.

»Ich versuche herauszufinden, wer da drüben wirklich das Sagen hat«, erklärte er. »Was meinst du?«

Auf den Fotos waren mürrisch dreinblickende Männer zu sehen, deren Gesichter von Pelzmützen und Schnurrbärten gerahmt wurden. Nach meinem Verständnis sah die Veranstaltung überhaupt nicht nach einer Parade aus. Ich zeigte mit dem großen Zeh auf einen der Männer.

»Ah, Tschebrikow«, sagte mein Vater. »Eine kluge Wahl. Du solltest Politikerin werden.«

»Ich werde Meeresbiologin«, sagte ich, nicht ahnend, dass daraus nichts werden würde.

»Wie du meinst«, sagte mein Vater ernst. »Tu, was du nicht lassen kannst. Aber weißt du, woran man noch erkennen kann, wer von ihnen die Fäden zieht?«

»Nein, woran denn?«

»An der Anordnung der Porträtbilder.«

»Weil das wichtigste Bild ganz oben ist?«

»Du hast es erfasst.«

»Das ist doch Quatsch.«

»Auch das hast du goldrichtig erfasst, Irina.«

Ich weiß nicht, was ihm das alles eigentlich bedeutete. Er war Pianist und Musiklehrer, und in der kurzen Lebensspanne, in der ich ihn kannte, war er immer am glücklichsten, wenn er am Klavier Stücke komponierte oder am Schachbrett eine Partie eröffnete. Soweit ich es beurteilen konnte, führte er ein schönes Leben. Doch vielleicht war es nicht das einzige, das zu leben er sich hätte vorstellen können.

Wenn wir spielten, holte er ehrfürchtig eine Figur nach der anderen aus seiner Schatulle – alte, klobige Holzfiguren, so groß wie meine Handflächen – und beugte sich feierlich vor. »Hiermit«, sagte er dann, und ich erfuhr erst später, dass er dabei Karl den Ersten zitierte, »wetteifern Herrscher und Untertan ohne Blutvergießen.« Vielleicht war es das – vielleicht waren diese sublimierten Kriegserklärungen, war diese atemlose Faszination für das geopolitische Geschehen ein angestrengter Blick über die Schulter auf einen Weg, den er bewusst nicht eingeschlagen hatte.

Doch solche Fragen stellen sich Kinder noch nicht, und als ich alt genug war, sie zu stellen, kamen keine Antworten mehr.

Es ist ein Jammer, dass mein Vater das Ende des Kalten Krieges nicht miterlebte; es hätte ihn beglückt, wie unsere CIA alles verschlief. (»Was meinst du, Irina, wie viele Leute fette Gehälter kassieren, nur damit sie versuchen, Tschernenkos Körpersprache zu deuten?«, sagte er manchmal zu mir. »Jedes Mal, wenn er niest, kriegen sie fünfzig Dollar. Wenn da ein Posten frei wird, heißt es zugreifen, mein Kind.«) Wie hätte er den Putschversuch von 91 geliebt (ihm ging nichts über einen ordentlichen Putschversuch) und sich über den Mauerfall in Deutschland gefreut. Meinen Vater rührten die Schicksale fremder Völker, die Geschichten anderer Nationen – vor allem aber faszinierte ihn die komplexe Choreographie aus Vorstoß und Rückzug, ob auf dem Schachbrett oder im wahren Leben. Wie Lear – oder wie jeder andere – wollte er sehen, wer verlor und wer gewann. Er wollte wissen, wie es ausgehen würde.

Und wenn ich ehrlich sein soll, macht dieser Wunsch auch einen Gutteil meiner eigenen Trauer aus. Nicht den Hauptteil – der besteht aus der guten alten Todesfurcht, aus dem tierischen Überlebenswillen, der gegen kalte wissenschaftliche Prognosen aufbegehrt. Aber ein nicht unerheblicher Anteil, fünfzehn Prozent vielleicht, ist das Bedauern, dass ich das Ende verpasse.

Ich wünschte also, mein Vater, der passionierte Russlandkenner, hätte das alles noch sehen können. In gewisser Weise hat er es sogar. Er war überall dabei. Als 89 die Mauer fiel, lebte er noch zu Hause und verbrachte die meiste Zeit in abgedunkelten Zimmern, wo sich das flackernde Mondlicht des Fernsehers in seinen Augen spiegelte. An Weihnachten wurden Ceauşescu und seine Frau hingerichtet und ihre bleichen Körper triumphierend im rumänischen Staatsfernsehen zur Schau gestellt. Mein Vater saß mit einem Lätzchen davor und scheiterte an dem Versuch, sich Möhrenbrei in den Mund zu schieben. 91 sah man Jelzin auf einen Panzer steigen – da fristete mein Vater seine Tage schon im Pflegeheim, mit offenem Mund, glasigen Augen und flatternden Händen, die ins Leere griffen. Der Kalte Krieg war vorbei, und die selbstzufriedene Erste Welt delektierte sich an seinen letzten visuellen Zuckungen. Auch wenn mein Vater sich zu dem Zeitpunkt herzlich wenig für diese Ereignisse interessierte, wäre es technisch gesehen nicht falsch zu sagen, dass er sie noch miterlebte.

Jeder »ist« natürlich sein Gehirn – und nach meinem nüchternen Weltbild sogar ausschließlich. Doch mein Vater war irgendwie *besonders* ausschließlich sein Gehirn. Seine Selbstwahrnehmung war von brillanten Schlussfolgerungen, einem herausragenden Gedächtnis und einem Sinn für Humor geprägt, der einem den Boden unter den Füßen wegzog, ohne dass man recht begriff, wie einem geschah – bis man sich zum Gehen wenden wollte. Manche Menschen haben einen Wesenskern, der Gehirnschäden widersteht – ihre Heiterkeit, ihre Güte, ihr Glaube –, so dass es eine Weile dauert, bis Chorea Huntington sie vollständig ausgelöscht hat. Bei einigen überlebt die Herzenswärme bis zuletzt und nährt den Glauben, sie seien noch immer irgendwo da drinnen, wenn man so etwas zu glauben geneigt ist. Bei meinem Vater war es anders. Er bestand in allererster Linie aus seinem Geist, und der Geist ist ein ausgeklügeltes System aus Kopplungen und Hebeln und empfindlichen Regelkreisen. Wenn ein Teil fehlt, ist das ganze System beschädigt.

Es begann damit, dass die kleinen Orientierungsverluste und Ausfälle, die jeder gelegentlich erlebt, ihm ständig passierten. Dann büßte er seinen Sinn für Kausalität ein – Erlebnisse lösten sich von ihren Kontexten und Konsequenzen. Er setzte sich ans Klavier, aber er spielte nicht mehr. Seine Persönlichkeit schnurrte zu einer verzerrten, vereinfachten Version seines früheren Selbst zusammen. Er wurde immer jünger, was seine Interessen und Ängste anging. Dann begann sich sein Gedächtnis von der Gegenwart rückwärts aufzulösen. Ich verschwand daraus. Und irgendwann meine Mutter.

Ganz zu Beginn seiner Erkrankung, in jenen verwirrenden ersten Monaten, nachdem ich ihn zum ersten Mal schachmatt gesetzt hatte, glaubten die Leute immer, mein Vater sei betrunken. Um neun Uhr morgens, an einem Dienstagabend, im Supermarkt oder der Bibliothek oder, noch schlimmer, bei einer Schultheateraufführung starrten sie ihn an, flüsterten und wechselten unbehaglich von einem Fuß auf den anderen. Meine Mutter blickte stur geradeaus, um nicht sehen zu müssen, wie peinlich berührt sie waren. Ich rutschte auf meinem Sitz hin und her, verdrehte die Augen und dachte, ich müsste sterben. Meine gesamte Pubertät hindurch war ich überzeugt, dass die Vererbung für mich keine Rolle spielte, weil ich diese Demütigungen ohnehin nicht überleben würde.

Später wirkte mein Vater wie die Karikatur eines Kranken, und manchmal glaubte wirklich jemand, seine ausladenden Bewegungen, seine rhythmischen Zuckungen und die kleinen korrigierenden Gebärden, mit denen er sie überkompensierte, seien ein geschmackloser Scherz. Sie verstummten indigniert, bis sie sein bleiches, eingefallenes Gesicht und die tief in ihre Höhlen gesunkenen Augen bemerkten. Dann blieben sie stumm.

Am Ende vollführten seine Arme mit flatternden Fingern wilde rudernde Bewegungen. Meine Mutter fütterte ihn mit unglaublicher Selbstverständlichkeit und Geduld. Sie machte den Mund weit auf, wie man es bei Babys tut, um sie zum Essen zu bewegen. Wenn ich in den Semesterferien zu Hause war, übernahm ich die Aufgabe manchmal und fühlte mich unwohl dabei – als könnte er jeden Moment zu sich kommen, mich streng anblicken und mich fragen, was zum Geier ich da tat.

Man sollte sich nicht einreden, die Psyche würde friedlich ihrem Ende entgegendämmern. Sie windet sich und sucht bis zuletzt verzweifelt nach Bedeutung. Mein Vater gab so viel repetitiven Nonsens von sich wie der endlose Strang immer gleicher Nukleotide in seiner DNA. Am Schluss erstickte er an seiner eigenen Spucke. So sollte man nicht sterben.

An dem Tag, an dem ich meine Testergebnisse erfuhr, war es windig. Ich ging auf die Straße hinaus, nachdem ich mit der Genetikerin gesprochen hatte – eigentlich hatte ich nicht allein gehen sollen, aber Claire hatte an meinen Blicken abgelesen, dass ich sie mit meinen eigenen, noch funktionstüchtigen Händen erwürgen würde, wenn sie mir folgte. Skelettierte Blätter kratzten an den Außenwänden der Häuser; die U-Bahn hielt am Massachusetts General Hospital, und Heerscharen von Medizinstudenten stiegen aus; der Charles River wirkte matt und schmutzig mit seinen wenigen Segelbooten. Der Himmel sah aus, als sei ihm schlecht. Zwei Dinge gingen mir durch den Kopf – erstens, dass das alles mir schon jetzt weniger bedeutete, und zweitens, wie wenig originell dieser Gedanke war.

In einem Durchgang übergab ich mich. Passanten erschraken bei dem Anblick – war ich eine Krebspatientin in Chemotherapie? War ich kurz davor, eine ungewollte Schwangerschaft abzubrechen? War ich drogensüchtig? Das waren die ersten von vielen ähnlichen Blicken und Fragen: Wie viel Mitleid verdiente ich genau? Und wie, wenn überhaupt, sollten sie es mir übermitteln?

Es war zehn Jahre her, dass ich meinen Vater im Schach besiegt hatte. Vererbung über die paternale Linie erhöht die Wahrscheinlichkeit eines frühen Krankheitsbeginns. In der Klinik hatten sie mir erklärt, dass die Anzahl meiner CAG-Tripletts, meiner krankhaft wiederholten chromosomalen Nukleotide, fünfzig betrug, was im Mittel einem Krankheitsbeginn mit zweiunddreißig entspricht. Die Hälfte aller Patienten mit fünfzig CAG-Tripletts entwickelt vor dem zweiunddreißigsten Lebensjahr Symptome und die Hälfte danach. Das nennt man einen Mittelwert.

Die Ärzte veranschaulichten mir diese Informationen mit Hilfe eines Diagramms, auf dem die Anzahl der Tripletts dem durchschnittlichen Krankheitsbeginn zugeordnet war – wie die Blätter, auf denen man das gesunde Verhältnis von Körpergröße und -gewicht bestimmt oder die Entwicklung eines Kleinkinds mitverfolgt.

Am Ende des Durchgangs wartete Claire mit meinem Mantel auf mich. An meinen Schuhen klebten Kotzespritzer. Sie legte mir den Mantel um die Schultern und hielt ihn während der U-Bahnfahrt dort fest. Ich zitterte, und die Harvard-Studenten auf dem Heimweg von ihren Praktika, die ihnen weltweite Karriereoptionen eröffnen würden, warfen mir finstere Blicke zu. Wir betrachteten die rauchgrauen Wolken im rosa Abendhimmel über dem Fluss. Wir zählten die Segelboote. Wir fuhren nach Hause und tranken und fluchten drei Tage lang.

Damals war ich noch auf dem College. Es hatte Vorbehalte dagegen gegeben, den Gentest so früh vorzunehmen, doch ich hatte alle davon überzeugt, dass es das einzig Richtige sei – damit ich überlegen konnte, ob ich Kinder wollte, und mir die Art kurzfristiger, erreichbarer Ziele stecken konnte, die Todkranke so mochten. Ich hatte innere Reife und aufgeblasenes Geschwätz aufgeboten, wie ich es mir selbst nie zugetraut hätte, hatte existenzialistisch und stoisch argumentiert und mein Gottvertrauen sowie meine positive Einstellung ins Feld geführt (die ich beide nicht besaß). Ich hatte eine Psychologin konsultiert und ihr Sätze aufgetischt wie »Ich lasse mich nicht unterkriegen« und »Es ist alles in Gottes Hand«. Nach den Tests war ich zusammengebrochen, hatte mich zurückgezogen und war in die tiefe Depression versunken, von der ich versprochen hatte, sie nicht zu bekommen.

Claire und ich lebten in jenem Jahr in einem großen, grauen zweigeschossigen Haus bei Somerville. Ich fürchte, ich machte es ihr nicht leicht. Ich hörte auf, Hausaufgaben zu machen. Claire schleifte mich durch die Tests in formaler Logik. Ich hörte auf, den Campus zu besuchen, und aß nicht mehr. Claire legte mir Bagel vor die Zimmertür. Ich schmollte. Ich verkroch mich. Ich besetzte stundenlang die Dusche, verbrauchte das warme Wasser und leerte das Grapefruitshampoo, weil das Badezimmer der einzige Ort war, wo mich niemand weinen hörte.

Ich brachte jedes Wochenende wechselnde Männer mit nach Hause, und Claire sagte nichts weiter dazu, als dass ich mir mehr Mühe bei der Auswahl geben könnte. »Ich weiß, dass es dir mies geht, und ich verstehe das«, sagte sie. »Aber in dem Bereich könntest du dich ein bisschen mehr anstrengen.«

Inzwischen ist natürlich alles anders, und ich blicke mit einer Art grimmigem Amüsement auf jene Zeiten zurück. Es grenzt an ein Wunder, dass ich mir auf dem College nicht mindestens eine ungewollte Schwangerschaft eingefangen habe – und schlimmstenfalls eine HIV-Infektion. Einer der Männer hat mich sogar danach gefragt – ein Burschenschaftler, ausgerechnet –, als ich schulterzuckend auf das Kondom verzichtete, das er mir hinhielt. »Hast du gar keine Angst vor Aids?« Nein, eigentlich nicht, antwortete ich und dachte insgeheim: Bitte, bitte, bitte lass mich Aids kriegen, damit ich an einer Lungenentzündung sterbe, damit mein Hirn zuletzt aussetzt und damit ich selbst diejenige bin, die stirbt, nicht irgendjemand sonst.

Irgendwie schaffte ich knapp meinen Abschluss. Mein Hauptfach war Philosophie. Eine falsche Prämisse, die zu einer falschen Konklusion führt, ist logisch gültig, wenn ich mich recht erinnere. Dann promovierte ich in Vergleichender Literaturwissenschaft. Ich befasste mich mit Nabokov.

Manchmal lachen die Leute bei dem Gedanken, ihr ganzes Leben im Elfenbeinturm zu verbringen: Sie brauchen eine Ewigkeit bis zum Abschluss, sagen sie, häufen Wissen an, das sie niemals werden anwenden können, und befassen sich mit Interpretationen von Interpretationen einer Welt, von der sie keinerlei Erfahrung haben. Der Akademiker lebt in einem System voller potentieller Energie, die nie kinetisch wird. Ich kann darüber weniger gut lachen.

Seit dem College bin ich ruhiger geworden. Ich gehe nicht oft aus, aber ganz selten – vielleicht ein, zwei Mal in den vergangenen fünf Jahren –, begegne ich jemand Interessantem, jemandem mit trockenem Humor und bissigem Intellekt, von dem ich objektiv weiß, dass ich ihn in einem anderen Leben begehrenswert gefunden hätte. Ich kann dieses andere Leben sogar sehen, wenn ich die Augen zusammenkneife, aber es fehlt mir nicht besonders. Ich betrachte es wie anderer Leute Urlaubsbilder. Und wenn doch Einsamkeit und Sehnsucht aufkommen, fühlt es sich an wie die Berührung einer Hand durch ein Stück Stoff hindurch – abgekoppelt und beinahe fremd.

Ich begann, samstags auf dem Harvard Square gegen die runzligen alten Männer Schach zu spielen, die dort für einen Dollar pro Partie jeden Herausforderer besiegten. Ich bin nicht zu einem Schachwunderkind herangewachsen – und habe übrigens auch sonst keine überragenden Talente. Aber irgendetwas an der Choreographie des Spiels fasziniert mich, an der Art, wie jeder Zug den nächsten nach sich zieht. Die Könige sind treffende Metaphern für uns Menschen: von einem rigiden Regelsystem zur Untätigkeit verdammt, wehrlos Angriffen von allen Seiten ausgesetzt und höchstens in der Lage, durch einzelne Schritte in eine beliebige Richtung vorübergehend den Kopf aus der Schlinge zu ziehen.

Die Schachmänner tauchten ohne jede Vorwarnung Anfang März an den Tischen auf, saßen im Dunst ihrer Kaffeebecher und warteten darauf, dass der Rest der Welt es ihnen nachtat und zum Leben erwachte. Sie kamen vor den Schaustellern – den lebenden Statuen, die sich gegen Kleingeld ruckhaft in Bewegung setzten, den silbrig-schwarzhäutigen Plastikeimertrommlern, den irren Propheten, die den Passanten bis ins letzte grauenhafte Detail das Ende der Welt ausmalten. Die Schachmänner kamen, bevor die nächste Ladung ambitionierter junger Akademiker die Straßen verstopfte, bevor die College-Schüler überall auf dem Square ihre unnatürliche Bräune und Lässigkeit zur Schau zu stellen begannen und bevor ganz Cambridge so weit zu sich gekommen war, dass es wieder gegen die jeweils aktuelle außenpolitische Katastrophe demonstrierte. Mein Lieblingsgegner war ein Mann namens Lars, der sich mit so viel heiligem Ernst dem Spiel widmete, dass ich immer wieder vergaß, wie leicht er hätte aufstehen und gehen können, wenn er nur gewollt hätte. Als ich ihn zum ersten Mal traf, musterte er mich kurz und sagte: »Du siehst aus wie jemand, der sich selbst mehr leidtut als unbedingt nötig.«

Ich war ziellos umhergewandert, wie ich es damals häufig tat. Das war zwei Jahre nach den Testergebnissen, und ich hatte meine Dissertation über dreisprachige Wortspiele in *Ada oder Das Verlangen* zur Hälfte fertig. Am liebsten war mir eisige Kälte; sie lenkte meine mäandernden, selbstbezüglichen Gedankengänge in eine klare Unzufriedenheit mit meiner unmittelbaren Umgebung um. Das war, wie ich zugeben muss, eine echte Verbesserung.

Ich setzte mich, Lars gewann, und dann legte er präzise dar, was ich falsch machte, sowohl im Spiel als auch ganz allgemein. Von da an waren wir Freunde.

Lars erzählte mir im Laufe der Zeit noch einiges mehr, auch wenn unmöglich alles davon wahr sein konnte. Er war in Stockholm als Sohn eines Großreeders geboren worden, der vom schwedischen Hochadel abstammte, sagte er. Seine Familie hatte während der Ölkrise 1979 ihr gesamtes Vermögen verloren. Er hatte in Philadelphia auf der Straße gelebt, ein Jahr in Hongkong verbracht und war aus Gründen, auf die er nicht näher einzugehen wünschte, unehrenhaft aus dem schwedischen Armeedienst entlassen worden. Seine Geschichten steckten voller Widersprüche, Rätsel und räumlicher oder zeitlicher Lücken, doch wenn ich ihn darauf ansprach, bestand Lars' einzige Reaktion darin, mich für meine neugierigen Fragen noch schneller vom Brett zu fegen. Also ließ ich es bleiben. Lars setzte auf dreiste Bluffs, unhaltbare Behauptungen, die nie nachprüfbar waren. Er erzählte, er habe in einer Mine am Schwarzen Meer gearbeitet, als blinder Eisenbahnpassagier Moldawien durchquert und von pakistanischen Immigranten in London gelernt, den Koran zu rezitieren. Wie hätte man ihm nachweisen sollen, dass das nicht stimmte?

Es hat etwas Intimes, sich Lügengeschichten anzuhören, finde ich – was jemand für wahr halten möchte, sagt mehr über ihn aus als alles, was wirklich geschieht. Manchmal gab es aber auch gezielte Provokationen – Anspielungen auf angebliche uneheliche Kinder, versuchte Attentate und dergleichen. Oder, noch schlimmer, Ratschläge. Analysen. Geistreiche Aphorismen. »Weißt du, was dein Problem ist?«, fragte er mich mehr als einmal. Und obwohl ich jedes Mal sagte, das wüsste ich nur zu genau – hochmoderne Gentests hätten es mir verraten –, schob er prompt seine eigene Antwort nach. »Du denkst zu viel«, oder »Du hast zu wenig Sex«, oder »Du denkst zu wenig an Sex«, erklärte er mir. Meistens ließ er seiner Diagnose eine instruktive Anekdote aus seinem eigenen Leben folgen, in der mehr Sex oder weniger Nachdenken ihm den Tag gerettet hatten.

Bei unserer letzten Begegnung, bevor er verstummte, erzählte Lars davon, wie man in der Türkei auf ihn geschossen hatte. Es war Ende März – in Neuengland die Zeit, in der allmählich der Lebenswille wieder erwacht. Der Himmel war weiß, und Menschen trieben über den Harvard Square dahin wie bunte Aquarienfische in allen möglichen Formen und Arten. Ich hatte uns Kaffee besorgt. Lars leerte fünf Tütchen Zucker in seinen und schickte mich zum Kaffeestand zurück, um Nachschub zu holen. Als ich ihn bei meiner Rückkehr missbilligend ansah, sagte er: »Weißt du, was dein Problem ist? Du hast Angst davor, Spaß zu haben.«

»Aber ich habe Spaß«, sagte ich, nippte an meinem Kaffee und kleckerte auf meinen Mantel. Das Schachbrett war noch unberührt. Jeder von uns hatte unendlich viele Möglichkeiten, zu gewinnen oder zu verlieren, wobei uns beiden einigermaßen klar war, worauf es hinauslaufen würde. »Ich habe jede Menge Spaß«, sagte ich. »Du hast ja keine Ahnung.«

»Oh, natürlich«, sagte Lars. »Insgeheim erlebst du ungeahnte Freuden.«

Ich eröffnete mit meinem Königsbauern. Lars tat es mir nach. »Du kannst es dir gar nicht vorstellen«, sagte ich. »Und das ist auch besser so.«

»Ich jedenfalls«, sagte Lars, »habe so manches Abenteuer hinter mir. Viele Male habe ich dem Tod ein Schnippchen geschlagen. Ich habe mir das Recht auf ein bisschen Zucker in meinem Kaffee redlich verdient.«

»Okay«, sagte ich.

»Habe ich eigentlich mal erwähnt, wie ich in der Türkei fast erschossen worden wäre?«

Ich durfte ihn nicht fragen, was er überhaupt in der Türkei zu suchen gehabt hatte; das hätte er als unverzeihlich aufdringlich und unhöflich angesehen. Die Spielregeln standen schon lange fest.

»Das war ein paar Autostunden außerhalb von Ankara«, erzählte er. Er schob ein paar Bauern vor und entwickelte seine Läufer. Lars' Einstellung zum Schach glich der zum Leben im Allgemeinen:

Bangemachen gilt nicht. Man muss sich reinstürzen, sich die Hände schmutzig machen und sehen, was dabei herauskommt. Zu viel Berechnung lähmt einen nur, und Lähmung ist Tod.

»Wann war das?«, fragte ich, weil ich wusste, dass es ihn verärgern würde. Lars zu verärgern gehörte zu meiner Strategie. Ich schob meinen Läuferbauern vor und wollte als Nächstes den Damenbauern ziehen, um ein Bauernzentrum aufzubauen und endlich einmal, hoffentlich, Lars in seine Schranken zu weisen.

»In den Siebzigern. Wer weiß das schon so genau? Vor deiner Zeit.«

»Ich bin dreißig.«

»Also bitte.« Lars verzog das Gesicht und entwickelte seine Dame. Das kam früh, auch wenn der Zug technisch gesehen in Ordnung war. Sie war nicht bedroht, und er wollte offenbar nur die Kontrolle über das Zentrum behalten. Ich redete mir ein, dass er beunruhigt war. »Es gehört sich nicht für eine Dame, ihr Alter preiszugeben«, sagte er.

Ich sondierte mit zusammengekniffenen Augen die Lage. Lars hatte seinen König hinter der Dame und ihrem Springer in Sicherheit gebracht. Meine Bauern und mein Läufer standen im Zentrum wie vor einem Erschießungskommando aufgereiht.

»Jedenfalls«, sagte Lars, »war ich in Begleitung. In Begleitung eines Mädchens.« In vielen seiner Erzählungen kamen Mädchen vor, jedes Mal ein anderes, wie Bond-Girls, die gerade lange genug auf der Bildfläche erscheinen, um verführt und gerettet zu werden, und dann sang- und klanglos wieder verschwinden. Lars erwähnte immer wieder, wie gutaussehend er als junger Mann gewesen war. Ich kannte ihn nur mit strähnigem, verfilztem grauem Haar und karierten Anzügen, aber seine blauen Augen hatten einen verschmitzten Glanz, der früher einmal attraktiv gewirkt haben mochte, wobei ich auf dem Feld nicht gerade eine Expertin bin. Von all seinen Geschichten wollte Lars an die von seiner jugendlichen Schönheit am meisten glauben.

»Okay«, sagte ich. »Und weiter?« Aus reiner Bosheit schlug ich einen seiner Bauern.

»Wir haben also außerhalb der Stadt diesen wunderschönen Fluss entdeckt und denken, ein herrlicher Ort für ein Picknick, für ein kleines Päuschen, du verstehst.«

»Ja, verstehe«, sagte ich. Den Bauern zu schlagen war ein Fehler gewesen. Ich hatte eine Diagonale auf meinen König eröffnet. Lars trieb mich wie immer kühl und berechnend in die Enge und wartete ab, dass ich von selbst Fehler beging.

»Wir wollten uns ein Weilchen hinlegen, einander näher kennenlernen«, sagte Lars. Er schlug meinen Bauern mit seinem Springer. Ich nahm seinen Springer mit meinem, der prompt von Lars' Dame geschlagen wurde.

»Ja«, sagte ich. »Schon kapiert.« Ich rochierte. Lars opferte einen Läufer, um mein Bauernzentrum aufzubrechen.

»Wir wollten mitten auf der Wiese vögeln.«

»Okay«, sagte ich. »Verstehe.« Ich weiß nicht, ob es ein Übersetzungsproblem war oder ein ausgeklügelter interkultureller Witz, aber Lars tat immer so, als hätte ich keinen Schimmer, worauf er hinauswollte – und er wollte immer auf dasselbe hinaus. »Verdammt, Lars«, sagte ich manchmal, »noch ist mein Gehirn nicht aufgeweicht. Du erfährst wahrscheinlich als Erster davon, wenn es so weit ist.« – »Wer weiß?«, antwortete er dann. »Du hast dein ganzes Leben an der Universität verbracht. Wann warst du das letzte Mal mit einem Mann zusammen?« Damit war das Gespräch dann meist beendet.

»Wir liegen also im Gras. Der Fluss ist so blau. Ein wahnsinnig intensives grünliches Blau, wie man es in der Natur überhaupt nicht vorkommen sieht. Wie sagt man dazu?«

»Türkis vielleicht. Aquamarin. Coelinblau.«

»Du kennst mehr Wörter, als du je gebrauchen kannst«, sagte Lars. Das sagte er mindestens einmal am Tag.

»Kann sein«, sagte ich.

»Und wir rammeln wie die Bisamratten«, sagte Lars stolz.

»Wie die Kaninchen.«

»Wie bitte?« Er funkelte mich mit gerunzelten Brauen an.

»Ich meine, man … rammelt … wie die Kaninchen. Du weißt schon. Öffentlich und ziemlich ausdauernd.«

»In Schweden ist genau das das Problem mit den Bisamratten.«

»Okay«, sagte ich. »Egal.«

»Und es ist herrlich«, tönte Lars. »Immer ist nur von der Politik des kurdischen Volkes die Rede und nie von der Schönheit seiner Mädchen.«

»Da ist was dran«, sagte ich. Lars' Dame rückte hoheitsvoll gegen meinen ängstlich hingekauerten König vor. Sie wirkte gebieterisch, unverwundbar. Ich starrte finster vor mich hin.

»Und als wir wieder aufstehen – viele Stunden später –, da schreckt Sinbil zusammen. Neben ihr ist etwas auf dem Boden aufgeschlagen und hat Staub aufgewirbelt. ›Lars‹, sagt sie, ›ich glaube, da wirft jemand mit Steinen.‹«

»Aber du weißt natürlich, dass es keine Steine sind.«

»Natürlich sind es keine Steine. ›Sinbil‹, sage ich, ›das sind keine Steine. Lauf, schnell!‹« Lars schlug mit seiner Dame meinen Läufer. »›Im Zickzack!‹, sage ich. ›Lauf im Zickzack den Berg hoch!‹ Übrigens, Schach.«

Ich zog meinen König auf das Ausgangsfeld des Turms, wo er einsam und machtlos hocken blieb. Und ich gähnte, mein liebstes Täuschungsmanöver.

»Der Hang, den wir eine halbe Stunde lang hinunterspaziert waren – plötzlich sind wir in wenigen Sätzen wieder oben. So ist es, wenn man unter Feuer steht.«

Ich blinzelte in meinen Kaffee und versuchte einzuschätzen, wie viel Prozent von Lars' Erzählung in diesem Fall Bullshit waren. Er schien eine ungewöhnliche Sorte Lügner zu sein. Offenbar glaubte er mehr oder weniger selbst an seine Geschichten, war aber, so ungern ich es eingestand, nicht einfach nur verrückt. Er log auch nicht, um etwas zu erreichen, um andere zu manipulieren oder sich aufzuspielen. Sondern er log, glaube ich, um sein Leben zu erweitern. Er ging von einem wahren Ereignis aus und dehnte es in alle Richtungen, machte es verrückter, exotischer, katastrophaler. Er erzählte nicht, wie es wirklich gewesen war, sondern wie es hätte sein sollen.

»In letzter Sekunde springen wir ins Auto«, fuhr er fort. »Ich verfluche diese Bastarde auf Türkisch. Wir rasen Richtung Stadt davon, aber es dauert Stunden, bis wir da sind. Stell dir vor, wenn sie einen von uns angeschossen hätten, dann wären wir bis dahin sehr, sehr tot gewesen. Der Autoverleih sagt noch zu mir: ›Ach ja, in den Bergen gibt es Räuber, haben wir nicht gesagt, dass Sie dort nicht ohne Leibwächter hinfahren sollen?‹ Aber ich, ich wusste es besser.«

Er fing an abzuschweifen, und das bedeutete, dass er den Weg zum Sieg genau vor sich sah. In dem Moment entspannte er sich immer ein wenig, und sein steter Redefluss uferte weiter aus. Er lächelte und stellte rhetorische Fragen.

»Und was, glaubst du, wusste ich? Ich wusste, was für eine dumme Erklärung das war. Warum hätten die Räuber uns, zwei einfache Reisende mit bescheidenen Mitteln, nicht einmal Amerikaner, verfolgen sollen? Wie hätten sie uns in den Bergen auflauern sollen, wenn sie uns nicht dorthin gefolgt wären? Warum blieben sie nicht in der Stadt, wo die Räuberei sich viel mehr lohnt?«

Ich schielte sehnsüchtig zu meiner eigenen Dame hinüber, die von all dem Material umstellt war, das ich nicht zum Einsatz gebracht hatte – einem Springer, einem Turm, dem schwarzfeldigen Läufer. Alle vergeudet.

»O nein, das war zu einfach. Verdächtig einfach. Räuber? Also bitte. Das ist ja beleidigend.« Lars senkte die Stimme. »Es war der türkische Geheimdienst.«

»Also wirklich«, wandte ich ein, um Zeit zu gewinnen, obwohl ich schon wusste, wie wenig es mir nützen würde. »Was sollte denn ausgerechnet der türkische Geheimdienst von dir wollen? Was sollte überhaupt irgendwer von dir wollen, außer deinem Reisepass?«

»Psst!«, mahnte Lars. »Weißt du nicht, dass sie auch hier ihre Agenten haben? Sie haben schon einmal versucht, mich umzubringen. Willst du, dass sie mich doch noch erwischen? Das ist keine sehr ehrenhafte Methode, eine Niederlage abzuwenden. Übrigens, Schach.«

Lars' Dame hatte einen isolierten Bauern aus dem Feld geräumt, und ich stellte meinen König wieder auf seine vorige Position. Lars ließ seinen Springer zur Verstärkung vorrücken, was inzwischen reichlich übertrieben wirkte. Ich holte meinen eigenen Springer dazu, doch es war zu spät. Die Dame war unangreifbar; sie umkreiste meinen König mit einer Vorsicht, die fast schon höhnisch wirkte. Dann preschte aus dem Nichts ein Läufer heran und schlug meinen letzten Verteidigungsbauern. Ich kippte meinen König um.

»Okay«, sagte ich. »Das war's.«

»Ein Musterbeispiel dafür, was passiert, wenn die Bauernkette vor dem rochierten König durchbrochen wird«, schniefte Lars. »Aber nächstes Mal, nächstes Mal. Du wirst schon besser. Ich habe mich mehrmals gefürchtet.« Das sagte er ebenfalls jedes Mal. Es war unerträglich. Ich würde einiges dafür geben, Lars schachmatt zu setzen, bevor ich sterbe.

Nachdem ich meine Testergebnisse erfahren und meine Dissertation abgeschlossen hatte und während mein Vater immer noch im Sterben lag – er lag schon so lange im Sterben, dass es mir manchmal schwerfiel, mich an eine Zeit davor zu erinnern –, entwickelte ich eine Art triste, einsame Alltagsroutine. Samstags spielte ich mit Lars Schach. Sonntags besuchte ich meinen Vater, der in ein Pflegeheim eingewiesen worden war, als er nicht mehr wusste, wer und wo er war. Ich streichelte ihm den Arm, fütterte ihn mit Pralinen aus der Drogerie und führte muntere einseitige Gespräche. Unter der Woche gab ich an einer Technischen Hochschule im South End eine Einführung in das wissenschaftliche Schreiben. Meine Studenten waren wechselweise schwer von Begriff oder brillant, je nach meiner Laune. Die meisten wirkten desinteressiert, mit halbgaren Meinungen, die sie halbherzig vertraten. Das verblüffte mich immer wieder, schließlich hatte ich selbst in dem Alter ein ziemlich enges Verhältnis zu meinen Ansichten gehabt. Abends blieb ich lange im Büro, während die Kollegen sich einer nach dem anderen zu ihren jeweiligen Verpflichtungen aufmachten – nicht zu ihren Familien, denn die meisten waren in meinem Alter oder jünger, aber zu ihren festen Partnern, ihren Pilatesabenden, Katzen oder Zimmerpflanzen. Ihren aufgezeichneten Fernsehsendungen, Spanisch-Konversationskursen, Tangostunden. Jede dieser Freizeitbeschäftigungen, oder auch alle – fast alle – hätte ich auch wählen können, aber ich habe den Charakterfehler, dass ich es nicht fertigbringe, mich für aussichtslose Fälle zu engagieren. Ein Problem, das ziemlich einsam macht, wenn man selbst so ein aussichtsloser Fall ist.

Bei der Heimkehr fand ich meistens mehrere Nachrichten von meiner Mutter auf dem Anrufbeantworter. Oft ging es darin um Antioxidantien, von denen meine Mutter besessen war. Sie helfen anscheinend gegen Alzheimer und gegen einige Arten Krebs, aber es gibt keinerlei Hinweise, dass sie Einfluss auf den Verlauf von Huntington haben. Doch meine Mutter brauchte ihren gewollten, sorgsam kalibrierten Optimismus zum Überleben – die Sorte positives Denken, die es als Erfolg wertet, wenn etwas langsamer schiefgeht als erwartet. Sie schickte mir Päckchen mit dunkler Schokolade oder getrockneten Blaubeeren oder der Anweisung, *sofort* eine bestimmte Sorte Spinat zu kaufen, und dazu Zeitungsausschnitte über Menschen, die ihren schweren Schicksalen trotzten. Meine Mutter war nicht verrückt oder verblendet, sie glaubte nicht an Heilkristalle oder Wahrsagerei oder so. Das Sterben meines Vaters hatte sie mit dem Pragmatismus einer Weltkriegs-Lazarettschwester durchgestanden. Aber sie war der Überzeugung, dass das Leben wie der Tod besser oder schlechter verlaufen kann und dass es größtenteils an einem selbst liegt, wie man lebt und stirbt – ein Gedanke, den ich natürlich entsetzlich fand.

Nachdem wir meinen Vater im Pflegeheim untergebracht hatten, zog meine Mutter nach Sedona, Arizona, um herauszufinden, was sich mit ihrem Leben noch anfangen ließ. Sie begann Schmuck herzustellen. Sie fand einen zutiefst sonnengebräunten neuen Partner. Sie holte Schlaf nach. Vermutlich betrachtete sie diese Zeit als kurzes Intermezzo zwischen zwei Tragödien. Ich weiß, dass sie zurückkehren wollte, wenn meine Zeit gekommen war. Der Gedanke, sie für weitere zwei Jahrzehnte Vollzeitpflege aus ihrem gerade erst begonnenen neuen Leben zu reißen, beglückte mich nicht gerade. Die Arme hatte Besseres verdient.

Ich hatte nicht viele Freunde. Das könnte ich meiner allgemeinen Verbohrtheit zuschreiben, und teilweise lag es wohl daran. Doch es kam noch etwas hinzu: Es macht einsam, wenn absolut niemand über die Dinge sprechen will, die einen am meisten beschäftigen. Mein Vater schien für meine Freunde all die Jahre ein Tabuthema zu sein, und selbst seinen Tod ignorierten sie im Großen und Ganzen. Meinen eigenen genetischen Status ließen sie bei Gesprächen geflissentlich außen vor, als sei er eine grauenhafte Missbildung und als seien sie höfliche Fremde. Wer noch niemanden verloren hat, glaubt die Trauer erst heraufzubeschwören, wenn er sie erwähnt. Wer sich nie mit seiner Sterblichkeit auseinandersetzen musste, spricht nicht über den Tod, weil er denkt, er werde erst dadurch real. Und in meinen jungen Jahren hatte keiner meiner Freunde jemand anderen begraben müssen als seine Großeltern oder seinen Hund. Also erkundigte sich niemand nach meinem Vater. Also erkundigte sich niemand nach mir. Und Trauer, die nie Ausdruck findet, geht irgendwann in Verbitterung über.

Auch mein Vater muss in den Jahren vor seinem endgültigen Verfall einiges an Einsamkeit und Verbitterung durchgemacht haben. Vielleicht hat er deshalb Alexander Besetow als eine Art Seelenverwandten angesehen. Oder vielleicht war es etwas anderes – die Vorstellung von Jugend, die der Vergänglichkeit trotzt, oder von einem Intellekt, der stärker ist als die Entropie. Mein Vater war ein Mann, der seinen Verstand liebte und wusste, dass er ihn eines Tages verlieren würde. Vielleicht war es das, was Alexander zu seinem Helden machte – hier war jemand, dessen neurologische Schaltkreise selbst über sieben Zeitzonen und einen Kalten Krieg hinweg ihre Strahlkraft nicht verloren. Hier war jemand, der um den Wert seiner eigenen Intelligenz ebenso wusste wie um ihre kurze Lebensdauer.

Eines Abends im Winter, als ich sieben Jahre alt war, hatte ich so hohes Fieber, dass die Schatten an der Wand sich in Tiere verwandelten und das Zimmer sich um mich drehte. Es schneite, und die Flocken wurden im Licht der Laternen rot, während ich an der diffusen, allumfassenden Angst eines kranken Kindes litt. Ich ging hinunter ins Wohnzimmer, wo mein Vater mit einem Glas Bourbon saß. Auf dem verrauschten Fernsehbildschirm waren zwei dunkle, wütend dreinblickende Gestalten an einem Schachbrett zu sehen.

»Dad?«, sagte ich mit fiebrig zitternder Stimme.

»Sieh dir das an«, sagte er. »Komm her.«

Ich setzte mich auf seinen Schoß und schwitzte in seinen Hemdkragen. Die Männer im Fernsehen waren vor lauter Rauschen kaum zu erkennen – graue, verschwommene Schemen, die sich bei jeder Bewegung verzerrten wie geisterhafte Relikte einer fremden Welt.

»Wo sind die?«

»In Russland. Das ist sehr weit weg. Ein riesiges Land östlich von Europa.«

»Es sieht auch weit weg aus«, sagte ich. »Ist es da kalt?« Der Raum, in dem die Männer saßen, hatte eine kühle Atmosphäre. Zwischen ihnen herrschte ein geladenes, intensives Schweigen, als könnte man, wenn man nur aufmerksam genug lauschte, durch das statische Rauschen ihre stummen Flüche, Beleidigungen und Grübeleien hören. Der jüngere der beiden Männer kratzte sich am Kinn und opferte einen Läufer.

»Schau dir den hier an«, sagte mein Vater und legte einen Finger auf die Mattscheibe, obwohl das gegen eine der Regeln meiner Mutter verstieß. »Er ist erst zweiundzwanzig.« Der Mann, den er berührte, wirkte grau und hager, doch seine Augen sprühten vor gespannter Intelligenz. Er packte die Figuren mit zornigem, fast schon aufsässigem Ungestüm. Sein Gegner ging behutsam mit den Spielfiguren um, legte beinahe zärtlich seine Hand um einen Läufer und ließ sie nach dem Zug noch einen Augenblick dort verweilen. Der Jüngere kratzte sich energisch am Kopf und zog mit beiläufiger Ungeduld seine Dame. »Bald ist er der jüngste Schachweltmeister der Geschichte«, sagte mein Vater nachdenklich.

Die beiden Männer starrten einander stumm an, und wir starrten die Männer an. Mein Vater strich mir über die Stirn, und ich wurde schläfrig, doch ich wollte wach bleiben, um zu sehen, was er mir zeigen wollte. Die Zeit schien wie eingefroren. Bis auf das Rauschen der Bildstörung war es ganz still, und wir saßen lange nur da und sahen zu, bis im Endspiel der Punkt kam, ab dem nichts mehr zu ändern war. Ich habe mich seither viel mit der Partie beschäftigt: wie Alexander seinen schwarzen Turm opferte, der beinahe gierig von Russajews weißem Springer geschlagen wurde, und dann den zweiten Turm – der reglos wie ein Tier am anderen Ende des Bretts gekauert hatte, vom Publikum und dem alten Mann unbemerkt – quer über das Feld zog. Damals begriff ich nur, dass mein Vater fasziniert war. Er lehnte sich unmerklich nach vorn. In dem monochromen, östlichen Licht ließ Alexander seine Knöchel knacken. Der König seines Gegners lag tot auf der Seite. Vielleicht war aus dem Publikum die Andeutung eines Überraschungslauts zu hören. Oder vielleicht habe ich es mir nur eingebildet. Aber ich erinnere mich noch an die Worte meines Vaters nach dem Spiel, auch wenn mir bis heute nicht klar ist, ob er die Wahrheit sagte.

»Siehst du«, sagte er und stellte den Fernseher ab, mit einem Lichtblitz, der in meinen Augen tanzende Flecken hinterließ. Die roten Schneeflocken sanken langsamer und immer langsamer zur Erde. Mein Vater sprach so leise, dass ich nicht wusste, ob er mit mir oder mit sich selbst redete. »Siehst du«, sagte er, und ich begann wieder zu zittern. »Du kannst eine Menge erreichen, bevor du dreißig bist.«

KAPITEL 3

Alexander
Leningrad, 1980

Als Alexander zum ersten Mal das Café besuchte, erkannten ihn Iwan und Nikolai nicht wieder. Er war im Laufe des Winters dünner geworden, weil seine Mutter nicht da war, um ihm Unappetitliches schmackhafter zu machen, und sah blasser aus. Die erbarmungslose Kälte hatte ihm einen hohläugigen, verlorenen Ausdruck verpasst. Selbst seine Bewegungen wirkten unbeholfen, mit steifen Gliedern, die Schultern bis zu den Ohren hochgezogen, als wollte jeder Muskel sich einwärts verkriechen. Er war nicht mehr der Alte, und selbst der war schon nicht sehr beeindruckend gewesen. Als er daher in einer pechschwarzen, verschneiten Januarnacht das Saigon betrat, schlug ihm von Iwan und Nikolai blankes Misstrauen entgegen. Sie saßen in einer Nische, vor sich winzige Wodkagläser und zwischen sich einen gewaltigen, ziegelsteinförmigen Aschenbecher. Die dunkelgrünen Vorhänge um ihren Tisch waren von Zigarettenrauch und verschwörerischen Blicken angegraut. Iwan hatte eine Zigarette zwischen seine langen Finger geklemmt und redete; Nikolai nickte eifrig und machte sich Notizen. Alexander stand unschlüssig dabei und mochte sie nicht stören.

»Was willst du?«, fragte Iwan schließlich. Er trug ein ausgefranstes Sex-Pistols-T-Shirt und das silberne Medaillon, das er schon bei der Hundertjahrfeier angehabt hatte. Alexander nahm die Mütze ab und ließ ein wenig Schnee auf den Cafétisch rieseln.

»Scheiße«, sagte Nikolai. Ein Schneewölkchen trübte seinen Wodka. »Wer zum Teufel bist du überhaupt?«

»Das wollte er uns bestimmt gerade erzählen«, sagte Iwan.

Alexander sah sich um. Das Café war dunkel und labyrinthisch, nur hier und da erhellte gedämpftes Licht eine Nische – ein Mann und eine Frau ohne Eheringe saßen sehr dicht beisammen und redeten; Gruppen junger Männer unterhielten sich stoßweise, in jähen Ausbrüchen von Lärm und Gelächter; ein einzelner Mann im Rollstuhl wiegte sich vor und zurück und zeichnete gestikulierend mit seiner Zigarettenglut Satellitenumlaufbahnen in das Dämmerlicht. Alexander schloss einen Moment lang die Augen und ließ die Stimmen zu einem Mosaik ineinanderlaufen. Sie klangen entspannt, fand er, ob sie lachten, lallten oder säuselten. Es klang wie in einem Schlafzimmer, nicht wie in der Öffentlichkeit. Später begriff er, dass dies der Klang von Stimmen war, die nicht logen.

»Also was?«, fragte Iwan streng. »Hast du dich verlaufen?«

»Ich bin Alexander Kimowitsch«, sagte Alexander. »Wir haben uns bei der Hundertjahrfeier kennengelernt. Sie haben dort Aufzeichnungen gemacht. Ich bin vor kurzem hergezogen.«

»Was?«, machte Nikolai. Sein katastrophal zerklüftetes Gesicht verzog sich zu einer Maske der Besorgnis; er sah, fand Alexander, wie ein sozialrealistisches Gemälde aus – *Der Inbegriff jugendlicher Angst und Sorge!*

»Sie haben mir diese Adresse gegeben«, sagte Alexander und kam sich sofort idiotisch vor. »Sie haben sie aufgeschrieben und gesagt, ich sollte vorbeikommen.«

»Wann war das?«, fragte Nikolai. Der Schnee in seinem Glas begann zu schmelzen. Alexander erinnerte sich, wie er einmal in der Volksschule einen Zettel bekommen hatte, der ihn einlud, eines der Mädchen mittags unter der großen Kiefer zu treffen, und wie er dort gewartet und nichts begriffen hatte.

»Jetzt weiß ich«, sagte Iwan und aschte seine Zigarette ab. »Du bist das Schachwunder, oder?«

Alexander wandte den Blick ab. »Ich bin nur an der Akademie.«

»Ich habe einiges über dich gelesen«, sagte Iwan. »Du hast dich gemacht.«

»Danke«, sagte Alexander und wusste nicht, was er sonst noch sagen sollte. Er wollte nicht den Eindruck erwecken, als sei er hergekommen, um sich gratulieren zu lassen.

»Aber bitte setz dich, setz dich doch«, sagte Iwan. »Nikolai Sergejewitsch, würdest du so gütig sein und dem jungen Mann Wodka bestellen?« Nikolai warf Alexander einen langen, prüfenden Blick zu und trollte sich, nicht ohne nach den jungen Frauen am Nebentisch zu schielen. »Also. Alexander Kimowitsch. Was hältst du von unserer Stadt?« Iwan lächelte wie ein sowjetischer Botschafter, der einen Drittweltdiktator zu becircen versucht.

»Sie ist sehr nett«, sagte Alexander.

Darüber lachte Iwan. In der aufglimmenden Glut seiner Zigarette verzog sich sein Gesicht zu metallisch glatten Ecken und Kanten. Er hob eine Augenbraue. »Keine Schwierigkeiten in deiner Wohnung?«

»Nein«, sagte Alexander, auch wenn er sich zuweilen wünschte, er hätte welche. Manchmal wünschte er, die Verwalterin oder einer der anderen Mieter würde in sein feuchtkaltes, flackernd erleuchtetes Zimmer platzen und fragen, was er triebe. Der Winter war so einsam gewesen, dass ihm jede Störung willkommen gewesen wäre.

»Wo ist der andere?«, fragte Alexander. Er erinnerte sich noch an den Dritten in dem Trio, der am verhärmtesten ausgesehen und erzählt hatte, sie befassten sich mit wirklicher Geschichte.

»Mischa.« Iwan zögerte und tippte sich mit den langen Fingern ans Kinn. »Du hast ein verdammt gutes Gedächtnis, wenn du dich an den armen Mischa erinnerst.«

»Danke«, sagte Alexander. Er hatte wirklich ein verdammt gutes Gedächtnis, auch wenn Andronow betonte, dass seine größte Stärke beim Schach darin lag, alles Gelernte zu vergessen und etwas ganz Neues zu versuchen.

Nikolai kehrte mit einem Tablett voller kristallin schimmernder Stoli-Gläser zurück. Alexander dankte ihm, und Iwan schwieg. Iwan hob sein Glas und stieß mit Nikolai an. »Auf Mischa«, sagte er.

Nikolai trank, ohne den Trinkspruch zu erwidern. Alexander nahm eins der Wodkagläser und betrachtete es. Bläulich schillernde Schlieren durchzogen die Flüssigkeit.

»Was ist?«, fragte Iwan. »Kennt man das bei euch im Osten nicht? Das trinkt man.«

»Schon klar.« Es zog ihm den Mund zusammen; Alexander presste die Lippen aufeinander und schluckte. Iwan lachte.

»Was macht ihr da drüben den ganzen Tag?«, fragte Nikolai.

»Es ist nicht so kalt wie hier. Und es gibt genug zu tun.« Alexander kippte den Rest seines Wodka hinunter, um zu beweisen, dass er es konnte, und Iwan reichte ihm den nächsten.

»Unser Freund Mischa«, sagte Iwan, »hat sich leider ein bisschen Ärger eingehandelt.«

»Das tut mir leid«, sagte Alexander. Die Sehnen an seinem Hals begannen sich zu entspannen, und er bekam Lust, sich umzusehen. Von der hohen, höhlenartigen Decke baumelten absinthfarbene Glühlampen. Oberhalb der Bar blitzten die silbrigen Fischbäuche der Flaschen. Der Mann im Rollstuhl fluchte noch immer vor sich hin und stach mit seiner Zigarette Löcher in die Luft.

»Wer ist das?«, fragte Alexander. »Mit wem redet er?«

»Du bist komisch«, sagte Iwan. »Du hast komische Prioritäten.«

»Alkohol bekommt mir nicht«, sagte Alexander. Er bereute allmählich, dass er gekommen war. »Er stört mich beim Denken und ist schlecht für mein Gedächtnis. Im Schach ist das Erinnerungsvermögen das Wichtigste. Und die Vorstellungskraft.«

»Erinnerungen und Vorstellungen sind praktisch illegal«, sagte Iwan. »Sollen wir dir lieber ein Bier bestellen?«

»Das Bier hier ist pures Wasser«, sagte Nikolai. »Beleidige ihn nicht. Bier ist was für Kinder.«

Sie reichten Alexander noch ein Glas Wodka, und er rollte es zwischen den Fingern hin und her. Es lag sauber und glatt in der Hand, und solange es voll war, hatte es fast dasselbe Gewicht wie der König eines guten Sets. Nikolai zog eine Zigarre aus seiner Tasche hervor und benutzte ein Streichholzheftchen des Café Saigon, um sie anzustecken. Süßliche Rauchschwaden kräuselten sich empor. Alexander fühlte sich, als sei sein Kopf an einem Faden befestigt und wippte im Takt mit seinen Gesten oberhalb des Körpers hin und her wie von einem unsichtbaren Puppenspieler bewegt.

»Was ist mit Mischa passiert?«, fragte Alexander. Das Sprechen fiel ihm schwer. Ein unsinniges Gefühl der Gelassenheit durchströmte ihn, eine angenehme Erschlaffung, in der nur Weniges noch denkbar schien: in tiefen Zügen den zimtenen Zigarrenduft zu atmen oder die grünen Leuchtbojen auf dem schwarzen Meer der Saaldecke schaukeln zu sehen.

»Tja«, sagte Iwan. »Mischa hat Dummheiten gemacht, Alexander Kimowitsch. Ich werde es dir erzählen, damit du nicht dieselben Dummheiten machst.«

»Okay«, antwortete Alexander dümmlich. Die Zunge lag ihm schwer im Mund.

»Wenn ich ehrlich sein soll, machst du nämlich nicht den allerhellsten Eindruck«, sagte Iwan.

»Nein«, sagte Nikolai. »Allerdings nicht.«

»Ich weiß, dass du ein brillanter Schachspieler bist«, sagte Iwan. »So steht es in der Zeitung. Und ich glaube alles, was in der Zeitung steht.«

»Alles«, sagte Nikolai.

»Aber man kann in einer Sache gut und in einer anderen schlecht sein«, fuhr Iwan fort.

»Oder in einer Sache gut und in allen anderen schlecht«, sagte Nikolai.

»Mischa hat Dummheiten gemacht«, sagte Iwan. »Er hat Unwahrheiten in Umlauf gebracht. Er hat Dinge gesagt, die nicht offiziell als Wahrheiten anerkannt sind.«

»Er hat diffamierende Behauptungen über die Sowjetunion und den Kommunismus verbreitet«, sagte Nikolai.

»Ach ja?«

»Er hat eine Petition unterzeichnet«, sagte Iwan, »und sie haben ihn in eine Psichuschka gesteckt. Wir wissen nicht, wann er wieder rauskommt.« Er rieb sich mit flatternden Händen die dunkel behaarten Schläfen.

»Er ist ein Idiot«, sagte Nikolai. Wenn er sich ins Licht drehte, wurden die Narben auf seinem Gesicht zu lilafarbenen Fingerabdrücken.

»Die Sache ist die«, sagte Iwan, »dass ich fürchte – und ich hoffe, du nimmst es mir nicht übel –, du könntest ihm ein bisschen zu ähnlich sein. Halte dich nicht an das, was die Leute dir sagen, es sei denn, sie sind von den zuständigen Stellen. Halte dich an die Verkehrsregeln.«

»Ich habe kein Auto«, sagte Alexander.

»Tu niemandem einen Gefallen. Ziehe nie voreilige Schlüsse. Du warst doch im Komsomol?«

Alexander schüttelte den Kopf. »In Ocha muss man das nicht unbedingt. Es ist so ein kleiner Ort. Sie etwa?«

»Alle waren dabei«, sagte Iwan schroff. Er hob die Brauen und presste die Lippen aufeinander. »Alle anständigen jungen Leute.«

»Verstehe«, sagte Alexander. Sein Kopf wurde allmählich wieder klarer, und die Deckenlampen pulsierten wie blassgrüne Himmelskörper gegen seine Augenlider. Nikolai und Iwan unterhielten sich ein wenig über Musik, dann über Frauen und dann über die Invasion Afghanistans und wie lange die sowjetischen Streitkräfte brauchen würden, um seine staubige, unkultivierte Landschaft und Bevölkerung zu unterwerfen. Alexander hatte das Thema kaum mitverfolgt, bis auf ein paar Überschriften, die ihm beim Blättern auf dem Weg zum nächsten Schachartikel ins Auge gesprungen waren – von »Interventionspflicht« war da die Rede und von der »Einladung unseres sozialistischen Brudervolks in Afghanistan« –, und hörte nur mit halbem Ohr hin. Er dachte an Mischa, der Pech gehabt hatte und in einem psychiatrischen Gefängnis gelandet war. Und an die unzähligen unverständlichen Formulare, die er für die Übersiedlung nach Leningrad gebraucht hatte, die er unterschrieben hatte, ohne sie überhaupt zu lesen. Er stand auf, um zur Toilette zu gehen.

Neben der Tür zu den Toiletten redete der Mann im Rollstuhl noch immer lebhaft mit sich selbst. »Arschlöcher«, schimpfte er und fuchtelte mit seiner Zigarette. Sein Kinn ruhte auf seiner Brust, als wollte er seinem Bauch ein Geheimnis erzählen. Die Beine des Mannes, oder was davon übrig war, wirkten verschrumpelt, und sein Gesicht war eingefallen. Als er den Kopf hob, erkannte Alexander, dass ihm Zähne fehlten, was nicht ungewöhnlich war, jedoch den beunruhigend ausgehöhlten Gesamteindruck verstärkte. Der Mann sah aus, als hätte man ihn in seine Einzelteile zerlegt und falsch wieder zusammengesetzt. »Verdammte Arschlöcher«, sagte der Mann noch einmal und sah Alexander direkt in die Augen. »Trau ihnen bloß nicht.« Das grünliche Licht umgab ihn mit einem radioaktiven Schimmer.

»Wem? Wen meinen Sie?« Alexander wollte es wirklich wissen, stellte er fest.

Der Mann bedeutete Alexander mit einem gekrümmten Zeigefinger näherzukommen. Alexander beugte sich zu ihm hinab; der Mann roch nach Rost und Alkohol und etwas, das Alexander traurig machte, ohne dass er hätte sagen können, warum.

»Wer sind die Arschlöcher?«, fragte Alexander noch einmal.

»Alle sind sie Arschlöcher«, flüsterte der Mann und brach in ein beängstigendes, halb ersticktes Lachen aus. Er vollführte eine weit ausladende Geste, die alle Menschen im Raum mit einbezog und Asche auf Alexanders Schuhe verstreute. »Jeder Einzelne!«

Als Alexander Stunden später auf die vereisten Straßen hinaustaumelte, war am östlichen Himmel ein aschfahler Streifen aufgetaucht. Das Licht sah aus, als sei es durch ein schmutziges Tuch gegossen worden, und die Schneeklumpen wurden flaumig wie Schimmelflecken. Ein zerfledderter Handzettel mit einer Warnung gegen den Teufel Alkohol klebte unter Alexanders Schuh, und er schüttelte ihn ab. In der Luft hing der Benzingeruch im Leerlauf wartender Schigulis. Leningrad rüstete sich für einen neuen Tag. In den dunklen Mauernischen versammelten sich die Straßenhändler: braun gekleidete Männer mit Gemüsekarren voller grauer Rüben und Kohlköpfe, denen die aufgehende Sonne allmählich Farbe verlieh. Eine frierende Frau mit Fischen, deren Bäuche zungenfarben glänzten. Bemützte Jungen kauerten an den Straßenecken und hielten nach der Polizei Ausschau, damit ihre Familien rechtzeitig die Ware zusammenraffen und fliehen konnten. Sie verschwanden so rasch wie die lichtscheuen Kakerlaken in der Kommunalka, wie einer, der in ein Auto steigt und nie mehr wiederkehrt.

Alexander ging den Newski-Prospekt entlang, am Museum für die Geschichte der Religion und des Atheismus vorüber. Leningrad war so ganz anders als Ocha, dies gesichtslose Kaff, das niemand gewollt oder geplant hatte. Leningrad strotzte vor weiser Voraussicht und geometrischer Präzision – der steingewordene Beweis, dass auch Russen mehr als eine Generation vorausplanen konnten. Es war eine schöne Stadt, wenn man im beißenden Wind lange genug die Augen aufbekam, um richtig hinzusehen. Doch Alexander sah auf seinem Heimweg von dem ersten Abend mit Iwan und Nikolai kaum von seinen Füßen hoch. Die neue Stadt, dachte er, hielt neue Bedrohungen für ihn bereit, subtiler und heimtückischer als KGB-Männer in weißen Wolgas. In Ocha hatte er die Spielregeln beherrscht; er war die Begrenzungen seines Lebensraums so oft abgeschritten, dass er selbst im Traum nicht daran dachte, sie zu überschreiten. Er hatte dort alle und jeden gekannt, jedermanns Großeltern, Pockennarben und lehmige Gemüsegärten, und wenn es Andersdenkende gegeben hätte, dann hätte er auch das gewusst.

In Leningrad, das begriff er jetzt, war es anders. Er war nie zuvor auf die Idee gekommen, sich vor alten Leuten zu fürchten, die Papier sammelten. Er hatte nie Angst vor den Rosenverkäuferinnen an den Straßenecken gehabt.

Als Alexander nach Hause kam, stand eins der Nachtmädchen im Flur, und der Schnee an ihren Stiefeln gerann zu öligen Flecken auf dem Teppichboden. Sie pochte heftig an die Zimmertür der Verwalterin, was seit Alexanders Ankunft noch nie geschehen war. Er blieb stehen, um zu sehen, was dabei herauskommen würde.

»Was gibt es da zu gucken?«, raunzte ihn das Mädchen an. Sie hatte dunklere Haare als die andere, und Alexander hatte sie schon oft im Flur laut fluchen gehört. Der Familienvater aus dem Nebenzimmer hatte sich schon einmal darüber beschwert, während er sich zu Alexander hinüberbeugte und in sein Waschbecken spuckte. »Es gefällt mir nicht, dass mein Kind Tür an Tür mit Bljadi aufwachsen muss«, sagte der Mann. »Es wird ihn dazu treiben, Fragen zu stellen, und je weniger Fragen er stellt, desto besser für ihn.«

Das Mädchen schnipste vor Alexanders Gesicht mit den Fingern. »Also, was?«, sagte sie. »Kannst du nicht sprechen?«

»Ich kann sprechen.«

»Ach.« Sie sah enttäuscht aus. »Dann habe ich eine Wette verloren.«

»Was machst du da?«, fragte Alexander. »Soweit ich weiß, kommt sie morgens nicht an die Tür.«

»Heute Morgen muss sie kommen. Mir egal, wie verkatert sie ist. Da waren Maden im Wasserhahn. So geht es nicht.«

»Was für Maden?«

»Was für Maden? Wen zur Hölle interessiert das? Ich habe das warme Wasser angedreht. Ich bin es gewohnt, dass keins kommt. Das hätte mich nicht überrascht. Wir kennen uns nicht, Towarischtsch, aber es gibt nicht vieles, das mich überrascht. Aber Maden? Das geht zu weit.« Ihr braunes Haar wogte ihr ins Gesicht, und sie fegte es so unwirsch beiseite, dass Alexander am liebsten dazwischengegangen wäre, um sie vor sich selbst zu schützen.

»Ja«, sagte er. »Das geht zu weit.«

»Also habe ich mir gedacht, ich unterhalte mich mal mit der alten Dame.« Sie hämmerte weiter auf die Tür ein, mit scharfen, unrhythmischen, möglichst nervtötenden Stößen. »Schließlich habe ich eine lange Nacht hinter mir. Ich arbeite nachts, weißt du?«

»Ich weiß.«

»Du weißt es.« Sie hämmerte noch lauter. »Natürlich weißt du es. Genauso wie ich weiß, dass du das Schachwunder aus Sibirien bist, das …«

»Aus Sachalin.«

»Auch gut«, sagte sie.

Trotz allem erstaunte es Alexander, wie rasend empört sie war.

Sie klopfte an die Tür wie jemand, dem ein furchtbares Unrecht widerfahren war. Maden im Badezimmer waren schlimm, keine Frage. Doch sie hatte sicher Schlimmeres erlebt.

»Welche bist du?«, fragte er.

»Was?« Sie drehte sich nach ihm um, und er hörte das leise Klimpern und Klackern dieser Bewegung, das unverwechselbar weibliche Geräusch von hohen Absätzen und Schmuck. Sie war ganz in Schwarz gekleidet, doch das Ensemble schien aus mehreren Schichten zu bestehen – vielleicht aus Bluse, Jacke und Rock? Ihr Gesicht war hübsch, wenn auch nicht hübsch genug, um die gesamte Aufmerksamkeit zu tragen, welche die schwarze Kleidung darauf lenkte. Es war ein Auftritt wie ein Trommelwirbel.

»Bist du Sonja oder die andere?«, fragte Alexander. Er wusste den anderen Namen nicht mehr und wusste auch nicht, was wahre Erinnerungen waren und welche er sich nur ausgedacht hatte. Prostituierte waren sie wirklich, dachte Alexander. Ob sie wirklich einen Wellensittich hatten, war eine andere Frage.

»Ich bin die andere. Elisabeta Nasarowna.« Sie lehnte resigniert ihren Kopf an die Tür. »Ich glaube, sie ist nicht da.«

»Ich heiße Alexander Kimowitsch Besetow.«

»Auch gut«, sagte sie, ohne ihm die Hand zu geben. Stattdessen wandte sie sich wieder der Tür zu und begann mit leiser Stimme Unflätigkeiten hervorzustoßen. »Du Schlampe. Du Hexe. Du verlogene, miese kollaborative Drecksau.« Sie hielt inne, und Alexander fragte sich, ob ihr die Beleidigungen ausgegangen waren.

»Solltest du nicht vielleicht versuchen, nett zu ihr zu sein?«, fragte er. Vielleicht würde die Verwalterin Elisabeta das Zimmer kündigen oder ihre Habe aus dem Haus werfen wie bei dem Universitätsdozenten. Er stellte sich Elisabetas über den Vorgarten verteilte Besitztümer vor: Bücher und Parfümflakons, schwarze Kleidung, silbernen Schmuck.

»Quatsch. Die verkauft jedes Jahr Wintersachen aus dem Keller. Ich weiß es, weil ich meine Handschuhe von ihr habe. Sie ist wie eine Spinne. Hat mehr Angst vor uns als umgekehrt.« Wieder wandte sie sich der Tür zu. »Und wie eine Spinne«, zischte sie, »verkriechst du dich den ganzen Tag in dunklen Ecken, bist ein widerlicher Anblick, und alle hassen dich. Übrigens«, sie drehte sich zu Alexander um, »rauchst du?«

»Zigaretten?«

»Ja.« Jetzt würde er damit anfangen müssen.

Elisabeta nickte. »Sonja und ich tun nämlich nichts anderes, als zu rauchen und Lügen zu erzählen. Wenn du uns dabei Gesellschaft leisten willst, nur zu. Ich weiß, dass du nichts zu tun hast.«

»Aber ich habe zu tun. Ich bin an der Akademie. Ich trainiere«, sagte er. Er hatte noch nie versucht, jemanden mit seinem Talent zu beeindrucken, und merkte selbst, wie schlecht es ihm gelang. Er räusperte sich, fixierte einen Punkt knapp oberhalb von Elisabetas Kopf und bemühte sich, intellektuell, beschäftigt und tiefgründig zu wirken. »Das Schachspiel hält mich ganz schön in Atem.«

»Klar«, sagte sie. »Dann also, wenn du mal einen Moment Zeit hast.« Hinter der Zimmertür waren Geräusche zu hören, ärgerliches Gemurmel und Geraschel. Grelles Licht drang unter dem Türspalt hervor und durch die Ritzen. Die Alte begann sich zu regen.

»Endlich, du Missgeburt«, murmelte Elisabeta, und dann säuselte sie: »Babuschka? Poschaluista? Bitte, Mütterchen, hier ist deine Mieterin Elisabeta mit einer Frage. Vielleicht springen auch ein paar Rubel dabei heraus.«

Bei diesen Worten öffnete die Verwalterin die Tür. Ihr fahles, behaartes Gesicht blinzelte verkniffen und giftig in den Flur hinaus. Um den Kopf hatte sie sich einen rostroten Schal geschlungen und roch nach billigem Tee und freudlosen Nächten.

»Was?«, schnauzte sie und starrte Alexander an, der rasch beiseitetrat. »Was gibt es, in Gottes Namen?«

»Maden im Wasserhahn, Babuschka«, sagte Elisabeta. »Bitte entschuldige die Störung. Ich weiß, wie beschäftigt du bist.« Sie blinzelte Alexander zu.

»Allerdings«, sagte die Alte und verschwand wieder in ihrer Wohnung, vermutlich, um das für Maden benötigte Werkzeug zu holen.

Elisabeta lächelte und zuckte mit den Schultern. »Vergiss nicht«, raunte sie Alexander zu. »Zimmer neun, wenn du Lust auf Zigaretten und ein bisschen Abwechslung bekommst. Vielen Dank, Babuschka!«, rief sie. »Ich bin so dankbar für deine Hilfe!«

»Gut«, sagte Alexander, lauschte im Gehen ihren blanken Lügen und staunte, wie routiniert sie Gefühle vortäuschte, die sie nicht empfand.

Nach einer kalten Dusche – den Warmwasserhahn hatte er gar nicht erst angerührt – und einem Tag voller lähmender Erschöpfung und dummer Fehler in der Schachakademie kehrte Alexander in sein Zimmer zurück und legte sich auf sein Bett. Es war erst fünf, doch wie immer schon dunkel, und sein Bett fühlte sich nach der langen Abwesenheit noch kälter an als sonst. Er dachte kurz an Elisabeta, wie sie sich in Zimmer neun auf die Nacht vorbereitete, und fragte sich, ob er hinübergehen, nach einer Zigarette fragen und sich erkundigen sollte, wie die Sache mit den Maden ausgegangen war. Vielleicht konnte er sich auf Elisabetas Bett setzen, das genauso ungemacht wäre wie seins, und sich eine Zigarette mit ihr teilen. Prostituierte mussten vermutlich genauso haushalten wie Schachstudenten. Vielleicht wäre auch ihre Mitbewohnerin Sonja da, und er könnte den beiden von seinem nächtlichen Ausflug erzählen. »Café Saigon«, würde er lässig einfließen lassen. »Mal davon gehört?« Wenn ja, wunderbar, und wenn sie es nicht kannten, umso besser. »Wie kannst du ganz ohne Schlaf so gut sein?«, würden sie ihn besorgt fragen. Und er würde einen tiefen Zug von seiner Zigarette nehmen, ohne zu husten, und würde ihnen zublinzeln und sagen: »Übungssache.«

Sein Bett wurde ein wenig wärmer, und er zog seine Hände in die Ärmel und rieb sie aneinander. Wenn er es sich recht überlegte, sollte er vielleicht doch nicht gehen. Er dachte an Mischa, der sich in der eiskalten Zelle einer Psichuschka hin und her wälzte, weil er einem Fremden einen Gefallen getan hatte. Er dachte an den Beinamputierten und seine Behauptung, dass alle, dass jeder Einzelne ein Arschloch war. Möglicherweise hatte er recht. Alexander drehte sich auf die Seite, rieb seine Füße aneinander und versuchte sich an alles zu erinnern, was er noch von seinem Elternhaus in Ocha wusste. Er stellte sich seine kleinen Schwestern vor, die ihm so ähnlich sahen und die schneller als der Blitz zwischen Glück und Verachtung hin und her wechselten. Er dachte an seine Mutter, die nächtelang aufblieb, undurchschaubare Gedanken wälzte und unerträglich traurige Lieder sang. Sicher war es besser, nicht in Elisabetas Zimmer zu gehen. Alexanders Stärke waren seine Erinnerungen, waren Gedächtnis und Vorstellungskraft. Und ob diese Fähigkeiten für ein Leben in der Sowjetunion nützlich waren oder nicht, sie hatten jedenfalls den Vorzug, dass man sie in aller Stille ausüben konnte, in einem kleinen gemieteten Zimmer, ganz für sich allein.

KAPITEL 4

Irina
Cambridge, Massachusetts, 2006

Eines Tages im Frühjahr, als ich mit Lars Schach spielte, blieb der Mann, der später Jonathan war, stehen und sah uns zu. Ich weiß nicht, warum er das tat; seine eigenen Antworten auf diese Frage habe ich nie so recht glauben können. Lars und ich müssen ein sehr ungleiches Paar abgegeben haben – ein verschlagener Alter und eine beunruhigend blasse junge Frau, die einander über eine phantasielose Konstellation hinweg niederzustarren versuchten –, und meine erste Vermutung war, dass der Mann mit sich selbst gewettet hatte, wer gewinnen würde. Ich ließ meinen Läufer quer über das Brett segeln, bis er Plastikauge in Plastikauge Lars' Springer gegenüberstand. Der Springer war gedeckt, also brachte der Zug mich nicht wirklich weiter. Doch aus unerfindlichen Gründen hatte ich das Bedürfnis, etwas besonders Dramatisches zu tun.

»Jemand beobachtet uns«, sagte Lars laut.

Der Mann hüstelte. »Ich hoffe, es stört Sie nicht.«

»Nein«, sagte Lars. »Aber hören Sie mit dem Husten auf.«

Ich schätze, diese erste Begegnung hat für mich im Nachhinein mythische Proportionen angenommen. Da ich ebenso areligiös wie krankhaft selbstbezogen bin, müssen wohl meine Erinnerungen dafür herhalten, dem Ganzen einen Sinn abzugewinnen. Der Mann blieb. Damals war es mir vermutlich eher unangenehm, wie er uns beobachtete, während sein Schal im Wind flatterte und seine Augen vor Kälte feucht wurden. Er war einigermaßen attraktiv, aber nicht auffallend schön. Und doch frage ich mich, ob ich nicht schon damals etwas ganz Besonderes, etwas eigenartig Passendes in seinem Gesicht gesehen habe – in seinem lockigen Haar, seinem leicht vorspringenden Kinn, den kohlschwarzen Stoppeln auf seinen Wangen, in seinem müden und zugleich beängstigend intelligenten Blick. Es könnte sein, dass mir sein Gesicht vertraut vorkam, und es könnte genauso gut sein, dass ich dieses Gefühl nur rückblickend hineininterpretiere. Ich vermied es, ihn anzusehen.

»Kann ich gegen den Gewinner spielen?«, fragte der Mann.

»Macht einen Dollar«, sagte Lars.

»Und wie viel nehmen Sie?«, fragte er mich.

»Ich nehme kein Geld«, sagte ich und sah ihn immer noch nicht an. »Und ich gewinne auch nicht.«

»Allerdings nicht«, schniefte Lars. »Wenn Sie gegen den Gewinner spielen wollen, spielen Sie gegen mich.«

»Ich lasse mich überraschen.«

Er sah uns zu. Man hört immer wieder von Blicken, die man angeblich spüren kann, und ich habe nie daran geglaubt, bis ich mich durch diese Schachpartie winden musste. Sogar meine Arme wurden rot.

»Lassen Sie ihn absichtlich gewinnen?«, fragte der Mann.

Lars schnaubte verächtlich.

»Nein«, sagte ich. »Ich lasse nie jemanden gewinnen.«

»Egal bei was?«

Ich war nicht mehr sicher, wovon die Rede war. »Nicht, wenn ich es verhindern kann«, sagte ich. Mir fiel selbst auf, wie sinnlos das klang, schließlich verlor ich gerade – wie immer – gegen Lars, und so wurde eine Art umgestülptes Eigenlob daraus.

»Und das kann sie nie«, sagte Lars. »Sie kann es nie verhindern. Sie verliert immer.« Offenbar wollte Lars in diesem Punkt für unmissverständliche Klarheit sorgen. Mir erschloss sich nicht ganz, warum. Immerhin gab es einen Dollar zu verdienen.

Wir spielten. Ich registrierte befangen, wie meine Hand den Springer umschloss, und ließ sie nach dem Zug befangen einen Moment lang dort verharren. Ich spürte, wie ich zwischen den Zügen ruhelos meine Hände knetete. Ich spürte, wie ich mein Haar zwirbelte (obwohl ich sonst keine sehr ambitionierte Haarzwirblerin bin). Herr im Himmel, dachte ich. Was ist denn jetzt los?

Ich verlor schneller als sonst.

»Bitte schön, Sie sind dran«, sagte ich zu dem Mann und stand ein wenig zu hektisch auf. Ich fühlte die Luft zwischen uns, die mir auf einmal zu dicht und zu dünn zugleich vorkam. Irgendwie, merkte ich, würde sich zwischen diesem Mann und mir nie eine akzeptable Distanz finden lassen; jeder Grad der Nähe und Entfernung würde gleichermaßen unerträglich sein. Ich stand auf, und er setzte sich. In meinen Ohren dröhnte es wie von einem sich nähernden Güterzug.

»Bleiben Sie doch«, sagte der Mann. »Damit Sie mal sehen, wie man es richtig macht.«

Die beiden spielten, und der Mann war grottenschlecht, viel schlechter, als ich es bin. Er kannte die Regeln kaum – anscheinend verwechselte er Schach mit Dame – und verlor dramatisch, mit viel Elan und bester Laune. Lars dagegen wirkte zunehmend verärgert, trotz des Dollars, den er gewinnen würde. Er schien zu ahnen, dass bei dieser Partie anderes auf dem Spiel stand als der Sieg auf dem Brett, und das störte ihn. Er nahm Schach sehr ernst und konnte es nicht leiden, wenn jemand es für niedere Zwecke missbrauchte. Nach dem letzten Zug ignorierte er die ausgestreckte Hand seines Gegners.

»Das ist kein Parcheesi«, sagte Lars.

»Ich weiß«, sagte der Mann.

»Kommen Sie erst wieder, wenn Sie geübt haben«, sagte Lars.

»Ich bin ein vielbeschäftigter Mann.«

»Ich danke Ihnen für Ihre Geduld.«

»Muss wohl Pech gewesen sein«, sagte ich zu dem Mann.

»Absolut«, sagte er und stand auf. »Ich bin normalerweise unschlagbar.«

»Das glaube ich sofort«, sagte ich.

»Ich heiße Jonathan«, sagte er. »Soll ich Ihnen vielleicht bei Gelegenheit ein paar Tipps geben?«

Ich weiß nicht, ich weiß nicht. Er war witzig, ja, und klug, aber in Boston gab es jede Menge witzige und kluge Männer. Witzige und kluge Menschen mit Hochschulabschlüssen, die in den U-Bahnen Zeitung lesen, sind der Exportschlager der Stadt. Ich will auch nicht allzu sehr ins grausige Detail gehen – ich persönlich finde anderer Leute Beziehungsgeschichten nur widerlich. Wenn die Kids in meinem Büro damit anfingen, setzte ich Kopfhörer auf und zog mir die neueste *Frontline*-Folge aus dem Netz.

Doch so viel soll gesagt sein: Es vollzog sich alles so zwangsläufig wie bei einer von vornherein verlorenen Schachpartie. Wir verabredeten uns zu unserem ersten Kaffee, der zum ersten Galeriebesuch führte, und der zum Sex – dem ersten nach langer, langer Zeit. Seine Lippen streiften meinen Hals, und vielfarbige Sonnensysteme barsten hinter meinen Augenlidern, und ich staunte über das ungewohnte Gefühl, meinen Körper nicht zu hassen. Danach zog ich mit den Fingerspitzen seine perfekten Rundungen nach, die kräftige Wölbung seines perfekten Gehirns – perfekt, weil es nicht verdammt war, nicht verdammter als andere jedenfalls – und stellte fest, dass ich ihm diese Normalität nicht einmal übelnahm. Und das, fürchte ich, war es dann.

Es war ein guter Frühling. Meine Abreise aus Boston hat ihn in ein bittersüßes Licht getaucht, in dem alles einen Hauch von Tragik bekommt, doch zu der Zeit war davon nichts zu spüren. Jonathan und ich tranken Kaffee und unterhielten uns und schwiegen wieder. Wir spazierten durch die regennassen roten Backsteinstraßen von Cambridge. Wir sahen zu, wie das Citgo-Schild vor dem Abendhimmel seine Farben wechselte. Irgendwann begannen wir, rein hypothetisch über die relativ kurzfristige Zukunft zu sprechen. Und da begriff ich – oder erinnerte mich daran –, dass ich ein Problem hatte.

Ich rief ihn nicht mehr an. Seine Anrufe ließ ich auf meinem Anrufbeantworter landen, obwohl mir die Vorstellung nicht gefiel, dass meine dämliche Anrufbeantworterstimme, so anbiedernd und piepsig wie Schlumpfine auf dem Straßenstrich, ihm wieder und wieder denselben Spruch aufsagte.

Bevor ich aus Versehen eine Beziehung zu Jonathan eingegangen war, hatte ich sorgfältig jede Form von romantischer Annäherung vermieden. Dieses Tabu war kein bloßes Gehabe von mir und nicht das Resultat einer mutwillig herbeigeführten sozialen Isolation. Es war der Versuch, mir den Freiraum zu schaffen, in dem ich mit meiner Situation fertig werden konnte, ohne dass jemand zusah. Der Versuch, nicht verrückt zu werden. Und – nicht zu vergessen – es war mein kleiner, armseliger, egoistischer Versuch, selbstlos zu sein.

Ich erinnerte mich daran, wie ich meinen Vater im Schach besiegt hatte. Man kann nicht sagen, dass ich an dem Tag aufhörte, ihn zu kennen, doch ich fing zumindest an aufzuhören. Ich fragte mich, wie der entsprechende Tag bei mir aussehen und was meine Abschiedsgeste werden würde. Und ich fragte mich, ob ich wirklich wollte, dass Jonathan sie sah.

Von da an träumte ich davon wegzulaufen. Ich stellte mir vor, durch die Kopfsteinpflasterstraßen europäischer Städte zu wandern, und sah mich auf dem Rücken eines Kamels vor einem klaren blauen Wüstenhimmel. Ich suchte nach einem Ausweg, irgendeiner Lösung, die es mir erlauben würde, bei Jonathan zu bleiben, ihn zurückzurufen, ihn zu lieben, ohne an den Tag zu denken, an dem nicht mehr ich es war, die ihn liebte, weil es dieses Ich nicht mehr gab.

Ich hatte es ihm noch immer nicht erzählt.

Weil ich es nicht fertigbrachte, es ihm zu erzählen, musste ich es ihm zeigen. Ich nahm Jonathan mit zu meinem Vater.

Im Auto erklärte ich ihm alles. Ich erzählte, dass das Schicksal, das ich mit meinem Vater teilte, keineswegs einzigartig war – vielleicht ist es ganz im Gegenteil als einziges wahrhaft universell. Immerhin ist der Tod universell. Auch dass wir den Verstand verlieren, ist nichts Besonderes – jeder tut es, nur dass einige ihren Verstand im Augenblick des Todes verlieren und andere davor. Alles, was wir verpassen, sind dreißig oder vierzig Jahre. Wenn man unsere Lebenszeit mit der unsagbaren Anzahl von Jahren vergleicht, die wir tot sind, machen dreißig bis vierzig Jahre keinen großen Unterschied. Doch wenn es die eigene Lebenszeit ist, mit den eigenen Erlebnissen angefüllt, kommt man nicht ganz umhin, ihnen eine unverhältnismäßige Bedeutung zuzumessen.

Ich erzählte ihm von den Nukleotiden, dem Gentest und der Prognose. Ich erklärte, dass die Atrophierung der Basalganglien etliche Jahre vor dem Auftreten der ersten Symptome beginnt und dass schon jetzt – in eben dem Moment, im Auto – Teile meines Gehirns sich zersetzten, Teile, von denen ich nicht einmal ahnte, wofür ich sie brauchte, und die doch unwiederbringlich verloren waren. Ich sagte, dass ich keiner meiner Emotionen, keinem Impuls, keiner Geste je ganz trauen konnte, dass eines Tages – wenn ich es zuließ – alles, was ich tat, sagte und dachte nichts weiter sein würde als die entropische Implosion eines abbruchreifen Gebäudes oder eines sterbenden Planeten.

Jonathan hörte zu. Er hielt sanft meine Hand. Ich weiß nicht, ob man das als Verständnis werten kann.

Das Pflegeheim roch wie immer nach gekochten Möhren, nach antiseptischen Putzmitteln und dem bitteren Kaffee, den die Frühschicht aufgesetzt und aus Zeitmangel nicht ausgetrunken hatte.

Einerseits war es mir zuwider, meinen Vater vorzuführen, als sei er ein wissenschaftliches Exponat und kein ehemaliger Mensch. Andererseits wusste ich: Wenn es eine Chance gab, Jonathan zu zeigen, was ich morgens im Spiegel sah, dann hier. Über den Zerfall der Hirnrinde konnte man endlose Vorträge halten, doch wahres Verständnis riefen nur dieser greisenhafte Mund, dies gelbliche, eingefallene Gesicht hervor. Dunkle Augen, die glänzten wie die eines Gefangenen, der wusste, dass er am nächsten Tag hingerichtet würde – wobei ich mich bemühte, nicht übermäßig zu dramatisieren. Ich glaubte nicht, dass mein Vater noch von seinem Schicksal wusste. Das war immerhin ein Vorteil.

Wir betraten sein Zimmer. Ich rieb meinem Vater die schmalen Schultern und gab ihm eine Praline. Er sah an uns vorbei. Seine Kiefer mahlten, und er produzierte Ploppgeräusche. Seine Finger krümmten sich wie die Krallen eines Dinosauriers, und er presste sie so fest auf den Tisch, dass sie weiß wurden.

»Guten Tag, Herr Ellison«, sagte Jonathan. Mein Vater sagte natürlich nichts.

»Alles Genetik«, sagte ich.

»Wirst du genauso?«

»Nicht, wenn ich es verhindern kann.«

Auf dem Rückweg schwiegen wir. Ich ließ Jonathan ans Steuer. Vor uns lag das Panorama der Stadt, silbrige Häuser, in denen sich das letzte Tageslicht verfing, und der Prudential Tower ragte bleich aus dem Dunst. Ich öffnete das Fenster und dachte an meinen Vater. Wie die meisten war ich mit zwölf nicht gerade eine beeindruckende Persönlichkeit gewesen. Manchmal störte mich der Gedanke, dass diese Version meiner selbst die letzte war, die mein Vater erlebte, bevor er den Verstand verlor – auch wenn das natürlich sinnlos war. Als stünde er seitdem am anderen Ende eines magischen Regenbogens und trüge ein verwischtes Abbild meiner Jugend mit sich herum. In Wirklichkeit war es umgekehrt. Aber in schwachen, sentimentalen Augenblicken hatte ich den Drang, ihm zu sagen: Siehst du, immerhin habe ich einen Sinn für Humor entwickelt. Du würdest mich mögen, wenn du das nicht sowieso schon tätest.

Womit nur gesagt sein soll, dass es mir nicht egal ist, wie man sich an mich erinnert.

Im April starb mein Vater. Es geschah sehr leise, und es war merkwürdig irreal, wie alles, das man lange genug herbeisehnt. Grauenerregend war es nicht. Es war friedlich, morphiumsanft und unausweichlich. In gewisser Weise war es das Einzige, was für meinen Vater in knapp zwei Jahrzehnten nicht schieflief. Ich ließ die ganze Zeit über die Hand auf seinem Kopf liegen, und er wurde kalt, noch bevor sein Herz aufhörte zu schlagen. Außerdem wurde er gelb, weil seine Leber versagte – und es wirkte tatsächlich wie ein natürlicher Prozess, wie eine Notwendigkeit, eine Quelle säkularen Trosts, wenn man nur von den achtzehn Jahren davor absah. Meine Mutter und ich standen dabei, und die Tränen blieben uns irgendwo im Rachen stecken, weil wir nur atmeten, wenn er es tat. Er starb erst eine Weile nach dem letzten Atemzug, nach dem letzten Pulsschlag, wenn ich auch nicht genau sagen könnte, wann. Zwei Jahrzehnte lang zu sterben nimmt etwas aus dem Leben fort, aber es nimmt auch dem Sterben etwas. Der Tod wird zu einer matten Asymptote, die immer näher kommt und immer unerreichbar bleibt. Bis er irgendwann doch erreicht ist.

Ich dachte an Jonathan – wie Jonathan auf meinen Vater gezeigt hatte, auf seine flatternden Hände und tief eingesunkenen Augen. Er hatte gefragt, ob ich genauso werden würde, und ich hatte gesagt, nicht, wenn ich es verhindern könnte. Was mich an Lars erinnerte, wie er sagte: »Das kann sie nie, sie kann es nie verhindern.«

Jonathan kam zur Beerdigung, und er hielt meine Hand und senkte den Kopf mit der angemessenen Dosis ernster Einkehr. Trotzdem begann sich schon damals ein Abgrund zwischen uns aufzutun, der immer unermesslicher wurde. Wir alle sind sterblich, ja, aber vielleicht sind einige von uns sterblicher als andere. Der Friedhof war beinahe schön mit seinem zartgrünen Hauch frischer Knospen und jungen Grases, das schüchtern den Boden zu erobern begann, mit einer kühlen Brise, in der die Schatten der Bäume halb anmutig, halb unheimlich über die Gräber wanderten. Jonathan betrachtete das alles – den Sarg, das Grab, den grünen Kunstrasen, der die bloßgelegte Erde verdeckte – mit dem Blick eines Zuschauers.

Rückschauend sage ich mir, dass diese Sache wie alles andere auch ihr Gutes hat. Wir heiraten also nicht, bekommen keine Kinder, werden nicht zusammen alt. Das alles verpassen wir. Außerdem hören wir nicht auf, miteinander zu schlafen, lassen uns nicht scheiden, werden einander nicht fremd, blicken nicht voller Trauer und Entsetzen auf jene ersten Tage zurück, um uns zu fragen, wie alles so den Bach runtergehen konnte. Diese ersten Tage, die Zeit in Boston, waren unsere einzigen. Ich meine, dafür kann ich durchaus dankbar sein.

Doch damals war ich es noch nicht. Ich sah in den Himmel, ich sah zu Boden. Alles war so zerbrechlich und roh und intensiv. Ich sah zu Jonathan hinüber. Wir gleichen einander nicht, dachte ich. Und du würdest auch nicht wollen, dass es so wäre.

Ein paar Wochen nach dem Tod meines Vaters räumte ich das Haus aus, und dabei fand ich die Kiste. Meine Mutter hatte das Haus all die Jahre behalten, einerseits, weil sie dort wohnen konnte, wenn sie zweimal im Jahr zu Besuch kam, und zum anderen, weil es der einzige Besitz war, den der Staat nicht einfordern konnte, als wir meinen Vater und seine Ersparnisse einer staatlichen Pflegeeinrichtung übereignet hatten. Nach seinem Tod konnte meine Mutter das Haus verkaufen und hatte mich gebeten, das Sortieren, Katalogisieren und Inventarisieren zu übernehmen, das am Ende eines Lebens fällig wird. Ich hatte einen Nachmittag Zeit, meinen Vater auf das zu reduzieren, an das wir uns am liebsten erinnern wollten: die geistreichsten Briefe, die rührendsten Andenken, die schmeichelhaftesten Fotos. Alles andere wurde entsorgt.

Die Kiste stand im Arbeitszimmer meines Vaters hinter einem

Stapel alter Postkarten und einem quietschenden Globus. Als ich sie öffnete, fand ich darin ein buntes Durcheinander von vergilbten, abgegriffenen Zeitungsausschnitten, und fast hätte ich den Deckel wieder geschlossen, hätte mich abgewandt und das Rätsel auf sich beruhen lassen.

Nein, das ist nicht wahr. Ich hätte ihn nicht beinahe geschlossen. Ich gehöre nicht zu der Sorte Mensch, die den Deckel wieder schließt. Ich ließ ihn offen und begann zu stöbern. In der Kiste befanden sich lauter Zeitungsartikel über Alexander Besetow, den Schachmeister.

Der erste Artikel war von 1980 und stammte aus der *Literaturnaja Gaseta*. Er handelte von einem frühen Erfolg Alexanders an seiner unaussprechlichen Leningrader Schachakademie. Auf dem Foto ist er herzzerreißend jung und unscheinbar – er hat nie ausgesehen wie jemand, der es weit bringen würde, selbst als er es weiter gebracht hatte als alle anderen – und wirkt ein wenig unglücklich darüber, fotografiert zu werden. Die nächsten Artikel begleiten ihn zu seinen regionalen und überregionalen Erfolgen und zu seinem ersten internationalen Triumph bei einem Turnier in Reykjavík. Auf den frühen Fotos sieht er hager und missmutig aus, mit kantigem Wesen und einem Ausdruck unterschwelliger Verbitterung. Dann kommen die achtziger Jahre. Die Berichterstattung klingt fast schon atemlos; es ist viel von seiner Jugend und von seinem Genie die Rede. Er habe einen subversiven Spielstil, heißt es. Eine individuelle Haltung. Es gibt Reportagen über Streitereien mit der FIDE. Besetow sieht nicht mehr in die Kamera, wenn er fotografiert wird. Er nimmt ein wenig zu und beginnt älter zu wirken. Er liefert sich ein endloses Duell mit Russajew. Das Match wird unterbrochen. Das Match wird fortgesetzt. Die letzte Partie wird gespielt. Das war die Partie, die ich mit meinem Vater angesehen hatte, und Besetows wild entschlossener Gesichtsausdruck versetzte mich in jene Nacht zurück – in den irren Tanz der Schatten an der Wand, die langsam erlöschenden Schneeflocken. Besetow gewinnt. Auf dem Foto, das ihn mit seiner Trophäe zeigt, wirkt er klinisch depressiv. Inzwischen sind die Artikel ein wenig zittrig ausgeschnitten, denn in den späten Achtzigern setzten bei meinem Vater die Symptome ein. Bald nach dem Ausbruch der Krankheit hören die Dokumentationsbemühungen ganz auf, wenn auch nicht so bald, wie ich gedacht hätte. Nach 1990 kommt gar nichts mehr – nichts über Besetows Buch, über seine viel betrauerte Niederlage gegen einen IBM-Computer und seinen Einstieg in die Politik nach dem Kalten Krieg. All das hat mein Vater verpasst. Er hat eine Menge verpasst.

Es war merkwürdig, diese Chronik eines fremden Lebens – nicht ganz das, was man in einer geheimnisvollen Kiste im Arbeitszimmer des verstorbenen Vaters erwarten würde. Aus narzisstischen Gründen hatte ich eher an alte Schulfotos, Auszeichnungen für gute Noten oder selbstgebastelte Weihnachtsgeschenke gedacht, während die Verschwörungstheoretikerin in mir auf Liebesbriefe, rätselhafte Schlüssel oder politische Korrespondenz gehofft hatte. Stattdessen fand ich die gewissenhafte, lückenlose Dokumentation der Karriere eines russischen Schachweltmeisters, eines Mannes, dem mein Vater nie begegnet war und dessen Geschichte er nicht bis zum Ende mitverfolgen sollte. Das kam unerwartet. Doch vollkommen überraschend war es nicht – nicht nur, weil sich mein Vater so sehr für Schach und für die Sowjetunion und für diesen speziellen sowjetischen Schachspieler interessierte. Ich erinnerte mich wieder an die verschneite Winternacht und die atemlose Faszination, mit der mein Vater jede unerwartete Wendung jener fernen Schachpartie beobachtet hatte. Besetow war für ihn mehr als ein vielversprechender junger Sportler. Er war der personifizierte Sieg der Ordnung über die Anarchie. Er verkörperte die Fähigkeit, sich mutig dem beinahe sicheren Untergang entgegenzustemmen. Und das Wichtigste war vielleicht, dass seine Geschichte den Glauben an unwahrscheinliche Ereignisse stärkte, für die sich mein Vater vermutlich schon zu interessieren begann, als er mich auf seinen Schoß setzte und mir zeigte, was man innerhalb kurzer Zeit erreichen kann.

Ganz unten in der Kiste lag ein Brief. Einen selbstzufriedenen

Augenblick lang glaubte ich, ich würde ihn nicht öffnen. Dann tat ich es doch.

Es war die Fotokopie eines undatierten und auf Russisch verfassten Schreibens. Damals, bevor ich nach St. Petersburg kam, war mein Russisch weniger gut als das meines Vaters, obwohl ich es im Zuge meiner Dissertation an der Uni gelernt hatte und er seine Kenntnisse dem Selbststudium verdankte. Ich brauchte drei Durchgänge, um den Inhalt des Briefes zu erfassen, und selbst jetzt, da ich Russisch ziemlich gut beherrsche, bin ich nicht sicher, ob ich nicht das eine oder andere falsch verstehe. Er lautete ungefähr wie folgt:

Sehr geehrter Herr Besetow,

vielleicht verwundert es Sie, dass Sie Fanpost von einem Amerikaner bekommen. Andererseits, wer weiß, könnte es auch sein, dass Ihnen das mehrmals täglich passiert. Vieles an Ihnen ist bewundernswert – Ihre originelle, radikale Spielstrategie, Ihr Durchhaltevermögen in scheinbar aussichtslosen Situationen, Ihre bemerkenswerte Intelligenz. Ganz besonders fesselnd sind diese Eigenschaften für jemanden, der sich seit Jahren sehr eingehend mit der Bedeutung von ersten Anfängen befasst; man darf davon ausgehen, dass Sie es noch weit bringen werden. Vermutlich fühle ich mich Ihnen auch deshalb in gewisser Weise verbunden, weil ich selbst derzeit ein schwieriges Match zu bestreiten habe, das, wie ich befürchte, schon bald in einer ausgesprochen bitteren Niederlage enden wird. Und daher frage ich mich, ob es Ihnen möglich wäre, mir eine Frage zu beantworten.

Sie wären gar nicht erst in Ihre jetzige Position gelangt, wenn Sie nicht in erster Linie ein Sieger wären – der Sieger jener Begegnungen, auf die es am meisten ankam. Und doch hat es auch Partien, Begegnungen und Turniere gegeben, die Sie verloren haben. Bei manchen dieser Spiele wiederum haben Sie sicher von vornherein gewusst, wie es ausgehen würde – Spiele, in denen Ihr Intellekt sich im Gegensatz zu sonst als beschränkt, schwankend und sterblich erwies. Wenn Sie so eine Partie, eine Begegnung, ein Turnier bestreiten, wie gehen Sie dann vor? Welche Geschichte erzählen Sie sich selbst, wenn Sie sich dieser absoluten Gewissheit gegenübersehen, wenn Sie das Gefühl haben, sich an den Grenzen Ihres Selbst wund zu reiben?

Bitte verzeihen Sie mir, dass ich so eigenartige Fragen stelle. Schreiben Sie es der Sentimentalität und Verwirrung zu – oder, etwas wohlwollender, der Klarsicht –, die es mit sich bringt, zu früh zu viel zu verlieren.

In dankbarer Erwartung
Prof. Frank Ellison

Ich las den Brief noch einmal und ließ mich auf die Heizung sinken. Es könnte sein, dass ich ein klein wenig weinte. Und dann las ich ihn wieder. Ich staunte, wie formell er klang. Die Formulierung »erste Anfänge« war meine Annäherung an eine schwer übersetzbare Phrase. Wörtlich stand dort in etwa »beginnende Eröffnungszüge« – ganz offensichtlich eine Anspielung auf die ersten Anzeichen der Krankheit, aber in einer eher untypischen Formulierung. Selbst nach der Übersetzung war der Idiolekt des Briefes ein anderer, als ich ihn von meinem Vater in Erinnerung hatte, wobei ich mir vor Augen halten musste, dass er mit mir als Kind vermutlich ein vereinfachtes Vokabular benutzte. Mein Vater hatte mit mir nie wie mit einer Erwachsenen gesprochen, weil er mich als Erwachsene nicht mehr kannte. Also war es unsinnig, darüber zu spekulieren, ob irgendein Tonfall für meinen Vater typisch war oder nicht. Ich konnte es nicht wissen.

Ebenso wenig wusste ich, was dieser Brief meinem Vater bedeutet hatte, wo er in der nebligen Landschaft seines Lebensentwurfs einzuordnen war. Vielleicht war er ungewöhnlich oder sogar einzigartig, oder vielleicht hatte es in seinem Leben immer wieder solche Briefe gegeben – an Schachweltmeister, an Squashspieler, Wirtschaftsexperten oder Zirkusartisten. Vielleicht war diese Wahlverwandtschaft nur eine unter vielen gewesen. Ich las den Brief noch einmal und verwarf diese Möglichkeit wieder.

Mein Vater wusste, dass es zu Ende ging, und vielleicht hatte dieser Umstand ihm eine tiefere Einsicht beschert – das unerklärliche Wissen, dass genau dies und nichts anderes der Weg war, den er beschreiten musste, das angemessene Ende seiner Geschichte. Mein eigenes Ende rückt ebenfalls näher, und ich habe noch keine solche Erleuchtung gehabt, aber darum geht es nicht. Wenn mein Vater seinen Weg gefunden hatte, freue ich mich für ihn.

Ich dachte über seine Fragen nach. Offenbar hatte er viel über das Schicksal nachgedacht, als er diesen Brief schrieb, und wollte von Alexander Besetow eine qualifizierte Auskunft zum Thema. Mein Vater war nicht religiös – wenn doch, wusste er es jedenfalls geschickt zu verbergen –, und ich glaube nicht, dass er sich unter dem Schicksal eine vorherbestimmte Ereignisfolge vorstellte, die eine grausame, selbstgefällige Gottheit ausgeheckt hatte. Ich glaube, wenn er über das Schicksal schrieb – das er ebenso gut Bestimmung oder sogar Zukunft hätte nennen können –, dann meinte er damit die bestehende Realität im Gegensatz zu all den anderen Realitäten, die hätten eintreten können. Wenn man eine fünfzigprozentige Chance hat, einer genetisch programmierten Katastrophe zu entgehen, bekommen solche Überlegungen eine besondere Bedeutung. Es ist ein ganz eigenes Gefühl der Niederlage, bei einer Wahrscheinlichkeit von 50 zu 50 zu verlieren.

Ich fragte mich, ob mein Vater eine Antwort bekommen hatte. Dass der Brief kopiert worden war, sprach dafür, dass er das Original abgeschickt hatte. Aber vielleicht auch nicht – vielleicht hatte ihn Befangenheit davon abgehalten, hatte er es sich anders überlegt, war abgelenkt worden, oder die Krankheit hatte ihn eingeholt.

Ich blätterte die Papiere noch zwei Mal durch, aber eine Antwort von Besetow war nicht dabei. Stattdessen fand ich eine kurze Notiz von jemand anderem:

Sehr geehrter Herr Prof. Ellison,
vielen Dank für Ihren Brief. Bedauerlicherweise ist Herr Bese-

tow im Augenblick nicht in der Lage, Ihre Fragen zu beantworten. Ich wünsche Ihnen jedoch alles Gute für Ihre Suche nach den Antworten.

Mit freundlichen Grüßen
Elisabeta Nasarowna

Ich las die Notiz noch einmal. Sie musste wohl eine Sekretärin sein, aber ihr etwas wehmütiger Tonfall klang, als hätte sie den Brief meines Vaters mit einem Interesse gelesen, das über die bloße berufliche Pflicht hinausging. Lange saß ich so da, betrachtete die Kiste, lauschte auf die im ganzen Haus widerhallende Stille und dachte nach. Offensichtlich hatte mein Vater keine Antwort von Alexander Besetow erhalten. Das kam mir ziemlich ungerecht vor, wo er schon sonst so wenig erhalten hatte.

Vielleicht dachte ich in dem Moment zum ersten Mal daran zu fahren. Ich suchte ohnehin nach einem möglichst eleganten Weg, aus Jonathans Leben zu verschwinden, und – das gebe ich offen zu – nach einer Chance auf ein letztes Abenteuer. Ich wollte meiner Mutter nicht noch einmal zumuten, was sie schon beim ersten Mal nur knapp überlebt hatte. Die Vorstellung, nach den Antworten auf die Fragen meines Vaters zu suchen, hatte etwas wohltuend Symmetrisches. Wie ein Zug auf dem Schachfeld wäre dieser Schritt eine Fortschreibung von Tendenzen, die es schon gab. Mir war durchaus bewusst, dass er alles andere als unausweichlich war und dass es an ein Wunder grenzen würde, wenn ich die Antworten – oder auch nur Besetow selbst – jemals fand.

Doch wie der von Nabokov so glühend gehasste Dostojewski schon sagte, haben Wunder einen wahren Realisten noch nie beirren können.

KAPITEL 5

Alexander
Leningrad, 1980

Den Rest des Winters über ging Alexander jede Woche wieder ins Saigon, und diese Ausflüge waren wie ein graues Dämmerlicht in der tristen Eintönigkeit seiner Tage. Es war keine herzerwärmende, rotglühende Morgendämmerung voller Hoffnung und Sonnenschein – Nikolai war abweisend und Iwan wichtigtuerisch, und Alexander begriff bald, dass sie ihn beide nicht besonders mochten –, doch immer noch besser als ewige Nacht. Samstags früh, wenn weniger Polizisten unterwegs waren, nahmen Iwan und Nikolai ihn mit zu dem Markt für verbotene Bücher, der jede Woche seinen Standort wechselte. Abends sahen sie sich manchmal im Kulturverein der Kirow-Werke inoffizielle Kunstausstellungen an, oder sie lauschten im Saigon einem Auftritt von Sankt-Petersburg und debattierten über die angeblichen monarchistischen Ansichten der Musiker. Sonntags verschanzte Alexander sich in seinem Zimmer mit schlecht übersetzten Werken von Kurt Vonnegut und Iris Murdoch, die ihm viel besser gefielen als die munteren Schnurren von unerschrockenen Jungen in widrigen Umständen, die er aus der Schulzeit in Ocha kannte. Die Wochentage verbrachte er in der Akademie oder in den Turnhallen von Universitäten, wo er jedes Spiel gewann und nach jedem Zug die Schachuhr mit dem Daumen stoppte. Das Vergehen der Zeit schien Alexanders Willen zu gehorchen, als setzte er alle seine Strategien gegen die Tage selbst ein, die ihm nachgeben und sich schließlich zurückziehen mussten.

Anfangs nahm niemand Alexander für voll – weil er so jung war, so provinziell und so grüblerisch und, stellte er fest, weil die anderen einfach glauben wollten, dass er dumm war, und diesen Glauben trotz aller Gegenbeweise ungern revidierten. Irgendwann jedoch konnten sie nicht umhin, ihn zu bemerken, erst innerhalb der

Akademie – wo seine endlose Siegesserie und seine verblüffenden Strategien ihm Aufmerksamkeit, Misstrauen und schließlich Hass eintrugen – und dann auch außerhalb, als die *Literaturnaja Gaseta* ihm ein kleines Porträt widmete. Er wusste, dass sich die Kunde früher oder später weiterverbreiten würde. Das Porträt war nur der Anfang. Wenn es ernsthaft aufwärtsging, würde er lernen müssen, selbstironisch und bescheiden zu sein. Am besten verhielt man sich zurückhaltend, wenn sich das ganze Leben änderte. Und er liebte es, sich diese Änderungen auszumalen. Die Verwalterin würde ihm morgens Tee und Saiki bringen. Sie würde vor den neuen Mietern mit ihm prahlen wie mit der günstigen Lage oder den Toiletten auf jeder Etage. Eines Nachts würde er vor seiner Zimmertür wie das Flüstern fallender Blütenblätter Elisabetas Stimme hören, die seinen Namen nannte. »Hier wohnt er«, würde sie sagen. »Alexander, das Schachgenie.« Dann sank er in den Schlaf zurück, und im Schlaf verwandelte sich das azurblaue Meer in ein endloses schwarzweißes Spielfeld und trug ihn bis ans Ende der Welt.

Auch bis zu einem Kräftemessen mit Andronow war es nur eine Frage der Zeit. Die anderen Jungen an der Akademie wussten das ebenso gut wie er. Wenn er neue, absonderliche Strategien einsetzte, fragten sie: »Willst du das auch an Andronow ausprobieren?« Wenn er einen Fehler machte, was selten genug vorkam, kreischten sie, das werde ihm Andronow niemals durchgehen lassen. Doch als ihn Andronow eines Tages am Ohr packte und von dem Spielbrett wegzerrte, war Alexander dennoch überrascht. »Habe ich etwas falsch gemacht?«, fragte er. Er spielte gerade gegen Oleg, einen intelligenten, hellhäutigen Jüngling, der offenbar den Ehrgeiz besaß, so wenig wie nur irgend möglich zu sprechen.

»Komm mit«, sagte Andronow.

Alexander sah Oleg schulterzuckend an, und Oleg räumte schweigend die Figuren ein. Andronow führte Alexander den Flur hinunter in sein Büro, wo er sich in einen Sessel fallen ließ. »Setz dich«, sagte er. Alexander gehorchte.

Zwischen ihnen stand Andronows vorsintflutlicher Schreibtisch, auf dem sich dicke Schachlehrwerke und uralte Spielsets türmten. Unter anderen Umständen hätte Alexander sich in dem Büro gern ein wenig umgesehen – besonders die Unterlagen, in denen sich bestimmt viele bewundernde Äußerungen über ihn fanden, hätte er gern studiert. Doch jetzt war nicht der richtige Zeitpunkt dafür, und Alexander, der sich vergeblich bemühte, Andronows Blick einzufangen, begann allmählich zu begreifen, dass dieser Zeitpunkt nie kommen würde.

Andronow ließ eine Ausgabe der *Literaturnaja Gaseta* auf den Schreibtisch klatschen. »So, man unterhält sich also mit der Presse«, sagte er.

»Na ja, eigentlich haben die sich mit mir unterhalten.«

»Wie ich sehe, hast du auch einiges zu der Spielstärke deiner Mitschüler an der Akademie zu erzählen.«

»Die haben danach gefragt!«

Andronow schob ein verschlissenes Spielbrett auf Alexander zu. »Spiel«, sagte er.

»Bin ich weiß?«

»Spiel.«

Alexander eröffnete mit einer bedächtigen Nimzo-Indischen Verteidigung. Es folgte ein ritualisierter, blutleerer Austausch von Figuren. Andronow schien zu zögern; seine Handflächen und seine Stirn glänzten, und Alexander fiel auf, dass er sich auf keine bestimmte Bauernstruktur festlegte. Von Zeit zu Zeit murmelte er angespannt vor sich hin, als nähme er dem Schachbrett sein unverfrorenes Verhalten übel, nicht seinem Gegner.

»Und?«, fragte Andronow schließlich. »Wo soll es danach hingehen?«

»Hingehen? Was meinen Sie damit?« Alexander fühlte einen trockenen Klumpen im Hals, der sich einen Weg bauchwärts bahnte. Wenn er so tat, als verstünde er nicht, vielleicht musste er dann nicht gehen. Die Zeichen standen auf Remis.

Als Andronow seine fetten Ellbogen auf die Bücher stützte, bildeten sich Grübchen, die Alexander betrübt zublinzelten. »Wenn du mich geschlagen hast, was tust du dann? Denkst du etwa, du könntest hierbleiben? Denkst du, wir lassen uns in so eine Farce einspannen?«

»Oh«, sagte Alexander. »Meinen Sie, ich werde gewinnen?« Doch er begann sich allmählich Sorgen zu machen. Andronow hatte seinen Läufer auf h2 vorgerückt, ohne zu beachten, dass Alexander ihn dort zwischen seinen Bauern festsetzen konnte.

»Könnte ich nicht, ich meine …«, sagte Alexander, »… könnte ich vielleicht hier aushelfen?« Er verrückte seinen Bauern nach g3 und schloss damit die Falle, in die der Läufer sich begeben hatte.

»Aushelfen? Bei was denn? Beim Putzen? Bei der Schmutzwäsche? Willst du unsere neue Waschfrau sein?« Er fuhr als letztes kleines Geschütz seinen h-Bauern auf.

»Könnte ich nicht vielleicht unterrichten?«

Andronow ließ seine Ellbogen mit einem satten Knall auf die Tischplatte fallen. »Unterrichten? Du willst unterrichten? Siehst du, Towarischtsch, das ist genau das, was ich meine. Diese Arroganz. Die können wir hier nicht brauchen. Niemand hat sie je gebraucht, und wir brauchen sie auch jetzt nicht.«

Alexander zog seinen König diagonal rückwärts, bevor er weitersprach. »Ich wollte nicht arrogant sein«, sagte er. »Ich weiß bloß nicht, wo ich sonst tagsüber hingehen soll.«

»Dann finde es raus, wenn du so schlau bist.« Andronow rückte seinen Bauern noch ein Feld vor, in der Hoffnung, er könnte den Läufer befreien. Alexander sah die feuchten Schlangenspuren, die der Schweiß auf Andronows Hals hinterließ.

Plötzlich wurde Alexander bewusst, wie wütend er war. Normalerweise bemerkte er es erst, wenn es zu spät war, doch diesmal konnte er genau dabei zusehen. Andronow verschwamm ihm vor den Augen, und er hörte tief in seinem Hinterkopf das Geräusch eines Tiers, das krachend durchs Unterholz brach. Er zog seinen König seitwärts, bedrohlich nah an Andronows Läufer.

»Ich dachte, es sei gut, Erfolg zu haben«, sagte er in möglichst neutralem Ton. Es war eine reine Feststellung. »Ich dachte, es sei gut für den Ruf der Schule. Ich dachte, Sie wären dann ... zufrieden.« Fast hätte er »stolz« gesagt.

»Zufrieden? Nein, Towarischtsch.« Andronow raufte sich die Haare, nahm seine Brille ab und sah Alexander – vielleicht zum ersten Mal überhaupt – direkt ins Gesicht. Seine Augen waren wie kleine Perlen in den zahllosen nackten Falten einer Auster. »Ich bin mit den Erfolgen und Misserfolgen meiner Schüler weder zufrieden noch unzufrieden. Ich bin nur dazu da, eine effiziente Schachakademie zu führen, und deine Anwesenheit ist dabei nicht förderlich.« Andronows Läufer zog sich vergebens um ein Feld zurück, und Alexander begriff, wie sehr Andronow sich gewünscht hatte, nicht zu verlieren.

»Verstehe«, sagte Alexander. Er schlug den Läufer mit seinem König.

»Gut«, sagte Andronow. »Dann wäre ja alles geklärt. Bis heute Nachmittag bist du hier raus.« Er nickte, dass sein Doppelkinn wackelte. Das Spiel war beendet.

Alexander trat in den Flur hinaus und sah zu der hohen Bogendecke auf. Durch die Fenster sickerte schmutziggraues Licht herein, als wollte es jeden Moment mitten im Gang zu regnen anfangen. Er hatte ja wirklich nicht viel gelernt. Doch es hatte ihm gefallen, das zu tun, wofür er nach Leningrad gekommen war, und er hatte die betäubende geistige Leere gemocht, die es ihm bescherte, die anderen zu besiegen. Er war nicht voller Verlangen aufgewacht, in die Akademie zu gehen, aber immerhin mit dem Gefühl, zu wissen, wo er hinmusste. Er konnte sich ein Leben in Leningrad ohne die Akademie nicht vorstellen, wusste nicht, wie er seine Tage strukturieren sollte, wofür er morgens aufstehen sollte, wer noch merken würde, ob er lebte oder starb, oder wozu er überhaupt hierbleiben sollte. Sicher würde es weitere Turniere, weitere Erfolge geben, aber ohne die Akademie gab es nichts, was ihn mit Leningrad verband. Er konnte sich treiben lassen, wohin er wollte – ins Weltall, in den erbarmungslosen äußersten Norden oder nach Ocha, wo er für seine Mutter die Hühner schlachten könnte. Nichts hielt ihn hier, und nichts zog ihn anderswohin. Da es keinen guten Grund gab, nicht dort zu sein, überquerte Alexander die Straße und setzte sich in die nächste Bar.

Eine selbstmitleidige, wodkagetränkte Stunde später bemerkte Alexander, dass sein Sitznachbar ihn anstarrte. Er tat, als wollte er seine Halswirbel knacken lassen, um sich den anderen anzusehen. Der Mann fing seinen Blick auf. Er wartete geduldig, und Alexander fragte sich, wie lange er das schon tat. »Zigarette?«, fragte der Mann.

Er wirkte gepflegt, doch seine Fingernägel waren nikotingelb verfärbt, und sein Atem gemahnte Alexander an die Vergänglichkeit allen Lebens. Der Mann war ein Apparatschik.

»Ich rauche nicht«, sagte Alexander und rückte ein wenig von ihm ab.

Eine Zeitlang musterte der Mann ihn amüsiert. Seine Nase lief, was irgendwie beunruhigend wirkte. »Ah, Sie rauchen nicht«, sagte er. »Natürlich nicht. Das habe ich ja gelesen.«

Einen flüchtigen Augenblick lang sonnte sich Alexander in der Vorstellung, der Mann beziehe sich auf sein Porträt in der Zeitung. Natürlich nicht.

»In meiner Akte«, sagte Alexander. Er hatte geahnt, dass es eine Akte über ihn gab – es schmeichelte ihm sogar ein bisschen, denn es hatte mit seiner Spielstärke zu tun. Doch es in aller Öffentlichkeit bestätigt zu bekommen war erschreckend. Man wusste von diesen Dingen und schwieg darüber wie über die Spezifika menschlichen Fortpflanzungsverhaltens.

»Ich dagegen trinke nicht«, gab der Mann gutgelaunt bekannt. »Wir sind also beide ungewöhnlich.«

»Sie trinken nicht?«

»Zumindest nicht bei der Arbeit. Das ist ungewöhnlich genug.« Der Mann lehnte sich zurück, und die spärliche Beleuchtung verlieh ihm einen Heiligenschein. »Sie trinken, zum Beispiel.«

»Ich habe jetzt Gründe dafür.«

»Alkoholismus ist ein Auswuchs des Kapitalismus.« Der Mann drückte seine Zigarette aus. »Aber Sie sind noch jung.«

»Ich bin neunzehn.«

»Grauenhaft jung.«

»Das höre ich nicht zum ersten Mal.«

Der Mann lachte laut los, als hätte jemand ihn vorgewarnt, dass Alexander versuchen würde, lustig zu sein, und dass es besser wäre, ihn bei Laune zu halten. Er strich sich theatralisch mit dem Handrücken über die Augen, wie um seine Lachtränen fortzuwischen. »Verzeihen Sie«, sagte er und streckte Alexander die Hand und seinen Ausweis hin. »Ich habe mich nicht vorgestellt. Peter Pawlowitsch Nikitin. Ich bin sozusagen das Bindeglied zwischen der Partei und dem Spiel.«

Der Ausweis bestätigte seine Mitgliedschaft in der KPdSU, die der schwere Anzugstoff und die manikürten Fingernägel bereits verraten hatten. Das Foto zeigte einen jüngeren und schlankeren Peter Pawlowitsch mit viel zu breiten Epauletten und einem überraschten, stolzen Gesichtsausdruck. Seine neue Position schien ihn damals begeistert, eingeschüchtert und verängstigt zu haben.

Alexander reichte dem Mann die Hand und ärgerte sich zugleich über seine krankhafte Höflichkeit. Der Mann hatte seidig weiche Hände; die Nikotinflecken wirkten deplatziert wie die Narben längst vergessener Verwundungen. Alexander ging auf, dass hier genau das Gespräch stattfand, vor dem Iwan ihn gewarnt hatte.

»Wir haben gehört, dass Ihre Laufbahn an der Akademie beendet ist«, sagte Peter Pawlowitsch. »Man sagt, Sie hätten Andronow geschlagen.«

»Das ging ja schnell. Hat er selbst bei Ihnen angerufen?«

»Na, na. Wir beide werden uns blendend verstehen, aber nur, wenn Sie keine direkten Fragen stellen.«

»Oder war es Oleg? Ich wusste gar nicht, dass er sprechen kann.«

»Beginnen wir noch einmal von vorn«, sagte Peter Pawlowitsch. Er bestellte noch eine Runde Wodka, dann zog er ein Feuerzeug aus der Tasche und starrte einen Moment zu lange in die kleine

Flamme, bevor er seine Zigarette ansteckte. Seine Lippen produzierten zwischen den Zügen ein schmatzendes Geräusch. »Also, von vorn. Ich habe mich unklar ausgedrückt. Ein Talent wie Ihres hebt das Ansehen der Sowjetunion. Sie zeigen dem Rest der Welt, wer die besseren Schachspieler sind.«

Alexander griff nach dem ersten seiner Schnapsgläser. Er trank normalerweise keinen Stoli, doch die staatlich hergestellten Wodkas schmeckten letztlich alle gleich. Am liebsten hätte er dem Mann gesagt, er solle sich verpissen, obwohl es schade gewesen wäre, seine gerade beginnende Karriere schon wieder zu beenden. Doch Alexander hatte noch nie jemanden weggeschickt. Höflichkeit war seine große Schwäche, und eines Tages würde er sie ablegen müssen, doch nicht heute, dachte er, nicht sofort. »Danke sehr«, sagte er.

»Mir ist aufgefallen, dass Sie noch nicht Parteimitglied sind.«

Alexander rollte sein Glas zwischen den Fingern. Er betrachtete die dicke, verzerrte Reflexion seines Daumens in der Flüssigkeit. »Nein«, sagte er. »Bin ich nicht.«

»Zweifellos ein Versäumnis, das Ihrer Jugend geschuldet ist.« Peter Pawlowitsch, der immer noch viel zu geräuschvoll rauchte, begleitete seine Feststellung mit einem zufriedenen Schmatzen.

Alexander schwieg, was neben dem Schach eine seiner größten Stärken war.

»Sie leben in der Kommunalka, habe ich recht?«

»Ja.«

»Ziemlich voll da, nehme ich an. Und immer Ärger mit den Wasserleitungen.«

Alexander dachte an die Maden im Wasserhahn. »Manchmal.«

»Sie hätten doch sicher gern eine eigene Wohnung?«

»Ich habe ein eigenes Zimmer.«

»Das ist natürlich eine große Errungenschaft«, sagte Peter Pawlowitsch großzügig. »Aber vielleicht ist Ihnen nach ein bisschen mehr Privatsphäre? Mehr Platz, vielleicht? Wie viel haben sie, acht Quadratmeter? Neun?«

Alexander dachte an sein feuchtkaltes, vollgestopftes Zimmer, an das unregelmäßige Zischen des altertümlichen Heizkörpers. Er dachte an die riesigen Stapel von Schachmagazinen, auf denen er nachts oft versehentlich zu liegen kam.

»Ein junger Mann wie Sie«, sagte Peter Pawlowitsch, »hat doch sicher schon ein Auge auf eine Dame geworfen. Sicher wollen Sie eine Familie gründen.«

Alexander schwieg. Wenn der Mann nur wüsste, wie weit er mit diesem Ansatz danebenlag.

»Oder irre ich mich?«, fragte Peter Pawlowitsch. »Vielleicht ist es nicht eine Dame, sondern mehrere? Auch dann könnte ein wenig mehr Platz nicht schaden. Und Privatsphäre. Eine kleine Datscha in den Wäldern vielleicht. Mit einem hübschen Ausblick und einer Sommerblumenwiese. Wo Sie mit ausgewählten Besuchern Schach spielen könnten. Ferien an der Wolga. Was halten Sie davon?«

Alexander nahm sich traurig seinen zweiten Wodka vor.

»Man hat mir gesagt, dass Sie schweigsam sind«, sagte Peter Pawlowitsch. »Aber Sie sind so gut wie stumm. Das werde ich in Ihrer Akte vermerken müssen.«

»Ich bin ganz zufrieden mit meinem Zimmer.«

»Das bezweifle ich. Doch selbst wenn, gibt es noch viel mehr, das wir für Sie tun können. Reisen. Visa. Einkäufe in unseren Parteigeschäften. Besseres Fleisch vielleicht? Mögen Sie Essen? Frauen? Irgendwas?«

Alexander dachte an die senfgelben Konserven mit zähem, faserigem Rindfleisch in den staatlichen Lebensmittelgeschäften, an die schrumpeligen Auberginen mit Schimmel an der Unterseite. Er dachte an die Kommunalka, wo die Luft nach ranzigem Fett roch und nach Füßen in zu vielen Socken. Dann stellte er sich eine Datscha unter schattigen, sommerlichen Bäumen vor, dazu Kaviar, Wein und frisches Gemüse auf einem breiten Holztisch unter sanft wogendem Geäst. Er stellte sich schöne Frauen vor, das genaue Gegenteil von Elisabeta – blond statt dunkelhaarig, unterwürfig statt gleichgültig, und austauschbar, während Elisabeta störrisch ihre Eigenarten bewahrte.

»Sie verstehen, worauf ich hinauswill. Sie sind ein herausragender Schachspieler, doch Sie können besser werden. Sie können der Stolz der Partei sein und die Partei Ihre Stärke.«

Alexander betrachtete nachdenklich sein leeres Glas. »Ich denke nicht, dass ich das kann.«

»Hören Sie«, sagte Peter Pawlowitsch schroff, und Alexander spürte, wie der Mann die Gangart wechselte. »Sie sollten aufhören, mit diesem Iwan Dimitrijewitsch anzubändeln.«

Alexander stellte viel zu laut sein Glas ab. »Wie bitte?«

»Noch mal dasselbe!« Peter Pawlowitsch klopfte auf den Tresen, und Alexander leerte noch ein Glas. Seine Augen wurden unangenehm feucht. Schmale Rauten mutlosen Lichts drangen zum Fenster herein. Peter Pawlowitsch erhob sich.

»Seien Sie vernünftig, Alexander. Lassen Sie sich nicht auf solche Dummheiten ein.«

Auch Alexander kam wackelig wieder auf die Beine. Er fingerte nach seinem Geldbeutel, doch Peter Pawlowitsch bremste ihn mit seinen weichen Händen.

»Bitte, Alexander Kimowitsch«, sagte er. »Denken Sie über mein Angebot nach. Aber die Getränke – sehen Sie sie als Zeichen unserer Bewunderung. Das geht auf uns.«

Zwanzig Minuten später stolperte Alexander über die Türschwelle des Saigon. Der Barmann musterte ihn skeptisch, sagte aber nichts. Wie immer war das Café bis unter die Dachbalken mit Rauch und konspirativen Gesprächen angefüllt. Der Rollstuhlfahrer hatte sich diesmal nahe der Tür postiert, und die Besucher wichen ihm und seinen finsteren Bemerkungen so gut wie möglich aus. Als Alexander sich ihm näherte, bemerkte er, dass hier und da Brotkrümel im Haar des Alten hingen. Ihn schickte niemand weg. Die Welt war ungerecht.

Als er Alexander kommen sah, erbleichte der Mann vor Aufregung, beugte sich vor und öffnete seinen schwarzen, klaffenden Mund. »Leonid Iljitsch ist hier, o Gott, er ist hier!«, kreischte er, dass Alexander vor Schreck zurückprallte. Er hatte ein Flüstern erwartet, irgendeine irrsinnige Geheimbotschaft, und die Stimme des Mannes war unerwartet schrill. Sie stülpte Alexander den Magen um wie eine Urangst, die aufsteigt, wenn etwas vielbeinig krabbelt oder jemand sich von hinten anschleicht.

»Was?«, fragte Alexander. Er versuchte sich an dem Mann vorbeizudrücken, der vergeblich nach seinen Händen grabschte. Einen Augenblick lang fragte Alexander sich, ob der Mann blind war.

»Breschnew. Er ist da.« Der Mann gestikulierte in Richtung der Nische, in der Iwan und Nikolai Rauchgirlanden aufsteigen ließen. »Er ist hier, ganz sicher. Er ist überall!«

Alexander wich den tastenden Händen des Alten aus, den dürren Fingern, die flatterten, als wollten sie Orgel spielen, und zog sich angewidert zurück. Nikolai und Iwan saßen an demselben Tisch wie immer, zwischen sich einen gewaltigen Stapel Zeitungen. Das Deckenlicht fing sich in ihren Wodkagläsern und tröpfelte auf die Tischplatte. Nikolai kritzelte in ein Notizbuch und lachte, was sein vernarbtes Gesicht in bizarre Falten legte. Er trug eine neue Lederjacke. Alexander fragte sich, ob er ihn je zuvor hatte lachen sehen. Er setzte sich zu den beiden an den Tisch.

»Dieser Mann«, sagte Nikolai und zeigte auf den Rollstuhlfahrer, der noch immer sein unsichtbares Publikum anschrie, »ist eindeutig verrückt.«

»Oder er ist ein Prophet«, schlug Iwan vor. »Ein Erbe Rasputins. Was sagst du, Alexander? Glaubt ihr im Osten an so was?«

»Also bitte«, sagte Nikolai. »Ein bisschen mehr Respekt. Der Junge ist jetzt wichtig, weiß du.« Er drückte seine Iskra aus, die sich wie ein Bakterium an die anderen in dem vollen Ascher lehnte.

»In unserer großen Sowjetunion«, sagte Iwan, »ist kein Mensch wichtiger als der andere. Also, was gibt es Neues, Alexander? Bist du nicht berühmt geworden? Solltest du nicht mit den Funktionären Brüderschaft trinken? Oder die nächstbesseren Nutten ausprobieren?«

»Also gut«, sagte Alexander. Scheiß auf Andronow. Scheiß auf alle anderen. »Dann gehe ich.«

»Warte, bleib«, beschwichtigte Nikolai. »Iwan, du solltest wirklich ein bisschen netter sein.«

»Du wirst also eine ganz große Nummer, ja?«, fragte Iwan gleichmütig und begann in dem Zeitungsstapel herumzublättern. »Wir haben gerade von dir gelesen. Oder, Nikolai? In der *Literaturnaja Gaseta*, nicht? Kann das sein, Alexander?«

»Ich weiß es nicht.« Er hatte gar nicht vorgehabt, so erbärmlich zu klingen, wie er sich fühlte. Im nächsten Moment ließ er den Kopf auf die Tischplatte sinken und kühlte sich an dem massiven Holz die Stirn. Er stellte sich den Baum vor, aus dem der Tisch gemacht war – in einem Wald am Schwarzen Meer vielleicht, wo das Salz ihm die Wurzeln zersetzte und das hellgrüne Laub im Wind unaufhörlich zitterte. Oder er kam aus dem Norden. Vielleicht war es ein kleiner, von den schneidenden Steppenwinden verkrüppelter Baum gewesen, der bucklig und schief den Elementen trotzte. Alexander schielte zur Seite und sah die Flaschen über der Bar wie eine Kette wässriger Edelsteine.

»Bist du betrunken?«, fragte Nikolai. Er wandte sich an Iwan. »Ist er betrunken?«

»Das wäre ja ganz was Neues. Bestimmt hat er nur den Verstand verloren. Alexander, hast du vielleicht den Verstand verloren?« Aus Iwans Stimme war eine Art verunglückte Zärtlichkeit herauszuhören, wie die eines ungeübten Vaters, der sein krankes Kind zu trösten versucht. Alexander hörte Nikolai gespannt mit den Kiefern mahlen.

»Ich bin aus der Akademie geworfen worden«, flüsterte Alexander der Holzplatte zu. Er beschloss, seinen Kopf so lange wie nur möglich auf dem Tisch liegenzulassen. Vielleicht, stellte er mit Entsetzen fest, weinte er sogar.

»Ich hab's ja gesagt«, sagte Nikolai. Er senkte die Stimme zu einem heiseren Bariton. »Ich habe dir gesagt, dass er labil ist. Dass man nicht auf ihn bauen kann.«

»Schon gut«, sagte Alexander. »Mir geht es gut, wirklich.« Doch sein Nacken lastete unerträglich schwer zwischen den Schultern, als sei er mit Sand oder Schuld angefüllt. War er arrogant? Er hatte versucht, es nicht zu sein; nach seinen Siegen war immer er derjenige gewesen, der mit ausgestreckter Hand stehen gelassen wurde, während sein Gegner ihm in einer Mischung aus Enttäuschung und Verachtung den Rücken kehrte. Doch wenn er sich vorzustellen versuchte, nach Ocha zurückzugehen – wieder bei seinen Hühnern und seinen Schwestern zu leben und sich an Leningrad zu erinnern wie an einen verblassenden Traum –, stieß ihn der Gedanke ab. Er musste zugeben, dass es ihm gefallen hatte zu siegen. Es hatte ihm gefallen, bescheiden und großmütig sein zu können.

»Ich dachte, du hast die Akademie nicht gemocht«, sagte Iwan. »Und dass du dich da gelangweilt hast.«

Alexander presste sein Kinn noch fester auf den Tisch. Über seinem Kopf hörte er tonlos gewisperte Worte und bemerkte ein heftiges Kopfschütteln. Schließlich legte sich eine anonyme Hand auf seine Schulter; so dick und rau, wie sie war, musste es wohl die von Nikolai sein.

»Hab ich auch nicht«, sagte Alexander. »Ich habe mich wirklich gelangweilt.« Das Holz war noch kälter geworden; von seiner Oberfläche schienen kleine Luftwirbel aufzusteigen, und Alexander spürte, wie er in eine angenehme Leere versank. »Ich weiß nur nicht, was ich jetzt tun soll.«

Ein erneutes Schweigen – in dem über Alexanders Kopf wieder tonlose Verhandlungen geführt wurden, unterbrochen von einigen Grunzlauten Nikolais – endete damit, dass Iwan sagte: »Dann musst du wohl für uns arbeiten.«

Alexanders Kopf füllte sich wieder, und er sah, wie sein Leben bedenklich schwankend um seine Achse rotierte und eine neue Richtung nahm. Schweißknospen drangen aus seinen Poren, und er schluckte mühsam gegen die rote Hitze an, die ihm den Rachen hochstieg. Er traute sich nicht aufzublicken.

»Also wirklich, Nikolai«, sagte Iwan. »Jetzt gib dem Mann endlich einen Wodka.«

Iwan und Nikolai gaben, wie sich herausstellte, eine monatlich erscheinende Flugschrift heraus, und sie nahmen Alexander mit, um sie ihm zu zeigen. Iwans Zimmer war winzig, und der Boden war von Wand zu Wand mit übereinandergeschichteten Büchern und Papieren und Abfällen bedeckt. Hier und da bemerkte Alexander den schwachen arktischen Geruch von Schimmelpilzen. In der Mitte des Raums stand eine Schreibmaschine auf einem hohen Bücherstapel. Von einem Poster über dem Fernseher blickte Brigitte Bardot wissend herab. Ihre Körpermitte war von vielen Umzügen ganz zerknittert. Iwan war Hochschuldozent gewesen, bis ihn die Universität wegen antisowjetischer Umtriebe hinausgeworfen hatte. »Dissidenten sind die einzigen Arbeitslosen in der Sowjetunion«, sagte er und goss Alexander ein Glas Kwas ein. Er war erst vor kurzem hier eingezogen, nachdem er fünf Jahre lang auf seine Propiska gewartet hatte, und war sich sicher, dass er noch nicht abgehört wurde. Iwan besaß Unmengen von Büchern, obwohl er nach der Quotenregelung für jeden Turgenjew mindestens fünf politische Abhandlungen kaufen musste. Sie standen in großen bunten Stapeln wie Möbelstücke im Raum verteilt. Dazwischen schlich eine einäugige dreifarbige Katze herum, die sich sogleich schnurrend und nasereibend auf die Ankömmlinge stürzte.

»Das ist Natascha«, sagte Iwan und kraulte das Tier mit einem Zeh. »Meine einzige wahre Freundin.« Er stellte einen Teller Schaschlik auf einem Stapel alter Ausgaben der *Sowetskaja Kultura* ab und zwinkerte der Katze zu. Nikolai hockte sich auf den Boden und machte sich an dem Schaschlik zu schaffen, und Alexander tat es ihm nach. Es war merkwürdig, Nikolai und Iwan außerhalb des Cafés zu sehen, wie sie bei Tageslicht auf dem Boden hockten und schmatzend ihr Schaschlik kauten, wo er sie sonst nur aus dem dämmrigen Café unter ihrer Dunstglocke aus Zigarettenrauch und gefährlichem Gedankengut kannte. Über ihren Köpfen thronte die Schreibmaschine, als sei sie das Gerüst, das den ganzen Raum zusammenhielt.

»Tippt ihr die Zeitung auf der Schreibmaschine?«, fragte Alexander.

»Genau«, sagte Iwan.

»Hast du sie aus der Universität gestohlen?«

»Ich habe einen Zollbeamten bestochen. Die Maschinen an der Uni sind alle registriert.«

Alexander nahm noch einen Bissen von dem Fleisch, das so salzig schmeckte wie Blut, und sah sich um. In den Ecken hatten sich faustgroße Staubballen angesammelt, und Alexanders Trinkglas hatte einen Milchrand.

»Und macht ihr die gesamte Zeitung hier?«, fragte Alexander.

»So ist es gedacht«, sagte Iwan. »Ein paar Freunde reichen ihre Beiträge bei uns ein. Lyrik, Prosa oder Meldungen über Verhaftungen. Diese Meldungen sind das Wichtigste. Nichts gegen die Schriftsteller natürlich. Wir vervielfältigen das Ganze mit Kohlepapier. Mehr als acht auf einmal geht nicht, sonst werden sie unleserlich. Davon machen wir mehrere Durchläufe, bis ich mit dem Farbband oder den Nerven am Ende bin. Jeder Leser soll weitere Kopien machen und verteilen. Bei jeder Ausgabe gehen uns ein paar Leute verloren, aber unsere Auflage ist insgesamt nicht schlecht.«

»Wie oft macht ihr das?«

»Alle drei Wochen ungefähr.«

Alexander sah zu Nikolai hinüber, der meditativ an seinem Schaschlik kaute und aus dem Fenster starrte. Er hörte nicht zu, oder zumindest tat er so. Er trug noch immer seine Lederjacke, und Alexander wunderte sich darüber. Sie war gut geschnitten, als käme sie aus dem Ausland – aus Italien vielleicht –, aber das konnte nicht sein.

»Kann ich sie mal sehen?«, fragte Alexander.

Sofort öffnete Iwan eine seiner Schubladen. Er hatte offensichtlich nur auf diese Bitte gewartet. »Natürlich«, sagte er und zog die Flugschrift hervor. »Hier.« Iwan beugte sich zu Alexander vor. Sein Atem roch säuerlich. Er errötete, als er Alexander das Pamphlet überreichte. Es war ungewohnt, dass Iwan so offensichtlich etwas von ihm wollte, und noch ungewohnter, dass dieses Etwas Alexanders Anerkennung war.

Die Titelseite des Blattes wirkte mit ihrer kleinen schwarzen Schrift eher langweilig. Es war keine Zeitschrift, die man aus Neugier aufgeblättert hätte, weil ihr Äußeres interessante Inhalte versprochen hätte. Eher wirkte es, als seien im Inneren metaphysische Traktate oder ein Abriss über die jüngsten Erfolge in der Agrartechnologie zu erwarten. Alexander blätterte trotzdem weiter. Der erste Text war eine anonyme Einleitung, die von Iwan stammen musste. (»Freunde«, stand da, »wir versammeln uns hier auf diesen Seiten, um wieder einmal eine Bestandsaufnahme unserer Situation und unserer selbst zu machen …«) Dann folgte ein blumiges Gedicht, das Alexander nach dem dritten Lesen immer noch nicht verstand, außer dass viel von »Kapitulation« die Rede war. In einem Essay wurde eine moderne Lesart von Bulgakow vorgeschlagen. Und dann gab es eine Aufzählung von Festnahmen, Verhaftungen, Hausdurchsuchungen in und um Leningrad im vergangenen Monat. Diese Liste war der längste Beitrag – Seite um Seite voller Namen und Daten und Maßnahmen, unkommentiert. Überschrieben war sie mit »Eine kleine Auswahl aussichtsloser Fälle«, was auch der Titel der Flugschrift war.

»Die Liste ist unvollständig«, sagte Iwan. »Wir versuchen nicht mal, sie vollständig zu bekommen. Es ist nur eine Auswahl, an der man die ungefähre Tendenz des Monats erkennen kann – wonach sie am meisten gesucht und was sie gefunden haben.«

Alexander überflog die Liste. Es gab Verhaftungen wegen Missbrauchs von Staatseigentum (Iwans illegal erworbene Schreibmaschine kam ihm in den Sinn), eine Festnahme wegen »Verbreitung von Falschinformationen« (er vermutete, dass auch der Eintrag, der diese Festnahme bekanntgab, offiziell als Falschinformation galt), eine Verhaftung aufgrund »sozialen Parasitentums« (damit war Arbeitslosigkeit gemeint, die Alexander neuerdings ebenfalls anzulasten war), und dann und wann hatte es Hausdurchsuchungen wegen Verdachts auf verschwörerische Umtriebe gegeben (Alexander musterte Iwan, wie er mit hervortretenden Halssehnen mühsam schluckte, und Nikolai, wie er überall hinsah außer zu ihm, und fragte sich, wie weit er ihnen vertraute). Er ließ die Zeitung sinken und beugte sich zu Iwan herüber. »Ich bin heute von einem Funktionär angesprochen worden«, sagte er. »Sie haben mir eine Datscha angeboten.«

Iwan nickte. »Sie wollen, dass du Mitglied wirst.«

»Ja.«

»Es gibt eine Akte über dich.«

»Natürlich.«

»Und du hast nein gesagt?«

»Natürlich habe ich das.«

»Dein Zimmer muss wirklich toll sein.«

»Er hat gesagt, ich sollte mich nicht mehr mit euch abgeben.«

»Ein kluger Rat.«

»Dann wissen sie, was ihr tut?«

»Es ist kein Geheimnis. Geheimnisse gibt es nicht. Vielleicht ist geheim, wer wir genau sind und was wir wollen. Und wer unsere Beiträger und Leser sind, ist auch geheim. Die Details, aber nicht die Tatsache an sich. Wir sind kein Geheimnis, und deine Teilnahme wird auch nicht lange eins bleiben. Der KGB hat dir eine Frage gestellt, und was du tust, wird deine Antwort sein.«

Alexander dachte an die seidig weichen Hände Peter Pawlowitschs und seine Mahnung, vernünftig zu sein. Wahrhaftig ein kluger Rat, wenn er so darüber nachdachte.

»Obwohl es kein Geheimnis ist«, sagte Iwan, »musst du immer so tun, als wäre es eins. Vor allem musst du sichergehen, dass dir niemand folgt, weil wir die Details nicht preisgeben wollen. Du und ich und Nikolai, wir sind wertlose Junggesellen, und wen kratzt es schon, was mit uns passiert?« Alexander war unsicher, ob er diese Gleichgültigkeit bewundern, verurteilen oder fürchten sollte.

»Aber einige unserer Beiträger und Abonnenten haben Familien«, sagte Iwan. »Wir müssen das Risiko, dass sie verhaftet werden, so klein wie möglich halten. Also müssen wir so diskret wie möglich vorgehen, ohne uns deswegen etwas vorzumachen. Okay? Zum Glück ist der KGB gar nicht so raffiniert, wie man denkt.

Manchmal schleichen sie allen Ernstes mit weißen Wolgas durch die Stadt und lauern den Leuten an den Straßenecken auf.« Er nahm einen Schluck Kwas und verzog das Gesicht. »Aber es geht auch ein bisschen subtiler. Am besten bewegst du dich also im Zickzack durch die Stadt. Geh nicht mehrmals hintereinander denselben Weg, und komm auf keinen Fall zu regelmäßigen Zeiten hierher. Du musst immer einen plausiblen Grund haben, da zu sein, wo du gerade bist – den Spezialitätenladen oder das Schuhgeschäft. Und wenn du den Verdacht hast, dass jemand dir folgt, langweile sie zu Tode.«

»Okay«, sagte Alexander zögernd. Er starrte in sein Glas, in dem faserige Wölkchen umherschwebten wie Algen im Brackwasser. »Ich bin ziemlich sicher, dass ich das kann.«

»Entscheidend ist, dass man es bemerken wird. Es wird in deiner Akte auftauchen. Trotzdem darfst du dich nie, nie verfolgen lassen, weil wir die anderen schützen müssen. Du darfst nie Informationen mit dir herumtragen. Keine Listen, keine Adressen, kein Kartenmaterial. Aber das sollte einem Mann mit deinem Gedächtnis ja nicht schwerfallen, oder?«

»Ich glaube, das kriege ich hin.«

»Wenn du verhört wirst, verschwindest du von der Bildfläche, klar? Und wenn du verfolgt wirst, setzt du dich ein Stündchen in den Park, nimmst die Metro nach Hause und kommst nie wieder.«

»Nie wieder«, sagte Nikolai ernst. »Wir trauern dir bestimmt nicht nach.«

Alexander starrte ihn an. »Schöne Jacke«, sagte er.

Nikolai nahm einen Schluck Kwas und sah zu Boden.

»Alexander«, sagte Iwan und ließ einen aufgespießten Fleischfetzen auf seiner Gabel kreisen. »Dein großer Vorteil ist, dass sich niemand an dein Gesicht oder deine Art erinnern wird. Ich bin zu groß, und Nikolai ist – verzeih, wenn ich das sage – zu hässlich, um in der Menge unterzutauchen. Du bist unauffällig. Natürlich nicht für die Behörden, aber für jeden, der gebeten werden könnte, dich zu beschreiben. Wenn sie einen unserer Leser in die Zange nehmen und wissen wollen, wer ihm die Zeitung gebracht hat, was soll er dann sagen? Tja, der Mann war nicht groß, nicht klein, hatte braunes Haar, ein normales Gesicht, zwei Augen, eine Nase? So finden sie nicht so leicht heraus, wie wir vorgehen und wo du überall warst. Und bei dir wird niemand misstrauisch. Du siehst zu dämlich aus, um verdächtig zu sein.«

»Vielen Dank«, sagte Alexander. »So viel Anerkennung tut gut.«

»Gern geschehen«, sagte Iwan und legte sein Fleischstück auf den Teller zurück. »Willkommen beim Vertrieb.«

Die Arbeit im Vertrieb bestand hauptsächlich daraus, früh aufzustehen, sorgfältig auswendig gelernten Wegbeschreibungen zu mehrfach überprüften Adressen zu folgen und dort anzuklopfen. Alexander trug dabei eine dicke Mütze, die bei Regen einen animalischen Geruch verströmte, und zog sie sich tief in die Stirn, damit sie sein dunkles Gesicht noch mehr verschattete. So würde ihn niemand erkennen – niemand würde morgens von seiner *Literaturnaja Gaseta* aufblicken und sich wundern, was Alexander Besetow in der Metro zu suchen hatte. Doch wenn er nachmittags auf eigene Faust durch Leningrad spazierte, wenn er seinen Rundgang beendet und die Mütze abgesetzt hatte und in die welke Sonne blinzelte, stellte sich heraus, dass er sich darum wenig Sorgen machen musste.

Alexander lernte interessante Leute kennen – die Liste der Abonnenten war kurz, aber bunt gemischt und voller Gestalten, mit denen er nicht gerechnet hätte. Nicht wenige Frauen waren darunter, ältere Menschen und der eine oder andere, der erst vor kurzem zu einer öffentlichen Selbstkritik gezwungen worden war. Zu allen hatte er eine genaue Beschreibung ihres Äußeren im Kopf. Wenn jemand anderes die Tür öffnete, erkundigte er sich in einem improvisierten gebrochenen Russisch umständlich nach dem Weg zur nächsten Metrostation, bis man die Tür wieder zuschlug. Es gab nie mehr als zwanzig Abnehmer. Manchmal kam jemand Neues hinzu, der im Saigon Iwans und Nikolais Vertrauen gewonnen hatte; manchmal wurde jemand paranoid oder befördert und bat

Alexander händeringend, nie, nie wiederzukommen. Und daran hielt er sich.

An manchen Tagen drehte er seine Runde zu Fuß, an anderen mit der Metro, und oft kombinierte er beide Möglichkeiten: Er fuhr ein paar Stationen und ging dann wieder zwei Kilometer zu Fuß bis zu einer anderen Station. Das war Iwans Idee gewesen, und die allmorgendlichen Botengänge gaben Alexander allmählich das Gefühl, die Stadt zu bewohnen und zu verstehen – das Eintauchen in die edlen Innereien einer reich verzierten, pompösen und atomkriegstauglichen Metrostation, dann der Aufstieg in die weißliche Morgendämmerung, wo Leningrad erst als Ahnung, dann als Schemen, dann als Silhouette aus dem Nebel tauchte, dann wieder der Abstieg in die Metro, wo Menschenmassen sich eilig vorwärtsdrängten und das Licht aus Kronleuchtern von der Decke tröpfelte wie auf der Titanic.

Bei einer seiner morgendlichen Metrofahrten im angeblichen Frühjahr sah Alexander Elisabeta bei der Arbeit. Er entdeckte sie auf einem Bahnsteig, um fünf Uhr morgens, wie sie schlaff am Arm eines Mannes mit der Statur eines Dinosauriers hing. Ihre Nachtschicht musste fast zu Ende sein, dachte Alexander. Ihre schwarze Kleidung, die sie wie ein eigenständiges Wesen mit seinen eigenen provokanten Ideen umspielte, wirkte ein wenig derangiert; ihr beinahe schönes Gesicht sah älter aus als sonst. Dunkle Ringe hatten sich unter ihren Augen gebildet, und ihr Make-up wirkte irgendwie missraten. Die Stirn des Mannes ragte wie eine Schublade nach vorn. Er beugte sich zu Elisabeta hinab und sagte etwas zu ihr, und sie lachte, wie sie es getan hatte, als sie mit der Verwalterin sprach.

Alexander sollte sich später einreden, er wäre fast zu ihr hingegangen. Er dachte zumindest darüber nach. Ernsthaft sogar. Er stellte sich vor, sie mitzunehmen, sie in seine Angelegenheiten einzuweihen, dem Mann das Geld, das er für sie ausgegeben hatte, mit Zinsen zurückzuzahlen und lachend durch die Straßen davonzulaufen, während der Mann ärgerlich und verwundert seine prähistorische Körpermasse von einer Seite auf die andere wälzte.

Doch er hatte zu tun – er musste arbeiten, und Elisabeta, das wusste er, ebenso. Und die Arbeit ging natürlich vor. Also wandte er sich ab und stieg weiter die breite, endlose Treppe hinauf in die Stadt und den neuen Tag.

KAPITEL 6

Irina
Moskau, 2006

Meine Maschine landete erst abends in Moskau-Scheremetjewo, aber beim Zoll gab es lange Schlangen. Als wir im Sinkflug durch die Landschaft kreuzten, betrachtete ich die matten Lichter, die Moskau in das All hinausschickte, und staunte, wie klein sie im Vergleich zu dem Rest erschienen, zu der Weite und der Dunkelheit. Ich hatte eine lange Reise hinter mir – sechs Stunden über dem wogenden Atlantik, drei Stunden mit überteuerten, undefinierbaren englischen Sandwiches in Heathrow und eine holprige letzte Etappe nach Russland. Die Stewardessen hatten sich gegen mich verschworen. Ich hatte mein Russischbuch Stufe drei hervorgekramt und versucht, eine Cola zu bestellen. Sie hatten die Augen verdreht, mich von oben bis unten gemustert und auf Englisch gefragt, ob ich lieber eine Diet Coke wollte. Ich hatte mein Gesicht an die kalte Fensterscheibe gepresst und mich gefragt: Wie? Warum? Und wofür?

Es hatte damit begonnen, dass Jonathan mich bat, mit ihm zusammenzuziehen. Wir waren schließlich verliebt, und das Zusammenziehen ist in unserer Kultur nun einmal Teil des dazugehörigen Krankheitsverlaufs. Ich hatte erst ja gesagt, dann vielleicht, dann sagte ich, dass ich für immer fortgehen würde.

Ich wusste, dass ich unmöglich bei ihm einziehen konnte. Ich wusste, es war alles nur gespielt. Das Gefühl mag ja echt gewesen sein, aber alles andere waren hohle Gesten, bloße Imitationen des Verhaltens von Menschen, die ein Leben lang Zeit haben, einander zu lieben und zu enttäuschen. Dass er mich überhaupt fragte, war beinahe schon beleidigend – entweder wollte er mich bevormunden, oder er verschloss die Augen vor der Wirklichkeit. Es war, als hätte er mir einfach nicht zugehört. Ich war dreißig. Ich hatte höchstens noch ein oder zwei körperlich und geistig intakte Jahre zu leben. Ich hatte nicht vor, mit Jonathan zusammenzuziehen, bloß damit er zusehen konnte, wie alles, was er zufällig an mir gemocht hatte, verschwand. Ich bin nicht romantisch genug, um zu glauben, dass die Liebe so einen Frontalangriff überstehen kann. Jemanden in seiner Abwesenheit zu lieben ist das eine, aber jemanden zu lieben, der deformiert und reduziert und immer, immer da ist – das ist etwas ganz anderes. Ich hatte meinen Vater geliebt. Liebte ich auch den Menschen, zu dem er durch seine Krankheit geworden war? Ich weiß es nicht. Was war das für ein Mensch?

Ich würde Jonathan verlassen. Als ich das beschlossen hatte, kam es mir nur folgerichtig vor, mich auch von allem anderen zu verabschieden.

Am Abend des Tages, an dem Jonathan mich gefragt hatte, kehrte ich allein in meine leere Wohnung zurück. Ich holte den Brief hervor, den mein Vater an Alexander Besetow geschickt hatte, und die knappe Notiz von Elisabeta Nasarowna. Ich dachte noch einmal daran, wie mein Vater gestorben war, ohne die Antwort auf seine besten Fragen je bekommen zu haben. Und ich dachte an Alexander Besetow und konnte nicht umhin, ihn ein klein wenig zu hassen. So viel Energie und Intelligenz und vor allem so viel Zeit – die gesamte durchschnittliche Lebenserwartung –, und er hatte es nicht einmal fertiggebracht, meinem armen sterbenden Vater ein paar Fragen zu beantworten, so abstrakt und zudringlich sie auch sein mochten. Was hätte es ihn schon gekostet, wenn er so viel besaß? Es kam mir so kleinlich vor, die Antwort – die Nichtantwort – an seine Sekretärin zu delegieren.

Ich sah mir den Brief der Sekretärin noch einmal an. Er hatte diesen leicht bedauernden, verlegenen Ton, als hätte sie gewusst, dass es so nicht richtig war. Elisabeta Nasarowna. Was für ein Name.

Ich setzte mich an den Computer. Ich tippte »Elisabeta Nasarowna« und »St. Petersburg« ein und hangelte mich von einem kyrillischen Wort zum nächsten. Es gab die Geburtsanzeige eines Kindes Jahrgang 1998. Dann den Verweis auf eine oppositionelle Schriftstellerin, die dem Großen Terror zum Opfer gefallen war. Dann kamen Fotos einer sehr jungen Frau auf einer Social-Network-Seite. Sie hatte eine perfekt gestylte Frisur und die langen, flaumigen Arme einer Magersüchtigen und hielt auf jedem der Bilder einen anderen grellbunt marmorierten Cocktail in der Hand. Dann fand ich eine Geschäftsfrau, die online kommunistische Andenken verkaufte. Ich fand unendlich viele Elisabetas, alte und neugeborene, angedeutete und ausgewiesene. Und dann begann ich, so peinlich es mir im Nachhinein auch ist, sie anzurufen.

Ich stellte mir Regeln auf: Nur Bewohnerinnen von Moskau oder St. Petersburg kamen in Frage (niemand, der je in Leningrad gelebt hatte, würde freiwillig aufs Land zurückgehen, dachte ich). Dann ließ ich alle weg, die zu alt oder zu jung waren, und alle, für die in den Siebzigern oder frühen Achtzigern ein Beruf angegeben war. Am häufigsten hörte ich am anderen Ende die Kein-Anschluss-Meldung, Freitöne und eine kaltherzige, unfassbar schnell sprechende Telefonistin, die mich wütend irgendeines mir unbegreiflichen Vergehens bezichtigte. Ich erreichte ein kleines Mädchen Elisabeta, eine Elisabeta, die mich nicht verstand, und den Witwer einer verstorbenen Elisabeta. Dann, irgendwann, erreichte ich eine Elisabeta mit einer leisen, seltsam zerbrechlichen Stimme, die sagte: »Da? Da?«

Das konnte sie auch nicht sein, dachte ich. Sie klang wie eine besonders technophobe Großmutter, die in das Telefon hineinsprach, als sei ihr Gesprächspartner im Hörer versteckt. Was zum Geier tat ich da überhaupt?

»Sdráwstwuite«, sagte ich langsam und deutlich. »Menja sowut Irina Ellison. Goworíte po anglíjski?« Ich hätte zwar auch den Rest auf Russisch sagen können, doch auf Englisch wäre es peinlich genug, dachte ich. Wenn es sich vermeiden ließ, musste ich es nicht noch schlimmer machen.

Das Schweigen in der Leitung war so lang und so eisig wie der Kalte Krieg.

»Ja«, sagte sie dann auf Englisch. »Was wollen Sie?« Sie glaubte offenbar, ich wollte ihr etwas verkaufen, was ja auch naheliegend war. Die meisten Menschen wollen irgendetwas verkaufen, auch wenn sie manchmal selbst nicht wissen, was.

»Das klingt jetzt vielleicht merkwürdig«, sagte ich. »Aber mein Vater hatte Briefverkehr mit Alexander Besetow. Erinnern Sie sich an ihn?« Ich bemühte mich um einen sanften, bittenden Tonfall – eine Haltung, die mir nicht besonders liegt. Ich wartete. Eine weitere Eiszeit verging, und ich fürchtete schon, ich hätte sie beleidigt. Sie war vermutlich alt, vielleicht schon vergesslich, hatte wer weiß was für eine Beziehung zu Besetow gehabt, und jetzt rief jemand an und verlangte von ihr, in alten Erinnerungen zu wühlen. Ich begann, elegante Rückzugsmanöver aus diesem Gespräch zu entwerfen – irgendetwas mit vertauschten Telefonnummern oder verwechselten Namen. Doch dann hörte ich durch das rapide anschwellende Rauschen meines Unbehagens plötzlich wieder ihre Stimme. Sie klang kräftiger als vorher. Selbstsicherer.

»Alexander Besetow«, sagte sie, und ich konnte hören, dass sie ein wenig aufzutauen begann. Ihre Stimme klang wie Eiswürfel im Glas, mit dem unmerklichen Glitzern eines Lachens im Hintergrund. »Ja, von dem weiß ich noch das eine oder andere. Der dumme Bengel.«

Ich hatte mir den berühmten Alexander Besetow nie als Bengel vorgestellt und hatte Mühe, mir eine Frau auszumalen, die ihn so sah. Sie musste alt sein, älter jedenfalls, als ich es je werden würde.

»Haben Sie für ihn gearbeitet?«, fragte ich.

»Nicht direkt.«

»Aber gekannt haben Sie ihn?«

Wieder folgte ein Schweigen. Es klang weniger leer – wie mit stillen Erinnerungen aufgeladen, die leise in der Leitung knisterten.

»Ja.«

Ich legte auf.

Wenn man sich aufs Sterben vorbereitet, blickt man auf sein Leben zurück und versucht die offenen Fragen zu klären. Man deutet sinnhafte Zusammenhänge in die chaotischen Abläufe hinein, wertet Zufälle als Omen. Man durchkämmt seine Vergangenheit nach den entscheidenden Weichen und fragt sich, ob man sie richtig gestellt hat. Es ist eine endlose Suche nach brüchigen Verbindungen, eine Jagd nach erkennbaren Mustern, von denen man nicht einmal weiß, ob es sie gibt. Wie ein Kind am Badestrand wühlt man panisch im Untergrund, während die Flut steigt und die Sonne sinkt, nach etwas, von dem man nicht mehr weiß, wo man es vergraben hat.

Als ich so mein Leben durchforstete, fand ich zu allererst einen erschreckenden Mangel an offenen Fragen. Besetow schien mir so etwas wie eine offene Frage zu sein.

Also stellte ich mir Russland vor: ein kaltes, gewaltiges Land, kriminell und korrupt und von einer unmöglichen Sprache beherrscht, gefährlich für Ausländer und allein reisende Frauen. Dann versuchte ich mir vorzustellen, wie ich die wenigen verbleibenden Wissenslücken füllen würde.

Ich kontrollierte den Stand meiner Ersparnisse: trotz eines bescheidenen Gehalts und wegen eines viel zu vernünftigen Lebensstils ziemlich hoch. Ich kontrollierte mein Alter: genau ein Jahr und vier Monate vor dem durchschnittlichen Auftreten der Symptome. Ich kontrollierte Elisabeta Nasarownas Namen und Adresse.

Logistisch war alles ganz einfach, beinahe zu einfach. Ich hatte nicht vor unterzutauchen; ich wollte nur reinen Tisch machen. Doch alles in allem dauerte es nicht einmal eine Woche, die gesammelten Verpflichtungen und Verbindungen meines kurzen Lebens abzuwickeln, und ich ertappte mich bei dem Wunsch, etwas mehr Chaos zu hinterlassen. Unwillkürlich hoffte ich auf irgendeine Altlast – einen rachsüchtigen verstoßenen Geliebten, ein anhängiges Gerichtsverfahren, Versäumnisse bei der Arbeit –, die meine Aufmerksamkeit fordern würde, die mich aufhalten und mich in mein Leben in Boston zurückholen würde. Doch die gab es nicht. Ich hatte ein relativ einfaches, geordnetes Leben geführt, ein Leben mit Blick auf den Notausgang. Und jetzt ging ich und hinterließ alles so wohlgeordnet wie eine Reisende, die im Hotel ihre Koffer nicht auspackt, weil sie weiß, dass sie nicht lange bleiben wird.

Ich löste meine Geld- und Sparanlagen auf. Ich schrieb die letzten Bewertungen für meine letzten Kursteilnehmer und reichte meine Kündigung ein. Ich überwies meinem Vermieter drei Monatsraten. Ich verbrachte ein bisschen Zeit im Internet. Ich verbrachte Zeit damit, mir meine bisherigen Eskapaden ins Gedächtnis zu rufen (es gab keine). Und ich verbrachte Zeit damit, mich zu verabschieden – was, wie alles andere, viel einfacher ist, wenn man einen Vorsprung hat.

Ich erzählte allen – der Mutter, dem Arzt, den Freunden und Kollegen –, dass ich verreisen wollte. Ganz spontan, sagte ich, ganz luxuriös und egoistisch und vor allem sehr, sehr lange. Ich sagte, ich wollte etwas von der Welt sehen, solange ich noch konnte, und ein kleines Abenteuer nur für mich erleben, solange ich allein zurechtkam. Meine Kollegen reagierten verständnisvoll. Meine Mutter war erleichtert, glaube ich. Menschen, die nie über meine Diagnose gesprochen hatten, die sich nie nach meinem Vater erkundigt hatten, waren begeistert, endlich einen konkreten, verständlichen und positiven Anlass zu haben, indirekt darüber zu reden. Sie redeten davon, wie bedeutend diese Entscheidung sei und wie gut es mir tun würde, unterwegs zu sein. Falls sie insgeheim fanden, dass ich mir für meine letzte Reise ein seltsames Ziel ausgewählt hatte, waren sie so höflich, es nicht zu erwähnen.

Jonathan erzählte ich mehr oder minder das Gleiche, auch wenn er mich gut genug kannte, um zu ahnen, dass ich log und wahrscheinlich nicht wiederkommen würde. Er war schockiert, fürchte ich, und traurig und wütend und all das. Er dachte, ich wollte nur bluffen; es sei nur eine Überreaktion. Er wollte, dass ich mich in Therapie begab.

Es war kein Bluff. Seelisch war ich vielleicht nicht in der allerstabilsten Verfassung meines Lebens. Aber ich dachte – und irgendwann, in einer dieser scheußlichen letzten Nächte, an die ich mich so wenig wie nur möglich erinnern will, sagte ich es auch: Ich bin hier nicht diejenige mit den Wahnvorstellungen. Ich bin nicht die mit dem verzerrten Blick auf die Realität.

Was hätte er letztlich auch tun sollen? Ich bin eine erwachsene Frau und eine Bürgerin der Vereinigten Staaten, finanziell unabhängig und in der Lage, mir einen Visa-Eilantrag zu leisten. Er konnte mich nicht aufhalten, so wie letztlich überhaupt niemand irgendwen vom Verlassen abhalten kann.

Ein paar Tage vor meiner Abreise wollte ich noch ein letztes Mal gegen Lars Schach spielen. Es war Mai, die Luft war seidig weich. Kein sehr passender Tag für eine Partie, doch ich brauchte jemanden zum Reden. Leider kam es nicht dazu. Lars hob die Augenbrauen, als er mich sah, und schwieg. »Hallo, alter Mann«, sagte ich und setzte mich. »Wie geht's?« Er zuckte mit den Schultern und wies mit großer Geste auf das Schachfeld.

»Was ist?« Ich kniff die Augen zusammen. »Stimmt etwas nicht?« Lars sah aus wie immer – spülwassergraues Haar, sonnenverbrannte Nase und die Gesamterscheinung eines Menschen, der regelmäßig unter Brücken schläft –, doch seine Augen strahlten bedeutsamer als sonst. Er reichte mir eine Karte.

Aus Protest gegen meine Festnahme durch FASCHISTISCHE POLIZEIKRÄFTE wegen Störung der öffentlichen Ordnung mittels Gesang habe ich ein Schweigegelübde abgelegt. Bitte unterstützen Sie mich in meinem Kampf gegen den Versuch dieser FASCHISTENSCHWEINE, alles LEBEN, die KUNST und die FREIHEIT in unserer Heimatstadt zu zerstören.

»Du bist verhaftet worden? Weil du gesungen hast?« Lars' Augen flackerten, und er legte den Finger auf das Wort »Festnahme« auf seiner Karte. »Festgenommen? Wegen Gesang?«

Lars nickte feierlich.

»Okay«, sagte ich. »Geschieht dir wahrscheinlich recht.«

Dann schwiegen wir und spielten das übliche Spiel. Ich war nicht mit dem Herzen dabei, also schonte er mich, wie ich vermute – ich hatte an dem Tag bessere Chancen auf einen Sieg als je zuvor. Doch ich besiegte ihn nicht. Und jetzt wird es wohl nicht mehr dazu kommen.

»Wenn du nichts sagst, bist du nicht gerade unterhaltsam«, sagte ich irgendwann. Lars streckte mir die Zunge heraus, wahrscheinlich, um zu zeigen, dass er zumindest ein bisschen unterhaltsam war.

»Wirklich schade, dass du nicht reden willst«, sagte ich. »Es gibt nämlich Neuigkeiten.«

Er wandte den Blick ab und kniff die Augen zusammen. Lars liebte es zu tratschen, und ich wusste, wie schwer es ihm fiel, abstinent zu bleiben, selbst wenn es seinen hehren politischen Idealen diente. Er griff nach einem Stift und drehte die Karte mit seiner Protestnote um. »Was?«, schrieb er.

Also begann ich zu reden. Ich verbreitete mich ohne Punkt und Komma, ungehemmt und vollkommen unzusammenhängend und noch viel selbstbezogener als sonst. Worauf ich hinauswollte war wohl, dass ich panische Angst hatte, doch das hätte ich nie geradeheraus zugegeben, weder vor Lars noch sonst irgendwem gegenüber. Aber Lars wusste es – seine privilegierte Position erreicht man nicht ohne eine gewisse Menschenkenntnis –, und je länger er mir zusah, wie ich in meinem Kaffee rührte, meinen Muffin liegen ließ und meine Spielfiguren umwarf, desto angewiderter sah er aus. Ich war gerade mitten in einem Monolog darüber, wie viel schonender es sei, mich leise aus Jonathans Leben zu schleichen, bevor er meinen Verfall mitansehen musste, als Lars es nicht mehr aushielt. Er hätte fast seinen Kaffee ausgespuckt und sein Schweigegelübde dazu.

»Oh, bitte«, sagte er. »Merkst du nicht, dass du es genießt, dich so zu fühlen? Du grübelst gern. Das macht, mit Verlaub, deinen bescheidenen Charme aus.«

»Du redest ja.«

»Du hast mich dazu getrieben.«

»Ich grüble nicht. Ich denke nach.«

»Was soll ich dir sagen?« Seine Augenbrauen wackelten bedenklich, und er opferte vor Verzweiflung seinen Turm. »Du hörst ja nie zu. Deshalb wirst du auch nicht besser im Schach.«

»Aber das werde ich doch«, sagte ich, beäugte den Turm und versuchte herauszufinden, in welchen ausgeklügelten Hinterhalt er mich locken sollte. »Oder?«

»Nein«, sagte Lars. »Wirst du nicht.«

»Oh.« Ich schlug den Turm und wartete – wartete, dass die Falle zuschnappte, die Welt über mir zusammenbrach, dass eine Bauernplage über mich kam. Doch nichts geschah. Lars rückte mit seinem Springer gegen meine Dame vor. Diesmal, dies eine Mal hatte ich einen kleinen Sieg errungen.

»Wenn du weglaufen willst, dann tu's. Ich halte dich nicht auf.«

»Das sehe ich.«

»Aber vielleicht solltest du ein bisschen bei diesem Mann bleiben. Er ist sicher sehr langweilig, aber wahrscheinlich nicht langweiliger als du. Du könntest ein bisschen Sex haben. Das würde dir guttun. Sex, weißt du? Schon mal davon gehört?«

»Nicht, dass ich wüsste.«

»Es würde dir guttun. Dich zum Lachen bringen. Du bist immer so ernst.« Er machte ein ernstes Gesicht, mit aufgeblasenen Backen und stierem Blick.

»Du siehst aus wie Kim Jong Il.«

»Oder lass es bleiben. Auch gut. Wenn du lieber schmollen willst, bitte. Bekommt vielleicht deiner Spielstärke besser.«

»Das ist eine meiner höchsten Prioritäten.«

»Ja, dachte ich mir. Übrigens, Schach.«

Als ich mich schon aus dem Spiel und dem Gespräch zurückzuziehen begann, packte mich Lars plötzlich am Kragen und zog mich zu sich herunter, bis dicht vor sein ergrautes, vorwurfsvolles Gesicht. »Hör mal«, sagte er. »Wenn ich sowieso schon rede, weil du sowieso schon mein Gelübde gebrochen hast, kann ich dir auch noch etwas sagen. Weißt du, was dein Problem ist?«

»Ich denke, ja.«

»Du hast Angst, dich auf etwas einzulassen, das du nicht verlieren willst«, sagte er triumphierend, als hätte er mich gerade zum tausendsten Mal in Folge schachmatt gesetzt – was er vielleicht längst getan hatte.

»Quatsch«, sagte ich. »Es gibt eine Menge, das ich nicht verlieren will.«

»Nein«, sagte Lars. Er setzte sich auf seinem Betonblock zurecht und klang auf einmal feierlicher und ernster. Normalerweise tänzelte seine Stimme schwerelos zwischen Berichten und Lügengeschichten, Ratschlägen und Anekdoten hin und her – das Geplauder eines Trickkünstlers, der letztlich nur von dem ablenken möchte, was er wirklich tut. Doch jetzt senkte sie sich um eine Oktave; sogar sein Akzent schien nachzulassen. »Bis jetzt gibt es nur eins, was du auf keinen Fall verlieren willst, und das bist du selbst. Vielleicht gibt es noch andere Dinge, die du magst. Vielleicht gibt es Menschen, mit denen du dich gut amüsierst. Deinen alten Kumpel Lars, zum Beispiel. Aber das Einzige, das zu verlieren du wirklich nicht ertragen kannst, ist dein – wie heißt es gleich? Selbstbewusstsein?«

Ich rutschte unbehaglich auf meinem Sitz hin und her. »Ichbewusstsein vielleicht.«

»Ichbewusstsein. Du liebst nur dein eigenes Ichbewusstsein.«

»Es ist mir wichtig, klar.« Ich bemühte mich, vernünftig und nicht defensiv zu klingen. »Geht das nicht allen so?«

»Manchen mehr, anderen weniger, würde ich sagen.«

Ich sah einen Moment lang auf und registrierte das Kommen und Gehen der kunterbunten Menschen auf dem Harvard Square, die Umlaufbahnen der zahllosen Individuen mit ihren je eigenen Vorstellungen und Träumen und Plänen. Die Mädchen in Businesskleidung, die internationale Telefongespräche führten, während sie über den Platz marschierten, kamen mir allmählich herzzerreißend jung vor. Eine von ihnen war gerade stehen geblieben. In einer Hand hielt sie einen Blumenstrauß und in der anderen ihr Telefon und sprach wütend auf jemanden ein, dem Klang nach auf Chinesisch.

»Dein Leben ist viel zu leise«, sagte Lars entschieden, und ich wandte mich ihm wieder zu. »Viel zu einsam.«

Ich blickte in meinen Kaffeebecher und stellte beunruhigt fest, dass ein schillernder Film auf der Oberfläche trieb.

»Also«, sagte ich und kämpfte gegen einen leichten Krampf in meiner Halsregion an. »Ich habe mir überlegt, nach Russland zu verreisen.«

»Nach Russland?« Lars lehnte sich zurück. »Dein heißgeliebter Pädophiler?« Er meinte Nabokov.

Ich schüttelte den Kopf. »Nein.« Ich sog die Wangen ein und richtete mich auf. »Ich will Alexander Besetow kennenlernen. Den Schachspieler.«

»Ah, so«, sagte Lars und musterte interessiert seine Fingernägel. »Willst du ihn zu einem kleinen Match herausfordern?«

»Mein Vater und er waren Briefpartner«, sagte ich von oben herab, in dem übertrieben beiläufigen Ton, mit dem man Dinge erwähnt, auf die man lächerlich stolz ist.

»Tatsächlich?«, sagte Lars. In seinen Augen tauchte ein vergnügtes Glitzern auf, das rührend gewirkt hätte, wäre es nicht so selbstzufrieden gewesen. Ich wartete auf Nachfragen, doch vergebens. Lars' Ausflug in den politischen Widerstand hatte ihn stoische Geduld gelehrt.

»Sie hatten einen Briefwechsel, bevor mein Vater krank wurde.«

Lars' graue Haarbüschel wurden inzwischen von der sinkenden Sonne von hinten angestrahlt, und es sah aus, als trüge er entweder Hörner oder einen Heiligenschein. »Weißt du«, sagte er, »in den Achtzigern bin ich einmal quer durch die Sowjetunion gefahren. Ein grauenhaftes Land. Aber die Frauen! Die Frauen waren erstklassig.« Ich war gespannt auf die Fortsetzung, doch sie kam nicht. Mit einer einzigen Handbewegung fegte er die Reise mit sämtlichen Gefahren und Bestechungsgeldern, die dazugehört haben mochten oder auch nicht, auf die riesige Halde von Dingen, von denen ich ohnehin nichts verstand.

»Schön«, sagte ich. »Ich würde mich nie mit Ländern abgeben, in denen die Frauen zweitklassig sind.« Lars' Gesicht hatte einen sentimentalen Ausdruck angenommen, einen abwesenden Blick und ein wehmütiges Lächeln, das an zwiespältige Reue und Staatsgeheimnisse denken ließ. Seine Aufmerksamkeit war längst anderswo. Er sank in das Reich der Fiktionen zurück – gleich würden sämtliche Wahrheiten, die gesagt worden waren, von Wellen des Sarkasmus, der Spekulation und Übertreibung fortgespült werden. »Genug jetzt«, sagte ich. »Hör sofort auf damit.« Ich stand auf, und diesmal meinte ich es auch so. Sein Blick öffnete sich kurz, wie der eines Pokerspielers, der begreift, dass sein Gegner Ernst macht. »Irina?«, sagte er.

»Ja?«

»So ein Abenteuer wird gut für dich sein.«

»Das glaube ich auch.«

»Du schreibst mir doch eine Postkarte?«

»Na klar.«

»Und stell dir vor«, sagte er, »wie viele Geschichten du mir erzählen kannst, wenn du zurück bist.« Er umarmte mich. Er roch nach Asche, nach Kaffee und Himmel und Alkoholgenuss am Vormittag. Dann klopfte er mir auf den Rücken, und ich lief die Massachusetts Avenue hinunter. Er blieb auf seinem Betonklotz sitzen und sortierte die Figuren, und auch wenn ich es nicht genau wissen kann, stelle ich mir vor, dass er bis heute dort sitzt.

Ich rückte am Flughafen Schrittchen für Schrittchen durch die Warteschlange, versuchte die kyrillischen Schilder zu entziffern und las mir leise die Worte vor. Am Schalter reichte ich meine Papiere über den Tresen, wo sie widerstrebend und misstrauisch gestempelt wurden. Um mich herum sah ich Horden nach Weißkohl riechender alter Frauen, jüngere Frauen mit klackernden Krallen und strohig gebleichtem Haar, verschlagen blickende Männer, die sich vordrängelten. Niemand beschwerte sich über sie.

»Geschäfts- oder Urlaubsreise?«, fragte der Zollbeamte mit schiefgelegtem Kopf und einer ungewöhnlichen Mischung aus paranoidem Misstrauen und Langeweile im Blick.

Ich dachte nach. Der Gedanke an Urlaub wirkte absurd, wenn ich an dem Beamten vorbei in das Flughafengebäude sah, auf die zerschlissene Wandbespannung und die verkrüppelten Skelette ehemaliger Sitzmöbel. Es war widerlich kalt. An den Fenstern hockten einsame alte Frauen. Andere, in meinem Alter, warteten an den Kiosken und ließen mit einem schmerzhaften Schnalzgeräusch Kaugummiblasen platzen. Ein Hund in der Größe und Statur einer Hyäne drückte sich in einem Winkel herum und machte nicht den Eindruck, zum Personal zu gehören.

»Geschäftsreise oder Urlaubsreise?«, fragte der Mann noch einmal, in einem Ton, als hätte ich die Wahl zwischen Erschießungskommando und Todesspritze.

»Geschäftsreise.« Kaum hatte ich es gesagt, wusste ich, dass es stimmte.

Draußen war es stickig und kalt zugleich. Es herrschte dieses irritierende Wetter, das einem unter die Kleider kriecht, einen zum Schwitzen bringt und dann den Schweiß gefrieren lässt. Eine Taxischlange schmiegte sich an die Bordsteinkante; die Fahrer hatten den lauernden Blick von Raubtierbändigern. Ich setzte mich auf eine der Rückbänke und zog den Namen meines Hostels und Elisabetas Adressdaten aus der Tasche. Meine Augen waren wie ausgetrocknet und saßen schief in ihren Höhlen. Ich bekam jetzt schon das Gefühl, auf einer ziemlich fragwürdigen Mission zu sein.

»Maly Slatoustinski, bitte«, sagte ich. Wir bogen aus dem Flughafenparkplatz aus. Am dunklen Horizont begannen sich Wolken zusammenzuballen, und unter ihnen zeichneten sich allmählich die bleichen Umrisse von Gebäuden ab. Die Landschaft außerhalb der Stadt wirkte so gesichtslos und trist wie jedes semizivilisierte Einzugsgebiet; als ich das Fenster herunterkurbelte, mir den schmutzigen Regen ins Gesicht wehen ließ, die grellgelben Werbeplakate der Mobilfunkanbieter an mir vorüberziehen sah und die Abgase roch, dachte ich, ich hätte genauso gut in New Jersey sein können. Doch je mehr wir uns Moskau näherten, desto mehr verdichtete sich das Gefühl, in der Fremde zu sein. Zu beiden Seiten der Straße tauchten Verkaufsstände auf, die auf kyrillischen, handbeschriebenen Pappschildern Gebäck anpriesen. Zwergenhafte, verwaschene Bäume duckten sich vor dem Wind. Auch der Wind war fremdartig: Er hatte etwas Ungebändigtes, als hätte er ohne Unterbrechung beängstigend lange Strecken zurückgelegt. Ich musste an die Landkarte denken, die im Arbeitszimmer meines Vaters über dem Regal mit den Schachsets gehangen hatte: Eine schmalzgelbe UdSSR, die wie ein Jaguar im Baum sprungbereit den Rest der Welt belauerte. Selbst jetzt, nachdem der Lauf der Geschichte die Landmasse um ein Drittel verkleinert hatte, bekam ich das Gefühl, etwas von ihrer ungeheuren Weite spüren zu können, wenn ich aus dem Fenster sah.

Nach und nach tauchte immer mehr von der Stadt aus der Dunkelheit auf. Der Verkehr war chaotisch, das Graffiti vielschichtig und ausdrucksstark. Die Männer strahlten mit ihren hellen, kantigen Gesichtern diese merkwürdig glatte Schönheit aus, die ich schon immer ein bisschen bedrohlich fand. In dem Aussehen der Frauen prallten die Jahrhunderte hart aufeinander. Die beinahe zahnlosen Alten sahen mit ihren koboldhaften Gesichtern und den straff gebundenen Kopftüchern wie Tolstoi-Figuren aus. Die Jungen waren so sorgfältig gestylt wie Frauen auf der Upper West Side, wobei es eine elegante Variante gab (gescheiteltes Haar, gedeckte Farben und sparsam hervorblitzender Schmuck) und eine prollige Variante (juwelenbesetztes Dekolleté, hochtoupierte Frisur, um den Hals die Bälger undefinierbarer sibirischer Wieselarten). Sie liefen durch die Straßen wie die konkurrierenden Sendboten verschiedener historischer Epochen. Vor einem Kaufhaus saß ein Mann auf einer Kiste, der einen Schimpansen an der Kette hielt. Ich ließ alles wie im Rausch an mir vorüberziehen und staunte über

das Wunder der Flugreise: Ich hatte nur mit den Fingern ge-
schnippt, überstürzt Geld ausgegeben, und schon war ich hier –
am anderen Ende der Welt, in einem unwirtlichen Land, in dem
ich niemanden kannte, und mein einziger Wegweiser war eine
zweifelhafte, hastig hingekritzelte Adresse. Niemand hatte mich
aufgehalten. Kaum jemand hatte es überhaupt bemerkt.

Das Taxi setzte mich vor meinem Hostel ab. Ich stieg aus und
klingelte. Auf eine der Wände hatte jemand mit großen Druck-
buchstaben SCHLAMPEN-IMPORT gesprayt. Ein monströses
Röhren signalisierte, dass die Tür geöffnet war. Ich stieg die knar-
renden Stiegen hoch und fand mich oben am Ende eines Flurs in
einem gelblichen Lichtkegel wieder. Ein junger Mann mit einer
Art windschiefer Rockabilly-Frisur saß hinter dem Tresen und
klopfte mit einem Fuß auf den Boden. Der Computerbildschirm
spiegelte sich in dem Glasschrank hinter ihm, und ich konnte eine
grüne Fläche mit Zahlen und Spielkarten erkennen.

»Moment«, sagte er auf Englisch, ohne aufzublicken.

Ich wartete. Er klickte mit seiner Maus. Ich sah mich um. An
den Wänden hingen zerschlissene Poster mit russischen Sehens-
würdigkeiten darauf – die Eremitage, die Basilius-Kathedrale, der
Baikalsee. Dazu gab es einen kryptischen Stadtplan, auf dem die
U-Bahnen farblich aufgetragen waren wie Adern und Nervenbah-
nen in einem Anatomielehrbuch. Daneben hing das Werbeplakat
einer Kunstausstellung aus dem Jahr 2002. Auf dem Glasschrank
wurde eine fünfte gespiegelte Karte umgedreht. Der Junge trat gegen den Tresen.

»Bljad«, sagte er. Dann wandte er sich mir zu. »Name?«

»Irina Ellison«, sagte ich und zeigte ihm meinen Reisepass. Er
nahm ihn entgegen und blätterte zu der Seite mit meinem veralteten, albernen Foto – noch aus Collegezeiten, vor den Gentests,
mit einem aufgesetzten Lächeln, von dem ich damals noch nicht
gewusst hatte, wie aufgesetzt es war. Ich hatte kurzes Haar, falten-
freie Mundwinkel, und meine Augen saßen genau richtig im Schädel, ohne die verdünnt teefarbenen Halbkreise um sie herum. Ich

sah jung aus, stellte ich erschrocken fest. Erst wenn man bemerkt, wie jung man einmal war, wird einem bewusst, wie alt man ist.

»Hm«, machte er und klappte den Reisepass zu. Er verstaute ihn als Pfand und zur Sicherheit hinter dem Tresen und reichte mir meine Schlüssel und einen Stadtplan, auf dem das Hostel eingekreist war. »Hier ist Pension Moskau«, sagte er und zeigte darauf. »Hier ist Metro. Hier ist Bar. Sie sind dreizehn.« Er zeigte den bedrohlich gekrümmten Flur hinunter. Rauch hing in der Luft und gilbte das hindurchsickernde Deckenlicht.

Ich nahm Stadtplan und Schlüssel entgegen und folgte dem Flur, den Koffer wie einen deformierten Hund immer auf den Fersen. Ich hatte mir ein Einzelzimmer gegönnt, und es sah aus, wie ich es mir vorgestellt hatte – trist, dunkel und kalt, aber zweckmäßig. Ich stellte mein Gepäck ab und schloss mich ein. Ich war angekommen, so merkwürdig der Gedanke auch war. In meiner Handtasche steckte der Brief, den mein Vater an Besetow geschrieben hatte. Morgen würde ich anfangen, die Antworten auf seine Fragen zu suchen. Doch heute wollte ich mich nur noch zusammenrollen, mich zur Wand drehen und einschlafen, ohne mich umzuziehen. Ich legte mich hin und schloss die Augen.

Als ich erwachte, waren vierzehn Stunden vergangen, doch es dauerte eine Weile, bis ich das begriff. Von meinen unruhigen, fiebrigen Träumen war nur ein Gefühl der Orientierungslosigkeit zurückgeblieben. Ich sah aus dem Fenster, um die Tageszeit zu erraten, doch es war ein seltsam zeitloser Ausblick. Feiner Nieselregen erfüllte die Luft wie statisches Rauschen. Der Himmel war weiß. Ein stockender Menschenstrom wälzte sich durch die Straßen, zu langsam für Berufsverkehr und für den Feierabend zu matt. Ich sah auf die Uhr und dachte nach. Es musste fast zwei Uhr nachmittags sein.

Bei Tageslicht konnte ich mir mein Zimmer genauer ansehen. Auf dem Boden gab es mysteriöse Flecken und am Ende des Flurs eine apokalyptische Toilette. In der Dusche hing der Duft von Gardenienshampoo über dem Geruch von feuchtem Schmutz. Auf dem Weg zum Ausgang kam ich an dem Rockabilly-Pokerspieler vorüber, der mit dem Daumen auf seinem iPod herumnavigierte. Vor der Tür schlug mir ein fürchterlicher Gestank entgegen, von dem ich lieber nicht wissen wollte, woher er kam.

Unten auf der Straße fand ich einen Kiosk, in dem es kleine Bärenanstecker und Mineralwasser gab. Auf Süßigkeiten ungewisser Herkunft waren in vierzehn winzigen Sprachen Zutaten aufgedruckt. Deprimierende Pornohefte standen neben Promimagazinen, der wenig einladenden *Prawda* und der internationalen Ausgabe der *Time*. Ich kaufte eine Tüte mit Schokolade überzogener Weingummibananen, setzte mich auf eine Parkbank und dachte zum ersten Mal seit der Landung ernsthaft darüber nach, was ich eigentlich vorhatte.

Bei Licht betrachtet, kam mir die Idee, Besetow um Antwort auf einen Brief zu bitten, den er vermutlich nicht einmal gelesen hatte, anmaßend und mehr als merkwürdig vor. Bei dem Versuch, zu begreifen, was ich mir davon versprach, fühlte ich mich seltsam unfähig, wie einer, der im Traum ein mathematisches Rätsel lösen soll. Ja, mein Vater hatte nach Antworten gesucht, aber er hatte es fertiggebracht, ohne sie zu sterben. Das konnte ich doch sicherlich auch. Selbst wenn ich Besetow fand, wusste ich nicht, wie ich ihn ansprechen sollte. Vermutlich wurde er ständig von Schachfans belagert, und vielleicht konnte ich so tun, als ginge es auch mir um Schach. Ich konnte so tun, als sei das ganze Unternehmen die letzte Marotte einer Mittelschichtsamerikanerin – war es nicht dasselbe, was reichere Leute mit normaleren Interessen auch immer taten? Sie nahmen Privatunterricht bei Sterneköchen, um Soufflés backen zu lernen. Sie erforschten ausgestorbene Sprachen. Sie waren es leid, die üblichen Fähigkeiten immer weiter zu perfektionieren, und suchten sich exotischere Hobbys – Windsurfen, Kräuterkunde, Ikebana. Ich konnte so tun, als sei es bei mir dasselbe, als sei das Ganze ein eitler, launenhafter Versuch, mein Ego zu befriedigen.

Doch eins war sicher: Besetow war derjenige, an den sich mein Vater gewandt hatte, als sein Stundenglas leerlief, als der Sand herausschoss wie bei einer arteriellen Blutung. Vielleicht hatte mein Vater etwas gewusst, das ich noch nicht wusste. Vielleicht würde ich dieses Wissen noch brauchen. Ich war nicht sicher, ob die Suche danach der beste Weg war, meine letzten zwölf bis vierundzwanzig Monate zuzubringen. Aber es würde mir genügen müssen.

Ich zog den Zettel mit Elisabetas Nummer hervor und fuhr mit dem Finger über ihren Namen. Ich rief sie an, stellte mich noch einmal vor und erinnerte sie daran, dass ich auf der Suche nach Besetow war.

»Oh, ja«, sagte sie. »Ich erinnere mich.«

»Tut mir leid, dass neulich die Verbindung unterbrochen wurde.«

»Ich habe mich seitdem nicht mehr vom Telefon wegbewegt.«

»Muss wohl ein Problem mit der Überseeleitung gewesen sein.«

Sie schwieg so lange, dass ihr Schweigen skeptisch klang. »Sind Sie Journalistin?«, fragte sie dann.

»Nein«, sagte ich und fragte mich, ob ich besser doch eine gewesen wäre.

»Mit denen redet er. Er liebt es, mit westlichen Journalisten zu reden. Aber ich nicht. Ich finde, das ist etwas für junge Männer.«

»Ich bin keine Journalistin«, sagte ich schon ein wenig überzeugter.

»Niemand ist heutzutage Journalist«, sagte sie etwas mysteriös. »Was wollen Sie dann von ihm? Sind Sie Schachliebhaberin?« Sie klang jetzt rein geschäftlich, kurz angebunden, und über das Stakkato ihres russischen Akzents legte sich ein leicht britischer Klang.

»Ja. Na ja. Kein ganz großer Fan. Eher gelegentlich.«

»Sind Sie politisch aktiv?« Ich hörte das leise Klicken und Zischen eines Feuerzeugs und einen pfeifenden Atemzug.

»Auch eher gelegentlich.«

»Niemand ist heutzutage politisch aktiv.«

Eine Weile war ihr leises Paffen zu hören. Dann hustete sie fürchterlich. Es klang tuberkulös und reißend, als wären sämtliche

Weichteile in ihrer Brust im Begriff, sich aufzulösen. Als sie fertig war, sagte sie: »Schauen Sie«, was in meinen Ohren merkwürdig amerikanisch klang. »Sie könnten ja versuchen, mit ihm persönlich zu reden. Aber dafür müssten Sie akkreditiert sein. Sie müssten irgendwo hingehören. Sie können nicht einfach so aus dem Nichts auftauchen.«

Ich dachte nach. »Wie wäre es mit einer Universität?«

»Vielleicht. Eine Universität könnte vielleicht passen.« Sie klang zurückhaltend, fast ein wenig spöttisch. »Wieso? Kommen Sie von einer Universität?«

»Ja«, sagte ich leichthin und nannte ihr den Namen meines Instituts. Meines ehemaligen Instituts. Was konnten sie schon tun – mich rauswerfen? Mich kaltstellen lassen? »Ich habe hier einen Brief von Ihnen. Mein Vater hat Alexander Besetow geschrieben, und Sie haben ihm geantwortet.«

»Daran erinnere ich mich gar nicht.«

»Könnte ich Sie vielleicht besuchen kommen? Dann bringe ich ihn mit.«

»Ich weiß nicht so recht.« Ihre Stimme wurde wieder schwächer, fragiler, wie zu dünn geblasenes Glas. »Warum wollen Sie ausgerechnet jetzt hier recherchieren, wenn Sie unpolitisch sind?«

Lügen machen es irgendwie leichter, eine harte Wahrheit auszusprechen. Es ist, als würde sich die Wahrheit unauffällig unter die Lügen mischen, und man vergisst, was wahr ist, was man gern für wahr halten würde und was man sich nur ausgedacht hat, damit die ganze Geschichte plausibler klingt. »Ich werde wahrscheinlich dieses Jahr sterben«, sagte ich.

»Ach wissen Sie«, sagte Elisabeta und hustete wieder. »Das ist aber keine besondere Auszeichnung.«

KAPITEL 7

Alexander
Leningrad, 1980

Und dann, eines Abends, aller Wahrscheinlichkeit zum Trotz und nach all dieser Zeit, klopfte es an der Tür. Ein gläsernes Klimpern war zu hören und das luftige Beinahe-Geräusch einander berührender fließender Stoffe. Und als Alexander die Tür öffnete, stand da Elisabeta. Die magnetische Kraft seiner wieder und wieder heraufbeschworenen Vorstellung eben dieses Augenblicks hatte sie endlich hergeführt.

Er hatte gerade bei Kerzenlicht seine Kleider ausgebessert, und auf dem Bett türmten sich löchrige Hosen. Alexander hielt noch immer die Nadel in der Hand und trug sein schlechtestes Hemd. Elisabeta trug das übliche vielschichtige Schwarz, und ihr Haar stand nach allen Seiten und schimmerte farbig in der trüben Flurbeleuchtung. Sie wedelte mit einem Stück Papier.

»Das warst du, habe ich gehört«, sagte sie und drückte ihm das Papier in die Hand.

Es war die neueste Ausgabe der Flugschrift, und auf der aufgeschlagenen Seite prangte das verwischte Schwarzweißfoto eines unglücklich aussehenden Mannes mit Bart.

»Das bin nicht ich«, sagte Alexander. »Das ist Scharanski.«

Elisabeta lachte – ein kompliziertes, mehrdimensionales Lachen voller Freude über einen schlechten Scherz, Spott darüber, wie schlecht er war, und Reue, weil sie dennoch lachte. Es war ein Lachen, über das man eine Doktorarbeit hätte schreiben können.

»Wo hast du das her?«, fragte Alexander. Elisabetas Daumen berührte seine Handfläche ein wenig länger als nötig, dachte er.

»Nirgendwoher«, sagte sie. »Jemand hat es mir weitergegeben. Ist doch egal. Hör mal.« Ihr Haar löste sich aus der Spange; Alexander hatte nicht den Eindruck, dass sich die Spange auch nur die geringste Mühe gab, ihren Auftrag zu erfüllen – ebenso wenig wie ihr Hemd übrigens, das viel zu dünn aussah, um seine Trägerin vor der Witterung zu schützen. Er hätte gern gefühlt, wie dünn es war, einfach den Stoff zwischen zwei Finger genommen und ganz leicht daran gezogen. Einfach nur so.

»Hörst du zu?« Sie hatte sich mit der Schulter an den Türrahmen gelehnt. »Kann ich reinkommen?«

»Äh …«, sagte Alexander, weil Kleiderstapel auf seinem Bett herumlagen, das nicht gemacht war, weil die Kerzen heruntergebrannt waren und seine Teetasse auf dem Tisch eine Pfütze gebildet hatte, doch da war sie auch schon drin, fuhr mit langen, schmalen Fingern die Wände entlang, schob die Kleidung beiseite und setzte sich ohne zu fragen auf sein Bett.

»Das ist doch Wahnsinn«, sagte sie und zeigte auf die Zeitschrift. »Hast du sie gelesen?«

»Ja. Sie ist sehr gut. Sehr klug gemacht. Ich frage mich bloß, ob du lebensmüde bist.«

»Lebensmüde nicht«, sagte Alexander. »Bloß ein Angeber.«

Und dann, plötzlich, berührten sich ihre Lippen, er wusste nicht, wie. Gerade hatte er noch geredet, und im nächsten Moment gab es keinen Zwischenraum mehr zwischen seinem Mund und ihrem. Er hob eine Hand an ihr Gesicht und erkundete mit der anderen die zarte Tastatur ihrer Rippen. Dann zog sie sich zurück, verschwand mit jedem Herzschlag ein wenig weiter, und Alexander dachte, dass er das hier nie vergessen würde: Eine Serie von Momentaufnahmen einer Frau, die mit niedergeschlagenen Augen lachte, und auf jedem Bild war sie ein wenig weiter entfernt.

»Entschuldige«, sagte sie. »Das war nur, falls du demnächst vom KGB ermordet wirst.«

»Oh«, sagte er, und dann schwieg er, weil ihm nichts Geistreiches einfiel. Sein Nacken wurde kalt, wo Elisabetas Hände ihn berührt hatten, und Alexanders Hirn war in einen Zustand der Lähmung verfallen, von dem er fürchtete, er könnte dauerhaft sein. »Wer hat dir gesagt, dass ich das war?«

»Niemand. Ich habe den Schachartikel gelesen, und mir ist in letzter Zeit dein komischer Zeitplan aufgefallen, und da … Aber hör zu, Alexander, mach keine Dummheiten, ja? Die haben das gelesen. Die aus der Partei.«

»Wieso haben die aus der Partei es gelesen?«

Elisabeta schüttelte den Kopf. »Ich meine, die wissen einfach alles.«

»Aber woher weißt du, dass sie es gelesen haben?«

»Alexander.« Elisabeta steckte ihr Haar hoch, ließ ihre Halswirbel so laut krachen, dass Alexander zusammenfuhr, und stand auf. »Du weißt, dass ich eine Menge Leute kenne. Tja. Ich muss los.« Schon stand sie in der Tür, und ihre Augen sahen irgendwo an Alexander vorbei. »Entschuldige die Störung.« Doch noch blieb sie, wo sie war, biss sich auf die Unterlippe und sah seltsam traurig aus.

»Du hast nicht gestört«, sagte Alexander, obwohl er selbst staunte, wie verstört er war. Behutsam und brüderlich legte er ihr eine Hand auf die Schulter. Sie griff danach und zog langsam, zärtlich, einen nach dem anderen seine Finger lang, bis die Gelenke knackten.

Eine Weile war nichts weiter zu hören als ihr leises Atmen, das Knacken von Alexanders Gelenken und das Zischen der Kerzen, die herunterbrannten, bis sie leise, ohne viel Aufsehens, erloschen.

»Sei vorsichtig, Alexander«, sagte Elisabeta und wandte sich zum Gehen. »Das war alles, was ich sagen wollte.«

So ging es eine Zeitlang weiter. Wenn Alexander später nachrechnete, kam er alles in allem auf sechs Wochen, doch zu der Zeit kam es ihm wie anderthalb Tage oder wie ein ganzes Leben vor. Sie besuchte ihn abends. Zuerst hatte sie Vorwände – einen neuen Artikel, der ihr aufgefallen war, oder eine neue Warnung –, doch bald verzichtete sie darauf. Bald verzichtete sie darauf anzuklopfen.

Vor Elisabeta hatte er nur mit einer anderen Frau geschlafen – der Tochter des einzigen Tankstellenbesitzers in Ocha, die stillhielt und nach Wolle roch –, und mit Elisabeta war es etwas ganz anderes: die Umkehr und Verwandlung einer bisher ziemlich freudlosen Angelegenheit. Mit Elisabeta erlebte er waghalsige Akrobatik und plötzliche glückliche Fügungen. Oft lagen sie lange Kopf an Kopf, bis er sich in ihrer Nähe verlor – bis das Zimmer sich drehte und die Zeit nicht mehr sie selbst zu sein schien. Sie bissen einander in die knochigen Schultern. Er leckte die fingerkuppengroße Mulde über ihrem Nabel. Sie fielen lachend aus dem Bett.

Dann erzählten sie einander Dinge, die Alexander noch lange im Nachhinein erröten machten – nicht, weil sie obszön gewesen wären; im Gegenteil. Er schämte sich später, so viel von sich preisgegeben zu haben, so schnell und für so wenig. Der Sex war das eine – darin wurde er später sogar gut, und es sollte noch viele Frauen, viele spielerische Raufereien und leidgeprüfte Betten und ruinierte teure Frisuren geben. Aber die langen Gespräche, die Vertraulichkeiten – es schüttelte ihn, wenn er daran dachte. Aber damals wusste er es nicht besser; er war ganz erfüllt von dem beglückten Schlingern und der zähneklappernden Panik einer frühen, undiagnostizierten Liebe. Elisabeta erzählte von ihrer Kindheit in Chabarowsk – von ihrem betrunkenen, stinkenden, cholerischen Vater, ihrer betrunkenen, stummen, bedrängten Mutter – und dass ihr das Leben in Leningrad nicht gefiel und das Leben in Chabarowsk ihr noch viel weniger gefallen hatte. Und Alexander erzählte von den Diskussionen mit seinem Großvater über den Kommunismus, von seinen Begegnungen mit Radio Free Europe, von seinen Fernschachpartien mit den Schülern von Andronows Schachakademie, bis man ihn schließlich in seine Zukunft abkommandierte. Und er erzählte vom Schach als seinem einzigen Ausweg aus der Einsamkeit und wie überwältigend diese Einsamkeit gewesen war, bis sie eines Tages an seine Tür geklopft hatte.

Elisabeta nahm ihre Hausschuhe mit in sein Zimmer, damit sie nicht vor der Tür den Nachbarn auffielen, doch wie die meisten Geheimnisse in der Kommunalka blieb auch dieses nicht lange geheim. Die Wände waren dünn. Alexander konnte seine Nachbarn niesen und sich nachts herumwälzen hören. Er versuchte, nicht daran zu denken, was sie von ihm und Elisabeta mitbekamen, doch das war nicht ganz leicht, wenn die Verwalterin ihn im Flur voller Genugtuung düster anfunkelte oder der Mann, der so ungern mit Prostituierten zusammenlebte, ihm männlich auf die Schultern hieb. »Hoffe, sie gibt dir Rabatt, Towarischtsch«, sagte der Mann.

Alexander zuckte zusammen, sagte aber nichts. Er war zu glücklich dazu.

Es war bemerkenswert, wirklich erstaunlich, wie er absolut ununterbrochen an Elisabeta denken konnte. Andere Gedanken kamen und gingen; sie titschten über die Oberfläche eines riesigen Bewusstseinsreservoirs, das ganz allein ihr gewidmet war. Alexander konnte sich zu seiner eigenen Verwunderung durchaus intelligent und tiefgehend mit anderen Dingen – vielen anderen Dingen – beschäftigen, ohne Elisabeta je zu vergessen. Sie hatte in seinem Kopf eine bestens befestigte militärische Besatzungszone eingerichtet. Das belebte Alexander. Es machte ihn schlagfertiger im Gespräch mit Iwan und Nikolai, trieb ihn an, sich bei allem mehr Mühe zu geben, brachte ihn dazu, sorgfältiger als je zuvor seine Knöpfe anzunähen, seine Haare zu kämmen und seine Kleidung auszuwählen. Iwan sagte einmal sogar, er sei offenbar darüber hinweggekommen. Es klang, als wollte er sagen, dass Alexander über seine gesamte frühere Persönlichkeit hinweggekommen war, und so fühlte er sich auch.

Eine merkwürdige Empfindung hatte sich in seinem Brustkorb festgesetzt, ein beinahe krankhafter Druck, als bewegte er sich ständig auf der Grenze zum Zusammenbruch, zum hysterischen Lachanfall, zum Herzinfarkt.

Alexander hatte an alles das nie geglaubt, doch jetzt war es da.

Einige Wochen darauf kehrte Mischa ins Saigon zurück. Es war ein regnerischer Abend Anfang April – der Himmel hatte seine Schleusen geöffnet und spülte alle Absonderungen des Winters in die Kanalisation und weiter in die Ostsee –, und als Alexander,

Iwan und Nikolai ihren üblichen Tisch ansteuerten, stellten sie überrascht fest, dass ein Mann sie dort erwartete. Es brauchte ein wenig Gewöhnung, diesen Mann anzusehen. Sein Gesicht sah aus, als hätte man es umgestülpt: rote Ekzeme leuchteten durch sein schütteres Haar und umrahmten es wie Koteletten; die Deckenbeleuchtung malte gelbe Pfützen in die Vertiefungen seines Schädels. In den Gruben unterhalb seiner Augen schien eine chronische innere Blutung durch die Haut zu schimmern. »Scheiße, Mischa«, sagte Nikolai. »Was ist denn mit dir passiert?«

Sie hatten über ihre nächste Ausgabe reden wollen, doch als sie Mischa dort sitzen sahen, verfielen Nikolai und Iwan in tiefes Schweigen.

Alexander hatte Mischa erst ein Mal gesehen und wusste daher nicht genau, wie der Mann normalerweise hätte aussehen sollen. Doch er war sicher, dass niemand normalerweise aussah wie er. Die Adern an seinen Schläfen waren beängstigend blau; seine Augen schienen einen Millimeter oder mehr hinter ihren Höhlen zu liegen. Er war so dürr, dass man an ihm Anatomieunterricht hätte nehmen können. Er grinste, was sein Gesicht nur noch mehr verunstaltete. »Wollt ihr euch nicht setzen, Jungs?«, fragte er.

»Natürlich«, sagte Nikolai, zog mit einem mörderischen Kratzen einen Stuhl hervor und setzte sich so hektisch, dass der Tisch wackelte. Alexander folgte seinem Beispiel. Iwan beugte sich zu Mischa hinüber, und zwischen seinen Augenbrauen bildeten sich tiefe Furchen.

Mischa saß lange nur da und schwieg. Er sah tief erschöpft aus, zu abgelebt, um sich je wieder zum Leben aufzuraffen. Iwan und Nikolai blieben stumm, und aus ihrem Schweigen war so etwas wie Verehrung herauszuhören – als sei Mischa ein entthronter König, der in sein Reich zurückkehrte, um es wieder in Besitz zu nehmen, oder ein betrogener Gott bei der Inspektion seiner aus den Fugen geratenen Welt.

»Tja«, sagte Mischa, nachdem ihn alle lange genug angestarrt hatten. »Und, was habt ihr so getrieben in meiner Abwesenheit?«

»Hör mal«, sagte Iwan. »Was können wir dir holen? Magst du essen? Oder einen Drink vielleicht?«

»Keinen Alkohol.« Mischa stieß ein bellendes, schmerzhaftes Husten aus. »Die Ärzte sagen, meine Organe sind wie Klopapier. Ein Wodka könnte mich auf der Stelle erledigen. Aber vielleicht soll er das ja?«

»Dann lass mich dir zumindest ein bisschen Brot holen«, sagte Nikolai. »Du siehst scheiße aus.«

»Ist das alles, was ihr gemacht habt? Trinken? Brot essen? Euch amüsieren?« Mischa drehte sich zu Alexander um, dem sofort ein elektrischer Schock durch das Rückenmark fuhr. So fühlte er sich jedes Mal, wenn er den deformierten Mann im Rollstuhl ansah oder unterwegs den weißen Wolgas begegnete. »Wer ist das?«, fragte Mischa. »Euer neuer Freund?« Er streckte seine welke Hand aus, und Alexander konnte nicht umhin, sie zu nehmen. Sie war rau und verschrumpelt, wie ein Organismus, der jahrtausendelang im Wüstensand gelegen hat.

»Ich bin Mischa«, sagte Mischa und starrte Alexander ins Gesicht. Kaum zu glauben, dass eine so schwache, eingeschrumpfte Gestalt durch bloßes Starren jeden niedermachen konnte.

»Wir kennen uns schon.« Alexander fühlte Mischas gekrümmte Hühnerkrallenfinger in seiner Hand.

»Ach ja? Bitte vielmals um Verzeihung. Mein Gedächtnis ist hinüber, fürchte ich. Das ist das Dumme daran, wenn man als geistig Gesunder in eine Irrenanstalt gesteckt wird. Man ist danach einfach nicht mehr derselbe.« Als Mischa zu Iwan herübersah, blitzte wie ein glänzender Fischbauch das Weiße in seinen Augen auf. Iwan, der sonst nicht auf den Mund gefallen war, brachte kein Wort heraus.

»Und?«, fragte Mischa fröhlich. »Ihr sagt ja gar nichts? Was gibt es Neues? Sagt nicht, ihr habt hier auf euren fetten Ärschen gesessen, während euer Kumpel im Irrenhaus schmoren musste.«

»Wir bringen eine Flugschrift raus«, sagte Alexander. Mischas Tonfall gab ihm das Gefühl, Iwan und Nikolai verteidigen zu müssen. Sie hatten monatelang Kopien ihrer Zeitung gemacht, bis ihre

Hände blau wurden, hatten ihr Leben und ihren Verstand riskiert, um sie auszuliefern. Man konnte es nicht genau wissen, doch Iwan vermutete, dass sie mehrere Hundert Leser hatten. Das war doch immerhin etwas, und Alexander begriff nicht, warum Iwan und Nikolai die Köpfe hängen ließen, ihre Servietten kneteten, ihren Wodka verschmähten und ängstlich vor sich hin starrten.

»Eine Flugschrift?«, fragte Mischa amüsiert. »Was für eine Flugschrift?« Iwan und Nikolai schwiegen, also zuckte Alexander mit den Schultern und holte seine Tasche hervor. Unter Mischas stechendem Blick und einem Grinsen, das von Sekunde zu Sekunde sarkastischer wurde, hatte er einige Mühe mit dem Reißverschluss, doch schließlich brachte er es fertig, eine der letzten Ausgaben herauszuziehen. Er schob das Papierbündel über den Tisch und zog rasch die Hand zurück, falls Mischa danach griff.

»Es sind hauptsächlich politische Kommentare drin«, sagte Alexander. »Und Philosophie. Artikel über Schach. Lyrik. Und manchmal Kunst.«

Mischa begann mit einem eingefrorenen Fotolächeln durch das Magazin zu blättern. »*Eine kleine Auswahl aussichtsloser Fälle?*«, sagte er. Dann blätterte er wieder und stieß dabei Laute aus wie ein Schläfer, der einen Alptraum durchlebt. Er blätterte schneller und schneller, und Iwan und Nikolai sahen wie gelähmt dabei zu, und als Mischa endlich die letzte Seite erreichte, schleuderte er die Zeitschrift mit der ganzen überraschenden Kraft seiner knochigen Arme Alexander vor die Brust. »Wirklich verdammt klein. Habt ihr wenigstens eine Kippe für mich?«

Nikolai reichte sie ihm. Als Mischa daran zog, verschwanden seine Wangen beinahe ganz. Alexander konnte Iwan und Nikolai denken hören und vor seinem inneren Auge die Kondensstreifen der vorwurfsvollen, anklagenden Blicke sehen, die sie über ihn hinweg austauschten.

»Ihr macht das falsch«, stellte Mischa schließlich unumstößlich fest. »Das Ding ist der letzte Dreck. Bildet ihr euch wirklich ein, eure Schulaufsätze könnten irgendetwas ändern?«

Alexander blickte auf seine Hände und studierte eingehend seine eingerissenen Nagelhäute und schwieligen Fingerkuppen. Iwan sagte leise: »Vielleicht.«

Mischa beugte sich vor, und Alexander wich instinktiv zurück. Ein Geruch von als Medizin getarnten Giftstoffen ging von Mischa aus, und wenn er mit der Zigarette im Mundwinkel sprach, klang seine Stimme hoch und angestrengt wie eine falsch gespielte Geige.

»Wisst ihr überhaupt, was sie mit mir gemacht haben?«, fragte Mischa. Iwan breitete zögernd seine Hände auf der Tischplatte aus und drehte eine Handfläche nach oben. Er schüttelte den Kopf. »Sie haben von den alten Kanülen den Rost abgekratzt und sie immer wieder benutzt. Haben mir Schwefel gespritzt. Elektroden an meine Schläfen gedrückt.«

Alexander schauderte. Mischas Adern verliefen so dicht unter der Hautoberfläche, dass sein Gesicht aussah wie eine Karte unterirdischer Wasserläufe.

»Manchmal haben sie mich in Laken eingewickelt, in eine Wanne mit Eiswasser gelegt und dann neben der Heizung abgeladen. Wenn die Laken trocken waren, hat es mir die Haut aufgerissen.« Mischa nahm den nächsten Zug und blies den Rauch ruhig und bedächtig in Richtung Iwan. Iwan hustete, drehte den Kopf weg und sagte nichts.

»Ich musste mit einem Mann im selben Bett schlafen, der mich Stalin nannte. Zuerst dachte ich, er wollte mich beleidigen, bis mir klar wurde, dass er mich wirklich für Stalin hielt. Nachts hat er geschrien und mit seiner eigenen Scheiße Flüche an die Wände geschrieben. Und mit dem musste ich im selben Bett schlafen, jede Nacht. Wisst ihr, wie viele Nächte das waren? Was denkst du, Nikolai, wie viele Nächte waren es wohl? Wie lange war ich weg?«

Nikolai wand sich. »Hundert? Hundert Nächte vielleicht?«

»Oh, Nikolai«, sagte Mischa. »Das klingt ja fast, als wäre es dir egal. Und ich dachte, du hakst jeden Tag in deinem Kalender ab. Ich dachte, du schreibst mir jeden Tag.«

Nikolai verzog das Gesicht.

»Es waren einhundertsiebenundfünfzig Nächte, die ich mit diesem Tier verbringen musste. Ist es etwa meine Schuld, wenn ich genauso bekloppt geworden bin wie er?« Mischa ließ seine Hände auf den Tisch klatschen, wo sie auf dem dunklen Holz liegenblieben wie zwei sonnengebleichte Schildkrötenskelette. »Glaubt ihr, eure verfickten Schmierereien ändern irgendwas daran? Glaubt ihr, die Leser sagen: ›Oh, ein unkonventionelles Gedicht, kommt Leute, schaffen wir den Kommunismus ab‹?«

»Bitte, Mischa, sei nicht so laut«, sagte Iwan. »Sogar hier. Ein bisschen mehr Diskretion.«

»Diskretion? Scheiß auf deine Diskretion! Weißt du, dass ich anfangs geknebelt schlafen musste, bis ich gelernt hatte, das Maul zu halten? Weißt du, dass sie Halbmenschen in Käfigen halten? Die meisten Leute da drin sind nämlich wirklich irre. Es sind nicht alles Intellektuelle und Dissidenten. Wir haben da nicht rumgesessen und uns in gelehrsamen Diskussionen ergangen. Und von diesen Viechern in den Käfigen haben viele geschrien. Das hat einem den Magen umgedreht, besonders am Anfang. Später wurde es weniger schlimm, aber das ist vielleicht auch Sinn der Sache. Am Anfang jedenfalls kamen mir diese Laute nicht mal menschlich vor. Es war, um es mal so zu sagen, nicht gerade angenehm, das zu hören.«

Nikolai biss sich auf die Lippe und umklammerte sein Glas so fest, dass seine Fingerkuppen violett anliefen. Iwan rührte geistesabwesend mit einem Finger in seinem Wodka herum und kaute hin und wieder an seinem alkoholisierten Fingernagel.

»Anfangs«, sagte Mischa, »habe ich noch versucht, denen klarzumachen, dass es alles ein Irrtum war. Ganz am Anfang vor allem, als sie mir die Knöpfe abgeschnitten haben. Ich dachte, wenn ich nur brav und vernünftig und verständig und ruhig blieb, dann würden sie einsehen, dass meine Einlieferung ein Fehler war.« Er stieß eine Rauchwolke aus, die einen Moment lang sein Gesicht verhüllte. Wenn man ihn nicht sah, konnte man fast glauben, er sei ein düsterer Prophet, der gekommen war, um der Gegenwart Kunde von der Zukunft zu bringen. »Aber so war es nicht. Alles, was ich sagte – einfach alles –, wurde als Unsinn abgetan. Manche Schwestern waren nett und gaben mir Bonbons, und andere waren gemein und verpassten mir mit dem Handrücken Ohrfeigen, wenn niemand hinsah und ich angebunden war. Die meisten interessierten sich nicht weiter für mich und gaben mir Tabletten – riesige braune Pillen, die mir im Hals stecken blieben und von denen alles verschwamm und verschwand. Aber eins hatten alle Schwestern gemeinsam, nämlich, dass sie mich wie einen Vollidioten behandelten. Und weißt du, was das Komische war, Iwan?« Er beugte sich vor, und Alexander bemerkte wieder den gelblichen Geruch nach Erschöpfung, flachen Atemzügen und Betäubungsmitteln.

»Nein«, sagte Iwan, der sich offenbar damit abgefunden hatte, rhetorische Fragen zu beantworten. »Was war das Komische?«

»Das Komische war, Iwan, dass ich mich irgendwann zu fragen begann, ob ich nicht tatsächlich verrückt war. Man sollte doch denken, dass man seine eigene geistige Gesundheit ganz gut einschätzen kann, aber dem ist nicht so. Von allen wie ein Irrer behandelt zu werden ist ein interessantes psychologisches Experiment, das sollte jeder mal ausprobieren. Dass ich an meinem Verstand zweifelte, brachte mich erst wirklich um den Verstand. Ich begann mich zwanghaft auf meine Worte und auf meine Aussprache zu konzentrieren. Ich übte stundenlang ein, was ich den Schwestern sagen wollte, schrieb es auf und feilte daran herum. Ständig zerbrach ich mir den Kopf über die Satzstellung und die Grammatik. Irgendwie hatte ich die Theorie entwickelt, dass die Ursache meines Problems, meiner Unfähigkeit, mich mitzuteilen, eine Art mechanische Fehlfunktion war.«

Iwan schüttelte den Kopf und presste sich die schweißnassen Hände an die Schläfen. Nikolai starrte in die grüne Deckenleuchte über Mischas Kopf. Alexander starrte Mischa an und versuchte, sein verheertes Gesicht im Geiste zu etwas zusammenzusetzen, an das er sich eines Tages würde erinnern können.

»Wenn ich dann abends mit den Schwestern redete«, sagte Mischa, »sahen sie mich nur an. Oder sie tätschelten mir den Kopf, wie einem dämlichen Hund, über den sich die ganze Familie lustig macht. Ich fing an, auf meinen Händen herumzukauen. Irgendwann gab ich es auf. Ich hielt den Mund, blieb ruhig und verbrachte die meiste Zeit damit, aus dem Fenster zu sehen. Ich dachte mir geistige Beschäftigungen aus, um die Zeit herumzukriegen, zum Beispiel ersetzte ich im Kopf alle Grüntöne im Hof durch Rot und alle Brauntöne durch Blau, bis ich einen neuen Ausblick hatte. Oder ich zählte die Wörter, die im Lauf eines Tages an mich gerichtet wurden – viele waren es nicht, kann ich euch sagen. Wenn mein Mitbewohner mich als Stalin ansprach, antwortete ich ihm.«

Iwan legte Mischa die Hand auf die Schulter, wo die Abbruchkante seines Schlüsselbeins unter dem Hemd verschwand.

»Irgendwann, wenn sie sicher sein können, dass deine geistigen Reserven aufgebraucht sind, laden sie dich auf ein kleines Pläuschchen ein. ›Es liegt ganz bei Ihnen‹, sagen sie. ›Wollen Sie Kaffee, Tee, Fleisch vielleicht? Sollen wir welches besorgen? Vielleicht können wir Zivilkleidung für Sie auftreiben. Dieser Ukrainer bei Ihnen im Zimmer – wissen Sie eigentlich, wie sehr er die Russen verachtet? Sie haben gute Heilungschancen, Mischa. Die anderen nicht, aber Sie, Sie sind was Besonderes.‹ Und dann führen sie dich aus, und du erzählst ihnen das eine oder andere, vielleicht auch das eine oder andere über deinen Mitbewohner, und was du sagst, mag wahr sein oder auch nicht, das kümmert dich längst nicht mehr. Alles, was dich noch interessiert, ist die versprochene Tasse Tee. Die ist der Höhepunkt deiner ganzen Woche. Du wartest darauf wie ein Schulmädchen auf ihren Liebsten. Wie ein Hund auf das Glöckchen.

Als ich dann also entlassen wurde – an einem Dienstag, ganz ohne Vorwarnung; sie gaben mir nur meine Anziehsachen und ein Entlassungsformular und keine Antworten auf meine Fragen –, klammerte ich mich an meinem Bettgitter fest. Es war kurz nach dem Mittagessen, müsst ihr wissen, und ich hatte mich schon so auf meine Tablette gefreut. Also vergebt ihr mir hoffentlich, wenn ich euren Bemühungen und eurer Diskretion gegenüber ein bisschen skeptisch bin. Bei allem Respekt, Wanja.«

Alexander wartete ab, was Nikolai und Iwan tun würden. Nikolai stürzte seinen letzten Schluck Wodka herunter. Iwan drückte mit beiden Händen Mischas Schultern, als wollte er ihm eine Art atheistische Segnung angedeihen lassen, und ließ wieder los.

»Tja«, sagte er, »ich glaube, ich verstehe, was du meinst.«

Eine Woche darauf, in Iwans Wohnung, zwischen hohen Stapeln matt glänzenden Kohlepapiers, erzählte Alexander Iwan, was Elisabeta gesagt hatte, und Iwan sagte, er solle sich keine Sorgen machen. »Ganz einfach«, sagte er. »Wenn sie uns kriegen wollen, kriegen sie uns.«

Mischa war bei seiner Mutter eingezogen, die bei seinem Anblick geweint und versucht hatte, alle Kartoffeln zu kaufen, die auf dem Markt zu bekommen waren. Ein paar Tage lang hatten sie die Arbeit an der nächsten Ausgabe ausgesetzt. Nikolai und Iwan hatten nervös und deprimiert in der Wohnung herumgehockt. Alexander hatte in einer Ecke so getan, als spiele er Schach gegen sich selbst, und in Wirklichkeit insgeheim an Elisabeta gedacht. Nach einer Woche war Iwan aufgestanden, hatte sich selbst ein paar kleine Ohrfeigen verpasst und gesagt, genug sei genug. Sie müssten weitermachen, hatte er gesagt, und sei es nur, weil sie nichts Besseres vorhatten.

Gerade spannte Iwan wieder Kohlepapier in die Schreibmaschine ein und machte die nächsten Kopien der Ausgabe. Diese Arbeit erforderte Konzentration, doch Iwan ließ sich selten daran hindern zu reden. »Sie haben wahrscheinlich andere Probleme. Und größere Exempel zu statuieren«, sagte er. Die Schreibmaschine stieß ein knarrendes Wiehern aus. »Scheiße, verdammt.« Er zerrte das ruinierte Papier aus der Maschine, warf es in hohem Bogen in den Müll und blickte zu Alexander, der auf einem Bücherstapel saß und mit einem Zeh Natascha kraulte. »Ich weiß wirklich nicht, wofür ich dich bezahle.«

»Du bezahlst mich gar nicht.«

»Ach, richtig. Wird wohl seine Gründe haben.« Iwan spannte neues Papier in die Maschine und tippte wieder rasch und rhythmisch drauflos, als spielte er eine Sonate. »Wer hat dir das überhaupt erzählt?«

»Elisabeta. Eine Freundin von mir. Was ist? Sie wohnt in meiner Kommunalka … Was??«

»Eine … Freundin?«

»Mitbewohnerin. Sagte ich doch schon.«

»Gibt es da etwas, das du mir sagen willst, Sascha?«

»Nein.«

Iwan strahlte vor Vergnügen, und Alexander wusste, dass das ein schlechtes Zeichen war. »Du hast doch hoffentlich die jüngste Berichterstattung zum Thema Geschlechtsverkehr in der Sowjetunion mitverfolgt.«

Alexander schüttelte kläglich den Kopf.

»Nein? Wie konntest du das verpassen? Es stand in allen Zeitungen. Die Partei hat herausgefunden, dass unehelicher Sex Impotenz, Neurosen und Frigidität verursacht. Und die Partei hat die empfohlene maximale Gesamtdauer des Geschlechtsakts auf zwei Minuten festgesetzt. Ich würde dir dringend empfehlen, dich mit diesen Erkenntnissen zu befassen, bevor du deine Freundin näher kennenlernst.«

»Hör auf.«

»Wenigstens wohnst du nicht im Intourist Hotel, wo alle Nutten vom KGB sind.«

»Du sollst bitte aufhören.«

»Na gut. Erst mal jedenfalls. Du hast es also von Elisabeta gehört. Und sie?«

Alexander schluckte und ließ sein Daumengelenk knacken. »Von jemandem, der es wissen muss.«

»Einem Funktionär?«

»Keine Ahnung.« Die Katze ließ einen schrillen Protestlaut hören, und Alexander merkte, dass er sie zu grob mit dem Fuß gekrault hatte.

Iwan zog die Augenbrauen hoch und klang etwas weniger amüsiert. »Okay«, sagte er. »Und woher wusste sie, dass du damit zu tun hast?«

»Wegen des Schachartikels. Und meiner Tagesabläufe.«

»Dann scheint sie dich ziemlich genau zu beobachten.«

Alexander schwang sich von dem Bücherstapel und stand auf. »Kann schon sein.«

»Sie wissen von uns. Natürlich tun sie das. Aber ich bin nicht so eingebildet zu glauben, dass wir ihre Aufmerksamkeit wert sind. Noch nicht.«

Die Schreibmaschine klapperte und schnarrte.

»Hast du Mischa mal getroffen?«, fragte Alexander nach einer Weile.

»Gestern habe ich ihm eine Pastete vorbeigebracht. Er ist immer noch verrückt vor Wut. Er phantasiert von irgendwelchen Plänen, ein großes Ding zu drehen, etwas, das wirklich Spuren hinterlässt. Sie haben ihm den Ausweis weggenommen, weißt du, und ihm einen Wolfspass gegeben. Er wird nie wieder Arbeit bekommen. Seine arme Mutter sitzt nur immer dabei und versucht ihn vom Reden abzubringen. Er wiegt immer noch fast nichts. Anscheinend ist er morphinabhängig. Ich habe keine Ahnung, wie er es überhaupt fertigbringt, so viel zu sprechen.«

»Und besorgt dich das nicht?«

»Ich mache mir nie Sorgen, falls dir das noch nicht aufgefallen ist. Mischa wird sicher nichts tun, was ihn zurück in die Psichuschka bringt.« Iwan stand auf und schaltete den Fernseher an. Es lief Wrémja, wie immer. Ein mürrisch dreinblickender Nachrichtensprecher ratterte die Themen des Tages herunter. Iwan stellte den Fernseher leiser und reichte Alexander einen Stapel Papier. »Hier, fünf Stück. Die sind für die Wassiljewski-Insel. Wenn du zurück bist, gebe ich dir die nächsten fünf. Und Alexander, du solltest deine Freundin Elisabeta vielleicht fragen, woher sie ihre Informationen hat. Reine Vorsichtsmaßnahme.« Iwan zwinkerte ihm zu.

»Hör schon auf«, sagte Alexander, doch allein schon die Erwähnung ihres Namens versetzte ihn in einen Zustand idiotischer Euphorie. Er arbeitete außergewöhnlich gutgelaunt seine Route auf der Insel ab und war wieder zurück, bevor Iwan den nächsten Stapel fertighatte.

Und dann hörte Elisabeta genauso plötzlich, wie sie begonnen hatte, wieder auf, ihn zu besuchen. Alexander traf sie nicht mehr im Flur und begegnete ihr nicht in der Küche. Er drückte sich vor dem Badezimmer herum, in der Hoffnung, dass sie früher oder später dort auftauchen würde, bis die Verwalterin ihn verscheuchte. Einige Male schlich er auch an ihrer Zimmertür vorüber, ohne anzuklopfen. Jedes Mal standen ihre Hausschuhe davor, was bedeutete, dass sie nicht zu Hause war.

Vielleicht sollte er besser klopfen, doch er war sich nicht sicher. Er wartete und schämte sich für seine Zögerlichkeit. Er wartete weiter. Er erwägte das Für und das Wider. Sie hatte mit der ganzen Sache angefangen, also war es nur recht und billig, ihr auch die Entscheidung über ihre Rückkehr zu überlassen. Besser, er setzte sie nicht unter Druck. Doch als aus Tagen Wochen wurden und aus Wochen eine endlose Abfolge quälender Augenblicke ohne Elisabeta, änderte er seine Argumentation. Sie hatte ihn zuerst besucht. Also geboten es Diplomatie und Ritterlichkeit, dass er ihren Besuch – oder ihre vielen Besuche – mit einem Gegenbesuch beantwortete. Es wäre unhöflich, das nicht zu tun, und Alexander hasste es, unhöflich zu sein. Nach weiteren philosophischen Erörterungen und Zweifeln – und nach dem Versuch, verklausuliert bei Iwan und Nikolai Rat einzuholen, der in Gelächter und Schamesröte endete – schluckte er seine Angst hinunter und ging zu ihrem Zimmer.

Vor der Nummer neun stand ein Mann mit dem Rücken an die Tür gelehnt. Sein Haar und seine Brauen waren beinahe schneeweiß und seine Augen von einem derart schönen Blau, dass sie für einen Mann viel zu schade waren. Vom Gesicht her hätte er slawisch sein können, doch nicht von seinem Verhalten. Er wirkte viel zu entspannt, betrachtete viel zu offen die vorbeigehenden Nachbarn und begegnete ohne Angst ihren Blicken. Ganz offensichtlich machte er sich keinerlei Sorgen darum aufzufallen. Ganz offensichtlich kam er aus dem Westen.

»Warten Sie auf Elisabeta?«, fragte Alexander. Er bemühte sich, langsam zu sprechen; er wusste, dass schnell gesprochenes Russisch wie ein einziges langes Wort klingen konnte.

»Ja«, sagte der Mann. Er war jung. Aus der Nähe waren seine Augen von einem noch unbändigeren Blau.

»Woher kommen Sie?«

»Aus Brüssel.« Der Mann nieste und wandte sich ab. »Entschuldigung.«

»Was tun Sie hier?«

»Das scheint ja alle mächtig zu interessieren, was? Jedes Mal, wenn ich im Verkehr stecken bleibe, kommt irgendwer im schwarzen Regenmantel und fragt mich, was ich hier will, warum ich nicht im Touristenviertel bin und ob ich zu keiner Reisegruppe gehöre. Ihr wisst schon, wie man jemanden zünftig willkommen heißt.«

Alexander trat einen Schritt zurück. Seit seiner Ankunft in Leningrad hatte er außerhalb des Saigon noch nie eine so lautstarke Beschwerde gehört. Es ärgerte ihn, wie nervös ihn das machte. »Fragen Sie mich nicht«, sagte er. »Ich spiele hier nur Schach.«

Der Belgier nickte. »Warten Sie auch auf das Mädchen?«

»Kann schon sein.«

»Dann spielen Sie also doch nicht nur Schach«, sagte der Mann. Ein Anflug von Belustigung durchzuckte seine Augen wie das Blaulicht eines Krankenwagens.

»Vermutlich nicht.« Der Mann war ganz schön neugierig und posaunte unangenehm schnell seine Meinung heraus. Alexander war es gewohnt, gleichgültig behandelt zu werden; er war es gewohnt, dass Menschen einander auswichen wie die falschen Enden zweier Magnete. Es war beängstigend, so zu leben, doch zumindest war es nicht ordinär.

Der Belgier blinzelte mit diesen Augen, deren Blau allmählich westlich aufdringlich wirkte: Es war das Blau der Kornblumen, der Van-Gogh-Gemälde, der UN-Blauhelme. »Sie ist ein nettes Mädchen«, sagte er. »Wirklich zu schade, dass sie heiraten wird.«

»Nein. Was? Nein.«

Der Belgier zuckte mit den Schultern und schob sich eine Zigarette zwischen die Lippen, um zu zeigen, dass es ihm gleichgültig war. Seine Augen waren so blau wie ein Erstickungsanfall. »Aber ja. Wussten Sie das nicht? Angeblich ist es ein Parteibonze, der aussieht wie ein Urzeitmonster. Ein Schrank von einem Mann. Ich habe ihn gesehen. Wie aus dem Museum entlaufen.« Alexander sagte nichts. Die Vorstellung, zu diesem Thema irgendetwas sagen zu wollen – oder überhaupt jemals wieder irgendetwas zu sagen –, kam ihm auf einmal unüberwindlich anstrengend vor. Der Belgier hatte einen Ausdruck der Verwunderung aufgesetzt, als sei Alexander das jüngste von einer ganzen Serie von Mysterien der Sowjetunion. »Schade, nicht?«, sagte er. »Ich mochte sie selbst ganz gern. Aber was soll man machen? Die Frau muss sehen, wo sie bleibt.«

»Ich glaube es nicht«, sagte Alexander, der allmählich anfing, es zu glauben.

Der Mann stieß einen rauchfreien Luftstrom aus und redete weiter an seiner Zigarette vorbei. »Ganz wie Sie meinen. Das ist typisch für Sie, oder? Für die Sowjets, meine ich.«

»Was?«, fragte Alexander kläglich.

»Dass Sie ungeachtet aller Fakten nur das glauben, was Sie wollen. Lassen Sie sich dabei bloß nicht stören. Ich will Ihnen auf keinen Fall im Wege sein. Es scheint ja eine Art traditioneller Volkssport zu sein.«

Vielleicht war es wirklich nicht wahr. Vielleicht hatte der Belgier sich geirrt, oder er meinte das andere Mädchen, die Mitbewohnerin, und hatte die beiden verwechselt. Erstens würde Elisabeta nie einen Funktionär heiraten, und zweitens – das hoffte Alexander inständig, und im nächsten Moment tat es ihm leid –

würde kein Funktionär auf die Idee kommen, Elisabeta heiraten zu wollen. Das konnte doch nicht gut für seine Karriere sein.

»Hey«, sagte der Belgier, »jemand zu Hause?« Er wedelte mit der Hand vor Alexanders Gesicht herum und schnippte ein paarmal mit den Fingern. Das Blau seiner Augen erinnerte Alexander an winterlich durchgefrorene Hände, die niemand wärmte und hielt. Elisabeta und ein Parteifunktionär. Vielleicht passte es gar nicht so übel. Vielleicht hätten die beiden sich eine Menge zu erzählen.

»Ihr Sowjets«, sagte der Belgier, »seid einfach zu komisch. Wenn es um eure Nutten geht, werdet ihr plötzlich sentimental.«

Alexander wurde von dem überwältigenden Verlangen gepackt, den Mann zu schlagen, und zwar weder intellektuell noch metaphorisch. Spiele waren sublimierte Kriegshandlungen, und für kein anderes galt das so offensichtlich wie für Schach. Doch manchmal brauchte es auch echte Gewalt und echte Niederlagen. Manchmal musste man etwas verteidigen, weil es wirklich zählte, und nicht nur, weil es etwas Wichtiges symbolisierte.

Außerdem war der Belgier kleiner als Alexander.

Alexanders Faust schnellte gegen den Wangenknochen des anderen. Der sah verdutzt aus, dann zutiefst verletzt, dann resigniert. Er boxte Alexander fast freundschaftlich vor die Brust. Alexander versuchte ihn bei den Haaren zu packen, streifte aber nur seinen Kopf. Der Belgier versuchte, seinen Oberkörper zu fassen zu kriegen und ihn mit einem Tritt in die Kniekehlen auszuhebeln. Alexander versuchte ihn mit dem Knie in die Weichteile zu treffen, traf aber nicht und war froh, dass er nicht getroffen hatte. In weniger als einer Minute war der Spuk wieder vorbei, und die beiden standen einander in gebührendem Abstand gegenüber, erleichtert, dass niemand sie beobachtet hatte.

»Tut mir leid«, murmelte Alexander.

Der Belgier schwieg. Seine buschigen weißen Brauen schienen unter dem Gewicht seiner Entrüstung beinahe einzuknicken. Er ließ rechts und links seine Halswirbel knacken, straffte die Schultern und prüfte, ob er unbeschadet sei. Alexander sah ihm zu. Ein

Schmerz begann sich in seinem Knie auszubreiten und ein Schweigen in seinem Herzen. »Kann ich … sind Sie verletzt?«, fragte Alexander.

»Bilde dir bloß nichts ein.«

»Ich gehe jetzt. Sie können ihr ja sagen, dass ich hier war.« Doch es war ihm egal, ob der Belgier es wirklich tat oder nicht.

Alexander wandte sich zum Gehen. »Hey«, sagte der Belgier, doch Alexander drehte sich nicht um. Da war nichts, was er sehen wollte, und nichts, was der Belgier ihm sagen könnte, wollte er hören. »Du musst mir überhaupt nicht glauben, du Wichser!«, rief der Mann ihm hinterher. Alexander ging schneller, er lief fast. Der Schmerz in seinem Knie pulsierte mit jedem Schritt, die Nachbarn knallten ihre Türen zu, Putz rieselte von der Decke, und er rannte, rannte den Flur hinunter. Doch nicht schnell genug, um zu überhören, wie der Belgier schrie: »Wenn du Augen im Kopf hast, sieh einfach nach ihrem Ehering!«

KAPITEL 8

Irina
Moskau, 2006

Elisabeta wohnte ein paar Kilometer nördlich von meinem Hostel, in einem betongrauen Wohnviertel mit lauter identischen Gebäuden, die sich ausbreiteten wie ein Virus. Je weiter wir nach Norden fuhren, desto enger und unwegsamer wurden die Straßen, also entließ ich irgendwann meinen gleichgültigen Taxifahrer aus der Pflicht und ging zu Fuß weiter. Auf der Suche nach Elisabetas Wohnung bog ich mehrere Mal falsch ab. Ich mühte mich, sechzehnstellige Straßennamen zu entziffern, die sich oft nur in einem Buchstaben unterschieden, und sah in den Gassen flatternde Wäscheleinen, Schwärme androgyner blonder Kinder, riesige Hunde, die niemandem zu gehören schienen. Über mir türmten sich die Wohnungen wie Klippenkolonien.

Ich hatte meine Suche fast aufgegeben, als ich endlich Elisabetas Laden entdeckte, über dem sie angeblich wohnte. Er lag direkt vor mir, zwischen lauter Häusern mit schnalzenden Russlandfahnen in den Fenstern, halb überfluteten Vorgärten und rauchenden Alten, die stumm auf den Eingangstreppen hockten. Ganz am Ende der Straße sprangen junge Männer mit ihren Fahrrädern von einer Betonrampe, und beim Klang ihrer Schreie fühlte es sich an, als sei die gesamte Nachbarschaft stummer Zeuge irgendeines Verbrechens.

Elisabetas Tür war, als ich sie endlich fand, unwahrscheinlich schmal. Ich klopfte und fragte mich in der folgenden lang anhaltenden Stille, ob ich gezwungen sein würde, mich würdelos seitwärts hindurchzuwinden. Dann drang unterdrücktes Stöhnen durch die Tür. Offenbar kostete es Elisabeta Kraft aufzustehen, und mich beschlich wieder der schreckliche Verdacht, dass dieses Treffen im Großen und Ganzen keine gute Idee gewesen war. Ein Husten war zu hören, als versuchte Elisabeta irgendetwas auszustoßen, das ihr Körper nicht hergeben wollte. Doch dann erschien keine welke Babuschka mit Sorgenfalten im Gesicht und zahnlosem Kiefer, sondern die Frau an der Tür wirkte einigermaßen kräftig und gesund. Sie war beiläufig hübsch, mit leuchtenden Augen und markanten Zügen – eine Art von Schönheit, die sich lange hält, weil sie es nicht übertreibt –, und ihr Make-up wirkte dezent, aber keineswegs unscheinbar. Sie war ganz in Schwarz gekleidet, machte jedoch nicht den Eindruck zu trauern. Um ihren Mund herum bemerkte ich etwas Spöttisches, den zittrigen Beinahe-Ausbruch eines Lächelns. Ich erkannte diesen Ausdruck, weil sich auch mein eigenes Gesicht manchmal so unvorteilhaft verzieht, wenn ich besonders ernst aussehen will, während ich etwas komisch, merkwürdig oder lächerlich finde.

»Ah«, sagte sie. »Sie sind Irina. Das Mädchen, das keine Journalistin sein will.«

»Ja.« Ich fragte mich, wann mich zuletzt jemand als Mädchen

bezeichnet hatte. Sämtliche Amerikaner, die auf die Idee kämen, mich so zu nennen, hätten wahrscheinlich Angst, verklagt zu werden. Selbst Lars, dem man so etwas noch am ehesten zugetraut hätte, ließ sich von meinem biblischen Alter und meiner vermeintlichen Sprödigkeit Männern gegenüber davon abhalten.

»Na dann, kommen Sie rein«, sagte sie. »Wenn Sie weiter da herumstehen und so hoffnungslos amerikanisch aussehen, wird Sie noch jemand sexuell belästigen.«

Sie führte mich durch den vollgestopften, staubigen Laden, dessen Wände fast vollständig mit Propagandaplakaten aus der Sowjetzeit tapeziert waren. Über der Kasse sah man auf einem von ihnen muskulöse Bauern auf einem leuchtend grünen Feld arbeiten, über dem ein Banner prangte: »Ihr seid die Erbauer des neuen Lebens!« Ich folgte Elisabeta eine klaustrophobisch dunkle Stiege hinauf in ihre Wohnung. Das Wohnzimmer war sauber und beinahe leer. Ein paar schwarz gerahmte Fotografien zierten die Wände, und die Bücher in den Regalen waren sorgfältig nach Farben sortiert: An einer der Wände zogen sich die Grüntöne entlang, an der nächsten gingen Blautöne in Schwarz über. Ein klappriger Schaukelstuhl in der Mitte des Raums bewegte sich gerade genug, dass es aussah, als säße ein besonders unterernährter Geist darauf. In einer der hinteren Ecken hing ein Drahtkäfig, aus dem ein smaragdgrüner Vogel hervoräugte.

»Werden Sie Tee haben wollen oder so?«, fragte Elisabeta und betrachtete mich misstrauisch von oben bis unten.

Ich nickte. Ich war erleichtert, dass sie so gut Englisch sprach; Verachtung ausdrücken zu können ist einer der zuverlässigsten Indikatoren fließender Sprachkenntnisse.

Sie öffnete eine Tür in die gelb eingerichtete Küche, und ich erhaschte einen Blick auf einen zischenden Gasherd, rosa Blumensträuße auf der fleckigen Tapete und ein paar Fotos, die mit Tesafilm an einem kleinen, nicht magnetischen Kühlschrank befestigt waren. Ich wartete. Im Wohnzimmer roch es nach Staub und künstlichem Zimt – dem Kerzenaroma, nicht dem Gewürz. Der kleine Vogel plusterte wichtigtuerisch sein Gefieder, und ich ging hin, um ihn mir anzusehen. Sein auf mich gerichtetes Auge war schwarzgefleckt wie Vulkangestein.

»Das ist Fjodor«, sagte Elisabeta, die mit einem Tablett zurück ins Wohnzimmer kam.

Fjodor blinzelte. »Ein netter Vogel«, sagte ich.

»Eigentlich nicht«, sagte sie. »Und er lässt sich ganz schön Zeit abzutreten. Er hat mehrere meiner sehr viel netteren menschlichen Freunde überlebt.«

Sie stellte den Tee und einen Teller staubig aussehender Kekse ab und setzte sich in den Schaukelstuhl. Ich nahm auf dem zerschlissenen Sofa Platz, auf dem sich ein grelles Rosenblütenmuster rankte. An der Wand gegenüber fiel mir das dunkel getönte Porträt einer ernst dreinblickenden, edel gekleideten Dame auf.

»Haben Sie Haustiere?«, fragte Elisabeta. Ihr Schaukelstuhl klapperte metallen auf den Bodendielen. Ich musste wohl bemitleidenswerter wirken, als ich gedacht hatte, wenn sie sich jetzt schon auf derart bodenlosen Smalltalk verlegte. »Es bringt eine Menge Verpflichtungen mit sich.«

»Ich habe es nicht so mit Verpflichtungen«, sagte ich und merkte selbst, wie kindisch es klang. Ich biss in einen Keks, um mich von weiteren Dummheiten abzuhalten. Er zerbarst in meinem Mund zu einer Staubwolke. Ich legte ihn zurück und drapierte meine Serviette über den Tellerrand.

»Tut mir leid«, sagte sie und blickte auf das verschmähte Gebäck, ohne übermäßig zerknirscht zu klingen. »Ich bin nicht sehr häuslich, wissen Sie.«

»Danke, dass Sie sich mit mir treffen«, sagte ich und nippte an meinem Tee. Elisabeta zuckte mit den Schultern. »Ich habe auch nicht besonders viele Verpflichtungen. Bloß den verdammten Vogel.« Sie stippte ein Stück Keks in ihren Tee und warf es Fjodor zu, der es gierig verschlang. »Zumindest hat er nichts gegen meine Kochkünste einzuwenden.« Der Vogel wippte milde mit dem Kopf, als wollte er halbironisch seine Zustimmung bekunden.

»Also«, sagte ich. Mir wurde allmählich bewusst, wie beklemmend absurd es war, um die halbe Welt zu fliegen, um in einem russischen Wohnzimmer mit einer alten Frau und ihrem wehrhaften Vogel Smalltalk zu betreiben. »Sie haben gesagt, Sie hätten nicht direkt für Besetow gearbeitet.«

Sie sah mich leicht amüsiert an. »Nicht wirklich, nein.«

»Woher kennen Sie ihn dann?«

»Eigentlich gar nicht. Wir haben damals im selben Gebäude gewohnt.« Ihre bis dahin kräftige Stimme klang auf einmal wie von Efeu erstickt. »Entschuldigung«, sagte sie und stürzte sich in einen so lang anhaltenden, heftigen Hustenanfall, dass ich wegsehen musste. Ihre schmalen Schultern bebten. Grauenhaft reißende Geräusche drangen aus ihrer Brust. Ihr Husten steigerte sich zu einem wilden, unversöhnlichen Heulen, wie der Ausdruck eines chronischen, universellen Schmerzes. Als sie sich allmählich wieder fing, hingen kleine Blutklumpen in ihrem Taschentuch.

»Ist alles in Ordnung?«, fragte ich, obwohl ganz offensichtlich nicht alles in Ordnung war. Ich kannte die Plattitüden, mit denen Menschen auf extremes Leid reagieren, die Trostfloskeln und phrasenhaften Nettigkeiten, aus eigener Erfahrung und ärgerte mich, dass ich nichts Besseres zu sagen hatte.

»Alles bestens«, krächzte sie.

»Ist das … Sind Sie … Ich meine …«, sagte ich und verpulverte damit meinen gesamten Vorrat an idiotischen Floskeln auf einmal.

Plötzlich hatte ich Mitleid mit Jonathan, mit meiner Mutter, mit den Ärzten, mit allen, die sich um mich bemüht und versagt hatten, und dann traf sie das unbarmherzige Urteil meines enttäuschten, weidwunden Blicks.

»Es ist keine Tuberkulose«, sagte sie. Ein glänzendes Fädchen Blut hing an ihrer Unterlippe, aber ich kannte sie nicht gut genug, um es ihr zu sagen. »Nichts Ansteckendes. Nur ein Emphysem. Verfluchte Raucherei.«

»Müssen Sie … Sollten wir nicht zum Arzt?«, fragte ich mit Blick auf das blutbefleckte Taschentuch.

»Noch nicht. Das Blut interessiert die Ärzte nicht. Ich gehe hin, wenn ich gar nicht mehr atmen kann. Es geht schon wieder.« In meinem Gesicht muss das nackte Grauen gestanden haben, denn sie fügte noch hinzu: »Ist nicht so schlimm, wie es aussieht.«

Ich habe genug Zeit in Krankenhäusern verbracht, um zu wissen, dass dieser Satz so gut wie nie wahr ist, doch ich wusste ihre Haltung zu schätzen.

»Wo waren wir gerade?«, fragte sie.

»Bei Besetow.«

»Ah, richtig, Besetow.« Ihre Stimme schien sich aus der Aschewolke des Hustenanfalls zu erheben – fedrig, kühl und beinahe unversehrt. »Ein netter junger Mann, soweit ich mich erinnere. Warum fragen Sie?«

»Na ja«, begann ich zögernd. »Ich würde mich gern mit ihm treffen.« Inzwischen kam es mir unpassend vor, dieses Thema anzusprechen – als würde ich meine liebe alte Großmutter auf ein Tässchen Tee besuchen, nur um sie über ihr Testament auszufragen.

»Glauben Sie mir, meine Liebe, wenn es so einfach wäre, sich mit Alexander zu treffen.« Sie verstummte, und ich fragte mich, ob dieser Abbruch mitten im Satz eine Art Übersetzungsproblem war. »Warum genau möchten Sie sich mit ihm treffen?«

»Mein Vater hat ihn bewundert, und die beiden standen in Kontakt«, sagte ich dümmlich. »Genauer gesagt hat mein Vater versucht, mit ihm in Kontakt zu treten, und Besetow hat nicht zurückgeschrieben. Aber Sie.«

»Ach ja?« Sie zog die Augenbrauen hoch.

Ich holte die kleine Notiz hervor und zeigte sie Elisabeta. Sie starrte den Zettel eine Zeitlang schweigend an.

»Das waren doch Sie, oder?«, fragte ich. »Ist das Ihre Unterschrift?«

»Ja. Mein Gott, hatte ich eine Sauklaue. Aber ich kann mich nicht erinnern, das geschrieben oder den Brief gelesen zu haben. Tut mir leid.«

Ich sah zu Boden.

»Was erwarten Sie denn von ihm?«, fragte Elisabeta und reichte mir den Brief zurück.

»Ich habe diese … diese Krankheit. Und ich interessiere mich für Schach«, sagte ich. Elisabeta zeigte keinerlei Regung. Sie sah mich nur an, rückte ihre schwarze Kleidung zurecht und wartete, dass ich etwas Verständliches von mir gab. »Ich konnte nicht mehr zu Hause bleiben«, schloss ich.

»Und dann sind Sie nach Russland gefahren, um einen Dissidenten durch den Schnee zu jagen? Eine merkwürdige Freizeitbeschäftigung. Er ist Tag und Nacht von Leibwächtern umgeben. Sie sind doch über die Situation informiert, oder nicht?«

»So halbwegs«, murmelte ich. Ich fühlte mich schockierend dämlich: eine ignorante Amerikanerin, die eine Schneise der Verwüstung durch einen Urwald zieht, oder durch einen Roman von Graham Greene.

Sie kniff die Augen zusammen. »Dann wissen Sie, dass er für die Präsidentschaft kandidiert?«

»O ja, natürlich«, sagte ich. »Natürlich weiß ich das. Sie freuen sich sicher sehr für ihn.« Ich hatte das Jahr über immer wieder davon gelesen – meistens in Form farbiger Textblöcke ganz am Ende der Sektion für internationale Politik, die mit selbstgefälligen Wortspielereien betitelt waren. »Staatstratege – Ein Schachgenie wagt den Sprung in die Politik« stand da, oder »Schach dem König – Ehemaliger Schachweltmeister fordert Putin heraus«. Gelegentlich – zwischen entsorgten Daseinsresten und gestempelten Visa, zwischen dem Abschied von meinem Liebsten und meiner Trennung von ihm – hatte ich durchaus daran gedacht, dass der Präsidentschaftswahlkampf ein Problem für mich darstellen könnte und dass aus Besetows Perspektive ein Treffen mit einer verstörten, in jeder Hinsicht ins Schlingern geratenen jungen Frau nicht unbedingt die allerhöchste Priorität genoss. Doch dann hatte ich beschlossen, diese Tatsachen weitestgehend zu ignorieren, wie so viele unbequeme Wahrheiten meines Lebens.

»Freuen trifft es vielleicht nicht so ganz«, sagte Elisabeta und verzog den Mund zu einem schroffen kleinen Komma. »Er wird nicht gewinnen, und außerdem führt es dazu, dass eine Menge einflussreiche Menschen ihn umbringen wollen. Leute, die wissen, wie man so etwas relativ diskret erledigen kann. Mit Giften oder Flugzeugabstürzen, Sie wissen schon. Putin hat es praktisch in sein Regierungsprogramm für den Rest der Legislaturperiode aufgenommen. Alexander fliegt nie mit Aeroflot, nicht einmal auf Inlandsflügen. Besonders nicht auf Inlandsflügen. Allerdings wird es für den FSB schwieriger, je bekannter Alexander im Westen ist. Deshalb redet er so gern mit Journalisten wie Ihnen.«

»Ich bin keine Journalistin.«

»Ist ja auch egal, wie Sie es nennen. Das Problem ist, wie gesagt, dass alle möglichen Leute ihn umbringen wollen. Frauen eher selten, und Amerikaner waren bisher auch nicht dabei, aber man weiß ja nie.«

»Ich will ihn doch nicht umbringen«, sagte ich ein wenig beleidigt.

»Selbst wenn nicht, kann ich Ihnen nicht weiterhelfen. Er wird sich nicht einmal an mich erinnern. Ich habe seine Kontaktdaten nicht.« Ihre Stimme begann wieder auseinanderzufallen, wie ein einzelner Ton, der sich in einen Vierklang auffächert. Ich dachte, sie würde jeden Moment wieder husten müssen, doch sie tat es nicht.

»Oh«, sagte ich und begriff, dass es dabei vielleicht bleiben würde. Vielleicht war das das Ende meines ausgefeilten, emotional anspruchsvollen und finanziell desaströsen Plans, aber es kam definitiv nicht in Frage, mit diesem Ergebnis wieder heimzukehren. »Ach, du lebst noch?«, würden die anderen sagen. »Wolltest du nicht irgendwo in den Weiten des wilden Ostens in den Tod gehen, und hattest du nicht eigentlich vor, unterwegs noch etwas zu lernen, zu finden oder zu tun? Natürlich kannst du deinen Job und deinen Partner wiederhaben, aber du verstehst hoffentlich, dass das jetzt ein bisschen unangenehm ist.« Zurückzugehen wäre ungefähr so, wie viel zu spät auf der Party von Leuten aufzuschlagen, die man kaum kennt, und dann dort hängenzubleiben und bei greller Deckenbeleuchtung und warmem Bier über gemeinsame Bekannte zu reden, die längst gegangen sind. Es wäre ungefähr so peinlich wie in der schlecht geheizten Wohnung einer halbtoten Russin einzufallen, ihr Informationen über einen längst vergessenen Bekannten abzuverlangen und dann schweigend an die Decke zu starren, weil sie diese Informationen nicht hat.

Aber was sollte ich sonst tun? Auf St. Petersburgs vielen Brücken umherstreifen, bis die Zeit reif war, in die Newa zu springen? Vielleicht den Schachmeister stalken, Steinchen an sein Fenster werfen und ihm Nachrichten in den Briefkasten stecken, bis seine Gorillas mich erschießen? Auch das kam mir eher antiklimaktisch vor.

Die scharfen Kanten meines Schweigens schienen Elisabeta allmählich Unbehagen zu bereiten, denn sie zeigte unvermittelt auf das Porträt der streng dreinblickenden Dame. »Kennen Sie die Geschichte Solomonijas?«, fragte sie. Solomonija funkelte mich unter ihren wuchtigen Augenbrauen missbilligend an.

»Nein. Wer ist sie?« Bestimmt hatte man sie wegen irgendwelcher hehrer Prinzipien oder wegen ihrer Enthaltsamkeit zu Tode gefoltert. Weibliche Heilige erwarben ihren Status fast immer durch tödlichen Sexverzicht. Vielleicht, überlegte ich, sollte ich versuchen, mich kanonisieren zu lassen. Dann hätte ich zumindest zu tun.

»Sie war die Ehefrau Wassilis des Dritten.«

»Ah, verstehe.«

»Sie konnte ihm keinen Stammhalter schenken – so ist es immer bei den Mächtigen, oder? Immer kriegen die falschen Frauen die Kinder, und dann wird wieder irgendjemand verbannt oder umgebracht. Solomonija wurde jedenfalls in ein Kloster verbannt, damit Wassili neu heiraten konnte. Und siehe da, neun Monate darauf gebiert sie einen Sohn.«

Ich zog die Augenbrauen hoch und versuchte schockiert auszusehen, obwohl ich eigentlich gar nicht in der Lage bin, schockiert zu sein. Elisabeta warf dem Vogel wieder ein Keksstückchen zu.

»Solomonija hat natürlich Angst um ihr Kind und lässt es für tot erklären. Niemand weiß, was aus dem Jungen geworden ist. Und dabei bleibt es, bis sie bei den Ausgrabungen 1934 Solomonijas Überreste finden – mit einer kleinen Babypuppe im Arm.«

»Also hat der Junge überlebt.«

»Er hat überlebt, und rein technisch gesehen hätten seine Erben Anspruch auf die Herrschaft über ganz Russland gehabt – nicht dass das unbedingt so wünschenswert wäre, und nicht dass heutzutage überhaupt noch jemand an solche Ansprüche glaubt.«

»Warum haben Sie sie dann dort hingehängt?«

»Sie sieht nicht so aus, als ob es ihr da oben gefällt, oder?«, sagte Elisabeta. Solomonijas Verachtung regnete förmlich von dem Bild auf uns herab. In ihren Augen lag die stumme reglose Wut der Verleugneten, Weggesperrten und Vergessenen der Geschichte.

»Nein, sieht sie nicht.«

»Ich weiß auch nicht. Ich interessiere mich eben dafür, wie die Dinge anders hätten laufen können. Für Augenblicke, in denen die Dinge sich in eine bestimmte Richtung entwickeln könnten und dann doch eine andere Wendung nehmen.«

Ich dachte an den Brief meines Vaters und an sein Interesse an jenem ganz anderen Augenblick, wenn man feststellt, dass sich die Ereignisse zwar in alle möglichen Richtungen entwickeln *könnten*, aber nur einen ganz bestimmten Weg einschlagen, dem man folgen muss, so unerträglich es auch sein mag.

»Ist das nicht in jedem beliebigen Augenblick so?«, fragte ich.

»Nicht gleichermaßen, würde ich inzwischen sagen«, antwortete sie leichthin und begann wieder zu husten. Als sie diesmal wieder zu sich kam, ließ ich einen Augenblick der Pietät oder Solidarität verstreichen und fragte dann: »Wie war Alexander denn so?«

»Wie er war?«

»Na, Sie wissen schon. Was hat er den ganzen Tag gemacht?«

»Wer weiß das schon so genau? Was tun Menschen überhaupt? Ich bin damals davon ausgegangen, dass er sich meistens die Zeit mit seinem Spiel vertreibt. Meine Freundin und ich – ich habe damals mit meiner Freundin Sonja zusammengewohnt – sind manchmal zu seiner Tür geschlichen und haben gelauscht. Sonja hatte alle möglichen Theorien über ihn; sie dachte, er wäre eine Art Perverser, ein Spinner oder ein Serienmörder. Oder vom KGB.« Elisabeta drehte sich zu Fjodor um und spitzte die Lippen, und ich wusste gleich, dass sie nur ihr Gesicht davon abhalten wollte, unwillkürlich etwas Verräterisches zu tun. Ich habe genug Erfahrungen mit mimischen und emotionalen Täuschungsmanövern gesammelt, dass ich sie sofort bemerke. Elisabeta und Alexander mussten ein Paar gewesen sein.

»Und was war Ihre Theorie?«

»Ich dachte nur, dass er ein netter Junge ist. Nein, nicht nett. Interessant und nicht ganz leicht zu verstehen. Ich mochte ihn.« Elisabetas Gesicht wechselte unmerklich die Farbe, und sie sah zu Solomonija hoch, die feindselig zurückstarrte. »Aber wir hatten nicht lange miteinander zu tun.«

»Was haben Sie damals gemacht?«

»Als Sekretärin gearbeitet«, sagte sie und wandte den Blick ab. Schlagartig kam mir die unangenehme Erkenntnis, dass sie sehr wahrscheinlich für die Partei gearbeitet hatte. Elisabeta wirkte so respektlos, dass ich nicht von allein daraufgekommen war. Doch damals war fast jeder Teil der Maschinerie gewesen – die Schlauen und die Zynischen, die lustlosen Durchlavierer genauso wie die glühenden Fanatiker. Also hatten ihr Männer mit abwegigen wirtschaftstheoretischen Ansichten Diktate gehalten – was hieß das schon? Und was wusste ich davon? Mir fiel auf, dass Elisabeta immer noch in eine unbestimmte Ferne sah.

Sie trank einen Schluck Tee. »Unsere Freundschaft währte nicht lang, und dann war es zu spät.«

»Zu spät?«

»Na ja, dann war er berühmt. Das waren andere Zeiten, wissen Sie. Als Sekretärin muss man ziemlich viel Egomassage betreiben, selbst in den Büros unserer großen sozialistischen Utopie. Das konnte ich nicht auch noch unbezahlt in meiner Freizeit tun.«

»Das klingt ja sehr prinzipienfest«, sagte ich. Es kam viel bissiger, als ich es gemeint hatte.

Ein schreckliches Schweigen folgte. »Bestimmt müssen Sie langsam in Ihr Hostel zurück«, sagte Elisabeta und stand auf. Ich tat es ihr nach. Ich wollte nicht sitzen bleiben und einer wütenden Russin – selbst einer schwachen, hustenden Russin – den Luftraum überlassen. Elisabeta war zierlich, aber sie gehörte zu den Leuten, bei denen einem unwohl werden kann, wenn sie einen mit so einem gewissen Blick ansehen.

»Es tut mir leid, wenn ich Sie verletzt habe«, sagte ich. Den Satz hatte ich mir von meinen Liebschaften am College geborgt.

Elisabeta lachte, und ihr Lachen klang wie rissiges Eis auf einem unentdeckten Planeten. »Mich verletzt man nicht so leicht. Aber warten Sie.«

Sie verschwand in die Küche und kam mit einer gelben Karteikarte zurück, die sie mir überreichte. »Das sind die Kontaktdaten eines Mannes in Petersburg.« Sie hatte den Namen in unsicheren, übertrieben deutlichen lateinischen Buchstaben aufgeschrieben.

»Ist es ein Freund von Alexander?«

»Ein Mann, der mit Alexander in Kontakt kommen wollte. Aus derselben Branche wie Sie wahrscheinlich. Immer wieder hat er angerufen. Vielleicht hat er ihn ja inzwischen erreicht.«

Ich wusste nicht, was sie mit »derselben Branche« meinte. War er ein entflohener Hochschul-Lehrbeauftragter? Jemand, der von Berufs wegen todkrank in fremden Ländern umherirrte? Ich las seinen Namen. Nikolai Sergejewitsch Tschernow, Wassiljewski Ostrow 132, St. Petersburg.

»Danke«, sagte ich, »das hilft mir bestimmt sehr weiter.« Wieder ein Wildfremder, den ich anrufen musste, dachte ich. Na toll. Ich wurde allmählich zur Spezialistin für Kaltakquise, zur hundeäugigen Telemarketing-Showmasterin in eigener Sache.

»Finden Sie zurück?«, fragte sie.

»Ich nehme ein Taxi.«

Elisabeta sah mich gleichmütig an. »Sie wissen hoffentlich, dass manche Taxifahrer gar keine sind.«

»Wie bitte?«

»Einige sind in Wirklichkeit Räuber.«

»Und woran erkennt man, welche welche sind?«

Sie zuckte mit den Schultern. »Das kann man wohl nur ausprobieren.«

Plötzlich hatte ich gründlich genug von Elisabeta, von ihren kaputten Lungen, ihrem verkniffenen Vogel und ihrem Bildnis einer Frau, die irgendwie ihr Schicksal verfehlt hatte. Ich fragte mich, warum ich dauernd mit Leuten zu tun bekam, die unbedingt in Rätseln sprechen oder in Sprichworten und Andeutungen kommunizieren mussten. Lars war genauso und konnte sich nicht einmal damit herausreden, in einem Polizeistaat aufgewachsen zu sein.

»Viel Glück«, sagte Elisabeta, und ich bedankte mich und trat in die Dämmerung hinaus. Vorbeifahrende Autos streiften mit ihren Lichtkegeln die Abfalltonnen. Ich musste eine ganze Weile im Kreis laufen, bis ich ein Taxi fand.

Am folgenden Nachmittag ging ich Moskau erkunden. Ich bewunderte die Jugendstilarabesken und die klassizistischen sonnenuntergangsfarbenen Fassaden der postkommunistischen Gebäude. Ich blickte zu der gigantischen Statue Peters des Großen auf, die über der Moskwa aufragte. Ich stromerte durch den Gorki Park und sah, wie Eltern Geld bezahlten, um ihren kleinen Peter oder ihre Iwanka mit einem deprimierten, flohgeplagten Tiger fotografieren zu lassen. Torffeuer im Osten hatten die Stadt aufgeheizt, und ich streifte abends schwitzend durch den Skulpturenpark und zählte die bleichen Rosen zu Füßen Lenins. Am Tag darauf rief ich Jonathan an.

Meine erste Begegnung mit der Telefonkarte war eine Katastrophe mit so vielen strengen Ermahnungen von der Vermittlung, dass ich mich schon elend fühlte, bevor Jonathan überhaupt abgenommen hatte. Als er es tat, hörte ich gedämpfte Unterwassergeräusche und war einen endlosen, quälenden Moment lang überzeugt, er sei nicht allein zu Hause.

»Hallo?« Er klang beunruhigt, und mir wurde klar, dass es bei ihm vier Uhr morgens sein musste.

»Tut mir leid«, sagte ich. Es war nichts zu hören, doch in dem Schweigen des Telefons schien sich eine bestimmte Haltung auszudrücken – Hohn oder Fassungslosigkeit oder die Erschöpfung eines Erwachsenen, der die egoistischen Albernheiten eines Kindes nicht mehr erträgt.

»Kommst du zurück?« In seiner Stimme lag das hölzerne Knarren eines Mannes auf der Grenze zwischen Schlaf und Wachen – mit dem ich, fiel mir auf, nie wirklich vertraut geworden war.

Ich überlegte, obwohl es nichts zu überlegen gab. »Ich weiß nicht, was ich sagen soll.«

Er schwieg, doch es klang nicht wie ein Schweigen kurz vor dem Auflegen. Es klang wie die Sorte Schweigen, die leise atmend abwartet und dich über die dunklen Weiten des Ozeans hinweg glühend hasst.

»Können wir nicht Freunde sein?«, fragte ich und hätte mir dafür beinahe selbst den riesigen Hörer aus der Breschnew-Ära über den Schädel gezogen.

»Was stellst du dir darunter überhaupt noch vor?«

»Ich meine, ob wir nicht miteinander im Reinen sein können.« Das war es, was ich mir wirklich wünschte, wurde mir bewusst. Es wäre zumindest erträglich, wenn wir Freunde waren, wenn wir in irgendeinem unsichtbaren kosmischen Kassenbuch einen Ausgleich erreichen konnten. Nicht erträglich wäre es, wenn er mich dort drüben in Boston hasste oder vergaß. Wenn er sein Bild von mir zurechtrückte, bis er unsere Beziehung mühelos als pathologischen Fehlgriff verbuchen konnte oder als Lehre fürs Leben oder als Krug, der an ihm vorübergegangen war.

»Das ist einfach nur beleidigend«, sagte Jonathan. »Was soll ich dazu noch sagen? Vergiss es. Ich will gar nicht wissen, was ich dazu sagen soll.«

»Es tut mir leid«, sagte ich, ein Satz, der mit jedem Gebrauch immer schaler und schaler wird. Wir schwiegen beide. Manchmal wünsche ich mir, ich hätte das Unwissen, den grausamen Optimismus auf mich genommen und auf die Diagnose verzichtet.

»Wie geht es dir so?«, fragte ich.

»Du glaubst doch nicht ernsthaft, dass ich das beantworte. Du hast gar nicht das Recht, mich so etwas zu fragen.«

»Okay.«

»Du hast diese ganze Sache nicht erfunden, weißt du«, sagte er.

»Was?«

»Du hast es nicht erfunden. Niemand zwingt dich, so damit umzugehen. Es gibt Leute, die es ganz anders machen. Wir beide hätten es anders machen können.«

Ich war nicht ganz sicher, ob ich wusste, wovon er redete, aber wahrscheinlich schon. Und wahrscheinlich hatte er recht. Es gibt Leute, die es anders machen, die beten und alternative Therapieformen ausprobieren und dankbar für alles sind, was ihnen bleibt. Dass ich das nicht konnte, lag nur an meinem Egoismus, meiner Unreife und meiner gottlosen Verehrung intakter menschlicher Hirntätigkeit. Ich war alles andere als stolz darauf. Aber ich konnte nicht heimfahren und es so machen wie die anderen – mich von meinen besten Eigenarten abwärts in Nichts auflösen und mich von einem Mann füttern lassen, der mich noch nicht einmal hatte weinen sehen.

»Ich habe dich wirklich geliebt«, sagte er.

»Tja«, sagte ich und wusste, dass ich gleich danach würde auflegen müssen. »Das war wohl der erste große Fehler.«

St. Petersburg war vollkommen anders als Moskau, ganz von Reißbrett-Straßen, prachtvollen Alleen und stilistisch einheitlicher Architektur geprägt. Auf der Teatralnaja Uliza sah es aus, als wollten die Gebäude tanzen. Lange Schnüre eiskalten Sonnenlichts folgten exakt den vorgeschriebenen Bahnen und drapierten sich in säuberlichen rechten Winkeln um die Gebäudeecken. Auch die Gerüche waren anders. In beiden Städten gab es Orte, die schlecht rochen – unverzeihlich, teuflisch, ausfällig schlecht. Der Gestank in einer Ecke nahe des Hostels in Moskau vernebelte beinahe die Sicht; die Knie sackten mir weg, und meine Seele lahmte, wenn ich ihm ausgesetzt war. Er wirkte wie ausgedacht, wie vorherbestimmt. So ein Geruch konnte unmöglich ohne übernatürliche Einflüsse organisch entstanden sein. Wie manche von der Komplexität des Universums auf das Wirken Gottes schließen, sehe ich die abstoßende Vielschichtigkeit dieses Pesthauchs als Indiz für die Existenz des Teufels. In St. Petersburg gab es den erdig-staubigen Geruch von Auberginen, darunter einen halbherzig salzigen Meeresgeruch wie von einem brackigen Aquarium und darunter wiederum den fleischlicheren, wilderen Geruch von Eisberg und Wal. In den Gassen roch es nach verklebtem Wodka und Bier, von dem nächtlichen Tau verdünnt und von dem indirekten Licht eines halben Tages vergoren, und dieser Geruch presste mir jedes Mal mit kalten dürren Fingern die Rippen zusammen, so sehr erinnerte er an fallengelassene Hoffnungen, umgestoßene Pläne, an die lehrreiche Konfrontation von Wünschen mit der Realität. Er bedeutete, dass ein festlicher Abend gekommen und unweigerlich wieder gegangen war.

Ich war kurz nach meiner Begegnung mit Elisabeta nach St. Petersburg umgezogen, hatte meine klammen Kleider und Nikolais Adresse in den Koffer geknüllt und mich in einen Nachtzug gesetzt. Von meinem Reisepass hatte ich zwei Kopien gemacht, die ich in meinem linken Schuh und einer Tamponschachtel versteckte. Im Zug fand ich einen Waggon für mich allein mit schmucken Antimakassars und einem satten Uringestank. Natürlich nahm ich mir vor, wach zu bleiben, und natürlich wachte ich mitten auf der Strecke davon auf, dass ein mittelalter Mann auf der anderen Seite des Ganges schnarchte und im Traum schmatzende Geräusche von sich gab. Am nächsten Morgen fühlte ich mich peinlich berührt und bloßgestellt, als hätte ich eine Nacht voller gravierender sexueller Fehltritte hinter mir. In St. Petersburg hatte ich ein Hostel gefunden, das mit seinen zugigen langen Fluren und dem leicht feindseligen Personal fast wie das in Moskau war. Dort blieb ich ein paar Tage lang und sammelte Mut für die neue Aufgabe, Nikolai ausfindig zu machen. Ich durchstreifte die Stadt, bewunderte die eindrucksvolle Architektur und die Statuen, verschwendete meine Zeit und mein Geld. Mein Russisch verbesserte sich ein wenig, wenn auch nicht so schnell, wie ich gehofft hatte. Ich war beinahe bereit, diesen Menschen anzurufen, ein Treffen auszumachen und mich den damit verbundenen Vergeblichkeiten, Absurditäten und Gefahren auszusetzen, als Nikolai mir zuvorkam.

Ich hatte mir angewöhnt, mich die Nachmittage über in einem winzigen Café unweit des Hostels fröstelnd in Zeitungen zu vertiefen. In dem Café war es immer einige Grad kälter als draußen, und draußen herrschte selbst jetzt im Juli manchmal eine stumpfe Nachmittagskälte. Also trug ich mehrere Pullover und ein verschlafenes Gesicht, als sich ein massiger Mann mir gegenüber auf einen Stuhl fallen ließ und in gebrochenem Englisch fragte, ob ich Irina Ellison aus Amerika sei.

Ich erschrak. Das Gesicht des Mannes sah aus wie mit Stahlwolle geschrubbt; sein Kopf hatte die Größe, Form und Härte eines Footballhelms. Ich sah nach, ob er eine Marke oder einen Ausweis in Händen hielt, und war erst erleichtert, dann verwirrt und schließlich beunruhigt, weil dem nicht so war. Ich wusste nicht recht, ob es klug war, einen Mann wie ihn zu belügen.

»Ja, so heiße ich«, sagte ich. »Und wer sind Sie?«

»Ich bin Nikolai Sergejewitsch«, sagte der Mann. »Sie haben nach mir gesucht, habe ich gehört.« Das feine Netzwerk länglicher Narben, das sein Gesicht überzog, machte ihn aus der Entfernung zu einer fast comichaft finsteren Erscheinung. Von nahem sahen sie einfach wie Aknenarben aus.

»Ich habe nach überhaupt niemandem gesucht«, sagte ich. »Ich habe es nur vorgehabt.«

Nikolai rieb seine Hände aneinander. Als er sich umwandte, um per Handzeichen einen Kaffee zu bestellen, sah seine Wange in dem veränderten Licht wie ein marmoriertes Stück Schinken aus.

Er war fett, und es war die Sorte Fett, die sich durch heftiges Atmen und schwer rollenden Speck deutlich bemerkbar macht.

»Soweit ich informiert bin, suchen Sie nach Alexander Besetow«, sagte er. »Ich will Ihnen helfen, ihn zu finden.«

»Warum?« Der Kellner brachte eine winzige Tasse Kaffee, und Nikolai bedankte sich mit einem Grunzlaut.

»Wir waren seinerzeit gute Freunde«, sagte Nikolai, nippte an seinem Kaffee und verzog missbilligend das Gesicht. »Sandkastenfreunde, sozusagen.«

»In Ocha?« Das kam mir unwahrscheinlich vor.

»Nicht ganz so früh«, sage Nikolai. »Eher von Jugend an. Wir haben uns zu Sowjetzeiten als junge Männer gekannt.«

»Ah«, sagte ich. Eine ganze Reihe naheliegender Fragen ging mir durch den Kopf: Woher wussten Sie, dass ich Ihre Adresse habe? Woher wussten Sie, dass ich auf der Suche nach Alexander Besetow bin? Woher kennen Sie meinen Namen? Mir kam der Rezeptionist im Hostel in den Sinn, dem ich so freimütig von meiner Mission und meinen Plänen erzählt hatte. Doch ich schwieg. Ich habe mich schon immer schwergetan, absurde Prämissen in Frage zu stellen, seien es die der anderen oder meine. Es wäre mir reichlich undiplomatisch vorgekommen, ihn zu fragen, wer zum Teufel er war und was zum Teufel er eigentlich wollte.

»Dann sind Sie von der Botschaft?«, fragte Nikolai. Aus seiner Stimme sprach eine verhaltene Aggressivität, die er nur vorübergehend aus schierer Willenskraft zurückzudrängen schien, als hätte ihn jemand im Vorhinein streng ermahnt, nett zu mir zu sein.

»Nein«, sagte ich.

Nikolai wirkte überrascht. »Verstehe.« Sein zerfurchtes Gesicht verzerrte sich zu einer sorgenvollen Grimasse, als fürchtete er, mich beleidigt zu haben. »Jedenfalls denke ich, wenn wir unsere Informationen austauschen, können wir einander helfen, meinen alten Kumpel Alexander Besetow zu finden.«

»Ich habe gar keine Informationen.«

»So«, sagte Nikolai und ließ sich mit einem fetten Schmatzen in seinen Stuhl zurücksinken. »Und wie würden Sie Ihre Rolle in der Botschaft genau beschreiben?«

Es war wirklich verwirrend.

»Ich gehöre nicht zur Botschaft«, sagte ich. »Ich bin hier nur im Urlaub.«

Nikolai musterte mich einen Augenblick – meine übereinandergeschichteten Pullover, den grauen Tee, der vom Tassenrand in die Zeitung sickerte. »Im Urlaub«, sagte er. »Verstehe. Sie sollten nur wissen, dass Sie sich registrieren lassen müssen, wenn Sie für die Botschaft arbeiten.«

»Aber das tue ich nicht.«

»Es ist uns nämlich nicht entgangen, dass Sie bis jetzt nicht registriert sind.«

»Ich weiß überhaupt nicht, wovon Sie reden«, sagte ich wahrheitsgemäß. »Wer sind ›wir‹?« Und dann, weil mir sein Gesicht nicht passte, das mich ansah wie ein sehr schlechtgelauntes Schnitzel, fragte ich endlich: »Und wer zum Teufel sind Sie?«

»Hören Sie«, sagte er und beugte sich vor. Er roch überraschend zart nach teurem Lavendelshampoo und betont maskulinem Aftershave. »Wir müssen uns ja nicht gleich heute entscheiden. Ich habe Ihnen schon gesagt, wer ich bin. Ich bin auf der Suche nach einem alten Freund.«

»Sie haben mir nicht wirklich gesagt, wer Sie sind. Warum suchen Sie nach ihm?«

»Und warum Sie?«, konterte er.

Ich schwieg einen Augenblick. »Hauptsächlich, weil mein Vater ihn fast persönlich kannte«, sagte ich. »Und weil ich nicht zu Hause bleiben konnte.« Mir wurde klar, wie das klingen musste – dämlich und verdächtig zugleich, wie das lose gestrickte Alibi einer dilettantischen Spionin.

»Okay«, sagte Nikolai. »Es geht um Ihren Vater. Na schön.« Er gab mir seine Visitenkarte, die aussah, als hätte er mehrere Adressen und unwahrscheinlich viele Telefonnummern. »Rufen Sie mich an, wenn Sie an einer Kooperation interessiert sind.«

Ich sagte nichts, weil mir nichts einfiel, was ich hätte sagen können. Nikolai stemmte seine Körpermasse in die Senkrechte. »Also. Vielleicht hören wir voneinander. Bis dahin«, er klatschte ein paar Rubel für seinen Kaffee auf den Tisch, »sollten Sie Ihren Auftraggebern sagen, dass Sie registriert sein müssen.«

Er stapfte davon und ließ seine halbvolle, noch immer dampfende Tasse auf dem Tisch zurück. Erst als er im grauen Nieselregen verschwunden war, begann ich mich zu fragen, wie er mich überhaupt hier gefunden hatte.

Von da an fiel es mir immer schwerer stillzuhalten. Die Mücken im Hostel hielten mich wach; ich verbrachte halbe Nächte damit, mich selbst zu ohrfeigen und wilde Beschimpfungen auszustoßen, was beides nicht half. Juckende Quaddeln bedeckten meine Füße, Unterschenkel und Knie. Ich sah versehrt aus, aussätzig. Vielleicht war es St. Petersburgs Art, mir zu verstehen zu geben, dass ich verflucht noch mal endlich heimfahren sollte. Doch das tat ich nicht. Die Stiche juckten und platzten auf und hinterließen kleine staubfarbene Narben, und ich fuhr immer noch nicht heim. Irgendwann wurde ich unempfindlich gegen sie – wie gegen manches andere auch.

Die Luft war schwer von auflandigen Winden. Es kam die Zeit der weißen Nächte, und der Himmel blieb bis zum Morgen perlgrau und wolkengestreift. Zu schlafen kam gar nicht in Frage. An den Ufern der Newa versammelten sich abends die Jugendlichen, rauchten und jonglierten mit Feuerfackeln, und ich gesellte mich zu ihnen – wanderte den Fluss entlang, verlor mich im Azurblau des Himmels und sah mir die Klappbrücke an, deren aufgestellte Seiten wie die Kiefer eines erschossenen Tiers in die Höhe ragten. Die Newa würde dieses Jahr nicht über die Ufer treten, hatte ich gelesen. Das geschah regelmäßig, wenn nordatlantische Tiefdruckgebiete sich landeinwärts bewegten und stehende Wellen aufschaukelten. In den Jahren 1824, 1924 und 1998 hatte es katastrophale Überschwemmungen gegeben. Oft betrachtete ich die Newa mit ihren Lichtreflexen unter der mitternächtlichen Abendsonne und versuchte mir vorzustellen, dass all ihre Schönheit nur Tarnung war. Aus irgendeinem Grund gefiel mir die Vorstellung sogar, wie sich das Wasser zu einer riesigen Spirale formierte und gewaltige Wellen übereinandertürmte, wie der Fluss die Brücke überspülte, bis sie sich aufbäumte und brach. Natürlich war jede Art von Katastrophe grauenerregend. Aber vielleicht waren die am schlimmsten, die man kommen sah und doch nicht verhindern konnte: ein Meteorit auf Kollisionskurs mit der Erde, eine kleingedruckte tödliche Diagnose oder ein Tiefdruckwirbel vor der Ostseeküste.

Spät nachts lag ich oft in meinem Bett und dachte zurück. Ich erinnerte mich an meinen Vater, und diese Erinnerungen liefen immer rückwärts ab, von den jüngsten zu den ältesten. Ich dachte an seine rasselnden, flachen Atemzüge, bevor wir den Morphintropf aufdrehten, dann an die geisterhaft umherstaksenden Männer aus seiner Abteilung in der Pflegeeinrichtung, dann an seinen wackelnden Unterkiefer, seine tief ausgehöhlten Augen und die Hände, die pausenlos in Bewegung waren, als wollte er einen unsichtbaren, unendlich langen Rosenkranz auffädeln. Daran, wie er am Klavier saß und gar nicht mehr spielte oder nur zusammenhanglose Triller oder fehlerhafte Mozart-Sonaten. Und dann, lange davor, an Fußballspiele im Wohnzimmer, wenn meine Mutter nicht zu Hause war, an abendliche Schachpartien und zärtlich umarmte Bäume, als es längst aus der Mode war, Bäume zu umarmen.

Ich erinnerte mich, wie ich am Ende seines Lebens meinem Vater in die Augen gesehen und versucht hatte, sie als die Augen des Mannes wiederzuerkennen, der mir Hauptstadtnamen und Harmonielehre beigebracht hatte. Doch es gelang mir nicht. Der Mann, der als mein Vater starb, war ein anderer als mein lebender Vater. Ich glaube, er selbst hätte das genauso gesehen.

Im Herbst würde ich einunddreißig werden und damit in das Zeitfenster von drei Jahren eintreten, in dem siebzig Prozent aller Betroffenen mit meiner Anzahl von CAG-Tripletts die ersten Symptome zeigen. Danach gibt es Variationen in der Geschwindigkeit, mit der sich die Symptome verstärken, in der Dauer, wie lange bestimmte Fähigkeiten erhalten bleiben, und in der Lebenserwartung. Doch ich hatte nicht vor, diese Spannbreiten auszureizen. Eine Krankheit, die einem die kognitiven Fähigkeiten nimmt, zerstört auch die Fähigkeit, diese kognitiven Fähigkeiten selbst einzuschätzen. Man kann zwar beschließen, nicht als Zombie vor sich hin vegetieren zu wollen, und kann sich sagen, dass man nicht mehr man selbst ist, sobald man keinen Witz mehr erzählen oder keinen vollständigen Satz mehr schreiben kann, dass dann der einzigartige, wiedererkennbare und menschliche Teil seiner selbst verschwunden ist und man ein Leben als Nicht-Person nicht lebenswert findet. Aber wenn der Punkt erst einmal erreicht ist, denkt man – wenn man überhaupt noch denkt – anders darüber. Dann interessiert man sich nur noch dafür, warm, satt und schmerzfrei zu sein. Man wird bescheiden.

Daher ist es nicht ganz leicht, seinen Abschied vorauszuplanen. Man muss klüger sein als das eigene zukünftige Selbst und irgendwie sicherstellen, dass die heutigen Prioritäten auch für die Entscheidungen von morgen gelten. Und dabei kann man sich auf niemanden verlassen, weil niemand – absolut niemand – bereit sein wird, einem zu helfen. Selbst der eigene Verstand wird einen früher oder später im Stich lassen.

Also lag ich in jenen frühen St. Petersburger Nächten, nachdem Nikolai mich gefunden hatte, wach und dachte zum ersten Mal ernsthaft über meine Optionen nach. Ich wusste nicht, wie es anfangen würde – mit einem Zucken, einem Taumeln oder einem Ruck in der Halsmuskulatur –, doch es würde mir nicht entgehen, wenn mein Körper anfing, ohne Auftrag zu handeln. Also begann ich – während die Tage immer länger und länger wurden, während mein Bankkonto wie ein verletztes Organ auszubluten begann, die Nächte bis nach Mitternacht unwirklich grell waren und die Trinker unter dem Fenster ihre rohe, jugendliche Lebensfreude in die Dämmerung hinausbrüllten –, vorauszudenken. Dann zitterten meine Hände so sehr, dass ich mich fragte, ob sie noch einmal damit aufhören würden, ehe es begann.

KAPITEL 9

Alexander
Leningrad, 1982

Ein Jahr verging, auch wenn Alexander im Nachhinein nicht hätte sagen können, wie. Er wusste noch, dass er angefangen hatte, auf eigene Rechnung Schach zu spielen; er hatte sich einen unfähigen Sekundanten zugelegt, Vadim, der wegen seiner ewigen Mittelmäßigkeit aus der Akademie ausgeschlossen worden war. Er hatte sich bei städtischen Turnieren angemeldet und war den Blicken der anderen Akademieschüler ausgewichen, die als Teilnehmer oder – immer öfter – als Zuschauer kamen. Im Laufe des Frühjahrs und des Sommers musste er einige brillante Partien gespielt haben – das wusste er, weil er ihren Verlauf auf Mikrofiche und später im Internet nachlesen konnte. Er hatte beim städtischen Schachturnier Tricks angewendet, mit denen niemand gerechnet hatte, und Gegner überrumpelt, die weit älter, erfahrener und bekannter waren als er selbst. Doch das Schachspiel war inzwischen bloß noch eine Funktion seines vegetativen Nervensystems – dass es so staunenswert komplex war, machte es kein bisschen schöner oder absichtsvoller. Er absolvierte seine Spiele wie einen besonders eindrucksvollen Partytrick. Irgendwie hatte seine Arbeit an der Flugschrift bewirkt, dass er die innere Bindung zum Schach verlor. Und weil er Elisabeta verloren hatte, war ihm dieser andere Verlust egal.

Es war verblüffend, wie vollständig eine abwesende Person jeden geistigen Freiraum ausfüllen konnte, wie die gesamte unbekannte dunkle Materie plötzlich aufleuchten und nur dieses eine Gesicht, diese eine Stimme reproduzieren konnte, wieder und wieder, wie unzählige Durchschläge eines verbotenen Kunstwerks aus dem Untergrund. Und es war erschreckend, wie eine entfernte Möglichkeit mit ihrem schieren Gewicht alles Reale erfasste, niederrang und erdrückte. Alexander wusste selbst, wie unsinnig es war, ein Jahr lang um eine Frau zu trauern, die so zufällig und kurz in sein Leben getreten war, so unwahrscheinlich wie ein Meteoritenschauer oder ein Hirnaneurysma. Sie war kurz an die Oberfläche gekommen und gleich wieder untergetaucht. Eine halbe Stunde lang hatte sie in dem See seiner Einsamkeit Wellen geschlagen, wie ein Urzeitmonster auf einer verwischten Fotografie, das es vermutlich nie wirklich gegeben hatte. Sie hatte kaum lange genug den Kopf über Wasser gehalten, um ihm zuzuwinken.

Und doch – wenn er auf jenes Jahr zurückblickte, war, so schrecklich es auch geendet hatte, seine lebhafteste Erinnerung die an eine unsichtbare weibliche Hand in seinem Nacken, die ihn daran hinderte, sich nach ihr umzudrehen.

Bevor sie umgezogen war, hatte sie ihn noch einmal besucht – um sich zu verabschieden, wie er später begriff. Als sie klopfte, war es Monate her, dass Alexander bei diesem Geräusch zuletzt hoffnungsvoll aufgeblickt hatte. In letzter Zeit war immer öfter der Mann aus dem Nebenzimmer vorbeigekommen, um ihn zum Trinken einzuladen, und einmal hatte die Verwalterin ihm einen Teller undefinierbaren Eintopfs mitgebracht, auf dem sich eine dicke Haut gebildet hatte, bis Alexander endlich auf die Idee kam, ihn zu essen. Es war ein wenig peinlich gewesen, dass die Nachbarn sein nächtliches Glück mitanhören mussten, doch dass sie sein Unglück mitbekamen, war fürchterlich. Sie hatten Mitleid mit ihm, und als er das begriff, tat er sich selbst nur umso mehr leid und zog sich ganz zurück. Als Elisabeta dann Anfang September vor seiner Zimmertür stand, war sein erster Impuls, ganz still zu halten und so zu tun, als sei er gestorben.

Doch Elisabeta ließ sich so leicht nichts vormachen. Er konnte sie vor der Tür mit ihrer Kleidung rascheln hören und wusste gleich, dass er nicht drum herumkommen würde aufzumachen. Immerhin konnte er sie warten lassen. »Alexander«, sagte sie. »Mach auf.«

Er tat es nicht, doch er richtete sich im Bett auf. Breite Lichtschlieren drangen zum Fenster herein und brachten den Staub zum Leuchten.

»Ich kann deine Hausschuhe sehen«, sagte Elisabeta. »Ich weiß, dass du da bist. Mach auf, ich bin's.«

Er stand auf und ging zur Tür. Er legte eine Hand auf den Knauf und dachte an das erste Mal, da er ihr die Tür geöffnet hatte. Es erschreckte ihn, wie schnell das Leben sich ändern konnte, nur um gleich darauf alles wieder rückgängig zu machen. Er öffnete, und da war sie. Sie sah aus wie immer. Er sah vermutlich hässlich aus, jedenfalls fühlte er sich so. Und er hatte nichts dagegen, wenn sie ihn so sah, schließlich war sie dafür verantwortlich.

»Tatsächlich«, sagte er. »Du bist es. Und wer bist du genau?«

»Kann ich reinkommen?«

»Nett, dass du fragst.«

Er trat beiseite, um sie hereinzulassen. Normalerweise hätte er den Stapel alter Ausgaben der 64 vom Bett geräumt, damit sie sich setzen konnte, doch diesmal ließ er es bleiben. Sie sah verlegen aus, und das freute ihn. »Was willst du hier?«, fragte er.

Sie berührte ihr Haar, dann ihre Stirn. Dann verschränkte sie die Arme. In einer Hand hielt sie einen Brief. »Du hast es schon gehört, nehme ich an«, sagte sie.

»Habe ich.«

»Ich hoffe, du verstehst, warum ich das tue.«

»Tue ich nicht.«

Sie kniff die Augen zusammen und wandte sich zum Fenster.

»Wann ist denn der große Tag?«, fragte er.

»Er ist ein guter Mann.« Eine Seite ihres Gesichts war wie von Schatten verschluckt.

»Gut? Das bezweifle ich. Erträglich vielleicht.«

»Er ist erträglich.«

»Na, wunderbar. Jeder sollte ein Leben führen, das er ertragen kann.«

Sie kramte nach einer Zigarette. »Hast du Feuer?«

Er holte ein Feuerzeug aus der Tasche und beugte sich vor, um ihr die Flamme hinzuhalten. Dann trat er drei Schritte zurück, damit sie nicht dachte, die Geste hätte sie einander näher gebracht.

»Was ist das?«, fragte er und zeigte auf den Brief. Er hoffte, er sei von ihr, voller liebevoller, tränenreicher Entschuldigungen, Erklärungen, Beschwörungen. Voller demütiger Bitten um Verzeihung und voller Versicherungen, dass sie ihn immer lieben werde. Er hatte ihr nie gesagt, dass er sie liebte, aber sie war ja nicht dumm. Oder vielleicht doch. Fast alles, was er zu Anfang von ihr gedacht hatte, hatte sich als falsch erwiesen, also hielt er sich besser mit seinen Vermutungen zurück. Er hoffte, sie würde ihm den Brief überreichen und ihn bitten, ihn zu lesen, so dass er sich die kleine, schmutzige Freude gönnen konnte abzulehnen.

»Du hast Post bekommen«, sagte sie. »Aus den USA. Der Leningrader Schachverein hat sie weitergeleitet.«

Es schmerzte ihn, dass der Brief nicht von ihr war, doch seine Gedanken blieben daran haften, und er wollte ihn nicht haben. »Ach ja?«, sagte er. »Das ist ja nett.«

»Ich dachte, ich könnte ihn dir vorbeibringen.«

»Auch das ist nett.«

»Glaubst du, es ist Fanpost?«

»Wohl kaum.«

Sie sah noch immer aus dem Fenster und rauchte – stand nur so da und wich seinen Blicken aus und wartete, aber worauf? Was für ein jämmerlicher Schlussakt das war. Er nahm ihre Beziehung immerhin wichtig genug, um zu finden, dass sie ein sauberes Ende verdiente. Das monatelange Schweigen kam ihm im Nachhinein angemessener vor, weniger erbärmlich. Der Unterschied war ungefähr wie der zwischen einer raschen Enthauptung und einer Steinigung – einer stundenlangen Steinigung, bei der man immer wieder aufstand und um sein Leben flehte. Doch im Grunde widerten beide Möglichkeiten ihn an. »Du solltest jetzt gehen. Ich habe zu tun.« Er wies vage in Richtung Bett und wollte damit zu verstehen geben, dass er sich mit Schachproblemen befasste, nicht, dass er damit beschäftigt gewesen war, die Wand anzustarren.

Sie hielt den Brief hoch. Es sah aus, als hätte sie eine weiße Fahne in der Hand. »Willst du ihn nicht lesen?«

Er setzte sich auf sein Bett und griff nach einer Ausgabe der *64*. Die Probleme darin hatte er längst alle gelöst. »Behalte du ihn doch«, sagte er. »Ich habe gerade keine Lust, Briefe zu lesen.«

Er dachte, sie würde vielleicht noch etwas sagen. Er wartete darauf. Doch sie sagte nichts. Sie stand noch eine Weile stumm da. Dann ging sie und schloss die Tür mit einer Sorgfalt, die ganz sicher geheuchelt war.

Die Heirat fand im Oktober in einem Hochzeitspalast im Stadtzentrum statt, und Alexander kam ungeladen gerade in dem Moment, da Elisabeta zu den Klängen der Nationalhymne den Saal durchschritt. Von da an verzog er bis zum Ende seines Lebens jedes Mal schmerzlich das Gesicht, wenn er diese Melodie hörte. Manchmal bemerkte es jemand und staunte, wie sehr Alexander das Regime noch immer hasste. Doch er dachte gar nicht an das Regime, wenn er die Hymne hörte, nicht an Stalins zwanzig Millionen Opfer oder den qualvollen Tod im Gulag oder an Mischas mit Pisse durchtränkte Irrenhauszelle. Er dachte an Elisabeta und den Parteifunktionär, der ihr in dem grellen, sirrenden Licht feist und erwartungsvoll entgegensah.

Alexander stand ganz hinten im Saal, neben ein paar weiteren Nachbarn, neben Passanten, die hereingekommen waren, um sich aufzuwärmen, und einigen Frauen, die vom Aussehen her vermutlich Elisabetas Kolleginnen waren. Elisabeta hatte ihr Haar an den Seiten zu zwei großen Schnecken aufgerollt. Der Mann sah aus, wie der Belgier ihn beschrieben hatte; selbst wenn er stillstand, ragte er bedrohlich schwankend in die Höhe. Es war merkwürdig, Elisabeta ganz in Weiß zu sehen, nachdem sie immer nur Schwarz getragen hatte. Sie sah aus wie eine domestizierte Blume, der man über Generationen eine falsche Blütenfarbe angezüchtet hat. Falls sie Alexander bemerkte, wusste sie es gut zu verbergen. Sonja, ihre Mitbewohnerin, stand mit welken Rosen und einem bestürzten Gesichtsausdruck dabei. Nationalistische Dankgebete wurden aufgesagt, Papiere gestempelt, und den Eheleuten wurden die Bedingungen für eine rechtskräftige Heirat vorgelesen. Alexander schlich sich davon, als die Fotos gemacht wurden.

Anschließend ging er ins Saigon. In seinem Schmerz nahm er die grünen Deckenleuchten wie die glimmenden Nachbilder war, die manchmal von innen vor den Augenlidern tanzen. Nikolai und Iwan stritten um irgendetwas – Iwan wollte in der nächsten Ausgabe eine Verteidigungsschrift für einen Pechvogel aus Litauen abdrucken, und Nikolai war vehement dagegen –, doch Alexander hörte gar nicht zu. Zum ersten Mal wünschte er sich, erwischt zu werden, nur um des Pathos willen, nur für den Hauch von Märtyrertum. Es war ein kindischer Wunsch. Aber irgendwie gefiel ihm die Vorstellung, in eine Art öffentliche Heldentat verstrickt zu werden, während Elisabeta den Weg in die privateste Form der Niedertracht wählte. Dann würde sie ja sehen, dachte er. Nur was?

Später schämte er sich dieser Gedanken. Obwohl er nicht abergläubisch war, konnte er nicht vergessen, dass er sich bei ihrem letzten gemeinsamen Abend im Saigon im Selbstmitleid gesuhlt hatte. Er konnte nicht vergessen, dass er bereit gewesen war, für einen Augenblick der Anerkennung durch dieses Mädchen alles hinzuwerfen. Deshalb konnte er in seinen düstersten Momenten, in den vielen schlaflosen Nächten, die folgen sollten, manchmal an Nikolai denken und ihm beinahe verzeihen.

An dem letzten Abend, den Alexander mit Iwan verbrachte, schneite es. Es war Mitte November, und dicke Flocken torkelten wie betrunkene Tauben durch die Luft. Seit Elisabetas Hochzeit konnte Alexander sein Zimmer kaum noch ertragen. Er hielt es dort nur aus, wenn er sehr spät dran oder sehr betrunken war oder beides zugleich. Er hatte sich angewöhnt, Wolschokoje-Wein aus den roten Verkaufsautomaten zu besorgen, weil die Supermarktware meistens aus Rohalkohol, Apfelsaft und petrochemischen Zusatzstoffen bestand. Ungefähr vier Minuten hielt er es bei voller Beleuchtung in seinem Zimmer aus – gerade lange genug, um seine Schachbücher vom Bett zu fegen, sich im Bad ein wenig Wasser ins Gesicht zu spritzen, den Großteil seiner Sachen auszuziehen und ins Bett zu fallen. Wenn er nur eine Minute länger blieb, fühlte er sich kränklich, nervös und niedergeschlagen; Kerzen ließen sein Zimmer noch dunkler wirken, als wenn er gar kein Licht machte. Also ging er abends immer öfter zu Iwan, trank mit ihm einen Wodka nach dem anderen, hörte Jazz auf Voice of America oder sah sich das grauenhafte Staatsfernsehen an. In jenem Herbst wurden auf Kanal eins wieder und wieder »Die Seelenschacherer« gezeigt, und manchmal lachten sie über den plumpen Antisemitismus der Sendung. Manchmal wurden sie sehr still und sehr betrunken.

Iwans Reaktionen auf Alexanders Besuche schwankten zwischen amüsierter Gleichgültigkeit und beinahe so etwas wie Zuneigung. Iwan lebte zwar ebenfalls allein, doch seine Wohnung strahlte keine Einsamkeit aus. Vielleicht lag es an der Katze, an den Büchern, an dem ständigen Schreiben, Recherchieren und Kopieren, an den wüsten Wortgefechten mit dem Radio oder den unfassbar vielen Zeitschriften, die Iwan immer irgendwo auftreiben konnte – der prokommunistischen Leningrader *Sowest'*, der *America* – dem Propagandablatt der US-Regierung – und der *Frauen und Russland*, dem ersten und, soweit Alexander wusste, einzigen feministischen Samisdat-Organ. Wie auch immer er es anstellte – irgendwie schien Iwan immer im Zentrum seines eigenen Lebens zu stehen, statt sich unbeholfen am Rande des Geschehens herumzudrücken und nicht zu wissen, wo er hinsehen sollte.

Als Alexander an jenem letzten Abend zu Besuch kam, saß Iwan vor dem winzigen Fernseher, in dem ein Mehrteiler lief, und machte Notizen für die nächste Ausgabe. Die abgehackten Gesten der Schauspieler wirkten hektisch, beinahe verzweifelt. Doch Iwan schlug sich vergnügt auf sein knochiges Knie und bot Alexander einen Wodka an. Die Katze schnurrte lauter als die Schreibmaschine. Im Fernsehen waren durch das schwarzweiße Schneegestöber plumpe Verwicklungen, überzogene Vorurteile und peinliche Missgeschicke zu sehen. Es war beinahe heimelig, wie Alexanders bessere Abende in Ocha, als sein Vater noch lebte und er ein kleiner Junge war. Als Alexander sich bei diesem Gedanken ertappte, richtete er sich auf, ließ seine Nackenwirbel knacken und kippte seinen Wodka hinunter. Manchmal hatte er fast das Gefühl, Iwan könnte hören, was er dachte, und das wollte er nicht.

»Soll der Litauer nun mit rein oder nicht?«, fragte Alexander.

Iwan zuckte mit den Schultern. »Wahrscheinlich schon. Trotz der Einwände unseres verehrten Freundes Nikolai Sergejewitsch.«

Auf dem Bildschirm war ein sturzbetrunkener Mann zu sehen, dessen hysterische, grobknochige Ehefrau erfolglos versuchte, seinen Zustand vor ihren teuer gekleideten Abendbrotgästen zu verbergen.

»Warum will Nikolai ihn nicht drinhaben?«, fragte Alexander.

»Kolja wird mir auf ewig ein Rätsel bleiben.« Iwan lachte kurz in Richtung Fernseher. »Er hat sehr feste, sehr undurchschaubare Prinzipien.«

Auf dem Bildschirm schien dem Betrunkenen übel zu werden. Er beugte sich in Richtung der Schuhe des teuer gekleideten Gastes. Die Ehefrau kreischte auf. Iwan lachte.

»Er hält es für zu provokativ«, sagte Iwan. »Finger weg vom Baltikum, sagt er immer. Er glaubt, es geht einen Schritt zu weit. Aber was weiß er schon? Er ist hier schließlich nicht der Zirkusdirektor, oder? Nicht gerade eine treibende kreative Kraft, wie?« Er stand auf und begann auf und ab zu gehen, wobei er eine Hand über die Bücherstapel gleiten ließ. »Er macht die Aufzeichnungen und übernimmt das Risiko dafür. Aber eigentlich ist es ihm egal. Nikolai Sergejewitsch ist mein Freund, aber eins lass dir gesagt sein: Er würde sich in alles Mögliche stürzen, was ihm gerade unterkommt. Er ist ein Radikaler auf der Suche nach einer Mission, und wir haben bloß Glück, dass es unsere ist.«

Alexander dachte über seine Worte nach. Draußen tippte der Schnee mit weißen Fingern an die Fensterscheiben. Manchmal lösten sich größere Klumpen, wirbelten in den Lichtkegel der Laterne und sanken wie glühende Asche zu Boden.

»Also«, sagte Iwan nach einer Weile. »Dein Mädchen hat geheiratet, habe ich gehört?«

»Ja.« Irgendwie sorgte der Blick hinaus in den Schnee dafür, dass es ihm weniger ausmachte; es war, wie wenn jemand die Schmerzen einer schweren inneren Verletzung unter Kontrolle bringt, indem er unwahrscheinlich, unmenschlich stillhält.

»Immer noch besser er als du.«

Alexander riss sich von den Schneeflocken los. »Wie meinst du das?«

»Bei einem Mädchen wie ihr ist es besser, sie denkt an einen zurück. Besser, auf der richtigen Seite der Bilanz zu stehen, verstehst du? Du willst bestimmt nicht der Mann sein, der zwischen ihr und ihren Verflossenen steht. Dann doch lieber ein Verflossener.«

»Vielleicht«, sagte Alexander, und dachte, dass er sich mit Iwans Formulierung anfreunden könnte. Vielleicht tauchte er gerade jetzt als schwarzweißer, holographischer Schemen in Elisabetas Hinterkopf auf und winkte ihr zu. Vielleicht suchte er sie gerade jetzt genauso heim wie sie ihn.

Iwan setzte sich, dass das Sofa quietschte und die Papiere durcheinanderflogen. »Man bewohnt einen Ort erst richtig, wenn man dort mindestens einen größeren Verlust erlitten hat«, sagte er. Alexander spürte eine plötzliche Veränderung der Atmosphäre, eine fast schon körperliche Energie, und fragte sich, ob Iwan etwas dazu sagen würde. Doch der Augenblick verstrich, und Iwan lehnte sich zurück und klopfte Alexander auf die Schulter. »Gratulation zu deiner offiziellen Ankunft in Leningrad, Towarischtsch.«

Alexander wollte ihm gerade scherzhaft danken, als das Fernsehbild sich plötzlich in schwarzweißes Rauschen auflöste. Als es sich wieder zusammensetzte, waren die Komödiendarsteller verschwunden, und statt ihrer blickte ein dunkel gekleideter Moderator starr in die Kamera und ließ eine Wortsalve los wie Gummigeschosse auf eine Horde Demonstranten.

»Was soll das denn jetzt?«, fragte Alexander.

»Psst.« Iwan drehte die Lautstärke auf und hockte sich direkt vor den Fernseher.

»Worum geht es überhaupt?« Der Sprecher kündigte eine Sendung über Stalins militärische Errungenschaften im Zweiten Weltkrieg an.

»Psst.« Iwan kroch fast in die Bildröhre hinein. »Leise jetzt.« Beide lauschten angestrengt, doch der Moderator verbreitete sich nur weiter über die Pracht und Größe der russischen Nation.

»Merkwürdig«, sagte Alexander.

»Er ist tot.«

»Was?«

»Breschnew ist tot.«

»Hat er das gerade gesagt?« Alexander fragte sich, ob ihm etwas entgangen war, und lauschte wieder.

»Nein«, sagte Iwan. »Aber sieh dir an, wie er gekleidet ist. Sieh dir sein Gesicht an. Warum sollten sie wohl eine Komödie für diesen pseudohistorischen Blödsinn unterbrechen?«

Jetzt fiel auch Alexander auf, dass der Sprecher leicht panisch wirkte. Irgendein geheimes Wissen verdüsterte von Zeit zu Zeit seinen Gesichtsausdruck, ehe er es wieder verdrängte.

»Er ist tot, jede Wette«, sagte Iwan. Er stand auf und lief mit hinter dem Rücken verschränkten Händen kopfschüttelnd auf und ab wie ein gereiztes Pferd. »Also.« Er blieb stehen, fluchte triumphierend und nahm die Wanderung wieder auf. »Also dann. Das wird ja interessant.«

»Sollen wir es veröffentlichen? Noch bevor es bekanntgegeben wird?«

»Wir bereiten uns jedenfalls vor. Es wird ja nicht ewig ungesagt bleiben. Eine Woche maximal. Aber sie wollen bestimmt in Ruhe die Nachfolge auskungeln.«

Alexander nickte und sah wieder zum Fenster hinaus. Der Schnee fiel jetzt in dichteren Schüben, kristallinen Wirbeln, die sich immer enger und enger um sich selbst drehten, bis ihm vom Zusehen schwindelig wurde. Er fragte sich, was als Nächstes kommen würde.

»Das Begräbnis wird eine Riesensache«, sagte Iwan. »Dafür werden sie schon sorgen. Es wird das größte Ding seit langem. Und es wird bestimmt sehr streng überwacht.«

»Und was sollen wir dann tun?«

Iwan sah beinahe träumerisch aus. Seine Augen wurden im schummrigen Licht bleigrau; ihr Ausdruck war sibyllinisch, als sähen sie durch Alexander hindurch in eine ferne, bedrohliche Zukunft.

»Sascha«, sagte er, »wir tapezieren die ganze Stadt.«

Auf dem Nachhauseweg vollführte Alexander einen kleinen Freudentanz. Wenn die Nachricht erst einmal offiziell war, verbat es sich von selbst zu feiern. Doch jetzt, vor der Bekanntgabe, konnte er unbesorgt durch den Schnee tanzen, konnte jubeln, gröhlen und große Hände voll Schnee hochwerfen und glitzernd auf sich herabregnen lassen, bis ihn fröstelte. Er wusste sehr wohl, dass es eigentlich nichts zu feiern gab. Nach Breschnew würde es einen neuen Breschnew geben, und danach noch einen. Doch jetzt, in diesem Moment, gab es keinen Breschnew, und Alexander war einer der wenigen, die davon wussten. Er hüpfte und schlitterte und stampfte gedämpfte Stiefelabdrücke in den Schnee. Die Sterne waren im Winter viel klarer zu sehen. Die früh hereinbrechende, tiefe Dunkelheit brachte die über den Himmel verstreuten Lichtkleckse zum Strahlen.

Alexander dachte darüber nach, was Iwan über den Verlust gesagt hatte – wie er einen an einen Ort binden, einen heimisch machen konnte. Er fragte sich, was Iwans eigene Verluste waren. Er hatte vorgehabt, ihn zu fragen, doch dann war die Sondersendung dazwischengekommen.

Er drückte seine bloßen Hände in den Schnee, bis ihm die Arme schmerzten. Er warf die Beine hoch und vollführte wüste Trittfolgen in der Luft. Die Fahrer der weißen Wolgas – wenn überhaupt welche vorüberfuhren – registrierten ohne besonderes Interesse einen sehr betrunkenen Mann auf dem Nachhauseweg.

Ein paar Tage darauf klopfte es bei Alexander an der Tür. Es war mitten in der Nacht, und einen schlaftrunkenen Augenblick lang fragte er sich, ob es Elisabeta war, ehe ihm klarwurde, dass sie gar nicht mehr hier wohnte und dass sie ohnehin nie so klopfen würde, mit fleischigen, fordernden Knöcheln, die über das Türblatt kratzten. Dann fragte er sich, ob ihm gekündigt worden war. Vielleicht hatte die Verwalterin von seinen Aktivitäten für die Flugschrift gehört und beschlossen, dass das Risiko nicht tragbar war, schließlich lebten Kinder im Gebäude, wusste er das denn nicht? Jetzt war sie hier, um ihn nachts aus dem Haus zu schleusen und ihm zu einem Vorsprung zu verhelfen, falls schon jemand hinter ihm her war. Und gleich würde sie ihm seine Sachen hinterherwerfen, dass die Koffer und Socken im Schnee ein chaotisches Schachbrett ergaben.

Doch das Klopfen wurde immer lauter und dringlicher, und er begriff: Er war erledigt. Es war der KGB. Sie wollten ihn töten, ihn bestechen, ihm den Willen brechen, und keines dieser Vorhaben wäre besonders schwierig durchzuführen.

Doch es war nicht der KGB. Es war Nikolai, der wie ein Tier im dunklen Flur kauerte.

»Lass mich rein«, keuchte er. »Scheiße noch mal, mach auf.«

Alexander öffnete, und Nikolai stolperte herein. Er zitterte am ganzen Körper, was sonst gar nicht seine Art war. Alexander trat zurück, und Nikolai taumelte zum Bett, ließ sich darauffallen – wobei er Alexanders Decke zerknüllte und überall schmutzige Schneeklumpen hinterließ – und blieb erst einmal eine Weile heftig atmend dort sitzen. Alexander fiel auf, wie ungern er wissen wollte, was passiert war.

»Tja«, sagte Nikolai. »Besser, ich sage dir gleich, dass Iwan Dimitrijewitsch tot ist.«

»Was?« Alexander konnte seine eigene Stimme nicht hören. »Was?«

»Er ist vom Bus überfahren worden.«

Nikolai atmete viel zu laut, mit verzweifelten Japsern, wie nach einem schlimmen Fall von Sauerstoffmangel – als hätte ihn jemand viel zu lange in die Newa getaucht oder als sei er ohne Helm aus seinem Raumschiff geworfen worden und hätte an die Fenster geklopft und an der Luke gerüttelt und sei weiß geworden, weil seine

Lungen kollabierten, seine Ohren dröhnten, weil sein Körper verstand. »Also wirklich«, sagte er. »Kannst du mir nicht wenigstens was zu Trinken geben?«

»Was sagst du da? Ein Bus? Wovon redest du überhaupt?«

»Ein Bus eben. Ein großes öffentliches Verkehrsmittel. Schon mal gehört? Mischa ist im Krankenhaus.«

»Dann sind sie beide überfahren worden? Vom selben Bus?«

»Sie waren betrunken. Es war spät. Du weißt, wie viel sie trinken.«

»War das jetzt gerade?«

»Natürlich jetzt gerade!« Nikolais Atmung klang hysterischer, als man bei seinem Gewicht erwartet hätte. »Würde ich sonst mitten in der Nacht hier vorbeischneien? Ich brauche doch sonst keinen Gutenachtkuss von dir, oder? Natürlich ist es jetzt gerade passiert.«

»Ein Bus? Mitten in der Nacht?«

Nikolai starrte ihn an. »Es war ein Nachtbus.«

»Und was ist mit dem Fahrer?«

»Wieso?«

»Ist er verhaftet worden? Wo ist er jetzt? Wie hat er es geschafft, mit einem verdammten Bus zwei Leute umzulegen?«

Nikolai blinzelte. »Es war spät. Die beiden waren sturzbesoffen. Da gab es keine großen Diskussionen.«

Er schwieg kurz, dann bat er so flehentlich um einen Schluck Wasser, dass Alexander wie von selbst eine seiner saubereren Tassen nahm, in die Küche lief und sie mit dem Wasser füllte, das immer ein wenig metallisch nach Blut und Sardinen schmeckte. Er brachte es Nikolai und setzte sich neben ihm aufs Bett, auf die Matratze, die nach so langer Zeit an der Nachtluft bestimmt nicht wieder warm werden würde. Dann begann Nikolai zu erzählen.

Sie kamen gerade aus dem Saigon, als es passierte, sagte Nikolai. Mischa wurde sieben Meter weit in einen abgestorbenen Busch geschleudert, der unter ihm splitterte und ihm mit seinen gefrorenen, gebrochenen Ästen das Gesicht aufriss. Iwan war fast sofort tot. Die Vorderreifen hatten ihm die Beine und mehrere Organe zerfetzt. Alexanders Vorstellungskraft kam nicht über dieses »fast« hinweg. Ein unerträgliches Wort. Seine eigenen Organe rebellierten, kollabierten und zuckten zurück, wenn er daran dachte.

Mischa würde überleben. Mischa war nicht totzukriegen, sagte Nikolai und stieß ein Lachen aus, das mehr wie Husten klang. Alexander lachte nicht. Er starrte auf einen Teefleck auf dem Boden. Irgendein entlegener Teil seines Verstandes fragte sich, wie er dort hingekommen war. War er von Anfang an dort gewesen? Hatte Elisabeta ihn bemerkt? Hatte er ihn in einer der letzten Nächte selbst produziert, als er betrunken und halbblind von einem Besuch bei Iwan zurückgekehrt war, zu einsam, um sich noch darum zu scheren, was alles zu Boden fiel? Nikolai verschwamm in seinem Augenwinkel. Er sackte in sich zusammen. Er atmete flacher und langsamer. Vielleicht, dachte Alexander, war er kurz davor einzuschlafen.

Alexander konnte es beinahe vor sich sehen. Wie die beiden auf die Straße hinaustraten, wie der graue Schneematsch ihnen in die Hosenbeine kroch, wie der Bus, eine verschwommene gelbe Masse, aus dem Nichts auf sie zugeprescht war. Es war einfach zu grauenhaft, auf einer vielbefahrenen matschigen Straße zu sterben. Iwan hätte Besseres verdient, weite Felder sauberen, weißen Schnees, mit Rillen und Dünen wie ein ausgetrockneter Salzsee. Er hätte Besseres verdient, als in einer Gasse in den Abgasen alter Autos zu sterben, zwischen Marktständen, die tagsüber blutige Fische und faulige Kartoffeln verkauften. Doch genau so, sagte Nikolai, war es gewesen, und Alexanders Vorstellungskraft war noch nie so eine Last gewesen wie in jener Nacht, in der Iwan starb. Er sah ihn vor sich: den Kiefer ausgerenkt, das Gesicht eine zerfließende Maske, in den Augen ein jenseitiger Ausdruck und, zum ersten Mal, seit Alexander ihn kannte, ein Ausdruck der Angst.

Als Alexander erwachte, war Nikolai nicht mehr da. Er hatte Mischas Zimmernummer im Krankenhaus auf ein Stück Papier geschrieben, und seine Socken lagen zusammengeknüllt unter dem Bett. Als Alexander sie aufhob, sah er, dass sie blutverkrustet waren. Angewidert ließ er sie fallen. Dann warf er sie aus dem Fenster.

Auf dem Weg durch Leningrad folgte er der Ligowski südwärts und umging das Stadtzentrum im weiten Abstand vom Saigon. Er wusste, dass es dort nichts mehr zu sehen gab; noch in der Nacht hatten sie die Marktstände wieder geradegerückt, das Blut fortgewischt, den Bus auf einen der Autofriedhöfe außerhalb der Stadt geschleppt. Dennoch kam mit jedem Blinzeln die Vorstellung wieder – das Kreischen rostiger Bremsen vielleicht und der dumpfe, viel zu harte Aufprall eines Körpers im Schnee.

Es war nicht so, dass er es nicht hätte glauben können. Er glaubte es, wie er glaubte, dass es kein Leben nach dem Tod gab, dass die Erde eines Tages in die Sonne stürzen würde, dass er vielleicht den Rest seines Lebens allein zubringen würde. Es war jene Art Wissen, bei dem einem, wenn man einmal daran glaubt, nichts anders mehr übrigbleibt, als sich auf den Boden zu legen und dort weiterzuglauben.

Das Krankenhaus war ein plumpes, feuersteingraues Gebäude mit Gittern vor den Fensterscheiben. An der Rezeption saß eine Frau mir blassrotem Haar, deren Haut sich so straff über die Knochen spannte, als hätte ihr Gesicht mehrere Jahre vor dem Schädel zu wachsen aufgehört.

»Ja?«, sagte sie, ohne aufzublicken.

»Ich möchte Michail Andrejewitsch besuchen. Er liegt in Zimmer 219.«

»Wenn Sie wissen, wo er liegt, gehen Sie«, sagte die Frau. »Wozu fragen Sie mich dann?«

Alexander ging den Flur hinunter. Die Wände und der Boden waren knochenbleich. An einigen der Türknäufe hingen grellbunte Plastikblumen, steifbeinige Plüschtiere oder kleine Fähnchen. Alexander dachte an die Menschen hinter den nicht geschmückten Türen.

Als er Zimmer 219 betrat, registrierte er erleichtert, dass Mischa schlief. Seine Augen waren geschlossen, sein Gesicht ein Mosaik aus unterschiedlich tiefen Wunden. Alexander trat ans Bett und beugte sich vor, um ihn sich genauer anzusehen. Ein besonders tiefer Schnitt verlief knapp unterhalb seines Auges, und es war deutlich zu sehen, wie leicht er es hätte verlieren können. Alexander berührte behutsam Mischas Hand. Die Haut fühlte sich an wie Wachspapier und hatte dieselbe Farbe wie die schmutzigen Krankenhauslaken. Dass er überlebt hatte, war beinahe komisch. Ausgerechnet Mischa, der ohnehin schon mehr tot als lebendig war – halb skelettiert, halb verrückt und fast schon ein Geist.

»Gute Besserung, Mischa«, sagte Alexander. »Viel Glück.« Er legte Mischa die Hand auf die Stirn.

Mischa riss die Augen auf. Plötzlich nahmen sie erstaunlich viel Raum ein, wie bei einem nachtaktiven Tier, das es gewohnt war, in die Dunkelheit zu blicken. »Wer sind Sie?«, zischte er.

Alexander zog rasch seine Hand weg und tat, als wollte er das Laken zurechtzupfen, das sich an den Ecken gelöst hatte. Aus der nackten, fleckigen Matratze lösten sich Schaumstoffflocken. »Ich bin Alexander Kimowitsch«, sagte er. »Ich bin ein Freund von Iwan. War ein Freund von Iwan.«

»Gehörst du zu Nikolai Sergejewitsch?«

»Nikolai ist nicht hier.«

»Nein.« Mischa richtete sich auf und stützte sich auf die Ellbogen. Durch seine Haut war zu sehen, wie sich Elle und Speiche teilten. Sein Brustbein stand vor wie ein drittes, abwärts gerichtetes Schlüsselbein. »Ich will wissen, ob du zu diesem *Abschaum* gehörst.«

»Wir kennen uns jedenfalls. Wir haben uns im Saigon getroffen und bei Stalins Hundertjahrfeier.« Mischa blinzelte nur mit seinen riesenhaften, vorwurfsvoll glänzenden Fledermausaugen.

»Ich weiß nicht, was du meinst«, sagte Alexander schließlich.

»Ich erinnere mich, wer du bist.« Mischa schloss die Augen. Alexander fühlte sich viel wohler in seiner Gegenwart, wenn er die

Augen geschlossen hatte. »Du bist ziemlich unscheinbar. Aber Iwan hat dir vertraut. Das hat er gesagt, als er mich bei meiner Mutter besucht hat. Ich persönlich verstehe nicht, warum. Du kommst mir nicht gerade helle vor.«

»Ich bin jedenfalls nicht an einem Gitterbett festgebunden«, sagte Alexander. Er hörte auf, das Laken zu richten, und ließ eine Ecke lose liegen. Er wünschte sich, dass Mischa nachts dorthin rollen und die kalte Matratze fühlen würde.

»Aber Iwan hat dir vertraut«, sagte Mischa. »Also komm her.«

»Wohin?«

»Komm dichter ran.«

»Nur, wenn es sein muss.« Mischa roch nach Formaldehyd und Zitronenreiniger.

Als Mischa die Augen wieder öffnete, sah Alexander die Schlängellinien der Kapillaren auf seinen Augäpfeln. Er sah das leichte Pochen seines Pulsschlags am Handgelenk. »Alexander«, sagte Mischa beinahe unhörbar. »Es war Nikolai.«

»Was?«, fragte Alexander, doch in seinem Hinterkopf hatte sich bereits etwas ratternd in Bewegung gesetzt. Es war ein Gefühl, das er vom Schach her kannte – wenn er wusste, was er als Nächstes tun würde, ohne noch zu verstehen, warum.

»Er war hinter uns. Er hat das Signal gegeben.« Mischas Stimme war beinahe ein Nichts, wie das Geräusch eines Schädels, der im Schnee versinkt.

»Wie denn? Was für ein Signal?« Alexander bewegte kaum die Lippen.

Mischas Augen sahen aus wie schief im Kopf befestigte Klumpen feuchten, blinden Vulkangesteins. Er hielt sie fest auf Alexander gerichtet. Dann ruckte er mit dem Kopf.

»So«, sagte Mischa. »So hat er gemacht.«

»Aber wenn du es gesehen hast«, sagte Alexander so ruhig wie möglich, »warum hast du dann nicht geschrien?«

»Ich wusste ja erst danach, dass es ein Signal gewesen war. Er hat mit dem Kopf geruckt. Ich habe es gesehen.«

»Okay«, sagte Alexander. »Okay.« Er blinzelte. Er sah Iwan und Nikolai über den Litauer streiten. Er blinzelte und sah Nikolais Lederjacke. Er blinzelte und sah Nikolai gestern Nacht, keuchend, mit blutigen Socken. Er blinzelte und sah Nikolai Notizen machen.

»Und was soll ich jetzt tun?«, flüsterte Alexander.

Mischa starrte ihn verächtlich an. »Das musst du mich nicht fragen. Ich schätze, für eure kleinen Ratgeberheftchen war es das wohl. Du hast jetzt ganz andere Probleme, Towarischtsch. Du solltest wohl besser den Ball flach halten.«

»Und du, was machst du?«

»Ich?«, schnaubte Mischa. »Ich müsste eigentlich tot sein, wie man sieht. Vielleicht sollte ich den Kreml in die Luft jagen. Oder ich könnte Breschnew kaltstellen. Hört ihr?« Er schrie jetzt. »Ich werde Breschnew die Lampe ausknipsen! Das wird ein Riesenspaß! Sie werden mich kriegen, aber erst, wenn ich Lenins Leiche geschändet habe! Scheiß auf euch! Scheiß auf euch alle! Hört ihr mich?« Alexander lauschte und hörte das Rascheln und Murmeln einer ganzen Phalanx von Schwestern, die mit Betäubungsmitteln bewaffnet den Flur entlangmarschierten.

»Wenn du so weitermachst, landest du in der Matrosskaja Tischina«, sagte Alexander, »weißt du das nicht?«

»Mach dir keinen Kopf«, sagte Mischa. »Aber versuch, weniger idiotisch zu sein. Denk immer an Nikolai.« Dann brüllte er wieder, warf sich hin und her, kippte eine Wasserflasche um und stieß obszöne Flüche aus. Die herablassende rothaarige Schwester von der Rezeption kam herein und verpasste ihm eine Injektion in den Nacken. Mischas Augen blieben auf der Stelle stehen, und seine welken Hände sanken auf das Laken zurück.

»Vielleicht haben die Medikamente ihm zugesetzt«, sagte Alexander.

Die Schwester verzog den Mund und sah Alexander ein klein wenig länger in die Augen, als er es gewohnt war.

»Ja«, sagte sie. »Vielleicht.«

Als Erstes brach Alexander in Iwans Wohnung ein. Das war nicht weiter schwer: Er schob seinen Ausweis zwischen Schloss und Rahmen, und die Tür sprang auf. Die Katze lauerte zitternd und sprungbereit auf den ungebetenen Besucher und stürzte sich mit mörderischer Wut auf seine Beine. Er hatte nicht daran gedacht, ihr irgendetwas mitzubringen, also fischte er ein paar fusselige Brotkrumen aus der Hosentasche und hoffte, dass es ihr nicht auffiel. Er zog an der Schnur für das Deckenlicht.

Die Wohnung war noch nie ordentlich gewesen, doch jetzt lag alles in Trümmern. Die Matratze war umgedreht worden. Aus den aufgerissenen Schubladen der Kommode quollen Anziehsachen hervor. Der Boden war dick mit Papieren bedeckt, die sich an Alexanders Knöcheln verfingen, als er den Raum durchquerte. Das Poster von Brigitte Bardot fehlte.

Okay, dachte Alexander. Verstehe.

Er entdeckte Notizen für die nächste Ausgabe und zog sie zwischen Staubmäusen, Münzgeld und einer undefinierbaren klebrigen Substanz unter dem Sofa hervor. Die alte Leica lag ausgeweidet, ihr Innenleben dem Licht preisgegeben, auf dem Wohnzimmertisch. Unter Iwans bestem Hemd fand Alexander ein paar Fotografien – eine Frau, einen kleinen Jungen, ein älteres Ehepaar –, auf denen er jedoch niemanden erkannte. Er dachte wieder an Iwans Worte über die Bedeutung des Verlusts und fragte sich, ob er einen dieser Menschen verloren hatte. Ihm fiel auf, dass Iwan nie von etwas anderem gesprochen hatte als der letzten oder nächsten Ausgabe, der Verkommenheit der Regierung, Alexanders und Nikolais Idiotie, Mischas Leiden oder den Bedürfnissen seiner Katze. Alexander ließ seine Erinnerungen noch einmal Revue passieren, doch da war nichts weiter – keine Kindheit, keine Liebschaften oder persönlichen Katastrophen. Keine Erklärungen für sein einsames Leben. Keine Schlüsselerlebnisse, die ihn dazu getrieben hatten, wieder und wieder sein Leben zu riskieren und ein System in Frage zu stellen, das, realistisch betrachtet, bis ans Ende aller Tage fortbestehen würde. Denn mehr hatten sie letztlich nicht getan, als Fragen gestellt. Sie waren, wenn es hoch kam, ein Ärgernis gewesen, wie ein Affe, der einen Elefanten reizt, der ihn jederzeit schnappen und unter seinen Füßen zermalmen kann. Für den Elefanten ist nur die Frage, wann. Er muss sich nur überwinden, die Energie aufzubringen.

Es konnte durchaus sein, dass Mischa recht hatte.

Sonst gab es in Iwans Wohnung nicht mehr viel zu finden. Der KGB hatte mehr mitgenommen, als sie je würden verwerten können. Selbst schmutzige Socken und alte Kaufbelege schienen verschwunden zu sein. Einiges von dem umherliegenden Kleingeld fehlte. Natürlich fehlten die Schreibmaschine und das Kohlepapier. Die auffälligste Leerstelle hinterließen die unzähligen Bücher.

Die Katze wimmerte, und Alexander hob sie hoch. Er fühlte das Surren in ihrem Rippenkasten und fragte sich, welcher Mechanismus sie so beharrlich am Laufen hielt.

»Dann gehörst du jetzt mir, wie?«, sagte Alexander.

Natascha biss ihm in den Daumen.

Er lieh sich eine Schreibmaschine von einem der akademischen Abonnenten. Er besorgte neues Kohlepapier. Er tippte vier Tage lang, bis seine Daumen und Ellbogen schmerzten. Alexander war gut darin, stillzusitzen und repetitive Bewegungen auszuführen, das, immerhin, hatte ihn das Schachspiel gelehrt. Im Morgengrauen, als seine letzte Kerze zu einer wächsernen Pfütze zerfloss, heftete er die Seiten zusammen und ließ Natascha mit ein paar getrockneten Pilzen auf dem Fußboden zurück.

Er fuhr allein mit dem Zug nach Moskau. Alle Abteile waren voll, und er stand im Gang und sah dem Eisenbahner zu, der vor der Abfahrt die Räder auf Materialermüdung abklopfte. Alexander trug zwei Mäntel untereinander, und unter dem unteren Mantel trug er fünfundzwanzig Exemplare der letzten Ausgabe der *Kleinen Auswahl aussichtsloser Fälle*.

In der Moskauer Metro wimmelte es von Sicherheitsleuten. Fahrgäste starrten, die Mützen im Schoß, aus den Fenstern in die vorüberdröhnende Dunkelheit. Unter den Kronleuchtern der Metrostationen und den lichtgetränkten Wandnischen trugen alle Passagiere Schwarz.

Zwei Straßen vom Roten Platz entfernt konnte er die viel zu heiteren, festlichen Blechbläser hören. Er wusste, dass er nicht sehr viel näher herankommen würde. Finster dreinblickende Soldaten in grauen Mänteln mit roten Flaggen über den Schultern und im Takt hochgeworfenen Knien würden überall den Weg versperren. Alles strebte zum Kreml und zu Breschnews Sarg, der düster im Zentrum des Geschehens kauerte. Im Kreml selbst würden sich die Staatsoberhäupter versammeln, arabische Nationalisten in Kefiyas oder traditionell gekleidete afrikanische Diktatoren, sie würden die Köpfe senken und nachdenkliche, traurige Gesichter machen.

Außerhalb des Rings aus Soldaten standen die Trauergäste: Im innersten Kreis die ausgewählten und bezahlten, weiter außen echte Trauernde und neugierige Passanten und Familien, die wollten, dass ihre Kinder Zeugen der Geschichte wurden, und Leute, die einfach noch nicht nach Hause mochten. Manche sahen richtig glücklich aus – sie reichten eine Feldflasche mit Alkohol herum, und ein alter Mann spuckte jedes Mal aus, wenn Breschnews Name fiel. Eine Frau heulte ungehemmt, mit verzerrtem Gesicht, wischte sich die Tränen mit dem Ärmel ab, bis ihre Wangen wundgerieben waren, und wiederholte immer wieder: »Er war ein guter Mann, ein guter Mann. Was soll jetzt bloß werden?«

Wenn die Massen in Bewegung gerieten, konnte Alexander hin und wieder einen Blick auf das Geschehen erhaschen: die grau-rot gekleideten Soldaten, die Marschkapelle, den goldgeränderten, schwarzen Sarg, der aus der Entfernung aussah wie ein schwankender Ozeandampfer. So viel Prunk und Eleganz wirkte beinahe unterkühlt, als würde der Tote weniger betrauert als öffentlich vorgeführt.

Alexander spürte, wie die Papierlagen auf seiner Brust die Erschütterungen seines Herzschlags dämpften. Er wusste nicht, was er als Nächstes tun sollte. Iwan hätte nie so etwas Unüberlegtes angestellt – er war immer äußerst diskret vorgegangen, mit akribisch überarbeiteten Listen der ersten Empfänger. Von diesem inneren Zirkel aus verbreitete sich die Flugschrift selbständig weiter; manche Leser vervielfältigten sie zwei, fünf, sieben Mal und gaben sie an ihre engen Freunde weiter. So ließ sich das Risiko ein wenig streuen, hatte er immer gesagt. Doch Risiken einzugehen musste nicht tödlich sein. Und Risiken zu vermeiden konnte einen nicht vor allem bewahren.

Alexander trat ein wenig zurück, bis die Menschen vor seinen Augen zu einer brodelnden Masse dunkler Wintermäntel wurden, die wie ein einziger Organismus witternd Ausschau hielt. Der Wind frischte auf, klopfte mit eisigen Fingern seine Wirbelsäule ab und zerrte ungehörig an seinen Hosenbeinen. Rost- und sandfarbene Blätter fegten vorüber, gefolgt von Programmheften mit Fotos von Breschnew, auf denen er unter zusammengewachsenen Brauen streng den Betrachter fixiert. Zarte, fedrige Schneefahnen materialisierten sich aus dem Nichts und rasten in wilder Flucht die Straße entlang.

Alexander zog die Flugschriften hervor. Er wartete. Er konnte noch immer das blecherne Stampfen der Musik hören und das Dröhnen im Gleichschritt marschierender Füße auf dem Kopfsteinpflaster. Der Wind packte und schüttelte ihn wie ein rachsüchtiger arktischer Geist, und er fühlte, wie sich sein Griff um die Papiere lockerte. Die Flugschriften stoben in vier Himmelsrichtungen davon, sie wirbelten durch die Luft wie eine Wolkenformation. Es sah schön aus, wie sich der Wind in ihnen fing – als wären es schlanke weiße Vögel, vielleicht, oder zitternde Brautschleier. Er wusste, dass sie bald am Boden landen und verschmutzt, zerrissen, von schweren Stiefeln zertrampelt werden würden. Doch vielleicht gäbe es ein paar Neugierige, die sie aufhoben und lasen.

Alexander wandte sich zum Gehen. Seine zwei Mäntel blähten sich im Wind, und seine Lungen schmerzten von so viel frischer Luft. Es begann jene Kälte, die für russische Abendstunden so charakteristisch ist, die einschüchternd und bedrohlich wirkt, weil sie so viel schlimmer werden wird. Und dort, in einiger Entfernung an eine Laterne gelehnt, stand Nikolai.

Einzelne Schneeflocken sammelten sich zu kleinen Wirbeln und Wölkchen. Sie färbten Nikolais Haar weiß, erinnerte sich Alexander später, als wäre er gerade Zeuge einer übermenschlichen Katastrophe. Er starrte Alexander an, da war Alexander beinahe sicher. Er stand da und starrte, bis die Menge sich, von den schrillen Tönen der Nationalhymne getrieben, aufzulösen begann und er im dichter werdenden Schneegestöber und Menschengewimmel verschwand.

Alexander fand Nikolai nicht wieder. Doch als er erst einmal begonnen hatte, Ausschau zu halten, sah er ihn überall.

KAPITEL 10

Irina
St. Petersburg, 2006

Und dann war der Sommer vorüber, und ich wusste nicht, wo er geblieben war. Es hatte lustlose Spaziergänge durch die Stadt gegeben, respektvolle, schweigsame Besuche der lange verlassenen Wohnstätten großer Dichter, die begierige Lektüre lange aufgeschobener russischer Klassiker. Ich schrieb Bruchstücke sinnloser Gedichte auf die Rückseiten von Servietten. Ich gewöhnte mir an, Tee zu trinken. Ich übte, auf Russisch Aussagen darüber zu treffen, was in der Vergangenheit geschehen war und was in Zukunft geschehen würde, was geschehen könnte und geschehen sollte. Ich lernte deklinieren. Unterdessen verblassten und fielen die Blätter und ließen nackte Äste zurück, die sich schwarz im weißen Schnee verzweigten. Es wurde kalt, so kalt, dass ich verstand, wie wenig ich bisher von Kälte verstanden hatte – im flauen Bostoner Winter, den der Atlantik mildert und der unangenehm schroff ist, aber nie so hart, dass man nicht aufrecht gehen, sich umsehen und bewundern könnte, wie die Möwen sich schütteln und die schneebedeckten Bäume die Stadt verschönern.

Die Kälte jenes russischen Winters – sie war in ihrer Absolutheit, ihrer Beispiellosigkeit wie ein Schlag ins Gesicht. Es war eine astronomische, unirdische Kälte, eine furchteinflößende Kälte, die mich krümmte und unterwarf und mich leise vor mich hin fluchen machte. Aber sie hatte auch ihr Gutes. Es erweiterte meinen Horizont, festzustellen, dass es jenseits des gefühlten Nullpunkts weiterging. Dass es Realitäten gab, die außerhalb des Vorstellbaren lagen.

Die Newa verkrustete und verstummte. Dem Mond wuchsen im Nachtfrost drei Lichtkreise. Die Kommunikationsversuche Claires und meiner Mutter ließen nach und tröpfelten nur noch, wie die unstillbare Blutung nach einer Amputation. Sie gaben sie nie ganz auf – in meiner Mailbox fand ich, wenn ich mir die Mühe gab, im Internetcafé nachzusehen, immer flehentliche Briefe, Schimpftiraden oder Versuche, ganz normal zu klingen, als könnte mich vorgespiegelte Beiläufigkeit dazu verleiten, zurückzuschreiben –, doch ich antwortete ihnen nicht. Es war grausam. Ich wusste, dass ich sie quälte, doch ich hatte einfach nicht die Kraft, es nicht zu tun.

Mit der Zeit wurde ich immer passiver und unbeweglicher. Die Kälte hatte mich fest im Griff; ich spürte eine Erschöpfung bis ins Mark, eine beginnende Gebrechlichkeit. Ich war dankbar, dass sich mir die Chance geboten hatte, dem Rest der Welt abhandenzukommen. Und ich begann mich zu fragen, ob ich auch mir selbst abhandengekommen war.

Ich fing an, Jonathan Briefe zu schreiben – langatmige, wirre Briefe, die ich ohnehin nie abschicken würde. Ich schrieb von unseren Anfängen, davon, wie die Tage nach unseren Begegnungen immer wie Heroinentzug gewesen waren, über das zittrige, ausgelaugte Gefühl, wenn sämtliches Serotonin im Körper auf einen

Schlag verausgabt worden war. Ich schrieb, dass er in meinem Leben eine singuläre Erscheinung gewesen war. Ich schrieb, wenn er mir irgendetwas glauben sollte, dann das. Ich schrieb, er sei das allerunwahrscheinlichste Plotelement in meiner ohnehin wenig plausiblen Biographie. Ich schrieb, dass wir uns selbst kaum kannten; wie sollten wir dann einander je verstehen? Ich verbreitete mich über Biologie, über Paarbindung und Pheromone. Ich schrieb von Rilkes Konzept der Liebe als Grenze zweier großer Einsamkeiten. Ich erörterte das Subjekt-Objekt-Problem. Ich schrieb über den Mythos der romantischen Liebe, die mittelalterliche Verblendung, an der wir, sowohl als Nation als auch kulturell, noch immer festhielten. Ich schrieb über Scheidungsraten. Ich schrieb über die metastasierende Trauer meiner verwitweten Mutter. Ich schrieb über meine eigene zellulare, atavistische, viszerale Angst. Ich schrieb von Selbstmord und wie viele Huntington-Patienten Selbstmord begehen – meist dann, wenn ihre Motorik geschädigt ist und ihr Verstand noch nicht. Sie schleppen sich in ihr Auto, um sich mit Kohlenmonoxid zu vergiften; sie schießen sich in den Kopf, wenn ihr Zustand es erlaubt. Ihre Hände zittern, ihre Arme zucken. Manchmal brauchen sie Hilfe bei diesem letzten Akt der Unabhängigkeit. Ich schrieb, dass ich für eine tödliche Krankheit einfach nicht geschaffen war. Ich schrieb, ich hätte ihn sofort erkannt, als wir uns zum ersten Mal sahen, das sei keine nachträgliche Verklärung, ich hätte es sofort gewusst. Ich schrieb, dass das nicht möglich war. Ich schrieb, er sei der schönste Mensch, der mir je begegnet sei. Ich schrieb, das läge an evolutionär verkabelten Neuronenverbindungen in meinem Gehirn, meinem funktionstüchtigen Gehirn. Ich schrieb, es täte mir leid. Ich schrieb, den freien Willen gäbe es nicht. Ich schrieb, dass ich ihn liebte. Ich schrieb, die Liebe gäbe es nicht.

Ich durchstreifte die Stadt – durchquerte die gewaltige Leere des Palastplatzes, schlenderte an dem weidengrünen Winterpalast entlang und weiter, bis die Kuppel der Isaakskathedrale vor mir aus dem Nebel ragte. Ich besuchte die Bluterlöserkirche mit ihren bezaubernd schizophrenen Zwiebelkuppeln. Ich folgte den Kanälen und zählte die pastellfarbenen Häuser. Die Kasaner Kathedrale schimmerte wie Manganerz im späten Novemberlicht. Ich sah halbwüchsige Mädchen Hand in Hand mit ihren Müttern durch die Straßen spazieren. Ich sah einen Passanten, wie er sich herabbeugte und tatsächlich der Bettlerin in der Metrostation etwas Kleingeld gab.

Ich stellte Recherchen zu Besetow an. Wie es aussah, diente sein Parteibündnis, Alternatives Russland, als Dachorganisation mehrerer Untergruppen, unter anderem Pomerancowo und Wahres Russland. Pomerancowo schien eine typische liberale Partei zu sein – pro-westlich, demokratisch, reformatorisch, für den Freihandel, für Bürgerrechte, gegen Korruption. Mit dem Wahren Russland war es komplizierter – die Partei war reaktionär und oppositionell, mit dem Status quo unzufrieden, aber voller vager, eher beunruhigender Alternativkonzepte. Sie mobilisierten Unzufriedene aus allen möglichen Lagern, bedienten Fremdenhass und Nationalismus und machten sich die Ressentiments gegen Wanderarbeiter aus Mittelasien ebenso zunutze wie die Abneigung gegen das Regime. Mir war nicht ganz klar, warum das Alternative Russland das Wahre Russland zu seinen Verbündeten zählte, doch einmal stieß ich auf ein YouTube-Video, auf dem Besetow einem Interviewer genau diese Frage beantwortete – er murmelte irgendetwas von den Vorzügen einer breiten, vielseitigen Koalition. Der Vorsitzende des Wahren Russland war ein Mann namens Michail Andrejewitsch Solowjow. Die Parteizentrale lag in der Konjuschennaja Uliza, einen Block von der Moika entfernt, die ich jeden Tag besuchte, um Münzen hineinzuwerfen.

Ich überlegte, ob ich ihm einen Besuch abstatten sollte. Ich ging an der Zentrale vorbei und ging noch einmal vorbei, trat näher und sah mir die Türklingel an, nur um sicherzugehen, dass sie eine hatten. Ich schlenderte die Fenster entlang, verlangsamte meinen Schritt und sah hinein – um was zu sehen? Alexander Besetow vielleicht, der zu einer Art Bündnistreffen gekommen war und gerade aus dem Fenster blickte und nur darauf wartete, von einer planlosen Amerikanerin belästigt zu werden? Ich sah ein paar schlechtgelaunte junge Menschen im Schein ihrer Computerbildschirme hocken. Alexander Besetow sah ich nicht. Und Michail Andrejewitsch Solowjow ebenso wenig.

Eines Tages tat ich es doch. Ich hatte keinen besonderen Entschluss gefasst; ich drückte mich wie üblich vor den Fenstern herum und spähte hinein, doch dann packte mich ein Anflug von Selbstekel, und ich marschierte geradewegs zur Tür. Ich klingelte und tat rasch ein paar Schritte rückwärts, als könnte der Abstand mich vor eventuell bevorstehenden Abwehrreaktionen bewahren.

Die Tür öffnete sich. Ein gelblich-blasser Mann starrte mir entgegen. Mit seinem Gesicht stimmte irgendetwas nicht, wenn ich auch nicht hätte sagen können, was – vielleicht waren die Winkel oder Proportionen kaum wahrnehmbar verschoben.

»Guten Tag«, sagte ich.

»Guten Tag.« Das Weiße in seinen Augen war blutrot entzündet. Ich fragte mich, warum sie ausgerechnet ihn zur Tür gehen ließen.

»Ist dies das Büro des Wahren Russland?«

Er ruckte ungeduldig mit dem Kopf zum Türschild.

»Könnte ich Michail Andrejewitsch Solowjow sprechen?«

Er trat zur Seite und bedeutete mir einzutreten. Die Büroräume waren feuchtkalt und bis unter die Decke mit Papieren und Krimskrams vollgestopft. Zwei junge Männer tippten lustlos auf riesigen, veralteten Computern herum. Die Rechner surrten und schnarrten bedrohlich; sie schienen kurz davor, endgültig den Geist aufzugeben. Ein Telefon klingelte einsam vor sich hin, doch niemand nahm ab.

Der Mann, der mich hereingelassen hatte, führte mich in ein Hinterzimmer. Er knipste das Licht an. Ein Mülleimer lag umgekippt auf dem Boden, und er beugte sich herab, um ihn aufzurichten. Dabei rutschte sein Hemd hoch, und ein Stück bleichen Fleisches mit spinnenbeinig schwarzen Haaren kam zum Vorschein. Ich verzog das Gesicht. Er rückte einen Drehstuhl zurecht. »Bitte«, sagte er. »Setzen Sie sich.«

Ich setzte mich. Aus der Nähe fiel mir eine silbrige, sichelförmige Narbe von einem Auge bis zum Wangenknochen auf. Eine merkwürdige Narbe; es war schwer zu sagen, was sie verursacht haben könnte, auch wenn mir ein Feuergefecht am wahrscheinlichsten schien. An der Wand hinter ihm forderte ein ramponiertes Wahlplakat: *Russland den Russen!*

»Soll ich hier auf Michail Andrejewitsch Solowjow warten?«

»Ich bin Michail Andrejewitsch Solowjow«, sagte er. »Sie können mich Mischa nennen.«

»Ach so?«, sagte ich. »Ach, natürlich.«

Er starrte mir mit einem unbeweglichen, unangenehmen Blick direkt in die Augen. Ich rutschte auf meinem Stuhl hin und her. Seine Narbe beschäftigte mich immer noch. Vielleicht war er Soldat gewesen; bei meiner Google-Suche war jedoch nichts dergleichen herausgekommen.

»Und jetzt wäre es vielleicht angebracht, mir zu sagen, wer Sie sind«, sagte er.

Seine Hose war zu kurz. Als er sich zurücklehnte, blitzte ein haariger, weißer Unterschenkel hervor. Ich beschloss, ihm erst einmal die Kurzantwort zu geben.

»Ich heiße Irina Ellison«, sagte ich. »Ich möchte mich mit Alexander Besetow treffen. In Moskau habe ich mich mit einer alten Bekannten von ihm unterhalten, die mir empfohlen hat, es über seine Kollegen zu versuchen.« Ich hätte gern hinzugefügt, dass ich hoffte, nicht zu stören, wenn es nicht so offensichtlich gewesen wäre, dass ich genau das tat.

»Mit wem genau haben Sie gesprochen?«

»Elisabeta Nasarowna. Sie war seine Sekretärin, glaube ich.«

Michail Andrejewitsch – ich hatte Schwierigkeiten, ihn mir als Mischa vorzustellen – schnaubte. »Seine Sekretärin? So nennt man das heutzutage?«

Ich beschloss, diese Bemerkung zu ignorieren. Ich starrte auf das Plakat über Michails Kopf. »Sie und Alexander Besetow sind doch Kollegen?«

»Ja, sind wir.« Er richtete sich auf, und sein spöttisches Gesicht glättete sich ein wenig. »Das kann man so sagen.«

»Heißt das, Sie könnten mir helfen, ein Treffen zu arrangieren?«

»Ein Treffen. Tja.« Er hustete. »Das dürfte schwierig werden.«

»Nur ein kurzes.«

Michail Andrejewitsch lehnte sich zurück. Er kaute einige endlose Sekunden an seiner Unterlippe herum und sah mich neugierig an – wahrscheinlich, um zu entscheiden, wie viel Zeit er mit mir verschwenden sollte. »Besetow ist ein Waschlappen«, erklärte er schließlich.

Damit hatte ich nicht gerechnet. »Ich dachte, Sie seien Kollegen.«

»Das heißt nicht, dass er kein Waschlappen sein kann. Ich habe noch nie jemanden gesehen, der dermaßen treudoof an seinem Leben hängt.«

Ich blinzelte. »Ist das der Grund, warum Sie mir kein Gespräch vermitteln können?«

Er feixte wieder, was in der Narbe unter seinem Auge einen Knick verursachte. »Er umgibt sich mit einer Horde Gorillas. Und er geht nie ohne Ganzkörperrüstung aus dem Haus.«

Ich stellte mir eine kugelsichere Weste vor. Und ein Kettenhemd. »Na ja«, sagte ich, »braucht er das nicht?«

Michail Andrejewitsch schnaubte. »Tja, was man nicht alles braucht. Aber nicht jeder bekommt es auch.«

Ich fühlte mich auf einmal hundeelend. Dieses Gespräch lief in die völlig falsche Richtung; es waren irgendwelche unterschwelligen Aggressionen am Werk, die ich nicht orten konnte. Ich hatte gedacht, Besetow würde von allen verehrt, wie mein Vater ihn verehrt hatte. Das war meine entscheidende Prämisse gewesen, meine einzige. Ich rutschte unbehaglich hin und her. »Also ist das Wahre Russland kein Bündnispartner des Alternativen Russland?«, fragte ich.

»Oh, doch. Wir sind einander sehr verbunden. Aber sie mögen

uns nicht. Wir sind das uneheliche Stiefkind der Familie. Sie halten sich lieber auf Distanz. Wir passen nicht dazu. Pomerancowo ist ihnen viel lieber, wissen Sie. Butterweiche, westfinanzierte Idealisten. Idioten.«

Ich beschloss, nicht überrascht zu sein, dass er mir all das erzählte. »Und wie ist Ihre Position?«, fragte ich, obwohl mir die Plakate den einen oder anderen Hinweis darauf gaben. »Haben Sie … politische Differenzen?«

»Wir haben ästhetische Differenzen.«

»Ist das nicht ziemlich oberflächlich?« Inzwischen war ich felsenfest davon überzeugt, dass es das einzig Richtige war, mich weiter durch dieses Gespräch zu bluffen.

»Oder sagen wir, spirituelle Differenzen.«

Ich schnaubte, bloß so, um des Schnaubens willen. Michail Andrejewitsch seufzte vernichtend. »Wir denken, dass Veränderungen authentisch und dauerhaft sein müssen. Sie müssen von innen heraus kommen. Deshalb sind wir Populisten. Besetow ist der hinterletzte Elitarist.«

»Ach ja?« Meine Laune besserte sich ein wenig. Elitarismus gefiel mir immerhin besser als Feigheit.

»Absolut. Er mag das russische Volk nicht einmal. Nicht mal für Geld würde er sich mit denen unterhalten. Er sitzt nur da in seiner Festung und schreibt Presseerklärungen und weiß nichts über das Land, das er regieren will.«

»Meinen Sie nicht, dass er einfach nur versucht, am Leben zu bleiben?«

»Meinetwegen. Jeder Idiot kann überleben. Jede verdammte Amöbe kann das. Das nennt man Evolution. Aber was man daraus macht, wenn man erst einmal überlebt hat – darauf kommt es an.«

Das gab mir zu denken. Es klang so einfach, wie er es sagte.

Plötzlich lehnte er sich entschlossen in seinem Stuhl zurück. »Wissen Sie«, sagte er. »Ich bin kein bisschen überrascht, dass Sie hier sind.«

»Sie sind … was?« Ich war ziemlich überrascht, hier zu sein.

»Ich habe es mir von Anfang an gedacht. Die Amerikaner haben alle Fäden in der Hand. Er hat keine einzige eigene Idee im Kopf.«

»Wovon reden Sie überhaupt?«

Er wedelte entnervt mit der Hand. »Verstehe, verstehe. Sie brauchen natürlich Diskretion. Na klar.«

»Ich habe nicht die geringste Ahnung, wovon Sie reden.«

»O nein. Nein. Ich auch nicht.« Er sah mich wissend an und lächelte beinahe freundlich. »Also sind Sie … ein Fan von ihm? Ist das die offizielle Version?«

»So ungefähr.«

»Natürlich«, sagte er. »Natürlich. Wir sind alle große Fans von Besetow. Und was genau möchten Sie mit ihm besprechen?«

Ich erklärte es ihm oder versuchte es zumindest. Allmählich wurde ich ein bisschen besser darin. Er hörte zu. Sein Gesicht wurde, falls das überhaupt möglich war, noch gelblicher und fahler. »Im Ernst?«, fragte er schließlich.

»Ja.«

»Wirklich?«

Ich starrte ihn an. Er kniff die Augen zusammen. »Das klingt eher, als bräuchten Sie einen Therapeuten.«

Ich zuckte zurück. »Nein.«

»Oder einen Priester.«

»Noch schlimmer.«

»Dann hat er symbolischen Wert für Sie.«

»Auch, äh, auch tatsächlichen Wert.«

»Glauben Sie, er könnte Ihnen irgendetwas erzählen, was Sie nicht schon wüssten?«

»Jeder könnte mir irgendetwas erzählen, was ich nicht weiß.«

»Auch das, was Sie hören wollen?«

Ich war erschöpft. Ein dumpf glimmender Schmerz nistete hinter meinen Augen. »Keine Ahnung. Ich weiß es nicht. Vielleicht nicht.« Zur Untermalung hüstelte ich schwach in meine Schulter.

Michail Andrejewitsch kaute wieder an seiner Lippe, die sehr mitgenommen aussah. Es stand ihm gar nicht gut. »Was wissen Sie von ihm?«

»Er ist … na ja, er ist Schachgroßmeister.«

»Ja. Sehr gut.«

»Und er ist Präsidentschaftskandidat.« Ich kam mir vor wie ein Kind.

»Sie wissen aber, dass seine Kampagne ein reiner PR-Gag ist, ja? Sie wissen, dass er weiß, dass er nicht gewinnen kann.«

Der Mann war frustriert, das war offensichtlich – also war die merkwürdige, scharfkantige Abwehrhaltung, die ich einzunehmen begann, vollkommen ungerechtfertigt. Besetow war moralisch unangreifbar. Ich bemühte mich, leichthin und unvoreingenommen zu klingen, als ginge es um politische oder philosophische Sachfragen, nicht um brutale persönliche Angriffe. Wie ich es einmal geliebt hatte, solche Diskussionen zu führen!

»Klar weiß er, dass er nicht gewinnen wird«, sagte ich, »aber das ist ja gerade das Eindrucksvolle, Mutige daran. Genau darum geht es.«

»Ach ja? Da wäre ich mir nicht so sicher.«

»Worum geht es denn sonst?«

»Es geht nicht darum, ob man eine schnelle oder langsame Revolution anstrebt, sondern ob sie wirken oder verpuffen soll. Besetow zieht die ganze Aufmerksamkeit, das Geld und die Unterstützung von pragmatischeren Leuten ab – Leuten, die eine ernsthafte Chance hätten, gewählt zu werden, und die das Land von innen heraus reformieren könnten. Besetow steht wegen seiner Scheiß-Schachkarriere immer im Mittelpunkt, und alle sagen, oh, wie aufregend! Wie beeindruckend! Geniale Schachzüge im nationalen Maßstab, das ist nun mal eine tolle Geschichte. Ich werde nie begreifen, wie die Öffentlichkeit auf diesen Mann reagiert. Es ist unglaublich. Egal, was er tut, die gesamte westliche Welt kriegt einen Ständer. Aber was ist für Russland am besten? Wenn es bloß wegen der Eitelkeit eines alternden Brettspielers wieder seine Chancen verpasst? Oder wenn es ernsthafte Männer wählt, die mit

Zähnen und Klauen und Kompromissen den Weg in ein humaneres Leben frei machen? Was ist mutiger?«

Meine Abwehrhaltung wich einem viel kleineren, traurigeren Gefühl. Alexander Besetow war jemand, der meinem Vater etwas bedeutet hatte. Ich wollte nicht, dass jemand ihn verunglimpfte. Meine Mission war bestenfalls absurd, so viel wusste ich schon. Selbst wenn Alexander Besetow ein Held war, ein Heiliger, war mein Vorhaben mehr als fragwürdig. Ich wollte es wirklich nicht wissen, wenn Alexanders Kollegen Beschwerden über ihn hatten oder unzufrieden mit ihm waren. Seine Aufgabe war nur, mir seine Lebensweisheiten zu übermitteln. Wenn er das nicht konnte, hatte ich keinen Grund mehr, hier zu sein. Und ich hatte keinen Grund, anderswo zu sein. Ich schwieg und sah mir Michail Andrejewitschs Plakate an.

»Aber, ich meine … Ich sehe hier Ihre Plakate und habe, wenn Sie erlauben, Ihren Wikipedia-Eintrag gelesen, und …«

»Und?«

»Und Sie sind selbst nicht gerade gemäßigt, oder?«

Er lachte. »Ich bin überhaupt nichts mehr.«

»Wie meinen Sie das?«

»Ich glaube an gar nichts. Ich versuche nur, ein interessantes Gespräch in Gang zu halten.«

»Ist das so erstrebenswert? Das Gespräch in Gang zu halten?« Ich hatte gar nichts gegen diese Vorstellung. Ich stellte nur reflektierende Fragen, weil ich beschlossen hatte, ihn nicht zu mögen.

»Wenn es siebzig Jahre lang überhaupt kein Gespräch gegeben hat, ist das sogar sehr erstrebenswert, würde ich sagen.«

Wir schwiegen beide. Ich fror und rieb meine Hände aneinander, um die Durchblutung anzuregen.

»Wissen Sie von dem Film, an dem er arbeitet?«, fragte Michail Andrejewitsch nach einer Weile.

»Natürlich.« Ich stockte. »Welchem noch mal?«

»Er versucht nachzuweisen, dass die Regierung in die Sprengstoffanschläge von 99 verwickelt war.«

Das klang vertraut. Ich erinnerte mich vage an Texte über den Beginn des zweiten Tschetschenienkriegs: eine Reihe merkwürdiger Zufälle, die oberflächlich betrachtet ein wenig zwielichtig aussahen. Doch ich war bis dahin immer der Meinung gewesen, solche Spekulationen seien dieselbe Mixtur aus Halbwissen und Paranoia, die meine schrilleren liberalen Kommilitonen in Cambridge dazu verleitet hatte, obskure Andeutungen über George W. Bush und den 11. September zu machen.

»Dann stellt er die These auf, dass es ein politisches Manöver war?«, fragte ich.

»Um Putin an die Macht zu bringen, ja. Putin hat sich von Anfang an als starker Mann positioniert.«

»Glauben Sie, es ist wahr?«

»Ich weiß es nicht. Aber ich hoffe, dass es wahr ist. Das könnte himmelschreiend genug sein, um wirklich etwas zu bewegen.«

»Um ein interessantes Gespräch in Gang zu halten.«

»Genau.«

Er stützte das Kinn auf seine Hand – eine merkwürdig gezierte, feminine Geste, die ihn in Geständnislaune zu versetzen schien. »Um ganz ehrlich zu sein«, sagte er, »bin ich von der Idee mit dem Film ziemlich beeindruckt.«

»Ja?«

»Ja. Und ich bin nicht von allem beeindruckt, was Besetow tut.«

»Das sehe ich.«

»Aber das hier, das könnte Wellen schlagen.«

»Und was haben Sie mit dem Film zu tun?«

Er hüstelte. »Das ist … tja. Das ist genau das Problem. Es ist schwer zu sagen.«

Ich lehnte mich zurück. »Dann hat man Sie nicht mit einbezogen?«

»Das hat mit einbeziehen nichts zu tun. Das Ganze ist ein riesiger Apparat mit vielen Hilfsstrukturen, vielen verschiedenen Aufgaben und Rollen. Sehr bürokratisch.«

»Verstehe.«

»Das Wahre Russland ist also nicht direkt beteiligt, aber wir sind an der Bewegung beteiligt, also im weiteren Sinne vielleicht auch an dem Film, wissen Sie?«

»So wie jeder irgendwie an allem beteiligt ist?«

»Jetzt werden Sie spitzfindig.«

»Würden Sie sich wünschen, mehr mit dem Film zu tun zu haben?«

Er lächelte unmerklich. »Wie schon gesagt – nicht jeder bekommt immer das, was er sich wünscht.«

Es war interessant, gleich beim ersten Kontakt auf ein Zerwürfnis im Bündnis gestoßen zu sein – wie wenn man eine Wiese betritt und gleich in ein Erdloch stolpert. Natürlich hätte ich damit rechnen sollen, Kleingeisterei und Flügelkämpfen, Ressentiments und Reaktionären zu begegnen. Natürlich hätte ich mit Splittergruppen rechnen sollen. Ich hätte nicht sagen können, mit was ich stattdessen gerechnet hatte, und je klarer mir das wurde, desto klarer wurde mir, dass ich mir generell nicht besonders viele Gedanken gemacht hatte.

Also lehnte ich mich nach vorn. Ich wusste – bestimmt wusste ich es –, dass es den Mann verärgern würde.

»Erzählen Sie mir von Alexander in den achtziger Jahren«, sagte ich. »Er hat damals eine Samisdat-Zeitschrift herausgegeben, oder?«

Michail schnaubte wieder. Ich begann mich zu fragen, ob es eine Art Markenzeichen von ihm war. »›Herausgegeben‹ wäre wohl zu viel gesagt. Er war daran beteiligt. Das muss man ihm lassen. Beteiligt war er schon.«

»Er hat die Zeitschrift selbst ausgeliefert, nicht?« Das war allgemein bekannt; ich war trotz meiner halbherzigen Recherche gleich darüber gestolpert. »Das muss gefährlich gewesen sein.«

»Gefährlich. Ja. Sicher. Er hätte Opfer eines Attentats werden können oder so.«

Seine Worte schienen irgendeinen Subtext zu haben, trotzdem sagte ich: »Also.«

Ich merkte sofort, dass ich ihn an den Rand eines Herzinfarks getrieben hatte. Er atmete bemüht langsam; man konnte ihn förmlich im Kopf bis *desjat* zählen hören. Er lehnte sich zurück. »Lassen Sie mich etwas fragen. Das hier ist für mich eine gute Gelegenheit, herauszufinden, wie Besetow allgemein wahrgenommen wird.«

»Von außerhalb, meinen Sie?«

»Ja, von außerhalb«, sagte er.

»Tja, ich weiß nicht.« Ich dachte nach. Ich versuchte zusammenzufassen, was mein Vater von Besetow dachte, was ich dachte, was CNN über ihn verbreitete und was die Welt im Allgemeinen von ihm hielt. »Ich würde sagen, man denkt über ihn, dass er viel für die Widerstandsbewegung getan hat …«

»Was getan hat?«

»Na ja, das mit der Zeitschrift eben.«

»Und was wäre das?«

Ich fand, dieser Punkt sei schon geklärt, und ignorierte seine Frage. »… und dass er trotz aller Rückschläge …«

»Rückschläge? Welche Rückschläge?«

»In seiner Karriere«, erklärte ich lahm.

»Tja«, sagte Michail. »Im Endeffekt scheint es ihm aber nicht sehr geschadet zu haben, wie?«

»Nein, wahrscheinlich nicht.«

Er fuhr sich mit der Zunge über die ramponierte Unterlippe. »Also wird er allgemein als Held angesehen?«

»So ziemlich.« Ich wand mich auf meinem Stuhl. »Jedenfalls soweit er überhaupt wahrgenommen wird.«

Michail lehnte sich wieder zurück. »Das hätte ich mir denken können.«

»Falls es Sie tröstet, kann ich sagen, dass der Westen sich gar nicht so sehr dafür interessiert. Insgesamt, meine ich.«

»Verstehe.«

»Wo waren Sie damals?«

»In einem psychiatrischen Gefängnis. Weil ich Behauptungen

verbreitet hatte, die nicht offiziell als Wahrheiten anerkannt waren.«

»Oh.« Allmählich begann ich zu begreifen.

Michail stand abrupt auf, wobei er fast den Mülleimer wieder umgestoßen hätte. »Mehr kann ich nicht für Sie tun, fürchte ich«, sagte er und ging zu seinem Computer, auf dem er ausschließlich mit den Zeigefingern tippte. »Das hier sind die Kontaktdaten seines Sprechers, des PR-Menschen. Er kümmert sich um sämtliche Anfragen.« Er schrieb einen Namen – Viktor Dawidenko – und eine Handynummer vom Bildschirm ab und reichte mir den Zettel.

Ich starrte darauf. »Ist das alles? Ich meine, das ist der Mann, an den sich jeder andere auch wenden würde, oder?«

»Und Sie sind nicht jeder andere?«

»Doch, ich dachte nur …« Ich verstummte und stand auf. Ich wusste selbst nicht, was ich gedacht hatte.

»Hören Sie. Sie haben zwei Möglichkeiten. Entweder können Sie ihn anrufen, ein Treffen ausmachen und sehen, ob er Ihnen weiterhilft, was er wahrscheinlich nicht tun wird. Oder …« Er musterte mich. »Oder Sie legen Make-up auf, kämmen sich die Haare, flattern an jedem beliebigen Nachmittag ab halb sechs in der Prawda-Bar vorbei und sehen, ob er Ihnen *dann* weiterhilft. Er ist jeden Tag da. Ich persönlich würde Ihnen die zweite Variante empfehlen. Wenn Sie es über sich bringen, sich die Haare zu kämmen. Aber entscheiden Sie selbst.«

Michail Andrejewitsch begleitete mich zur Tür, an den jungen Männern vorüber, die erschrocken aufblickten und dann weiter auf den Tastaturen klapperten. Vor der Tür war es lächerlich kalt in der jämmerlich frühen Dämmerung. Michail sah mich aus zusammengekniffenen Augen an. »Und wenn Sie es tatsächlich schaffen, zu Besetow durchzukommen«, sagte er, »sagen Sie ihm, er soll mich anrufen, okay? Ich muss noch das eine oder andere mit ihm besprechen.«

Ich lief den Newski-Prospekt hinunter, vom Flussufer weg. Die Begegnung mit Michail Andrejewitsch hatte mich verbittert und verunsichert zurückgelassen. Und wütend – ich platzte fast vor narzisstischem Verlangen, dass die Welt sich meinen Bedürfnissen beugte, und kindischer Empörung, weil sie es nicht tat. Ein Gefühl der Ruhelosigkeit trieb mich um, ein Gefühl, als könnte ich die ganze Nacht über rennen oder mit bloßen Händen Scheiben einschlagen oder mich im Nachtfrost nackt ausziehen und überleben. Ich wusste sehr wohl, dass es nicht darum ging, ob Alexander der war, für den ich ihn hielt oder für den mein Vater ihn gehalten hatte. Er musste für Russland Gutes tun und für das Volk, dem er angehörte, nicht für einen senilen Musiklehrer, der seit sechs Monaten unter der Erde lag. Es sprach von einem absurden Anspruchsdenken – einem absurd amerikanischen Anspruchsdenken –, wenn ich versuchte, ihn irgendwie für mich zu vereinnahmen.

Und doch – wenn ich an mein bisheriges Leben dachte, sah ich als Erstes die riesige Anzahl von Dingen, die ich mir gewünscht und nicht bekommen hatte. Meine Wünsche waren bescheiden; ich wollte durchaus nichts Außergewöhnliches. Nur ein normales Leben mit einer normalen Lebenserwartung und normalen Annehmlichkeiten und einer normalen Liebe, die unausweichlich nach der normalen Frist vor die Hunde gehen würde. Das alles waren keine skandalösen Forderungen. Vielleicht hatte ich geglaubt, meine eine skandalöse Forderung – diesen Mann zu treffen, an seiner Weisheit teilzuhaben, ein einziges gestohlenes Geheimnis mit ins Grab zu nehmen –, würde mir im Ausgleich für all die anderen gewährt. Sobald ich mir das klarmachte, stellte ich allerdings fest, dass diese Vorstellung eine Instanz voraussetzte, die gewährte und nicht gewährte Wünsche gegeneinander aufrechnete, was eine verkappte religiöse Überzeugung war. Also versuchte ich es mir aus dem Kopf zu schlagen.

Aber merkwürdig war es schon: Ich hatte oft an meiner Mission gezweifelt; ich hatte bis zum Abwinken meine Motive in Frage gestellt, meine Hoffnungen zurückgeschraubt und meine unausgesprochenen Prämissen ausgesprochen. Aber ich hatte nicht ein einziges Mal daran gedacht, dass Besetow vielleicht kein würdiges Ziel all dieser Sorgen und Hoffnungen war. Ich selbst mochte eine unwürdige Bittstellerin sein – ignorant, fehlgeleitet, arrogant und fordernd. Aber Besetow war unanfechtbar. Wenn er nicht die Lösung aller Probleme in Händen hielt, gab es keine.

Peinlicherweise trugen mich meine Beine ausgerechnet zur Kasaner Kathedrale, wenn auch aus rein ästhetischen Gründen (der Implizite Assoziationstest hatte ergeben, dass mir alle Weltreligionen gleichermaßen gleichgültig waren). Ich ging hinein. Die Kuppel war fast so groß wie die des Petersdoms und leitete bunt gescheckt es Licht ins Innere. Eine schwarzweiße Katze lag ungerührt auf einer Kiste in der Ecke. Ihr gegenüber blickten farbsatte Heilige sehnsüchtig aus ihren vergoldeten Rahmen hervor, auf ewig in der zweiten Dimension festgebannt.

Blasphemisch wie immer, dachte ich nur an Jonathan. Es ist keine große Tragödie, jemanden zu verlieren. Jede zweite Ehe wird geschieden – was für eine langweilige, überstrapazierte Statistik –, und ich bilde mir nicht ein, dass es mit uns anders gekommen wäre. Dem entgangen zu sein hat immerhin sein Gutes: Es ist eine große Lebensniederlage weniger. Jemandes Abwesenheit kann einen so sentimental werden lassen, aber in seiner Gegenwart dauerhaft sentimental zu sein ist unmöglich, in dem ganz alltäglichen Egoismus und dem Schweigen, aus dem angeblich der Großteil eines Lebens besteht. Trotzdem – er und ich waren noch so neu. Wir standen am rückhaltlosen, glücklichen Anfang, von dem aus man all die kommenden Erniedrigungen weder ahnt noch sieht. Wir wussten noch nicht, was uns je davon abbringen könnte, einander zu lieben.

Zuerst hatte ich gehofft, der Trennungsschmerz könnte sich als heilsam erweisen, könnte mich stärken und bessern wie einen Diamanten, der unter Druck aus Kohle entsteht, oder eine Perle, die sich der ständigen Reibung eines Sandkorns verdankt. Aber wenn ich ehrlich war, fand ich es – besonders jetzt, nach der Begegnung mit Michail Andrejewitsch – einfach nur ermüdend.

Ich blieb eine Weile dort sitzen und starrte in die Kerzen, die in ihren roten Halterungen für anderer Leute Hoffnungen brannten, für Gebete und für aussichtslose Fälle. Ich erinnerte mich, wie ich einen anderen Fluss entlanggegangen war, mit anderen Neigungen und Ängsten im Herzen.

KAPITEL 11

Alexander
Leningrad, 1982-1986

Als Alexander endlich aus Moskau wieder in Leningrad ankam, stand jemand vor seiner Haustür und erwartete ihn. Im Zug hatte Alexander die ganze schlaflose, paranoide Nacht hindurch jedes Mal, wenn er eindöste, Nikolais grinsende Fratze vor sich gesehen, und als er eine Gestalt unter dem ausgemergelten Baum am Eingang entdeckte, erstarrte er. Doch es war nicht Nikolai. Es war Peter Pawlowitsch Nikitin, der sich dort in den Wind lehnte.

Peter Pawlowitsch sah Alexander entgegen. Er warf seine Zigarette zu Boden und sah zu, wie sie im Schnee verlosch. Doch er rührte sich nicht vom Fleck. Alexander begriff, dass Peter Pawlowitsch warten würde, bis er zu ihm kam.

Er überlegte umzudrehen. Er überlegte, sich wieder in den Zug zu setzen und wegzufahren – aber wohin? Zu wem? Nach Moskau, in den Untergrund? Ins Saigon an den Tresen?

Er ließ es bleiben. Mit vor Angst gebleckten Zähnen ging er auf Pawlowitsch zu. »Was wollen Sie hier?«, fragte Alexander.

»Raten Sie mal.«

Alexander sah hoch. In seinem Fenster zeichnete sich die verzerrte Silhouette eines Mannes ab – ein Arm, ein Rücken, ein deformierter Kopf –, der sehr methodisch nach etwas zu suchen schien. Alexander stellte sich vor, wie die Verwalterin die Hände rang und sich auf die Lippe biss und sich alles, alles ins Gedächtnis rief, was sie gegen ihn vorbringen konnte. Er war zu unmöglichen Zeiten gekommen und gegangen, würde sie sagen. Er hatte zweifelhaften Umgang gepflegt. Er hatte mit einer Nutte angebandelt und sich nicht einmal die Mühe gemacht, diskret zu sein. Alexander wusste, dass es der Verwalterin jetzt leidtat, ihn nicht längst vor die Tür gesetzt zu haben.

»Das war ein hübscher kleiner Auftritt in Moskau«, sagte Peter Pawlowitsch. In dem kalten Licht sah er hohlwangig und gelbsüchtig aus, und seine Nase lief. Insgesamt wirkte er nicht wie jemand, der eine ganze Existenz zerstören könnte.

Alexander sah sich nach allen Seiten um.

»Erwarten Sie jemanden?«, fragte Peter Pawlowitsch.

»Wo ist Nikolai?«

»Woher soll ich das wissen? Ich bin doch nicht sein Kindermädchen.« Pawlowitsch zog mit Nachdruck die Nase hoch. »Das mit Ihren Freunden tut mir leid.«

»Sicher.«

»Das war bedauerlich. Zwei so junge Männer. Äußerst bedauerlich.«

»Für wen bedauerlich? Ich meine, wer bedauert das genau?«

Pawlowitsch kniff sich in die Nase und sah Alexander wohlwollend an. Schnee hatte sich in seinen Augenbrauen verfangen, sie sahen wie die haarigen Beine einer Albino-Tarantel aus. »So eine Tragödie«, sagte er, »kann jeder nur bedauern.«

Alexander wandte sich von ihm ab und stapfte auf die Haustür zu. Das Eis unter seinen Füßen gab ein hohles Knirschen von sich.

»Ich würde an Ihrer Stelle nicht hineingehen.«

Alexander drehte sich um. »Ach, nein?«

»Sie sind noch nicht fertig.«

Alexander stellte sich vor, wie sie seine Unterhosen und Schachsets, seine Bücher und seine wenigen Briefe durchwühlten, die dürftige Ausbeute seiner gesamten einsamen Existenz. Er fragte sich, wie viel sie tatsächlich begriffen, wenn sie sein Zimmer nach verbotenen Veröffentlichungen durchforsteten; vielleicht vermaßen und fotografierten und archivierten sie gerade das ganze Durcheinander von Einsamkeit, Sehnsucht und Enttäuschung – seinen einzigen persönlichen Besitz.

»Da oben ist nichts.«

»Nicht? Na, mag sein.« In Peter Pawlowitschs Atemwegen war ein sattes Gurgeln zu hören. »Verzeihen Sie. Ich habe Polypen. Ziemlich unangenehm, so was.«

Das Gurgeln machte Alexander Mut. »Seit wann arbeitet Nikolai schon für Sie?«

»Werden Sie nicht drastisch. Wenn Sie so weitermachen, werden Sie nie die Karriere haben, die Sie verdient hätten.«

»Seit wann hatten Sie vor, Iwan umzubringen?«

»Er ist bei einem Unfall gestorben.«

»Klar.«

»Es war ein Unfall. Und außerdem ist das nicht mein Ressort. Das wissen Sie hoffentlich. Ich halte mich strikt an Sport und Propaganda.«

Alexander schwieg und starrte stumpf vor sich hin – auf die bleigraue Gebäudeflanke, die gefrorene Wäsche an der Leine im Hof. Licht sickerte von oben auf sie herab.

»Ich muss zugeben«, sagte Peter Pawlowitsch, »dass es mich beeindruckt, wie lange Sie es in diesem Drecksloch ausgehalten haben. Und die Kollegen auch. Ich war nicht gerade davon ausgegangen, einen Palast vorzufinden, aber nachdem Sie so darauf bestanden haben, hierzubleiben, dachte ich, es sei zumindest ein bisschen erträglicher.«

Alexander sah wieder zu seinem Fenster auf. Er konnte noch immer Schemen erkennen, die sich im schwachen Gegenlicht der Glühlampe rätselhaft hin und her bewegten.

»Aber das hier«, Peter Pawlowitsch deutete auf das Gebäude, »das ist grauenhaft. Sie müssen Ihr kleines Projekt wirklich ernstgenommen haben, um es hier auszuhalten. Wer weiß, mit wem Sie da unter einem Dach gelebt haben? Mit Huren, möchte ich wetten.« Alexander wurde mit einem Schlag in die Magengrube klar, dass Elisabeta in seiner Akte stand. »Sie müssen an diesen Blödsinn wahrhaftig geglaubt haben.«

»Habe ich.«

Peter Pawlowitsch sah ihn mit einem beinahe zärtlichen Ausdruck an, den Alexander unerträglich fand. Er schniefte triumphierend. »Tja, bestimmt haben Sie einer Menge Menschen den Kopf verdreht.«

In dem Moment kamen die Männer die Treppe herunter. Es waren zwei, einer mit der Muskulatur eines Bärenmarders und einer mit einem Gesicht, das aussah wie abgekocht. Ohne Alexander anzusehen, trugen sie ihre magere Ausbeute davon, und Alexander erkannte einige der Sachen wieder – ein Hemd, ein paar Briefe, ein Buch, ein schmuddeliges Bettlaken. Er hätte das Laken wechseln sollen, dachte er. Andererseits hatte er nicht damit gerechnet, Gesellschaft zu bekommen.

Peter Pawlowitsch sah ihn an und wechselte den Tonfall. »Also. Demnächst ist ein Turnier in Moskau, habe ich recht?«

»Ja.«

»Und Sie möchten weiterhin teilnehmen?«

»Ja.«

»Natürlich möchten Sie. Kluger Junge. Schließlich sind Sie ein Schachwunderkind. Eine politische Leuchte sind Sie nicht. Ich denke, darauf können wir uns einigen. Der Kreml ist ausgesprochen großzügig und sehr beeindruckt von Ihren Fähigkeiten, und wenn wir zwei uns einig werden, ist man bereit, trotz allem über ihre früheren Fehltritte hinwegzusehen. Vielleicht finden wir ja zu einer Übereinkunft.«

Peter Pawlowitsch sah Alexander besorgt an, wie ein Arzt, der hofft, dass sein minderjähriger Patient eine bittere, aber lebensrettende Pille schlucken wird.

»Die städtischen Meisterschaften sind Kinderkram, meinen Sie nicht? Für einen Spieler wie Sie? Sie sollten überregional spielen. International, wenn Sie mich fragen. Sie wollen weiterhin für die

Sowjetunion spielen, und wir wollen, dass Sie weiterhin für die Sowjetunion spielen.«

Alexander wurde bewusst, dass Pawlowitsch von Angebot und Nachfrage sprach.

»Aber es liegt ganz bei Ihnen – ob Sie an Ihrer Einstellung arbeiten. Ob Sie ideologisch lernfähig sind.«

Und vielleicht war Alexander das. Vielleicht. Die Frau, die er liebte, hatte beschlossen, einen Parteifunktionär zu heiraten; der Mann, den er am meisten bewunderte, war tot; die einzigen anderen Menschen, denen er vertraut hatte, waren ein Irrer und ein Verräter. Es gab immer weniger Alternativen für ihn. Wer würde es ihm vorhalten? Wer war überhaupt noch übrig, der es ihm vorhalten konnte?

»Und wenn nicht?«, fragte Alexander. Vielleicht wusste er schon, dass die Frage reine Effekthascherei war.

»Wenn nicht, war es das mit dem Schachspielen. Und vielleicht mit ein paar anderen Dingen. Wer weiß? Aber Schach würden Sie nicht mehr spielen, so viel ist sicher. Man hat Ihnen viel Toleranz und Geduld entgegengebracht. Aber ich denke, darüber müssen wir uns nicht weiter unterhalten. Ich denke, Sie wissen schon, was Sie zu tun haben.«

Vielleicht hatte Peter Pawlowitsch recht. Vielleicht würde Alexander in sein Zimmer gehen, auf die braunen Flecken am Boden starren und es sich überlegen. Er hatte versucht, in Leningrad ein ehrbares Leben zu führen. Er hatte versagt. Vor dem Fenster würde er die Schneeflocken im Laternenlicht verglühen sehen. Auf dem Bett hätte der KGB sein Schachspiel stehen lassen. Sie hätten gewusst, dass er es mitnehmen würde und dass es das Einzige war, was er mitnehmen würde. Sie hätten gewusst, was er tun würde. Wenn er ginge, würde er an der Tür Nummer neun vorbeigehen, ohne hinzusehen.

»Sie können jetzt gehen«, sagte Peter Pawlowitsch gutgelaunt. »Sie wollen doch sicher packen.«

Die neue Wohnung hatte tadellose Wasserleitungen, einen gerahmten Spiegel und ein zweites Schlafzimmer (»für Gäste«, hatte Peter Pawlowitsch mit großer Geste gesagt). Es gab ein Wohnzimmer mit Kamin und mit eingebauten Bücherregalen voller offiziell anerkannter unlesbarer Lektüre. Im Kühlschrank lagerten frisches Fleisch und importierter Wein. Eine Schüssel auf dem Tresen war bis über den Rand mit tropischen Früchten gefüllt, darunter eine Banane, so gelb und halbrund wie eine Mondsichel. Alexander hatte noch nie eine Banane gegessen, nur eine Orange, als Kind in Ocha, als ein Güterzug mit Waren für die Parteielite entgleist war. Vor seinen Fenstern blühten in jenem Frühjahr Schachblumen und die prallen, leuchtenden Herzen der Wolfsmilchpflanzen.

Er hatte nicht einmal geahnt, wie schmutzig er war, bis er eine halbe Stunde mit Unmengen Seife unter einer brühend heißen Dusche verbrachte. Er dachte an die ewig kratzenden Dreckkrümel in seinem Bett in der Kommunalka zurück und begriff beschämt, dass er sie selbst dort hinterlassen hatte. Er trank armenischen Cognac. Er rauchte ohne jeden Anlass kubanische Zigarren. Dass er Elisabeta und Iwan verloren hatte, hatte ihn rachsüchtig gemacht. Er fand, er hätte alles verdient, was er an sich raffen konnte. Er wälzte sich nachts in seinem neuen Bettzeug herum, das eine ganz andere Gattung zu sein schien als das, was er von früher her kannte. Dass Decken seidenweich und nachgiebig sein könnten, hatte er gar nicht gewusst. Zum ersten Mal in seinem Leben heilten die Ekzeme an seinem Hintern vollständig ab.

Er trat in die KPdSU ein und wurde offiziell Mitglied des Komsomol. Sein Lächeln auf dem neuen internationalen Reisepass verrutschte zu einem höhnischen Grinsen. In seinem neuen Wohnzimmer schlug er freudlos ein Rad, nur weil genug Platz dazu war.

Er bekam einen neuen Trainer zugewiesen, einen Mann, der unerklärlicherweise immer eine Art Damen-Kopftuch um den Hals trug – außer bei Turnieren, wo ein dicker, sehniger Nacken darunter zum Vorschein kam. Er war ein einfallsloser Spieler, und seine Halssehnen vollführten akrobatische Kunststücke, wenn Alexander Züge ausführte, die er nicht kannte oder nicht verstand. Und dann gab es noch den allgegenwärtigen, den zudringlichen Peter Pawlowitsch, der sich mitten in Alexanders Leben breitmachte, ihn in Hotels und Restaurants begleitete und ihm warnende Blicke zuwarf, wenn er zu redselig wurde, was nur noch selten geschah.

Innerhalb weniger Wochen hatte Alexander ein neues Leben begonnen. Es war nicht zu spät dazu, stellte er fest.

Alexander wurde dicker – langsam, doch so stetig und unausweichlich, wie er älter wurde. Manchmal sah er in seinen gerahmten Spiegel und war sicher, dass er Falten bekam, auch wenn andere ihm versicherten, das sei nicht der Fall. Elisabeta, die bisher sein gesamtes Bewusstsein ungebeten in Beschlag genommen hatte, lauerte jetzt düster im Epizentrum seines Hirns wie ein metastasierendes Krebsgeschwür. Er bemühte sich nach Kräften, sie aus seinem Kopf zu verdrängen. Er versuchte sich mit anderen Dingen zu beschäftigen – hauptsächlich mit Schach, aber auch mit der bestmöglichen Rationalisierung für sein eigenes Verhalten oder der bestmöglichen Ordnung in seinem neuen, eigenen Kühlschrank (der ihm ein ständiger Quell der Freude war). Viel Zeit verbrachte er auch damit, an Sachalin zurückzudenken, an die leuchtend weißen Birkenschonungen, die Ausflüge nach Juschno-Sachalinsk, wo es nach Schlamm und Zwangsarbeitern roch, an die koreanischen Schiffe, die im Schutz der Nacht im Hafen einliefen und illegal Kohle für die Kraftwerke anlieferten. Er aß riesige Salate mit viel echter Mayonnaise (statt der bisherigen Mischung aus Essig und Möbelpolitur). Er versuchte Liegestütze. Er versuchte, Wert auf seine Kleidung zu legen. Er versuchte, sich in die ganz eigenen Details seines eigenen Lebens zu vertiefen, statt sich obsessiv mit jedem Detail jenes anderen Lebens zu befassen.

Jeden Tag, jeden einzelnen Tag führte er einseitige stumme Zwiesprachen mit Iwan. Er versuchte ihm zu erklären, dass ihm gar nichts anderes übriggeblieben war. Dass er den einzig pragmatischen Schluss gezogen hatte – und waren sie nicht immer schon pragmatisch gewesen? Pure Ideologie hatte noch nie jemandem gutgetan. Er versuchte zu erklären, wie leid es ihm tat. Manchmal wurde er defensiv und erklärte, wenn Iwan wirklich so überragend darin gewesen wäre, Menschen und Situationen zu beurteilen, dann wäre er heute nicht tot. Dann wieder erklärte er, im Leben ginge es nur darum, wie man am besten überlebte. Für die Toten war es leicht, sich moralisch überlegen zu fühlen. Alle anderen mussten sich irgendwie durchschlagen.

Alexander erklärte und erklärte, doch Iwan schien gar nicht hinzuhören. Antworten tat er jedenfalls nicht.

Alexander begann zu siegen. Er begann an allem, dem er ausgesetzt war, Geschmack zu finden. Er begegnete Russajew, der schon seit einem Jahrzehnt Schachweltmeister war (allerdings nach einem kampflosen Sieg, nur aufgrund von Fischers theatralischem Getue), und Peter Pawlowitsch plapperte drauflos, was für eine *Ehre* es für ihn sei, einem derart brillanten Spieler zu begegnen, während Alexander lustlos an seiner Räuchermakrele herumstocherte. Russajew war älter als er, trug einen Schnurrbart und vergaß innerhalb von Minuten Alexanders Namen. Alexander siegte weiter. Er bekam ein höheres Gehalt. Erinnerungen an Elisabeta ließen ihn noch immer vor Scham zusammenfahren, aber nicht mehr vor Schmerz. Wenn er am Telefon mit seiner Mutter sprach, die er seit drei Jahren nicht gesehen hatte, und noch jemand im Raum war, senkte er die Stimme. Er siegte weiter. Als er Russajew zum zweiten Mal begegnete, vergaß dieser Alexanders Namen nicht mehr.

Er besuchte Cocktailpartys, er besuchte Abendgesellschaften, er besuchte Feste, immer in Gesellschaft von Peter Pawlowitsch, der ihn mit dem besitzergreifenden Stolz eines Vaters oder Sporttrainers anstrahlte. Alexander wurde mehr und mehr zum Trinker, und es gefiel ihm, sich in einen Schleier der Gleichgültigkeit, Wirrnis und Wortkargheit zu hüllen, wenn Pawlowitsch ihm männlich auf die Schulter klopfte. »Ich finde, du hast dich goldrichtig entschieden«, sagte Peter Pawlowitsch auf der Feier nach Alexanders Sieg im UdSSR-Halbfinale 1982. »Ich habe gewusst, dass du rehabilitationsfähig warst. Ich habe es gewusst.« Auf der Silvesterfeier 1983 sagte er: »Weißt du, wir modernisieren uns jetzt. Alles wird moderner. Auch die Partei. Es geht nicht immer um ideologische Reinheit und so weiter. Stalin ist zu weit gegangen, da sind sich alle einig.« Er fuchtelte mit einem winzigen Kanapee herum, auf dem in der Mitte ein Klecks schwarzen Kaviars saß. »Wir sind ein praktisches Volk, und wir vertreten eine praktische Weltanschauung.« Auf einer Maifeier im Frühjahr darauf stürzte er verschwitzt und nach dem würzigen Tomatensaft riechend, den er getrunken hatte, auf Alexander zu und sagte: »Es geht um Gerechtigkeit, stimmt's? Es geht um ein Mindestmaß an sozialem Ausgleich.« Er schniefte und blinzelte; in seinem Gesicht lag der bittende Ausdruck eines untauglichen Lehrers, der seinen klügsten Schüler anfleht, keine Meuterei anzuzetteln. »Wir müssen nicht alle radikal sein. Alles, was wir brauchen, ist ein gewisser Grundkonsens, stimmt's? Die Parteilinie entwickelt sich weiter. Wir alle entwickeln uns weiter. Nur das Grundprinzip ist nicht verhandelbar. Und ich bin so froh, dass du einsichtig geworden bist.«

War Alexander einsichtig geworden? Nein, war er nicht. Aber vielleicht sah er ein, dass ein begütertes Leben auch seine Vorzüge hatte; vielleicht hatte er die Sicherheit, Saturiertheit und Einsamkeit schätzen gelernt. Er sah ein, dass er nicht für den Widerstand geschaffen war. Er sah ein, was für einen schrecklichen Fehler er begangen hatte. Iwan war tot, und das allein bewies, wie tödlich es war, unschuldig zu bleiben. Was hatte er damals schon gewusst? Er hielt sich besser an sein Spiel, an das Hin- und Herschieben von Holzfiguren auf einem Brett. Die Einsätze waren auf internationaler Ebene hoch genug, und meistens starb niemand dabei.

Er spielte im Interzonenturnier. Im Kandidatenturnier. Er siegte und siegte, und er siegte weiter, und er genoss die Aufmerksamkeit, die er bekam – das Geschnatter der Kameraverschlüsse, die Interviews in kleinen Textkästen in den Tageszeitungen. Vielleicht genoss er sogar die kleingeistige, beschränkte Befriedigung, genau das zu tun, was man von ihm erwartete. Er war der lebende Beweis, dass Schach eine Spezialität der Sowjetunion war, wenn schon nicht die Geopolitik, und das bisschen Nationalgefühl, das er besaß, wurde – wenn überhaupt – von dieser Vorstellung angefacht. Er las jedes seiner Interviews, und sie klangen immer distanziert und lächerlich, immer sehr viel selbstzufriedener, als er sich je gefühlt hatte. Das Leben war erträglich. Er dachte nie an Elisabeta. Er hielt die meiste Zeit den Mund. Wenn er hin und wieder bei feierlichen Anlässen zu viel trank und sarkastische Bemerkungen über die FIDE oder die Partei fallenließ, schien sich kaum jemand etwas daraus zu machen. Die Funktionäre blieben höflich. Falls sie von seiner Vergangenheit wussten – und das taten sie bestimmt –, wussten sie dieses Wissen geschickt hinter ihrem Dauerlächeln und ihrem leberkranken Blick zu verbergen. Falls sie es wussten, hatten sie freundlicherweise beschlossen, es zu verdrängen.

Alexander tat das Einzige, in dem er je gut gewesen war, und er tat es mit Erfolg. Er war allein – immer allein, und am allermeisten dann, wenn er jemandem unmittelbar gegenübersaß und spielte –, doch er hatte sich mit seiner Einsamkeit ausgesöhnt; er lebte in ihrem Mittelpunkt und stieß sich nur selten an ihren Grenzen. Im Jahr 1983 hatte er es so weit gebracht, dass man ihn nach Pasadena, Kalifornien, schicken wollte, um die Amerikaner im Halbfinale der Weltmeisterschaft zu besiegen. Als Preisgeld waren fünfzigtausend Dollar ausgelobt. Er dachte nie an Elisabeta. Nachts träumte er von Palmen und von festen Währungen.

Zu den Festen kamen hin und wieder Frauen, mit denen Alexander allerdings selten ein Wort wechselte. Die Frauen der Parteimitglieder waren meist ältere, matronenhafte Damen, abweisend in ihren hochgeschlossenen Sekretärinnenblusen und umgeben von einem Hauch von Dogmatismus und Deodorant. Die meisten anderen Frauen waren für die Funktionäre vorgesehen – sie waren aus Elisabetas Branche, makellos gekleidet, überschminkt, mit enganliegenden Kleidern und opernreifen Lachsalven im Koloratursopran. Für Alexander waren sie tabu, und er hielt sich von ihnen fern, wenn er nicht gerade an ihnen vorbeimusste, um sein Glas aufzufüllen. Eines Abends jedoch kam er mit einer Frau ins Gespräch, die er nicht recht zuordnen konnte – sie war zu jung für eine Alibi-Parteifrau und zu unattraktiv, um eine der Hostessen zu sein. Ihr Gesicht war gerötet und ihre Lippen prall, eher grotesk als erotisch. Sie trank Rotwein, der ihren Mund grellrot verfärbte.

»Sind Sie nicht Alexander Besetow?«, fragte sie. »Das Schachwunderkind?«

»Ein Wunderkind?« Alexander war schon ziemlich betrunken, spürte den sanften Auftrieb, mit einem Ölfilm der Verzweiflung überzogen, und zählte die anbrandenden Wellen in seinem Kopf. »Bin ich nicht langsam zu alt für ein Wunderkind?«

»Wie alt sind Sie denn?«

»Zweiundzwanzig.«

»Das ist nicht so alt.«

»Und wie alt sind Sie?«

Sie drehte sich ins Profil. Um ihre Augen hatte sich eine Entzündung ausgebreitet, die ihr ein chronisch erschöpftes Aussehen verlieh. Ihre Haut war schlecht, doch ihr Haar ausgesprochen schön. Alexander entwickelte sich allmählich zum Connaisseur.

»Ein Gentleman fragt so etwas nicht«, sagte sie.

»Wer sagt denn, dass ich ein Gentleman bin?« Sie hatte sich den Teller mit importierten Käseecken vollgeladen. Er beugte sich darüber und schnappte sich ein Stück Brot. »Sie sind älter als ich, würde ich schätzen. Vierundzwanzig, fünfundzwanzig. Zu alt, um hier einen Mann abzugreifen, falls Sie deshalb hier sind. Woher ich das weiß? Weil ich ein Wunderkind bin? Nee, bin ich nicht. Und kein Held, und wenn Sie noch so drauf bestehen.«

»Tue ich nicht.« Sie hatte nicht gelächelt, also konnte sie auch kein Lächeln dramatisch ersterben lassen.

»Irgendwer muss ja die Schachwelt vor der internationalen Mafia retten, oder?« Er hickste.

»Ach ja? Und wer wäre das?«

Er tippte sich mit dem Zeigefinger an die Schläfe und nickte feierlich. »Ich wäre das. Mit meiner geistigen Unabhängigkeit, wissen Sie? Mit meinem subversiven Spielstil. Ich könnte zur ernsten Bedrohung für Russajew werden, haben Sie vielleicht schon gehört.«

»Vielleicht.«

»Russajew ist ein Dinosaurier. Ein Apparatschik. Waren Sie mal in Kalifornien?«

»Natürlich nicht.«

»Aber ich fahre da hin. In drei Wochen. Nach Pasadena. Was glauben Sie, wie da die Frauen aussehen, in Pasadena?« Er erkannte seine eigene Stimme nicht wieder. Er hörte sie kaum.

»Das weiß ich nicht.«

»Wollen Sie 'nen Witz hören?«

»Eigentlich nicht.«

Er hob sein Glas. »Adam und Eva haben bestimmt in der Sowjetunion gelebt, denn sie hatten zu zweit nur einen Apfel und nichts anzuziehen und dachten, sie wären im Paradies!«

In dem Moment packte ihn eine Hand am Kragen; sie war so unnatürlich weich, dass Alexander gleich Peter Pawlowitsch erkannte. Mit der anderen Hand griff er nach Alexanders Glas. »Entschuldigen Sie«, sagte Peter Pawlowitsch. »Herr Besetow wird leider anderswo verlangt.«

Eine Woche vor der geplanten Abreise nach Pasadena erschien Nikolai auf einem der Feste. Alexander hatte gewusst, dass es früher oder später dazu kommen würde, doch es überraschte ihn, wie gelassen er blieb, als es schließlich so weit war. Nikolai trat hinter einem der Kunstblumenarrangements hervor, die bei diesen Feierlichkeiten den Großteil der Dekoration ausmachten. Alexander hatte einen Angstschock erwartet, der ihm wie ein Skalpell sauber den Brustkorb auftrennte; stattdessen musterte er Nikolai stumpf, mit demselben Gefühl der Taubheit, mit dem man wiederkehrenden Alpträumen begegnet. Nikolai war, ebenso wie Alexander, dicker geworden – sein Hemd spannte bedenklich –, aber sein Gesicht sah jetzt weniger hässlich aus. Vielleicht war er auch nur in seine Hässlichkeit hineingewachsen.

»Hallo Alexander«, sagte Nikolai. »Eine eindrucksvolle Leistung war das in Kaliningrad.«

Alexander sah auf den Heringssalat auf seinem Teller herab. So oft hatte er sich vorgestellt, wie er Nikolai fragen würde, ob er Iwan von Anfang an hintergangen hatte. Und Nikolai würde antworten: »Von Anfang an hintergangen? Da gab es nicht viel zu hintergehen.« Je mehr er darüber nachdachte, desto mehr fand Alexander, dass dies das eigentlich Beleidigende an Nikolais Verrat war: wie wenig er sich bemüht hatte, ihn zu verbergen, weil er wusste, dass er es nicht nötig hatte. Er hatte direkt vor ihren Augen Notizen gemacht, verdammt noch mal – und was hatte Alexander sich eigentlich dabei gedacht? Dass Nikolai ihrer Sache derart treu ergeben war, dass er einen steten Fluss neuer Inspirationen zu Papier bringen musste? Das hatte er nicht gedacht; er hatte immer gedacht, dass Nikolai ein Spießer und ein Arschloch war. Doch Iwan hatte er so blind vertraut – Iwan, der jetzt auf ewig der kluge, aufrechte einundzwanzigjährige Junge bleiben würde, der in so vielem recht hatte und sich in der einen Sache irrte, auf die es am meisten ankam –, dass er gar nicht auf die Idee gekommen war, dessen Bild von Nikolai zu hinterfragen. Iwan war immer der gewesen, der sich auskannte, der Vordenker und Visionär, der Kopf des Ganzen. Und jetzt war er tot, und niemand konnte mehr seine Meinungen hinterfragen, weder die über Nikolai noch sonst irgendeine. Alexander hatte sich mit seinen eigenen Stärken und Schwächen abgefunden und vertrat jetzt die Auffassung, dass man in dem, was man am besten konnte, sein Bestes geben sollte, und konnte daher Nikolai neidlos zugestehen, dass er von ihnen dreien der Kompetenteste war. Kompetenz war in Alexanders neuem Leben das höchste Gut. Nikolai hatte sie damals ausmanövriert; er hatte verdient gewonnen, und Alexander wollte ganz gewiss kein schlechter Verlierer sein.

»Das war nur das Aufwärmtraining für Pasadena«, sagte Alexander. Er sah zu, wie Nikolai länger auf einem Cornichon herumkaute, als es unbedingt nötig schien.

»Ach, dann glaubst du immer noch, dass du fährst?«, fragte Nikolai milde. Er tunkte seinen Pfannkuchen in die saure Sahne.

Alexander klappte den Mund zu. »Ja«, sagte er, »das glaube ich.«

»Hmm.«

»Was?«

»Da habe ich aber anderes gehört.«

Und dann war er doch da, der Hass, ein Krampf in der Kiefermuskulatur, der nur schlimmer wurde, weil Alexander wusste, wie ungerechtfertigt er war. Er verdiente es nicht, Nikolai zu hassen. Er hatte den moralischen Standpunkt, der diesen Hass erst möglich machte, längst aufgegeben. Sie waren Kollegen. Verbündete. Genossen. Die Unterschiede zwischen ihnen waren quantitativ, nicht qualitativ. Nikolai mochte ein wenig engagierter sein als er, doch das konnte in ein, zwei Jahren anders aussehen. Und sein neuer Genosse Nikolai hatte ihm etwas Schreckliches, aber Wichtiges zu sagen.

»Wovon redest du?«, fragte Alexander.

»Na ja, angeblich soll es politische Bedenken geben.« Nikolai wand sich, als sei es ihm unangenehm, doch Alexander wusste, dass es ihm nicht leidtat.

»Was für politische Bedenken?«, fragte Alexander. Er fragte nur widerstrebend. Wenn ihm noch etwas anderes geblieben wäre als Schach, hätte ihn die Antwort nicht interessiert. Doch wenn ihm etwas anderes geblieben wäre, wäre er auch nicht hier – dann wäre er nicht so käuflich gewesen, nicht so pflegeleicht, und würde nicht dieses Pläuschchen mit Nikolai Sergejewitsch halten, während seine Cornichons labbrig wurden.

Nikolai hob die Brauen und lächelte süßlich. »Ich an deiner Stelle würde mal Peter Pawlowitsch fragen.«

Alexander marschierte im Zickzack zwischen den Gästen hindurch. Peter Pawlowitsch stand in einer Ecke und erzählte einer kleinen Schar gelangweilter Zuhörer eine langweilige Anekdote.

Alexander zerrte an seinem Ellbogen, bis Peter Pawlowitsch die Gruppe mit einem gereckten Zeigefinger warten hieß und sich geduldig lächelnd zu ihm umdrehte wie zu einem geliebten, aber anstrengenden Kind. Sie zogen sich in eine Ecke zurück, und Alexander begann sofort zu flüstern.

»Ich soll nicht nach Pasadena? Ist das wahr?«

Pawlowitsch wackelte mit dem Kopf und antwortete, ohne die Lippen zu bewegen. »Psst. Man wird dich noch hören.«

»Wer hat das beschlossen?«

»Das, äh, das ist eine ziemlich neue Entwicklung.«

»*Warum* wurde das beschlossen?«

»Sei doch leise. Ich habe nichts dagegen, weißt du. Ich will gern, dass du fährst. Aber es geht hier nicht um mich.«

»Sie ziehen einen Spieler zurück? Zum ersten Mal in der Geschichte? Ich verstehe nicht, wie das im Interesse der Sowjetunion sein soll.«

»*Ich* ziehe doch keinen Spieler zurück. Ich mache überhaupt nichts.«

»Dann eben die FIDE.«

»Hör auf, so mit den Kiefern zu mahlen. Du könntest ruhig ein bisschen dankbarer sein. Es geht schließlich um deine Sicherheit.«

»Geht es nicht.«

»Dann geht es um die Olympiade. Die haben Moskau boykottiert. Deshalb können wir dich nicht hinschicken.«

»Russajew würden Sie schicken.«

Pawlowitsch rollte mit den Augen. »Das reicht jetzt.«

»Ich weiß es.«

»Das reicht. Das mit Russajew ist etwas anderes. Du bist jung. Du kannst problemlos noch drei Jahre warten.«

Alexander ließ seinen Teller fallen. Triefende Klumpen Fisch und eingelegte Gemüsehappen verselbständigten sich und legten erstaunliche Strecken über den Marmorboden zurück.

»Ihr seid alle so begeistert von Russajew«, zischte Alexander. »Dabei wisst ihr, dass er nur dem Namen nach Weltmeister ist. Er hat den Titel kampflos von Fischer übernommen. Aber ihr, ihr verehrt ihn. Ihr würdet alles tun, damit er den Titel behält.«

»Arroganz passt so gar nicht zu dir«, sagte Peter Pawlowitsch und beugte sich herab, um mit seiner Serviette das Essen aufzuklauben. »Und Alkohol auch nicht.«

»Kann ich es mir nicht leisten, arrogant zu sein?«

»Du könntest besser sein.«

Alexander schnaubte. »Ich stehe in der Rangliste dieses Jahr über Russajew.«

Peter Pawlowitsch richtete sich auf. »In anderen Bereichen, meine ich.«

Alexander starrte in sein Wodkaglas. Ihm dröhnte der Kopf. Er erinnerte sich an seine sarkastischen Kommentare zu Oleg Tschasow, dem FIDE-Präsidenten, in Hörweite eines Verbandsfunktionärs. Er erinnerte sich, wie er bei einem Diavortrag zu der Überlegenheit russischer Athleten die Augen verdreht hatte. Er erinnerte sich an den Witz, den er der dicklippigen, wenig beeindruckten Frau erzählt hatte, die nicht gelacht hatte, weil es nicht einmal ein guter Witz gewesen war.

»Wenn du im Herbst bei der Weltmeisterschaft gegen Russajew antreten willst, musst du lernen, dich besser zu benehmen. Noch ist es nicht zu spät, Alexander. Ich setze mich jeden Tag für dich ein, jeden Tag, wirklich.«

Alexander sah einen Teil seiner runden, uneleganten Nase in seinem Wodkaglas gespiegelt. Er stellte sich ungern vor, wie Peter Pawlowitsch sich gegenüber der Partei für ihn einsetzte, wie er mit dieser schmeichlerischen Stimme, in diesem entschuldigenden Ton um mehr Zeit und mehr Nachsicht bettelte. Alexander begriff, dass er längst einer dieser armseligen kleinen Diktatoren geworden war. Wahrscheinlich gab es eine ganze Armada von Denkern und Strategen, die sich damit befassten, wie sie ihn dazu bringen konnten, genau das zu tun, was sie wollten. Und wahrscheinlich gelang es ihnen jedes Mal.

»Weißt du das überhaupt? Natürlich weißt du das, oder?«, fragte

Peter Pawlowitsch. Er klang zutiefst verletzt. Alexander hatte keine Lust, auf rhetorische Fragen zu antworten. »Du kannst nicht nach Pasadena«, sagte Peter Pawlowitsch. »So leid es mir tut. Du kannst im Herbst gegen Russajew antreten. Aber nur, wenn du mich nicht hängenlässt.«

Alexander sah Peter Pawlowitsch nicht an; er wusste, dass er diesen falschen Ausdruck nachsichtiger Zärtlichkeit im Gesicht haben würde, den er nicht sehen wollte.

»Du musst lernen, dich zu benehmen«, sagte Peter Pawlowitsch. »Bitte lass das da mit den Kiefermuskeln. Ich hole einen neuen Teller.«

Den ganzen ausgefransten Frühling und den grausigen Sommer hindurch benahm Alexander sich vorbildlich. Er hörte aufmerksam zu. Er heuchelte Interesse, wann immer es nötig war, und schwieg, solange es ging. Er stellte keine Forderungen. Er hakte nie nach. Auf Empfängen stellte er sich an die Panoramafenster und schaufelte große Mengen teures Essen in sich hinein, und wenn jemand aus der Partei sich mit ihm unterhalten wollte, tat er immer so, als kaute er noch.

Das Spiel um die Weltmeisterschaft begann im September. Moskaus Hochhäuser schnappten mit einer modernen, monolithischen Unersättlichkeit nach den Wolken; die Kommunalki ragten monumental und bleich in unregelmäßigen Reihen nebeneinander auf wie schiefe Zähne im Rachen eines riesigen Tiers. Leningrad konnte schon aufgrund seiner Architektur nicht umhin, sich mit seiner Vergangenheit auseinanderzusetzen, seinen Triumphen und Niederlagen und seinen Ursprüngen in Rationalität und Euklidischer Geometrie. In den langen Alleen und kurvigen Kanälen Leningrads waren die Hoffnungen der Vergangenheit für die Zukunft aufbewahrt. In Moskau hatte man die Zukunft an sich gerissen, zerlegt und der Gegenwart dienstbar gemacht. Gigantische Spruchbanner verschandelten die Fassaden: *Hilf dem Mutterland – diene dem Kommunismus*; *Die Gedanken Lenins leben und siegen*. Auf seinem Weg durch die Gorki Uliza registrierte Alexander, dass die Straße ein Gefühl des unbeschwerten Pragmatismus hätte ausstrahlen können, wenn man geneigt war, so zu denken.

Am Tag der ersten Partie begleitete ein Gehilfe Alexander und seinen von der Partei zugeteilten Sekundanten Dimitri zum Austragungsort. Der Gehilfe führte sie in die Säulenhalle mit ihren kunstvoll gearbeiteten Leuchtern und reich verzierten Tapeten und wartete vor der Tür, als Alexander einen Abstecher in die prachtvollen Toilettenräume machte und sich übergab. Vor der Tür hörte er das Scharren und Murmeln von fünfhundert Reportern aus siebenundzwanzig Ländern. Er wünschte, niemand hätte ihm je diese Zahlen genannt. Er zog die Spülung und wusch sich das Gesicht. Der Gehilfe hämmerte an die Tür.

Als er die Stufen zur Tribüne hochgestolpert war, fand sich Alexander endlich Russajew gegenüber. Russajew war schon immer ein imposanter Mann gewesen, und auf der anderen Seite des Spielbretts wirkte er noch massiger und einschüchternder. Die Zuschauer kamen allmählich zur Ruhe und richteten sich auf die kommende Enttäuschung ein. Russajew hatte vier Jahre in Folge die sowjetischen Schachmeisterschaften gewonnen, und es war beinahe anstößig, fanden die Gäste, diesen obszön jungen Mann gegen ihn antreten zu lassen – einen ungelenken, unbeholfenen Jungen mit buschigen Augenbrauen. Alexander schien sich mit jeder seiner Bewegungen entschuldigen zu wollen, dass er überhaupt existierte. Er gab keinen sehr vielversprechenden Gegner ab, und man erwartete einen mühelosen Sieg. Die Zuschauer mochten keine mühelosen Siege.

Alexander hätte gern vor Beginn des Spiels das Brett berührt, um sich zu sammeln, aber das war nicht erlaubt. Die Schachuhr war bereits gestellt. Russajew rang sich ein beinahe respektvolles Lächeln ab. Alexander waren die weißen Figuren zugelost worden, und als er mit dem Springerbauern eröffnete, ließ er alles – das Publikum, den großen Saal, seine Gedanken – im reinen Schwarz-Weiß des Schachbretts versinken. Das Spiel begann.

Wie Schachberichterstatter und -studenten, Sozialgeschichtler und Anekdotensammler immer wieder angemerkt haben, wurde das Spiel fast bis zum Ende von Russajew dominiert. Alexander spielte anfangs viel zu nachlässig und aggressiv (mit der ganzen Respektlosigkeit der Jugend, wie man sich im Zuschauerraum zuraunte). Nach je zwei Remis verlor er eine Partie, und dann verlor er zwei in Folge. Das war ihm noch nie passiert, aber jetzt war es so weit (was bewies, dass der Emporkömmling mindestens halb so dämlich war, wie er aussah, sagte man sich). Als Sekretärinnen die Abschriften der Wertungsbögen in den Presseraum brachten, stampften die Reporter der *Sowjetski Sport* vor Ärger mit den Füßen auf und schimpften, die ganze Veranstaltung sei einfach peinlich. Seit Fischer auf dem Weg zu Spasski Taimonow überrollt hatte, hatte man keinen so klaren Sieg mehr gesehen (und kein so offensichtliches Ungleichgewicht, murmelte man). Selbst die Jungen am Demobrett langweilten sich sichtlich.

Dann folgten siebzehn Remis hintereinander. Viele der Pressevertreter gingen. Das Turnier wurde von der prachtvollen Säulenhalle in das baufällige Hotel Sport verlegt. Alexander knirschte beim Essen mit den Zähnen. Er wachte nachts mit furchtbaren Beinkrämpfen auf und hüpfte, sehr zum Missfallen von Dimitri, im Halbschlaf im Zimmer auf und ab. Tagsüber durchstreifte er Moskau, bewunderte das Oktjabrskaja-Hotel gegenüber der französischen Botschaft und zählte die metallenen Muskelstränge des Eisernen Felix vor dem KGB-Hauptquartier. Auf dem Roten Platz starrte er sehnsüchtig auf die schönen Lichter des Staatlichen Kaufhauses und stand vierzig Minuten Schlange, um den wächsernen Lenin zu bestaunen.

Nie hatte sich Alexander so weit weg von Ocha gefühlt wie in diesen ersten Tagen in Moskau. Er spürte, wie ihm die Weite Russlands den Nacken hinaufkroch. In der weißen Morgendämmerung stand er am Fenster seines Hotelzimmers und glaubte das endlose Flachland im Osten vor sich zu sehen, die immergleichen Dörfer und Weiler, die wie Mondkrater die Landschaft sprenkelten, bis sie seltener und seltener wurden und sich schließlich in der stoischen, steingrauen Einöde des Kontinentalschelfs verloren. Er stand am Ende der Welt, und die erschreckende Leere des Alls lastete auf ihm. Ihm wurde schwindelig davon, wie wenn man zu dicht an einem steilen Abhang entlangläuft oder wenn man in den Nachthimmel sieht und sich vorstellt, man sähe gar nicht hoch, sondern nach unten, in die Tiefen eines Ozeans voller phosphoreszierender Lebewesen, deren Leuchtorgane aus einem unerforschlichen Meeresgraben zu uns emporblinken.

Er träumte so oft davon, gegen Russajew zu spielen, dass er manchmal nicht mehr wusste, welche Fehler er begangen und welche er im Schlaf erfunden hatte. Es wurde Winter. Zwei Monate nach Beginn des Turniers gewann Russajew noch eine Partie.

Und dann, endlich, als fast niemand mehr hinsah, gewann Alexander eine Partie. Danach folgten vierzehn Remis. Und als die Zuschauer – und einzelne über die Welt verstreute Interessierte – sich reckten und sich die Augen rieben, um sich dem Turnier wieder zuzuwenden, fanden sie am Brett zwei ganz andere Männer vor.

Alexanders drohende Niederlage hatte ihn entschlossener gemacht. Wenn er in den Spiegel sah, blickte ihm ein halbwaches nachtaktives Tier entgegen. Er vergrub sich tiefer und tiefer in das Spiel, bis alles andere nur noch verschwommen und verwässert zu ihm vordrang. Die Nebensächlichkeiten des Lebens – der Weg zum Austragungsort und zurück, die vom Staat gestellten Mahlzeiten, die kalten Nächte im Hotel mit Dimitri – kamen ihm zunehmend irreal vor, wie Schatten der platonischen Realität seines Spiels. Abseits des Bretts wirkte er unartikuliert, verschlossen und benommen. Er gab den Journalisten, die ihn zu seiner Strategie befragten, zutiefst unbefriedigende Antworten. Er hatte keine bahnbrechenden Erkenntnisse anzubieten, keine faszinierende Biographie, nur die eine oder andere kleine Anekdote von seinen Schwestern auf der Insel. In mehr als einem von der TASS verbreiteten Portrait hieß es, trotz seiner bemerkenswerten Spielstärke sei er nicht gerade der hellste Kopf.

Doch bei dem Spiel selbst verfolgte er lebhaft und aufmerksam jede Zuckung, jeden Lidschlag seines Gegners. Alle Straßen verwandelten sich für ihn in die Felder eines Schachbretts, und er begann jeden seiner Wege in die Algebraische Notation zu übertragen. D3: Er ging geradeaus zur Speisentheke, um sich Braten, Borschtsch und Pepsi-Cola zu holen, schüchtern und bescheiden wie ein Bauer. De7: Er überquerte majestätisch und selbstgewiss die Bühne bis zum Brett, die Augen mit tödlicher Sicherheit auf das Ziel gerichtet. Sc4: Er sprang mit rassiger Eleganz beiseite, um einem Regierungswagen auszuweichen.

Russajew ging es weniger gut. Er hatte im Laufe des Turniers fünf Kilo abgenommen, rang hinter seinem vorgehaltenen Taschentuch nach Luft und aß bei den Mahlzeiten fast gar nichts mehr. Seine Haut hing schlaff und überflüssig an ihm herab; er sah zunehmend wie ein Elefant aus, der im Begriff war, seine ritualisierte letzte Reise anzutreten. Manchmal, wenn er einen Zug ausführte, kippte er beängstigend weit nach vorn, und die ohnehin stille Zuschauerschar wurde noch stiller und wartete mit angehaltenem Atem darauf, dass er zusammenbrach. Er tat es nicht, aber hier und da wurden Bemerkungen laut, in weniger modernen Zeiten hätte das ungebildete Landvolk seine Verwandlung sicher irgendeinem Hexenwerk zugeschrieben und einen finsteren Verdacht gegen Alexander gehegt. Aber dies hier war die Zukunft, und so etwas dachte niemand mehr.

Im Papierwald raschelte es, denn die Berichterstatter liebten es zu rascheln. Alexander ist der jüngste Spieler auf diesem Niveau seit Michail Tal, raschelte es. Er ist fast so jung wie dieser autistische Amerikaner, raschelte es. Er wird nicht gewinnen, natürlich nicht, es wäre Unsinn, über so etwas zu spekulieren. Aber vielleicht, raschelte es, vielleicht, vielleicht ja doch.

Dann gewann Alexander die siebenundvierzigste Partie. Dann gewann er die achtundvierzigste. Russajew führte noch immer mit zwei Punkten, aber das Blatt hatte sich gewendet. Alexander richtete sich in seinem Sessel auf. Er schlief nachts besser. Russajew hustete in seinen Hemdsärmel und funkelte ihn aus wässrigen, rotgeränderten Augen an. Am frühen Morgen vor der neunundvierzigsten Partie klingelte Alexanders Telefon.

Es war fünf Uhr morgens, und Dimitri nahm den Hörer ab. Er lauschte eine Weile und reichte das Telefon an Alexander weiter. »Peter Pawlowitsch ist dran«, sagte er.

»Wer auch sonst«, sagte Alexander. Es war für einen Februar recht warm, also weiterhin sehr kalt, und Alexander blieb, ohne Licht zu machen, in seinem Bett. Vor den Fenstern hörte er das schmelzende Eis durch die Kanaldeckel tröpfeln. »Was ist?«, fragte er.

Peter Pawlowitsch schniefte. »Du bist morgens nicht gerade ein Sonnenschein, weißt du?«

»Was wollen Sie?«

»Noch nicht ganz ausgeschlafen, wie?«

»Was?«

»Keine Sorge, du kannst dich wieder hinlegen. Das Turnier wird unterbrochen.«

»*Was?*« Alexander setzte sich auf und spürte, wie die seltsam feuchte Kälte des Hotelzimmers sich ihm um Rumpf und Schultern legte. Dieses verdammte Zimmer hatte anscheinend ein weltweit einzigartiges Mikroklima.

»Die FIDE hat beschlossen, das Turnier vorerst zu unterbrechen. Bis die Unregelmäßigkeiten ausgeräumt sind.«

»Unregelmäßigkeiten? Was für Unregelmäßigkeiten?«

Dimitri streckte eine Hand nach dem Lichtschalter aus und blinzelte aus schlaftrunkenen Augen interessiert zu ihm herüber.

Peter Pawlowitsch nieste. »Gewisse …. Abweichungen eben.«

»Wovon reden Sie überhaupt?«

»Reg dich doch nicht auf.«

»Meinen Sie, weil ich jetzt gewinne?«

»Natürlich nicht. Und du gewinnst auch nicht.«

»Es war nicht vorgesehen, dass ich ihn schlagen würde, oder?«

»Also weißt du, es ist doch immer dasselbe mit dir.«

»Aber warum *jetzt*?«

»Du hast Russajew ja gesehen, oder? Der Mann ist schwer krank.«

»Er ist nicht krank!« Alexander trat gegen Dimitris Bett, und sein Sekundant zog sich rasch Richtung Wand zurück. »Er ist bloß alt! Er ist ein Wrack. Er ist erschöpft, weil er verliert und weil Verlieren so anstrengend ist. Ich muss es schließlich wissen, ich habe selbst fünf Monate lang verloren. Da haben Sie sich allerdings keine Sorgen gemacht.«

»Du wirst immer kindischer.«

»Und Sie werden immer korrupter. Ich habe dem Mann achtundvierzig kostenlose Lektionen erteilt.«

»Diese Farce hat jetzt sechs Monate gedauert. Es wird allmählich peinlich.«

»Peinlich für wen?«

»Für alle Beteiligten. Nicht zuletzt auch für dich. Wir haben mehr von dir erwartet, Alexander.«

»Haben Sie nicht. Offensichtlich nicht.«

»Für morgen ist eine Pressekonferenz angesetzt«, sagte Peter Pawlowitsch. »Dort wird verkündet, dass das Turnier ergebnislos abgebrochen wird. Es ist zu einem physiologischen Leistungstest verkommen.«

»Ist es nicht.«

»Die Pressekonferenz ist morgen, und du wirst dabei sein.«

Dimitri war aufgestanden und zog die Vorhänge auf, um die triste, spärliche Dämmerung hereinzulassen.

»Werde ich nicht«, sagte Alexander.

Peter Pawlowitsch lachte. »Du vergisst, dass ich dich kenne, Alexander. Besser als jeder andere vielleicht.« Er nieste wieder. »Du wirst kommen. Natürlich wirst du das.«

Am Tag der Pressekonferenz erwachte Alexander früh. Dimitri lag noch mit halboffenem Mund, die Hände wie bei einem Neugeborenen zu Fäusten geballt, schlafend im Bett, und Alexander starrte auf ihn herab und fragte sich, wie Dimitris bisheriges Leben verlaufen war. Die Vorstellung, dass Dimitri die gleichen Kompromisse gemacht und die gleichen Probleme durchgestanden hatte, nur um neben Alexander am Tisch sitzen und seinen Geisteszustand im Auge behalten zu dürfen, stieß ihn ab. Wenigstens hatte er, Alexander, seine Seele für ein etwas ruhmreicheres Leben verkauft.

Dimitri schlug die Augen auf und fuhr hoch. »Was tun Sie?«

Alexander trat einen Schritt zurück. »Wir müssen bald los.«

Andererseits saßen sie jetzt in demselben muffigen Hotelzimmer fest, sahen Abend für Abend dieselben langweiligen Fernsehsendungen, kauten wieder und wieder dieselben Schachzüge durch – und Dimitri hatte, wenn alles vorbei war, zumindest eine Verlobte, ein Leben, in das er zurückkehren konnte.

Dimitri sah ihn verständnislos an.

»Zur Pressekonferenz.«

»Brauchen Sie mich dort?«

Alexander gab ungern zu, dass er Dimitri überhaupt jemals brauchte, und wollte nicht ausgerechnet jetzt damit anfangen.

»Das gehört zum Protokoll«, sagte Alexander. Dimitri hegte eine geradezu religiöse Ehrfurcht vor allem, was mit dem Protokoll zusammenhing.

Zwölf Minuten darauf eilten sie durch den Schneematsch die Straße hinunter. Dimitri hatte eine chronisch laufende Nase, und heute war es nicht anders. Immer wieder legte er den Kopf in den Nacken und tat, als gäbe es dort oben etwas zu sehen, oder fand einen Vorwand, sich mit dem Ärmel über das Gesicht zu wischen. Alexander fragte sich, seit wann die rhinologischen Probleme seiner Mitmenschen eine so wesentliche Rolle in seinem Privatleben spielten.

Bei der Pressekonferenz stand Alexander unbeholfen neben dem FIDE-Präsidenten Oleg Tschasow auf der Bühne. Auf dessen anderer Seite stand Russajew. Die Reporter wirkten erschöpft, Vitamin-D-depraviert und wahnsinnig gelangweilt. Im Blitzlicht der Kameras blinkten ihre Namensschildchen. Peter Pawlowitsch saß in den hinteren Reihen und betrachtete Alexander mit der bitter-süßen Ergriffenheit einer Mutter, die ihren soldatischen Sohn in den sicheren Tod schicken wird.

Tschasow hielt einen längeren Monolog über das endlose Turnier. Er wies auf Russajew, der sich, schwach lächelnd, mit den leuchtenden Augen eines religiösen Eiferers die Lippen leckte. Alexander bemühte sich, keine Grimassen zu ziehen.

»Wie Sie alle wissen, dauert dieses Spiel bereits mehrere Monate«, sagte Tschasow. »Die Spieler haben sich bis zur Erschöpfung und darüber hinaus verausgabt.«

Alexander sperrte die Augen weit auf. Er wollte keinesfalls erschöpft aussehen. Er versuchte den Zuschauern klarzumachen, dass er jung und voller Leben war, intelligent und – was das Wichtigste war – ein potentieller Sieger, wenn das Turnier fortgesetzt würde.

»Unsere Spieler haben sich ehrenvoll geschlagen. Alexander Besetow hat sich trotz seiner anfänglichen Schwierigkeiten« – die Zuschauer ließen ein leises, wissenden Lachen hören, und Alexander bemühte sich nicht mehr, nicht zu grimassieren – »als ... nun, als sehr ausdauernder Gegner erwiesen. Und Igor Russajew, unser verehrter Meister, hat während dieser Begegnung einige seiner bisher besten Partien gespielt. Ihm zuzusehen war uns allen eine Ehre und ein Privileg.«

Russajew senkte bescheiden den Kopf. Das kam Alexander nicht richtig vor. Nur ein Sieger durfte derart demütig sein. War es nicht beschämend (ein bisschen, ein kleines bisschen nur), den Titel kampflos zuerkannt zu bekommen und dann die Chance zu verschenken, ihn zu verteidigen? Alexander hatte ihm mit seiner Herausforderung einen Gefallen getan; er hatte Russajew die Chance gegeben, seine gesamte lächerliche Karriere im Nachhinein zu rechtfertigen, und das konnte er nicht allein erledigen.

»Doch jetzt«, fuhr Tschasow fort, »müssen wir diese Veranstaltung beenden, bevor sie vollends zur Farce verkommt.«

Russajew lächelte tapfer.

»Das Turnier ist nur noch eine Prüfung des körperlichen Durchhaltevermögens, nicht der geistigen Fähigkeiten. Dies sind keine fairen Bedingungen mehr, um die Spielstärke dieser Männer zu ermitteln.«

Vielleicht lag es an der Erwähnung von Fairness – solche Abstrakta trieben Alexander in letzter Zeit zur Raserei. Oder vielleicht lag es daran, wie Russajew dastand – bleich und übermäßig wohlerzogen.

»Entschuldigung«, sagte Alexander. »Ich habe … Entschuldigen Sie.« Die Reporter wirbelten herum, um Alexander anzusehen, als sei ihnen gerade erst aufgefallen, dass es ihn gab. Sie hoben ihre Kameras. Sie zückten ihre Notizblöcke.

»Bitte?« Tschasow starrte ihn entsetzt an.

»Also«, sagte Alexander, »wir wollen beide weiterspielen. Oder irre ich mich?«

»Was sagen Sie da?« Über Tschasows Kopf blickten Lenin und Gorbatschow gleichgültig aus gerahmten Portraits hervor. Gorbatschows Muttermal hatte die Farbe rohen Fleisches und die Form des Königreichs Thailand.

»Also«, sagte Alexander. Seine Stimme klang fremdartig – zu unterwürfig, eine halbe Oktave höher als normal. »Ich verstehe nur nicht, warum die FIDE eingreifen und das Spiel unterbrechen sollte, wenn beide Spieler weitermachen möchten.«

Die Reporter begannen zu schreiben. Pawlowitsch schüttelte nachdrücklich den Kopf. Eine Kamera blitzte Alexander ins Gesicht. Es war zu spät für einen Rückzieher.

Alexander räusperte sich und versuchte, seine normale Tonlage wiederzugewinnen. »Wir wissen alle, dass er seinen Titel nicht ehrenhaft gewonnen hat. Vielleicht möchte er ihn ja ehrenhaft verteidigen?«

»Genug jetzt«, sagte Tschasow streng.

»Ich frage mich nur …«, sagte Alexander. Er sah die Filmkameras an. Ihm fiel ein, dass man immer der mit dem Licht folgen sollte. Pawlowitsch starrte ihn fassungslos an. »Ich frage mich nur, ob das hier mit Korruption zu tun hat. Vielleicht sollten wir Russajew direkt fragen, was er vorziehen würde.«

Tschasow bedeutete den Reportern, die Kameras abzuschalten. Er machte Gesten, als wollte er sich die Kehle durchschneiden und als zöge er Stecker aus der Wand. Er schob sich zwischen Alexander und das Mikrophon. »Es hat ein kleines Missverständnis gegeben«, sagte er. Peter Pawlowitsch hielt sich mit beiden Händen den Kopf, und Alexander hoffte einen Moment lang, dass er ihn nicht in Schwierigkeiten gebracht hatte. »Zeit für eine Mittagspause«, sagte Tschasow hastig. »Wir werden Sie in Kürze über alles Weitere informieren.«

Am nächsten Morgen rief Peter Pawlowitsch bei Alexander an. Vor dem Fenster hupten Autos; von irgendwoher stieg ein moosiger Geruch auf. Alexander wusste kaum noch, wie es war, dort draußen zu leben.

»Tja, Alexander«, sagte Peter Pawlowitsch. »Ich weiß nicht, was ich dir jetzt sagen soll.«

»Ist es nicht Ihre Aufgabe, immer genau zu wissen, was Sie mir sagen sollen?«

Alexander hörte, wie Peter Pawlowitsch sich eine Zigarette ansteckte und geräuschvoll ausatmete.

»In ihrer Großmut haben sie beschlossen, die Fortsetzung des Turniers zu erlauben.«

»Weil es im Fernsehen war.«

»Du darfst so etwas nie, nie wieder tun. Ich weiß, dass du keine Ahnung von meiner eigentlichen Aufgabe hast. Du denkst, ich habe es auf dich abgesehen. Aber ich sage dir das hier als Mitstreiter – nicht als Freund, aber als Mitstreiter, der deine Fähigkeiten respektiert. Du darfst das nie, nie wieder tun.«

»Im Fernsehen?«

»Auch sonst nicht. Überhaupt nicht. Es ist vollkommen inakzeptabel.«

»Ich verstehe gar nicht, warum es denen so wichtig ist, wer gewinnt. Sie kriegen so oder so ihre fünfzig Prozent der Einnahmen.«

»Du machst so viel mehr Mühe, als du wert bist.«

»Immerhin werde ich Weltmeister, oder?«

»Du bist nicht bereit dazu. Du bist nicht bereit, die Sowjetunion als Schachnation zu repräsentieren.«

»Aber ich werde doch Weltmeister, oder?«

»Begreifst du denn überhaupt nichts?«

»Oder?«

»Begreifst du wirklich *gar nichts*? Irgendjemand muss Weltmeister sein.«

Darüber dachte Alexander erst einmal nach. »Und ihr wollt wirklich, dass es dieser vorgestrige Hanswurst ist?«

Ein Schniefen war zu hören, und Alexander versuchte seinen emotionalen Gehalt einzuschätzen. Im Laufe der Jahre hatte er die ganze Bandbreite von Peter Pawlowitschs Schnief- und Schnüffelgeräuschen kennengelernt; er konnte sie diagnostizieren und interpretieren; er kannte sie, wie eine Mutter jede Nuance der Schreie ihres Neugeborenen kennt. Peter Pawlowitsch hatte ein Schniefen, wenn er verärgert, und ein anderes Schniefen, wenn er enttäuscht war – bizarrerweise hatte er sogar ein verschleimtes, glucksendes Schniefen, das Zufriedenheit ausdrückte. Und er hatte ein Schniefen, das bedeutete, dass er in einer passiv-aggressiven Stimmungslage war. Dieses Schniefen äußerte er am häufigsten, und es war auch dasjenige, das er jetzt von sich gab.

»Werden Sie jetzt rausgeworfen?«, fragte Alexander.

»Nicht von dir, mein Lieber. Das steht nicht in deiner Macht.«

»Von der Partei.«

»Jedes Mal, wenn du einen Wutanfall bekommst, kriege ich eine Gehaltserhöhung, weißt du. Die wissen, wie schwer meine Aufgabe ist, und, Towarischtsch, das ist ein großes Glück.«

Seine Worte ratterten wie Fehlzündungen. Alexander zuckte zusammen.

»Jedes Mal, wenn du dich wie ein undankbares Kind aufführst, begreifen sie noch besser, was für ein Vergnügen – ein reines Vergnügen – es ist, sich mit dir herumzuzanken. Wenn das also deine einzige Sorge ist, nur weiter so.«

Schweigen. Alexander wartete darauf, dass Pawlowitsch wieder schniefte, doch er tat es nicht.

»Du scheinst nie begriffen zu haben, dass ich ehrliches Interesse an deiner Karriere habe. Wenn ich ein Talent wie deines sehe, will ich es beschützen. Ich will es fördern. Ich will helfen, es innerhalb des Systems voranzubringen. Ich will verhindern, dass es gewissen zersetzenden Einflüssen ausgeliefert ist.«

Durch das Fenster beobachtete Alexander, wie ein Auto Schmutz an eine Gebäudewand spritzte.

»Aber ich interessiere mich nicht für dich, Towarischtsch. Nur für dein Gehirn. Dass das klar ist.«

Alexander, der lange geglaubt hatte, er und sein Gehirn seien ein und dasselbe, wusste selbst nicht, warum er das als beleidigend empfand. »Gut«, sagte er. »Ich denke nicht, dass ich das je verwechselt habe.«

»Du kannst also weiterspielen«, sagte Peter Pawlowitsch. »Das ist die gute Nachricht. Ich hoffe, du bist glücklich. Überglücklich.«

»Begeistert.«

»Gut. Das hoffe ich doch. Dein Glück hat eine solche Strahlkraft, weißt du? Es erhebt uns und macht uns zu besseren Menschen. Es ist eine wahre Freude, das zu erleben. Eine Inspiration für sämtliche Generationen.«

»Schon gut. Das reicht.«

»Am Dienstag geht das Spiel weiter.«

»Verstanden.«

»Im Voraus gern geschehen«, sagte Peter Pawlowitsch mit einem traurigen Schniefen. »Bestimmt liegt die Dankeskarte schon in der Post.«

Das Spiel ging weiter, und Alexander spürte zersetzende Paranoia in sich aufsteigen. Er begegnete Dimitri mit tiefem Misstrauen. Er

beobachtete, wie Dimitri sich unbewusst auf den Lippen herumkaute oder sein dummes Gesicht rasierte (unnötig, immer unnötig) oder am Telefon über Nichtigkeiten sprach – mit seiner langweiligen Freundin angeblich, aber Alexander war sich nicht mehr
sicher, dass das stimmte. Bei einigen Eröffnungen hatte Russajew
ein wenig zu schnell, ein wenig zu sauber reagiert, und Alexander
begann sich zu fragen, ob Dimitri bestochen worden war, seine Eröffnungszüge an Russajew durchzugeben. Sobald Alexander sich
das fragte, war er überzeugt. Die Theorie bewegte sich in seinem
Hirn wie ein mechanischer Apparat. Das Getriebe schaltete; die
Riemen zogen an.

Als Alexander den Parteiarzt besuchte – um gewogen und begutachtet und betastet zu werden wie ein wertvolles Stück Vieh –,
wurde er nach seinem Belastungsniveau, seinen Alpträumen, seinen Sorgen, seinen Ängsten befragt. Alexander saß auf der Stuhl-
kante und weigerte sich zu antworten. Diese Fragen waren zu zielgerichtet; Alexander hätte sich nicht gewundert, wenn auch der
Arzt in der Sache mit drinsteckte. Egal – er war nicht umsonst ein
Schachgenie. Alexander baumelte mit den Beinen und sprach gutgelaunt über die Annehmlichkeiten des Spiels: den Trost, den die
Siege boten, die Weisheit, welche die Niederlagen mit sich brachten. Der Arzt presste die Lippen flach wie eine Klinge aufeinander.
Er machte sich eine Notiz.

Am Ende dauerte das Spiel dreiundfünfzig Partien – eine unendliche, undenkbare Zahl. Die Reporter waren abwechselnd ehrfürchtig und schadenfroh und gelangweilt und fassungslos. Als die
letzten Züge ausgeführt wurden – als Alexander seine Dame den
offenen Armen von Russajews wartendem Läufer überließ –, beugten die Zuschauer sich vor, konzentriert, atemlos. Die Kameras
schnappten wie konsternierte Schildkröten. Alexander ließ die
Knöchel knacken und lockerte seine Finger. Er rückte seine Schultern zurecht. Er sah als Erster, wie Russajews Blick sich trübte –
nicht mit Tränen, sondern mit der matten Verwirrung eines Kindes, das erklären soll, wie es eine abgeschriebene Matheaufgabe

gelöst hat. Die Zuschauer sahen es nicht, also beugten sie sich weiter vor, hielten still und mühten sich gemeinsam, zu begreifen, was da vor sich ging – war es verrückt, selbstmörderisch, ein Wunder? Auf Lichtwellen, die jede Grenzkontrolle unterliefen und jedes Protokoll missachteten, strahlten die steifen Gestalten Alexanders und Russajews ins All hinaus. Staubkörner rieselten von der Decke, fingen das spärliche Lampenlicht ein und verliehen dem Raum eine matte, traumgleiche Atmosphäre. Alexander trommelte mit den Fingern; er wusste, wie grausam und theatralisch das war. Russajews Gesicht übergoss sich mit ungläubigem Staunen, dann nahm es den beinahe dankbaren Ausdruck eines Menschen an, dessen bittere Enttäuschung endlich tiefer Erschöpfung weicht. Er hatte begriffen. Er machte seinen nächsten Zug mit resignierter Anmut. Der Rest war reines Ritual, war das herrschaftliche Reglement, das ein Heer auf dem Rückzug befolgt. Russajew lächelte leicht und schluckte. Alexander blinzelte und sah die Zukunft vor sich aufblitzen. Seine Hände zitterten, sein Kopf leerte sich, ein arktisch kalter Draht zog sich ihm von der Kehle bis in den Magen, und es verblüffte ihn, wie sehr der größte Augenblick seiner Karriere einem Moment absoluten Grauens glich.

Und dann war es vorbei. Russajews König lag auf der Seite, und Russajew unterschrieb den Punktestand, und Alexanders Ohren versagten ihm den Dienst. Ein Mann kam mit einem Raubtierlächeln auf die Bühne gestürmt, mit ausgestreckter Hand und einem Pokal.

Später saß Alexander in der Hotelbar, während Dimitri die Koffer packte. Im Staatsfernsehen sprach ein hässlicher Nachrichtensprecher über Alexanders Sieg. Es war viel von seiner Jugend die Rede, als sei es das Beste, was man über ihn sagen konnte, dass er den Anstand besessen hatte, nicht allzu lange auf der Welt zu sein.

Am nächsten Morgen wurde Alexander wie so oft vom Klingeln des Telefons geweckt. »Geh ran, Dimitri«, ächzte er, bis ihm wieder einfiel, dass Dimitri nicht da war; er war am Abend davor mit hochroten Ohren abgereist, beglückt, dass seine Arbeit getan war und er zu seiner albernen Verlobten zurückkehren würde – Galina, hieß sie nicht so? Alexander wurde bewusst, dass er nie danach gefragt hatte. Er stand auf. Auf dem Fußboden hatte Dimitri ein paar verstreute Habseligkeiten hinterlassen, die angesammelten Kleinigkeiten seines halben Jahrs als besserer Hausdiener auf der Flucht. Stifte und Kleiderbügel waren darunter und rätselhafte Zettel – Quittungen für Einkäufe, an die Alexander sich nicht erinnern konnte, obwohl sie immer zusammen gewesen waren. Wer war Dimitri? Wo war er jetzt? Warum ging er nicht ans Telefon?

Einen kurzen, erhebenden Moment lang überlegte Alexander, wer wohl anrief, um ihm zu gratulieren – am wahrscheinlichsten seine Mutter, wenngleich sie in letzter Zeit meistens wartete, bis er sie anrief. Ein Kommilitone von der Schachakademie war es eher nicht; ihre unverhohlene Missgunst hatte ihm etwas ausgemacht, als er noch das Gefühl hatte, Besseres verdient zu haben. Jetzt kam sie ihm angemessen vor. Er fragte sich nicht, ob es Elisabeta sein könnte, denn er dachte nicht mehr an sie.

Das Telefon klingelte weiter. Er wusste – und eigentlich hatte er es von Anfang an gewusst –, dass es nur einer sein konnte.

Peter Pawlowitsch schniefte glücklich in den Hörer. »Herzlichen Glückwunsch, mein Freund«, sagte er.

»Ihnen habe ich das nicht gerade zu verdanken.«

»Gerade mir, wenn du mal darüber nachdenkst.«

»Tue ich nicht.«

»Wie fühlt es sich an?«

Alexander trat ans Fenster und blickte in das Morgengrauen hinaus. Der Tag sah jetzt schon aus wie ein Requiem. Ein ekelhafter Geschmack haftete in seiner Kehle. »Nach gar nichts. Es fühlt sich nach gar nichts an.«

»Komm schon. Sei nicht so verbittert.«

»Es fühlt sich an wie immer.«

»Tut es nicht.«

Peter Pawlowitsch hatte recht. Es fühlte sich nicht an wie immer. Jetzt, da er bekommen hatte, was er wollte, hatte Alexander sein ganzen Leben gerechtfertigt – jede einsame und egoistische und seltsame kindliche Marotte, den Mangel an Freundschaften, den Mangel an Liebesbeziehungen. Den Entschluss, mit der Flugschrift aufzuhören, den Entschluss, sich die vergangenen vier Jahre lang mit diesen Leuten abzugeben und jede importierte Delikatesse zu schlucken, die sie ihm auftischten. Alles hatte sich gelohnt; alles ergab einen Sinn. Er war quer durch ein gewaltiges Land seinem Ego nachgejagt, und hier, in Moskau, im Hotel Sport, hatte er es endlich eingeholt. Er war für den Augenblick der beste Schachspieler der Welt – auch wenn mit jeder Minute der Tag näherrückte, wo dem nicht mehr so war, und wer konnte schon sagen (selbst jetzt, in eben dieser Sekunde), ob es nicht irgendwo auf der weiten Welt jemanden gab, der ihn schlagen konnte? Ein manisches, prophetisches Genie in irgendeiner Höhle vielleicht oder eine bessere Version seiner selbst in einem Paralleluniversum, die es nicht über sich gebracht hatte, so viele Kompromisse zu machen wie er. Es war ein bitterer Sieg – damit hatte er gerechnet. Wie seltsam, dass er sich zugleich so flüchtig anfühlte. Alexander sah zu, wie der Minutenzeiger zuckend über das Ziffernblatt zurückwich, und fragte sich mit jedem Augenblick: War er jetzt wirklich Weltmeister? War er es *jetzt*? Man konnte es nie wissen. Seltsam, dass er daran nie gedacht hatte, als er entscheiden musste, ob er den Rest seines Lebens gegen diese Chance eintauschen sollte. Er konnte sich seines Erfolges nie sicher sein. Selbst wenn er wirklich der Weltmeister war, war der Mann, der ihn einmal besiegen würde (und natürlich wäre es ein Mann), zweifellos schon geboren – er schrieb schon Aufgaben in den Sand oder riss Schachrätsel aus der Zeitung aus oder starrte stundenlang die Wände an. Er war schon einsam. Seine Eltern machten sich schon Sorgen um ihn. Sie sahen in ihm schon die Anlagen zu Größe oder Wahnsinn oder zu beidem zugleich; sie sahen, wie ihr Kind einen Keil in die Welt trieb und eine Kluft aufriss, in der er einmal gesalbt und gepriesen sitzen würde, wenn Alexander alt und vergessen war.

»Bist du noch da?«, fragte Peter Pawlowitsch.

»Ich weiß es nicht.«

»Jetzt werd nicht philosophisch.«

Draußen wandten die Blätter an den Bäumen ihre blasse Unterseite nach oben. Es sah aus, als wollten sie sich ergeben.

»Du hast dein Leben lang auf diesen Moment hingearbeitet. Du solltest radschlagen vor Freude. Wofür war denn alles gut, wenn nicht dafür?«

Alexander glaubte nicht, dass Peter Pawlowitsch seine Worte freundlich meinte. Doch er hatte niemanden sonst, dem er das hier sagen konnte – das hier oder sonst irgendetwas.

»Ich weiß es nicht«, sagte er. Die Fensterscheibe kühlte seine Stirn; sie vermittelte ihm ein Gefühl beruhigender, pragmatischer Gegenwart. Alexander dachte kurz an seine Mutter. »Ich weiß nicht, wofür es gut war.«

Peter Pawlowitsch schwieg. »Bist du angezogen? Es wird Zeit für die Fotos.«

»Was für Fotos?«

»Mit dem Pokal natürlich.« Peter Pawlowitsch schniefte grausam. »Ein Familienportrait.«

KAPITEL 12

Irina
St. Petersburg, 2006

Und so zog ich, als mir nichts Besseres einfiel, mein einziges tief ausgeschnittenes Top an und ging in die Prawda-Bar. Drinnen war die Atmosphäre unerbittlich schmuddelig; die Luft war trüb vor Staub und von einer halsstarrigen Verdorbenheit, die fast schon wieder erfrischend wirkte. Ich rutschte auf einem Barhocker hin und her, trank Weißwein, buchstabierte mir die Worte in der *Kommersant* vor und musterte potentielle Kandidaten für Viktor Dawidenko, wenn sie zur Tür hereinkamen. Es fühlte sich dekadent, verdorben, krankhaft an, vor Einbruch der Dunkelheit zu trinken. Ich trommelte mit den Fingern auf dem Tresen. Dafür war ich schließlich hergekommen, oder? Um in Bars herumzusitzen und auf wildfremde Männer zu warten? Eigentlich war es nicht ganz das, was mir vorgeschwebt hatte.

Nach mehreren Fehlalarmen kam der Mann herein, der Viktor Dawidenko sein musste. Er war recht groß, knapp eins neunzig vielleicht, eine Körpergröße, die je nach der eigenen Einstellung gewaltig oder beinahe normal wirken konnte. Er trug einen Bart, was ich ihm gar nicht mal übelnahm. Ich fragte mich, ob jemand, der nach mir suchte, Schwierigkeiten hätte, mich zu erkennen. Oder war ich in der ganzen Bar die einzige Kandidatin für mich selbst? Das mochte ich nicht glauben; ich wollte lieber denken, ich könnte jede Beliebige sein. Aber dann sah ich mich um – sah die Kampflesben, die Femmes fatales mit ihren dicken Schutzschichten aus Augen-Make-up, und musste den Tatsachen ins Gesicht sehen. Ich war weit und breit die einzige, die nervös und wohlerzogen aussah, und hätte jemand nach mir gesucht, er hätte mich sofort entdeckt.

Ich trat zu Viktor Dawidenko an den Tisch. Ich verschränkte die Arme und ließ sie wieder sinken. Dann sprach ich ihn an.

»Ja?« Seine Stimme klang ein wenig rau, ein wenig mürrisch, ganz so, wie man es sich vorstellen würde. Er hatte vorspringende Brauen und darunter erstaunlich blaue Augen. Sein Haar war gelockt und offenbar kaum zu bändigen.

Ich stellte mich vor. Er musterte mich von oben bis unten, wie Mischa es vorhergesagt hatte.

»Sind Sie Journalistin?« Er hatte auf Englisch umgeschwenkt. Sein Akzent, das war selbst an diesem einen Satz zu hören, war eine komplexe Angelegenheit, zu der etliche Erfahrungen und Existenzen und höhere Lehranstalten beigetragen hatten.

»Nein.«

»Bloggen Sie?«

»Nein.«

»Sind Sie in den sozialen Medien aktiv?«

»Eigentlich nicht, nein.«

Er seufzte. Es war ein zutiefst betrübter, gequälter, demonstrativer Seufzer, und ich mochte ihn sofort dafür.

»Kann ich trotzdem kurz mit Ihnen sprechen?« Eine leichte Panik stieg in mir auf. Dies war meine erste Begegnung mit einem Vertreter von Besetows eigentlichem Team, und ich scheiterte kläglich daran, zu sagen, was ich zu sagen hatte.

»Meinetwegen.«

»Wann denn? Soll ich in Ihr Büro kommen?«

»Büro? Ah. Nein. Wie wäre es jetzt gleich?«

Das kam mir ein wenig unprofessionell vor, auch wenn man meine eigenen Gründe, hier zu sein, nicht ganz – nicht einmal teilweise – professionell nennen konnte. Allerdings hatte ich im Laufe der letzten Monate begonnen, meine Suche nach Alexander Besetow als eine Art Job zu betrachten – ich drückte mich jedenfalls davor wie vor der Arbeit, und ich stellte mich ihr mit Stressgefühlen, gelegentlichem Pflichtgefühl und erheblichem Widerwillen.

»Ja«, sagte ich. »Okay.«

Er nahm meine Hand, und einen kurzen, absurden Augenblick lang dachte ich, er würde sie küssen.

»Viktor Dawidenko«, sagte er und ließ meine Hand los. »Bitte setzen Sie sich.«

Das tat ich. In seinem Auftreten war eine Vornehmheit, die mir fast ein bisschen albern vorkam, aber zugleich sehr reflektiert. Ich richtete mich auf, um für die Darbietung, die mich erwartete, gerüstet zu sein. Viktor bestellte drei Wodka, was ich beeindruckend und beängstigend fand, bis er mir eins der Gläser herüberreichte. Ich nahm einen Schluck und hustete.

»Wo haben Sie Englisch gelernt?«, fragte ich.

»Zuletzt in Oxford.«

»Was haben Sie davor gemacht?«

»Ich habe japanische Videorekorder importiert.«

»Wirklich?«

»Wirklich.«

»Und jetzt sind Sie der PR-Mensch.«

»Der bin ich. Und Sie?« Er wirkte amüsiert.

»Wo ich Englisch gelernt habe?«

»Was Sie machen.«

»Nichts.«

»Natürlich. Wäre das eher ein diplomatisches Nichts? Oder ein kommerzielles Nichts?« Sein quasi-britischer Akzent klang, als sei er immer kurz davor, sich zu entschuldigen. Sein Gesichtsausdruck war der eines Menschen, der sich in seinem ganzen Leben nicht entschuldigt hat.

»Ich weiß nicht, wovon Sie reden«, sagte ich.

»Oder akademisch? Einfach nur verquer?«

»Ich weiß es wirklich nicht.«

»Ah. Na schön.«

Ich wusste, dass er mich nach einem verworrenen sozialen Koordinatensystem beurteilte, das ich nicht durchschaute. Ich nippte noch einmal an meinem Wodka und ließ den Alkohol meine Schleimhäute beizen.

»Also, was dann? Was wollen Sie?« Er hielt sein zweites Glas in der Hand und fuhr den feuchten Ring nach, den es auf dem Tisch hinterlassen hatte. »Soll ich Ihnen ein Schachbrett signieren lassen oder so?«

Ich wandte den Kopf zur Seite. Der Mann hatte irgendetwas an sich, dass ich ihm nicht alles auf einmal sagen mochte. »Mein Vater war ein Fan von Besetow«, sagte ich. »Ich würde mich einfach gern mit ihm treffen.«

»Ihr Vater war sein Fan?«

Ich nickte. Mir war klar, wie das klang; ich wusste, was für unappetitliche Gebrechen dieser Mann jetzt in meiner Psyche sah oder zu sehen glaubte. Ich wollte diesen Teil der Unterhaltung so schnell wie möglich hinter mich bringen.

»Besetow hat viele Fans«, sagte Viktor.

»Klar.«

»Wahrscheinlich haben viele Menschen Väter, die seine Fans waren.«

»Bestimmt.«

»Und sie kommen nicht alle her und wollen ihn sprechen.«

»Sicher nicht.«

Er lehnte sich zurück und nahm einen Schluck, und gleich darauf einen kräftigeren Schluck von seinem Wodka. »Es ist eine Art sentimentale Mission, oder?«

Ich zuckte zurück. Ich hasse es, wenn man mir Sentimentalität vorwirft. Aber ich wusste, dass es nicht half, sie abzustreiten; mit jedem Versuch machte man sich erst recht verdächtig. »Kann sein. So kann man es vielleicht ausdrücken.« Ich hielt inne, um großspurig noch einen Schluck zu trinken. »Er ist sicher sehr beschäftigt.«

»So beschäftigt auch wieder nicht.«

»Nein?« Ich wartete lange genug auf eine Erläuterung, um zu begreifen, dass es keine geben würde. »Wie lange arbeiten Sie schon für ihn?«

»Seit zwei Jahren.«

»Und wie kam es dazu?«

»Ich bin zu einer Kundgebung gegangen.«

»Und dann?«

»Dann habe ich ihn angesprochen und ihm meinen Lebenslauf in die Hand gedrückt.«

»Verstehe. Sie sind also einfach hingegangen?«

»Ich habe einfach einen eindrucksvollen Lebenslauf.«

»Daran zweifele ich bestimmt nicht. Stellt er sein Personal immer so ein?«

»Welches Personal?«

»Wer arbeitet denn für ihn?«

»Da wäre erst einmal ich. Dann Nina, Besetows Frau. Ein echter Sonnenschein. Dann Vlad, der Leibwächter, der zu zwei Dritteln verblödet ist. Und Boris, mein Assistent. Er selbst würde sich nicht so nennen, aber genau das ist er.«

»Wie würde er sich denn nennen?«

»Er würde vermutlich behaupten, mein Kollege zu sein. Besetows Personalentscheidungen haben nicht viel mit Logik zu tun. Wenn Sie seine Frau kennten, wüssten Sie, was ich meine. Sagen Sie niemandem, dass ich das gesagt habe.«

»Natürlich nicht.«

Viktor bestellte mit einem Fingerschnipsen die nächste Runde. Er lehnte sich zurück und sah mich lange an. »Also – das ist alles? Ihr Vater war ein Fan von ihm, und Sie wollen sich mit ihm treffen?«

»Ja.« Ich wusste selbst nicht, warum ich ihn belog. Ihm die Wahrheit zu sagen konnte meiner Sache nur nützen – vielleicht betrieb Besetow ja eine Wunscherfüllungsstiftung für todkranke Amerikaner. Aber Viktor Dawidenko war attraktiv, schätze ich, und sein Blick war ungewöhnlich klar, und ich wollte nicht sehen, was mit seinem Gesicht passierte, wenn wir dieses spezielle Gespräch führen mussten. »Ja«, sagte ich. »Ich schätze, das ist alles.«

Er schien skeptisch zu sein. »Manchmal verstehen wir uns wohl nicht einmal selbst.«

»Ziemlich oft sogar, würde ich sagen.«

»Aber – wirklich? Ist das wirklich alles? Sind Sie nicht hier, um ihn zu interviewen oder so? Ihm zu sagen, was er anders machen soll? Ihre politische Expertise anzubieten?« All das ratterte er herunter, ohne im Mindesten ironisch zu klingen.

»Was? Ob ich … was? Nein. Nein.«

»Hm.« Er nahm die Speisekarte und begann darin zu lesen. Ich wartete darauf, dass er weitersprach, und bemerkte distanziert die Welle der Angst, die sich in meinem Brustkasten aufzutürmen begann. Es ist interessant, wenn man beobachten kann, wie die einzelnen Bestandteile eines Gesichts zu Schönheit verschmelzen. Wenn etwas an dem Gesicht dieses Mannes ungewöhnlich war, dann seine Strenge, die von der Lieblichkeit seiner Augen gebrochen wurde. Ich wollte unser Gespräch unbedingt wieder in den Bereich beantwortbarer Fragen lenken. Ich sagte das Einzige, was ich zu sagen hatte.

»Ich habe mich neulich mit Michail Andrejewitsch Solowjow getroffen.«

Er ließ die Speisekarte sinken und sah mich mit einem Ausdruck an, den man nur als Weltschmerz beschreiben konnte. »Mischa. Verstehe. Und wie war's?«

»Es sieht so aus, als wäre er auf einem Rachefeldzug.«

Viktor riss mit einem gespielt verletzten Ausdruck die Augen auf. »Ach ja?«

»Ich hatte den Eindruck, es gäbe, na ja, Flügelkämpfe.«

»Flügelkämpfe? Um Himmels willen. Erzählen Sie mehr davon.«

»Er wirkte verbittert.«

»Er ist von einem Bus überrollt worden. Das würde jeden verbittern, würde ich sagen.«

»Das wusste ich nicht. Aber, ich meine, das war nicht Besetows Schuld, oder?«

»Schuld ist ein ziemlich verschwommener Begriff, finden Sie nicht?«

»Eigentlich nicht«, sagte ich. Viktor Dawidenko zuckte mit den Schultern und wandte sich wieder der Speisekarte zu. Ich zwang meine Stimme, tiefer zu klingen, als sie es normalerweise tat. »Wie würden Sie die Beziehung zwischen dem Wahren Russland und dem Alternativen Russland genau beschreiben?«

Er verzog das Gesicht. »Stumme Gleichgültigkeit. Nein, das stimmt so nicht. Widerwillige Duldung.«

»Von dem Anderen Russland aus, meinen Sie?«

»Ja, klar.«

»Also ist das Wahre Russland ein PR-Problem?«

»In mancher Hinsicht schon, in anderer nicht.«

»Wie alles andere auch. Aber warum duldet Alexander Mischas Fraktion? Hat Mischa etwas gegen ihn in der Hand?«

»Sie meinen, ob er ihn erpresst?«

»Schuldet Alexander ihm einen Gefallen oder so? Oder weiß Mischa etwas über ihn?«

Viktor warf mir einen amüsierten Blick zu. »Über eine Geliebte, meinen Sie?«

»Oh, das würde ich nie …«

»Darauf wäre ich gar nicht gekommen«, sagte er. »Aber … nein. Ich denke nicht, dass Besetows Geheimnisse sexueller Natur sind. Dann wäre er wahrscheinlich ein besserer Chef.«

»Aber warum dann das Bündnis mit dem Wahren Russland?«

»Darüber darf ich mit Ihnen nicht sprechen«, sagte Viktor gutgelaunt. »Aber ich habe einen Vorschlag. Nächste Woche ist er auf einer Kundgebung. Am Samstag. Am Gostiny Dwor.«

»Ich weiß.« Ich hatte in den Nachmittagsstunden zwischen Lesen und Schlafen, die ich mit ziellosen, trüben Wanderungen durch die Stadt verbrachte, die Plakate gesehen. »Versammlung der Unzufriedenen« stand darauf. Dazu waren die winzigen Flaggen und Symbole verschiedener Interessengruppen abgebildet, die mir teilweise vertraut waren – Umweltschützer waren dabei, Menschenrechtler, Wirtschaftsliberale, Marktregulierer und viele, die mir überhaupt nichts sagten –, und ich fand es interessant, in einer einzigen Demonstration so eine Bandbreite politischer Splittergruppen versammelt zu sehen. In der Mitte des Plakats war ein Bild von Alexander Besetow: Er starrte mir angewidert entgegen, als wüsste er schon, dass ich vorhatte, ihm auf die Nerven zu fallen. Über ihm war in surrealen Farben ein verzerrter, durchgestrichener Putin abgebildet. Sein spitzes, reptilienhaftes Gesicht trug den Ausdruck fortwährender Missbilligung.

»Da sollten Sie hin«, sagte Viktor, »und wieder dieses Top anziehen.«

Mir dämmerte allmählich, dass er mit mir flirtete. Ich bin wirklich schlecht darin, so etwas wahrzunehmen. »Soll ich mich da wieder an Sie wenden?«

»An mich? Nein, bloß nicht. Mit mir reden Sie überhaupt nicht mehr. Mir können Sie nichts vormachen, aber Alexander ist eben, sagen wir mal, vorsichtig. Dieses Gespräch hat nie stattgefunden. Ich darf mich mit Leuten wie Ihnen gar nicht treffen.«

»Mit Frauen?«

»Sehr witzig.«

»Amerikanern?«

»Schon wärmer.«

»Wen soll ich dann ansprechen?« Mir wurde klar, dass Viktor mir möglicherweise kein Wort geglaubt hatte, und dann kam ich zum ersten Mal auf die Idee, mich zu fragen, ob es klug sei, ihm zu glauben.

Viktor beugte sich vor. »Wenden Sie sich an Nina. Die Ehefrau. Sie hat rotes Haar. Sie können sie gar nicht verfehlen.«

»Okay.«

»Die können Sie um einen Termin bitten.«

»Sie sind der PR-Mensch, und Sie raten mir, bei einer Kundgebung seine Frau zu belästigen?« Genau das hatte ich vermeiden wollen.

»Sie fühlt sich wichtig, wenn sie Dinge arrangieren kann«, sagte Viktor. »Sie gibt Ihnen bestimmt einen Termin.«

»Wie ist sie so?«

Er blickte hoch. »Wieso? Sind Sie auf ihre Stelle aus?«

Mir klappte der Mund auf. Ich klappte ihn wieder zu. »Nein. Nein. Natürlich nicht.«

»Es wäre nicht gerade professionell, mich über die Frau meines Vorgesetzten zu äußern.«

»Nein. Natürlich. Tut mir leid, dass ich danach gefragt habe.«

»Aber meine ganze Karriere beruht darauf, berufliche Grenzen zu überwinden. Also kann ich sagen, dass sie … dass sie ihn nicht glücklich macht.«

Ich verdrehte die Augen. Dieses Thema langweilte mich jetzt schon. War sie vielleicht dominant? Beraubte sie ihn seiner Männlichkeit? War sie geschmacklos? Ich wollte nichts mehr von den Defiziten irgendwelcher Ehefrauen hören, nie mehr, und war plötzlich froh, dass ich nie eine werden würde.

»Was ist?«, fragte Viktor.

»Ach, ich weiß nicht. Jemanden glücklich zu machen ist heutzutage ganz schön viel verlangt.«

»Finden Sie?« Er sah mich an, fiel mir auf, wie Männer mich damals angesehen hatten, als sie das noch taten. Im College hatte es eine kurze, komische Phase gegeben, in der man mich für tiefgründig hielt. Die Leute meinten damit nur, dass mein Gesicht beim Zuhören nicht besonders lebhaft wirkte. Ich merkte, wie Viktor Dawidenko anfing, mich für eine Art Rätsel zu halten, und das kann nicht gutgehen – nicht einmal deshalb, weil Leute dieses Rätsel lösen, sondern weil sie herausfinden, dass es gar nicht viel zu lösen gibt. Sich selbst durch die Augen eines anderen zu sehen ist, als würde man jemanden durch die lange unbesuchte eigene Wohnung führen. Teile der eigenen Persönlichkeit, die einem selbstverständlich geworden sind, wirken wie Souvenirs aus einer Zeit, an die man sich nur ungern erinnert. Ach, das alte Ding?, würde man am liebsten von seinem unnützen Wissen, seinen politischen Ansichten, seinem Körper sagen. Habe ich in Barcelona für vier Euro gekauft. Das ist gar nicht echt. Dieser Witz? Den reiße ich ständig. Der langweilt dich bald. Mich langweilt er. Aber das weiß der neue Bekannte noch nicht, und man hat nicht wirklich vor, es ihm zu erzählen.

»Und Sie?«, fragte ich.

»Und ich was?«

Mir fiel auf, dass ich nicht wusste, was ich eigentlich fragen wollte. »Was … motiviert Sie? Glauben Sie an Besetow?« Ich fragte leichthin, obwohl ich verzweifelt auf ein Ja hoffte.

»Ja.« Er beugte sich vor. »Das tue ich.«

»Warum?«

»Warum? Die Dame fragt warum. Weil es etwas bewegen wird, im Wesentlichen. Ich glaube schon, dass es etwas bewegen wird. Denken Sie an den einundneunziger Putsch, wie da die Demonstranten nicht mit Gewalt vertrieben werden konnten, weil es einfach zu viele waren. Es ist ein gewaltiges Land. Er wird nicht gewinnen. Natürlich wird er nicht gewinnen. Aber ich glaube, dass er etwas in Bewegung setzt.«

In diesen Worten fand ich endlich den spezifischen Grund für mein unbestimmtes Hingezogensein: Hier war jemand, der daran glaubte, dass Alexander etwas bewegen konnte. Vielleicht hatte ich mich schon vorher zu Viktor hingezogen gefühlt, aber jetzt ließ sich dieses Gefühl auf etwas ganz Konkretes, Eigennütziges zurückführen: eine gemeinsame Vision.

»Haben Sie zu Hause jemanden?«

»Hatte ich.«

»Dann haben Sie ihn verlassen?«

»Habe ich.«

»Für das hier?«

Ich ließ meine Zunge über die untere Zahnreihe gleiten und spürte die Unebenheiten, die in den letzten Jahren wiedergekommen waren. All diese Kieferorthopädie, so eine Investition, und wofür? Aber ich wusste, dass dieser Gedanke es nicht wert war, weiterverfolgt zu werden. Wenn man so darüber nachdachte, konnte man alles – das ganze Leben – als Abfolge unnützer Vorbereitungen ansehen. Warum treiben wir Sport, und warum essen wir jeden Tag die erforderlichen Unmengen Gemüse? Und warum sind wir so eitel, was unseren Körper oder unser Hirn angeht oder worauf wir uns sonst so viel einbilden? Und warum schluchzen wir eine Woche lang, weigern uns zu essen, liegen falsch herum im Bett und sehen das nekrotische Licht am Horizont heraufkriechen, bloß weil ein Junge, der uns nie geliebt hat, es immer noch nicht tut? Solche Qualen, so viel Narzissmus, so viel Geschichtsblindheit. All die großartigen Vorhaben sind am Ende doch nicht so groß. Es sind alles läppische kleine Anwandlungen, Stückwerk zur Abwehr des Unausweichlichen, müßige Versuche, uns abzulenken, die allein dazu da sind, diese eine Tatsache zu entschärfen – die zentrale Tatsache, die unglaubliche, unumstößliche Tatsache unserer Vergänglichkeit.

»Ich denke schon«, sagte ich zögernd.

»Das hat ihn bestimmt nicht glücklich gemacht.«

Ich zuckte ruckartig, ausweichend mit den Schultern. Ich imitierte die Art, wie er kurz davor mit den Schultern gezuckt hatte.

»Wahrscheinlich nicht.«

»Hat es Sie glücklich gemacht?«

»Bis jetzt nicht. Ich bin verhalten optimistisch.«

»Das ist wahrscheinlich zu optimistisch.«

Etwas Durchtriebenes regte sich in seinem Gesicht, wie ein Penimento, ein Echo früherer Absichten. Die ganze Zeit schon hatte eine Spannung das Gespräch durchzogen, hatte die Oberfläche mit einem synkopischen Kontrapunkt unterlegt. Wir waren kämpferischer als nötig, das war es.

Er verlangte per Handzeichen nach der Rechnung und bezahlte sie, bevor ich auch nur angefangen hatte, in meinem Portemonnaie zu wühlen. Ein Gefühl der Zuneigung bahnte sich an, schwenkte sich, wie so oft, auf eine neue, unerwartete Richtung ein. Ich dachte kurz an meine Serie von Männergeschichten am College: insgesamt eher unerheblich; es fiel mir schwer, mir einzelne Gesichter oder Persönlichkeiten ins Gedächtnis zu rufen, während ich mich an die Enttäuschungen, Missverständnisse und Erniedrigungen nur allzu leicht erinnerte. Ich fragte mich, wie halbgare Mini-Affären im Jahr 2006 überhaupt aussehen mochten – wahrscheinlich fragten sich die Leute ständig, ob sie verlassen wurden, weil sie nicht genug Präsenz im Internet zeigten oder so. Das Internet: ein komplett neuer Schauplatz der existentiellen Bedeutungslosigkeit. Sobald mir klar wurde, worüber ich da nachdachte, wusste ich, dass ich betrunken war.

Draußen auf der Straße waren die Gebäude zu klar umrissen, als seien sie eben frisch skizziert; die Sterne waren ein Stück heller, als es glaubhaft gewesen wäre; ich fühlte mich insgesamt, als hätte ich vor kurzem neue Kontaktlinsen bekommen. Das – das alles, ich wusste es ja – war albern. Was mir am Betrunkensein gar nicht gefiel, war, dass es das gesamte Selbstmitleid auf einmal freisetzte – und in meinem Fall war dieses Selbstmitleid gewaltig, nagend und unersättlich; es war ein ständiger Kampf, es im Zaum zu halten. Wenn ich trank, brach meine Verteidigung in sich zusammen, und ich konnte ohne weiteres eine Stunde vor dem Spiegel zubringen und denken, ich sei zu hübsch, um zu sterben.

»Also dann«, sagte ich unvermittelt hölzern, unvermittelt professionell. »Danke, dass Sie sich Zeit genommen haben.«

Ich reichte ihm die Hand und wusste sofort, dass das ein Fehler war.

»Sehr gern geschehen«, sagte er, nahm meine Hand und schüttelte sie kunstvoller als unbedingt nötig. »Dann sehen wir uns bei der Kundgebung.«

»Ja«, sagte ich, nahm all meine Selbstachtung zusammen und versuchte einen stimmigen Abgang hinzubekommen. »Wir sehen uns auf der Kundgebung.«

Ich ging langsam, in immer weiter werdenden Kreisen zurück. Die Newa wirkte kälter als sonst; sie zitterte mit ihren Blättern und Treibgutstückchen. Ich hielt an und starrte hinein, um den Kopf freizubekommen. Dass ich ins Wasser sah, rief aus irgendwelchen Gründen – oder auch ohne Grund – ein Bild meines Vaters in mir wach. Vielleicht war es die Erinnerung an eine Erinnerung oder die Erinnerung an ein Foto. Jedenfalls starrte ich ins Wasser und konnte ihn beinahe vor mir sehen, einem Ostfenster zugewandt, seinen harten Schatten im schräg einfallenden Licht. Ich konnte beinahe seinen gebeugten Rücken, seine hängenden Schultern sehen. Beinahe erkannte ich darin seine vorzeitige Resignation. Als dieses Bild aufgenommen wurde oder diese Erinnerung entstand, wusste er es schon. Er wusste es, musste es gewusst haben. Und doch ist es so schwer, den Moment abzupassen, wenn der Scheideweg erreicht ist. So schwer zu wissen, ob es Zeit ist zu gehen. Es ist ein Strategiespiel, das niemand gewinnen kann. Vielleicht hatte er darüber nachgedacht, hatte sich verschätzt, und dann war es zu spät. Oder vielleicht hatte er darüber nachgedacht und sich edelmütig dagegen entschieden, hatte mit klarem Verstand, bewusst und mutig die Erniedrigungen des geistigen und körperlichen Verfalls als Bestandteil des Lebens in Kauf genommen. Oder vielleicht, vielleicht hatte er einfach zu große Angst. So oder so kam es mir nicht zu, darüber zu urteilen.

Ich sah den Frauen nach, die am Fluss entlang nach Hause eilten: Sie waren alle gleichermaßen dünn und trugen billige Kleider mit grellen Mustern. Unter ihren Mänteln schlugen, das wusste ich, winzige Kreuze gegen vorstechende Brustbeine.

Aber es fällt leicht, zu urteilen, wir sind dazu geschaffen; wir leben dafür. Indem wir urteilen, entscheiden wir uns für unser eigenes Selbst statt all der anderen, die wir hätten sein können. Ich jedenfalls urteilte mit Begeisterung und Freude, selbst über ihn, den Mann, dessen Lebenskatastrophe die genaue Vorlage meiner eigenen war – vielleicht ging ich mit ihm sogar besonders hart ins Gericht. Als ich jung war, dachte ich, dass ich genug Entschlusskraft aufbringen würde, um es zu tun, dass die vorherrschende Ethik und Ästhetik sich durchsetzen würden und dass, wenn man sich nur bewusst und rational zum Selbstmord entschloss, nicht mehr und nicht weniger als die universelle Katastrophe geschah – wenn man nur seine Handlungsfreiheit behielt, wenn das Bewusstsein das letzte Wort hatte, dachte ich, konnte ein Mensch nicht mehr von seinem Leben verlangen. Ich verurteilte ihn dafür, dass er es nicht getan hatte. Ich trug es ihm nach, als er schließlich vollständig verschwunden war und sich nicht mehr damit auseinandersetzen musste, und ich unterstellte ihm einen Mangel an Mitleid mit uns, einen Mangel an Ehrgefühl – nicht sein einziger Charaktermangel vielleicht und vermutlich nicht der größte, aber doch der, mit dem wir am längsten leben mussten und den wir daher nie vergessen würden. Der Mangel war sein Vermächtnis. Der Mangel war alles, was blieb.

Am Ufer der Newa sah ich einer älteren Frau nach, die ihre geistig behinderte Tochter im Rollstuhl vor sich her schob. Die Tochter trug Eyeliner, und ich musste daran denken, wie viel Mühe es gekostet haben musste, das wahr werden zu lassen – wie die Mutter den Stift angeleckt und mit dem Daumen die Wimpern der Tochter gehalten hatte.

Während ich das Versagen meines Vaters in harte Worte fassen konnte – seine Weigerung, auf die letzten kläglichen Augenblicke seiner Existenz zu verzichten; dass er sich gierig und klein an das Wenige klammerte, das übrig war –, während das meine Definition von Versagen war, hatte ich von Erfolg, das wusste ich selbst, eine sehr viel verschwommenere Vorstellung. Zumindest versuchte ich es zu vermeiden, meiner Mutter dieselbe Art Qualen zu verursachen, die mein Vater uns zugefügt hatte – den speziellen Schmerz, wenn man sich rasend nach dem Tod eines Menschen sehnt, den man einmal verzweifelt geliebt hat. Aber wenn ich ehrlich zu mir war, wusste ich, dass ich mit meiner Flucht etwas Ähnliches, nicht nachweislich Besseres tat. Glaubte ich denn wirklich, dass sie mich vergessen hatten? War ich wirklich so wenig selbstbewusst? Nein, war ich nicht. Jonathan würde eines Tages über mich hinwegkommen – er würde sich neu verlieben, würde neue Erinnerungen sammeln; diese Erinnerungen würden die Erinnerungen an mich überlagern und mich immer weiter in den Hintergrund drängen; Zeit würde vergehen, große Strecken Zeit, so viel Zeit!, und die Zeit, die er mit mir verbracht hatte, würde im Vergleich dazu immer kürzer werden, bis sie eines Tages vielleicht nebensächlich, anekdotisch wirkte. Aber ich wusste, dass dieser Tag noch nicht gekommen war, und fürs Erste hatte ich ihn schlichtweg traumatisiert. Und meine Mutter … Ich dachte nicht so schlecht über sie, dass ich mir eingebildet hätte, ich hätte ihr mit meiner Flucht einen Gefallen getan. Ich glaubte nicht, dass sie sich jetzt endlich entspannen, die Wärme Arizonas und die Liebe eines naiven Mannes in sich aufsaugen und das Leben genießen würde. Das alles tat sie hoffentlich auch, aber ich konnte nicht so tun, als seien die großen Schwierigkeiten wirklich überwunden. Dazu hätte es ein Ausmaß von groteskem Märtyrergehabe gebraucht, das nicht einmal ich aufbringen konnte. Nein, es ließ sich nicht romantisieren: Diese Reise war im Grunde ein Trotzanfall. Aber vielleicht zieht

Wahnsinn eben Wahnsinn nach sich, und Irrationalität zeugt Irrationalität. Es gab einfach keine richtige Antwort. Es gab keinen richtigen Weg, nur unzählige falsche, ein jeder so einzigartig wie eine Schneeflocke.

Ich wusste nicht, was die humane Lösung gewesen wäre, nur, dass ich sie nicht praktizierte.

Ich wandte mich von der Newa ab und lief auf die Brücke zu. Die Luft war unnachgiebig kalt, die Stadt in eine Dunkelheit gehüllt, die nicht enden zu wollen schien.

Einmal, glaube ich, habe ich aus der Krankheit meines Vaters etwas gelernt. Meistens lernte ich nichts; meistens grollte ich nur und opponierte und machte unmissverständlich klar, wie wenig mir persönlich das alles gefiel, wann immer jemand mir zuhörte, was praktisch nie geschah. Aber ein Mal vielleicht, als mir vor Überdruss die Kiefer schmerzten, in einem dieser heillosen, größtenteils vergessenen Jahre, hatte ich eine Art kleine Erleuchtung. Ein Mal vielleicht sah ich ihm in das erschütterte, erlöschende Gesicht und wusste etwas, von dem ich keine Wahl hatte, als es zu wissen.

Hinter mir verdämmerte die Newa. Der Himmel verausgabte sein letztes Fädchen Licht.

Persönlichkeit ist Kontinuität. Persönlichkeit ist der Mythos der Kontinuität. Und die Person geht verloren, wenn ihr nie etwas alt erscheint, wenn nichts ihr vertraut ist, wenn alle Parallelen, alle Symbole, alle Analogien fehlen; wenn die Welt fortwährend staunenswert ist; wenn wir endlich, endlich wieder Neugeborene sind.

TEIL ZWEI

KAPITEL 13

Alexander
St. Petersburg, 1986–2006

Die Achtziger gingen in die Neunziger über, und Alexander wurde wieder schlanker. Sein Ansehen bei den Frauen stieg, und es gab eine Art Volksaufstand in seinem Privatleben. Plötzlich waren sie überall – mit ihren schmalen Brauen, ihren schmalen, blassen Gesichtern und langen Gliedmaßen, mit warmen Hintern, die sie die ganzen langen Winter über gegen seine Schenkel pressten. Sie fanden seine Witze umwerfend und seine breite Nase distinguiert und sein Schachgerede *faszinierend*. Als er dann auf CNN auftrat und Vorträge an renommierten amerikanischen Universitäten hielt, wurde er geradezu überschwemmt: Er begann ihnen ihre Schönheit, ihre selbstverständliche Verfügbarkeit beinahe übelzunehmen. Er gewöhnte sich an, mit Frauen zu schlafen, deren Nachnamen er nicht kannte, dann gewöhnte er sich an, mit Frauen zu schlafen, deren Vornamen er nicht kannte. Er fragte nicht danach, und er versuchte es zu vergessen, wenn sie es ihm sagten. Eine Zeitlang wurde Sex langweilig; manchmal sehnte er sich, nur zur Abwechslung, nach einer Abfuhr.

Er dachte daran zurück, wie Elisabeta ihn verlassen hatte, als er ihre Liebe noch verdient hatte und es wert gewesen wäre. Jetzt, das wusste er, verdiente er keine Liebe mehr.

In dem anderen Leningrad – dem, in dem Alexander nicht mehr lebte – standen Menschen für Toilettenpapier bis zur Straßenecke Schlange. Im Fernsehen stellte dieser lächelnde, affenähnliche amerikanische Präsident weiter seine Forderungen. Als die Satellitenstaaten wegbrachen – beinahe mühelos, als sei die Sowjetunion ein verrottendes Ding, das nur allzu gern alles Unnötige abstieß – richtete er sich gerade auf und erlaubte sich dreißig Sekunden Optimismus. Er unterstützte Gorbatschow von Anfang an; er wartete in der Kälte, bis seine Ohren rot waren, und weinte, als er seine Stimme für Jelzin abgab. Das Museum für die Geschichte der Religion und des Atheismus wurde wieder zur Kasaner Kathedrale. Die Kommunistische Partei wurde verboten; der Rubel wurde eine konvertierbare Währung; staatliche Betriebe wurden von der gewaltsamen Privatisierung erfasst; die Inflationsrate stieg auf zwanzig Prozent. Die Ladenregale füllten sich wieder, aber niemand konnte die Waren kaufen. Als sich die Preise verdreifachten, begannen die Menschen ihre Hunde fortzujagen, die wie Bettler räudig und verdrossen durch die Straßen zogen. Die Bevölkerung schrumpfte um sechshunderttausend Menschen pro Jahr. Ja, für das einfache Volk war es sicherlich eine harte Schocktherapie, aber das waren eben die Geburtswehen des Kapitalismus, der Sockel, auf dem das überragende neue Russland errichtet werden würde. Und in der freien Marktwirtschaft schrieb Alexander ein Buch über Schach und Unternehmertum, das fünf Millionen Dollar einspielte. Er beabsichtigte, sich dankbar in den verschwenderischen Reichtum der nagelneuen postkommunistischen Oligarchie fallenzulassen – mit Whirlpools, Frauen und der Sorte Reisen, bei denen man an der Datumsgrenze ein dampfendes Erfrischungstuch gereicht bekam.

Er besuchte Nachtklubs. Er tanzte nie, sondern sah nur zu. Er traf Blondinen. Er traf Brünette. Er traf Zentralasiatinnen, die, wie sich herausstellte, überhaupt keine Schambehaarung hatten. Und eines Abends, als er bis spät unterwegs war, etwa fünf Jahre nach seinem Sieg in der Weltmeisterschaft, traf er eine Rothaarige, die still in sich hineinlächelte.

»Hallo«, sagte er. »Was wissen Sie, das ich nicht weiß?«

Sie zuckte mit den Schultern, und damals wertete er es als Zeichen, dass sie tatsächlich etwas verbarg. Später wusste er, dass er besser seinen Augen getraut hätte.

»Sie sind der Schachweltmeister.«

»Ja.«

»Aber das wussten Sie schon.«

Er zog den Kopf ein. »Vermutlich.«

Sie trank Sekt. Er fragte sich, ob sie etwas zu feiern hatte. Sie legte den Kopf schief; ihr rotes Haar war bei dem Licht unbeschreiblich schön. Nein, beschloss er, sie hatte nichts zu feiern. Sie brauchte keinen Grund.

»Und wer sind Sie?«

»Nina«, sagte sie und streckte ihm die Hand hin. Ihr Handgelenk war unfassbar zart und feminin, von erstaunlicher Qualität. Sie schien ein Mensch zu sein, mit dem sich jemand Mühe gegeben hatte, während Alexander gern von sich sagte, Gott habe ihn im Dunkeln erschaffen, einhändig und wahrscheinlich betrunken. Natürlich glaubte Alexander nicht wirklich an Gott, aber er mochte diesen Witz und erzählte ihn oft. Er überlegte, ihn jetzt wieder zu erzählen, betrachtete dann aber noch einmal ihr Handgelenk und überlegte es sich anders.

Sie lächelte ihn an. »Das war mutig, wie Sie die bei der Weltmeisterschaft dazu gebracht haben, das Spiel fortzusetzen.«

»Mutig?«

Es war lange her – zu lange –, dass irgendjemand ihn als mutig bezeichnet hatte. Nein, vielleicht hatte das überhaupt nie jemand getan. Höchstens Elisabeta, wegen der Flugschrift, aber das war vor Ewigkeiten, in einem anderen Leben. War Ninas Einschätzung unverdient? Vielleicht. Das Risiko, das er mit der FIDE eingegangen war, war kalkulierter, eigennütziger gewesen; schließlich hatte er sich nicht gegen sie aufgelehnt, weil sie so moralisch bankrott war – er hatte sich gegen sie aufgelehnt, weil sie ihn über den Tisch ziehen wollte und er schon zu viel verloren hatte, um sich so spät noch über den Tisch ziehen zu lassen. Also bewunderte sie ihn für einen Impuls, der so banal, oberflächlich und reflexhaft war, wie wenn man die Hand von jemandem fortschiebt, der einem in die Tasche greift.

»Ja«, sagte sie. Sie ergriff seine Hand. »Es war waghalsig. Nicht jeder hätte sich das getraut.«

»Na ja«, sagte Alexander. Er spürte das Knirschen sich verschiebender Kräfteverhältnisse; er wusste, dass er sich mit seiner Antwort Zeit lassen konnte, dass sie warten würde. »Es war eigennützig, wissen Sie.«

Sie lachte ein wenig. Er roch den Sekt, den sie getrunken hatte, die leichte Essignote darin; ein billiges Gesöff, dachte er. Er wollte ihr etwas Besseres kaufen. »Rational egoistisch«, sagte sie. Als er später daran zurückdachte, fiel ihm auf, wie sie anfangs oft Schlagworte oder Versatzstücke aus einem akademischen Fachjargon benutzt hatte, am liebsten im falschen Kontext und leicht schief; ihre Art zu sprechen schien auf ein tiefes Verständnis breiter Wissensbereiche hinzudeuten. Es stellte sich bald heraus, dass sie nur eine Anzahl Begriffe auswendig gelernt hatte, die, mit einem wissenden Gesichtsausdruck kombiniert, bei Männern den Eindruck erweckten, sie besäße so etwas wie Intelligenz, wenn sie schon geneigt waren, darauf zu hoffen.

»Genau«, sagte er. »Rational egoistisch. Sagen Sie es nicht meinen Beratern.«

»Im Leben nicht. Dieser Russajew – sagen Sie, ist der wirklich so hässlich, wie er im Fernsehen aussieht?«

Sie lachten. Er erzählte ihr teils ausgeschmückte Anekdoten über Russajews Körperhygiene, seine Angewohnheiten und Ticks und Forderungen. Er machte nach, wie Russajew sich manchmal vorbeugte, einen mit der irrationalen Hoffnung quälte, er werde endlich seinen Zug machen, sich dann aber wieder zurücklehnte, dann wieder vor, dann zurück, bis einen nervöse Erschöpfung überkam. Außerdem hatte er die Angewohnheit, seine Figuren ewig lange festzuhalten; mit einer Drehung des Handgelenks ließ er erst alle Finger darauf ruhen, dann zwei Finger, dann einen und zog sich langsamer zurück als die Amerikaner aus Vietnam, sagte Alexander, und Nina lachte. Es war ein wunderbares Lachen, hell und glockenklar. Es klang nicht unbedingt so, als drücke es wahres Vergnügen aus, aber das störte Alexander in dem Moment nicht.

Irgendwann im Laufe des Abends begann er sie sich genauer anzusehen. Er begriff, dass er sich einmal an diese erste Begegnung würde erinnern wollen, also versuchte er sich einzuprägen, was sie anhatte, wie sie aussah und was ihre ersten Worte gewesen waren. Wenn sich die Geschichte weiterentwickelte, würden diese Details bedeutsam sein.

Am Ende des Abends begleitete er sie zur Tür und sah sie liebevoll an, küsste sie aber nicht. Er hätte es tun können, das wusste er, er hätte tun können, was immer er wollte; vor einer Abfuhr hatte er keine Angst. Aber er wollte später die Möglichkeit haben, ihr zu erzählen, wie er sie habe küssen wollen und zu schüchtern gewesen sei. Es sollte Teil der Geschichte werden, die sie einander einmal erzählen würden.

Am nächsten Abend küsste er sie dann und nahm sie mit nach Hause. Und von da an waren sie ein Paar.

Er führte sie in Privatklubs mit reservierten, abgesperrten Logen aus, in denen schimmernde Wodkakrüge und frische Obstsäfte bereitstanden. Er ging mit ihr tanzen. Er ging mit ihr ins Ballett. Sie war keine Intellektuelle, aber auch kein Kulturbanause – sie liebte Malerei und Gesang. Sie kannte sich weder mit Kunst- noch Musikgeschichte aus, aber das hinderte sie nicht daran, Kunst und Musik zu mögen; sie war keine Theoretikerin, und das war ja so erfrischend. Für sie quälte er sich – zwei Mal sogar – durch eine Oper, und es war beinahe der Mühe wert, nur um Nina so ergriffen zu erleben: die schöne Leere ihres erschütterten Gesichts.

Sie begann sich für Biorhythmen zu interessieren und für Energiefelder. Sie sah sich gern Kaschpirowskis Massenheilungen im Fernsehen an. Für Politik interessierte sie sich nicht. Sie fand öffentliche Auftritte peinlich. Die beiden sahen sich offenen Mundes den Putschversuch an, aber als es vorüber war und Jelzin die Nation gerettet hatte, wollte sie nicht hinaus auf die Straße. Er versuchte sie zum Juri-Schewtschuk-Konzert zu schleifen, wo 120 000 Menschen sich auf dem Palastplatz im Takt wiegten, doch sie verdrehte nur die Augen. Sie würde eher in aller Öffentlichkeit weinen, sagte sie, als öffentlich einen Popmusiker anzuhimmeln. Und damit war die Diskussion beendet, denn Alexander hatte Nina in all den Monaten nie – nicht ein einziges Mal – weinen sehen, auch wenn er ein, zwei Mal den Verdacht gehabt hatte, dass sie hinter den Kulissen Tränen vergoss.

Das machte nichts. Das machte überhaupt nichts. Endlich war da eine Frau, die ihn als das liebte, was er war, nicht was er – unbeholfen! – zu sein versucht und worin er – erbärmlich! – versagt hatte. Wenn diese Frau Sachkompetenz wollte – die hatte er reichlich. Wenn sie Skrupellosigkeit wollte – daran arbeitete er. Es war besser, für das eigene elende Ich geliebt – oder was auch immer – zu werden als für eine entstellte Version dessen, was man hätte werden können. Genau solche Diskrepanzen führten immer zu Enttäuschungen.

Und noch etwas kam hinzu: Er war zweiunddreißig. Es musste nicht unbedingt Nina sein, aber irgendeine musste es sein, um des Anstands willen. In Familiendingen war er immer anständig geblieben: Er hatte seine Mutter und zwei seiner Schwestern aus ihrer altertümlichen Hütte in Ocha gerettet (die dritte hatte einen beinahe zahnlosen Störfischer geheiratet und sich geweigert zu kommen).

Nina und Alexander mochten ein ungleiches Paar sein, aber in ihrer Ungleichheit lag eine gewisse Symmetrie: Sie war so viel schöner als er, er war so viel talentierter und erfolgreicher als sie, und war das nicht das typische Tauschgeschäft mächtiger Männer? Es war ein prekäres Einvernehmen, ein wackeliges Gleichgewicht des Schreckens – jeder der beiden konnte den anderen verletzen, indem er ihm vorwarf, nicht das zu sein, was einmal gewünscht worden war. Wenn er sie hätte verletzen wollen, hätte er darauf hinweisen können, dass es zahllose schöne Frauen gab, aber nur einen Schachweltmeister (bis auf weiteres: ihn). Er hätte sagen können, wie vergänglich Schönheit war. Aber sie hätte antworten können, dass alles vergänglich war – Schachfähigkeiten hielten sich nur unwesentlich länger als Schönheit; beides waren Spiele, in denen die Jungen bessere Chancen hatten. Und überhaupt – was bedeutete die Vorherrschaft auf dem Schachbrett im Vergleich zu der im Bett? Schach war eine Metapher für den Krieg; Sex dagegen stand für sich selbst. Wer hatte also am Ende die größere Macht?

Sie verfielen in eine Routine, bei der sie ihn fortwährend spielerisch kritisierte und er ihr unendliche Toleranz entgegenbrachte, und das schien die Verwerfungen in ihrer Beziehungslandschaft ein wenig einzuebnen. Alexander mochte ein Schachmeister sein, aber er war auch einfach nur ein Mann und hatte als solcher die ständigen Vorwürfe schöner, anspruchsvoller Frauen verdient. Das sah er ein; er hatte in seinen eigenen Augen sogar mehr Vorwürfe verdient, als selbst Nina ihm je machen konnte, wenn auch aus Gründen, über die er nie mit ihr sprach.

Er kaufte ihnen beiden eine prachtvolle Wohnung mit Blick auf den Newski-Prospekt (teuer). Er kaufte einen pflegeintensiven kleinen Hund mit Silberblick (ebenfalls teuer). Nach einer angemessenen Zeitspanne heirateten Nina und Alexander.

Ein Jahrzehnt verstrich, erst in Zeitlupe und dann schneller und schneller. Wenn Alexander zurückblickte, kamen die Erinnerungen bruchstückhaft und verzerrt, in Wiederholungsschleifen und Sprüngen, wie von einer zerkratzten Schallplatte. Es hatte gute Zeiten gegeben, das wusste er genau – manche Nächte mit Nina, besonders anfangs, auch wenn sich im Nachhinein nicht leicht sagen ließ, wie viele Nächte wirklich schön gewesen waren. War es eine Nacht gewesen, zwei, ein halbes Dutzend oder ein ganzes? Oder war es typisch für sie, war es üblich gewesen, engumschlungen vor dem gewaltigen Panoramafenster zu tanzen, St. Petersburg zu ihren Füßen, das im Mondlicht in der gleichen Pracht erstrahlte wie das Alte Rom? Was man sich ausmalt, daran erinnert man sich, und woran man sich erinnert, ist alles, was einem bleibt. Warum sollte man es sich also nicht ein wenig anders ausmalen? Es war immerhin möglich, dass die Ehe nicht von vornherein ein grauenhafter Fehler gewesen war. Es war möglich, dass sie glücklicher waren, als er es manchmal glaubte.

Doch wenn er sich an das Gute zu erinnern versuchte, kamen ihm vor allem Banalitäten in den Sinn: Da war Nina, wie sie 1993 vor dem Spiegel ihr Haar kämmte; da war sie noch einmal, 1997 ungefähr, mit etwas längerem Haar und einer etwas tieferen Zornesfalte. Er erinnerte sich an den evolutionären Wandel ihrer Schlafbekleidung, an die zyklischen Abfolgen ihrer Schuhe im Rhythmus der Jahreszeiten und der Gestirne. Er erinnerte sich an Dinge, die sie gekauft hatten: die Stereoanlage, die im Dunkeln zu vibrieren schien, mit einer Fülle von Reglern, Knöpfen und Schaltern, die in Alexanders Augen wie das Kontrollfeld eines Raumschiffs aussahen; die Computer, die anfangs bedrohlich aufragende Kolosse waren, halb so groß wie Alexander selbst, und dann langsam zu boshaft glänzenden, verwirrend unaufdringlichen Objekten zusammenschrumpften. Er erinnerte sich auch an Ninas lange Reihe von Freundinnen, die sich farbenfroh kleideten und verschwörerisch die Köpfe zusammensteckten. Sie kamen zum Mittagessen, zum Abendbrot und blieben ewig auf ein Gläschen da. Sie kamen in wechselnder Besetzung: Er konnte sich nie ihre Namen merken, verwechselte immer eine mit der anderen, wurde immer zurechtgewiesen, gelobte immer Besserung und vergaß im nächsten Moment doch wieder ihre Namen. Die Frauen lästerten oft wegen irgendwelcher Mängel übereinander, die Alexander nie aufgefallen wären – wer ein Treffen verpasste, galt als Freiwild. Egal, wie gründlich eine der Frauen in ihrer Abwesenheit von den anderen auseinandergenommen wurde – wenn sie wiederkam, begrüßte man sie mit derselben atemlosen Anteilnahme, demselben falschen Lächeln, demselben erstaunten Heben der Augenbrauen wegen derselben erbitterten Klagen über unverschämte Kinder und abgestumpfte Ehemänner. Dann folgten dasselbe herzliche Einvernehmen und dasselbe Gläserklirren.

Und Alexander erinnerte sich an die halbherzigen Versuche, ein Kind zu bekommen. Im Laufe der Jahre nahm Nina drei verschiedene chemische Verhütungsmittel und setzte sie halbherzig wieder ab; 1994 verzichtete sie wieder darauf – diesmal ernsthaft und absichtsvoll –, und sie warteten. Nichts geschah. Sie warteten weiter. Es geschah immer noch nichts. Alexander erinnerte sich an die allmähliche Erkenntnis, dass es länger dauerte als gewöhnlich, dann viel länger als gewöhnlich, und dann die Einsicht – die sie, wenn auch unausgesprochen, ganz sicher beide hatten –, dass sie nicht so enttäuscht waren, wie man es hätte erwarten können. Er beobachtete, wie Nina beim nächsten negativ ausgefallenen Test – dem elften oder zwölften – die Lippen schürzte und wusste, dass sie etwas verblüfft, aber nicht verzweifelt war. Sie beide und ein Baby: Was hätten sie denn damit anstellen sollen? Nina war gut darin, sich um Dinge zu kümmern – um die Stereoanlage zum Beispiel und ihre stetig wachsende Sammlung heikler Seidenkleider –, aber Dinge waren still und stumm und verhältnismäßig leicht sauber zu halten. Eine Schwangerschaft, eine Geburt, ein plärrendes Kind, das ständig den Schnabel aufsperrte – das klang nicht nur ermüdend, sondern peinlich. Nach ein, zwei Jahren standen wieder Verhütungspillen im Badezimmerschrank, und Alexander beklagte sich nicht.

Sie stritten sich nicht. Nie. Manchmal wechselten sie tagelang kein Wort, aber selbst das musste kein Zeichen des Unfriedens sein – er vergaß manchmal einfach, mit ihr zu reden. Ihr Liebesleben siechte leise und klaglos, mit dem ganzen demütigen Ernst eines religiösen Märtyrers dahin: Erst wurde der Sex Routine, dann selten, dann gereizt und unwillig und, wie Alexander verbittert feststellte, verbittert. Und dann wurde er ein seltener Glücksfall, ein undeutlich durch einen Sternennebel erspähter Komet – er kam nur vor, wenn sie getrunken hatte oder er ihr schmeichelte oder wenn sie (selten, selten) gemeinsam lachen konnten. Manchmal vollführte er eine Art Ritual, das sie wieder zu dem machen sollte, was sie einmal gewesen waren, aber gerade dann wusste er am wenigsten, was das eigentlich war. Er versuchte es trotzdem: Er legte grauenhafte Liebeslieder aus den frühen Neunzigern auf, die sie zu Beginn ihrer Beziehung beim Ausgehen gehört hatten. Die Geste war ironisch gemeint, aber wie jede Ironie hatte sie etwas Sentimentales – und da Nina weder für Ironie noch für Sentimentalitäten empfänglich war, starrte sie Alexander nur mit geschürzten Lippen an und lächelte nicht.

Anstelle des Sex begann Alexander fernzusehen. Er sah, wie Jelzin rotgesichtig und betrunken und zunehmend inkompetent durch seine Amtszeit stolperte: Man mochte kaum glauben, dass er derselbe war, der einmal einen Staatsstreich niedergeschrien, der Russland vom Abgrund des Polizeistaats zurückgerissen hatte. Die durchschnittliche Lebenserwartung der Männer sank – vor allem aufgrund der Alkoholismus- und Selbstmordraten – auf 58 Jahre. Das organisierte Verbrechen hatte die Hälfte aller Wirtschaftsbetriebe in der Hand. Spät abends lief Alexander in seiner Wohnung auf und ab und dachte über sein Land nach, das seine eigene Bedeutung überlebt zu haben schien. Darin, fand er, hatten sie etwas gemeinsam.

Alexander verfolgte weiter die Schachberichterstattung; nachts, wenn Nina schlief, schlich er zu den immer kleiner werdenden Computern und besiegte gnadenlos die besten schlaflosen Schachgenies der Welt. Aufregung waberte durch die Onlineforen, wenn sie ihn an einer Verteidigung oder einer Eröffnung erkannten, und er spürte den Nachhall einer entscheidenden Wendung, wenn er daran zurückdachte, wie er selbst einmal die vielversprechenden Eröffnungszüge seiner Karriere und seines Lebens ausgeführt hatte. Jetzt hatte er alle in ihn gesetzten Hoffnungen erfüllt, und ihm blieb nichts weiter zu tun, als die Zusammenkünfte der Online-Enthusiasten heimzusuchen. Seine Errungenschaften beim Schach kamen ihm vor wie die endlosen Erfolgsgeschichten sowjetischer Führungspersönlichkeiten, die er in der Schule eingetrichtert bekommen hatte.

Im echten Leben spielte er selten. Peter Pawlowitsch arrangierte 1995 ein glanzloses Match im World Trade Center in New York. Alexander spielte gegen einen indischen Schachmeister und gewann mühelos. Der Sieg fühlte sich billig an, hohl, wie der Abklatsch eines Triumphes. Draußen konturierte zitronengelbes Licht den Himmel. Die Zwillingstürme ragten mit unheilvoller Klarheit vor den blankgeputzten Fenstern auf.

Danach hörte Alexander nur noch selten von Peter Pawlowitsch. Er hatte andere, um die er sich kümmern musste, wenn auch weniger als früher. Die FIDE war jetzt weniger mit der Bürokratie verbandelt – nicht mehr von der Korruption erstickt –, und es gab ohnehin weniger zu verlieren, weniger zu beweisen, weniger Hoffnung, den Kalten Krieg durch einen kulturellen Triumph, durch die vernichtende Überlegenheit im edelsten Wettstreit der Welt gewinnen zu können. Am Ende war es ein Wettstreit der Raketen und Diplomaten und des nationalen Stolzes, vor allem aber ein Wettstreit darum, wer ständigen Nachschub an Toilettenpapier und erschwinglichen Proteinen sicherstellen konnte, und diesen Wettstreit hatte Russland definitiv verloren. Sie brauchten keinen Schachspieler mehr als Standartenträger, und Alexander konnte sie nicht mehr so bloßstellen, wie er es früher gekonnt hatte. Sie stellten sich schon selbst genug bloß.

Manchmal richteten Nina und Alexander Partys aus, zu denen auch Peter Pawlowitsch kam, immer schlechtgelaunt und meistens allein. Er drückte sich in den Ecken herum und griff jedes Mal zu, wenn ein Tablett mit Häppchen in Reichweite kam. Alexanders Gefühle ihm gegenüber schwankten, je nachdem, wie er am entsprechenden Tag sein ganzes Leben sah. Manchmal war Peter Pawlowitsch für ihn der unverzichtbare Mittelsmann, der ihm das Überleben gesichert hatte – sie hatten eine parasitäre, bestenfalls symbiotische Beziehung gehabt, und Alexander wusste, er sollte dankbar sein. Dann wieder dachte er an sein Leben – seine riesige Wohnung, sein leeres Herz, seinen glänzenden Pokal, den die Putzfrauen jeden zweiten Tag vom Staub befreiten – und fragte sich, ob er nicht ein authentischeres Leben, ein authentischeres anderes Ich hätte haben können. Wenn er dann versuchte, sich dieses Leben vorzustellen, war da nichts – was hätte er denn anderes tun sollen? Vielleicht hätte man ihn eine Weile unterrichten lassen, wenn auch nicht in Leningrad. Er hätte nach Ocha zurückkehren können, um dort alle aussichtsreichen Talente zu fördern, die der Ort hervorbringen mochte, und er hätte den Status eines Jungen genossen, der draußen in der Welt etwas aus sich gemacht hatte, selbst wenn ein Rückkehrer nie so hochgeschätzt wird wie einer, der fortbleibt. Seine Familie wäre ganz fraglos stolz auf ihn gewesen, auch wenn sie vermutlich das Gefühl gehabt hätten, er hätte sich zu viel entgehen lassen, und wofür? Für irgendein vages Ideal, das ebenso unklar wie unerreichbar blieb. Das Leben war voller Unhaltbarkeiten, voller Unüberwindbarkeiten und Absurditäten; die Frage war nicht, ob man in seinem Leben irgendeine Form von Reinheit erreichen konnte (konnte man nicht), sondern ob man die Stolpersteine umgehen und sich mit den Voraussetzungen arrangieren konnte (der Staatsform, den eigenen Raum-Zeit-Koordinaten, der eigenen Sterblichkeit) und trotzdem etwas erreichte. Das hatte Alexander eine Zeitlang getan, und war Erwachsensein nicht immer so? War so nicht das Leben? War es nicht pure Realitätsflucht, wenn man sich dem zu entziehen versuchte? Natürlich konnte man passiven Widerstand leisten; natürlich konnte man protestieren. Aber war das nicht so ähnlich, als weigerte man sich, morgens aufzustehen, nur weil man wusste, dass man eines Tages sterben würde?

Aber trotz allem hätten sie sich natürlich gefreut, ihn wiederzuhaben.

Im Januar 1997 rief Peter Pawlowitsch bei Alexander an. Dank der Rufnummernerkennung – einer von Ninas neuesten Errungenschaften, die sie nutzte, um keine Anrufe ihrer jeweils gerade in Ungnade gefallenen Freundinnen beantworten zu müssen – leuchtete sein Name auf dem Display auf. Alexander zuckte zurück und wollte den Anruf ignorieren, doch dann gewann seine Neugier Oberhand. Er hatte seit Monaten nicht mehr ausführlich mit Peter Pawlowitsch gesprochen. Er fragte sich, ob er endlich etwas gegen seine Polypen unternommen hatte.

»Hallo, Peter Pawlowitsch«, sagte Alexander und genoss das darauf folgende verwirrte Schweigen.

»Rufnummernerkennung«, sagte Peter Pawlowitsch schließlich.

»Genau.«

»Sehr fortschrittlich von dir.«

»Das ist alles die Gattin.«

»Wie geht es der Gattin?«

»Fabelhaft, wie immer.«

Alexander versuchte sich zu erinnern, ob Peter Pawlowitsch verheiratet war. Vor ein paar Jahren war auf einer der Partys eine Frau aufgetaucht, das wusste er noch – sie war zierlich, rauchte Kette und lächelte und schien Pawlowitsch sehr glücklich zu machen. Alexander wusste nicht, ob sie eine Ehefrau gewesen war, eine Geliebte oder Partnerin oder eine Bekannte, um die Peter Pawlowitsch erfolglos warb. Er vermutete Letzteres.

»Sind Sie verheiratet, Peter Pawlowitsch?«

»Ich war es. Danke der Nachfrage. Sie ist vor drei Jahren gestorben. Speiseröhrenkrebs. Ging ganz schnell.«

Alexander erschauderte. »Tut mir leid.«

»Bestimmt liegt die Beileidskarte schon in der Post.«

Alexander hüstelte sich einen etwas sanfteren und demütigeren Tonfall zurecht. »Haben Sie Kinder?«

»Oh, aber nein, Alexander Kimowitsch. So ein Ausbruch großzügiger Anteilnahme von deiner Seite ist beispiellos. Ich hoffe, du nimmst keine Antidepressiva. Das wäre nicht gut für dein Spiel.«

»Ich nehme keine Antidepressiva.«

»Da bin ich aber erleichtert.«

Peter Pawlowitsch schniefte, und Alexander fürchtete stark – und vorübergehend –, er hätte zu weinen angefangen.

»Und du, Alexander? Willst du Kinder? Von deiner bezaubernden Frau – wie heißt sie doch gleich?«

»Nina.«

»Nina. Natürlich. Und?«

»Äh, nein.« Alexander hielt das Telefon an sein anderes Ohr. »Erst einmal nicht.«

»Verstehe. Du bist vermutlich viel zu beschäftigt.«

»Weshalb haben Sie angerufen?«

»Also.« Alexander hörte, wie Peter Pawlowitsch sich auf den geschäftlichen Teil des Gesprächs vorbereitete und seine Stimme von ihrem üblichen müden Sarkasmus befreite. »Ich weiß, wie sehr du dich für Technik interessierst. Du bist immer *up to date*. Mit Rufnummernerkennung und so weiter.«

»Hmm«, machte Alexander. Er schielte nervös zu der Stereoanlage hinüber.

»Wie du wahrscheinlich gehört hast, hat IBM einen Computer entwickelt, der Schach spielen kann.«

»Ich weiß«, sagte Alexander. Davon hatte er allerdings schon gehört.

»Big Blue, Deep Blue Sea oder so ähnlich. Er soll inzwischen sehr gut sein. Sie testen ihn schon seit Jahren. Er besiegt jeden. Sie programmieren jede denkbare Reaktion auf jeden denkbaren Zug in sein … was auch immer … sein Gehirn wahrscheinlich, und dann programmieren sie ihn so, dass er weiß, welcher Zug in jedem denkbaren Szenario der vielversprechendste ist. Im Wesentlichen tut er also, was dein Hirn wohl auch tun muss. Du bist auf genau dieselbe Sorte Reaktionen programmiert.«

»Ja, aber ich muss erst darüber nachdenken.«

»Dieses Ding denkt auch. Es denkt nur schneller. In, äh, Algorithmen, nicht? Was weiß ich, das ist nicht mein Fachgebiet. Jedenfalls wollen sie, dass du gegen ihn antrittst.«

»Sollte ich das?«

»Natürlich. Glaubst du, du kannst ihn nicht schlagen?«

»Ich weiß es nicht.«

»Er ist ein Haufen Röhren. Du bist der beste lebende Schachspieler der Welt. Die Jungs vom MIT sind bestimmt nicht dumm, aber für dich wird das eine Partie Tetris, meinst du nicht?«

»Wahrscheinlich. Woher soll ich das wissen?«

Ein Schweigen folgte. »Als du jünger warst, hättest du bestimmt nicht gezögert, weißt du.«

Alexander trat an das Panoramafenster. Draußen hatte sich

St. Petersburg in blaue und graue Falten gehüllt, in denen man die neuen Bauprojekte, die neuen Werbetafeln, die neuen Früchte einer sich rasch etablierenden neuen Kleptokratie nicht sah. Das war die Zukunft. Sie wollten, dass er gegen einen Computer antrat. Alexander hätte nicht gezögert, als er jünger war, aber er war nicht mehr jünger.

»Wenn ich verliere, ist es eine Katastrophe.«

»Wenn du verlierst, ist es gute Publicity. Aber du wirst nicht verlieren.«

»Ich weiß nicht.«

»Alexander«, sagte Peter Pawlowitsch fröhlich. Alexander konnte ihn beinahe lächeln hören. »Du vergisst, dass du der Weltmeister bist. Hab ein bisschen Selbstvertrauen.«

Alexander sollte sich an das Spiel so erinnern wie an den Rest des Jahrzehnts, wenn er überhaupt daran dachte, was selten geschah. Es tauchte verzerrt, bruchstückhaft vor seinem inneren Auge auf – die aufgeblasenen Backen des Mannes, der für den Computer spielte, die sich mit jedem bestürzten kleinen Atemzug aufblähten und wieder zusammensackten; das Schweigen der Zuschauer – ruhig, dann angespannt, dann fassungslos. Danach war da die erstaunte Grimasse Peter Pawlowitschs – Alexander hatte ihn oft überrascht, aber nie auf diese Weise. Dann erinnerte er sich an das fröhliche Geschnatter der MIT-Leute, der Internetenthusiasten, der IT-Journalisten – den Triumphalismus, mit dem alle fröhlich diese brandneue Form der Apokalypse begrüßten. Alexander wusste – noch während er spielte, während er verlor, während er in der Limousine auf dem Weg nach Hause war –, dass er mit diesem Abend würde umgehen müssen wie mit seiner Ehe. Er würde versuchen, nicht darüber nachzudenken. Er würde versuchen, die Details, die Abfolgen, die aufgetürmten Erniedrigungen zu vergessen.

Nina hatte das Ereignis online mitverfolgt, und als er nach Hause kam und sie dasitzen sah, die Beine unter sich eingeklappt, ihr seidenes Nachthemd im Mondlicht schimmernd (Nina trug so viel Seide, dass er sich fragte, ob sie irgendwo im Schrank eine ganze Seidenraupenarmee besaß), wusste er, dass sie gerade dabei gewesen war, die Ergebnisse, die Analysen, die obsessiven Spekulationen im Internet zu lesen. Die Details verstand sie vielleicht nicht, aber der Tonfall – die Schlagzeile, das Fazit – war unmissverständlich.

»Es tut mir leid, Alexander.« Sie klappte rasch den Computer zu.

»Ja.« Er ging geradewegs zum Wandschrank und goss sich ein Wasserglas voll Whiskey ein.

»Es tut mir wirklich leid.«

Alexander dachte über Eiswürfel nach, entschied sich dann aber dagegen. »Mir tut es auch wirklich leid.«

»Willst du mit mir darüber reden?«

Er wollte nicht mit ihr darüber reden. Er wollte mit niemandem darüber reden. Er wollte nicht einmal mit sich selbst im Stillen darüber reden. Jeder, der zugesehen hatte, hatte es verstanden. Was gab es da noch zu reden? Niemand würde dieses Ding je besiegen. Niemand würde je wieder mit einem Abakus Zahlen addieren. Und durfte er das bedauern? Wer würde schon bedauern, dass die Geschichte voranmarschierte, dass Fortschritte gemacht und Probleme gelöst wurden? Ja, ja, ein bisschen Romantik war verloren, seit der gesamte Erdball kartographiert war, aber trotzdem. Man konnte nicht dagegen sein; das war, als würde man sich wünschen, dass jedes winzige Dorf seine unübersetzbare, nutzlose Sprache und seine grauenhaften sanitären Gewohnheiten behielt, nur damit man hinfahren und es sich anschauen und denken könnte, wie authentisch und malerisch es sei. Alexander hatte durchaus ein Ego, aber nicht so eins. Er würde nicht fordern, dass die Welt weniger können sollte, nur damit er am meisten konnte.

»Du siehst furchtbar aus«, sagte Nina.

Er schenkte sich nach. »Mir geht's gut.«

»Du siehst aus, als würdest du dich gleich umbringen.«

»Werde ich nicht.«

»Oder mich.«

»Keine Sorge.«

Nina ging zur Couch und zog von irgendwo eine Nagelfeile hervor. Alexander füllte sein drittes Glas. Auf der Couch fing Nina lebhaft zu feilen an, und er sah ihr eine Weile dabei zu. Er würde nie begreifen, wie sie es schaffte, sich nicht in die Finger zu feilen. Alexander setzte sich an den Computer.

Nina blickte hoch. »Du brauchst die Sachen über das Spiel nicht nachzulesen.«

»Hatte ich nicht vor.«

»Wirklich nicht.«

»Hatte ich wirklich nicht vor.«

»Da stehen Sachen, die du gar nicht wissen willst.«

»Verdammt, Nina!«, brüllte Alexander. »Ich weiß!«

Sie sah ihn mit vor Mitgefühl feuchten Augen an. Er war nicht sicher, ob er je zuvor Mitleid an ihr wahrgenommen hatte. Aber er wusste genau, dass es ihm nicht gefiel.

»Wirklich, Sascha«, sagte sie. »Es ist nur ein Spiel.«

Danach folgte eine Phase der Entspannung – es musste sie gegeben haben. Ein paar betäube Jahre, ein Eingeständnis der Entfremdung, das merkwürdigerweise mehr Wohlwollen mit sich brachte. Als er aufgehört hatte, Nina zu seiner Frau machen zu wollen, wusste er sie besser als eine Art Freundin zu schätzen; als jemand, für den und mit dem er gern Geld ausgab. Es gibt ebenso viele Facetten der funktionierenden wie der gescheiterten Ehe, und ihre Ehe, glaubt er jetzt, hat funktioniert. Er weiß es, weil er sicher ist – absolut sicher –, dass er am Tag des Sprengstoffattentats liebevoll zu Nina hinübersah.

Es war der letzte Augusttag 1999, und sie verbrachten das Wochenende bei Freundinnen von Nina in Moskau. Er wartete auf Nina, die in einem Laden am Manegeplatz Schuhe anprobierte. Er stand draußen und beobachtete sie durch das Schaufenster – er sah die strenge Linie ihrer gerunzelten Brauen, als sie ihre porzellanzarte Ferse in ein Folterwerkzeug von einem Schuh zu zwängen versuchte – und er weiß, dass es ihnen beiden besser gegangen sein muss, weil er noch weiß, dass er sie bewunderte, dass er daran dachte, wie schön sie war, und dass er stolz war, eine so anspruchsvolle Frau zu haben, die genau wusste, was sie von einem Schuh erwartete. Gestreiftes Licht sickerte durch das Schaufenster hinein. Nicht weit von ihm entfernt kreischte ein kleines Mädchen auf einem Fahrautomaten aus Plastik – einem blauen, schnurrbärtigen Walross, das sich langsam auf und ab bewegte –, und Alexander fand, dass die Welt gut sei. Sie hatten vor, später Sushi zu essen und den Rest des Abends in einem Nachtklub zu verbringen, und Alexander freute sich auf seine Sashimi und seinen Vollrausch. Das Licht im Laden berührte Ninas Haar, und es leuchtete beinahe golden. »Mama, Mama, Mama, es ist ein Walross!«, schrie das Kind auf dem Fahrautomaten.

Und dann war irgendwie das halbe Gebäude nicht mehr da. Das Licht war nuklear, der Lärm zyklonisch – und alles, alles schien kurz nach dem Moment zu passieren, als Alexander sich bei seinem Aufprall auf dem Boden das Schlüsselbein brach. Nina taumelte aus dem Laden, den Fuß noch in dem unbezahlten Schuh. Dem kleinen Mädchen neben ihm fehlte die Hälfte einer Hand. Ihr Mund stand offen, vermutlich, weil sie schrie, und Alexander war schon den halben Weg zu ihr hingekrochen, ein Fegefeuer des Schmerzes in der Brust, als er begriff, dass er nichts mehr hörte.

Sein Gehör kehrte im Laufe des Tages zurück, und das kleine Mädchen überlebte, und nur ein Mensch starb. Sie kehrten nach St. Petersburg zurück, und Alexander schaltete den Fernseher an, um zu sehen, was als Nächstes geschehen würde.

Eine Woche darauf traf es Buinaksk, dann wieder Moskau, dann Wolgodonsk – Einkaufspassagen, Schnellstraßen, Wohnhäuser. In den Wohnhäusern zündeten sie die Sprengsätze nachts, um die Zahl ziviler Opfer zu maximieren. Die Regierung gab den Anschlag in Buinaksk bekannt, zwei Tage bevor er geschah, was Alexander persönlich beleidigend fand: Ein Regierungskomplott, wenn es denn eins war, sollte zumindest professionell durchgeführt werden. »Siehst du das, Nina?«, rief Alexander von der Couch aus und fuhr zusammen. Das Atmen tat ihm noch weh. »Interessiert es dich überhaupt?«

»Was hast du, Alexander? Brauchst du mehr Kodein?«

Auf der Couch heilte Alexanders Schlüsselbein, aber er blieb sitzen und sah weiter fern. Er sah, wie die Tschetschenen beschuldigt wurden; er sah, wie der zweite Tschetschenienkrieg begann. Er sah die Kriegstreiber in die Duma einziehen und sah Putin – Jelzins rückgratlos-selbstgefälligen Ministerpräsidenten, der bloß KGB-Oberstleutnant war – zum Präsidenten aufsteigen. Er sah, wie die Regionalwahlen abgeschafft wurden.

»Alexander.« Nina hustete. »Meinst du nicht, du solltest ein bisschen Sport machen gehen?«

Alexander hasste Putin mit einer Inbrunst, die sich persönlich anfühlte. Wenn er an die anderen dachte – an Breschnew und die Riege hinfälliger, taumelnder Greise danach –, erinnerte er sich nicht, je so intensiven Hass verspürt zu haben wie Putin gegenüber. Putins erste Amtshandlung bestand darin, die sowjetische Nationalhymne wiedereinzuführen. Als Alexander nach neun Jahren die Melodie wiederhörte, sah er Elisabeta unter dem Applaus der Bürokraten den Mittelgang hinunterschreiten und musste sich beinahe übergeben.

»Alexander«, sagte Nina, »meinst du nicht, dass du das alles ein bisschen zu ernst nimmst?«

Nach dem Anschlag – nach dem Anblick von arteriellem Blut auf dem blauen Pinguin-T-Shirt des kleinen Mädchens und nachdem er über den zerborstenen Marmorboden zu ihr gekrochen war – war er weniger duldsam seinem eigenen Lebenswandel gegenüber. Nina bewegte ihn dazu, seine alten Gewohnheiten wiederaufzunehmen, aber sie verfingen nicht mehr. Der Kaviar blieb ihm im Hals stecken. Die Nächte in den Klubs erschienen ihm leer. Er musste mehr und mehr an Iwan denken und daran, wie Iwan sein Leben geführt hätte, hätte er denn überlebt. Iwan hätte sich nicht ein Jahrzehnt lang mit dem Regime arrangiert. Iwan hätte nicht die Anfangsjahre der Demokratie damit zugebracht, sich mit je einer gleichgültigen Schönheit links und rechts im Whirlpool langsam pochieren zu lassen. Jeden Morgen stand Alexander auf, sah in den Spiegel und versuchte sich daran zu erinnern, wer er gewesen war, als er mutig war.

Seine Freunde – seine reichen Freunde, denen der Kaviar noch schmeckte – sagten, wenn ihm das alles so wichtig sei, solle er sich hinter die gerade neuaufgekommene Reformbewegung stellen. Schließlich war er ein Nationalheld, die Ikone eines Spiels, das reiner war als die Religion und eleganter als jeder Sport. Er hatte Geld. Wenn er Ideen hatte, konnte er eine echte Persönlichkeit werden. Hatte er denn Ideen?

Ja, die hatte er, wenn sie auch vage waren – er war unternehmensfreundlich, gegen Korruption, für Transparenz, für Bürgerrechte. Er war ein Kapitalist. Ein Realist. Aber zunächst wollte er ein Netzwerk oppositioneller Gruppen unterstützen – den Aufbau einer breiten Opposition hielt er für den ersten und wichtigsten Schritt –, und er begann damit, jeden zu kontaktieren, der gewillt war, öffentlich Widerstand zu leisten, seien es ernsthafte Reformer, Verschwörungstheoretiker, Phrasendrescher oder linke Spinner. Bei den ersten Versammlungen tauchten regelmäßig Bilder von Trotzki neben Zitaten von Milton Friedman auf. Sie gaben sich den Namen Alternatives Russland.

»Ich mag es nicht, wenn sie hier drin rauchen«, sagte Nina.

Zu Anfang redeten sie nur. Sie waren sich einig, dass die postkommunistische Kleptokratie in mancher Hinsicht nur unwesentlich besser war als die wankende Inkompetenz des untergehenden Kommunismus – und in anderer vielleicht schlimmer. Sie waren sich einig, dass die Indifferenz des Regimes so kaltschnäuzig war, dass man sie fast schon nicht mehr Indifferenz nennen konnte. Im Laufe der Zeit lieferte ihnen Putin weitere Gesprächsthemen. Nach den Sprengstoffanschlägen kamen die im Stich gelassenen Matrosen der Kursk, eines Atom-U-Boots, das während Putins erstem Sommer im Amt leise in der Barentssee versank. Später wurde aus den Aufzeichnungen, die sie auf ihren eigenen Körpern hinterlassen hatten, deutlich, dass einige von ihnen tagelang überlebt hatten, während der Kreml darauf bestand, sie seien längst tot, während Hilfsangebote aus Norwegen und Großbritannien ignoriert wurden, während Putin seinen Strandurlaub fortsetzte.

Dann waren da die als Geiseln genommenen Theaterbesucher, die im Herbst 2002 einem grauenhaft verpfuschten Befreiungsversuch zum Opfer fielen. Sie waren, von staatlich verabreichtem Morphium halb erstickt, aus dem Gebäude gekrochen und im Schnee gestorben, weil der Kreml es versäumte, Notärzte zu rufen. Alexander sprach bei den Treffen des Alternativen Russland darüber. Er sprach auch außerhalb häufig davon.

»Hör auf, dauernd über solche Sachen zu reden«, sagte Nina. »Du bist total morbide.«

»Ich bin nicht morbide. Das Leben ist morbide. Die Realität ist morbide. Unser Regierungssystem ist morbide.«

»Wenn du noch ein Mal ›unser Regierungssystem‹ sagst, sterbe ich vor Langeweile.«

»Bitte, nur zu.«

Im Jahr 2004 kam dann die Geiselnahme von Beslan: Schulkinder wurden tagelang gefangengehalten und starben, als die Regierung die Schule mit Panzern und Aerosolbomben stürmen ließ. Ein Jahr darauf zogen die Eltern der toten Kinder nach Moskau und forderten ihre eigene Festnahme – sie hatten Putin gewählt, sagten sie, und waren damit mitschuldig am Tod ihrer Kinder.

Obwohl Alexander gut im Rechnen war – gut im Abwägen der Konsequenzen rational egoistischen Handelns –, konnte er das alles nie ganz begreifen. Was hatte der Staat davon, Hunderten dabei zuzusehen, wie sie sich in Moskaus Prunkstraßen würgend auf dem Boden wälzten und starben, oder zuzulassen, dass Matrosen sich Abschiedsbotschaften auf den Körper schrieben und am eigenen Kohlendioxid erstickten? Sicher war Unfähigkeit im Spiel, aber das konnte wohl kaum alles sein: Es war eine mörderische Apathie, die an Sadismus grenzte. Es erinnerte Alexander daran, wie die Partei zu Zeiten des Kommunismus, als die Kindersterblichkeitsrate bedrohliche Höhen erreichte, kurzerhand Geburten bezuschusst hatte.

Nina kam und setzte sich zu Alexander auf das Bett. »Es ist traurig, Alexander. Natürlich ist es traurig. Aber es ist wirklich nicht unser Problem.«

Dann kamen die Attentate. Erst traf es Anna Politkowskaja von der *Nowaja Gaseta*, die einen Giftanschlag und einen Einsatz in Tschetschenien überlebt hatte, nur um dann im Treppenhaus ihres Wohnhauses erschossen zu werden.

Dann war da der Ex-KGB-Agent in London, der mit radioaktivem Sushi vergiftet wurde, von Männern, die gleich darauf wieder im wabernden englischen Nebel verschwanden; ein Mann, der in Farben angelaufen war, die bei Menschen gar nicht vorkommen sollten, und der noch im Sterbebett einen anklagenden Finger gen Osten richtete.

Und es gab den Mitarbeiter eines russischen Wirtschaftsmagazins, der über Putins Versuche berichtet hatte, illegal Waffen nach Syrien und in den Iran zu verkaufen, indem er sie über Weißrussland umleitete. Er hatte einen Sohn im Hochschulalter und eine Tochter, die gerade mit seinem ersten Enkelkind schwanger war. Eines Tages war er ausgegangen, um Orangen zu kaufen, war wieder nach Hause gekommen und hatte sich aus dem Fenster zu Tode gestürzt, so die offizielle Version.

»Siehst du das, Nina? Hast du das gelesen?«

Nina verdrehte die Augen und ließ sich auf das Bett fallen. Doch Alexander dachte nach.

»Hör auf«, sagte sie. »Ich höre genau, dass du wieder nachdenkst.«

Im Laufe der Jahre hatte Alexander begonnen, Putin als launenhaft und ein wenig unberechenbar anzusehen. Er war nicht puritanisch; er erstickte nicht jeden Widerspruch im Keim. Zeitungen gegenüber war er tolerant, großherzig fast. Die symbolträchtigste von ihnen, die *Nowaja Gaseta*, war besonders vorlaut – selbst nach dem Tod Anna Politkowskajas –, wobei Alexander sicher war, dass

Putin es nur zuließ, um sich den Anschein demokratischer Glaubwürdigkeit zu geben. Bestimmt brachte er das Blatt nach Brüssel mit und sagte: Seht ihr? Seht ihr, was ich sie über mich schreiben lasse? Aber wo es wirklich zählte, griff Putin hart durch, und was wirklich zählte, war das Fernsehen. Alexander hatte einmal bei einer Konferenz Seite an Seite mit einem in Ungnade gefallenen Wirtschaftswissenschaftler einen Vortrag gehalten, und als er sich die Übertragung im Fernsehen ansah, hatte man den Unglücklichen digital ausradiert – seine Hände waren noch da, sein geisterhafter Schatten, aber sein Kopf und seine unbequemen Worte fehlten. Und es war nicht bei pubertären Kraftmeiereien geblieben. Einmal war Alexander von dem Klang berstenden Glases und einem Übelkeit erregenden dumpfen Aufprall auf dem Boden aufgewacht. Als er nachsah, fand er in einem Plastikbeutel eine blutige menschliche Ohrmuschel.

Nach diesem Ereignis bat ihn Nina, das Alternative Russland aufzugeben oder zumindest um Himmels willen das Hauptquartier nach außerhalb der Wohnung zu verlagern.

»Ich weiß, dass du das hier tust, weil du damals mit der Partei zu tun hattest«, sagte sie. Sie nahm sein Gesicht in beide Hände und beugte sich vor. Er sah den flackernden Pulsschlag an ihrem Hals. »Und du sollst wissen, dass du überhaupt keinen Grund hast, dich schuldig zu fühlen.«

»Habe ich nicht?«

»So war es damals. Das waren andere Zeiten. Jetzt ist doch alles vorbei.«

»Ist es das?«

»Du hast uns alles so schön eingerichtet, Alexander.«

»Schön für wen?«

Sie lehnte sich zurück. »Oh, bitte. Für uns beide natürlich. Magst du die Wohnung etwa nicht? Oder deine Geräte?«

»Es sind deine Geräte.«

»Du bist ein wohlhabender Mann. Du bist wohlhabend und einflussreich und gefragt.«

»Vom FSB vielleicht.«

»Und wenn du mit deinem Leben unzufrieden bist, hast du die Möglichkeit, es zu ändern.« Er spürte das Unglück, das von ihr abstrahlte.

»Genau das habe ich vor.«

»Bist du in der Midlife-Crisis?«

»Hör auf, mich zu analysieren.«

»Machst du das, weil du gegen den Computer verloren hast?«

Er schlug mit der Faust gegen die Wand, wenn auch nicht so fest, dass es der Wand oder seiner Faust geschadet hätte.

Nina gab nicht nach. »Wenn du dir die Hand brichst, schreiben sie in der Zeitung darüber.«

»Hör auf.«

»Ich bin hier nicht diejenige, die analysiert.«

»Hör verdammt noch mal endlich auf, bitte.« Nina feilte weiter ihre Fingernägel. Er sah sie an, und er staunte über das paradoxe Gefühl, jemanden so genau zu kennen, wie er Nina kannte – zu wissen, wie ihre Zehen aussahen, wenn sie die Zehennägel zu lang werden ließ (was Nina allerdings fast nie tat), wie ihr Husten in der Dusche widerhallte, wenn sie krank war, wie ihr Gesicht aussah, wenn es nach dem Erwachen blass und ausgezehrt war – und sie zugleich wirklich, wirklich gar nicht zu kennen. Er dachte an Situationen auf Partys und Empfängen zurück, wo er sie aus dem Augenwinkel gesehen hatte, in Licht oder Schatten gehüllt, und sich gesagt hatte, was für ein Mysterium sie war – diese Person inmitten von drei Pfund Neuronenmasse, was auch immer, wer auch immer sie war, unergründlich, unerreichbar und nicht weniger rätselhaft, nur weil Alexander nicht an außerphysikalische Kräfte glaubte.

»Du grübelst so viel in letzter Zeit.«

»Ninotschka«, sagte er. »Du bist sträflich naiv, sträflich schizophren, wenn du bei alledem nicht ins Grübeln kommst.«

»Ninotschka mag ich nicht, weißt du. Es klingt herablassend.«

Das musste man Nina lassen: Sie konnte ihn immer noch überraschen. Allerdings konnte er selbst sich auch immer noch überraschen, nach so vielen Jahren, die er sich schon kannte (und vielleicht niemanden sonst; vielleicht hatte er das nie).

Drei Wochen darauf gab er seine Absicht bekannt, sich als Präsident der Russischen Föderation zur Wahl zu stellen.

KAPITEL 14

Irina
St. Petersburg, Dezember 2006

Am Samstag fuhr ich mit der Metro Richtung Innenstadt. Eine strenge, blecherne Lautsprecherstimme ermahnte die Fahrgäste, dem Gostiny Dwor fernzubleiben, also wusste ich, dass ich auf dem richtigen Weg war. Oben erwartete mich eine erstaunlich große Menschenmenge: Tausende, glaube ich, vielleicht zehntausend standen auf dem Platz zu Füßen blassgelber Gebäude, die aussahen wie mit Zuckerguss überzogen. Rote Fahnen flatterten über einer Masse brauner Mäntel, so wollig, dicht und dunkel wie eine Armee wütender Otter. Es gab verschiedene Banner mit kantigen kyrillischen Schriftzügen – Ultranationalisten schienen dabei zu sein, radikale Linke, Trotzkisten. Treue Anhänger des Kommunismus gab es auch, mit all ihrer krankhaften Nostalgie. Jemand reichte mir ein Fähnchen, und ich schwenkte es ein wenig. Irgendwo hinter mir hörte ich leise ein paar Worte in amerikanischem Englisch, doch als ich mich umdrehte – mit vor idiotischer Begeisterung, einen Landsmann zu treffen, überquellendem Blick vermutlich –, verstummten sie, und es blieb ein Rätsel, wer sie gesprochen hatte. Ich sah mich um, konnte aber Viktor nirgends entdecken.

Auf einem Podest mitten in der Menge stand Alexander Besetow. Ich hatte Bilder von ihm gesehen, denen er auch ähnlich sah. Daher weiß ich nicht, was mich an ihm so überraschte. Vielleicht hatte ich mir vorgestellt, er hätte eine Art Aura – das jenseitige Erkennungsmal eines Menschen, der eine unerklärliche Verbindung zur Zukunft oder zu den Toten unterhält. Stattdessen sah er normaler aus als normal; er war kleiner, als ich erwartet hatte – mir fiel auf, wie viele Porträtaufnahmen es von ihm gab –, und seine Nase war unschön gerötet. Beim Sprechen stieß er schneeweiße Dampfwölkchen aus.

»Meine Freunde«, rief er. Die wimmelnde Menschenmenge richtete sich bei dieser vielversprechend familiären Anrede erwartungsvoll auf. »Wir haben keine Chance zu gewinnen.« Zu meiner Überraschung brach die Menge in Jubel aus.

Ich spähte durch den winterlichen Nebel, die wabernden Massen, die bunten Fahnen, die knatterten wie Pistolenschüsse. Ich verglich diesen Mann mit dem, den ich vor so vielen Jahren mit meinem Vater im Fernsehen gesehen hatte. Dieser Besetow wirkte kompakt und solide, während er während des Turniers dünn gewesen war, mit höckerigen, knackenden Fingerknöcheln. Aber die schweren Augenlider waren gleich geblieben, die fleischige Nase, wie eine aussortierte Kartoffel. Der Mund, der für die Härten des Wettkampfs zu träge und unartikuliert aussah.

»Es bringt gar nichts, so zu tun, als hätten wir eine Chance auf den Sieg«, sagte er. »Das wäre eine Lüge. Wir sind nicht angetreten, um zu siegen.« Die Menge jubelte lauter – die rotwangigen, blassstirnigen jungen Frauen mit ihrem unglaublich kantigen, knochigen Körperbau, die mattgesichtigen Männer, die wohl alternde, unbedeutende Dissidenten sein mussten. Den Horizont säumte ein Streifen Polizisten, grimmig, breitschultrig und unübersehbar, obwohl Besetow für diese Veranstaltung sicher eine Genehmigung hatte.

»Wir sind angetreten, um zu verlieren«, rief Besetow. »Und wir sind angetreten, um, während wir verlieren, bemerkt zu werden. Wir sind angetreten, damit man uns aufhält. Wir sind angetreten, damit man uns entgegentritt.« Die Menge wurde lauter und Besetows Stimme heiserer.

»Wir sind angetreten, damit man uns unterdrückt«, schrie er.

»Damit man uns systematisch ignoriert, uns totschweigt. Wir sind angetreten, damit man uns ermordet.« Wieder tobte die Menge. »Wir sind angetreten, damit man uns terrorisiert, ignoriert und tötet, und damit alle Welt es sieht. Wir sind angetreten, damit es eines Tages Aufzeichnungen gibt. Damit es Erinnerungen gibt.«

Die Leute schrien und schwenkten ihre Fahnen. Eine Frau hinter mir stieß einen Triller aus, der mich zusammenfahren ließ. Die Menge trug eine oberflächliche Patina des Triumphgefühls, aber es gab auch Hinweise auf unterschwellige Raserei, als würden sie im nächsten Moment Heugabeln hervorholen und die Bastille stürmen. Neben mir hüpfte ein Kind auf der Stelle auf und ab. Ein Mann schwenkte eine Frau herum, und beide schrien zusammenhanglose Worte. Ein junger Mann stand allein da, zitterte und lächelte so heftig, dass ich dachte, er werde in Stücke brechen und über den Platz auseinanderschlittern. Ich zog ein Notizbuch hervor und tat, als sei ich voll darauf konzentriert. Mir fiel zum ersten Mal auf, dass mir Ausbrüche aufrichtiger politischer Gefühle zutiefst unangenehm waren.

Am Rand der Menge, unweit des Podiums, stand eine Frau, die Alexander zusah und gelangweilt wirkte. Sie war schmal und leicht und hatte mit ihrer effizienten Art die Ausstrahlung eines Fensterbriefumschlags. Sie sah zu gleichgültig aus, um eine Ansprechperson zu sein, und zu funktional, um nicht dazuzugehören. Sie hatte rotes Haar. Das war Nina. Ich schob mich in ihre Richtung – eine meiner Zehen wurde von einem verblüffend schweren Kind gequetscht, eine meiner Brüste von einem alten Mann begrapscht, der in die Luft starrte, als ich mich umdrehte. Als ich die Frau erreichte, betrachtete sie erst alles um mich herum – das schneidende Sonnenlicht, den festgestampften Schnee, die Horden junger Männer, die johlend mit Eissplittern warfen –, ehe ich ihre Aufmerksamkeit auf mich lenken konnte.

»Entschuldigung«, sagte ich und wedelte mit der Hand.

»Ja?«, sagte sie. Sie klang überrascht, ganz so, als hätte sie mich tatsächlich gerade erst bemerkt.

»Ich heiße Irina Ellison«, sagte ich. »Ich wollte fragen, ob ich einen Termin mit Herrn Besetow haben könnte.«

Sie sah mich ungeniert von oben bis unten an, als wollte sie meine physische Fitness ermitteln und sei mit dem Ergebnis unzufrieden. »Und wer sind Sie, Irina Ellison?«

»Niemand«, erklärte ich eifrig. Ninas Blick trübte sich. »Ich bin eine amerikanische Dozentin«, verbesserte ich mich. »An der Universität.«

Sie schwieg. Winzige Furchen gruben sich in ihre Mundwinkel. Sie sah aus, als saugte sie sehr fest an etwas Bitterem. »Ist das alles?«

»Das ist alles.« Ich wusste nicht genau, was sie meinte, aber ich wusste, dass das ganz sicher alles war. »Denken Sie, ich könnte einen Termin bekommen?«

»Eher nicht. Er ist sehr beschäftigt.«

Nina begann sich abzuwenden; die Fehlzündung eines Motorrads lenkte ihre Aufmerksamkeit auf sich. Ich hätte Recherchearbeiten vorschützen sollen, fiel mir ein, irgendeinen akademischen Vorwand für mein Anliegen. Vielleicht hätte es dafür mehr Verständnis gegeben.

»Bitte«, sagte ich. »Mein Vater und Mr. Besetow waren Briefpartner.«

»Dann lassen Sie Ihren Vater ein Treffen vereinbaren.«

»Er ist schon tot«, sagte ich. »Mein Vater.« Normalerweise sage ich aus Rücksicht auf meine Gesprächspartner immer »von uns gegangen«. Nicht, weil ich fände, »von uns gegangen« sei der passende Ausdruck – wohin gegangen?, fragt man sich, von wem gegangen? Sondern ich sage es, weil »tot« so konfrontativ klingt, so ordinär. Aber im Russischen kannte ich kein anderes Wort.

Nina wandte mir ihren schiefgelegten Kopf zu, aber ich konnte nicht erkennen, wo sie hinsah. »Tut mir leid«, sagte sie. Falls in ihrem Tonfall so etwas wie Mitleid lag, konnte ich es nicht hören. »Aber Alexander hat mit allen möglichen Leuten korrespondiert.«

Sie blickte sich nach einem breitschultrigen Mann mit Sonnenbrille um, der ein paar Schritte entfernt stand. Er nickte leicht. Ich hatte Sorge, im nächsten Moment abgeführt zu werden.

»Könnten Sie ihn nicht einfach fragen?«, sagte ich. »Ich habe einen sehr weiten Weg hinter mir.«

Sie neigte wieder den Kopf, und plötzlich konnte ich mich selbst mit ihren Augen sehen: mit geröteter Nase, ungekämmtem Haar und wirrem Blick und mit jenem amerikanisch klingenden Russisch, das die Leute wechselweise als komisch, tragisch oder als Zeichen minderer Intelligenz auffassten.

»Wer ist Ihr Auftraggeber?«, fragte sie schließlich.

»Mein Auftraggeber?« Dasselbe hatte Nikolai auch wissen wollen, und ich fragte mich, ob es irgendeine Fehlübersetzung war, die immer wieder zu diesem Verständigungsproblem führte.

Die Frau presste die Lippen aufeinander, als hätte sie es mit der vorgetäuschten Blödheit eines unwilligen Schülers zu tun. »Für wen arbeiten Sie?«

»Für niemanden mehr.«

»Niemanden *mehr*?«

»Ich habe an der Universität gearbeitet«, sagte ich, obwohl ich einen Moment lang unsicher war, ob das stimmte. »Das ist schon einige Zeit her.«

»Verstehe«, sagte sie und sah mich verständnislos an. »Dann sind Sie also als Touristin hier?«

»Könnte man sagen«, sagte ich. »Ja.«

Sie musterte mich angestrengt, dann zuckte sie mit den Schultern. »Vielleicht geht es«, sagte sie. »Am Mittwoch hat er frei. Vielleicht hat er eine Viertelstunde Zeit für Sie. Sie werden natürlich nicht allein sein.«

»Natürlich nicht«, sagte ich, obwohl ich in dem Moment nicht sicher war, was sie damit meinte.

»Kommen Sie Mittwochvormittag zu dieser Adresse, dann sehen wir weiter. Okay? Sie werden warten müssen. Ich kann Ihnen nichts versprechen.« Sie steckte mir eine Visitenkarte zu, an der ich mir sofort den Finger schnitt.

»Okay«, sagte ich. »Ich kann warten.« Warten war in letzter Zeit mein Spezialgebiet, meine größte Stärke. Ich war eine Meisterin, Profiligistin, eine Weltklasseathletin des Wartens, konkurrenzlos, ungeschlagen. Auf meine Wartefähigkeiten war Verlass.

»Gut«, sagte sie. »Sie sind eine seltsame junge Frau.«

Irgendetwas an ihren Worten – an dieser Urteilsverkündung einer quasi-feindseligen Europäerin – führte dazu, dass ich Lars so sehr vermisste, dass mir fast die Tränen kamen. Ich weine nicht oft – es ist für mich eine Beschäftigung, die ich in Betracht ziehen und dann doch wieder verwerfen kann, meistens, weil mir die Kraft dazu fehlt –, aber gelegentlich wurde ich in den merkwürdigsten Augenblicken von Emotionen überwältigt: auf Parkplätzen, in Supermärkten, wenn ältere Paare gemeinsam Obst auswählten oder ein kleines Kind nach dem Kleid seiner Mutter griff. Die Frau sah mich alarmiert an.

»Ich weiß«, sagte ich. »Danke für Ihre Hilfe.«

Sie schniefte und wandte sich ab, wofür ich dankbar war, denn der Anblick vor mir – die brodelnde Menge mit ihren winzigen Fahnen, ihren unverständlichen Rufen und ihrer enormen Wut – begann zu verschwimmen, und ich wollte keine Zuschauer bei meinem Versuch, dort hindurchzugehen.

Ich wählte den weiteren Weg zurück – über das Schlossufer, an der Kanone der Peter-und-Paul-Festung vorbei, bis ich die bucklige Krone der Sphinx als unförmigen Schatten in der Ferne sah, dann über die Dworzowy Most zu meiner Insel zurück. Mein Kopf füllte sich mit Kriegen und Revolutionen. Ich dachte an den Überfall auf Nikolaus II. – das mörderische Kratzen an den Palasttüren, die Schüsse, die den Männern das Brustbein durchschlugen, die Frauen, die zusammenbrachen und in ihre Taftkleider weinten. Ich dachte an Stalins Säuberungsaktionen – die zitternden, rotgesichtigen Intellektuellen, die weinten oder ihre Peiniger anspuckten. Ich dachte an die Juden, die in den Achtzigern Schlange standen, um ihre Ausreisevisa zu bekommen, die sich nach der trostlosen

Landschaft umdrehten, die einmal ihre Heimat gewesen war; ich dachte an Jelzin auf dem Panzer, wie er einen Militärputsch niederschrie; ich dachte an die Geiselnahme von Beslan, den Terrorismus, die Vabanquespiele, die Bluffs des letzten Jahrzehnts. Und dann dachte ich an Alexanders Kundgebung, daran, wie sich tausend Köpfe drehten, wenn er in eine Richtung wies, und wie tausend Rufe antworteten, wenn er sprach.

Ich ging nach Hause, nickte dem Rezeptionisten mit den eisigen Augen zu und setzte mich auf mein Bett. Ich sah zu, wie die kühlen Sterne in der herabsinkenden Dunkelheit deutlicher hervortraten. Im Laufe der Wochen hatte ich in meiner Unterkunft ein gewisses Zugehörigkeitsgefühl entwickelt: Mein Handtuch mit den einst knallblauen, jetzt grau verblassten Fischen hatte seinen Stammplatz im Gemeinschaftsbadezimmer; meine salzverkrusteten Stiefel standen im Flur vor der Zimmertür wie Spuren einer Gräueltat. Ich hatte so oft den Boden angestarrt, dass ich begonnen hatte, aus den Flecken eine absurde Topographie herauszulesen: Neben dem Nachttisch gab es einen indischen Subkontinent; am Fenster war ein ganzes Afrika, komplett mit Madagaskar.

Ich musste an die Weltkarte meines Vaters mit der gelblichen Sowjetunion denken, daran, wie ich jetzt mitten in dieser gewaltigen Masse war. Es war, als wäre ich auf den Schreibtisch meines Vaters geklettert, hätte seine Papiere beiseitegeschoben, seine Souvenirs durcheinandergebracht und wäre in die Karte hineingekrochen. Es war, als wäre ich durch den Fernsehbildschirm auf die andere Seite gezogen worden: ein Ort, wo die Zeit die Welt im ewigen Zustand potentieller Energie festhielt, wo das statische Rauschen die Luft in Stücke zerbrach und alles schachbrettfarben war.

Alexanders Wohnung war sonnig und weitläufig und mit derselben leicht schrägen Geschmackssicherheit eingerichtet wie ein Museum für Moderne Kunst. Im Salon stand ein schwarz-weißes Sofa, und die komplizierten Akkorde einer Klaviersonate – dissonant und in Moll – rieselten leise von irgendwo über meinem Kopf herab. Makellos gekleidete Frauen und etwas nachlässigere Männer gingen sehr zielstrebig in der eigentlichen Wohnung ein und aus. Wenn die Tür aufging, konnte ich einen Flachbildfernseher sehen, auf dem ohne Ton ein staatlicher Nachrichtensender lief, und eine Espressomaschine kreischen hören.

Ich wurde von einem bulligen Leibwächter abgetastet, der sich unziemlich lange mit meiner Innennaht befasste. Dann durfte ich, wie Nina versprochen hatte, warten. Jedes Mal wenn die Tür geöffnet wurde, blickte ich erwartungsvoll auf und begegnete den misstrauischen Blicken der Besucher, die gerade gingen – ein ziegengesichtiger Mann mit dicken Brillengläsern, ein sehr junger Mann mit einem Klemmbrett, mehrere markige Kerle mit Headsets und grimmigen Gesichtern. Viktor ließ sich nicht blicken. Niemand rief mich auf. Niemand redete mit mir. Es erinnerte mich an die Arztbesuche damals am College, wo ich, mit Broschüren über Vitamine und Selbstmanagement und das »Leben mit Chorea Huntington« versorgt, ganze Äonen, ganze Epochen mit Warten verbrachte und den Schwestern nachsah, die gelegentlich mitfühlend zusammenzuckten.

Irgendwann kam Nina. Zu dem Zeitpunkt schlief ich fast; alle dreißig Sekunden nickte mich mein Kopf unsanft wieder wach. Meinem ohnehin immer etwas missratenen Haar hatte die lange Wartezeit nicht gutgetan. Nina runzelte die Stirn. Sie trug diesmal eine beigefarbene Bluse mit kunstvoll gekräuseltem Kragen und einen orange getönten Lippenstift. Sie war blasser, als ich sie in Erinnerung hatte, und hatte ihr Haar zu einem strengen Dutt hochgesteckt. Ihre Wangenknochen standen aus dem Gesicht hervor wie eine Kunstinstallation.

»Sie sind immer noch da?«, fragte sie.

»Scheint so.«

»Also gut. Kommen Sie rein.«

Sie führte mich einen Flur mit hohen Decken entlang. An den weißen Wänden hingen kleine Druckgraphiken von Ansichten aus Moskau und St. Petersburg in Rot- und Blautönen. Über mir wand sich die Newa in tintigem Kobaltblau; die Basiliuskathedrale erhob sich seltsam drohend über einen blutroten Horizont.

»Eine schöne Wohnung«, sagte ich. Ich spürte, wie sie die Augen verdrehte, obwohl sie mir den Rücken zuwandte.

»Herr Besetow hat ungefähr fünfzehn Minuten Zeit«, sagte Nina. »Ich habe ihm erklärt, eine seltsame Amerikanerin wolle ihn sprechen, und er schien interessiert zu sein. Ich gehe davon aus, dass Sie ihm Ihr Anliegen genauer erklären können. Er ist sehr beschäftigt.«

»Natürlich«, sagte ich, und dann mündete der Flur in ein Zimmer. Es war so groß, dass es darin hallte; zarte Schnüre aus Sonnenlicht fielen in einer Ecke schräg durch ein verschneites Oberlicht, und in einer anderen kauerte ein kleiner Konzertflügel. In der Mitte des Raums saß Alexander Besetow an einem schwarzen Schreibtisch und tippte eilig auf einem Laptop.

»Alexander«, sagte Nina. »Dein Besuch.«

»Einen Moment«, sagte Alexander auf Russisch. Nina war schon wieder verschwunden. Er war legerer gekleidet als bei der Kundgebung und trug eine Nickelbrille, die westlich und ein klein wenig zaghaft aussah. Sein Gesicht, das bei seiner Rede energiegeladen, lebhaft ausgesehen hatte, mit buschigen Brauen, die hin- und hergingen, als hielte er Ausschau nach politischem Sprengstoff, wirkte jetzt leicht gelangweilt. Er befühlte mit der Zunge gedankenverloren seine Unterlippe. Seine Ärmel waren hochgekrempelt.

Nach einer Weile sah er zu mir hoch und hob eine Augenbraue. Das war mein Stichwort.

»Guten Tag«, sagte ich auf Russisch, und Alexander verzog das Gesicht.

»Oh, bitte«, sagte er auf Englisch. »Ich spreche jetzt lange genug Russisch, dass mir das in den Ohren weh tut.«

Sein Englisch war glatt und professionell und sehr artikuliert. Es erinnerte mich an Steine, die über eine Wasseroberfläche titschen.

»Also«, sagte er. »Sie fragen sich wahrscheinlich, warum ich mich mit Ihnen treffe.«

»Sicher«, sagte ich, obwohl das nicht stimmte. Ich hatte gehofft, dass er sich mit mir treffen würde, und war dankbar, dass er es tat. Aber ich wäre nie auf die Idee gekommen, dass der Grund dafür etwas anderes sein könnte als wohlwollende Nachsicht und der Umstand, dass er zufällig gerade Zeit übrig hatte.

»Tja«, sagte er. »Ich weiß, dass Ihnen das vermutlich gar nicht klar ist, aber Sie haben mich ganz schön in Schwierigkeiten gebracht. Sie können sich übrigens setzen.« Er wies auf einen zierlichen Stuhl ihm gegenüber. Während ich meinen Schal abwickelte und mich setzte, nahm er seine Schreibarbeit wieder auf.

»Habe ich das?«, fragte ich.

Er hörte auf zu tippen. »Ja.«

Ich schwieg und wartete auf eine Erläuterung. Ich hatte keine Ahnung, wie ich es geschafft haben könnte, Alexander Besetow in Schwierigkeiten zu bringen, wenn es mir nicht einmal gelungen war, mir selbst Schwierigkeiten zu bereiten.

»Sie sind nicht zufällig von einem Nikolai Sergejewitsch angesprochen worden?«

In meinem Hinterkopf pingte es leise. »Doch.«

»Und hat er vielleicht versucht, Sie zu überzeugen, Sie und er hätten gemeinsame Interessen? Hat er behauptet, er sei mein Freund?«

Das Ping-Geräusch ging in ein misstönendes Vibrato über. Ich kam mir allmählich wie ein Idiot vor. »Es war ein bisschen verwirrend«, sagte ich.

»Das glaube ich gern.«

So hatte ich mir unsere Begegnung nicht vorgestellt. Ich wusste selbst nicht genau, was ich erwartet hatte, aber vermutlich hatte ich gedacht, Alexander wäre gütig und sanft und vielleicht ein ganz klein wenig professoral, würde geduldig meine Fragen beantworten, sich höflich nach meinen Wünschen erkundigen und mich dann milde, mit den allgemeingültigsten guten Wünschen für die Zukunft, wieder verabschieden. In meinen kühnsten Träumen wäre er tatsächlich in der Lage gewesen, mir ein paar Fragen zu beantworten, die meinen noch intakten Geist und mein Herz beschäftigten – er hätte irgendein tiefgründiges Geheimwissen über einen würdevollen Weg in den Untergang preisgegeben, und dieses Wissen hätte mir irgendwie die Vergangenheit oder die Zukunft erhellt. Jedenfalls hatte ich nicht damit gerechnet, ins Kreuzverhör genommen zu werden.

»Es tut mir leid«, sagte ich. »Ich habe nur eine alte Freundin von Ihnen besucht, um an Ihre Kontaktdaten zu kommen. Ich wusste nicht, dass das irgendwelchen Ärger verursachen würde.«

Alexander seufzte müde, als hätte man ihn gebeten, Trainer eines Highschool-Schachteams zu werden. »Natürlich wussten Sie das nicht. Ich erkläre es Ihnen. Die russische Regierung vermutet, ich sei ein Strohmann des amerikanischen Geheimdienstes. Das haben sie von Anfang an geglaubt. Und da kommen Sie hierher und suchen nach mir und wirbeln jede Menge Staub auf, und das haben die natürlich mitbekommen. Sie glauben, dass Sie mich steuern oder es zumindest versuchen oder wie auch immer. Verstehen Sie?«

Er atmete schwer vor Anstrengung, höflich zu bleiben. Sarkasmus brach an die Oberfläche seiner Stimme durch wie eine lange zurückgehaltene unterirdische Substanz. »In Wirklichkeit werde ich, nur falls Sie sich das fragen, nicht von Ihrer CIA gelenkt. Aber wenn die CIA so etwas vorhätte, würde sie es sicher sehr viel subtiler anstellen, als Sie es sind.«

»Und wer ist Nikolai?«

»Er ist ein sehr angesehener Bürokrat unserer sehr legitimen Regierung.«

»Oh.« Ich begann zu verstehen. »Okay.«

Ein Schweigen folgte, und Alexander begann wieder zu tippen, und ich fragte mich, ob unser Gespräch irgendwie plötzlich beendet war. Ich versuchte mich zu erinnern, was ich getan hatte, als Nikolai Wochen zuvor in dem Café aufgetaucht war. Hatte ich etwas Verdächtiges getan, etwas, das auf finstere, illegale Aktivitäten schließen ließ? Ich begriff einfach nicht, wie ich das fertiggebracht haben sollte, ohne es selbst zu merken. In den letzten paar Wochen konnte ich mich überhaupt an so gut wie keine bedeutsamen Ereignisse erinnern – und die, die doch an die Oberfläche kamen, wenn ich danach tastete, waren eher klein und persönlich und merkwürdig sentimental: Einmal hatte ich aus meinem Zimmerfenster im Hostel zugesehen, wie der aufgewirbelte Schnee die Sterne verwischte, einmal bei der alten Frau Gebäck gekauft, die mir immer ein Bialy extra »für meine Kinder« mitgab, einmal war ich an der Newa entlanggelaufen, bis meine Haut gerötet war, bis mir die Augen tränten und mein Kopf sich mit einer Symphonie russischer Lyrik füllte.

»Ich verstehe das nicht«, sagte ich. »Ich verstehe nicht, warum ich überhaupt irgendwem aufgefallen sein sollte. Ich tue doch gar nichts, außer in Cafés herumzusitzen und zu lesen.«

»Tja«, sagte er. »Die werden auch nicht so richtig klug aus Ihnen. Aber sie halten Sie für eine Beauftragte der amerikanischen Regierung, wenn auch eine unwissentliche.«

»Eine unwissentliche Beauftragte?« Jetzt war ich beleidigt.

Alexander musterte mich, und ich konnte sehen, wie er nacheinander meinen halboffenen Mantel, meinen schlechtsitzenden Pullover und die dünnen Haarsträhnen registrierte, die aus meiner Frisur ausbrachen wie politische Flüchtlinge.

»Ja«, sagte er.

Ich befühlte meinen Mantelsaum und sah zu Boden. Ich war sehr müde. In letzter Zeit war da diese bis ins Mark reichende Erschöpfung, in dunklen Wellen, die sich anfühlten, als rotierten meine Augen im Schädel herum. Ich wusste nicht, wie ich es deuten sollte oder ob ich mich überhaupt bemühen sollte, es zu deuten. Es war kein Vorbote der ersten Symptome – ich hatte genug Berichte gelesen, um das zu wissen –, aber vielleicht war es eine psychologische Vorbereitung darauf, und ich war beinahe dankbar dafür.

»Das alles«, sagte er, »bereitet mir nur weitere Schwierigkeiten. Ihnen übrigens auch. Ihnen vielleicht sogar mehr als mir. Ich habe längst größere Sorgen.«

»Ich auch«, sagte ich, ohne aufzublicken.

Alexander schniefte. »Ich weiß, dass Sie nicht vorhatten, Ärger zu machen.«

»Ich hatte ja keine Ahnung.«

»Das glaube ich Ihnen ohne weiteres.« Er starrte mich an. Es sah aus, als hielte er seine Augen absichtlich weit offen und still, was auf dasselbe hinauslief, als hätte er sie verdreht. »Warum sind Sie dann hier«, fragte er, »wenn Sie nicht auf Ärger aus sind?«

Eine gute Frage.

»Erinnern Sie sich«, fragte ich behutsam, »an einen Brief, den Sie in den Achtzigern von einem amerikanischen Akademiker bekommen haben?«

Er lehnte sich in seinem Sessel zurück. »Ich habe in meinem Leben viele Briefe bekommen.«

»Natürlich«, sagte ich schnell. »Ich weiß. Aber es war ein ziemlich seltsamer Brief.«

»Wie seltsam?«

»Er handelte nicht wirklich vom Schach. Es ging darin um die Frage, was man tun soll, wenn man weiß, dass man verlieren wird.«

»Wenn man verliert?«

»Ja.«

»Bin ich hauptsächlich als Verlierer bekannt?«

Ich hatte nicht damit gerechnet, dass er arrogant sein könnte. Es hätte mich nicht verwundern sollen – er war der beste Schachspieler aller Zeiten. Der beste Hamsterdompteur aller Zeiten hatte vermutlich auch seinen Stolz. Aber irgendwie hatte ein Teil von mir gehofft, er würde sich bei meiner Frage aufrichten, in seine Jackentasche greifen und ein maschinengeschriebenes Manifest daraus hervorholen. Hier, bitte, würde er sagen. Ich habe Sie schon erwartet. Hier steht alles drin, was Sie wissen müssen.

»Nein«, sagte ich. »Natürlich nicht. Er wusste nur, dass es in Ihrer langen Karriere auch … Momente gegeben haben muss, in denen Sie wussten, dass Sie verlieren würden. Und er wollte wissen, wie Sie es dann schafften weiterzuspielen.«

»Ich glaube nicht, dass ich auf so einen Brief geantwortet hätte«, sagte er. »Falls er überhaupt bei mir angekommen ist.«

»Das haben Sie auch nicht«, sagte ich. »Deshalb bin ich hier.«

Er sah mich lange an. Dann nahm er seine Brille ab und massierte sich die Nasenwurzel. »Wann ist Ihr Vater gestorben?«

Ich sah ihn an.

»Wenn er nicht tot wäre, wären Sie nicht hier, oder?« Es war eine herausfordernde Frage, aber er brachte es fertig, dabei freundlich zu klingen.

»Im Februar«, sagte ich. »Aber davor war er schon sehr lange krank.«

Besetow nickte. Er setzte seine Brille wieder auf. Ich bemühte mich, einen bewundernden Kommentar zu der modernen Kunst an den Wänden zu machen, aber mein Blick blieb an den dunkel gekleideten breitschultrigen Männern an der Tür hängen. »Sie haben ziemlich viele Sicherheitskräfte«, sagte ich.

»Allerdings.« Er gestikulierte in ihre Richtung. »Sie kosten mich Zehntausende Dollar, und am Ende werden sie mir wahrscheinlich doch nichts nützen. Ich kann die Risiken minimieren, aber letztlich ist es alles vergeblich. Es ist nur eine Frage der Zeit.«

»Das kenne ich«, sagte ich. Die Heizung begann zischende Geräusche von sich zu geben und verbreitete den Geruch von etwas Verkochtem im Raum. Alexander sah zum großen Panoramafester hinaus, obwohl es nicht viel zu sehen gab: Im spätnachmittäglichen Dunkel waren da nur die Spiegelungen seiner vergoldeten Lampenkugeln, des Flackerns auf seinem Computerbildschirm und die unangenehme Blässe meines Gesichts.

»Sie haben gesagt, Sie hätten eine alte Freundin von mir getroffen«, sagte Alexander. »Wer war das?«

»Elisabeta Nasarowna. Erinnern Sie sich an sie? Sie hat mit Ihnen zusammen gewohnt. Sie sagte, Sie wüssten es vielleicht nicht mehr.«

Er schwieg und sah weiter aus dem Fenster. Ich bildete mir ein, dass seine Halsmuskeln sich ein klein wenig anspannten. Draußen durchdrang eine an- und abschwellende Brandung von Scheinwerferlichtern die Dunkelheit.

»Das eine oder andere weiß ich noch von ihr.« Er ließ den Satz wirken; die Stille dämpfte ihn ein wenig. »Und, wie geht es ihr?«

Ich dachte an ihr mörderisches Husten, an ihre Schultern, die bebten wie Baumwipfel im Orkan. Und ich dachte an das Glitzern in ihrer Stimme, daran, dass man sich beim Zuhören fühlte wie in einem Spiegelkabinett.

»Nicht so gut, fürchte ich.«

»Verstehe.« Er wartete. Ich spürte, dass er sich noch etwas von mir erhoffte, wusste jedoch nicht, was. »Lebt sie allein?«

Ich dachte daran, wie sie meine Hand gepackt hatte, an die Nacktheit ihrer dürren Finger. Ich dachte an die Größe ihrer Wohnung und daran, wie der Vogelkäfig die gesamte Einrichtung dominierte. Mir fiel auf, dass es kein Schlafzimmer gegeben hatte – nur das enge Wohnzimmer und die Puppenhausküche. Sie musste auf dem Sofa geschlafen haben.

»Ich glaube schon.« Dann begriff ich, als ich sah, wie Alexander die Zähne zusammenbiss, wie er den Ausdruck seiner Augen löschte und wie seine Worte zitterten wie Hochseiltänzer, dass er sie geliebt hatte. Und ich begriff, wie unverzeihlich dumm es war, Liebe zu verweigern. Und ich begriff außerdem, was für einen brutalen Fehler ich selbst begangen hatte, und war dankbar dafür, wie wenig Zeit mir bleiben würde, ihn zu bereuen.

»Sie sollten sie besuchen«, sagte ich. Dann kam ich mir aufdringlich vor. »Vielleicht. Wenn Sie möchten.«

»Vielleicht. Ich bin ziemlich beschäftigt in letzter Zeit.«

»Das sehe ich«, sagte ich. Mir fiel auf, dass ich diesen Ansatz noch gar nicht ausprobiert hatte. »Vielleicht könnte ich Ihnen ja behilflich sein?«

Er stand auf, und es verblüffte mich wieder, wie klein er in Wirklichkeit war. Die Autorität, die er ausstrahlte, verdankte sich seinen dichten Augenbrauen, seinem energischen Unterkiefer, der muskulösen Kompaktheit seiner Schulterpartie, der müden Intelligenz seines Blicks. Er wirkte nicht wie jemand, der sein Leben damit zugebracht hat, Spielfiguren auf einem Brett hin und her zu schieben.

»Sie möchten einen Job«, sagte er brüsk.

Ich hustete. »Keinen Job. Ich möchte mich nützlich machen.«

Ein ungeduldiges Schweigen folgte. Ich stand ebenfalls auf, weil es das Gebot der Stunde zu sein schien. Er sah mich an. »Und Sie sind in Ihrer Heimat Akademikerin?«, fragte er schließlich.

»War ich mal.«

»Sie können auf Englisch schreiben, oder?«

»Ja.«

»Und Sie werden sich nicht wieder mit unserem Freund Nikolai unterhalten?«

»Nein.«

»Also gut«, sagte er. »Sie könnten uns mit der amerikanischen Presse behilflich sein. Mit der E-Mail-Korrespondenz. Okay? Sie könnten Texte zusammenschreiben. Nichts Aufregendes. Nichts Glamouröses.«

»Aufregung brauche ich nicht.«

»Schön«, sagte er. »Wenn die sowieso schon denken, dass Sie Ärger machen, warum sollten Sie es nicht wirklich tun? Sie können Montag anfangen. Wie lange planen Sie im Lande zu bleiben?«

Ich überlegte, wie ich antworten sollte. »Das weiß ich noch nicht«, sagte ich. »Wahrscheinlich nicht sehr lange.«

»In Ordnung«, sagte er und manövrierte mich in Richtung Tür. »Dann nutzen wir Ihre Fähigkeiten, solange wir können.« Er öffnete die Tür, und vor mir schwebte wieder der Duft teuren Kaffees über einem weißen Sandstrand von einem Teppichboden, der sich von Wand zu Wand erstreckte. Ich reichte Alexander die Hand. Er ergriff sie.

»Danke«, sagte ich.

»Bitte. Und, Irina?« Er wies mir den Weg hinaus. »Wenn man weiß, dass man verliert, ist es das Vernünftigste, aufzugeben, habe ich gehört.«

Der Rest der Woche schmolz ungefähr so dahin wie die Wochen davor: in einem verträumten, fast trunkenen Zustand stillgestellter Erregung, die durch jedes noch so winzige Fragment einer Erinnerung oder Einbildung in Schwingung geriet. Oft fühlte ich mich krankhaft unempfindlich und beobachtete mich selbst mit der distanzierten Außenperspektive eines Menschen, der heftige Schmerzmittel schluckt. Dann wieder war ich seltsam aufgekratzt, und mein Kopf füllte sich mit Satzfetzen und bedeutungslosen Bildern. Ich erinnerte mich aus dem Nichts an die Strichzeichnung eines Stinktiers auf dem Umschlag eines Malbuchs aus den siebziger Jahren; an einen Tag in meiner Schulzeit, den ich mit einem Jungen, in den ich verliebt war, in einem Obstgarten verbracht hatte; an den gelben Hund in dem Haus gegenüber von meinem Kinderladen, der eines Tages auf geheimnisvolle Weise verschwunden war. Ich staunte über die Fähigkeit meines Gehirns, dermaßen viele Informationen abzuspeichern, die ich nie im Leben brauchen würde.

Ich schrieb weiter an Jonathan, unabschickbare, unlesbare, unverzeihliche Briefe. Ich schrieb, dass mir bewusst war, was ich in den Monaten ohne ihn verpasste. Ich schrieb, dass ich Abendessen und Spaziergänge und Sex und Gelächter verpasste und gemeinsames Duschen und leidenschaftliche Diskussionen im Flüsterton und die Sorte Streit, die man sucht, weil man es sexy findet, wenn der andere ein klein wenig wütend wird. Aber dann schrieb ich ihm auch, was ich noch verpasste und was ich ihn zu verpassen zwang. Das erste Zucken eines Ellbogens oder einer Hand. Den unaufhaltsamen Verlust von Fähigkeiten. Den unerbittlichen Rückzug meines Gehirns über eine abgeriegelte Grenze. Ich schrieb von seiner wachsenden Verbitterung und wie schuldig er sich ihretwegen fühlen würde und wie sie ihn überwältigen würde. Denn das würde sie, schrieb ich, ob er es mir je glauben würde oder nicht. Die Lebenden reagieren seit jeher mit Verbitterung auf die Forderungen der Toten, besonders, wenn die Toten noch lebendig sind. Ich schrieb, ich kenne mich da aus. Ich schrieb, ich wüsste, dass ich die richtige Entscheidung getroffen hatte, auch wenn ich es für ihn gleich mit wissen musste.

Durch mein Fenster kam morgens rosafarbenes Licht: Wenn ich zu einer bestimmten Zeit aufwachte, war das ganze Zimmer in das Rosa der Sixtinischen Kapelle getaucht, in das Rosa eines eben wieder zum Leben erweckten Gesichts. Dann setzte ich mich auf und horchte auf gezupfte Harfentöne, auf den sich regenden Chor, und wenn nichts kam, legte ich mich wieder hin und versuchte noch einmal einzuschlafen. Es überraschte mich immer wieder, wie wenig Angst ich vor dem Schlaf hatte, obwohl er die größtmögliche Annäherung war.

Seltsame Dinge passierten mit meinem Zeitgefühl. Augenblicke bündelten und krümmten sich; manchmal starrte ich stundenlang nur vor mich hin, in einer Art Anfall, aus dem ich desorientiert und aufgelöst erwachte. Dann wieder ballte sich eine ganze qualvolle Ewigkeit in dem Umrühren meines Kaffees, in dem Umblättern einer Buchseite zusammen.

Meine Nächte waren ruhelos und fieberhaft. Ich streifte die Grenze zum Schlaf und lauschte auf den Widerhall sarkastischen Gelächters, auf das Geklapper der Zimmerschlüssel. Schatten malten Fasern und Spitzenmuster an die Wand. Wenn ich erwachte, murmelte ich vor mich hin, halb noch in Träumen, die mich danach den ganzen Tag verfolgten. In ihnen kamen weitere stumme Erinnerungen hoch: Meine Eltern, wie sie an einem Baumstamm lehnten, inmitten von langsam zu Boden sinkendem gelbem Laub. Schachspiele aus Boston verschmolzen mit denen meiner Kindheit. Ich erinnerte mich an die Triumphe der immer siegreichen Dame meines Vaters. Ich erinnerte mich an den Aufprall des geborstenen Schädels seines Königs auf dem Brett.

Dann erinnerte ich mich an den Aufprall seines Arms auf dem Herd, den seines Kopfes auf den Badezimmerfliesen.

Als ich in der Woche darauf wieder in Alexanders Wohnung kam, war Viktor dort. Sein Blick huschte kurz zu mir herüber. Dann fuhr er fort, über einen kleineren Mann mit Notizblock in der Hand energisch den Kopf zu schütteln. »Das nimmt Naschi sofort auseinander«, sagte Viktor. »Die machen uns platt. Das Layout muss besser werden.«

»Sei still«, sagte der andere.

»Guck dir doch an, wie es beim G8 war. Du verschwendest deine kostbare Tinte.«

»Sei jetzt bitte still.«

Viktor schielte zu mir herüber und nickte mit dem Kinn in Richtung des Sitzenden. »Assistent«, formte er stumm mit den Lippen.

Ich zog mich schnell in den Flur zurück und beschäftigte mich damit, mir die Drucke an den Wänden anzusehen. Mir war bewusst, wie verloren ich aussah, obwohl man mich hergebeten hatte. Ein Bild von meinem vierzehnjährigen Selbst blitzte vor mir auf, wie ich am ersten Tag der neunten Klasse auf der aussichtslosen Suche nach dem Geometrieraum durch die Gänge irrte. Ich starrte angestrengt auf einen bernsteinfarbenen Newski-Prospekt und bemühte mich, ganz vertieft auszusehen.

Kurz darauf gab es eine Veränderung der Luft. Alexander stand hinter mir. »Mögen Sie die?«, fragte er.

»O ja«, sagte ich und drehte mich um.

»Die hat ein Freund von uns gemacht. Ein sehr reicher Mann. Er war im Ölgeschäft. Die Drucke hat er gemacht, um sich zu zivilisieren.«

»Ist er hier?«, fragte ich.

»Er verbringt acht Jahre in einer Strafkolonie in Sibirien«, sagte Alexander. »Er hat uns finanziell unterstützt. Aber Putin setzt klare Prioritäten. Er ist gar nicht daran interessiert, jeden aus dem Weg zu räumen. Nur jeden, der seiner Ansicht nach wirklich zählt. Dieser Freund von mir, der die Drucke hergestellt hat, war sehr, sehr reich. Ein Milliardär. Wissen Sie, wie reich man sein muss, um einen Milliardär ins Gefängnis abzuschieben?«

»Ziemlich reich«, sagte ich.

»Ja«, sagte Alexander, »ziemlich reich. Niemand redet je davon, wie unanständig reich Putin eigentlich ist, aber ich erwähne es immer wieder gern. Wissen Sie, wie viele Milliardäre wir insgesamt in Russland haben?«

»Wie viele?«

»Einundsechzig. Einundsechzig Milliardäre, und Putin könnte jeden einzelnen ins Gefängnis stecken lassen, wenn sie seine Geschäftsinteressen gefährden. Das ist etwas, das die Leute nicht verstehen. Er ist kein Ideologe. Er ist nur pragmatisch. Nur gierig. Er könnte genauso gut liberal wie konservativ sein – das ist ihm egal. Syrien und Iran unterstützt er, weil die Spannungen den Ölpreis hochtreiben. Und Sie lassen ihm das durchgehen.«

»Ich?«

»Der Westen. Sie lassen sich von seiner Fassadendemokratie blenden. Schließlich veranstalten wir hier etwas, das man Wahlen nennt. Aber das heißt nicht, dass wir keinen Polizeistaat haben. Und inzwischen gibt es hier etwas zu holen. Also lässt der Westen die Oligarchen ihre zweifelhaften Produkte exportieren, und Putin stellen sie zu dem Zweck ein gutes Zeugnis aus. Wenn die USA es ernst meinten mit dem Anspruch, Putin in seine Schranken zu weisen, würden sie anfangen, Visaanträge abzulehnen. Einen neuen Kalten Krieg könnte sich die Oligarchie nicht leisten.«

Ich sah ihn an. »Was würden Sie denn als Präsident dagegen tun?«

Er winkte ab. »Das ist nicht so ein Wahlkampf, wie Sie ihn sich vorstellen, nach dem Motto: Ich werde mich für den und den Gesetzesentwurf einsetzen. Ich gewinne ja nicht. Ich will eine breite Agenda koordinieren, nicht meine eigenen Ambitionen verfolgen.«

»Das ist ein bisschen unspezifisch, oder?«

Er zog die Augenbrauen hoch, und da wusste ich, wenn ich es nicht schon vorher gewusst hatte, dass ich ihm Kontra geben musste, wenn ich ihn für mich einnehmen wollte. »Also, wenn Sie es genau wissen wollen: Wir müssen sehr sorgfältig prüfen, welche

Bestandteile des bestehenden Apparats für den Aufbau des neuen Staates brauchbar sind. Sonst bricht Chaos aus.«

Ich atmete tief durch und stürzte mich ins Gefecht. »Des bestehenden Apparats? Das klingt ja sehr zurückhaltend.«

»Es ist zurückhaltend.«

»Wissen Ihre Unterstützer, dass es das ist? Wissen sie, wie extrem vorsichtig Sie sind? Diese Leute scheinen nämlich von außen betrachtet nicht die Allerzurückhaltendsten zu sein.«

Er sah mich an, und ich rechnete jeden Moment damit, dass er seine Sicherheitsleute rufen und bitten würde, mich zur Tür zu begleiten. Ich hätte das jedenfalls getan, hätte ich einen ganzen Sicherheitsapparat zu meiner Verfügung gehabt. Doch er tat es nicht. Er lächelte, als hätte er einen Schachgegner entdeckt, der ein klein wenig besser war als angenommen, wenn auch nicht annähernd gut.

»Wir brauchen wieder Gouverneurswahlen. Wir müssen eine neue Verfassung entwerfen, weil die jetzige viel zu autoritär ist.«

»Aber im Alleingang die Verfassung zu kassieren – ist das nicht auch ein klein wenig autoritär?«

Seine Augen blitzten. Er amüsierte sich offenbar. »Das wird auf der Basis eines nationalen Konsens passieren.«

»Welcher Prozentsatz der russischen Bevölkerung sieht sich noch einmal als Anhänger Stalins?«, fragte ich. »Fünfundvierzig Prozent?«

Er grinste. »Fünfundfünfzig, um genau zu sein. Sie sehen also, womit ich es aufnehmen muss.«

»Ja«, sagte ich. Ich wandte mich wieder den Bildern zu. Auf einem war in sattem Grün ein kleines Café am Ende einer langen Straße zu sehen.

»Das ist das Saigon«, sagte Alexander. »Da waren wir damals oft. Vielleicht haben Sie es gesehen? Es ist inzwischen ein Hotel. Ein Zimmer kostet so um die sechshundert Rubel, glaube ich. Also. Mögen Sie anfangen?«

»Ja.«

»Die hier könnten Sie lektorieren«, sagte er und gab mir einen

Stapel Papiere. »Sie sind schon übersetzt, aber es braucht noch einen Muttersprachler, der den Feinschliff macht.«

Ich überflog die erste Seite. *Unter Mithilfe der Demokratischen Union wird Alexander Besetow in der Staatlichen Universität St. Petersburg einen öffentliche Debatte teilnehmen und der Frage nachgehen, in welchen Maßen der Staat in einer modernen Wirtschaft die Ölmonopole abschwächen sollte.*

»Okay«, sagte ich. »Das kriege ich hin.«

»Ich habe auch mal so was gemacht«, sagte er. »Einfache Handlangertätigkeiten. Ich bin damals durch die Stadt gelaufen und habe den Leuten illegale Flugschriften in die Hand gedrückt.«

»Sind Sie je erwischt worden?«

»Man hatte uns von vornherein erwischt. Schon bevor wir wirklich wussten, was wir da taten. Aber wir hielten uns für ziemlich schlau.«

»Waren Sie schlau?«

»Nicht besonders«, sagte er. »Ich war prominent. Nicht so wie jetzt, aber trotzdem. Ich stand schon auf irgendeiner Liste, bevor ich mich überhaupt in der Stadt umgesehen hatte. Sie haben uns von Anfang an gehabt. Und diesmal …« Er richtete sich gerade auf. »… diesmal weiß ich das immerhin schon. Ich weiß, dass ich längst erwischt worden bin. Ich versuche nicht, mich zu verstecken. Und ich bilde mir nicht zu viel ein. Egal wie man es dreht und wendet, es ist ein aussichtsloses Unterfangen.«

»Warum tun Sie es dann?«

»Mir bleibt nicht viel anderes übrig. Schach langweilt mich inzwischen.«

»Spielen Sie noch?«

»Nicht oft. Ich musste mir ein neues Hobby suchen.« Er steckte die Hände in die Taschen und runzelte die Stirn, als sei ihm gerade eine unangenehme Möglichkeit in den Sinn gekommen. »Spielen *Sie*?«

»Habe ich mal. Als Kind habe ich mit meinem Vater gespielt.« Ich sah zu Boden. »Und in Boston hatte ich einen Freund, mit dem ich manchmal eine Partie gespielt habe. Aber ich war nie besonders gut darin. Ich konnte nie mehr als einen Zug vorausdenken.«

»Da können Sie sich glücklich schätzen. Mehr als einen Zug vorauszuplanen hat mich im Leben nie weitergebracht. Nur im Schach. Und selbst da konnte es manchmal eine Last sein. Einmal, in Norwegen, habe ich fünfzehn Züge vorausgedacht, aber es hätte einen viel einfacheren Weg zum Sieg gegeben, und den habe ich übersehen. Sich zu sehr auf die Zukunft zu konzentrieren kann lähmend sein, habe ich festgestellt.«

»Das habe ich auch festgestellt.«

Alexander sah mich skeptisch an. »Also«, sagte er und klopfte mir auf die Schultern. »Dann lasse ich Sie mal arbeiten.«

Ich nahm den Papierstapel – die Pressemitteilungen, die E-Mail-Entwürfe, die lieblos getexteten Flyer – und setzte mich in eine Ecke. Um mich herum wurde gestritten und gelacht und wurden Worte in die Computer gehackt. Ich begann die erste Mail zu überfliegen, fand den ersten Rechtschreibfehler und die erste unelegante Formulierung. Ich fühlte mich wacher als sonst. Nach so vielen Wochen im Morast der Nutzlosigkeit war es sehr befriedigend, etwas Praktisches zu tun zu bekommen. Ich dachte darüber nach, was Alexander über Schach gesagt hatte, über die lähmende Wirkung der Einbildungskraft. Ich wusste, wie recht er hatte. Immer wenn ich meine Gedanken mehr als drei Schritte in die Zukunft tun ließ, erreichten sie die Grenzen des Verstehbaren und stürzten ab. Aber jetzt hatte ich konkretere Sorgen – kleine, bewältigbare Probleme: Tippfehler, grammatikalische Regelverstöße. Damit konnte ich leben. Ich beugte mich über die Seiten und begann zu arbeiten.

KAPITEL 15

Alexander
St. Petersburg, Dezember 2006

Alexander stand am Gostiny Dwor auf einem Podest und schrie in die Menschenmenge. Es waren ansehnlich viele Teilnehmer – vielleicht nicht die größte Gruppe seit seinen Anfängen, aber doch annähernd so groß. Er würde Nina nach den Zahlen fragen müssen. Heute waren sie ein bisschen frenetischer als sonst: Ein paar Jungs traten Hagelkörner wie Fußbälle vor sich her; die Menge stampfte auf dem unnachgiebigen Schnee herum wie eine Huftierherde, die im nächsten Moment ausbrechen würde. Er wusste, er sollte dankbar sein für so viel Energie. Aber der Wind wand sich durch seine Kleidung – das tat er immer, egal, wie viele Lagen Alexander trug; immer fuhr ihm der Wind mit spitzen Fingern provozierend die Hosenbeine entlang und in den Kragen –, und Alexander erschrak bei dem Gedanken, dass er (jetzt schon!) begann, das alles sattzuhaben. Die Menschenmassen, die Parolen, die gen Himmel gerufenen Worte – als ob es am Ende von Bedeutung wäre. Er stand hinter seiner Sache, ja, doch, und er würde weitermachen, bis sie ihn erwischten, bis sie ihm Polonium in das importierte Sushi schmuggelten, den Motor seines Flugzeugs auseinandernahmen, ihn im Treppenhaus seiner eigenen Wohnung erschossen, wie sie es im Oktober mit Anna Politkowskaja getan hatten. Aber es gab Zeiten – wie jetzt, und jetzt war kein guter Zeitpunkt dafür –, wo ihm alles wie vorherbestimmt vorkam. Sie waren nicht die erste Gruppe, die sich zusammenrottete und schrie und Forderungen stellte.

Er nahm einen Schluck eiskalter Luft. »Wir sind angetreten, um zu verlieren«, rief er. Dieser Spruch erntete immer die lautesten Rufe, und das musste ihm doch zu denken geben. »Und wir sind angetreten, um, während wir verlieren, bemerkt zu werden. Wir sind angetreten, damit man uns aufhält. Wir sind angetreten, damit man uns entgegentritt. Wir sind angetreten, damit man uns ermordet.« Er sah sich um. Dieser Satz war seine Herausforderung, vielleicht seine Einladung an das Universum. Irgendwann würde er wahr werden, das wusste er, also konnte es genauso gut kunstvoll inszeniert aussehen. Aber die Fahnen flatterten, und die Menge jubelte. Heute war es noch nicht so weit.

Er warf einen Blick in seine Notizen. Alexander bemühte sich, seine Reden immer wieder abzuwandeln, wenn er sie hielt – heute vor soundso vielen Jahren, stellt euch vor, hat Puschkin seinen *Eugen Onegin* fertiggestellt, hat Polen seine Unabhängigkeit von Russland erklärt! –, damit man ihm auch mehrmals zuhören und immer noch etwas Neues erwarten konnte. Er sah wieder auf und in die Menge; er verlieh seinem Gesicht einen Ausdruck überraschten Interesses, um möglichst überzeugend die Freude an der Entdeckung zu vermitteln, dass sich heute der Tag jährte, an dem Chruschtschow einen Hund dem Tod im Weltall überantwortet hatte. Während er das tat, fiel sein Blick auf eine junge Frau, die schräg gegenüber seines Podests stand und sich Notizen machte. Er sagte seinen Satz auf und sah noch einmal hin. Es fiel ihm jedes Mal auf, wenn sich jemand bei seinen Kundgebungen Notizen machte – eine Marotte, die sicher mit Nikolai zu tun hatte –, auch wenn Nina ihm oft versichert hatte, dass nichts Schlimmes dabei sein musste: Es konnte ein Bürgerjournalist sein, ein europäischer Blogger oder die richtige westliche Presse. »Was hast du bloß?«, fragte sie dann und schlang in ihrem riesigen schwarz-weißen Bett ihr Bein um seins. »Willst du nicht, dass die Leute sich für dich interessieren?« Und er antwortete, ja, doch, das wollte er, obwohl er wusste, dass sich zumindest manche aus sehr schlimmen Gründen für ihn interessierten. »Du machst dir zu viele Sorgen«, sagte Nina und verzog das Gesicht zu einem monströsen aufgesetzten Schmollen (das wohl sein Gesicht darstellen sollte, wenn er sich Sorgen machte, also immer). Und weil es würdelos gewesen wäre, eine Frau zu bitten, sich Sorgen um ihn zu machen, wenn sie von Natur aus nicht dazu neigte, zuckte er dazu nur mit den Schultern, drehte sich um und schlief mit dem Gesicht zur Wand ein.

Aber diese Frau – was war es nur, das an ihr ganz und gar nicht journalistisch wirkte? Sie sah so unaufdringlich, so unsicher aus, dass man sich fast schon fragte, ob es eine Fassade war. Vom Äußeren her hätte sie Russin sein können – sie hatte braunes Haar, einen finsteren Gesichtsausdruck und eine Hautfarbe wie Speisesalz –, aber er wusste sofort, dass sie keine war. Etwas stimmte nicht mit ihrer Haltung; sie hielt sich zu fern von den anderen, als dass sie sich unter ihnen wohlgefühlt hätte, und zu nah, um offen feindselig zu sein. Sie war nicht hübsch – sie war zu monochrom, ihre Blicke und Gesten zu schüchtern, fand er –, aber in ihren Augen lag eine verschlagene Intelligenz, die ihn zweimal hinsehen machte. Sie sprach Nina an. Nina würde sie sofort abwimmeln, das wusste er; die Fähigkeit, Menschen abzuwimmeln, war eine von Ninas größten Stärken, und Alexander setzte darauf, dass sie an seiner statt unfreundlich war. Irgendjemand musste es tun, und Alexander war nach all den Jahrzehnten, all den Frauen immer noch ein wenig zu nett dafür. Es war gut für Nina, wenn sie dann und wann anderes zu tun bekam, als auf High Heels durch die Wohnung zu klackern, sich die Haare rot zu färben und ihren Körper so kunstvoll hygienisch auszuhungern, dass Alexander es kaum noch fertigbrachte, sie als Produkt der natürlichen Auslese zu begreifen. Nina sprach mit der Frau mit dem Notizbuch.

Er sah, wie Nina den Kopf schüttelte, sich nach Vlad umblickte – dem Chef der Leibwache, weil er der Größte war – und sich dann wieder der Frau zuwandte. Aus den Blicken der Frau sprach Verzweiflung, stellte er fest, nicht das ganz große Pathos, aber doch ein leiser Hinweis, dass hier jemand etwas nicht bekommen hatte, das ihm sehr, sehr wichtig war. Alexander zog sich Handschuhe über. Er ertappte sich dabei, zu hoffen, dass Nina der Frau das geben konnte, worum sie bat.

Nach der Kundgebung, abends im Bett, strich Alexander Nina mit seinen kalten Füßen über die Beine.

»Hör auf«, sagte sie. »Du bist ein grausamer Mensch.«

»Findest du, die Kundgebung ist gut gelaufen?«

»So gut wie immer«, sagte Nina, was so gut wie gar keine Antwort war. Alexander wünschte sich manchmal, es wäre ihm weniger wichtig, was Nina von ihm hielt; sie waren verheiratet, und er war reich, und sie war schön, und das sollte ihm genügen, und doch zerbrach er sich manchmal den Kopf über die Distanz zwischen ihnen, steckte seine Finger in die Bruchstellen und riss sie nur noch weiter auf. Heute schaffte er es, den Mund zu halten.

»Ich wünschte, du könntest den Satz mit dem Ermorden weglassen«, sagte Nina.

»Du sagst doch immer, ich mache mir zu viele Sorgen.«

»Machst du ja auch. Mit dem Satz machst du dir in aller Öffentlichkeit Sorgen. Das ist nicht männlich.«

»Soll ich jetzt gleich mal etwas Männliches tun?«

»Heute lieber nicht.« Sie küsste ihn trocken auf die Wange und drehte sich weg. »Tut mir leid, Grib.« Er hatte es noch nie gemocht, dass sie ihn »Pilz« nannte – erst, weil er fürchtete, dass er wie ein Pilz aussah (dunkel, pausbäckig und untersetzt), und dann, weil er fürchtete, sich wie ein Pilz zu verhalten (verstohlen im Dunkeln vor sich hin zu brüten, wo niemand es sah). Aber Nina antwortete nur, das sei Unsinn – sie liebe Pilze, und sie liebe ihn –, und fuhr fort, ihn »Grib« zu nennen, und er hörte auf zu protestieren.

»Wer war denn die Frau da bei der Kundgebung?«, fragte Alexander.

»Weiß ich nicht genau. Eine ziemlich seltsame Amerikanerin.«

Alexander legte sich auf die Seite und stützte seinen Kopf mit der Hand. »Ein Fan von mir?«

»Vermutlich«, sagte Nina und zog gähnend ihre Nase kraus. Das war wieder so etwas: Sie hätte doch ein winziges bisschen Eifersucht durchblicken lassen können, wenn eine junge Amerikanerin um die halbe Welt reiste, um ihn zu treffen, hätte zumindest flüchtig den Gedanken streifen können, dass viele, viele Frauen einiges für so eine Gelegenheit hergegeben hätten, dankbar gewesen wären, mit ihm sprechen zu dürfen, und sich nicht wegdrehen würden, wenn sie neben ihm lägen.

»Ging es um Schach oder Politik?«, fragte Alexander.

»Weiß ich nicht.« Ninas Stimme rutschte knarrend und widerstrebend in den Schlaf. »Ich habe ihr für Mittwoch einen Termin gegeben. Nimm Vlad mit.«

»Ich nehme immer Vlad mit«, sagte Alexander. Eine Besucherin aus Amerika war ungewöhnlich. Seine Schachfans waren normalerweise Russen und fast immer männlich. Aber er hätte gleich gemerkt, wenn sie die Vertreterin irgendeiner NGO gewesen wäre; dann hätte sie ein professionelleres Auftreten gehabt und hätte nicht seine liebe Frau damit verschreckt, ihr kläglich im Schnee etwas vorzuzittern.

»Sie ist eine amerikanische Hochschuldozentin«, sagte Nina noch.

»Ach ja?« Alexander setzte sich auf. In seinem Hinterkopf begann sich etwas zu verknüpfen – irgendetwas begann Form anzunehmen, wie Teeblätter, die ein Symbol ergeben.

»Was ist?«, fragte Nina, doch in ihrer Stimme lag die tiefe Gleichgültigkeit der Erschöpfung.

»Ich bin gleich wieder da.«

»Was ist denn?«

»Ich komme gleich wieder.«

Er ging in sein Arbeitszimmer, knipste das Licht an und begann seine Notizen durchzusehen. Letzte Woche bei der Sicherheitsbesprechung war von einer amerikanischen Dozentin die Rede gewesen. Alexander hatte ein paar Jahre zuvor Geld investiert, um einen niedrigrangigen FSB-Agenten umzudrehen – Grigori, einen bubengesichtigen Hanswurst aus Nischni, der beim ersten Mal gezittert hatte wie Espenlaub und versucht hatte, eine höhere Summe auszuhandeln –, der seitdem regelmäßig Alexanders Akte fotokopierte. Im Großen und Ganzen hatte sich die Aktion als gewaltige Geldverschwendung erwiesen. Doch bei dem letzten Treffen hatte Grigori etwas Merkwürdiges gesagt – man hatte ihm gleich angesehen, dass er mehr in petto hatte als das übliche vorhersehbare Gewäsch, weil er noch selbstzufriedener und widerwärtiger wirkte als sonst – und sich mit ausgestreckten Beinen in seinem Stuhl zurückgelehnt.

»Die denken, du hast einen neuen Boss«, hatte er gesagt und dabei gegrinst.

Alexander hatte gegen das Tischbein getreten. »Ich habe keinen verdammten Boss«, sagte er. Vlad brachte ihn mit seinem starren Blick zum Schweigen. Alexander hatte sich nie daran gewöhnt, Verleumdungen ausgesetzt zu sein, und bestand meistens darauf, sie zu widerlegen, obwohl es weder Vlad noch den Doppelagenten zu interessieren schien, was die Wahrheit war, solange er sie bezahlte.

»Sie glauben, dass die Botschaft eine neue Mitarbeiterin hat, eine irgendwie komische junge Frau, und dass sie auf dich angesetzt ist.«

»Also bitte«, hatte Alexander gesagt. »Allein so was anhören zu müssen ist schon peinlich.«

Der kleine Kriecher hatte gelächelt und sich das glatte Kinn gekratzt. »Ich sage ja nur, was in ihrer Akte steht.«

Wo waren seine Aufzeichnungen von dieser Sitzung? Alexander blätterte in seinen Papieren – den Recherchen für seine Ansprache, Statistiken über die Entvölkerung Sibiriens, Notizen zum Filmprojekt –, bis er das Protokoll gefunden hatte. Die Botschaftsangestellte war angeblich eine »unbeholfene amerikanische Akademikerin«. Wie viele davon konnte es in einer Stadt schon geben? Bestimmt war es dieselbe Frau.

Die CIA hatte sie nicht geschickt, so viel war klar. Im Laufe der Jahre hatten sie mehrmals Kontakt zu ihm aufgenommen, hatten ihm den einen oder anderen Gefallen getan und auch welche von ihm angenommen, aber im Großen und Ganzen war ihnen klar, dass er seine Glaubwürdigkeit verlieren würde, wenn er sich von ihnen vereinnahmen ließe. Er verfolgte auch nicht dieselben Ziele wie sie. Oder wie irgendjemand sonst. So sehr sie ihn bei CNN mochten – weil er sarkastisch und skeptisch war und gern über Bürgerrechte sprach –, war er doch ein radikaler finanzpolitischer Konservativer. Er wollte die Einheitssteuer. Er wollte totale Deregulierung. An den amerikanischen Universitäten würden sie ihn nicht besonders mögen, wenn er darüber redete, aber meistens ging es bei seinen Vorträgen um Pressefreiheit und Demokratie, also rissen sich diese Kids aus Princeton in ihren Che-Guevara-Hemdchen um sein Autogramm.

Aber das Entscheidende waren die Gerüchte. Sie waren entscheidend, weil er, wenn er die Provinz bereiste, wenn er sich in Jekaterinburg, in Nischni Nowgorod und Irkutsk die Sorgen der Bevölkerung anhörte, auf ihr Vertrauen angewiesen war. Die Leute redeten gern mit ihm und mochten ihn meistens; er hatte ein gewöhnliches Gesicht und eine ungewöhnliche Energie und erinnerte Mütter offenbar an ihren talentiertesten Sohn. Sie beklagten sich gern bei ihm und mochten es, wie er Putin lächerlich machte – indem er parodistisch boshaft die Wangen einzog und seine Augen flach und leer werden ließ –, aber wenn sich Gerüchte verbreiteten, würden sie ihm nicht mehr trauen. *Der arbeitet für die Amerikaner, habe ich gehört. Der ist ein CIA-Agent.* Das konnte er sich nicht leisten – es richtete zu viel Schaden an, riss zu große Löcher in das zarte Netz der Vertrauensverhältnisse, das er überall in diesem weiten, einsamen Land geknüpft hatte –, und er musste dafür sorgen, dass diese Frau, wer immer sie war, aufhörte zu tun, was sie tat.

Er überlegte, sich wieder hinzulegen – den Arm um Ninas knochige Schultern zu legen, mit den Fingerspitzen die Hügelkette ihrer Wirbelsäule entlangzufahren –, doch dann entschied er sich anders. Er war viel zu wach. Er blätterte zu den Notizen für seinen Film über die Sprengstoffanschläge zurück. Obenauf lag ein Foto: Eine Schwarzweißaufnahme des ersten Anschlags auf ein Wohnhaus, dessen Dach fehlte, von dessen Wohnzimmereinrichtungen und Schlafsofas und Küchentresen nur graue Aschehaufen geblieben waren. In einer Ecke des Bildes lief ein kleiner Junge mit weit aufgerissenem Mund eine rauchverhangene Straße entlang.

Der Junge erinnerte ihn immer an das Mädchen – sein Mädchen, sein handloses Mädchen mit dem lautlosen Schrei. Und wenn er an sie dachte, dachte er an die Gebäude, die sich in faserig orangefarbene Feuerbälle verwandelten, deren Rauchpilze die Stadt beinahe unbewohnbar machten. Dann kam die Angst: panische Verzweiflung wie bei einer Belagerung, Hamsterkäufe, Wetten, Durchhalteparolen. Dann kam die Meinungsmache: Terrorismus wurde es genannt; ganz sicher die Tschetschenen, wurde beschlossen; ganz sicher im Rahmen des globalen islamischen Dschihad, der ein Jahr zuvor Amerikas Botschaftsgebäude heimgesucht hatte, wobei die Amerikaner, da war man sich einig, zumindest teilweise selbst schuld waren. Dann kam Putin, ausgerechnet Putin, und hüpfte leichtfüßig von Sieg zu Sieg – selbstzufrieden, siegesgewiss verordnend und verurteilend. Die Menschen waren froh, dass jemand das Ruder übernahm. Es lag nur daran, dass sie so verängstigt waren – gefangen im eisernen Würgegriff des Terrors, im metallischen Geruch des Todes (wobei Mischa, der öfter als die meisten dem Sterben nahegekommen war, sagte, der Geruch des Todes erinnere eher an Sassafras).

Alexander kannte diese Angst. Er hatte sie damals gekannt, als rotznäsiger Schachidiot, der mit klappernden Zähnen und einem breiten, dummen Grinsen vor seinen Aufpassern stand und zu dem Gott, an den er nicht glaubte, betete, er möge nicht so werden wie Iwan (weniger mutig, meinte er damit, und weniger tot). Und er kannte die Angst jetzt, als Erwachsener, der schmerzhafte erwachsene Entscheidungen traf und schmerzhafte erwachsene Risiken einging. Es war eine machtvolle Angst.

Das wusste Putin natürlich auch. Alexander fragte sich oft, ob nicht etwas von derselben primitiven Todesangst in Putin steckte, hinter seiner glatten Fassade und seinem reptilienhaften Lächeln. Sicher lag der Mann nachts in seinem seidenen Bett und wusste, dass er sich den Platz an der Spitze des größten Landes der Erde mit Lüge und Betrug, Unterdrückung und Mord erobert hatte, und dass dieses Land ihm im Nacken saß, wenn er sich beim Einschlafen gen Sonnenuntergang wandte – und sicher wachte er manchmal morgens auf und erstickte fast an dem Geruch von Sassafras.

Alles in allem hatte es aber funktioniert. Putin hatte das Land gewonnen. Selbstzufrieden, mit diesem säuerlichen halben Lächeln, hatte er das Vertrauen der Nation und das demokratische Mandat an sich gerissen. Es war schon merkwürdig. Diese Terroristen, diese Anschläge. Diese Tschetschenen, die von so weit her angereist waren. Nett von ihnen, Putin kurz vor der Wahl so einen Gefallen zu tun. Merkwürdig war es schon.

Also wollte Alexander einen Film produzieren, in dem gewisse Erkenntnisse, gewisse Fragen des Volkes zur Sprache gebracht wurden. Zuerst hatte er einen Artikel darüber schreiben wollen, aber Boris und Viktor – seine postpubertären, aber bestialisch intelligenten Berater – hatten nur gelangweilt vor sich hin gestarrt, als er ihnen die Idee vorstellte. Sie hatten kürzlich eine Dokumentation über die Vorgeschichte des elften September gesehen, hatten sie gesagt. Ein verlotterter amerikanischer Filmemacher interviewte darin mit zu Tode betrübtem Gesicht Politiker und Passanten. Er war höflich. Er stellte liberal gesinnte Fragen. Er schaffte es irgendwie, die anderen als Idioten dastehen zu lassen.

»So was sollten wir machen«, sagte Viktor. »Was Zugängliches.«

»Du weißt aber, dass der Mann Sozialist ist, oder?«, sagte Alexander.

»Er macht effiziente Filme.«

»Er macht Filmmontagen. Er schneidet Schnipsel von schrecklichen historischen Ereignissen zu Popmusik zusammen. Das sind Musikvideos.«

»Das ist das, was die Leute sehen wollen. Diese Filme ändern die öffentliche Meinung«, sagte Boris.

»Bushs zweite Amtszeit hat der Film nicht gerade verhindert.«

Viktor hatte ihn angesehen und das Einzige gesagt, das Alexander hätte überzeugen können: »Wann war je ernsthaft die Rede davon, Putin zu verhindern? Oder wen auch immer er als Nächsten ernennt? Ich sage bloß, der Film wird ihnen *unangenehm* sein.«

Seit mehreren Monaten arbeiteten sie jetzt an diesem Film, und Alexander konnte nicht umhin zu denken: Wenn irgendetwas ihn das Leben kosten würde, dann das. Aber er erwartete nicht, dass der Film magische Wirkung entfalten würde. Er erwartete nicht, dass nur dieser Film veröffentlich werden müsste, und dann kämen die Dezentralisierung, das Ende der Zensur, der Zusammenbruch des gegenwärtigen Regimes oder freie und faire Wahlen von allein. Alles, was er sich erhoffen konnte, war, dass ein paar Leute den Film auf YouTube sahen und dass er der Regierung, wie Viktor sagte, unangenehm war. Unabhängige Fernsehsender wären etwas ganz anderes. Nur ein Monat unabhängiges Fernsehen, und es gäbe einen Staatsstreich.

Alexander ging wieder ins Bett. Nina schlief, ihr rotes Haar wie eine Flutwelle über das Kissen aus ägyptischer Baumwolle gebreitet, die Arme dicht an den Körper gelegt, als hielte sie eine Yogaposition. Es war erstaunlich, wie reglos sie schlief, mit welch kompromissloser Zielstrebigkeit. Diese Frau tat nichts ohne Kalkül. Aber dafür hatte er sie schließlich auch geheiratet. Er war es leid gewesen, sich mit albernen Mädchen abzugeben, die den Kopf verloren und ihre Drinks auf ihren teuren Blusen vergossen, die zu laut und an den falschen Stellen lachten. Nina mochte oberflächlich sein, aber sie stand dazu, und sie war souverän und pragmatisch und hielt es nicht für nötig, ihm zu schmeicheln. In seinem Alter, in seiner Einkommensklasse war das das Beste, was einem Mann passieren konnte.

Allerdings dachte er manchmal noch an Elisabeta – nicht oft, nicht obsessiv, aber öfter als an jede andere Frau außer Nina. Es war ihm peinlich, es zuzugeben, sogar vor sich selbst, und die Erinnerung an sie war, als erinnerte er sich an alle besonders beschämenden Episoden seines Lebens gleichzeitig: an den Tag, als er gegen ein Computerprogramm verlor; an die Tatsache, dass er einmal auf Lehmböden geschlafen und mit bloßen Händen Hühnern das Genick gebrochen hatte; an sein persönliches Verhalten in den gesamten 1980er Jahren. Warum sollten, wenn er neben einer schönen, in edle, verführerische Stoffe gekleideten Frau im Bett lag, seine Gedanken zu einer drei Jahrzehnte alten Nicht-Beziehung zurückkehren? Aber manchmal taten sie es, selten, selten, und dann war er wieder in der Kommunalka und sah, wie sie mit wild fliegendem Haar gegen die Tür der Verwalterin trommelte, und hörte, wie sie ihre temperamentvollen Flüche ausstieß.

Solche Gedanken waren Energieverschwendung, und Alexander wusste, dass er seine Kräfte für komplexere Schwierigkeiten, für interessantere Probleme aufsparen musste. Er legte eine Hand um Ninas Hüfte und hielt sie fest, bis sie ihn im Schlaf abschüttelte.

Als Alexander an dem Tag, an dem der Termin mit der Amerikanerin angesetzt war, das Büro betrat, spielte Boris gerade ein Computerspiel. Boris spielte oft während der Arbeitszeit; dabei habe er die besten Ideen, sagte er. (»Und welche wären das?«, stichelte Viktor dann oft.) Neben ihm schrieb Viktor Stichworte auf eine Papierserviette.

»Was kritzelst du schon wieder?«, fragte Boris, ohne Viktor anzusehen. Auf dem Bildschirm hüpfte etwas, das für Alexander wie ein pausbäckiger Zwerg aussah, durch eine gelbgrüne Landschaft.

»Nur ein Dankeschön an deine Mutter für letzte Nacht«, sagte Viktor.

»Freut mich zu hören, dass du deine Potenzprobleme in den Griff bekommen hast.«

Alexander hatte sie vor anderthalb Jahren bei einer Demonstration aufgesammelt und hatte sie Botengänge erledigen lassen, bis er sicher war, dass sie es ernst meinten. Viktor hatte vorstehende Brauen und blaue Augen; Boris war ein Stück kleiner und hatte eine schiefe Nase, die Alexander merkwürdig fand, die aber bei Frauen herzzerreißend gut anzukommen schien. Beide waren arrogant, brillant und ständig in Rivalitätskämpfe verstrickt; Alexander sagte gern, wenn sie seine Söhne wären – wenn er Söhne bekommen hätte –, hätte er sie mit achtzehn zu den Landstreitkräften der Russischen Föderation geschickt. Doch sie waren nicht seine Söhne, Gott sei Dank, also ließ er sie einander triezen und sich übertrumpfen, so viel sie wollten, solange es sie auf Trab hielt.

»Wer hat dir den Stift gekauft, Golubó?«, fragte Boris. »So was Affektiertes habe ich ja noch nie gesehen.«

»Du bist bloß neidisch, dass ich schreiben kann.«

Nina hatte ihn für verrückt erklärt, weil er Viktor und Boris so bereitwillig in sein Team aufgenommen hatte. Er redete oft davon, wie seine Sache durch sie endlich Fahrt aufgenommen hatte und dass er selbst dann, wenn sich herausstellte, dass sie für den FSB arbeiteten, einen fairen Tausch gemacht haben würde. Alexander verstand inzwischen – jetzt, da er älter war, als Iwan es je sein würde –, wie verzweifelt Iwan in Nikolai einen Vertrauten hatte sehen wollen, wie sehr er sich nach Bestätigung gesehnt hatte. Alexander ließ Viktor und Boris zusammenarbeiten, weil er wusste, dass sie sich bekriegen würden: Seit er erlebt hatte, wie Nikolai sklavisch an Iwans Lippen hing, hielt er eine gewisse Feindseligkeit unter Kollegen für unverzichtbar. Außerdem waren sie jung – zu jung, um die Bürde ihres eigenen Fehlverhaltens während der Sowjetära zu tragen – und ärgerten alle anderen mit ihrem wohlfeilen Idealismus, ihrer Ignoranz den bedrückenden moralischen Abwägungen gegenüber, die sie nie hatten anstellen müssen. Andererseits konnte das Alternative Russland, wie Alexander oft betonte, ein paar Leute gut gebrauchen, die ethisch unkompromittiert waren. Es gab etliche, die öffentlich ihren Verrat eingestanden hatten, und solche, die stillschweigend so taten, als hätten sie nie einen begangen (unter anderem ihn selbst); dann gab es ehemalige treue Parteigänger, die offiziell abgeschworen hatten, und solche, die immer, immer taten, was gerade opportun war, und es heutzutage für angezeigt hielten, oppositionell eingestellt zu sein. Und es gab Leute wie Mischa – Mischa, der auf seine alten Tage ultranationalistisch geworden war und der nichts unternahm, um die rassistischen, fremdenfeindlichen, antisemitischen Kräfte im Wahren Russland im Zaum zu halten, und der manchmal auf Alexanders Kundgebungen auftauchte, um störende Zwischenrufe zu machen und Schilder mit unmöglichen Parolen zu schwenken.

»Du scheinst nicht gut voranzukommen. Hast du Rechtschreibprobleme?«, fragte Boris. Das Computerspiel gab fröhliche Synthesizer-Geräusche von sich.

»Wahre Männer können ihre Aktivitäten auch länger als dreißig Sekunden durchhalten, weißt du.«

Viktor trat gegen Boris' Stuhlbein und fuhr fort, den Reiseplan für die Fahrt nach Moskau auszuarbeiten, die in einer Woche anstand. Sie waren schon in Wolgodonsk und Buinaksk gewesen und wollten in Moskau einen ehemaligen Soldaten interviewen, der sein Geld inzwischen mit Dingen verdiente, die, wie Alexander sofort eingesehen hatte, nicht filmisch dokumentiert werden sollten. Die Interviews sollten das letzte und wichtigste Drittel des Films ausmachen – nach der Analyse der Vorteile, die Putin aus den Anschlägen gezogen hatte, und einer Darstellung der Versäumnisse in der Presseberichterstattung –, und Alexander beneidete die beiden sehr um ihre Mobilität. Er selbst ging schon lange nirgendwo mehr hin.

Viktor und Boris fingen an, Fragen und Nachfragen für das Interview zusammenzutragen, und der Nachmittag verging wie im Flug. Vlad überbrachte eine ziemlich zahnlose Morddrohung; einer der Assistenten überbrachte die Einladung zu einem Vortrag an der Yale-Universität. Um Punkt vier Uhr, als Alexander gerade anfing, müde zu werden, wurde ihm ein perfekt gebrauter, winziger Espresso serviert, der ihn wieder auf die Beine brachte. Dann ging die Tür auf, und Nina kam herein, gefolgt von einer seltsamen, überrascht dreinblickenden Amerikanerin. »Dein Besuch«, sagte sie und stöckelte davon.

»Einen Moment«, sagte Alexander.

Die Amerikanerin nahm ihre Mütze ab, was zur Folge hatte, dass ihr Haar nach allen Seiten abstand. »Sdráwstwuite«, sagte sie in so schlechtem Russisch, dass er zusammenfuhr.

»Oh, bitte«, sagte er. »Ich spreche jetzt lange genug Russisch, dass mir das in den Ohren weh tut.«

Anschließend hätte er nicht sagen können, was genau ihn dazu getrieben hatte, sie zu engagieren. Mitleid war es nicht, auch wenn er unwillkürlich Empathie empfunden hatte, und es hatte nichts mit ihrer Intelligenz (die sie allerdings besaß) oder ihrer Schönheit zu tun (die sie nicht besaß). Es war, wie er letztlich beschloss, die Art, wie sie von Elisabeta gesprochen hatte und wie sie vor seinen Augen mit tastenden, stolpernden Schritten zu einer sehr grundlegenden Erkenntnis über ihn gelangt war. Er redete sich ein, das sei eine gute Eigenschaft für eine Mitarbeiterin: die Fähigkeit, Rückschlüsse zu ziehen, eine Narration zusammenzufügen, sich intuitiv in das Innenleben ihrer Mitmenschen hineinzuversetzen. Und er war absolut sicher, dass sie in der Lage sein würde, die Pressemitteilungen in Ordnung zu bringen (was Viktor nach seinem Studium in Oxford allerdings ebenso gut konnte). Aber wenn er ganz ehrlich war, hatte er sie nicht wegen ihrer Englischkenntnisse angeheuert. Nicht, weil sie lektorieren und korrigieren konnte. Er hatte sie angeheuert, damit sie einfach nur da war und sein einziges unentdecktes Geheimnis mit ihm teilte.

An jenem Abend – als die ganze Armada der Schreiberlinge und Redenschwinger wieder gegangen war und als Alexander sein Abendessen aus Gemüse und exquisitem Fisch beendet hatte und der Himmel vor dem Wohnzimmer aussah wie ein beinahe abgeheilter blauer Fleck – klackerte Nina quer über das Eichenholzparkett und setzte Teewasser auf. Alexander bestaunte oft ihre vielfarbige Sammlung verschiedenster Teebeutel in den Regalen – fremdartige, unbegreifliche Tinkturen, oft mit obskuren südamerikanischen Knollengewächsen darin – und dachte dann, dass sie der einzige greifbare Beweis in der gesamten Küche waren, dass Nina eine auf Nahrungszufuhr angewiesene kohlenstoffbasierte Lebensform war.

Sie wedelte mit einem übelriechenden Teebeutel vor seinem Gesicht herum. »Magst du auch davon?«, fragte sie, obwohl er dieses Angebot noch nie angenommen hatte.

»Nein, danke«, sagte Alexander. »Wozu ist er gut?«

»Für die Verdauung.«

»Was hast du schon zu verdauen? Du isst doch gar nichts.«

»Ich esse reichlich«, sagte Nina müde. »Wie war dein Treffen mit der seltsamen Amerikanerin?«

»Ganz gut.«

»Ja?«

»Ich habe sie eingestellt.«

»Du hast was?«

»Sie eingestellt«, sagte er. »Ich will sie ins Team eingliedern, weißt du? Sie wird uns noch nützlich sein.«

Ninas Wasser kochte, und sie goss es über die Teeblätter. Ein bitterer Geruch wölkte hoch, beißend und unangenehm, und Alexander wich zurück. »Wirst du sie bezahlen?«, fragte Nina.

»Sie sagt, sie bräuchte kein Geld. Ich zahle ihr irgendeinen symbolischen Betrag.«

»Das ist sehr merkwürdig.« Nina nippte an ihrem Tee. »Was, wenn sie dich aushorchen will?«

Daran hatte Alexander auch gedacht. Doch nach dreißig Jahren der Paranoia – nach all den Spionen in dunklen Ecken, Geistern im Schatten, Mördern im öffentlichen Nahverkehr und Terroristen in der Mitte der Gesellschaft – war er vollkommen sicher, dass sie keine Agentin war.

»Was, wenn *du* mich aushorchen willst?«, sagte er und griff in Ninas volles Haar.

»Hör auf damit, Grib«, sagte sie. »Ich habe sie gerade geföhnt.«

In der Nacht konnte Alexander – schon wieder; hoffentlich war es kein Trend – nicht einschlafen. Er lag im Bett, neben sich die reglose Nina, und bemühte sich, die Beine still zu halten. Er atmete tief durch, aber die Luft verfing sich irgendwo in seiner Kehle, wühlte kleine Wellen der Sorge auf und strudelte durch tiefe Seen der Ruhelosigkeit. Er wollte nach Moskau. Er wollte einen Marathon laufen. Er wollte, stellte er fest, endlich einmal die Wohnung verlassen.

Eine Zeitlang, bis vor wenigen Jahren sogar, war Alexander noch hin und wieder spazieren gegangen. Aber er hatte wie amerikanische Staatsoberhäupter, die auf sportliche Betätigung unter freiem Himmel nicht verzichten wollten, immer einen kleinen Tross schwarzgekleideter Leibwächter dabeigehabt. Das war für ihn ermüdend, für sie langweilig, und in Sachen Freiheit und Muße war damit überhaupt nichts gewonnen. Also hatte er es in den vergangenen Jahren mehr oder weniger aufgegeben. Seine Wohnung war seine Welt geworden – geschmackvoll eingerichtet (alles Ninas Verdienst), und wohlorganisiert: Um fünf Uhr fünfzehn standen Toast und Tee auf dem Tisch, um Punkt vier Uhr ein dampfender Espresso, und sein Laptop wartete aquatisch blau blinkend in der Dunkelheit darauf, ihn mit der Außenwelt in Kontakt zu setzen. In dieser Wohnung lebte es sich wie in einem Museum, dachte er manchmal; alles war so makellos sauber, alle Gegenstände wie von einem Kurator sorgfältig zusammengestellt. Jedes Zimmer hatte seinen eigenen unaufdringlichen Duft – Zitrone in der Küche, Lavendel im Schlafzimmer und im Badezimmer eine Art Meeresbrise, die ihn zum Niesen reizte. Manchmal durchstreifte er die Wohnung abends von einem Ende zum anderen, und wenn er den Fuß auf den nachgiebigen weißen Teppichboden setzte, stieg ihm der rohe Geruch des Lehms in Sachalin in die Nase. In seinem erhabenen, gewaltigen, vielschichtigen Bett fühlte er die tödliche Kälte des Zimmers in der Kommunalka.

Kein Wunder also, dass er manchmal beim Erwachen an etwas würgte, das sich wie Angst anfühlte. Manchmal hielt er es einfach nicht aus – den subtilen Prunk, die übernatürliche Ruhe, wie verdammt *geordnet* immer alles war, wie in einer Planwirtschaft.

Er setzte sich auf. Er schlüpfte aus dem Bett und zog sich den Mantel über seinen Schlafanzug, dann stieg er in seine Laufschuhe – ein Weihnachtsgeschenk von Nina, die ihn bei der Bescherung grinsend in die kräftige Körpermitte gezwickt hatte –, dann gab er neben der Wohnungstür den Sicherheitscode in den unterirdisch grün blinkenden Kasten ein, und dann stand er draußen auf dem

Gehweg. Er versuchte sich zu erinnern, wann er zuletzt allein draußen gewesen war. Früher hatte er es manchmal aus Unbesonnenheit getan, bis das Ohr zum Fenster hereingeflogen war, und danach aus Trotz. An einem vergessenen Hochzeitstag, als es zu spät war, ein Geschenk zu bestellen, war er frühmorgens hinausgeschlichen und war sehr stolz auf seinen Sinn für Romantik gewesen – seine Bereitschaft, Leib und Leben zu riskieren, um seiner Frau ein diamantenes Armband zu besorgen. Hatte sie es je getragen? Er wusste es nicht mehr.

Die Kühle der Morgenluft, das Knarren des Schnees unter seinen Schuhen – sie waren bald durchnässt, und ein brandiger Schmerz kroch ihm die Beine hoch – erinnerten ihn an die quälend kalten frühen Morgenstunden Anfang der Achtziger, als er, noch bevor die Dämmerung am Himmel zu zerfließen begann, durch die Stadt gelaufen war und die Freiheit seiner schrumpfenden Anonymität genossen hatte. Beinahe beneidete er diese sonderbare Amerikanerin um jene Wunde, die sie dazu getrieben hatte, allein ihre Heimat zu verlassen und umsonst für ihn arbeiten zu wollen. Was immer es war, was immer sie gebrochen hatte – es hatte auch den Mechanismus zerstört, der klein war und geduckt, der immer ängstlich über die Schulter sah.

In der Ferne konnte Alexander beinahe die tintenschwarzen Grate der modernen Bürogebäude sehen, den abblätternden Glanz der zerfallenden Paläste, die schieferfarbene Windung der Newa. Niemand wusste, dass er unterwegs war, und mit seiner dicken Mütze konnte er stundenlang unerkannt umherwandern. Seit Jahren riskierte er alles für die großen Grundfreiheiten – das Recht auf freie Wahlen, auf einen freien Markt, das Recht, das Führungspersonal grausam zu karikieren. Aber es gab auch diese kleine Freiheit, unbeaufsichtigt durch die verschneiten Straßen zu laufen. Alexander ging den Newski-Prospekt entlang. Die ersten Bäckereien öffneten gerade, und durch die Fenster der Kasaner Kathedrale troff Licht. Alexander bog in die Nabereschnaja reki Moyki ein. In der mürrischen, nachtschattigen Dämmerung sah die

Moika aus wie Aluminium. Bald würde Nina aufstehen und auf das Laufband steigen, und vielleicht würde sie sich wundern, wo er war, und bald darauf würde sie vielleicht anfangen, sich Sorgen zu machen. Vielleicht würde sie zwei schroffe, aufgebrachte Nachrichten auf seinem Handy hinterlassen, und die dritte würde vielleicht lang, bittend und zärtlich werden. Vielleicht würde sie Vlad anrufen, und er würde sich vielleicht ins Auto setzen und Alexanders schlammige Turnschuhabdrücke quer durch die Stadt verfolgen. Aber im Augenblick war Alexander weit weg von alledem. Im Augenblick war er hier draußen, allein, und der Wind schnitt ihm in die Lungen, und mit jedem Schritt näherte er sich seiner Stadt.

KAPITEL 16

Irina
St. Petersburg, 2006

Alexander war brillant; natürlich war er das. Jeder konnte es sehen, und jeder sah es auch. Aber er war nicht ganz so, wie ich ihn mir vorgestellt hatte, oder besser gesagt nicht ganz so, wie ich mir vorstellte, dass mein Vater ihn sich vorgestellt hatte. Wenn das Dienstmädchen ihm seinen Nachmittagsespresso hinstellte, bedankte Alexander sich nie bei ihr – meistens blickte er nicht einmal auf. Wenn seine Mitarbeiter ihn enttäuschten, blaffte er sie an; wenn er etwas zu hören bekam, das er für unsinnig hielt, zog er mit derart vernichtender Geringschätzung eine Augenbraue hoch, dass im ganzen Saal jedes Gespräch verstummte. Die Wohnung war absurd: Sie war so dekadent wie Versailles, mit unzähligen albernen kleinen Apparaturen, die dazu dienten, das Leben einfacher zu machen, als es sein sollte – ein Gerät, das gleichzeitig Brötchen toasten und Spiegeleier braten konnte, Parfümfläschchen mit Holzstäben darin, die rund um die Uhr ihren frischen Duft verbreiteten. Und die Ehe war genau so, wie Viktor sie beschrieben hatte. Es war eine jener Beziehungen, die in ihrer Durchschaubarkeit jeden Unbeteiligten peinlich berühren – ihre kleingeistige Eigendynamik, ihre festgefahrene Verbitterung sprachen aus jeder Geste, wenn Nina Alexander eine Kaffeetasse überreichte oder wenn er ihr nachblickte, wenn sie den Raum verließ. Alexanders Mitarbeiter respektierten ihn – und nicht wenige bewunderten ihn zutiefst –, aber auf Ninas Auftritte folgten unweigerlich ein paar angespannte, klamme Sekunden, in denen alle den Blick in ihre Papiere senkten, um ihr Mitleid zu verbergen. Ich hielt mich nicht weiter damit auf, darüber nachzugrübeln. Ehen zerbrechen so oft und auf so viele verschiedene qualvolle Weisen, dass der Versuch, bei einer davon den genauen Ursachen nachzuspüren, ungefähr so aussichtsreich ist, als wollte man die Todesursache von jemandem ermitteln, der keinerlei Immunsystem hatte. Aber manchmal war da eine Spur von Müdigkeit in Alexanders Blick oder von Ironie in seinen Worten, die mich an Elisabeta denken ließ und daran, wie Alexander ausgesehen hatte, als er ihren Namen hörte.

Allerdings kann es gut sein, dass ich einiges hineinprojizierte. Wer kann schon Geschichten von alten, verflossenen Liebschaften widerstehen. Wenn ich an Jonathan dachte – falls ich an ihn dachte –, kamen die Erinnerungen bruchstückhaft, ohne Ton und verrauscht. Unsere gemeinsame Zeit hatte die surrealen Dimensionen eines Traums oder einer Kindheitserinnerung angenommen.

Ich gewöhnte mir an, länger und länger zu arbeiten, weil es nichts gab, das mich davon abgehalten hätte. Ich hatte den Eindruck, dass Viktor und Boris in einer ähnlichen Lebenssituationen steckten – sie gehörten vermutlich zu der Sorte junger Leute, die auf durchgelegenen Matratzen schliefen, ihre Bücher auf dem Boden aufstapelten und ihre Gerätschaften gar nicht erst auspackten. Sie führten die Flüchtlingsexistenz von Studenten, die noch nicht begriffen haben, dass sie den materiellen Dingen Bedeutung beimessen sollen, nicht nur den Ideen.

Doch obwohl ich so viel Zeit in Alexanders Wohnung zubrachte

– zwölf, vierzehn, sechzehn Stunden am Tag –, obwohl ich immer später in die bittere Dunkelheit hinausstolperte, an der Tür des Hostels klingelte und von dem Rezeptionisten mit mal missbilligenden, mal gleichgültigen, mal wissend-amüsierten Blicken empfangen wurde, sprachen Alexander und ich nie wieder über meinen Vater. Manchmal kam er mit einem entschlossenen Gesichtsausdruck auf mich zu, und ich war beinahe sicher, dass er etwas gefunden hatte – den Originalbrief meines Vaters vielleicht oder eine schlüssige Antwort auf dessen Fragen oder eine magische Formel für das Leben und den Tod. Aber das hatte er nicht. Er gab mir keine Antworten. Stattdessen gab er mir Pressemitteilungen, E-Mail-Entwürfe, Plakate. Grauenvolle Zahlen zu den Sprengstoffanschlägen: 300 Tote, 108 zerstörte Gebäude, Hunderte festgenommene Tschetschenen und 17 Verurteilte. Es waren Fakten, angesichts derer einem die eigene Suche nach Erleuchtung beinahe peinlich war. Und das war gut so, denn diese Erleuchtung kam nicht. Stattdessen vergingen Wochen, bevor Alexander und ich überhaupt wieder ein längeres Gespräch führten.

Es war spät, und ich wollte mich gerade widerstrebend auf den Heimweg machen. Ich hatte einen Kommentar für eine britische Zeitung neu übersetzt und zeigte ihn Alexander. »Hier, fertig«, sagte ich und schwenkte den Papierstapel durch die Luft. Er saß an seinem Laptop. In dem Panoramafenster hinter ihm erkannte ich das Spiegelbild einer Partie Online-Schach. Auf dem Schreibtisch stand ein echtes Set, ein teures, vermutlich, das sehr alt und sehr schön aussah. Ich stutzte. Ich hatte ihn noch nie spielen sehen.

»Danke«, sagte er und entließ mich mit einem Winken.

Ich konnte die Augen nicht von dem Spielbrett lassen. »Spielst du gerade?«, fragte ich.

»Schach.«

»Das sehe ich.«

Er zog einen Läufer in die Mitte des Bildschirms und führte den entsprechenden Zug auf dem Spielbrett aus. »Du hast zu Hause auch gespielt, nicht?«, sagte er. Er klang heiser, als hätte er in letzter Zeit sehr viel geredet oder als hätte er tagelang geschwiegen. Es musste wohl Ersteres sein.

»Nicht viel. Mit einem der Schachspieler auf dem Harvard Square. Und mit meinem Vater, wie gesagt.« Ich wartete auf einen Kommentar von ihm. Es kam keiner.

»Weißt du, was ein Narrenmatt ist?«, fragte er.

»Nein.«

»Der kürzestmögliche Weg zum Schachmatt. Es geht so.« Er stellte die Figuren auf dem Brett in ihre Ausgangspositionen zurück. »Zwei verbundene Bauern und eine gut platzierte Dame. Das war's.«

»Passiert das jemals im echten Leben?«

»Nein, nie. Es ist nur eine theoretische Möglichkeit. Schach ist ein rein theoretisches Spiel.« Er klang ein wenig verbittert, fand ich.

Ich betrachtete seine Figuren. Die Mähnen der Springer schwangen sich nach hinten wie auf einem mythischen Schlachtfeld vom Wind bewegt; die Könige waren gebeugt, knorrig, majestätisch. Sie waren prachtvoll, eher wie Statuen auf einer mittelalterlichen Brücke als wie das, was sie im Grunde genommen waren – bloße Spielzeuge. Das Aussehen der Könige gab mir Mut.

»Wie hast du spielen gelernt?«, fragte ich.

Alexander kratzte sich an der Nase. »Ich habe ein Schachproblem in der Zeitung gesehen und es gelöst.«

»Ja, aber wie hast du es gelernt?«

»Genau so habe ich es gelernt. Ich war vier Jahre alt.« Er kippte mit dem Daumen den König des besiegten Narren um. Die Figur landete klappernd auf dem Brett. »Dann hat meine Mutter mir einen Lehrer gesucht. Dann habe ich einen Fernlehrgang gemacht. Dann bin ich hier gelandet. Ende der Geschichte.«

»Ah«, sagte ich und wusste nicht, was ich noch sagen sollte.

»Wusstest du, dass sie in Saudi-Arabien ohne Damen spielen?«

»Klingt irgendwie einleuchtend.«

»Es ist eigentlich ein ziemlich subversives, radikal feministisches Spiel, wenn man mal darüber nachdenkt.«

»Wer war dein letzter ebenbürtiger Gegner?«

Er sah mich an, wie um einzuschätzen, ob ich absichtlich grausam war. »Ein Computer«, sagte er. »Wusstest du das nicht?«

»Oh.« Ich schlug die Augen nieder. Jetzt erinnerte ich mich wieder, ungefähr jedenfalls – an die amüsierten Schlagzeilen, die Zeitungen, die mit munterer Häme über die Erkenntnis stolperten, dass der Mensch seinen eigenen überlegenen Gegner geschaffen hatte. Das größte Schachgenie der Welt war von einem Computer besiegt worden; wofür brauchte man da noch Schachgenies oder überhaupt das menschliche Genie? Ich war beinahe froh, dass mein Vater nicht lange genug bei Verstand geblieben war, um das mitzuerleben. »An das eine oder andere erinnere ich mich noch, glaube ich«, sagte ich.

»Bestimmt tust du das. Die Newsweek hat das Spiel ›Das Rückzugsgefecht des Gehirns‹ genannt.« Er lachte reumütig. Dann begann er mir davon zu erzählen.

Die Pointe an dieser Niederlage, sagte er, war folgende: Wenn Schach überhaupt je einen Sinn gehabt hatte – und Alexander hätte jederzeit zugegeben, dass das vielleicht gar nicht der Fall war –, war es damit nach der Erkenntnis, dass alle Schachprobleme der Welt durch unbewusste, ins Leere feuernde Roboterneuronen gelöst werden konnten, endgültig vorbei. Großes Schach als eleganteste Errungenschaft des menschlichen Geistes gab es nicht mehr; die wahre Leistung bestand darin, etwas Größeres und Besseres zu erschaffen als sich selbst und ihm staunend zuzusehen. Menschen mussten sich zur Ruhe setzen oder sich bescheidenere Beschäftigungen suchen. Jeder wusste das. Selbst aus den Witzen, die man sich hinterher in den Bars, in den Nachrichten, im Internet erzählte, sprach diese Erkenntnis. »Passend dazu«, hatte einer der Talkshow-Moderatoren gesagt, »erreicht uns soeben die Meldung, dass die New York Mets von einem Mikrowellenherd besiegt worden sind.«

Das Schlimmste aber war die Geschwindigkeit, mit der das Programm spielte – Alexanders Züge wurden unmittelbar durch den Computer gekontert und übertrumpft, ohne das Zögern, Schwitzen und Zweifeln, das einem bei jedem brillanten menschlichen Spielzug das Gefühl gab, es hätte auch anders laufen können. Der Computer agierte nüchtern und rücksichtslos, und Alexander begriff mit beklemmender Gewissheit, dass es nichts gab, was er sich hätte ausdenken können, ohne dass der Computer es im Voraus mitbedacht hatte. Er war effizient wie eine Guillotine.

Der Mann, der für den Computer spielte, hatte weiche Gesichtszüge, Pausbacken, Hände wie Hähnchenschnitzel und ein breites, unschuldiges Hasengesicht. Er vollführte bei jedem Zug eine kleine Geste, ein fast unmerkliches halbes Schulterzucken (Alexander hätte nie sagen können, ob es auf den Filmaufzeichnungen erkennbar war oder nicht), als wollte er sich davon distanzieren – ich nicht, schien es sagen zu wollen, ich bin es nicht, der dir das hier antut, der dich erniedrigt, der den menschlichen Geist entzaubert. Ich bin nur das Medium, der Bote, der Mechanismus. Ich bin, ganz bescheiden, nur eine Spielfigur.

Am Ende dauerte es kümmerliche neunzehn Züge – die schnellste Niederlage in Alexanders ganzer Karriere. Er hatte mit einer Caro-Kann-Verteidigung eröffnet – die er gegen menschliche Gegner selten einsetzte, aber eine Zeitlang schien alles unter Kontrolle zu sein: Er setzte den zwei parallel vorrückenden Bauern des Computers eine Zweierkette entgegen, und es kam zu einem kurzen Schlagabtausch. Dann folgte die ritualisierte Entwicklung der Springer. Er hatte seine eigene Regel gebrochen – führe nie während der Eröffnung dieselbe Figur zwei Mal –, aber insgesamt war der Beginn der Partie konventionell und aussichtsreich gewesen. Der Computer schickte seinen Springer vor, und Alexander entwickelte seinen zweiten. Die drei Springer formierten sich zu einer leicht gebogenen Postenkette. Der Computer rückte seinen Läufer vor. Alexander zog einen Bauern auf e6 und stellte ihn seinem Springer zur Seite. Der Computer reagierte, indem er seinerseits den zweiten

Springer entwickelte. Dann rückte Alexander den Randbauern auf h6 vor, und sobald er die Hand von der Figur löste, wusste er es. Die aufmerksamen Zuschauer wussten es. Er hatte den Bauern zu früh eingesetzt – er hätte erst seinen Läufer entwickeln, dann den großen Auftritt der Dame des Computers abwarten sollen, und dann wäre es Zeit gewesen, mit dem Bauern auf h6 den Springer des Computers anzugreifen. Dieser Springer hätte sich in die Brettmitte zurückgezogen, und Alexanders Springer hätte ihn dort angreifen können. Der h6-Zug gleich nach dem Springer des Gegners war ein Fehler. Er war ein Fehler, aber kein strategischer Fehler – es war kein Trugschluss, keine inkorrekte Prognose. Es war ein Gedächtnisfehler, ein Versagen ganz grundlegender Kompetenzen – wie wenn man seine Autoschlüssel verlegt oder einen Teller fallenlässt.

Der Springer des Computers schlug einen anderen Bauern auf e6 und setzte sich Alexanders König in den Nacken. Hätte er diesen Springer gleich nehmen sollen? Vielleicht. Später sagten viele, viele Menschen – anonym zumeist, im Internet, nachdem sie jahrelang in aller Ruhe darüber nachgedacht hatten –, er hätte gleich zuschlagen sollen. Er hatte es nicht getan. Er hatte seinem König ein weiteres Feld zum Manövrieren lassen wollen. Er hatte das Springeropfer zugelassen, das kein Anzeichen für eine besonders brillante Strategie des Computers war; das Opfer war ein langweiliger, beinahe kindlicher Zug, den die Schachwelt zur Genüge kannte. Er hatte ihn selbst einmal während seiner dreiundfünfzig Partien gegen Russajew eingesetzt – damals, als er das neue Faszinosum gewesen war, der brillante neue Kopf, den alle bestaunten.

Zu dem Zeitpunkt, hieß es später in den Zeitungen, hatte Alexanders Gesicht einen »Ausdruck des Grauens« angenommen, den es bis zum Ende des Spiels beibehielt.

Also hatte er die Möglichkeit verloren, zu rochieren, was der Computer gleich darauf tat – stillschweigend und brutal, ohne Kommentar, und die Stirn des weichen Mannes blieb trocken und glatt.

Alexander tat den notwendigen nächsten Schritt, indem er den Springer schlug, und der Läufer segelte in die Lücke, die sein zu früh gezogener Bauer hinterlassen hatte, und bot ihm Schach. Er führte den König ein Feld nach rechts; etwas anderes blieb ihm nicht übrig. Es war erst der zehnte Zug der Partie.

Der zweite Läufer des Computers pirschte sich über das halbe Brett vor und legte sich auf die Lauer. Alexander drohte ihm halbherzig mit seinem Springer, und der Läufer zog sich vorübergehend um ein Feld zurück.

Wieder gab es einen Bauernabtausch, diesmal schon schmutziger und verzweifelter. Alexanders Hals war klitschnass, und er blickte sich instinktiv nach einem Ausgang um. Der fette Mann ihm gegenüber wirkte gelassen; seine Wangen bliesen sich mit jedem selbstzufriedenen Atemzug auf und schwollen wieder ab. Dieser Mann – wer war er überhaupt? Hatte er an dem Computer mitgebaut? Hatte er sich jahrelang in Schachtheorie und Programmiersprachen vertieft, hatte er eins in das andere zu überführen gelernt, um eine Maschine zu erschaffen, die extrapolieren und rückschließen konnte? Wahrscheinlich nicht. Wahrscheinlich war er ein Niemand, einfach irgendwer, der in der Lage war, ein, zwei Knöpfe zu drücken. Alexander dachte verbittert, dass er nicht nur Verrat am Schach beging, wie einige der Kritiker im Internet schrieben. Er beging Verrat an der Menschheit.

Alexander hatte die Augen geschlossen und seine Dame für einen Läufer und einen Turm geopfert. Den Läufer des fetten Mannes nahm er gierig, als kleine, vorübergehende Genugtuung. Es war ein verzweifelter Zug: Er fühlte, wie er in einen Brunnenschacht stürzte, hörte das Kratzen seiner Fingernägel am Beton. Jeder fühlte es. Der fette Mann hustete. Die Zuschauer murmelten, wandten den Blick ab.

Und dann hatte er aufgegeben. Er war vielleicht nicht klug genug, um einen Computer zu besiegen, aber sehr wohl klug genug, zu merken, wenn er besiegt worden war. Er hatte nicht vor, sich der unausweichlichen Erniedrigung auszusetzen; er hatte nicht vor, sich in immer neue, immer hoffnungslosere Rückzugspositionen drängen zu lassen, während die ganze Welt ihm zusah. Er stand auf. Er verließ den Saal. Er schüttelte dem fetten Mann nicht die Hand.

Später fragten ihn die Leute immer wieder nach dem Bauern – dem etwas verfrühten Zug auf h6. Er konnte nur sagen, er wisse es nicht, er wisse es nicht. Es war ein Fehler gewesen, und er wusste nicht, wie oder warum er ihm unterlaufen war. Im Internet fragten sich Verschwörungstheoretiker, ob er die Partie absichtlich verloren hatte, damit er eines Tages eine Revanche fordern und ein höheres Preisgeld gewinnen könnte. Aber so war es nicht. Vielleicht war der Computer auch gar nicht unschlagbar. Vielleicht stimmte es nicht, dass seine Brillanz die menschliche Vorstellungskraft überstieg. Vielleicht lag es einfach daran, dass Alexander vierzig war. Dass er müde war.

Der Computer stand seitdem im Smithsonian in Washington, D. C., und ließ für die Besucher eine Simulation jener letzten Partie in Endlosschleife laufen.

Das alles erzählte Alexander, und dann schwiegen wir. Es war eins dieser Geständnisse, nach denen man sich so unwohl fühlt, dass einem nichts übrigbleibt, als selbst eins zu machen.

»Tja«, sagte ich. »Ich habe eine Krankheit, die mich den Verstand kosten wird.«

Alexander hob die Augenbrauen. »Was?« Die Andeutung eines Lachens lag in seinem Tonfall. Auf haarsträubende Informationen reagieren Menschen häufig mit Gelächter.

»Man nennt sie Chorea Huntington«, sagte ich. »Daran ist auch mein Vater gestorben. Man kann testen lassen, ob man es hat. Erst trifft es die motorischen Fähigkeiten, dann die geistigen. Vom Cortex abwärts.«

Alexander wandte den Blick ab, was jeder zuerst tut. Dann hob er den Blick wieder, und ich konnte dabei zusehen, wie er seine Reserven an Mitgefühl, Pragmatismus und emphatischer Vorstellungskraft mobilisierte, um eine passende Antwort zu formulieren.

Ankündigungen wie diese haben die Tendenz, ihre Adressaten aus der Fassung zu bringen, und dann rücken die Verwirrung und der Schock in den Mittelpunkt des Gesprächs. Ich habe lange Zeit gehabt, mich mit der Krankheit auseinanderzusetzen, und die anderen nicht. Trotzdem stört es mich manchmal, wie sehr ihre Reaktionen in dieser Art von Gespräch in den Vordergrund rücken, und ich wusste es zu schätzen, dass Alexander diesen Effekt zu vermeiden versuchte.

»Und das passiert dir … bald?«, fragte er. Ich hörte, wie er absichtlich ebenmäßig und deutlich sprach.

»Dieses Jahr. Oder nächstes vielleicht.«

»O Gott.« Er senkte den Blick. Er nahm seine Brille ab und massierte sich die Nasenwurzel, eine Geste, die er so oft und aus so alltäglichen Gründen vollführte, dass ich wusste, dass sie nicht aufgesetzt war. »O Gott. Irina. Es tut mir so leid.«

Es war mir immer schwergefallen, es anderen zu erzählen. Ich fühlte mich jedes Mal schuldig dafür, meinem Gesprächspartner den Tag zu verderben, und er fühlte sich schuldig, wenn sein Tag nicht ausreichend verdorben worden war. Ich gebe zu, dass es sich manchmal seltsam anfühlte, wenn ich es jemandem gestand und ihn später dabei ertappte, wie er lachte, flirtete oder ein Sandwich aß, statt mit der Ungerechtigkeit der Welt zu hadern oder in tiefe, stumme Trauer zu versinken. Meine Lebenskatastrophe war für die anderen vielleicht nur das Unangenehmste, was sie an jenem Nachmittag zu hören bekamen; vielleicht hatten sie es beim Abendbrot schon wieder vergessen; vielleicht setzten bestimmte Kinofilme ihnen viel schlimmer zu. Ich werde dabei ziemlich gnadenlos damit konfrontiert, welchen genauen Wert ich für andere habe – je nachdem, ob sie weinen, sich setzen müssen oder gramvoll den Mund verziehen, während ihre Augen ganz woanders sind.

»Herrgott«, sagte Alexander. »Hast du Angst?«

Ich war nicht sicher, ob mir je jemand diese Frage gestellt hatte. Die Leute hatten immer gestaunt, wie tapfer ich sei, waren davon ausgegangen, dass ich Mut bewies, wenn ich lächelte, wenn ich zur

Arbeit kam und mir die Zähne putzte. Ich war davon weniger überzeugt. Ich ging zur Arbeit, wie jemand aufrecht geht, dem man eine Pistole an die Schläfe hält: Es gab absolut keine Alternative. Ich hätte mich natürlich hinlegen und sterben können. Aber das war gerade das, was ich vermeiden wollte.

»Ja«, sagte ich. »Furchtbare Angst.«

Er nickte, wie um zu sagen, dass das die richtige Antwort war. Er griff nach seinem gefallenen König und rollte ihn zwischen Daumen und Zeigefinger hin und her. »Deshalb bist du hergekommen.«

Es war nicht als Frage formuliert, trotzdem sagte ich: »Ja.«

»Deshalb stellst du diese Fragen nach dem Verlieren und den sicheren Niederlagen.«

»Genau.«

Er legte den König mit dem Gesicht nach unten auf den Tisch. »Lass mich dir etwas zeigen.«

Er stand auf und holte eine große Zigarrenkiste aus dem Regal über dem Schreibtisch. Dann setzte er sich wieder und stellte die Kiste zwischen uns ab. Er öffnete sie, und zum Vorschein kam ein großer Haufen Zettel. Es müssen Hunderte gewesen sein – manche abgegriffen und vergilbt, andere frisch und weiß, wieder andere aus schwerem, cremefarbenem Papier, wie man es nur für besonders wichtige Geschäftskorrespondenz verwendet. Manche Zettel trugen handschriftliche Notizen – Kratzspuren aus verblichenem Graphit; dicke Tintenschwünge, die an den Enden verschwammen und verschmierten; die labyrinthischen Kringel kyrillischer Schreibschrift, die für ungeübte Leser kaum zu entziffern sind –, und andere waren bedruckt. Einzelne waren sogar unheilverkündend aus Wörtern zusammengesetzt, die jemand aus der Zeitung ausgeschnitten hatte.

»Was ist das alles?«

»Morddrohungen«, sagte er. »Alle an mich.«

»Oh.« Ich sah ihn an. Ich begriff, dass er nicht erreichen wollte, dass ich mich besser fühlte – oder auch schlechter –, sondern nur eine Erfahrung mit mir teilen wollte, die wir gemeinsam hatten. Es war ein wortkarger Austausch von Erinnerungen zwischen zwei Veteranen eines aussichtslosen Krieges. Es war die Anerkennung der unausweichlichsten, schrecklichsten Tatsache unseres Daseins – nicht der einzigen, aber derjenigen, die jeder andere zu ignorieren versucht. »Darf ich?«, fragte ich.

»Bitte«, sagte er. »Nur zu.« Ich begann, einzelne Zettel herauszugreifen. *Ich lauere dir nachts auf und reiße dir die Eier ab*, stand auf einem davon. *Sie sind eine Schande für Ihr Land und Ihr Volk*, stand auf einem anderen. Einige waren subtil – mit Andeutungen über Menschen und Orte, die Alexander besser meiden sollte –, und andere beschrieben explizit, bis ins letzte grausige Detail, wie Alexander getötet werden sollte. Manche wirkten amateurhaft und wirr, als hätten geistig labile Männer mit verfilzten Bärten sie bei Kerzenlicht verfasst. Andere sahen professionell und zielgerichtet aus und ließen auf ganz andere Absender schließen: Menschen in schwarzen Anzügen, die alle nötigen Mittel besaßen, um ihre Drohungen in die Tat umzusetzen. Menschen, die ernst meinten, was sie schrieben.

»Unglaublich«, sagte ich, denn das war es wirklich. Und dann fragte ich: »Hast du Angst?«

Er nickte zu schnell, und ich fragte mich, ob er genau wie ich nur darauf gewartet hatte, dass einmal jemand fragte.

»O ja«, sagte er. »Die habe ich allerdings.« Mit einer Sorgfalt, die an Zärtlichkeit grenzte, faltete er die Blätter wieder zusammen und packte sie in die Kiste zurück. »Aber Angst ist nicht gleich Angst, oder?«

»Wie meinst du das?«

»Na ja, wir haben beide Angst. Aber deine Angst ist befreiend. Meine ist einengend. Deine hat dich hergeführt. Meine hält mich in dieser Wohnung fest.«

»Es ist eine schöne Wohnung.«

Er kniff die Augen zusammen. »Ja. Eine sehr schöne Wohnung.«

»Du gehst doch zu deinen Kundgebungen. Oder auf Reisen. Du gehst große Risiken ein.«

»Ich fliege nicht. Ich esse nie auswärts. Dafür spreche ich dauernd mit der Westpresse, und was denkst du, warum? Nicht, weil ich Larry Kings Show bereichern will, kann ich dir versichern. Sondern wenn ich im Westen bekannt genug bin, werden unangenehme Fragen gestellt, wenn mir etwas passiert.«

»Das ist vernünftig. Wirklich vernünftig.«

»Und du?«

»Und ich was?«

»Wem sollen wir es sagen, wenn dir etwas passiert? Hattest du zu Hause jemanden?«

Ich sah ihn an. Mir wurde klar, was er mich da fragte. »Wäre ich dann weggefahren?«

»Ja«, sagte er und nickte nachdenklich. »Ich glaube allmählich, das wärst du.«

An jenem Abend ging ein ganz unwinterlicher Regen nieder: Mild und schlammig stürzten gewaltige Wassermassen vom Himmel herab. Ich nahm meine Mütze ab und dann meinen Mantel, und dann, als ich in die Straße mit meinem Hostel eingebogen war, zog ich mir die Schuhe aus. Vielleicht würde ich mir Hepatitis einfangen. Oder eine Lungenentzündung. Einen Moment lang konnte ich es so sehen wie Alexander: Ich sah die Schönheit, das verrückte, eigenartige Glück, das darin lag, allein und unbeachtet und barfuß irgendwo draußen in der weiten Welt zu sein. Vielleicht war es ein Segen, irgendwie. Es war wie der freie Fall von jemandem, dessen Fallschirm nicht funktioniert: Wer weiß, was er auf seinem Weg nach unten erlebt, wenn die Sonne in einem ganz bestimmten Winkel die Landschaft streift, wenn er die Hände nach den Wolken ausstreckt. Wer weiß, was er in dieser jenseitigen Schwerelosigkeit alles lernt.

Aber dann lag ich im Bett, vollkommen durchgefroren, und meine Lage sah weniger romantisch als kläglich aus. Ich drehte mich zur Wand, zog die Arme und Beine an mich und versuchte einzuschlafen. Es war kurz vor Weihnachten, fiel mir auf. Irgendwann in dem Monat, der hinter mir lag, war ich einunddreißig geworden.

Von da an waren Alexander und ich so etwas wie Freunde. Oder vielleicht sollte man besser sagen, es hatte sich zwischen uns eine Spannung aufgebaut – eine Energie, die weder romantisch noch sexuell, aber doch intensiver als bloße Zuneigung war. Wir wussten beide immer, wo sich der andere im Raum befand. Wir beobachteten, wie der andere bestimmte Informationen aufnahm oder bestimmte Witze. Wir vertrauten einander plötzlich, mit unseren Morddrohungen und tödlichen Diagnosen.

In Wirklichkeit war es natürlich einfach zu erklären: Wir waren beide, jeder auf seine Weise, vom Tod gezeichnet. Und uns war beiden, egozentrisch, wie wir waren, nie ernsthaft in den Sinn gekommen, dass auch andere sterben mussten. Und jemanden zu treffen, dem es genauso ging, war eine Erleuchtung für uns.

Ob dieses neue Einverständnis zwischen uns dazu führte, dass ich mehr mit dem Film zu tun bekam, weiß ich nicht, würde es aber vermuten. Meine einzige Qualifikation war mein muttersprachliches Englisch, wobei Alexander durchaus schon auf weniger soliden Grundlagen Berater engagiert hatte. Boris und Viktor schien er nur deshalb aus der Masse ähnlicher junger Männer herausgefischt zu haben, weil er in ihnen eine gewisse bodenständige Zähigkeit bemerkt zu haben glaubte. Für jemanden, dem so viele den Tod wünschten, wählte Alexander seine Vertrauten ziemlich willkürlich aus – und ich fragte mich, warum. Ich fragte mich, ob er damit das Schicksal herausforderte oder es zu verleugnen versuchte. Allerdings schien er bis jetzt noch keinen Fehlgriff getan zu haben.

Der Film, den das Alternative Russland produzierte, handelte von der Serie von Sprengstoffanschlägen in russischen Städten im Herbst 1999. Ich hatte nur sehr vage Erinnerungen an die Ereignisse selbst. Die Anschläge waren verübt worden, als ich an meiner Dissertation schrieb, und ich konnte mich noch so eben daran erinnern, die Berichterstattung gesehen zu haben, während ich die Nächte durcharbeitete. Sie fielen in Amerika in die Kategorie von Nachrichten, mit denen sich nur Spezialsender oder die Auslandsseiten der Zeitungen befassen. Nachrichtensprecher mit glänzendem Haar schüttelten missbilligend den Kopf. Sie stolperten über die Namen der Städte und setzten Gesichtsausdrücke auf, in denen sich die generelle, leicht verwirrte öffentliche Missbilligung gegenüber Sprengstoffanschlägen im Allgemeinen spiegelte, und leiteten wieder zu Geschichten über tote weiße Kinder oder lebensrettende Hunde über.

Viktor und Boris, die ich inzwischen als Alexanders Schildknappen betrachtete, sichteten und bearbeiteten das Filmmaterial. Ich korrigierte die Grammatikfehler im Voiceover-Skript. Tagelang sahen wir wieder und wieder dieselben grauenvollen Bilder ablaufen: den schartigen, rot und schwarz schwelenden Schlund eines zerstörten Gebäudes; ein Rinnsal zerlumpter Menschen mit erschütterten, überraschten Gesichtern; die rauchenden Trümmer einer Schnellstraße. Der Film vertrat die These, dass Putin die Anschläge angeordnet oder zumindest stillschweigend gebilligt hatte, damit die verängstigte Bevölkerung ihn wählte und seinen Feldzug in Tschetschenien guthieß. Diese These wurde hauptsächlich mit zwei Tatsachen gestützt. Erstens hatte die Regierung in einer Stellungnahme ihr tiefes und aufrichtiges Bedauern über den Anschlag in Buinaksk zum Ausdruck gebracht – und zwar zwei Tage bevor dort eine Bombe detonierte. Zweitens hatte die Regierung ursprünglich bekanntgegeben, bei den Anschlägen sei der Sprengstoff Hexogen, auch genannt RDX, verwendet worden. Hexogen wurde nach Aussagen der Regierung nur in einem einzigen, streng bewachten Militärstützpunkt in Perm produziert – kein sehr wahrscheinliches Ziel fanatischer Tschetschenen, wie Boris anmerkte. Sobald die Medien von diesem merkwürdigen Zufall berichteten, zog die Regierung ihre ursprünglichen Aussagen zurück.

In jenen ersten Wochen bei Alexander begann ich mich lebendiger zu fühlen. Ich wachte morgens in meinem satt nach Frost

riechenden Zimmer auf und erlebte jeden Tag wieder die uner-
hörte Erleichterung, zu wissen, wo ich hinsollte. Ich wappnete
mich mit drei Jacken übereinander und langer Unterwäsche, dann
packte ich eine Tagesration Texte, Korrekturbögen und Pressemitteilungen ein. Ich rutschte über den vom Nachtwind leicht ange-
nagten Schnee. In der Unterführung vor der Metrostation Wassiljewski-Insel stolperte ich über die Händler, die ihre Stände mit
DVDs, Pornoheften und Souvernir-Nippes bestückten. Bis die
Metro kam, beobachtete ich die klammen Hunde und ihre Besit-
zer mit den vom Ketamin ausdruckslosen Augen. Manchmal war
es noch dunkel, wenn ich vor Alexanders Haus ankam, und manchmal wartete ich dann, starrte in den Himmel und bewunderte die
reine Brutalität der Sterne. Manchmal dachte ich an Jonathan.
Manchmal dachte ich an meinen Vater. Manchmal dachte ich an
Alexanders Morddrohungen und daran, wie er die Antwort auf die
Fragen meines Vaters lebte. Am häufigsten kreisten meine Gedanken um mich selbst: darum, wie dankbar ich für ein paar mehr wa-
che Augenblicke war und für eine Aufgabe, die diese Augenblicke
erfüllte.

Wenige Tage vor Boris' und Viktors Abreise nach Moskau wurde
in der Wohnung eine Sitzung einberufen, um die jüngsten politischen Skandale zu besprechen. Einer von Alexanders Konkurren-
ten, ein Oppositionskandidat mit einem etwas nationalistischeren
Programm, als Alexander es vertrat, war kürzlich verschwunden.
Seine Mitarbeiter hatten nicht gewusst, wo er war. Seine Frau hatte
nicht gewusst, wo er war. Nach einer Woche war er wieder aufgetaucht, mit einer großen Sonnenbrille, auf seine Leibwächter gestützt, und hatte sofort eine defensive Pressekonferenz abgehalten.
»Was ist?«, hatte er gesagt. »Kann man nicht mal eine Woche unterwegs sein? Habe ich nicht das Recht auf ein bisschen Urlaub,
ein bisschen Privatsphäre?« Seine Frau hatte ihn sofort verlassen.
Es gingen Gerüchte, dass der FSB ihn nach Kiew verschleppt und
ihm psychotrope Substanzen eingeflößt hatte, bis er jedes letzte

bisschen Schmutz und strategische Informationen von sich gab, und ihn dann kotzend, torkelnd und ohne jede Erinnerung an das Geschehene in einer anonymen schwarzen Limousine wieder nach Hause verfrachtet hatte. Dann war da der Menschenrechtsanwalt, der erst vor wenigen Tagen in Moskau auf offener Straße erschossen worden war. Er hatte versucht, die angebliche Vergewaltigung einer Tschetschenin durch einen russischen Soldaten aufzuklären. Er war am hellichten Tag auf der Straße gestorben, und hinterher hatte niemand etwas gesehen. Außerdem war da die Geschichte eines der reichsten Oligarchen Russlands – eines Mannes, der mit Öl ein Vermögen gemacht hatte, dann aber bei der Regierung in Ungnade gefallen war, als er etwas zu vorlaut gegen die grassierende Korruption gewettert hatte. Man erzählte sich, er stünde ganz oben auf der Verhaftungsliste, und sofort kaufte er auf dem internationalen Kunstmarkt sämtliche Fabergé-Eier aus der Sammlung Nikolaus II. auf, um sie wieder in russischen Besitz zu übergeben. »Für meine Heimat«, hatte er mit verklärten Augen vor den Kameras gesagt.

»Alles läuft bestens in diesem Land«, sagte Boris. Alle schweigen. Ich malte einen Rand um meine Notizen.

»Also«, sagte Alexander. »Ihr Jungs freut euch hoffentlich auf Moskau? Ihr fahrt mit dem Auto.«

»Gut«, sagte Viktor.

»Und nehmt die Kreditkarte mit.«

»Klar.«

»Und ihr übernachtet natürlich im Moskowsko. Auf keinen Fall im Rossija, da vergiften sie euch nur das Frühstück.«

»Okay«, sagte Viktor. »Ist klar.«

Auf Alexanders Gesicht machte sich ein schelmischer Ausdruck breit, als hätte er uns allen einen großartigen Streich gespielt, den wir im nächsten Moment bemerken würden. Er nickte in meine Richtung. »Und Irina fährt natürlich auch mit.«

»Was?«, sagte ich.

»Was?«, sagte Boris. Er zog die Kappe von seinem Kugelschreiber, und ich fürchtete einen Moment lang, er wollte jemanden damit erstechen.

»Ihr nehmt sie mit.«

Viktor grinste, und Boris stand der Mund offen.

»Ach ja?«, sagte Viktor. »Spricht sie überhaupt Russisch?«

»Spricht sie überhaupt?«

»Njet«, sagte ich in einem Versuch, witzig zu sein.

»Sie kann für euch Notizen machen.«

»Wir können selbst Notizen machen«, sagte Viktor. »Wir sind funktionale Alphabeten, falls dir das entgangen ist.«

»Ihr zwei seid so hölzern, und ihr seid Kindsköpfe«, sagte Alexander. »Es kann nicht schaden, eine harmlos aussehende Frau dabeizuhaben – entschuldige, Irina. Dann fühlen die Leute sich wohler. Dann erzählt der Soldat mehr von sich.«

»Nein«, sagte Viktor. »Das glaube ich eher nicht, nein.«

Alexander sah mich an, während er antwortete. »Doch«, sagte er bestimmt. »Ich glaube doch.« Zwischen Alexander und den beiden Jungen knisterte die Luft. Viktors Halsmuskulatur zuckte. Boris öffnete und schloss eine Faust. Sie schienen kurz vor einer Meuterei zu stehen.

Doch dann erschien Nina in der Tür, den Kopf schief gelegt, das Haar zu einem strengen Dutt hochgebunden. »Mein Pilzchen«, sagte sie. »Dein Gemüse ist fertig.«

Damit war Alexander verschwunden, und Viktor und Boris ließ er allein zurück – mit offenen Mündern, die Augen so weit verdreht, wie es anatomisch möglich war.

Für die Reise überließ Alexander uns eine glänzend schwarze Limousine, so groß wie eine Segelyacht. Die Sitze waren ringförmig angeordnet, so dass Viktor, Boris und ich uns die gesamte Fahrt über ansehen oder aus dem Fenster schauen mussten. Ich hielt mich überwiegend an die Fenster. Wir waren mit dem Soldaten in einem Klub verabredet, und Alexander hatte Nina gebeten, mich mit passender Expeditionskleidung auszustatten. Was sie mir herausgesucht hatte, war hauchdünn und orange und viel zu klein; immer wenn ich die Arme ausstreckte, spannte es unvorteilhaft, also hielt ich sie eng an den Körper gepresst. Außerdem war es für das Wetter viel zu leicht, und ich rieb meine Oberschenkel am Ledersitz, um mich zu wärmen. In dem Auto gab es Flaschen mit Nobelwasser aus geheimnisvollen sibirischen Mineralquellen und grüne Sektkelche. Ich fühlte mich abwechselnd, als sei ich auf dem Weg zu einer Hochzeit oder zu einer Beerdigung. Ungefähr in der Oblast Nowgorod fingen Viktor und Boris an, Witze zu reißen.

»Stalin erscheint Putin im Traum«, sagte Viktor. »Und er sagt zu ihm: ›Putin, wenn du an der Macht bleiben willst, musst du zwei Dinge tun: den Kreml grün anmalen und alle deine politischen Gegner töten.‹ Putin sieht ihn an und fragt: ›Warum denn grün?‹«

»Den kannte ich schon«, sagte Boris.

»Du kennst sie wahrscheinlich alle schon«, sagte Viktor.

»Den hat mir deine Mutter im Bett erzählt.«

Die Interviews, die Viktor und Boris bis dahin geführt hatten, waren federleichte, substanzlose Angelegenheiten gewesen – als persönliche Schicksale waren sie interessant, als Beweise aber nicht gerade zwingend. Die Interviewten hatten Geschichten erzählt, die so einprägsam und vertraut wie Mythen waren, aber solide Schlüsse konnte man nicht aus ihnen ziehen. Während der Fahrt sahen wir uns die Zusammenschnitte im DVD-Player der Limousine an. Die erste Zeugin war eine nervöse Studentin, die ihre feinen Gesichtszüge hinter einer klobigen Brille verbarg und immer wieder ihren Rock über die Knie zupfte. Sie hatte in der Nacht vor dem ersten Anschlag die Stimmen zweier Männer unter ihrem Fenster gehört – eine tiefe, dumpfe Stimme hatte darauf bestanden, etwas *hier* zu platzieren, nicht da. Die Frau hatte schabende Geräusche gehört und erst an ein Tier gedacht, aber dann waren da wieder die Stimmen gewesen, das gepresste Atemgeräusch eines übergewichtigen Mannes, ein unterdrückter Fluch.

War das alles?, fragte Boris hinter der Kamera. Seine Enttäuschung war ihm deutlich anzuhören.

Die junge Frau blinzelte und rückte ihre Brille zurecht. Ja, sagte sie, das war alles.

Bei der Detonation hatte sie ihre Mutter und ihren jüngeren Bruder verloren, und erst Wochen später – erst als das Klingeln in ihren Ohren nachließ und die blutroten Verbrennungen auf ihren Beinen abzuheilen begannen – erinnerte sie sich an die Männer und daran, dass sie nicht wie Tschetschenen geklungen hatten.

Im nächsten Interview sah man eine unglaublich dicke Frau, deren ältester Sohn am Abend vor dem Anschlag etwas in einer Bar mitgehört hatte. »Wird ein großer Tag morgen, was?«, hatte jemand gefragt, und ein anderer hatte ein bisschen zu grausam darüber gelacht. Der Sohn hatte es der Frau erzählt, als er im Krankenhaus lag, um sich von seinem Wirbelsäulenbruch zu erholen, was jedoch nicht geschah. Er war Turner von Beruf. Als er erfuhr, dass er sein Leben lang querschnittsgelähmt sein würde, hatte er sich als letzte sportliche Glanzleistung in eine selbstgeknüpfte Schlinge gewunden und sich erhängt.

Sie starrte in die Kamera, während sie sprach. Die Kamera zoomte näher heran. Tränen wallten in ihren Augenwinkeln auf, liefen aber nicht über ihre Wangen. Es war ein berührender Moment. Aber ihre Geschichte bedeutete gar nichts, wenn man mehr als dreißig Sekunden darüber nachdachte.

Der letzte Interviewpartner war ein lebhafter, beinahe elfengleicher älterer Herr. In der Nahaufnahme erinnerte er an einen halbverhungerten Polarfuchs. Er erzählte von etwas, das er während des Anschlags beobachtet hatte: In dem Tumult, wo jeder rannte und schrie und sich die schwelenden Kleider vom Leib riss, hatte er einen Mann gesehen, der sich an einen Baum lehnte. Er hatte gedacht, der Mann stünde unter Schock, und war auf ihn zugegangen, um ihm zu helfen. Doch im Näherkommen hatte er gesehen, dass der Mann eine Zigarette rauchte und dass seine Lippen zu einem Ausdruck verzogen waren, den man als Lächeln hätte interpretieren können. Der ältere Herr hatte sich abgewandt, um einer Frau zu helfen, die unter einer Fensterbank aus Zement feststeckte.

Später, erzählte er der Kamera, war er über den Mann unter dem Baum ins Grübeln gekommen. Er war während der Explosion dort gewesen, während die Journalisten erst nach dreißig Minuten vor Ort waren und die Polizei nach fast einer Stunde. Er hatte einen dunklen Mantel angehabt, und das Auffälligste an ihm war seine Gleichgültigkeit gewesen.

Das Bild des Mannes wich einem bildschirmfüllenden Blau, und Viktor schaltete den DVD-Player aus. »Das ist nicht besonders überzeugend, oder?«, sagte er.

»Es ist bewegend«, sagte ich. »Herzzerreißend, wirklich.«

»Das bringt uns nichts. Wir haben nichts davon, noch mehr Herzen zu zerreißen.«

»Es ist überzeugend, wenn man überzeugt werden möchte.«

»Das typische Kennzeichen eines schwachen Arguments.«

Wir fuhren durch Dörfer mit feucht aussehenden Holzhäusern, und ich spürte fast die Kälte, die dort von der Decke tropfte, und die Zugluft, die durch die roh gezimmerten Wände drang. Es gab auch ein paar Andeutungen des romantischen Ostens, wie man ihn sich vorstellt, wenn man überhaupt eine Vorstellung davon hat: Die Türme der orthodoxen Kirchen, die aus winterlichen Nebelschwaden ragten, ein Gefühl der Fremdheit, das nicht nur aus dem Ortswechsel entsprang, sondern auch irgendwie aus einer Verschiebung der Zeit. Es war ein Gefühl, als reiste man nicht zurück oder in die Ferne, sondern auswärts – auswärts auf einer Art Z-Achse und in eine Märchenzeit hinein, die es nie wirklich gegeben hat. Ich muss ein wenig verträumt ausgesehen haben, denn ich bemerkte, wie Boris mich voller Abscheu anstarrte. »Du glaubst, das hier ist irgendwie romantisch, oder?«

»Was?«

»Genau das glaubst du. Das sehe ich doch. Du denkst, du erlebst hier ein hübsches kleines Abenteuer. Also hör mir mal gut zu. Das hier ist nicht romantisch, okay? Und es geht nicht um Abenteuer. Es geht um abgerissene Köpfe in den Nebenstraßen. Ich weiß nicht, was du hier willst, aber das ist kein Studienaustausch, okay?«

Ich nickte. Ich war überrumpelt und ein bisschen benommen – wie in dem ersten Augenblick, nachdem man sich verbrannt oder verwundet hat, bevor der Körper den Schmerz registriert. Vielleicht konnte ich hilfreich sein, vielleicht nicht, und ich konnte verstehen, dass meine Anwesenheit für Verärgerung sorgte. Aber ich wusste sehr wohl, dass ich nicht beim Studienaustausch war. Worum auch immer es bei dieser Reise ging – es ging nicht um Fotos und Postkarten. Es ging nicht um Anekdoten, die man bei ersten Dates erzählt, um Souvenirs, die man Jahrzehnte später seinen Dinnergästen zeigt, oder um Weisheiten, die man seinen Kindern mitgibt, wenn sie eigene Wege gehen. Es ging nicht um eine Vorlage oder eine Landkarte oder eine Wissensquelle für die Zukunft, denn die würde ich mit einiger Sicherheit nie erleben.

Aber das alles konnte ich unmöglich sagen, und es hätte auch nicht überzeugend gewirkt. Vielleicht wäre es berührend gewesen, aber das ist nicht das typische Kennzeichen eines starken Arguments – da sind sich wohl alle einig. Also schwieg ich, spitzte die Lippen und wandte mich ab, um aus dem Fenster zu sehen.

Und dann krachten wir in den Glanz und die Herrlichkeit der Moskauer Innenstadt bei Nacht. Überall waren schöne Frauen, mit grellem Make-up und nicht viel anderem angetan, die vor pulsierenden Nachtklubs Schlange standen. Sie sahen beängstigend aus und außerdem so, als sei ihnen furchtbar kalt. Ich starrte sie an. Die Frauen warfen ihr Haar zurück. Ihre silbernen High Heels streuten Licht auf die Gehsteige. Gewaltige IKEA-Werbeschilder dominierten die Skyline. Wir kamen am Puschkin-Theater vorbei, das im Laternenlicht glomm wie eine beleuchtete Eierschale. Wir sahen das Nord-Ost auf der Melnikow-Straße, und ich musste an das Geiseldrama von 2002 denken: wie Spezialeinheiten Geiselnehmer und Gefangene gleichermaßen mit Gift einnebelten und alle qualvoll im Schnee verendeten. Dann kamen mehr Klubs, mehr Restaurants, mehr triefende, ornamentale Opulenz. Der funkelnde Wagankowski-Friedhof zog an uns vorüber, wo die Opfer der Pestepidemie im achtzehnten Jahrhundert lagen. Dann sahen wir ein hell erleuchtetes Café mit dem Namen »Gaben des Meeres«.

»Für Homosexuelle«, sagte Viktor, vertraulich zu mir herübergebeugt. »Boris, sollen wir anhalten?«

Der Fahrer brachte uns zu einem Klub namens Absinth. In den höhergelegenen Fenstern konnte ich gerade eben einen Stapel pinkfarbener Würfel ausmachen und einen Hauch lilafarbenen Lichts. An der Tür wurde eine bezaubernde Frau abgewiesen; wutentbrannt schleuderte sie ihre Handtasche in eine Schneewehe.

»Wie kriegen wir bloß Irina durch die Gesichtskontrolle?«

Ich streckte die Zunge heraus.

»Nett«, sagte Boris. »Das erhöht deine Chancen erheblich.«

»Zum Glück gibt es ja auch noch Bestechungsgelder«, sagte Viktor. Er zeigte auf die obere Fensterreihe. »Da oben sitzen sie und sehen den anderen zu.«

»Wer?«

»Die reichen Männer. Die haben da oben Privatkabinen mit Spiegelglas und sehen den Frauen beim Tanzen zu. Wenn sie eine entdecken, die ihnen gefällt, laden sie sie auf einen Drink ein.«

Wir reihten uns hinter rotsamtenen Absperrbändern in die Schlange ein. Ich stampfte mit den Hacken in den Schnee und verflocht meine Hände ineinander, um mich warm zu halten. Ich fragte mich, ob die für dieses Wetter vollkommen ungeeignete Frauen-Abendkleidung nicht das Resultat einer patriarchalen Verschwörung war.

»Und es ist vermutlich keine bloße Einladung, würde ich denken«, sagte Viktor und rieb sich die Nase. Sein Englisch war nach der Zeit in Oxford mit typisch britischen Manierismen durchsetzt – Arabesken, die in Zusammenhang mit seinem Akzent komisch klangen. »Unser Blatnoi ist auch da oben, möchte ich wetten.«

»Warum trifft er sich ausgerechnet hier mit uns?«, fragte ich mit zusammengebissenen Zähnen.

»Ich glaube, hier verbringt er seine meisten Abende. Wir wollen ja nicht seinen Terminplan umwerfen.«

Wir sahen weiter hinauf. Dort oben brach irgendetwas das Licht; etwas grün Phosphoreszierendes schwebte auf das Fenster zu und schnellte wieder davon.

»Haben die – ist das da oben ein Aquarium?«, fragte ich.

»Würde mich nicht wundern«, sagte Viktor. »Es würde mich auch nicht wundern, da eine komplette Zirkusmanege vorzufinden.«

»Da oben servieren sie nur Sushi«, sagte Boris. »Das ist der wahre Grund, warum die Weltmeere leergefischt sind.«

»Wart ihr schon mal in so einem Klub?«

Sie lachten. »Nein«, sagten sie. »Aber heute ist es so weit.«

»Und irgendwann machen wir es uns zur Gewohnheit«, sagte Viktor.

»Wann ist irgendwann?«

»Wenn wir reich sind«, sagte Viktor. »Wir sind Männer, also brauchen wir nicht hübsch zu sein. Nur reich.«

»Ach ja?«, sagte ich. »Und wann genau gedenkt ihr reich zu werden?«

»In der neuen Weltordnung, schätze ich«, sagte Boris.

»Ich dachte, die haben wir längst«, sagte ich, weil ich fror, was mich in eine schwierige Stimmung versetzte.

»Wenn Besetow Präsident ist, macht er uns zu seinen wichtigsten Beratern«, sagte Boris.

»Ha. Wenn Besetow Präsident ist, kürzt er wahrscheinlich als Erstes die Bezüge der Staatsbediensteten«, sagte Viktor.

Ich sah die beiden an. »Glaubt ihr das wirklich?«, fragte ich.

Sie sahen mich an. »Welchen Teil davon?«, fragte Viktor.

»Glaubt ihr ernsthaft, dass Alexander irgendwann Präsident wird?«

»Klar«, sagte Boris. »Nicht dieses Jahr, das ist auch klar. Aber irgendwann. Denk an die Ukraine. Irgendwann ist es hier auch so weit. Und dann ist er die einzig logische Wahl, oder?«

Viktor nickte. »Er ist immer die Stimme der Vernunft gewesen. Er ist Vaclav Havel. Nur dass er nicht der dichtende Präsident wird, sondern der schachspielende Präsident. Typisch russisch eben.«

»Und er ist noch jung«, sagte Boris. »Einigermaßen jedenfalls. Es kann noch eine Menge passieren, wenn er nicht aufgibt. Das Leben ist groß.«

Ich sah sie wieder beide an. Wenn man sich Alexanders Ansprachen anhörte – sein Lob auf die Vergeblichkeit, auf den Mut, gegen den Strom zu schwimmen –, konnte man denken, dass niemand ernsthaft mit seinem Erfolg rechnen würde. Man konnte denken, dass der Misserfolg das war, worauf es ihm eigentlich ankam.

»Ja«, sagte ich. »Für manche ist es das wohl.«

»Was ist?«, fragte Viktor. »Hast du auf ein anderes Pferd gesetzt? Hast du selbst Ambitionen? Wer sollte es wohl sonst sein?«

Ich kniff die Augen zusammen, und als ich das tat, konnte ich kleine Bruchstücke der Zukunft sehen – Alexander, wie er im Kreml alle Fenster aufriss, wie er den Sicherheitsapparat auflöste, während die Menschen auf den Straßen jubelten –, die ich alle, wenn sie denn wahr wurden, nicht miterleben würde. »Ich weiß es nicht«, sagte ich. »Ich weiß es wirklich nicht.«

Am Eingang steckte Viktor dem Türsteher ein Bündel Scheine zu. Das war vorab telefonisch so abgesprochen. Der Türsteher musterte amüsiert mein durchscheinendes Gewand, nahm das Geld aber an. Er ließ uns ein. Drinnen war die Musik so laut, dass es in meiner Brust vibrierte. Das Aquarium war, wie sich herausstellte, in die Wand und einen Teil der Decke eingebaut. Wässriges Licht flutete durch es hindurch auf die Tanzfläche, und wenn ein Fisch dicht an der Scheibe vorüberschwamm, sprenkelten die psychedelischen Farben tropischen Meeresgetiers den Boden. Der Türsteher zeigte auf eine geschwungene Treppe an der Rückwand des Raumes. »Er ist da oben«, sagte er. »Er ist immer da oben.«

In der Luft überschrien sich die widerstreitenden Botschaften ausgefallener Deodorants; Werbespots mit Alpenlandschaften und

Wildbächen tauchten vor meinem inneren Auge auf. Der Boden war mit einer undefinierbaren Substanz überzogen, die farblich an Blei und in ihrer Konsistenz an Schlick erinnerte. An der Bar schoben sich Cocktails in Technicolor durch eine dichte Nebelwand. Das ganze Ensemble wirkte, als sei der Moderne die Sicherung durchgebrannt, wie der ambitionierteste Club des Weltalls, obwohl es hier und da barockere Ecken gab: Die geschwungene Treppe und die schweren samtenen Tapeten an der Rückwand wirkten auf mich, als müssten oben hinter den Balustraden Opernbesucher sitzen, die entsetzt durch ihre Lorgnetten das nackte Treiben verfolgten. In der Mitte des Raumes tanzten Frauen in riesigen durchsichtigen Würfeln. Es lief »SexyBack«. Die Mädchen krochen an den Seitenwänden hoch und leckten die Scheiben. Sie trugen silberne Brustwarzenschoner, schimmernde Ganzkörperfarbe und, soweit man sehen konnte, sonst nichts. Boris starrte sie an, doch Viktor zog ihn weiter.

»Ein andermal«, sagte Viktor.

»In der neuen Weltordnung?«, fragte ich.

Unser Soldat, Valentin Gogunow, saß oben in einer der VIP-Logen. Wie Viktor vorhergesagt hatte, sah er durch einen Einwegspiegel den Mädchen zu, während er seinen schillernden Cocktail trank. Als wir die Tür hinter uns schlossen, verkorkte Stille den Raum. Wir warteten. Unter unseren Füßen waren die Vibrationen des Popsongs zu spüren, aber hören konnten wir nichts mehr. Gogunow saß lange mit einem Finger im Mund stumm da und ignorierte uns, bis vermutlich Justin Timberlakes verzerrtes Gestammel verklungen war und die Mädchen aufhörten zu tanzen. Dann begann er zu sprechen. »So«, sagte er, ohne uns anzusehen. »Ihr seid also Besetows Gang.« Eine Frau in einem pinkfarbenen Fetzen tanzte um einen finsteren Leibwächter herum. »Wie wär's, wenn du uns ein paar Drinks besorgst«, sagte Gogunow zu ihr. Sie machte einen Schmollmund und verschwand.

»Die Gang«, sagte Viktor. »Ja, das könnte man sagen.«

»Eine ziemlich buntgemischte Truppe, oder?«, sagte Gogunow

und drehte sich auf seinem Stuhl zu uns um. Irgendetwas an seinem Verhalten wirkte wie einstudiert, und das war mir nicht unsympathisch. Das war mal ein Drogendealer, der sich wirklich bemühte, einen guten Eindruck zu hinterlassen, und so etwas sieht man nicht alle Tage. »Ihr seht aus wie Doktoranden«, sagte er. Viktor zuckte zusammen.

»Gefällt euch eins der Mädchen da draußen?«, fragte Gogunow ihn. »Ich könnte sie hochschicken lassen.«

»Jetzt gerade nicht«, sagte Viktor. »Wir würden gern erst filmen.«

Gogunow musterte mich. »Was hat es mit der Amerikanerin auf sich?«

Mir war nicht ganz klar, woher er wusste, dass ich eine Amerikanerin war, bevor ich den Mund aufgemacht hatte.

Viktor sah mich an. »Was hat es mit dir auf sich, Amerikanerin?«

»Herr Besetow hat mich eingestellt«, sagte ich. »Ich korrigiere die englischen Untertitel.«

Gogunow betrachtete mich einen Moment und wandte sich wieder an Viktor. »Vögelt er sie? Das kann er besser.«

»Schon gut«, sagte Viktor. »Das reicht. Sie ist unsere Mitarbeiterin.«

»Eure Mitarbeiterin? Na, großartig«, sagte Gogunow. »Soll sie vielleicht die neue Präsidentin der Zentralbank werden? Meinetwegen, mir egal. Behaltet eure Amerikanerin. Das gehört bestimmt zu Besetows brillantem Entwurf für die Weltherrschaft. Oder die kapitalistische Utopie. Was auch immer es jetzt wieder ist. Hey, ihr habt doch diese Möglichkeit, dass man das Gesicht nicht erkennt, oder?«

»Ja.«

»Und so ein Dings, das die Stimme verzerrt? Meine Stimme ist ziemlich markant. Ich will diese Technik, mit der sie tief und gefährlich klingt.«

»Klar«, sagte Boris. »Kein Problem.«

»Euer Dokumentarfilm geht mir am Arsch vorbei«, sagte Gogunow. »Nur dass ihr es wisst.«

»In Ordnung«, sagte Viktor müde. »Wir brauchen Ihren Arsch nicht. Wir bezahlen Sie nicht für Ihren Arsch.«

»Das könnt ihr unter meinen Namen setzen. Nicht unter den echten natürlich. ›Exsoldat, dem das am Arsch vorbeigeht.‹ Das könnt ihr schreiben.«

»Wird gemacht, Soldat«, sagte Boris.

»Ich glaube nicht, dass euer Besetow damit irgendwas erreicht«, sagte er. »Das muss klarwerden. Ich will klarmachen, dass ich nicht bekloppt bin. Wenn Besetow Selbstmord begehen will, kann er das billiger haben. Ohne die ganze Ausrüstung. Ohne Lizenzgebühren für amerikanische Popsongs. Es sind doch Popsongs dabei, oder?«

»Wenn das hier eine Selbstmordmission ist, freue ich mich, dass Sie sich uns anschließen«, sagte Boris.

»O nein, ich schließe mich ganz bestimmt nicht an«, sagte Gogunow. »Meine Jungs kennen alle Tricks. Aber warum macht ihr euch überhaupt die Mühe, einen Kleinunternehmer zu behelligen?«

»Tja, warum, wenn wir es nicht längst getan haben?«

Gogunow verzog das Gesicht. »Ich will mich bloß an der verfickten russischen Armee rächen. Das waren die schlimmsten Jahre meines Lebens. Die Hälfte von denen waren Kriminelle, bevor sie sich eingeschrieben haben, wisst ihr? Nicht ganz leicht, sich mit denen kultiviert zu unterhalten. Ich bin ein Literat. Und du weißt nicht, was echter Spaß ist, bevor du mal in Sibirien Dünnschiss gehabt hast. Ist euch je die Scheiße am Arsch festgefroren? Das gibt's. Also, was zahlt ihr mir?«

»Wie viel können Sie uns erzählen?«

»Kommt drauf an, wie viel ihr zahlt.«

»Sie scheinen ja so schon ganz gut über die Runden zu kommen«, sagte Boris. »Für einen Kleinunternehmer.«

Gogunow runzelte die Stirn. »Unternehmer sind das Rückgrat der Gesellschaft.«

»Ich hoffe nur, dass Sie die Steuerlast stemmen können«, sagte ich.

»Gerade so«, sagte Gogunow. »Aber das ist eben meine Bürgerpflicht.«

»Tja«, sagte Viktor, »dann betrachten Sie das hier einfach auch als Ihre Bürgerpflicht.«

»Aus Liebe zum Vaterland?«

»So ungefähr.«

»Ihr könnt loslegen«, sagte Gogunow gutgelaunt. »Ich sollte euch bloß noch daran erinnern, dass meine Schutztruppe mindestens so groß ist wie Besetows und wahrscheinlich viel weniger rücksichtsvoll. Und sie können sehr, sehr defensiv werden.«

»Ja«, sagte Boris mit zusammengebissenen Zähnen. »Verstanden.«

»Ich weiß nicht, wie sie reagieren, wenn es Pannen gibt, wenn mein Gesicht oder meine Stimme nicht unkenntlich sind, wenn ich nicht bezahlt werde oder ihr die Diskretion nicht wahrt.«

»Okay«, sagte Viktor. »Alles klar.« Er baute die Kamera auf, und Gogunow setzte sich in seinem Stuhl zurecht.

»Wie sehe ich aus?«, fragte er.

»Sie sollten im Bild sein«, sagte ich.

»Falsche Antwort«, sagte Gogunow.

»Es ist egal, wie Sie aussehen«, sagte Viktor, »weil man im Film nur Ihre Umrisse sieht.«

»Richtige Antwort«, sagte Gogunow. Er beugte sich vor. »Ihr versteht doch, dass ich es ernst meine, oder? Dich meine ich auch, Hübsche. Habt ihr Kinder, Freundinnen, lesbische Geliebte? Kleine teure Haustiere?«

»Nein«, sagte Boris. »Aber wir haben uns selbst unheimlich gern.«

»Gut«, sagte Gogunow. »So sollte es sein. Ich tue das hier nicht für die Demokratie. Denkt also nicht, dass ich euch nicht ausschalten lasse, wenn ihr mich verarscht.«

»Wir werden Sie nicht verarschen«, sagte Viktor. »Und uns ist egal, wofür Sie es tun.«

»Ich bin so weit«, sagte Gogunow.

Viktor schaltete die Kamera ein, die ein klinisch rotes Licht ausstrahlte. Gogunow blickte auf seine Fingernägel und dann ins Objektiv. Plötzlich wirkte er ein bisschen verlegen – er achtete offenbar bewusst auf seinen Gesichtsausdruck, obwohl er uns zu glauben schien, dass das keine Rolle spielte. »Kann ich anfangen?«

»Wann immer Sie die Muse küsst«, sagte Viktor.

Gogunow wartete noch ein paar Augenblicke, dann fing er an. »Ich war Wachmann auf dem Militärstützpunkt«, sagte er. »In der Nacht hätte ich normalerweise keinen Dienst gehabt.«

»Und welche Nacht war das?«, fragte Viktor.

»Das war am 30. August 1999.« Dass er vor laufender Kamera sprach, ließ Gogunow – obwohl weder sein Gesicht noch seine Stimme zu erkennen sein würden – höflicher, beinahe unterwürfig werden. Ich begriff, dass dieser Mann – dieser Drogendealer, dieser Soldat – an leichter Vortragsangst litt.

»Die Nacht vor dem ersten Sprengstoffanschlag«, sagte Viktor.

»Genau.«

»Dem in der Einkaufspassage.«

»Genau«, sagte Gogunow. »Ich hatte die Schicht mit einem der anderen Wachmänner getauscht, der an dem Abend krank war. Er war andauernd krank – vielleicht hat er simuliert, das weiß ich nicht –, aber mir war es so oder so recht. Wir hatten einen Deal. Ich war nicht für das RDX-Silo zuständig, aber ich hatte es gut im Blick. Meistens verbrachten wir die halbe Schicht damit, Cognac zu trinken und einander zu verarschen. Aber an dem Abend hatte ich darauf verzichtet und stand an der Tür. Ich war stocknüchtern, und ich weiß, was ich gesehen habe.«

»Warum haben Sie an der Tür gestanden?«

Gogunow wand sich. »Weil ich meiner Frau texten wollte, um ehrlich zu sein, und nicht wollte, dass die Jungs es mitkriegten. Ich hatte gerade erst mit SMS angefangen, und sie wollte dauernd, dass ich ihr schreibe. Da hätte ich es schon wissen müssen. Wir waren sieben Jahre verheiratet, und das mit den SMS hätte mich warnen müssen. Nehmt das nicht mit rein, okay? Das schneidet ihr doch raus?«

»Ja«, sagte Viktor müde. »Wahrscheinlich.«

»Also. Es war ungefähr gegen Viertel vor drei morgens. Da kam ein Lastwagenkonvoi, und jemand machte ihnen das Tor auf.«

»Was haben Sie sich zu dem Zeitpunkt dabei gedacht?«

»Der Stützpunkt gehört dem Militär. Von denen wird er genutzt. Es ist nichts Besonderes, dass sie solche Materialien bestellen – auch wenn das vor dem zweiten Krieg seltener passierte und noch seltener mitten in der Nacht.«

»Und?«

»Und es tauchte nicht im Protokoll auf, was, wie man sich denken kann, ein ziemlich ernstes, ziemlich ungewöhnliches Versäumnis war.«

»Und dann?«

»Dann weiß ich nicht, was weiter mit dem RDX passiert ist. Ich weiß nur, dass es um drei Uhr nachts vom Stützpunkt abgeholt wurde, und zwar von Militärs. Es hat keinen Einbruch gegeben. Keine Tschetschenen.«

Wir ließen die Kamera alles sehen. Wir ließen jeden, der den Film einmal ansehen würde, alles hören, was er sagte. Gogunow beugte sich vor.

»Und da war noch was«, sagte er. »Einer meiner Kollegen hat mir gegen Viertel nach drei, nach der halben Schicht, einen Tee gebracht. Er hat ihn mir gegeben, und ich habe einen Schluck getrunken und ihn sofort ausgespuckt. Er schmeckte widerlich – schlimmer als ranzig, also nicht, als wäre was Pflanzliches vergammelt, sondern wie etwas, das man überhaupt nicht trinken sollte. Ich hätte ihm fast vor die Füße gekotzt. ›Was zum Teufel ist das?‹, habe ich ihn gefragt. ›Tee‹, hat er gesagt. ›Was hast du da reingetan?‹, habe ich gefragt. ›Das schmeckt wie pures Gift.‹ Das tat es wirklich. ›Wieso?‹, fragt er. ›Ist die Milch schlecht geworden? Es ist bloß Tee mit Milch und Zucker.‹ – ›Was für Zucker denn?‹, frage ich, weil uns der Zucker ausgegangen war. ›Aus dem Lastwagen‹, sagt er. ›Ich habe ihn aus einem der Säcke genommen. Nur ganz wenig.‹ – ›Aus welchen Säcken?‹, habe ich gefragt. Und dann bin ich nachsehen gegangen. Auf den Säcken im Lastwagen stand tatsächlich ›Zucker‹ drauf. Am nächsten Tag ging in Moskau die Einkaufspassage hoch.«

Er nahm einen Schluck von seinem Cocktail. Er entspannte sich allmählich. Die Kamera begann ihm zu gefallen.

»Ich weiß nicht, was aus dem RDX geworden ist. Nicht sicher jedenfalls. Aber ich weiß genau, dass der Stützpunkt in Perm nicht, zu keinem Zeitpunkt, auf die bewaffnete Verteidigung von Zuckervorräten ausgelegt war.«

Er sah in die Kamera. »Das war's«, sagte er. »Ihr könnt ausmachen.«

Viktor schaltete die Kamera ab. »Das war sehr hilfreich«, sagte er. »Das war uns wirklich eine große Hilfe.« Er begann, die Spinnenbeine der Kamera einzuklappen.

Gogunow beugte sich wieder nach vorn. »Das war noch nicht alles«, sagte er. »Ich habe gelogen, als ich gerade sagte, das wäre alles gewesen.«

»Ach ja?«

Gogunow nippte an seinem Glas und lächelte. »Die entscheidende Frage ist doch: Wer hat den Transport autorisiert? Wer hat das RDX rausgegeben, und was haben die gedacht, wo es hingeht? Warum haben sie die Säcke falsch beschriftet? Ich war bloß ein einfacher Soldat. Und uns haben sie keine Schutzwesten gegeben, also neige ich zur Verbitterung. Was ich sage, ist vielleicht nicht so viel wert, wie wenn einer da draußen in Perm was weiß. Jemand, der das Kommando hat und der euch diese Fragen vielleicht beantworten kann. Wenn einer von denen was dazu sagen kann, hängt das Militär mit drin. Dann geht es nicht bloß um stillschweigende Duldung oder um grobe Inkompetenz. Sondern um Militärbeteiligung – um Regierungsbeteiligung. So sehr ich die russische Armee hasse – und ich *hasse* diese verfickte Armee –, glaube ich nicht, dass die solche Tricks aus Spaß durchziehen. Und so lächerlich ich euch auch finde – und ich kann gar nicht in Worten ausdrücken, wie lächerlich ihr seid –, kann ich doch einer guten

Verschwörungstheorie nicht widerstehen. Das liegt in der Natur des Menschen. Dazu gibt es wissenschaftliche Studien.«

»Okay, okay«, sagte Viktor. »Können Sie uns Namen nennen?«

»Es gibt da diesen Mann«, sagte Gogunow. »Den Leutnant, der den Stützpunkt leitet. Andrei Simonow. Er weiß bestimmt Bescheid. Aber ich weiß nicht, wie ihr ihn zum Reden bringen könnt. Ich glaube nicht, dass ihr ihn kaufen könnt. Erpressen auch nicht. Aber ihr seid ja so charmant. Besonders die hier.« Er zeigte auf mich. »Die ist ein Traum.«

»Genug jetzt«, sagte Viktor.

»Wisst ihr«, sagte Gogunow. »Ich bin kein besonderer Fan von eurem Besetow. Seine Nase passt mir nicht.«

»Das erwähnten Sie schon«, sagte ich.

»Er würde sich wahrscheinlich besser machen als Putin, aber das ist kein großes Kompliment. Und ich glaube nicht, dass er die Wahl gewinnt. Aber wer weiß. Selbst wenn der Dorfidiot den Drachen tötet, jubeln die Leute. Sie feiern ihn. Sie machen ihn zum König.« Er zwinkerte mir zu. »Das ist ein Aphorismus. Eine Metapher. Putin ist hier der Drache, und Besetow ...«

»Schon verstanden.«

»Denk darüber nach.«

»Mache ich.«

»Natürlich machst du das. Das Denken hat dich schließlich hergeführt, oder? Dein gutes Aussehen kann es nicht gewesen sein.«

»Das reicht jetzt«, sagte Viktor, und ich wechselte Blicke mit ihm.

»Ihr könnt gern bleiben«, sagte Gogunow. »Aber ich bestelle mir jetzt einen Lap Dance.«

»Wir gehen«, sagte Boris, und das taten wir – die Treppen hinunter, unter dem Coelinblau des Aquariums hindurch, an den abgemagerten Frauen vorbei, die in ihren Kästen Fellatio simulierten. Silberne Lichtpixel blieben in meinem Mantel hängen, und ich hielt mich an Viktors Schulter fest, um nicht zu ertrinken.

Draußen wartete der Wagen auf uns. Viktor legte die Ausrüstung in den Kofferraum. Wir fuhren los. Ich drehte mich wieder zum Fenster, während wir durch die Stadt jagten. Wie Gogunow es befohlen hatte, dachte ich über seine Worte nach. Und überall um uns herum waberte Licht wie unentdeckte Zivilisationen jenseits eines Ozeans, und Musik hämmerte auf die Straßen hinaus, und betrunkene Mädchen fielen leise in den Schnee.

KAPITEL 17

Alexander
St. Petersburg, 2007

An Silvester bestand Nina darauf, eine Party zu geben. Sie hatte einen Catering-Service bestellen wollen, aber das fand Alexander zu riskant; stattdessen hatte sie die Zutaten einzeln eingekauft und den Nachmittag über die Bediensteten beaufsichtigt, die riesige Häppchenplatten zusammenstellten – Hering in Sahnesoße, gekochte Ochsenzunge, Lachskaviar, vor Mayonnaise triefende Salate, eingelegte Gurken zum Wodka. Vlad stand im Anzug an der Tür, tat, als wollte er die Gäste willkommen heißen, und tastete sie mit Blicken ab – nach unerwünschten Gesichtern, nach ausgebeulten Taschen, nach zuckenden Augenlidern. Er hatte eine Liste, mit der er ihre Namen und Ausweise abglich, und wenn er sie auf der Liste gefunden hatte – aber erst dann –, lächelte er und bedeutete einem der Bediensteten, ihnen Hors d'œuvres anzubieten.

Nina nickte großmütig allen Eintretenden zu. Sie nahm ihnen die Jacken ab und reichte sie heimlich an eins der Dienstmädchen weiter. Alexander hielt sich etwas abseits – außerhalb des Sichtfelds durch die Eingangstür, außerhalb der Schusslinie – und begrüßte seine Gäste. Die meisten waren Freunde und deren Freunde und enge Mitarbeiter, aber ein paar entferntere Bekannte waren auch dabei. Alexander duckte sich hinter einen Wäscheschrank und tat, als suchte er nach Stoffservietten, als er Mischa hereinkommen sah. In den letzten Jahren hatte Alexander es möglichst vermieden, mit Mischa allein in einem Raum zu sein. Das Wahre Russland war mit der Zeit nur noch schriller geworden; Mischa duldete immer armseligere Gestalten in seinem Umfeld, und Alexander bemühte sich, so wenig wie möglich mit ihnen zu tun zu haben. Alexander hatte sogar Vlad gebeten, die Fanatiker von ihm fernzuhalten, damit er nicht mit ihnen reden musste, aber Vlad hatte gesagt, das sei nicht seine Aufgabe.

Jedenfalls musste Alexander zugeben, dass Nina alles bestens organisiert hatte. Die Lichter waren heruntergedimmt, die Tische waren mit Arrangements aus einer blassen winterlichen Blume geschmückt, und auf den Fensterbrettern standen winzige Teelichter aufgereiht. Draußen war das blinkende, freudetaumelnde St. Petersburg, in silvesterlichen Glanz gehüllt, von den diamantenen Fenstern ihrer fünfzehntausend heruntergekommenen Herrenhäuser erleuchtet. In einer Ecke stand Irina mit einem Glas Weißwein und redete mit Viktor und Boris, die ihre Anwesenheit seit der Rückkehr aus Moskau besser zu ertragen schienen. Um halb zwölf machten Bedienstete mit gekühlten Champagnerflaschen die Runde. Alexander trank selten, und wenn, dann meistens allein. Alkohol war ein zu leichtes Angriffsziel; man konnte nur schwer etwas Bitteres herausschmecken, und eine beginnende Vergiftung war leicht mit Trunkenheit zu verwechseln. Aber heute war Silvester, und Alexander fühlte sich ein klein wenig verwegen – es war keine feierliche Stimmung im engeren Sinn, aber die Art gedämpfte, bittersüße Zärtlichkeit, die einen dazu bewegt, allein durch dunkle Räume zu streifen und auf die wunderschöne nächtliche Stadt hinauszusehen. Also griff er sich ein Glas Champagner und ging ins Arbeitszimmer. Vor dem Fenster sah er die leuchtenden Zwiebelkuppeln, die kantigen Bürogebäude, die indigoblaue Falte des Himmels, die neonbunten Lichter der Klubs. Aus dem Wohnzimmer waren der Triller eines Frauenlachens zu hören und das raue Arpeggio eines Mannes, der eine Anekdote erzählte. Alexander gefiel es, diese Geräusche in seiner Wohnung zu hören, aber es gefiel ihm auch, von ihnen fort und in ein leeres Zimmer zu gehen.

Irina und die Jungs waren Anfang der Woche aus Moskau zurückgekehrt, und er hatte mit einem kindischen Gefühl des Neids zugehört, als sie erzählten, wie sie durch die Straßen gefahren waren, den Frauen zugesehen und das kapitalistisch vitale Arbat bestaunt hatten, auch wenn sie dort selbst nicht einkaufen konnten. Es hatte Schwierigkeiten gegeben – Hotels, die wussten, wer sie waren, hatten sie nicht beherbergen und Restaurants sie nicht bewirten wollen –, aber eine gewisse Anonymität hatte sie beschützt, und sie waren nur aufgehalten worden, wenn Gerüchte ihnen vorauseilten. Sie hatten unbehelligt in Museen gehen können; sie hatten vom Auto aus das großartige Moskauer Nachtleben miterlebt.

Alexander fröstelte. Draußen flackerte verfrühtes Feuerwerk in eisigem Silber vor dem blauen Himmel; das Licht der Sterne strich über den Fluss und glitzerte wie die Augen von Tieren in einem dunklen Wald.

Manchmal fragte er sich, so ungern er es zugab, wie sein Ende aussehen würde. Er hoffte – wenn er überhaupt hoffte –, dass es ein Schuss sein würde oder ein Sturz aus einem hohen Gebäude. Vor Vergiftungen fürchtete er sich am meisten, obwohl ambitionierte Giftattentate teuer waren – mit Polonium zum Beispiel, das nicht konkret zurückverfolgt werden konnte, zu dem es kein Gegenmittel gab (im Gegensatz zu Thallium, einer billigeren Alternative, der man mit einer Dosis Preußischblau entgegenwirken konnte), waren es zwei oder drei Millionen Dollar in bar für eine tödliche Dosis. Also hatte er zumindest die Finanzen auf seiner Seite.

Alexander hatte ohnehin die durchschnittliche männliche Lebenserwartung seines Landes erreicht, und manchmal fragte er sich, ob es nicht ein bisschen anmaßend, ein bisschen elitär war, mehr Zeit zu wollen. Bei seinen Reisen über Land hatte er ganze

Dörfer gesehen – die Überreste staatlich finanzierter Agrarkooperativen –, die fast nur von Trinkern, Sterbenden und Behinderten bevölkert waren, wo die Jungen in die Städte flohen, die Scheunen ungestrichen blieben, das Gemüse reihenweise verfaulte und die Alten ihre Herzinfarkte mit Unmengen stinkendem selbstgebranntem Fusel behandelten. Wie konnte Alexander sich anmaßen, leben zu wollen, wenn andere so lebten?

Als ein Finger ihn an der Schulter berührte, wäre Alexander fast aus dem Fenster gesprungen.

»Du bist aber schreckhaft«, sagte eine Stimme.

Alexander drehte sich um. Mischa hatte den Kopf auf die Seite gelegt, und sein Hemd hing über der Anzughose. Er hielt mit zwei Fingern ein Glas Wodka und ließ es sich so weit zur Seite neigen, dass Alexander sicher war, dass es herunterfallen und den Teppich beflecken würde.

»Mischa. Wie geht es dir?« Alexander streckte ihm die Hand hin, obwohl er Mischa nur ungern berührte. Die Jahre hatten es nicht gut mit ihm gemeint – da war noch immer diese kränkliche Ausstrahlung, dies Gefühl, dass seine Gesichtskonturen das Licht unnatürlich reflektierten, allen physikalischen Gesetzen zuwider.

»Wie es mir geht?« Mischa feixte. Er gab Alexander nicht die Hand.

»Genau, Michail. Das ist eine höfliche Frage. Höfliche Menschen fragen einander so etwas.« Alexander fragte sich, wie Mischa zu einer Einladung gekommen war. Nina musste eine ältere Liste benutzt haben.

»Na gut, wenn höfliche Menschen so etwas sagen. Danke, dass du einem Bauern Manieren beibringst.«

Alexander starrte ihn an. Als Mischa aus der Psichuschka zurückgekehrt war, hatte Alexander erst üben müssen, ihn anzusehen – er hatte sich zwingen müssen, Mischas Blick standzuhalten und ihn direkt anzusprechen. Damals hatte Mischa furchteinflößend gewirkt; er war ein monströser Anti-Prophet, und seine Botschaft war so grauenhaft wie sein Gesicht. Jetzt kam er Alexander bloß noch reduziert vor. Er war nicht hässlicher oder paranoider als die meisten. »Was willst du jetzt wieder?«, fragte Alexander.

»Warum denkst du, ich wollte irgendwas? Warum sollte ich nicht einfach meinem alten Freund hallo sagen wollen?«

»Wir sind nie Freunde gewesen.«

»Dagegen kann ich wohl nichts sagen.« Mischa ließ seine Hand über Alexanders Schreibtisch gleiten. Trapeze aus künstlichem Licht fielen durch das Panoramafenster und kreiselten über den Teppichboden. In der Ferne konnte Alexander das Schmettern verfrühter Partytröten hören. »Wenn ich so drüber nachdenke, will ich tatsächlich etwas, Alexander. Jetzt, da du es sagst.«

»Ja?«

»Ihr macht einen Film, habe ich gehört.«

»Das ist kein Geheimnis.«

»Ich möchte, dass das Wahre Russland mit beteiligt wird.«

»Beteiligt?« Alexander lachte ein strategisches, freudloses Lachen. Er fragte sich, ob jemals jemand unabsichtlich so lachte.

»Assoziiert. Ich will, dass wir damit assoziiert werden. Ich finde, der Film klingt nach einer wirklich guten Idee.«

»Das weiß ich zu schätzen, Mischa.«

»Und?«

»Muss ich erst betonen, dass ihr überhaupt nichts für uns getan habt?«

»An uns hat es nicht gelegen. Ihr ladet uns weder zu euren Kundgebungen ein noch zu euren kleinen Konferenzen. Ich weiß, dass wir euch peinlich sind.« Er kramte eine Zigarette aus seiner Hosentasche hervor und zündete sie an.

»Würdest du die bitte ausmachen?«

»Rauchst du nicht mehr?«

Alexander wand sich. »Nina mag das nicht.«

»Na so was! Der Erlöser aller Slawen raucht nicht mehr, weil seine Frau es verboten hat.«

»Also wirklich, Mischa.«

Mischa kniff die Augen zusammen, dann paffte er. »In all den

Jahren«, sagte er, »bei all euren Foren, euren Versammlungen, euren ganzseitigen Zeitungsanzeigen habt ihr uns nie mit einbezogen. Es wird Zeit für ein bisschen Kooperation.«

»Kooperation? Red keinen Blödsinn, Mischa. Ich muss glaubwürdig bleiben. Und das Wahre Russland ist … nicht glaubwürdig, sagen wir mal so. Lassen wir es dabei.«

»Und ihr?«

Alexander sah wieder aus dem Fenster. In ganz Petersburg öffneten die Leute Sektflaschen und pirschten sich an den Menschen heran, den sie um Mitternacht am liebsten küssen wollten. Und er stand hier mit diesem gelbsüchtigen, faltigen, vorwurfsvollen Kampfhahn. Alexander schloss die Augen. »Mischa«, sagte er und machte sich darauf gefasst, lächerlich zu klingen. »Es liegt nicht an dir, weißt du, du bist nicht gemeint. Aber einige von deinen Leuten sind ein bisschen neben der Spur. Von wegen ›Russland den Russen‹ und so.«

»Das ist nur ein Slogan.«

»Nur ein Slogan? Ein Viertel der Bevölkerung hält ihn für faschistisch.«

Mischa sog wieder an der Zigarette, und Alexander konnte seinen mühevollen, stockenden Atem hören. »Willst du jetzt Politik nach Umfragewerten machen? Weißt du, wie es dann hier aussehen würde?«

»Es ist eine sträflich fremdenfeindliche Haltung. In ihrem Namen werden Leute umgebracht.«

»Beschuldigst du uns jetzt, Mörder zu sein?«

»Werd doch nicht hysterisch. Ich beschuldige euch, dämlich zu sein. Und schlechtes Marketing zu betreiben. Mit meinem Film sollt ihr nichts zu tun haben.«

Mischa nahm den nächsten nachdenklichen Zug und setzte einen übertrieben beeindruckten Gesichtsausdruck auf. Er sah auf den Teppich hinunter und starrte aus dem Fenster. Er pfiff bewundernd durch die Zähne. »Eine tolle Wohnung hast du. Habe ich das überhaupt schon gesagt?«

Alexander schwieg. Es gab keine passende Antwort.

»Ganz schöner Kontrast zu deiner alten Bruchbude, wie? Schon erstaunlich, oder, Alexander? Wie weit du gekommen bist?«

Alexander nahm einen Schluck Champagner.

»Wo kommst du noch mal her? Wo deine Schwester noch lebt? Irkutsk, oder?«

»Aus Ocha. Sachalin.«

»Richtig. Stimmt ja. Sachalin.« Mischa schwieg einen Moment und strich mit der Fußspitze über den Teppich. Schmutzkrümel rieselten von seinem Schuh, und er trat sie fest. »Ich finde«, sagte er, »das bist du mir schuldig.«

»Schuldig? Was bin ich dir schuldig? Wofür?«

Mischa zog die Augenbrauen hoch. »Du weißt doch sicher noch, dass ich weiß, was mit Iwan passiert ist.«

Alexander starrte ihn an. »Was weißt du, was mit Iwan passiert ist?«

»Es wundert mich, dass du das vergessen haben willst. Ich weiß, dass du ihn hast sterben lassen.«

Alexander dachte an Iwan – wie schmerzhaft dünn er war, wie er sich beim Gehen dem Schnee entgegenstemmte, wie sehr er daran glaubte, immer davonkommen zu können. Rückblickend konnte Alexander sehen, wie verletzlich Iwan gewesen war, obwohl er damals so unbesiegbar erschien. Er schien derjenige zu sein, der die Zeichen erkannte und wusste, wofür sie standen; er schien die Realität zu erahnen, die unterhalb der Fiktionen verlief wie eine Wasserader unter einer Stadt. Aber wenn Iwan schon fragil war, dann konnte Alexander kaum aufrecht stehen – er sah im Rückblick, wie naiv, wie erschütternd angreifbar er gewesen war. Er hatte Iwan nicht sterben lassen. Sein halbes Leben hatte er damit zugebracht, darüber nachzudenken, und jetzt war er sich sicher. Man konnte etwas nur geschehen lassen, wenn man wusste, was auf einen zukam; man konnte etwas nur geschehen lassen, wenn man wusste, wie man es verhindern konnte.

»Das habe ich nicht«, sagte Alexander.

»Natürlich hast du. So muss es gewesen sein. Meinst du, sie hätten ihn erwischt und dich nicht? Meinst du, sie hätten dich ohne Grund all die Jahre in Ruhe gelassen? Es ist nicht so, dass Nikolai nicht gewusst hätte, wo du wohnst – sogar bevor du deren liebstes nationales Schachwunderkind geworden bist und draußen im Wald residiert hast. Nein, das glaube ich nicht. Ich glaube, du hast ihnen einen Gefallen getan. Ich glaube, du hast Kompromisse gemacht. Noch vor den vielen anderen Kompromissen. Ich habe lange gebraucht, um es mir zusammenzureimen, aber jetzt weiß ich es.« Mischa ließ ein seltsam gutmütiges Lächeln sehen. »Und deshalb denke ich jetzt, dass du mir etwas schuldig bist.«

Alexander atmete tief durch. »Ich weiß nicht, Mischa«, sagte er. »Ich weiß es wirklich nicht. Ich habe viel darüber nachgedacht. Ich weiß nicht, warum sie Iwan erledigt haben und mich nicht. Wahrscheinlich war ich nicht wichtig genug, um sich mit mir abzugeben. Ich war nur im Vertrieb. Wahrscheinlich haben sie es versucht und mich verfehlt und beschlossen, das sei Warnung genug gewesen.«

Mischa sah ihn mit einem befremdlichen Ausdruck an. »Nein. Ich bin sicher, dass sie dich nicht verfolgt und verfehlt haben.«

»Oder vielleicht war ich zu wichtig«, sagte Alexander. Er hörte, wie flehentlich er zu klingen begann. »Vielleicht hat es mich beschützt, dass ich relativ bekannt war. Und mit meinem Schachtalent war ich ein nationales Aushängeschild. Das haben damals alle gesagt. Vielleicht wollten sie mich deshalb nicht verlieren. Vielleicht wussten sie damals schon, dass sie mich protegieren würden. Und ja, du hast recht, vielleicht wussten sie auch damals schon, dass ich es zulassen würde. Es gab keinen expliziten Kompromiss, Mischa. Wirklich nicht. Aber vielleicht haben sie gedacht, mein Tod könnte auffallen.«

»Auffallen? Alexander, wann hat es sie je interessiert, was irgendwem auffällt? Vielleicht beschützt dich das heutzutage – dein Ruhm, wenn man es so nennen will. Vielleicht hält es sie jetzt davon ab, zu plump vorzugehen und die westlichen Intellektuellen gegen sich aufzubringen. Aber damals? Nein, mein Freund. Ich glaube nicht, dass das der Grund war.«

Alexander dachte an die Nacht zurück, in der Nikolai in sein Zimmer gestürzt war, die entsetzten Augen tiefgerändert, mit zitternden Händen, als hätte ihn der Rückstoß eines Gewehrs getroffen. Da hätte Alexander es wissen müssen. Natürlich hätte er es wissen müssen.

»Ich weiß nicht«, sagte Alexander. »Ich weiß nicht. Ich weiß nicht. Wahrscheinlich hätte es besser mich treffen sollen.«

»Immerhin darin sind wir uns einig.«

Sie schwiegen eine Weile. In seinen finstersten Nächten wollte Alexander tatsächlich manchmal nichts einfallen, was Iwan nicht auch getan und besser gemacht hätte als er, wenn er noch lebte. Egal, wie berühmt und mächtig und beliebt er war, egal, wie die Westpresse ihn verehrte, egal, wie hässlich und verrückt Mischa wurde, wie stigmatisiert seine Vereinigung war – nichts würde etwas daran ändern, dass Mischa etwas Entscheidendes über ihn wusste. Er wusste, dass sie mit Iwan den besseren Menschen getötet hatten.

»Jedenfalls«, sagte Alexander, »bleibt es dabei, dass ich euch nicht an dem Film beteiligen kann. Es tut mir leid, Mischa.«

»Ja«, sagte Mischa mit einem jungenhaften Grinsen. »Ja, ich denke, das wird es.«

Mischa ging, und als er die Tür öffnete, hörte Alexander das An- und Abschwellen flirtender, spielerisch streitender Stimmen. Er erhaschte einen Blick auf Nina, der Strähnen ihres roten Haars über den Rücken wogten. Sie hatte ihren Arm auf den Arm eines rebellischen Wirtschaftswissenschaftlers gelegt und warf amüsiert den Kopf zurück. Mischa schloss die Tür hinter sich.

Im dunklen Zimmer ging Alexander zum Fenster zurück und lehnte die Stirn an das kühle Glas. Durch die Tür konnte er den Countdown hören, die Jubelrufe, das Ploppen und Zischen des Champagners, der geöffnet und eingeschenkt wurde. Er hob sein Glas und trank auf das Jahr 2007.

Ende Januar war Alexander eingeladen, in einer Universitätsbibliothek Bücher und Schachbretter zu signieren. »Ein bisschen klein, findest du nicht?«, hatte er gesagt, als er die Beschreibung des Veranstaltungsortes durchlas. Nina hatte die Augenbrauen gehoben und gefragt, ob er auf die Gelegenheit verzichten wollte, mit einer Gruppe gleichgesinnter junger Leute zu sprechen, bloß weil der Saal zu klein war. Dann hatte sie die Augen verdreht und mit den Fingern auf den Schreibtisch getrommelt, und er hatte fast hören können, wie sie sich fragte, für wen oder was er sich neuerdings hielt – obwohl er nicht ganz begriff, seit wann *sie* eigentlich die Anwältin des Volkes war. Also war er hingegangen und hatte am Pult gestanden und zugesehen, wie die Sicherheitsleute an der Tür Pässe kontrollierten und Besucher nach Waffen abtasteten. Vlad und die anderen hatten sich reglos und massiv wie griechische Säulen neben den Türen postiert. Als ein träges Häufchen Studenten eingetrudelt und als Alexander sicher war, dass niemand mehr kommen würde, obwohl der Saal erst halbvoll war, setzte er seine Brille auf, holte seine Notizen hervor und begann zu sprechen.

Von dem Podium aus konnte er im Publikum Textnachrichten aufleuchten sehen. In den hinteren Reihen reichten sich zwei struwwelhaarige Männer ein Kreuzworträtsel hin und her; ganz vorn flüsterten ein junger Mann und eine junge Frau einander hörbar wütende Worte zu.

Alexander versuchte es trotzdem. Er wollte ihnen die Vorzüge der Demokratie nahebringen und die Gefahren der Untätigkeit. »In diesem Land«, sagte er, »werden die Profite privatisiert, und die Kosten werden sozialisiert.«

Überall im Saal sah er gelangweilte Blicke und hörte Knöchel knacken. Ein Mann in der ersten Reihe sah mit leuchtenden, unübersehbaren Augen zu ihm auf. Er beugte sich vor und schien sich Notizen zu machen. Alexander beschloss, den Rest seiner Rede an diesen jungen Mann zu adressieren.

»Putin«, tönte Alexander, »treibt keine fehlgeleitete Ideologie.

Ihn treibt das Geld, der Selbsterhaltungstrieb, die Gleichgültigkeit – was genauso gefährlich sein kann wie eine Weltanschauung.«

Vom Publikum war unterdrücktes Gähnen zu hören. Die Augen des jungen Mannes in der ersten Reihe leuchteten. Alexander blickte in seine Notizen. Normalerweise machte er Pausen für den Applaus; heute würde sein Vortrag kürzer dauern als sonst, kürzer als angekündigt.

»Er ist die humorloseste Führungspersönlichkeit seit langer Zeit«, fuhr Alexander fort. »Bestimmt erinnern Sie sich, dass *Kukly*, unsere beliebte Puppen-Satiresendung im Fernsehen, sogar Breschnew aufspießen durfte. Aber sobald es eine Putin-Puppe gab, wurde sie abgesetzt. Wenn unser Recht auf Satire dermaßen beschnitten wird, wie können wir da so tun, als hätten wir seit dem Kommunismus echte Fortschritte gemacht?«

In der hintersten Reihe spuckte eine Frau ihr Kaugummi aus, wickelte es in ein Taschentuch und steckte es in ihre Handtasche.

»Aber wenn Putin ein Tyrann ist, sind wir vielleicht mitschuldig an seiner Tyrannei. Fünfundachtzig Prozent der Bevölkerung haben in Umfragen gesagt, sie würden sofort emigrieren, wenn sie ein anständiges Gehalt bekämen. Diese alarmierende Statistik trägt sicherlich zu dem Gefühl der Apathie bei, mit dem die jungen Leute sich eine Erniedrigung nach der anderen gefallen lassen.«

Die Zuschauer sahen zu Boden; sie wandten den Kopf ab. Der junge Mann grinste frenetisch, wild entschlossen.

»Und so«, schloss Alexander, »sind wir zu einem Volk verkommen, das sich damit zufriedengibt, in der warmen Küche auf dem Allerwertesten zu sitzen. Wir werden so lange dort sitzenbleiben, bis sie uns die Küchen auch noch nehmen. Ich danke Ihnen.«

Das Publikum applaudierte in abgehackten Stakkato-Schüben. In den hinteren Reihen musste jemand niesen.

Danach wartete ein klägliches Grüppchen Studenten darauf, dass Alexander ihre Bücher oder Schachbretter signierte. Eine langhaarige Frau wollte ein Autogramm »für ihre Freundin«; ein gedrungener junger Mann wollte eins »für seinen Dozenten«. Schließlich tauchte der junge Mann aus der ersten Reihe auf, der nervös sein Schachbrett an sich presste.

»Guten Tag«, sagte er ernst.

»Ich bin froh, Sie zu sehen, junger Mann«, sagte Alexander. »Ich glaube, Sie waren der Einzige, der heute wach geblieben ist.«

Der junge Mann lächelte. »Herr Besetow«, sagte er, »Sie sind für mich der größte Schachspieler aller Zeiten. Würden Sie mir die Ehre erweisen, mein Brett zu signieren?«

»Natürlich.«

Alexander lächelte, griff nach seinem Stift und spürte, wie ihm ein stumpfer Gegenstand seitlich gegen den Kopf knallte. Ein roter Schleier überzog seinen Blick; ein Augenblick der Taubheit folgte und dann ein überraschend scharfer Schmerz. Alexander griff sich an den Kopf und wandte sich gerade rechtzeitig nach dem jungen Mann um, um zu sehen, wie er mit dem unsignierten Schachbrett in der Hand zu einem zweiten Schlag ausholte.

»Als Schachspieler habe ich Sie so bewundert«, stieß er wütend hervor. »Und jetzt sind Sie bloß noch ein dreckiger Politiker!«

Eine Frau schrie, und Vlad stürzte sich auf den jungen Mann und überwältigte ihn. Der junge Mann bebte vor Zorn, umklammerte sein Schachbrett mit einer zitternden Hand und zeigte mit dem anderen knochigen Zeigefinger auf Alexander.

»Sie haben Russland verraten, und Sie haben das Schachspiel verraten!«, rief er, und Alexander sollte nie vergessen, dass es die zweite Beleidigung war, die zählte, ein bisschen zumindest.

»Ruhe jetzt!«, bellte Vlad.

»Verräter!«, schrie der Mann. Speichelfäden hingen zwischen seinen Lippen; seine Augen – die eben noch vielversprechend idealistisch gewirkt hatten, voller Sehnsucht nach Demokratie, Pressefreiheit und Transparenz – strahlten jetzt eine milde Form von Wahnsinn aus.

»Mund halten«, sagte Vlad und rammte ihm einen Ellbogen in den Bauch.

»Schon gut«, sagte Alexander. »Lass ihn schreien.« Das war schließlich der Sinn der ganzen Veranstaltung.

Also schrie der Mann weiter seine heiseren Anschuldigungen heraus, während Vlad ihn aus dem Saal bugsierte. Und als er draußen war und die Tür sich hinter ihm schloss, holten alle Studenten ihre Telefone hervor und begannen zu tippen.

Am selben Abend hielt Nina ihm einen kalten Umschlag an den Kopf und servierte ihm eine Portion Eis, obwohl sie es sonst nicht leiden konnte, wenn er Süßes aß.

»Mein Pilz«, sagte sie. »Du bist so tapfer.«

Und er hatte beinahe das Gefühl, dafür hätte es sich gelohnt – für das Mitgefühl in Ninas Stimme und die Berührung ihrer kühlen Hände an seinem Hals.

»Hört mal«, sagte Alexander ein paar Wochen später. »Wir müssen etwas ganz anderes machen.«

Irina, Viktor und Boris saßen mit ihm am Tisch. Boris hielt eine Fernbedienung in der Hand und schaltete zwanghaft zwischen Rossija, NTW und Kanal 1 hin und her. Irina starrte vor sich hin und ließ eine Kopeke zwischen ihren Fingern kreisen. Sie schien in letzter Zeit ein wenig nachzulassen: Ihre Haut wurde beinahe durchscheinend blass, und ihr Blick verhärtete sich zu einem grimmigen, stumpfen Ausdruck, der Alexander an die sepiabraunen Fotos sibirischer Mütter im Kopftuch mit ihrem halben Dutzend noch lebender Kinder denken ließ. Er fragte sich, ob es eine Folge gesundheitlicher Probleme war, eine Folge der Einsamkeit oder des endlosen russischen Winters – der unerträglichen Kombination von Kälte und Dunkelheit und den ständigen Angriffen von Salz und Sand.

»Nur weil du ein Mal ein Schachbrett abbekommen hast«, sagte Viktor.

»Es geht hier nicht um das Schachbrett«, sagte Alexander. »Boris, könntest du den Fernseher ausschalten? Irina, könntest du damit aufhören?« Sie sah ihn düster an und steckte die Kopeke weg. Alexander fühlte sich in letzter Zeit zunehmend unwohl in ihrer

Gegenwart, und nicht nur deshalb, weil ihre Haltung und ihr Aussehen ihn an den nahen Tod erinnerten, an den er ohnehin schon bis zur Erschöpfung dachte. Noch mehr als das bedrückte ihn, wie wenig er sich in der Lage sah, ihre Fragen zu beantworten. Er war alle seine Briefe, Kalender und Notizen aus der Zeit durchgegangen, und Irinas Vater war nirgendwo aufgetaucht – er war ein Geist, der seine Ausgaben der *Kleinen Auswahl aussichtsloser Fälle* heimsuchte (die brüchig geworden waren wie trockenes Laub) und durch Alexanders alberne, wirre Gedichte an Elisabeta spukte (die noch genauso banal klangen wie damals). Alexander wollte Irina unbedingt etwas von ihrem Vater geben – irgendein Zeichen, einen Segen. Aber was sollte er sagen, wenn er nichts zu sagen hatte? Der Mann hatte ihm angeblich einen Brief geschrieben. Das wusste Irina schon selbst.

Und dann gab es noch die gewichtigere Frage – die Frage, was man tun soll, wie man weiterspielt, wenn man weiß, dass man verloren ist. Irina hatte bei ihrer Ankunft in St. Petersburg vermutlich nicht geahnt, wie sehr seine gesamte Existenz zu einer Antwort auf eben diese Frage geworden war. Aber es war keine befriedigende Antwort, und Alexander fühlte, wie enttäuscht Irina war, und das verletzte ihn. Was tut man also angesichts der unausweichlichen Niederlage? Man dreht einen kleinen Film, trifft vernünftige Sicherheitsvorkehrungen und versucht sich an seinem Espresso, seiner frigiden Ehefrau, seinem Frühstück zu erfreuen. Ist das etwa inspirierend? Ist es nobel? Man putzt sich die gottverdammten Zähne. Das, dachte Alexander, wusste Irina ebenfalls schon selbst.

Viktor grinste und ließ seine Fingerknöchel knacken. »Vielleicht hat es doch ein bisschen mit dem Schachbrett zu tun.«

Alexander befühlte seine Beule. Sie heilte erstaunlich langsam; wenn er in einer seiner immer häufigeren schlaflosen Nächte den Kopf hin und her warf, schmerzte sie so sehr, dass er vor sich hin fluchte, bis Nina ihn vorwurfsvoll ansah und mit ihrer Decke ins Wohnzimmer umzog.

»Vielleicht«, sagte er. »Vielleicht hat es teilweise mit dem Schachbrett zu tun. Aber das Schachbrett steht für ein grundlegenderes Problem, meint ihr nicht?«

»Du bist doch zufrieden mit den Kundgebungen, oder? Sie sind doch gut besucht, oder?«, sagte Boris. »Es war nur ein einziger Vorfall.«

»Ja, ja, die Kundgebungen«, sagte Alexander. Er kratzte sich wieder am Kopf. Natürlich war die Signierstunde eine Ausnahme gewesen, ein Ausrutscher, der viel mit schlechtem Marketing zu tun gehabt hatte. Normalerweise waren die Teilnehmerzahlen bei seinen Veranstaltungen ansehnlich, wenn auch nicht überwältigend; er wusste, dass sich die Leute für ihn interessierten, aber dieses Interesse hatte noch längst nicht die kritische Schwelle überschritten, den Punkt, an dem es von allein exponentiell weiterstieg. Aber sie kamen. Sie kamen auch, wenn Putin Alexander gerade persönlich beschuldigt hatte, eine Marionette der Amerikaner zu sein; sie kamen und brachten Transparente mit der Aufschrift *Wir sind die fünfte Kolonne des Westens* mit. Sie kamen auch bei Kälte, was Alexander besonders beeindruckte, wenn er an seinen unwahrscheinlich bitteren ersten Winter in St. Petersburg dachte, als er noch nicht in der Lage gewesen war, sich von der Kälte freizukaufen. Derart extreme Kälte war wie Sauerstoffmangel – sie wurde schnell zum einzig entscheidenden Faktor –, und Alexander wusste, dass die Menschen, die kamen und die Kälte ertrugen, es ernst meinten. *Trotzdem*, dachte er.

»Die Kundgebungen sind ja schön und gut«, sagte er. »Aber ich finde, wir sollten mal etwas anderes ausprobieren. Frischen Wind reinbringen, versteht ihr? Wir sollten unseren Unterstützern wieder etwas zu unterstützen geben. Und Putin etwas, das er verurteilen kann.«

Boris knipste mit seinem Kugelschreiber und schloss die Augen.

»Wir wollen, dass die Leute unseren Film zu sehen kriegen«, sagte Alexander. »Und ich weiß, dass alle hart daran arbeiten, aber davon bekommt ja niemand etwas mit. Wir sollten so lange das Interesse wachhalten. Wir sollten Guerilla-Marketing betreiben.«

»Na ja«, sagte Boris in geduldigem Ton, als wollte er ein Klein-kind oder einen Paranoiker beruhigen. »Es gibt ja noch den Hun-gerstreik. Wenn man nicht reden kann, kann man in Hungerstreik treten, um darauf aufmerksam zu machen, dass man zum Schwei-gen gebracht worden ist.«

»Das hat Chodorkowski im Gefängnis auch gemacht«, sagte Viktor. »Er hat sogar Wasser verweigert.«

»Das könnten wir auch probieren«, sagte Boris. »Darauf stehen die Leute.«

»Nicht gerade originell, oder?«, sagte Alexander.

»Du hängst bloß zu sehr an deinem Abendessen«, sagte Boris.

»Oder vielleicht könnte Nina an deiner Stelle in Hungerstreik treten«, sagte Viktor. »Ich wette, sie hat sogar schon angefangen.«

»Das reicht jetzt«, sagte Alexander, und Viktors Lächeln erstarb. »Gibt es andere Vorschläge?«

Eine Weile blieb es still. Das Klicken von Boris' Kugelschreiber klang wie ein Insekt, das ganz leise seine Mundwerkzeuge öffnete und schloss. Am anderen Ende des Tisches richtete Irina sich plötz-lich auf. »Also …«, sagte sie.

»Ja?«, sagte Alexander. Es überraschte ihn, dass sie sich zu Wort meldete. Ihre Verzweiflung umgab sie wie eine Elektronenwolke.

»Das klingt jetzt wahrscheinlich albern.«

»Ziemlich sicher sogar«, sagte Boris.

»Immer raus damit«, sagte Alexander.

»Ich habe in letzter Zeit öfter an eine Beerdigung gedacht.«

Im ersten Moment wusste Alexander nicht, was sie meinte, und dann fürchtete er einen schrecklichen Augenblick lang, er wüsste es doch. »Eine Beerdigung?«, fragte er behutsam.

»Ja«, sagte sie. »Eine Trauerfeier für die Demokratie.«

Alexander merkte erst beim Ausatmen, dass er den Atem ange-halten hatte.

»Eine Trauerfeier für die Demokratie?«, fragte Viktor. »Ziemlich freudlos, oder?«

Alexander beugte sich vor. »Was stellst du dir darunter vor?«

»Na ja«, sagte Irina. »Man könnte eine lebensgroße Puppe besorgen, die die Demokratie darstellen soll. Die könnte man aufbahren – vielleicht unter ein paar Transparenten, auf denen unsere Forderungen stehen. Und dann könnte man sie in einem Trauerzug durch die Straßen tragen.«

»Ein bisschen melodramatisch, meinst du nicht?«, schniefte Boris. »Ein bisschen plakativ vielleicht. Ein bisschen übertrieben.«

»Es war nur so eine Idee.«

»Interessant«, sagte Alexander. »Ich glaube, sie könnte interessant sein.« Auf den ersten Blick gefiel ihm die Idee sogar ganz gut. Sie war ausgefallen, aber dagegen hatte er nichts. Sie war polarisierend und bizarr. Vielleicht würden sich besonders die Jüngeren davon angesprochen fühlen.

»Ich finde sie nur irgendwie hysterisch«, sagte Boris. »Aber vielleicht ist das ja unsere neue Masche? Hysterie pur?«

»Mir gefällt, dass es gute Bilder abgeben würde«, sagte Alexander. »Ein Foto von so einer Aktion wäre ziemlich aussagekräftig, meint ihr nicht? Ganz anders als die Kundgebungen, wo man erst das Redemanuskript durchforsten müsste, das sowieso nirgends abgedruckt wird, bevor man die Kernaussage versteht.«

Viktor fuhr sich mit dem Fingernagel über die trockene Haut auf seinem Handrücken. Boris kaute auf seiner Unterlippe herum.

»Habe ich nicht recht, Männer? Einen Redner kann man jederzeit überhören – ihr macht ja gerade vor, wie es geht. Und man kann sich weigern, zu lesen, was einem unter die Nase gehalten wird. Aber wenn der Blick zufällig auf ein Foto fällt, kann man überhaupt nicht anders, als es zu verstehen. Es setzt sich direkt im Kopf fest, ob man will oder nicht.«

»Ja, aber ist das nicht ein bisschen zu theatralisch für uns? Zu dramatisch?«, fragte Boris. »Unsere Unterstützer sollen doch nicht denken, dass wir neuerdings nur noch PR-Stunts betreiben.«

»Vielleicht kann ein Stunt gerade jetzt gar nicht schaden. Vielleicht ist ein bisschen politisches Theater gar nicht verkehrt. Ich jedenfalls habe unsere üblichen Tricks allmählich über. Irina, schreib uns doch mal einen Ablaufplan.«

»Ich?«, fragte Irina. Viktor und Boris tauschten finstere, vielsagende Blicke aus, aber das kümmerte Alexander nicht. Immer wenn Irina etwas Sinnvolles zu tun hatte, schien es ihr besser zu gehen; ihre Depression schien, soweit er das einschätzen konnte, eine rein pragmatische zu sein. Vielleicht war so ein Projekt gut für sie – nicht dass er gewusst hätte, was für einen Menschen in ihrer Lage, worin auch immer sie bestand, gut oder schlecht war.

»So«, sagte Alexander. »Und jetzt raus mit euch.«

Am selben Abend lief Alexander in seinem Arbeitszimmer auf und ab und dachte an die Zukunft. Am Himmel blinkten die kosmisch grünen Lichter eines winzigen Flugzeugs. Er dachte daran, was passieren würde, wenn der Film herauskam. Wenn es so weit war, dachte er, konnte er sich offiziell von dem Alternativen Russland zum Kandidaten küren lassen. Und von da an hätte der Kreml Angst vor ihm, und er hätte noch immer Angst vor dem Kreml, und sie würden in einem Zustand nervöser gegenseitiger Hochachtung erstarren. Wie ein beidseitiger Zugzwang beim Schach, wenn es für jeden der beiden Spieler von Nachteil ist, am Spiel zu sein.

Aber ganz so stimmte es nicht. Gegen Putin anzutreten war eher wie der Kampf gegen diesen grauenhaften Computer – man konnte nichts tun, das er nicht längst vorausgesehen hatte. Die Wahl war längst entschieden, Putins Nachfolger längst ausgewählt und hergerichtet; offen blieb nur, welcher seiner Lakaien es sein sollte und wann es offiziell bekanntgegeben würde. Kein russisches Kino würde den Film zeigen, und Alexander bildete sich nicht ein, ihn im Fernsehen platzieren zu können. Er setzte seine bescheidenen Hoffnungen in das Internet, in YouTube, raubkopierte DVDs und Mund-zu-Mund-Propaganda. In Menschen, die auf den Straßen Schmuggelware von einem zum Nächsten weiterreichten. So hatte es schon einmal – beinahe – funktioniert.

Das Flugzeug zog jetzt seine Bahn mitten über der Stadt. Ein Gefühl der Einsamkeit ging von seinem Anblick aus: Die kalt aufblitzenden Farben des Flugzeugs, das Gewirr der Gebäude unter ihm und dazwischen der gewaltig leere Himmel.

Das wäre alles, dachte er: Eine Woche, zehn Tage vielleicht würde es aussehen, als hätte er eine Chance. Er hätte sie nie, natürlich nicht, aber vielleicht könnte er – eine Woche, zehn Tage lang – genug Menschen vormachen, er hätte sie. Vielleicht würden sie endlich wütend werden, und vielleicht würden sie anfangen, ernsthaft Unruhe zu stiften.

Aber vielleicht, dachte er, vielleicht auch nicht. Vielleicht würde die eine Woche kommen und gehen, der Film würde angesehen und vergessen werden, seine Kandidatur würde ignoriert und Putins handverlesener Nachfolger – der Mann, der ihm vier oder acht Jahre lang den Stuhl frei hielt, bis Putin ihn wieder in Besitz nahm – würde seelenruhig dem Sieg entgegengehen.

Draußen vor dem Fenster blinkten die Lichter der Büros wie Leuchtfeuer, und die Newa färbte sich in der winterlichen Dämmerung silbergrau. Das kleine Flugzeug glitt aus Alexanders Sichtfeld – aus dem Umkreis der Stadt, aus der Reichweite der Lichter – in eine andere, tiefere Dunkelheit.

KAPITEL 18

Irina
St. Petersburg, März 2007

Zwei Monate vor dem angesetzten Termin begannen Viktor und ich die Trauerfeier für die Demokratie anzukündigen. Wir benutzten das Internet – hauptsächlich VKontakte –, was uns das Interesse einiger Studenten einbrachte. Wir drehten ein Video, das sich mäßig viral verbreitete. Aber das Entscheidende waren die Plakate.

Wir fanden die Idee lustig, uns verschiedene Piktogramme für die tote Demokratie auszudenken – mit einem Messer im Rücken, einer Kugel im Kopf oder X-förmigen Augen. Die druckten wir aus und verteilten sie in Cafés, Studententreffs und Wohnheimen. Die Plakate wirkten ironisch und brachten Alexander tatsächlich ein bisschen Prestige ein. Schon bald rissen die Studenten sie von den Wänden, um sie in ihren Wohnheimzimmern aufzuhängen, so dass ich dieselben Orte mehrfach besuchen und für Ersatz sorgen musste.

Die Trauerfeier für die Demokratie war Teil eins eines dreiteiligen Aktionsplans, den Alexander für den Sommer ausgearbeitet hatte. Nach diesem Ereignis sollten Viktor, Boris und ich nach Perm fahren und versuchen, mit dem Leutnant ins Gespräch zu kommen, den Valentin Gogunow erwähnt hatte. Wenn dieser Leutnant zugab, dass an dem Diebstahl in Perm das Militär beteiligt gewesen war, waren die Ermittlungen zur Beteiligung der Regierung an den Anschlägen abgeschlossen. Dann hatte der Film seinen Zweck erfüllt. Und dann würde Alexander – als Reaktion auf die aufkeimende Wut, getragen von einer Welle intensiver populistischer Gefühle – die Kandidatenwahl des Alternativen Russland gewinnen. Davon, die Präsidentschaftswahl zu gewinnen, konnte keine Rede sein.

Und danach? Was würden wir tun, wenn Alexander nominiert worden war? Wenn er sich in einem Land, in dem es keine echten Wahlen gab, als Gegenkandidat hatte aufstellen lassen? Wenn er sich mittig im Fadenkreuz eines Gegners platziert hatte, der das Monopol auf die Munition besaß?

Wir wussten es nicht. Was nur heißen soll, dass wir glaubten, es zu wissen, und zu höflich waren, darüber zu reden.

Im Hostel wurde ich mittlerweile als wunderliche, tendenziell unbequeme Eigenart des Hauses angesehen, wie der immer leicht verstopfte Abfluss oder die Kaffeebecher im Küchenschrank, die immer schmutzig aussahen. Ich weiß nicht, was die Betreiber von mir hielten. Sie hatten noch nie einen Gast gehabt, der so lange blieb; bestimmt dachten sie, ich würde überhaupt nie wieder gehen. Seit ich dort wohnte, hatte ich Hunderte junge Leute kommen und gehen sehen. Ich hatte sie in Dutzenden Sprachen turteln und streiten und einander kennenlernen sehen; sie diskutierten über Literatur, ließen ihre Philosophiekenntnisse durchblicken und gaben ätzende Kommentare zum politischen Geschehen in den Herkunftsländern ihrer Gesprächspartner ab. Da war eine weißrussische Stripperin (»Ich arbeite in der Klubbranche«, sagte sie, »verstehst du?«). Da waren zwei Verlobte, die sich mitten in einer grauenhaft kalten Februarnacht auf der Straße vor dem Hostel für immer zerstritten. Da war eine ältere Dame aus Japan, die mit niemandem dieselbe Sprache sprach, jeden Tag dieselben Anziehsachen trug und sich jede Nacht zum Schlafen an ihren Rucksack schmiegte. Da war eine junge Frau, die ihr Kind verlor, ohne vorher bemerkt zu haben, dass sie schwanger war. Da war eine Dreiundzwanzigjährige, eyeliner-umkränzt und multilingual, die ewig auf ihr Visum wartete, weil sie an der Sorbonne studieren wollte. Da waren zwei gegelte italienische Männer, die mich ununterbrochen anstarrten – der Versuch, sie nie meine Brüste sehen zu lassen, erwies sich letztendlich als aussichtslos. Da war ein junger Mann, der sich pausenlos vor- und zurückwiegte und Zuckerpäckchen aus der gemeinschaftlichen Teeküche neben dem Ausgang stahl. Er sei seit vierzehn Monaten auf Achse, behauptete er.

Dann verschwanden alle wieder, und es kamen neue. Einmal hörte ich, wie einer von ihnen den Rezeptionisten nach mir fragte. »Diese Frau«, sagte er. »Diese ältere Frau, die schon die ganze Zeit hier ist. Wer ist das?«

Ich glaube, er hat »ältere Frau« gesagt. Es hätte auch »alte Frau« sein können. Und was war dagegen einzuwenden? Hatte ich den Titel etwa nicht verdient?

»Ach, die«, sagte der Rezeptionist. »Keine Ahnung. Die wohnt hier.«

Es überraschte mich, das zu hören, aber es stimmte natürlich, dass ich dort wohnte – sofern man überhaupt noch behaupten konnte, dass ich irgendwie irgendwo wohnte.

Zuerst hatte es mir etwas ausgemacht, von Alexanders Wohnung aus spätabends nach Hause zu laufen – es war eher die Ausnahme, wenn ich einmal keinem pöbelnden Betrunkenen, keinem aggressiven Bettler und keinem Verrückten begegnete, der dringend hätte eingewiesen werden sollen. Ich war allen möglichen Belästigungen ausgesetzt, weil ich so offensichtlich weiblich war, so offensichtlich fremd (besonders anfangs), und weil ich zu jeder Tages- und Nachtzeit allein unterwegs war. Aber irgendwann im Laufe des Winters verlor der Heimweg seinen Schrecken. Vielleicht lag es daran, dass ich selbst mich unmerklich zu verändern begann – vielleicht wurde meine Haltung selbstsicherer, aggressiver, weniger ängstlich. Vielleicht lag es an der Kälte, die mir immer wieder das Gefühl gab, die Witterung sei letztlich eine größere Bedrohung als alles andere. Oder es kam daher, dass ich inzwischen – mehr noch als zuvor – das Gefühl hatte, es sei nicht wichtig, was mit mir geschah, und dass diese Gleichgültigkeit mir einen quasi-ironischen Schutz vor allen echten Gefahren bot. So oder so hatte ich auf allen meinen Wegen, in all diesen Nächten nie ernsthaft Angst vor etwas, bis Nikolai mich wiederfand.

Es war früh am Abend, Ende März, in jener Jahreszeit, in der man tiefe Dankbarkeit empfindet, bloß weil der Himmel am späten Nachmittag noch blass aussieht. Die Jahreszeit, in der man noch die allerkleinsten Freuden genießt – worin ich nie besonders gut gewesen bin. Aber an jenem Tag gab ich mir zumindest Mühe, es zu tun – ich war früh bei Alexander aufgebrochen und hatte einen langen, mäandernden Spaziergang am Fluss gemacht, hatte die Eremitage besucht und Stunden später am Ufer zugesehen, wie sich die Klappbrücke hob. Es war schon spät, als ich schließlich in die Metro stieg, unter der Newa hindurch auf die Wassiliewski-Insel fuhr und den kalten Heimweg in mein Stadtviertel antrat.

Als ein Mann kurz vor dem Hostel aus dem Schatten eines Gebäudes trat, war ich fast zu müde, um mich zu erschrecken.

»Irina?«

Etwas umfing mein Handgelenk wie ein eingetrockneter Aal. In meiner Kehle durchlief ein stummer Schrei sämtliche Stadien seiner irdischen Existenz.

»Wer sind Sie?«, zischte ich.

Er bewegte sich, und die Leuchtröhren des Spätkauf-Ladens erhellten ein Stück rohe, rote Haut. Ich erinnerte mich.

»Junge Frau«, sagte Nikolai. »Ich glaube, wir kennen uns schon.«

»Ich weiß, wer Sie sind«, sagte ich. Die Begegnung im Café im letzten Herbst fiel mir wieder ein, noch bevor ich Alexander kennengelernt hatte. Und mir wurde unabwendbar klar, dass er mich kaum bis hierher hätte verfolgen können – durch das Labyrinth der Metro, an den drei Millionen Kunstwerken der Eremitage vorbei –, ohne bemerkt zu werden. Nein, es war schlimmer. Er hatte mich hier erwartet.

»Da überschätzen Sie sich aber«, sagte er. Ich starrte ihn an und versuchte auszumachen, was in seinem Gesicht vor sich ging. Es sah aus, als hätte man ihm sorgfältig und präzise die Haut abgezogen, vielleicht im Rahmen eines wissenschaftlichen Experiments.

»Sie arbeiten jetzt für Alexander Besetow«, sagte er.

»Das beantworte ich nicht.«

»Das war keine Frage.«

Ich wandte den Blick ab. Eine gebeugte Alte zuckelte vorüber und murmelte vor sich hin. Ich versuchte ihren Blick aufzufangen, aber sie sah nicht vom Boden hoch.

»Hören Sie«, sagte Nikolai. »Ich weiß nicht, was Sie da treiben. Vielleicht haben die Amerikaner ja beschlossen, Besetow auszuspionieren, und wenn es das ist, dann nur zu.«

Ich schwieg.

»Aber in letzter Zeit zweifle ich eher an dieser These. Wir zweifeln daran. Wir glauben, Sie sind einfach eine – eine unabhängige Akteurin, freundlich ausgedrückt, oder ein Querschläger. Es sieht tatsächlich danach aus, dass Sie ganz allein hier sind, aus Ihren eigenen unerfindlichen Gründen, so unglaublich es ist. Daher haben wir uns gefragt, ob wir Sie nicht davon überzeugen können, Ihren Ansatz zu überdenken.«

Ich schwieg. Ich konnte es kaum glauben, dass es allen Ernstes Leute gab, die so redeten, und ich hatte keine Antwort parat – weder eine würdevoll-herablassende noch sonst irgendeine –, die nicht abgedroschen geklungen hätte.

»Sie sagen nichts? Auch gut«, sagte Nikolai. »Die meisten Menschen kann man kaufen, aber ich nehme an, das gilt nicht für alle.«

Ich wollte mich an ihm vorbeischieben, aber er versperrte mir mit seinem breiten Brustkasten den Weg.

»Nicht so eilig«, sagte er. »Wir sind noch nicht fertig mit unserem Gespräch.«

In dem Moment bekam ich Angst. Mir kam in den Sinn, dass sich Nikolai, wenn er sein Ziel – was immer es war – nicht im Gespräch erreichte, auf andere Methoden verlegen könnte.

»Sie halten Alexander bestimmt für sehr mutig, oder?«, fragte Nikolai. »Wie er der Gefahr ins Gesicht sieht? Und alles nur für seine Ideale. Sehr poetisch, nicht? Sehr tapfer. Sie bewundern ihn. Und warum er Sie so dicht ranlässt, weiß ich nicht. Vielleicht bespringt er Sie ja, wenn mir auch nicht einleuchten würde, warum. Aber warum auch immer – jetzt sind Sie eben hier. Sie respektieren den Mann. Sie halten ihn für moralisch unfehlbar. Sie würden für ihn alle möglichen Opfer bringen. Vermutlich haben Sie das schon.«

Ich sah zu Boden. Das stimmte nicht ganz. Ich hatte keine Opfer gebracht, jedenfalls keine, die ich nicht ohnehin hatte bringen wollen.

»Dabei gibt es eine Menge, was Sie über Alexander noch nicht wissen. Zum Beispiel ist sein bester Freund aus den Achtzigern vom Bus überfahren worden. Wussten Sie das? Sein bester Freund und Mitarbeiter, der ihn beschützt hat, der ihn bei seinen ersten Schritten hier in Petersburg an die Hand genommen hat. Der

Mann, dem er sein Interesse an der Politik verdankt. Das wussten Sie aber, oder? Sie wussten doch, dass Alexander bloß ein Schachwunderkind war? Er konnte kaum rechts von links unterscheiden. Er wusste nichts mit sich anzufangen. Hat immer nur diese Figürchen auf einem Brett hin und her geschoben und sich nach einer Nutte aus seiner Kommunalka verzehrt. Es war wirklich armselig. Und dann wurde sein Freund Iwan vom Nachtbus überfahren. Ein schrecklicher Unfall. War wohl unvorsichtig, als er über die Straße gegangen ist. Total besoffen, möchte ich wetten. Der Mann war ein hoffnungsloser Säufer.«

Ich starrte Nikolai an.

»Das hat er Ihnen nie erzählt, oder?«, fragte Nikolai.

»Was wollen Sie mir damit sagen?«

»Haben Sie sich nie gefragt, warum Alexander nie so einen Unfall hatte? Er ist auf seine Weise auch ziemlich unvorsichtig gewesen, kann man sagen.«

»Sie meinen, ob ich mich gefragt habe, warum Sie ihn noch nicht umgebracht haben? Sicher nicht aus Mangel an Motivation.«

Nikolai schnalzte missbilligend mit der Zunge und zog in einer seltsam manierierten, aufgesetzten Geste die Wangen ein. »Also bitte«, sagte er. »Wir wollen doch nicht ordinär werden.«

Ich schloss die Augen. Ich hoffte, dass er verschwinden würde, aber er tat es nicht. Stattdessen beugte er sich zu mir herüber. Er stank nach kurzgebratenem Fleisch, nach billigem Fusel, nach drohender Gewalt. Ich hatte das Gefühl, ich würde im nächsten Augenblick aus schierer Charakterschwäche in Ohnmacht fallen.

»Hören Sie«, sagte er. »Ich will ehrlich mit Ihnen sein. Die Wahrheit ist folgende, Irina: Wenn Ihr Freund Besetow seine Kundgebungen abhalten will, seine kleinen öffentlichen Aussetzer oder was das ist – kein Problem. Das stört uns nicht im Geringsten. Es nützt uns sogar. Wenn er in seinem goldenen Käfig sitzen und sein Ego streicheln will – auch gut. Und die Beerdigung, die Sie planen, mit den lustigen kleinen Plakaten – ganz reizend. Wunderbar. Nur zu.«

Er öffnete und schloss seine Faust, wie ein Tier, das seine ausfahrbaren Krallen lockert. »Aber der Film. Der ist ein bisschen zu viel, meinen Sie nicht?«

»Zu viel?« Mich packte – nachträglich und unnütz – das Entsetzen. Mir bebten wahrhaftig die Knie. Meine Wirbelsäule krümmte sich unter dem gewaltigen Ansturm der Angst.

»Das geht zu weit. Wir haben lange Geduld gehabt.« Er zog mich dicht zu sich heran, und es fiel wieder ein Lichtstrahl auf sein Gesicht. Ich konnte erkennen, wo er sich beim Rasieren geschnitten hatte. Ich erkannte die einzelnen Haare zwischen seinen Augenbrauen, die aussahen wie die Beine massakrierter Käfer. »Der Kreml hat viel Geduld und viel Toleranz bewiesen. Er hat großzügig ein Auge zugedrückt und sich einiges an Beleidigungen und Albernheiten gefallen lassen. Aber eins sollten Sie wissen, Irina, und sagen Sie es auch Ihrem Chef: Diese Großzügigkeit hat Grenzen. Der Film geht zu weit. Und Ihr Alexander ist vielleicht berühmt. Vielleicht ist er beliebt. Aber selbst Berühmtheiten leisten sich Fehler im Straßenverkehr. Selbst Berühmtheiten haben manchmal Unfälle.«

Ich versuchte mich loszumachen, und diesmal ließ er es zu.

»Ich denke, Sie verstehen mich schon. Aber Alexander scheint es leider vergessen zu haben. Erinnern Sie ihn doch bitte daran, ja?«

Ich tat einen ersten Schritt, dann einen zweiten, und dann knickten mir die Knie ein, und ich rannte.

»Sie werden es tun!«, rief Nikolai. »Ich kenne Leute wie Sie, auf Sie ist Verlass!«

Am nächsten Tag war ich vor Sonnenaufgang auf den Beinen, als die Bäckereien gerade ihre Lichter einschalteten. In der Metrostation saßen Betrunkene zitternd in den Alkoven, bis die Polizisten sie wegstießen. In der Bahn kehrten hohläugige junge Leute von ihren langen Klubabenden heim, mit Pupillen so groß wie ein Daumenabdruck.

Ich erreichte Alexanders Wohnung, als der Himmel sich gerade fleckig grau verfärbte. Ich wartete unten vor der Tür, bis ich das Licht angehen sah, und dann ließ ich noch eine Viertelstunde verstreichen. Vlad drückte für mich auf den Summer, und ich klopfte bei Alexander an der Tür, hörte eine Stimme und trat ein.

Nina hielt einen Schuh in der Hand, die Kiefer wild entschlossen aufeinandergepresst. Vielleicht lag es daran, wie das Licht auf sie fiel, aber ihr rotes Haar und ihre rasende Wut und ihre schwer atmende Brust ließen sie unschön wirken. Zorn kann schöne Frauen noch hinreißender machen, habe ich gehört, aber bei Nina war es anders. Die Wut verzerrte ihr Gesicht, bis es irgendwie ihres und doch nicht ihres war – es war dasselbe kunstvolle Arrangement derselben objektiv feinziselierten Züge, nur dass jetzt insgesamt etwas Hässliches dabei herauskam. Es war, wie wenn man von einem Gemälde zurücktritt und sieht, wie die Farbkleckse eine grauenvolle neue Bedeutung gewinnen.

»Du«, sagte Nina, »bist ein erbärmlicher Mensch.« Es klang, als meinte sie es auch so. Alexander saß mit gesenktem Kopf, mit hochgezogenen Schultern da. Ich hob instinktiv die Hände vor die Augen, versuchte mich zurückzuziehen und stieß dabei eine antike hölzerne Schale um, auf der eine orthodoxe Kathedrale abgebildet war.

Nina sah mich an. Ihr Gesichtsausdruck änderte sich unmerklich – einen Augenblick lang schwappte Verachtung darüber hinweg und verschwand sofort wieder. Und in Alexanders Blick: tiefste Erniedrigung. Ich muss ja wissen, wie das aussieht. Dann nickte Nina mir kurz zu und dematerialisierte sich lautlos im Flur.

»Also dann«, sagte Alexander etwas überartikuliert. »Guten Morgen.«

»Es tut mir leid. Ich habe angeklopft. Ich dachte, ich hätte jemanden antworten hören.«

Er wedelte mit der Hand, als wollte er die unausgesprochenen Fragen verscheuchen. »Schon okay. Das kann passieren.«

»Du bist nicht glücklich«, stellte ich geistesgegenwärtig fest.

Das erinnerte mich an Jonathan. Ich dachte wieder, dass es sein

Gutes hatte, die schlechten Seiten nicht kennenzulernen – die kleinen, hässlichen Dinge, die man irgendwann über einen Menschen erfährt, so sehr man sich auch bemüht, es nicht zu tun. Die kleinen Anflüge von Egoismus und Herzlosigkeit. Die letztendliche, unausweichliche Unfähigkeit, einander zu verstehen.

»Glücklich? Ach, ist das der eigentliche Sinn der Sache?« Es war seltsam intim, ihn das sagen zu hören, wie wenn man jemanden im Schlaf reden hört. Er trommelte mit dem Stift auf einen Stapel Papier und schwang sich freudlos in seinem Bürostuhl zu mir herum. »Sollten wir die zusätzliche Zeit nutzen, um Perm noch einmal durchzusprechen?«

»Alexander, ich …«

»Der Aufseher trifft sich im Café mit euch. Von dem Stützpunkt selbst haltet ihr euch fern. Ich komme nicht mit, wie du weißt.«

»Alexander.«

»Ich bleibe einfach hier und genieße die Freuden des trauten Heims. Aale mich in der Sonne meines ehelichen Glücks.«

»Bitte.«

»Bitte«, echote er. »Bitte lass uns nicht darüber reden. Es ist ein ziemlich banales Problem, meinst du nicht?«

»Ja.«

»Es gibt wichtigere Dinge zu besprechen.«

»Ja!«, sagte ich mit Nachdruck.

Alexander zog die Augenbrauen hoch.

»Nikolai hat mich wieder angesprochen. Er wollte, dass ich es dir sage.« Ich musste an Nikolais Gesicht denken und daran, wie nah es mir gewesen war. »Er hatte schrecklichen Mundgeruch«, sagte ich.

Alexander nahm seine Brille ab. Er massierte seinen Nasenrücken. Er sah ein wenig mitgenommener, ein wenig abgekämpfter aus als sonst.

»Hat er mir gedroht oder dir gedroht oder so was in der Art?«

»Woher weiß er immer, wo ich bin?«

Alexander kniff die Augen zusammen. »Du wohnst seit einem Jahr in ein und demselben Hostel. Du machst es ihm nicht gerade schwer.« Er presste sich den Zeigefinger gegen die Stirn, dass sich eine kleine Wulst bildete. »Was hat er gesagt?«

»Er sagt, das mit dem Film geht zu weit.« Plötzlich wurde mir klar, wie viel Angst ich um Alexander hatte. Es erstaunte mich, weil ich mich kaum noch erinnern konnte, wann ich zuletzt um jemand anderen Angst gehabt hatte als um mich selbst.

»Ich bin schon oft zu weit gegangen«, sagte er müde. »Ich war schon immer zu weit.«

Das stimmte, das wusste ich. Er ging zu weit, und er lebte mit den Konsequenzen. Es war anders als bei mir – bei ihm kamen die Bedrohungen von außen, und sie würden ihn den Verstand und das Leben gleichzeitig kosten. Trotzdem waren wir einander in mehr als einer Hinsicht ähnlich. Der Tod belauerte uns; jeden Tag erhaschten wir Blicke auf ihn aus den Augenwinkeln, eine grinsende Hyäne im Gesträuch. Wir wussten nie, wann er kommen würde, und an besseren Tagen konnten wir uns einreden, er würde gar nicht kommen. Alexander konnte sich einreden, niemand würde ihm jemals bis nach Hause folgen, die Schatten in den Ecken würden Schatten bleiben, die lauten Geräusche wären immer Fehlzündungen von Motorrädern und die Kopfverletzungen immer ungefährlich und fast ein bisschen zum Lachen. Und ich konnte glauben, die Testergebnisse seien vielleicht falsch, die Zahlenkolonnen auf einem zehn Jahre alten Stück Papier hätten nichts mit meinem wirklichen Verstand, meinem realen Erinnerungsvermögen zu tun, die Prophezeiung sei fehlgedeutet oder umkehrbar. Ich konnte mir einbilden, wenn ich sowieso schon zu statistischen Anomalien neigte, konnte ich vielleicht auch das statistisch Unmögliche erreichen. Ich konnte mir Zeitungsartikel über den einzigen bekannten Überlebenden voll ausgeprägter Tollwut ausschneiden (mit künstlich induziertem Koma und Steroiden) oder Zeitungsartikel über die Wiederbelebung eines klinisch Toten. Eigentlich glaubte ich nicht an Wunder. Aber irgendwie fühlt es sich nicht wie ein Wunder an, einfach weiterexistieren zu dürfen. Es ist die Alternative dazu, die jeder Logik widerspricht, die jeden Glauben zerstört.

»Sie werden dich töten«, sagte ich.

»Das hat er bestimmt nicht gesagt.«

»Er hat in einem ziemlich beängstigenden Tonfall über ›Unfälle‹ schwadroniert.«

Alexander nickte geistesabwesend, als hielte ich ihm stundenlange Vorträge über irgendwelche Nichtigkeiten. Er sah aus dem Fenster. »Weißt du, man sollte doch meinen, dass sich meine Frau Sorgen um mich macht«, sagte er.

»Tut sie das nicht?«

»Es ist komisch, weißt du. Sie tut es nicht. Wirklich, wirklich nicht.«

»Vielleicht kann sie den Gedanken daran nicht ertragen. Oder sie glaubt fest daran, dass alles gut wird.« Ich wusste selbst, was für eine seichte Vorstellung das war. Sie war mir oft genug begegnet – bei Freunden von Freunden und bei älteren Tanten, die mit beiden Händen meine Hand ergriffen und sagten: Irina, es wird alles gut, ich weiß es, ich weiß es einfach. Im Klartext bedeutet das: Ich habe nicht so richtig darüber nachgedacht – habe es mir nie klar und brutal vor Augen geführt –, weil es unangenehm ist und weil es mir letztendlich nicht so viel bedeutet.

»Mit Glauben hat es bei Nina nichts zu tun. Und sie verleugnet es auch nicht. Sie weiß, was wir an Versicherungsbeiträgen zahlen. So oder so glaube ich nicht, dass diese Sache mit Nikolai besorgniserregender ist als all das, womit ich ohnehin schon fertig werden muss.«

»Eben doch«, sagte ich. »Das sagte er ja gerade. Er hat gesagt, sie haben dich absichtlich laufen lassen. Und dass sie das zukünftig nicht mehr tun würden.«

»Ach ja?« Er hob milde die Augenbrauen. »Kaum zu glauben. Kaum zu glauben, was ich mir alles hätte erlauben können, wenn ich das gewusst hätte. All die Restaurants, in denen ich hätte essen können. Die Urlaube, die ich hätte machen können. Ich habe noch nie den Baikalsee gesehen, weißt du.«

»Du nimmst es nicht ernst.«

»Ich nehme es sehr ernst. Fürchterlich ernst. Was soll ich denn deiner Meinung nach noch tun? Wie sehr soll ich mich noch verstecken? Wo soll ich noch überall nicht hingehen? Fahre ich etwa selbst nach Perm, um meine eigenen Interviews zu führen? Nein. Ich schicke meine Assistenten hin. Ich sitze hier den ganzen Tag am Laptop. Wenn ich aus dem Haus gehe, tauche ich überall mit einem Trupp Gorillas auf und kriege trotzdem ein Schachbrett über den Schädel gezogen. Ich nehme es ernst. Ich nehme es ernst. Wenn ich es noch ernster nehmen würde, würde ich mich auf der Stelle hinlegen und sterben, bloß um es hinter mir zu haben.«

Wir schwiegen beide. Mein Blick fiel auf Ninas Schuh, der noch immer auf dem Tisch kauerte. Er sah aus, als würde er sich jeden Moment aufrichten, einen Knicks vollführen und quer durch den Raum Pirouetten drehen.

»Entschuldige«, krächzte ich. »Ich will doch bloß, dass du vorsichtig bist.« Und das wollte ich. Ich wollte unbedingt, dass er sich vorsah – Alexander, der seinem Schicksal durch die richtigen Strategien, Vorsichtsmaßnahmen und Vorhersagen entgehen konnte. Alexander, der mit seiner Angst leben musste – sie ignorieren, verdrängen, überlisten musste –, solange es ihm zu überleben gelang.

»Ich bin ja vorsichtig«, sagte er. »Das bin ich. Wirklich. Ich verspreche es. Also. Können wir jetzt über Perm reden?«

Als ich am selben Abend in das Hostel zurückkehrte, sprach der Rezeptionist mich zum ersten Mal seit Menschengedenken freiwillig an.

»Fräulein«, sagte er und wedelte mit einem Briefumschlag. »Ich glaube, Sie haben Post.«

»Post?« Das war neu. Das hatte noch niemand aus meinem früheren Leben ausprobiert. Sie hatten es mit E-Mails versucht, bis ich meinen Account gelöscht hatte. Ich konnte mir nicht vorstellen, wie mich jemand aus der Ferne hätte finden sollen, ohne selbst herzukommen.

»Sieht ganz so aus.« Er zog die Nase hoch und gab mir den Brief. Ich spürte etwas Schweres, Fingerdickes in dem Umschlag liegen. Blassblaue, handschriftliche kyrillische Buchstaben überzogen das Papier wie Krampfadern. Irgendetwas an der Handschrift ließ mein Herz stocken und sich überschlagen, bevor ich überhaupt begriff, wie mir geschah – es war wie der namenlose Geruch aus dem Kinderladen, wie die herzzerreißende Melodie deiner allerersten Spieluhr.

Der Brief war von Lars.

Ich riss den Umschlag auf und holte den höckerigen Gegenstand heraus. Es war ein König. Ich hielt ihn umklammert, während ich das Schreiben las.

Liebe Irina,

ich hoffe, dieser Brief erreicht Dich bei bester Gesundheit, aber vor allem hoffe ich, dass er Dich überhaupt erreicht. Ich weiß noch, dass in den Achtzigern, als ich die Sowjetunion bereiste, die Post recht unzuverlässig war. Und davon abgesehen weiß ich nicht, ob er richtig adressiert ist – ich habe mich bei mehreren Herbergen erkundigt, und in dieser hier wohnt angeblich eine Frau Deines fortgeschrittenen Alters mit Deinem unauffälligen Erscheinungsbild. Ich hoffe, dass Du den Aufenthalt in Leningrader Herbergen als angenehmer empfindest als ich es damals empfunden habe! Ich hatte meinerzeit einige, sagen wir, interessante Erlebnisse. Anstand und Sitte verbieten es mir, näher darauf einzugehen.

Auf dem Harvard Square ist alles beim Alten, und ich sitze wie immer an meinem Brett. An Gegnern herrscht kein Mangel, denn die jungen Studenten mit den klobigen Brillen und den engen Hemden haben es sich zur Angewohnheit gemacht, an den Wochenenden gegen mich anzutreten. Sie spielen natürlich besser als Du, aber ich finde sie weniger amüsant, und sie interessieren sich weniger für meine Geschichten als Du es getan hast. Als Männer sind sie weltgewandter und erfahrener und lassen sich weniger leicht beeindrucken. Aber als Studenten halten sie es außerdem für eine Art ironischen Zeitvertreib, gegen mich zu spielen. Da war mir Dein ehrliches, wenn auch unerklärliches Interesse lieber, obwohl Du leider keinerlei Fortschritte gemacht hast.

Ich denke, Du solltest wissen, dass Dein Freund Jonathan Dich sehr vermisst hat. Nach Deiner Abreise hat er mich recht häufig besucht und hat viele Male gefragt, wie er Dich wiederfinden könnte. Ich habe lange überlegt, ob ich es ihm sagen soll. Aber ich fand, dass Du das Recht hättest, davonzulaufen, wenn Du es wolltest. Ich hoffe, Du hast nicht die ganze Zeit darauf gewartet, gefunden zu werden.

Übrigens kommt es mir seltsam vor, an jemanden zu schreiben, ohne zu wissen, ob er den Brief liest oder nicht, ob er überhaupt da ist oder nicht. Es ist, wie wenn man mit sich selbst oder mit den Toten redet, und beides habe ich in meinem Leben oft genug getan. Also komme ich zum Schluss.

Ich weiß, dass das, wovor Du davongelaufen bist, Dich früher oder später einholen wird, wenn es das nicht schon getan hat. Lass mich Dich daran erinnern, dass Du mehr Wörter kennst, als Du je gebrauchen kannst – das war schon immer so – und Dich daher nicht allzu sehr grämen solltest, wenn Dir welche fehlen.

Dein Freund

Lars Bergquist

PS: Anbei schicke ich Dir meinen König. Du hättest ihn nie mit herkömmlichen Mitteln erwischt, aber jetzt möchte ich, dass er Dich bekommt. Allerdings möchte ich es nicht so verstanden wissen, dass er sich ergeben hat. Vielleicht ruht er sich einfach nur ein bisschen aus.

Ich starrte auf den Brief, bis das Papier vor meinen Augen verschwamm und in meinem Kopf ein vollbesetztes Orchester einsetzte. Irgendwo in der Ferne hinter mir spürte ich Laub aufwirbeln, fühlte ich den Wind auffrischen, und ein schrecklicher Frühling verdichtete sich zu einem Orkan.

Ich hatte nicht gedacht, dass noch jemand an mich dachte. Ich hatte nicht gedacht, dass je jemand an mich denken würde – bruchstückhaft zwar, ein wenig spöttisch und verzerrt. Aber doch.

»Junge Dame«, sagte der Rezeptionist. »Wenn ich Sie bitten dürfte, im Empfangsbereich nicht zu weinen.«

Ende Mai war die Trauerfeier für die Demokratie angesetzt. Das Wetter wurde endlich milder; eine bedrohliche Feuchtigkeit lag in der Luft, und die Wolken hockten tief und schwer am Horizont. Sie sahen wie die Schaumkronen tödlicher Wellen aus – wie der Ansturm eines beispiellosen Unwetters mitten auf dem Atlantik, eines gewaltigen Zyklons, den nur die Seesterne und die ängstlich weggeduckten Haie zu Gesicht bekommen. Unter der siruppartigen Schwere der Luft regte sich stumpfe Kälte. Es war dieselbe stickige Kühle wie an dem Tag meiner Ankunft in Moskau vor einer halben Ewigkeit. Ich war seit fast einem Jahr hier.

Viktor stand in Sonnenbrille, mit einem Megaphon in der Hand auf einer Eierkiste. Ich hielt mich am Rand der Menge und verkaufte Plakate zu 150 Rubel das Stück. Auf der anderen Straßenseite liefen Polizisten wie eingesperrte Tiere auf und ab und klopften mit ihren Schlagstöcken auf den Boden. Die Genehmigung für die Veranstaltung war erst am selben Morgen gekommen. Vielleicht warteten sie auf einen Vorwand, jemanden zu verhaften, oder sie hatten Weisung, die Protestaktion eine festgelegte Zeitlang laufen zu lassen – gerade lange genug, um Putin als geduldig, als liberal, als gnädig dastehen zu lassen. Ich sah sie mir genau an, aber Nikolai konnte ich nirgends entdecken.

Die Menge war erfreulich groß. Einige der Demonstranten schwenkten Fahnen, andere hüpften auf und ab, und die vieldimensionale Bewegung ihrer sommerlichen Kleider sah aus wie die Flaggen friedfertiger Völker bei einer Sportveranstaltung. Manche hatten sich schwarz angezogen; ein paar nahmen das Thema der

Kundgebung sogar so wörtlich, dass sie Leichenhemden trugen und Krokodilstränen vergossen. Manche streuten Blumen. Manche hielten feierlich Bilder hoch – von Anna Politkowskaja, von Sacharow, sogar von Alexander – und paradierten sie mit todernsten Gesichtern herum. Andere sahen die Feier eher als vergnügliche Veranstaltung: Sie zogen Flachmänner aus ihren Taschen und Stiefeln hervor, drehten sich mit fliegenden Mänteln um sich selbst oder skandierten die Parolen von verrückteren, alberneren, abwegigeren Anliegen als unseren. Alexander stand, von Leibwächtern flankiert, auf einem Podest. In der Menge waren eigens angeheuerte Scharfschützen postiert. Ich blickte über sie hinweg in die Wolken, deren kumulierte Flanken sich wie Wildbret aufeinandertürmten.

Alexander winkte der Menge zu. Die Menge schrie sich heiser.

Und dann winkte ich zurück, ohne es zu wollen. Ich meine, ich wusste nicht, dass ich winken würde, bis ich es tat. Mein Arm winkte ohne meine Erlaubnis.

Es war nichts Dramatisches. Es fühlte sich an, wie wenn ein Augenlid unkontrollierbar zuckt, nur kraftvoller. Schließlich kostete es Kraft, die Knochen, Muskeln und Sehnen eines ausgewachsenen menschlichen Arms in Bewegung zu setzen; es war ein aggressiver Akt, die normalen mechanischen Vorgänge – die verblüffende, grazile, komplexe Kunst der Bewegung – zweckzuentfremden und einem anderen, dunkleren Ziel dienstbar zu machen. Und einen Moment lang lag ein Lächeln auf meinem Gesicht; einen Moment lang amüsierte es mich, wie seltsam es sich anfühlte. Und dann bohrte sich ein eisiger Dorn in mein Herz und schlug dort Wurzeln, und ich hatte Angst.

Denn jetzt war es da. Das war es.

Aber sobald ich mir sicher war, war ich es schon wieder nicht. Ich hatte auf das hier so lange gewartet, so viele Jahre lang, dass ich es mir möglicherweise nur einbildete. Die Szenerie um mich herum – die Skandierenden, die Marschierenden, die unauffälligen Inlandsgeheimdienstleute, Alexander – verschwamm vor meinen Augen. Das Gebrüll wurde zu einem gedämpften Vibrieren, wie das Rauschen von Blut in den Ohren oder das unhörbare elektrische Pulsieren des Weltalls. Ich beobachtete meine Hand. Ich starrte sie an. Ich forderte sie heraus, sich zu bewegen. Sie blieb still.

Vielleicht auch nicht, dachte ich. Vielleicht wirklich nicht.

Ich ließ die Plakate fallen, wo ich stand. Ich schleuderte wie ein Idiot meine Mütze weg. Ich rannte durch die Straßen, und die Newa kräuselte sich unter mir, und ich wich wütend fluchenden alten Frauen aus – und plötzlich zog mein kurzes, wenig beeindruckendes Leben in bewegten Bildern an mir vorüber, als hätte ich die gesamte Zeit mit Laufen verbracht: Ich rannte in den Nächten nach der Diagnose den Charles River entlang; dann rannte ich mit meinen unbeschwerten Highschool-Freunden durch den Schnee; dann lief ich durch das rostrote Laub eines vergessenen Herbsttages hinter meinem Vater her. Ich preschte quer durch die Stadt, und ich hatte das Gefühl, wenn ich mich so schnell, so vollständig bewegen konnte, musste ich mich getäuscht haben, was das Zucken anging. Ich sprintete, und ich fluchte, und ich dachte, selbst wenn ich mich nicht getäuscht hatte – wenn ich es wirklich gesehen hatte, wirklich gespürt –, hatte ich es jetzt ganz sicher hinter mir gelassen, es auf dem Platz zurückgelassen, wo eine aufgebrachte Menschenmenge es zu Tode trampeln würde.

Ich polterte die Treppe zum Hostel hinauf, und ich rannte in mein Zimmer, und ich warf mich auf das Bett. Das flatterige Pochen meines Herzens wirkte beinahe beruhigend. Ich starrte an die Decke, und ich starrte die Wand an, und dann starrte ich auf die sieben Flecken-Kontinente auf dem Teppichboden. Ich dachte an Afrika – das wirkliche Afrika, nicht das auf dem Teppich – und daran, wie gern ich dort hingefahren wäre, um mir die Pyramiden anzusehen und die Sphinx und lauter Dinge, die mir nicht gehörten, von denen ich aber immer (heimlich zwar und respektlos) geglaubt hatte, sie seien für alle da. Ich redete mir frenetisch ein, vielleicht würde ich ja doch noch eines Tages fahren; vielleicht würde mein Leben genauso weitergehen wie gerade jetzt (so nomadisch, unwahrscheinlich und interessant), bis ich mich eines Tages hinsetzte und meine Memoiren schrieb. Dass ich schon vor Jahren zum Tode verurteilt worden war, würde ich lachend als verrückte Anekdote aus meiner Jugend abtun. Vielleicht, vielleicht. Mein Herz beruhigte sich allmählich, das Blut rauschte mir in immer sanfteren Strudeln durch den Kopf.

Dann passierte es wieder. Meine Hand ruckte – wenig nur, maßvoll, aber vollkommen unabsichtlich. Ich sah voller Abscheu zu, wie sie sich gegen meinen Willen bewegte; es war, wie wenn man die postmortalen Zuckungen eines geköpften Huhns beobachtet. Es war meine Hand, aber zugleich war sie es ganz eindeutig nicht: Sie hatte mich verraten, wie es schien, sich gegen mich aufgelehnt. Sie war gekommen, um mich im Burgfried zu ermorden.

Ich rammte meine Faust gegen die Wand und ließ das Gewebe meiner Hand in den Schmerz meiner Hand übergehen und den Schmerz meiner Hand in den Schmerz überall sonst.

Draußen vor dem Fenster spielte ein kleiner Junge mit einem Windrad, und ich erinnerte mich an den Ausblick durch das U-Bahn-Fenster am Tag meiner Diagnose: wie die Farben plötzlich etwas Gedämpftes an sich hatten, die Szenerie etwas Eintöniges und zugleich eine neue Eigentümlichkeit – es war, als überzöge eine graue Lackschicht ein Gemälde, von dem jemand behauptete, es sei das schönste der Welt, und es sei wirklich zu schade, dass man es nicht richtig sehen könne.

Ich hatte jahrelang – jahrelang! – darüber nachgedacht, wie ich es tun würde, wenn es Zeit wurde, es zu tun. Meine derzeitigen Aussichten, das war mir immer klar gewesen, waren keine. Weder zu Hause, wo mein schleichender Abschied Stück für Stück mitverfolgt und betrauert werden würde, nicht zuletzt von mir selbst, noch hier – anonym und einsam, in einem Land, das mich in einer pissegetränkten staatlichen Anstalt abladen würde, wo ich brabbelnd, in meinem eigenen Kopf gefangen, erlosch.

Also hatte ich nachgedacht. Ich hatte an die saubere Zuverlässigkeit von Schusswaffen gedacht; ich war schaudernd vor den panischen, erstickten letzten Minuten beim Erhängen zurückgeschreckt. Dann gab es Ertränken, aber das ist keine Option, wenn man weiß, wie jemand am Ende aussieht, der sich ertränkt. Ich hatte mit den verweichlichten femininen Lösungen geliebäugelt – Tabletten und dergleichen. Optionen, die einem Zeit für Interventionen von außen nach dem Abraham-Isaak-Muster lassen, wenn die Götter beschlossen haben, man sei genug gestraft und hätte seinen Glauben bewiesen. Und dann das: Sobald die Entscheidung unmittelbar bevorstand, suchte ich nach Gründen, sie zu verschieben. Sofort ließ ich mich auf einen grauenvollen Tauschhandel ein. Mein ganzes Leben hatte ich nur unter dem Vorwand gelebt, dass die Entscheidung schon gefallen sei: Sobald ich etwas bemerkte – irgendetwas –, wäre es das. Dann würde ich handeln müssen. Es gab zwar eine Gnadenfrist mit guten kognitiven Fähigkeiten zwischen den ersten Symptomen und dem Beginn des mentalen Verfalls – und sie war alles andere als vernachlässigbar: Der Verstand meines Vaters hatte nach dem Auftreten der ersten Symptome noch jahrelang mehr oder weniger funktioniert –, aber ich würde mich nie darauf verlassen können. Das Risiko war viel zu groß, dass die Geistesschwäche meinen Willen zersetzte, dass ich mich hinter dem näher rückenden Vergessen verkroch und dem einzig möglichen Ausweg den Rücken kehrte.

Ich konnte diese Abläufe in einem intellektuellen Sinn verstehen. Ich hatte mir den wissenschaftlichen Hintergrund angeeignet und die Artikel gelesen; ich hatte die Grammatik und das Vokabular der Krankheit auswendig gelernt. Und ich kannte sie auch im nicht-intellektuellen Sinn. Ich hatte die Arme meines Vaters wie Windmühlen kreisen sehen, hatte die Angst und die Wut von seinen Augen abgelesen und gesehen, wie er sich an Wasser und Worten verschluckte.

Aber es gibt einen Unterschied zwischen Dingen, von denen man objektiv weiß, dass sie wahr sind, und Dingen, die man subjektiv spürt; zwischen Dingen, die man irgendwo im Kopf versteht, und Dingen, die man von innen heraus begreift, intuitiv, hinter dem Herzen. Wir wissen, dass das Weltall unendlich ist, und wir verstehen die Kontingenz der Zeit, und wir haben eine wissenschaftliche Notation für die Größe eines Atoms. Aber wenn wir versuchen, diese Dinge auf irgendeine Art und Weise wirklich zu erfahren, versagen wir. Wir haben die Grenzen unseres Verständnisses erreicht und müssen uns mit der unbequemen Tatsache abfinden, dass es Wahrheiten gibt, die ziemlich weit jenseits unseres Vermögens liegen, und sie für wahr zu halten.

Dann folgten mehrere Tage im Bett. Ich weiß nicht, wie ich sie zugebracht habe.

Ich weiß doch, wie ich sie zugebracht habe. Im Fenster: ein Keil aus weißem, geschwächtem Licht. Am Boden: Schatten, die vom Morgen bis zum Abend durch das Zimmer schlichen. Ich begann mir vorzustellen, Licht und Schatten seien in eine Art Wettkampf verstrickt, in ein Strategiespiel. Aber die Schatten gewannen jedes Mal, und es wurde langweilig zuzusehen.

Ich glaube, nach den ersten paar Tagen fing der Rezeptionist an, mir Brot und Tee vorbeizubringen. Und einmal, glaube ich, tauchte Viktor im Empfangsbereich auf – vermutlich auf Alexanders Anweisung hin – und erkundigte sich nach meinem Gesundheitszustand.

Es war kein körperliches Fieber, aber doch ähnlich: das Gefühl, mein Kopf schwebe meterweit über dem Rest meines Körpers; meine hingebungsvolle Faszination für die Risse in der Zimmerdecke und die alternden Schmutzflecken am Boden. Die Art, wie Träume die Realität verdrängten, bis ich nicht mehr auseinanderhielt, welches welches war.

Und hin und wieder – nicht oft, aber immer regelmäßiger – eine Zuckung im Arm, im Bein. Meine Finger schnellten gegen die Bettdecke. Meine Beine traten, traten wütend, immer ins Leere.

Vielleicht dauerte es eine Woche, so genau weiß ich es nicht. Dann stand ich auf, stellte mich unter die Dusche und aß vier Sandwiches vom Spätkauf-Laden nacheinander.

Ich erinnerte mich daran, warum ich nach St. Petersburg gekommen war. Ich dachte an die Fragen meines Vaters – meine Fragen: wie man angesichts der Katastrophe weitermachen soll, wie man würdevoll die letzten Züge eines verlorenen Spiels ausführt. Ich dachte an Alexanders Morddrohungen und an Nikolais frostigen Atem auf meinem Gesicht und an den Film, der so oder so gedreht werden würde. Alexanders Leben war eine Art Antwort auf diese Fragen, eine Art Vorlage für das Weitermachen. Ich wusste, dass mein Leben dasselbe würde leisten müssen.

Ich beschloss, trotzdem nach Perm zu fahren. Es war meine Pflicht. Und es war meine letzte Frist. Was konnte ich über mein kurzes Leben sagen, wenn ich ehrlich war? Ich hatte ein paar Schülern die korrekte Verwendung des Semikolons erklärt. Ich hatte ein paar Menschen, die mich liebten, furchtbar unglücklich gemacht. Wenn ich nach Perm fuhr und wenn wir dort etwas Wichtiges zu Tage förderten, gäbe es zumindest das. Es gäbe zumindest eine Rechtfertigung für diese Reise. Eine Rechtfertigung für dieses Leben. Es gäbe eine Geschichte, die sich für eine schöne Grabrede eignen würde, wenn jemand auf die Idee käme, eine zu halten.

In ferner Vergangenheit hatte es Momente gegeben – in Träumen, in fiebrigen Alptraumschüben, in Tagträumereien (ängstlichen und unruhigen, rachsüchtigen, kleinlichen, selbstmörderisch depressiven, gespannten, verhalten optimistischen) –, in denen ich mich fragte, ob es nicht auch eine Erleichterung wäre, wenn es geschah. Ich hatte zehn Jahre lang jeden Tag, jeden einzelnen Tag daran gedacht. Ich hatte es beim Aufwachen vergessen, besonders anfangs, und mich dann wieder daran erinnern müssen. Ich hatte geweint. Ich hatte Beziehungen abgebrochen. Ich hatte Angst vor meinem eigenen Schatten gehabt. Ich war weggelaufen. Würde es nicht am Ende, hatte ich mich gefragt, auch befreiend sein? Würde es mir nicht letztendlich helfen, meinen Frieden zu finden?

Das war es nicht, und das tat es nicht. Es war grauenvoll. Es war unvorstellbar grauenvoll. Es war so ungeahnt grauenvoll, wie ungeahnte Schönheit schön ist. Es war eine Neuerfindung, eine Umkehrung, eine Offenbarung.

Ich kehrte zu Alexander zurück, und ich lernte wieder zu tippen und mich normal zu unterhalten und morgens aufzustehen und zu tun, was man mir sagte. Aber es war eine andere Welt – an dem Tag und an jedem Tag, der folgte: fehlübersetzt, entstellt, verkehrt. Die Welt hatte sich so verändert, dass ich sie kaum noch wiedererkannte. Wir hatten nichts gemeinsam, sie und ich, und schwiegen uns manchmal stundenlang nur an. Irgendwann gab ich es auf, mich mit ihr verständigen zu wollen. Und ich sagte zu mir selbst, während ich mich Schritt für Schritt von ihr entfernte, dass sie mir sehr schnell sehr fremd geworden war.

KAPITEL 19

Alexander
St. Petersburg, Juni 2007

Der Sommer schwebte still und leise auf St. Petersburg herab, wie jemand, der unbemerkt in ein Zimmer zu schlüpfen versucht. Eschen und sibirische Birken blühten an den Straßenrändern; die Kanäle erzitterten unter immer milderen Winden. Am Horizont ballten sich die Wolken zusammen, spalteten und zogen sich auseinander wie träge Pupillen. Alexander sah vom Fenster aus zu.

Manchmal konnte er an Ninas Geruch das Wetter erraten, wenn sie, mit raschelnden Taschen behängt, von einer Shoppingtour mit ihren Freundinnen wiederkehrte – er roch die Sonne, die milde Luft, die längeren Tage in ihrem Haar, auch wenn sie sich ihm schnell entwand, sobald er sich ihr näherte. Manchmal fand Alexander an der Tür zart sonnenbehauchte Blätter, Zweige oder Blütenblätter, Überbleibsel eines Lebens, das sich draußen in der Welt abspielte, und dann nahm er ein Blütenblatt zwischen Daumen und Zeigefinger, um das Öl darin zu fühlen und zu sehen, wie es sich unter dem Druck verfärbte. Und manchmal saß Alexander nachts am Schreibtisch wach, riss das Fenster auf und trank in tiefen Zügen die Luft, die in mal lieblichen, mal ranzigen Brisen hereinwehte. Es roch nach Hortensien und Bittersüßem Nachtschatten und Maiglöckchen, und es roch nach all den Dingen, die im Winter in den Schnee gefallen und festgefroren waren und die jetzt als unkenntliche schwarze, zähe Fossilien wiederkehrten: verlorene Schuhe und Büstenhalter und Liebesbriefe, empörte Zeitschriften mit strengen Lettern, leuchtend pinkfarbene Klatschmagazine.

Er erinnerte sich daran, wie er die Flugschriften ausgetragen hatte, damals, als die Stadt noch Leningrad hieß, als er noch ausgehen durfte. Unter der Herrschaft eines maroden Regimes hatte er sich eine Art schlechtberatene Freiheit erlaubt. Damals hatte er zumindest frühmorgens oder in frostkalten Nächten vor die Tür schlurfen können. Er hatte im brüchigen Licht des nageldünnen Mondes gestanden, war an gewaltigen Denkmälern vorüberspaziert, die sich heroisch und monströs dem Strom der Zeit entgegenstemmten. Damals hatte er Verbündete gehabt und den Überschwang der Jugend. Und eine Frau, die er aus der Ferne lieben konnte, was ihn auf seinen langen Wegen durch die Stadt beschäftigt hielt. Elisabeta hatte etwas in ihm ausgehebelt, das er sein Leben lang nicht würde einrenken können; und auch darin, auch in diesem ganz speziellen aussichtslosen Fall, hatte eine bittersüße Freude gelegen.

Er schüttelte sich und ließ seine Halswirbel knacken. Es war beschämend genug, derart lange ein und dieselbe Frau zu lieben. Noch schlimmer war es, voller deplatzierter Nostalgie auf den Kommunismus zurückzublicken. Er begegnete solchen Gefühlen oft in den Beschwerdebriefen griesgrämiger alter Herrschaften, für die Breschnew und Andropow und Tschernenko den Hintergrund ihrer ersten Liebschaften, ihrer Heirat, ihrer jungen Familie abgegeben hatten. Für die Briefeschreiber waren die alten Zeiten mit einer Süße, einer Unschuld, einem Optimismus getränkt, der – so verfehlt er vielleicht gewesen war – immer noch besser schien als die Alternative. Alexander antwortete ihnen dann: *Sehr geehrte Dame, sehr geehrter Herr, danke für Ihren Brief. Ich kann Ihre Gefühle nachvollziehen. Aber ich glaube, dass es nicht das Regime ist, das Sie vermissen, sondern Ihre Jugend.*

Er sollte es doch schaffen, seinem eigenen Rat zu folgen.

Alexander schlug sich leicht mit der flachen Hand auf die Wange. Er hatte gerade an einer Liste von ungefährlichen Unterkünften und Restaurants für Irinas, Viktors und Boris' Fahrt nach Perm gearbeitet. Er ging davon aus, dass Irina nach wie vor fahren würde, obwohl sie vor kurzem eine Woche lang verschwunden war und er nicht aus ihr hatte herausbekommen können, warum. Er hatte Viktor in ihr Hostel auf der Wassiliewski geschickt, und Viktor hatte berichtet, es sei ein alberner Laden, eine Absteige für verschrobene Westler, die unnötige, vorübergehende Entbehrungen suchten, um hinterher etwas zu erzählen zu haben. Es war wahrhaftig kein Ort, an dem man leben sollte, wie Irina es offenbar tat. Aber das Entscheidende war, wie Viktor feststellte, dass sie Irina nicht bezahlten und nicht behaupten konnten, ihre Arbeitgeber zu sein, und dass es sie deshalb letztendlich nichts anging. Vielleicht war sie zurück nach Hause gefahren. Vielleicht war sie weitergezogen. Und Alexander wurde schlagartig bewusst, dass er nicht wusste, wo Irina hingehen könnte – wo »zurück« war und was »weiter« bedeutete.

Irgendwann war sie wiedergekommen, hatte bleich und panisch ausgesehen und jeden, der ihr Fragen stellte, mit tödlichen Blicken gestraft. Alexander hatte sie eine Woche lang durch die ganze Wohnung verfolgt, um einen Moment unter vier Augen abzupassen und sie zu fragen, wie es ihr ging, aber sie war ihm konsequent ausgewichen. Einmal hatte er es Nina gegenüber erwähnt, und sie hatte gefragt: »Dieses Mädchen? Ist sie immer noch dabei? Bezahlst du sie inzwischen?«

»Nein.«

»Dann kannst du wohl kaum erwarten, dass sie hier aufkreuzt, oder? Das ist Kapitalismus, Grib. So läuft es nun mal.«

»Das ist es nicht. Ich mache mir Sorgen um sie.«

Nina hatte ihn desinteressiert angesehen und ihn geradeheraus gefragt, ob er sich in die Amerikanerin verliebt habe. Alexander hatte wahrheitsgemäß nein gesagt und hatte sich zur Wand gedreht, enttäuscht von Ninas Mangel an Phantasie.

Jetzt biss er sich auf die Lippe und beugte sich über seine Notizen für Perm. Er hatte keine Ahnung, wie sie den Leutnant zum Reden bewegen sollten. Weitere Gespräche mit Gogunow hatten reichlich Informationen zu Tage befördert, mit denen man ihn hätte erpressen können, aber Alexander schreckte vor solchen Methoden zurück, und Gogunow hatte ohnehin durchblicken lassen, dass sie nicht wirken würden. Der neueste Ansatz bestand darin, dass sie sich als Filmstudenten ausgeben sollten, aber es gefiel ihm nicht, sie mit so wenig Rückhalt loszuschicken. Er hatte ihnen eine Liste mit möglichen Fragen, Standpunkten und Ideen zusammengestellt, aber es war nicht leicht, weil er den Tonfall und den Wortlaut nicht einschätzen konnte und nicht die Möglichkeit hatte, ihnen bei improvisierten Nachfragen oder beim Erkennen von Lügen zur Seite zu stehen. Sie allein loszuschicken war, wie wenn man eine Sonde auf den Mars katapultiert – er sah es vor sich, wie sie auf ihren Insektenbeinen in die Hocke ging und ihren motorisierten Kopf hin und her schwenkte. Man konnte sie dazu programmieren, zu tun, was man wollte, aber es war kein Ersatz dafür, selbst vor Ort zu sein und die Hände in den roten Sand zu graben.

»Grib.« Nina stand in der Tür. Sie trug ein seidenes Nachthemd, das sie im Mondlicht mit einer zittrigen, fahlen Aura umgab. Sie legte den Kopf schief. »Was machst du da?« Es klang, als wollte sie es wirklich wissen.

Er schwang sich im Drehstuhl herum und nahm die Brille ab. »Ich arbeite daran, die Kids auf Perm vorzubereiten.«

»Ah.« Ihr Mund schien irgendwie zu verschwinden. Sie stellte sich hinter Alexander und strich über das raue Gewebe seines Polohemds. Er zog den Bauch ein, bevor sie ihn erwischen konnte. »Dauert das die ganze Nacht?«, fragte sie.

»Was? Wieso? Hast du etwas vor?«

Nina warf ihr Haar über die schmale Schulter zurück und setzte einen Ausdruck auf, der wohl schelmisch wirken sollte. »Ich langweile mich«, sagte sie. »Lass uns ausgehen.«

»Ausgehen?«

»Du und ich. Nur dies eine Mal. Mit dem Auto. Wir könnten irgendwo hinfahren, und den Sicherheitsleuten sagen wir einfach nichts davon.«

»Das geht nicht.«

»Alexander.«

»Ich kann nicht.« Er rieb sich die Augen. »Du weißt, dass ich das nicht kann. Es wundert mich, dass du überhaupt fragst. Wenn ich nicht nach Perm fahren kann, wie könnte ich dann alles aufs Spiel setzen, um tanzen zu gehen?«

Nina sah zu Boden. Ihr Gesicht wurde ausdruckslos.

»Es tut mir leid«, sagte er. »Es ist nicht so, dass ich keine Lust hätte, mit dir auszugehen. Es ist nur einfach nicht machbar. Ich weiß, dass du das auch verstehst.« Er versuchte ihre Hände zu ergreifen, aber sie hielt sie zu unnachgiebigen Knospen geballt. Eine ganze Weile stand sie nur schweigend da.

»Ninotschka«, sagte er. »Bitte.«

»Glaubst du wirklich, dass du die Wahl gewinnen kannst?«, fragte sie heiser.

»Gewinnen?« Er hörte auf, nach ihren Händen zu greifen. »Nein, Nina. Nein, natürlich nicht.«

»Natürlich nicht?« Sie hob den Kopf und sah ihn an. Durch ihre Haut schimmerten Adern hindurch, blau, ein wenig erhaben und von all den Gefühlen durchpulst, die zu ihrem fernen, rätselhaften Herzen flossen. Es musste merkwürdig sein, wenn einem die Verletzlichkeit so offen ins Gesicht geschrieben stand.

»Wie«, fragte er zögernd, »wusstest du das denn nicht?«

»Ich wusste nicht, dass du dir so sicher bist.«

»Ich hätte es sagen sollen.«

Sie senkte wieder den Blick. Eine leichte kinetische Spannung lag in der Luft, die er aus seiner Zeit als Schachspieler kannte – von jenen Momenten, wenn er irgendwo tief unten in der Großhirnmasse wusste, was geschehen würde, ohne noch zu verstehen, weshalb.

»Du hältst das alles für einen Witz«, sagte sie. »Aber als ich dich kennengelernt habe, warst du ein ganz anderer Mensch. Du hast das Leben genossen. Du hattest Spaß daran, Leute zu treffen und auszugehen und dich zu amüsieren. Aber so ist es jetzt nicht mehr. Wir können nirgendwo hin, wir können überhaupt nichts unternehmen, und wenn ich eine Party geben will, kann ich kein Essen liefern lassen und muss jeden Gast abtasten, bevor er in die Wohnung darf. Das ist doch kein Leben, Grib.«

Er schielte sehnsüchtig zu seinen Notizen hinüber. Es würde inzwischen eine ziemlich lange Nachtschicht werden. »Es tut mir leid, Nina.« Und das tat es. Es tat ihm furchtbar leid. Aber er hatte sich seit fast einem Jahrzehnt mit jeder Geste, jedem Vorstoß und jedem Rückzug bei ihr entschuldigt. Gab es noch kreativere Methoden, zu Kreuze zu kriechen, noch einfallsreichere Varianten der Selbstgeißelung? Vielleicht, aber er brauchte seine Kräfte für andere Dinge. Nina würde sich mit ihrer kleinen Auswahl prosaischer Racheakte zufriedengeben müssen.

»Dann tun wir das alles für nichts und wieder nichts?«, fragte sie. »Und du sagst einfach so: ›Natürlich gewinne ich nicht‹? Das ist nicht leicht für mich, Grib.«

»Ich weiß.« Es ergab durchaus Sinn, was sie sagte. Er konnte die Augen zusammenkneifen, den Kopf schief legen und ihren Standpunkt nachvollziehen. Aber sobald er sich in sie hineinversetzte, sah er auch schon die Lösung für ihr Problem. Er kniff die Augen noch fester zusammen, bis sich strahlenförmige Falten um die Lider legten. Dann geh doch, dachte er. Na los. Er schwieg. Er lauschte. Geh, beschwor er sie stumm. Geh. Schließlich tat sie es – aber nur bis ins Schlafzimmer, von wo er das Quietschen der Schranktür hörte und das gedämpfte Wispern des Nachthemds, das die Bettdecke streifte. Eine Weile blieb es still. Und dann war unterdrücktes Schluchzen zu hören, das so ehrlich klang, dass es Alexander vorkam wie das Weinen einer Fremden.

Alexander blieb im Arbeitszimmer, schlief die halbe Nacht beinahe ein und lag die zweite Hälfte beinahe wach. Als sich am Horizont die Morgendämmerung andeutete, rot wie eine schwärende Wunde, gab Alexander es auf und versuchte zu arbeiten. Irina und Boris kamen um neun Uhr leise herein und trugen ihre Papierstapel in zwei gegenüberliegende Ecken des Raums. Um zehn kam mit angespanntem Unterkiefer und abgehackten Bewegungen Viktor ins Arbeitszimmer. Er hielt eine Ausgabe der *Nowaja Gaseta* in der Hand. »Hier, Boss«, sagte er. »Hast du das gesehen?«

Er gab Alexander die Zeitung. Auch für Irina und Boris hatte er zwei Exemplare mitgebracht. Sie schlugen die Zeitungen auf der Leserbriefseite auf. In großen Lettern stand dort die Überschrift: *Alexander Besetow – der richtige Oppositionskandidat für unser Land?* Während Alexander las, spürte er das Toben und Pulsieren der Adern in seinem Hinterkopf. Er erkannte darin die Physiologie kalter Wut.

Sehr geehrte Damen und Herren,

viele Unterstützer der Reformbewegung sehen in Alexander Besetow einen bedeutenden Vertreter der Opposition; viele hoffen sogar, er könnte eines Tages der zweite demokratisch gewählte Präsident unseres Landes werden. Ich kenne Besetow seit vielen Jahren, und ich denke, es wird Zeit, meine tiefen Zweifel an seiner Eignung für dieses Amt zum Ausdruck zu bringen.

Welche Opfer hat Besetow eigentlich für unser Land gebracht? Was hat er riskiert oder verloren? Hat er sich seinen Status als verehrte Galionsfigur der Opposition wirklich verdient? Natürlich braucht Russland Veränderungen. Natürlich braucht Russland einen neuen Regierungsstil. Aber es tut mir in der Seele weh, mitzuerleben, wie viele Menschen ihre Hoffnungen in einen so korrupten, so trägen und – so unpopulär diese Meinung sein mag – so verängstigten Menschen setzen.

Es ist bekannt, dass Besetow einen Film über die Sprengstoffanschläge von 1999 drehen will, und das ist durchaus ein lobenswertes Projekt. Aber wer hat die Interviews geführt? Wer hat die gesamte Arbeit gemacht? Nicht etwa Besetow selbst – lieber schickt er eine Gruppe Zwanzigjähriger überall hin, die für ihn die Recherchen übernehmen. Besetow begibt sich nur ungern außer Haus und unter das Volk, und zwar letztendlich deshalb, weil er vor dem Volk Angst hat. Genau diese Arroganz und Kälte sind der Grund, warum Besetow die gesammelte Aufmerksamkeit der Reformbewegung nicht wert ist.

Möglicherweise kann Besetow sich noch rechtfertigen. Von Insidern ist zu hören, dass er Nachforschungen auf einem bestimmten Militärstützpunkt plant und dass er wieder seine Assistenten dorthin schicken will. Sicher ist ihm bewusst, dass er diesmal selbst fahren muss, wenn ihm daran gelegen ist, in den Augen der Bürger seiner zukünftigen Demokratie seine Glaubwürdigkeit zu wahren. Russland braucht keinen zweiten mächtigen Milliardär, der sich um das einfache Volk nicht schert. Russland braucht einen Mann, der im Namen des Volkes echte Entscheidungen trifft – und echte Risiken eingeht.

Mit freundlichen Grüßen
Michail Solowjow

Alexander las, und seine Schultern fühlten sich so unbeweglich an, als hätte man sein Hemd an die Wand genagelt. Er zog sich auf das Sofa zurück und räumte eine Gartenschere beiseite, um sich setzen zu können. Irgendeins seiner abgelegenen Hirnareale beschäftigte sich mit der Frage, wozu Nina eine Gartenschere besaß – schließlich hatten sie keinen Garten, nicht einmal einen Vorgarten, und selbst wenn sie einen gehabt hätten, wäre es zu riskant gewesen, darin zu arbeiten. Manchmal baute sie auf den Fensterbänken Basilikum an, und vielleicht hatte sie gehofft, sie würden irgendwann ihre Sommer in einer riesigen, wunderschönen Datscha irgendwo außerhalb der Stadt verbringen und ihre Horde von Kindern zum Spielen nach draußen schicken. »Tja«, sagte er. »Das ist schlecht.«

»Schlecht? Wir sind erledigt«, sagte Boris.

»Noch nicht ganz«, sagte Viktor.

»Du weißt, dass uns das hier das Leben unendlich viel schwerer macht, oder?«, sagte Boris. »Du weißt, dass es unser Risiko, umgebracht zu werden, unberechenbar erhöht? Wenn die wirklich denken, du würdest mitkommen, war's das für uns. Und genau das will Mischa sie glauben machen – dass du nach Perm fährst. Dass du jetzt fahren *musst*, um deine Kandidatur zu retten.«

»Das muss ich auch«, sagte Alexander. »Ich muss wirklich fahren.«

»Das kannst du nicht tun«, sagte Irina.

»Ich muss.«

»Soll das etwa lustig sein?«, fragte Boris.

»Was soll daran lustig sein? Es ist meine Bewegung, oder? Und meine Idee. Es ist meine verdammte Kandidatur, oder etwa nicht?«

»Das geht nicht. Das kannst du nicht tun.«

»Dieser Idiot hat nicht unrecht, oder?«, sagte Alexander. »Das denkt ihr doch alle. Ihr habt Angst, es zu sagen, aber ihr denkt es. Was hat er schon riskiert?, fragt ihr euch. Woher nimmt er seine Autorität, wenn er sich nicht einmal traut, draußen eine Bratwurst zu essen, in sein Heimatdorf zu fliegen oder ohne seine verdammten Gorillas einen Fuß vor die Tür zu setzen? Das soll ein Held sein? Nein, denkt ihr. Der Mann ist ein Feigling, ein Weichei, und er schickt junge Leute los, um für ihn die Drecksarbeit zu machen, und dann lehnt er sich zurück und genießt den Applaus.«

Ein Schweigen folgte, und Alexanders Worte wirbelten in immer weiter werdenden Kreisen durch die Stille, bis ihr Echo den ganzen Raum erfüllte.

»Nein«, sagte Irina schließlich. »Das denken wir nicht. Du hast Hunderte Morddrohungen bekommen. Bei dir sind Körperteile durchs Fenster geflogen. Wenn sie dich ein einziges Mal allein im Treppenhaus erwischen, würden sie dich sofort umbringen.«

»Habt ihr das gelesen?«, fragte Alexander. »Habt ihr es gelesen?« Ihm wurde bewusst, dass er auf und ab lief und vielleicht sogar brüllte. »Das hier wird die neue Verteidigungslinie. Das wird das Mantra. Ich muss hin. Er lässt mir keine andere Wahl.«

Boris schüttelte heftig den Kopf. »Nein. Nein«, sagte er. »Nein, das glaube ich kaum. Ich mache das nicht mehr. Ich steige aus. Ich fahre da nicht hin. Das kannst du nach so einer Nummer nicht von mir verlangen. Nachdem er uns so zum Abschuss freigegeben hat.«

»Du musst das relativ sehen«, sagte Viktor. »Es ist ein kalkulierbares Risiko, so wie alle anderen auch.«

»Schwachsinn«, sagte Boris. »Glaubst du, die lesen die *Nowaja Gaseta* nicht? Glaubst du, sie kriegen das nicht mit? Also bitte.«

»Krieg dich wieder ein«, sagte Viktor.

»Herrgott noch mal«, sagte Boris. »Was zur Hölle hast du ihm angetan, dass der Mann solche Sachen schreibt?«

Alexander wand sich. »Ich wollte nicht, dass er an dem Film beteiligt ist.«

»Du wolltest nicht, dass er an dem Film beteiligt ist?« Boris trat gegen das Sofa. »Vielleicht, weil er dir ein bisschen zu rechts von der Mitte ist? Ein bisschen zu nationalistisch? Es sind nicht die Nationalbolschewiken, verdammt noch mal. Du hättest doch einen Deal machen können. Und wenn du ein halbwegs fähiger Politiker wärst, hättest du das auch.«

»Boris«, sagte Viktor. »Hör auf damit.«

»Aufhören?«, sagte Boris. »O ja, das tue ich. Und ich gehe. Ich könnte mir schon vorstellen, mein Leben für etwas herzugeben, irgendwann mal, aber nicht für so was Idiotisches.«

»Er hat recht«, sagte Alexander. »Ihr solltet nicht fahren. Keiner von euch. Ihr seid jung. Keiner von euch sollte die Risiken eines alten Mannes tragen. Sich zwischen ihn und seine Feinde stellen. Ich fahre selbst. Ihr könnt alle bezahlten Urlaub nehmen.«

»Das war's dann«, sagte Boris und stand auf. »Ich hab genug.« Er verließ das Zimmer. Kurz danach warf Viktor noch einen finsteren Blick auf Alexander und Irina und folgte ihm.

Alexander ließ seinen Kopf auf den Schreibtisch sinken. Er spürte, wie Irina ihn anstarrte, wie ihre Blicke Zwillingskrater in seinen Nacken bohrten, und es gefiel ihm nicht. Seit sie aus ihrem unangemeldeten Urlaub zurückgekehrt war, hatte sie diesen erschütterten, trauernden, wissenden Blick, den Alexander unerträglich fand, ohne zu wissen, wie er darauf reagieren sollte. Man konnte schlecht jemanden bitten, mit etwas aufzuhören, was offenbar unabsichtlich geschah. Und da war noch mehr – in unregelmäßigen Abständen wurde ihr Gesicht ganz leer, als würde sie sich an etwas Schreckliches erinnern, es wieder vergessen und sich dann doch wieder erinnern. Sie war zittriger als sonst. Ihre motorischen Fähigkeiten – die nie herausragend gewesen waren – wurden immer schlechter, und sie hatte sich angewöhnt, von teuren und zerbrechlichen Gegenständen einen Sicherheitsabstand einzuhalten. Außerdem war sie zum ersten Mal, seit Alexander sie kannte, zu dünn. Sie hatte immer wie eine Bohnenstange ausgesehen, aber jetzt wirkte es, als wollte ihr Knochengerüst seinen Protest kundtun, indem es sich durch die Haut davonmachte. Ihr Schlüsselbein stand vor wie eine Abbruchkante.

»Hör auf«, sagte er. »Bitte hör auf, mich so anzusehen.«

»Was soll das werden?«, fragte sie. »Was tust du?«

»Nichts«, sagte er. »Ich denke bloß, dass dieser gelbsüchtige Schizophrene recht hat, so sehr es mich schmerzt, das zuzugeben. Ich muss nach Perm. Sonst bin ich nicht glaubwürdig.«

»Dieses Land darf dich nicht verlieren.«

»Wer sagt mir das? Was habe ich denn schon vorzuweisen? Alles, was ich zu sehen kriege, sind unzuverlässige Umfragewerte und schlecht ausgeführte Studien.«

»Du siehst doch die Menschenmassen. Du siehst, wie sie deinetwegen kommen. Daran muss ich dich wohl kaum erinnern. Du weißt es. Du benimmst dich absichtlich schwierig.«

»Ich werde nicht gewinnen.« Er hörte selbst, wie bejammernswert er klang – hörte das Aufstampfen eines heulenden, untröstlichen Kleinkinds in seiner Stimme –, aber er konnte nichts dagegen tun.

»Dieses Jahr wirst du nicht gewinnen. Das ist klar«, sagte Irina. »Und vielleicht gewinnst du in überhaupt keinem Jahr. Weißt du noch, wie Anna Politkowskaja gesagt hat, dass du nicht Thomas Paine bist, sondern Johannes der Täufer? Du hast recht – vielleicht wirst du nicht selbst derjenige sein. Aber wer immer es ist, wird es dir zu verdanken haben. Du hast es denkbar gemacht. Du machst es mit jedem Tag wahrscheinlicher. Und damit du das weiterhin tun kannst, musst du am Leben bleiben.«

Er schwieg. Am Leben, was hieß das schon? Er würde nie wieder wirklich am Leben sein – nie das berauschende Gefühl erleben, wenn ihm Windböen in die Lunge fuhren, nie in dem wilden, anonymen Glück schwelgen, jung und allein in einer gewaltigen Stadt zu sein. Es gab zwei Möglichkeiten, wie es enden würde, dachte er: Entweder beobachtete er am Ende das Leben durch die Panzerglasfenster des Kreml, oder er war am Ende tot. Er sah verschwommen vor sich, wie er, in einem reichverzierten Grab eingepfercht, griesgrämig zuhörte, wie das Leben in der Stadt über ihm und um ihn herum weiterlief. Es wäre ein verstecktes Grab, zum Schutz vor Vandalismus. Einmal im Monat käme Nina, säße im strömenden Regen da und begutachtete ihre Fingernägel.

Aber nein, in Wirklichkeit wäre es anders. In Wirklichkeit würde er am Ende hier landen, genau hier – immer älter werdend und immer am selben Fenster. Vielleicht wüssten die Leute nicht, dass er noch am Leben war, wenn sie überhaupt an ihn dachten. Und irgendwann käme dann der Tag – wenn es wichtigere Anschlagsziele gab und Gras über seine Kampagnen gewachsen und er ein alter Mann geworden war, an den niemand mehr eine Kugel oder ein Komplott verschwenden wollte – an dem er wieder gefahrlos ausgehen konnte. Nur würde er es leider nie erfahren, wenn dieser Tag gekommen war.

»Du kannst es dir nicht leisten, dich so zu benehmen«, sagte Irina. »Hör auf damit.«

Er starrte aus dem Fenster, wo eine untertriebene Sonne höflich abwartete. Er starrte auf den Tisch, auf den Zettelstapel, der vor ihm lag. Er starrte Irinas Hände an, eine halbe Armlänge von seinem Gesicht entfernt. Es waren robuste, unelegante Hände; unmanikürt, aber mit Fingern, denen man ansah, dass sie über Klaviertasten oder Schreibmaschinen geglitten waren. Auf diese Hände starrte er, das sollte er nie vergessen, weil er es nicht über sich brachte, Irina ins Gesicht zu sehen. Und dann, plötzlich, tat eine ihrer Hände einen Satz – man konnte es nicht anders sagen, weil sie so offensichtlich nicht mit Absicht bewegt worden war. Die Hand erhob sich in die Luft und platschte wieder herunter, schlaff und schwer, wie ein Frosch, der sich in einen Teich katapultierte. Irina wurde weiß wie eine Zwiebel und versteckte die Hände unter dem Tisch. Alexander starrte sie an.

»Was war das?«, fragte er, obwohl er es wusste und obwohl es schrecklich war, diese Frage zu stellen, und noch schrecklicher, die Antwort hören zu müssen.

»Es ist nichts«, sagte sie mit einer Stimme, die nicht wie ihre eigene klang.

Er musste es gewusst haben, aber es mit eigenen Augen zu sehen war überraschend und grausig und um einiges schmerzhafter, als er erwartet hatte. Er hatte gedacht, die Unausweichlichkeit dieses Augenblicks hätte ihn irgendwie gegen seine Auswirkungen immun gemacht. Andererseits hatte er sein ganzes Leben mit dem Versuch – dem vergeblichen Versuch – zugebracht, sich mit dem Unausweichlichen abzufinden. Er wusste längst, dass das Unausweichliche oft auch das Schlimmste war; umso schlimmer, weil es sich so lange angekündigt hatte, weil es ein Ende war, das seiner eigenen Geschichte vorausging.

»Irina«, sagte er. Er wollte ihre Hand ergreifen, aber sie ließ es nicht zu. Er konnte beinahe ihr gequältes, faustgroßes Herz flattern sehen. Er hörte ihren rauen, schneidenden Atem. »Ich habe es gesehen. Ich habe das eben gesehen. Das hast du nicht absichtlich gemacht.«

Sie blickte zu Boden. Sie sah aus dem Fenster. Ihr Atem klang wie Flügelschläge. Ihr Gesicht sah wächsern aus, unwirklich fast, als sei sie der Versuch eines Hobbymalers, einen Menschen darzustellen. Es war einfach zu schrecklich, zu intim – zu sehen, wie diese arme Frau auseinanderfiel. Es war fast eine Art Ehre, eine Art Verpflichtung.

»Das ist es, oder?«, fragte er.

»Ja«, sagte sie. »Das ist es. Genau das, fürchte ich, ist es.«

Er schüttelte instinktiv den Kopf, obwohl er wusste, dass er dabei aussah, als trauerte er um etwas Kleines, Albernes, über das man am ehesten »so ein Pech« sagen würde. Was war die angemessene Geste? Was war die angemessene Antwort? Er rückte seine Brille zurecht, in der Hoffnung, kompetent und professoral auszusehen. »Was genau bedeutet das?«

Sie sah ihn finster an und schwieg. Er richtete sich in seinem Bürostuhl gerade auf. Irgendwo ganz hinten, in den verborgenen Kammern hinter seinem Gesicht – hinter den Wangenknochen und den Augenhöhlen, in jenem innersten Kern, von dem er immer das Gefühl gehabt hatte, er beobachte von dort aus die Ereignisse seines Lebens – spürte er die latente Drohung aufsteigender Tränen. Er hustete.

»Tja«, sagte er schroff. »Hier kannst du selbstverständlich nicht bleiben. Die staatlichen Kliniken sind grauenvoll. Wir würden dir eine private bezahlen, aber in Amerika wäre es trotzdem besser für dich. Wir besorgen dir ein Flugticket nach Hause.«

»Ich fahre nicht nach Hause.«

»Irina, du musst. Du musst fahren.« Er war erleichtert, dieses Gespräch führen zu können – es war so enorm viel besser, über etwas zu debattieren, zu dem er feste Ansichten hatte und halbwegs selbstsicher Weisungen geben konnte. Es gab ihm einen festen Rahmen vor. Es begeisterte ihn, dass Irina nicht nach Hause wollte, denn damit konnte er sich ganz auf das Projekt konzentrieren, sie zu überzeugen.

»Nein«, sagte sie. »Das kann ich nicht. Du verstehst das nicht.«

Obwohl sie recht hatte – er verstand es wirklich nicht –, bedrängte er sie blindlings weiter.

»Aber hast du denn niemanden dort?«, fragte er. Er wusste, dass sie Angehörige hatte und dass sein Ansatz verfehlt war. Er wusste, dass er, indem er dieses Thema anschnitt, mit jener achtlosen Grausamkeit handelte, die Menschen immer an sich haben, wenn die Umstände sie so überwältigen, dass sie lieber etwas Schreckliches sagen, als ganz zu schweigen.

»Nein«, sagte sie. »Also, ja, doch, aber ich will nicht zu ihnen zurück. Darum geht es ja gerade. Darauf kommt es mir doch die ganze Zeit an.«

Er wusste, dass sie hergekommen war, um wegzukommen – er wusste, dass es bei dieser Erfahrung teilweise darauf ankam, die überschüssige Energie eines verkürzten Lebens loszuwerden. Neben all den hehren Fragen nach Würde angesichts der Katastrophe hatte auch, vermutete er, der Sinn für Abenteuer eine kleine Rolle gespielt – für ein Abenteuer, das dieses eine kurze Leben zumindest ansatzweise von anderen, ähnlichen unterscheiden würde. Aber er hatte auch gedacht – wenn er überhaupt darüber nachdachte, was so selten geschah, wie sein Mitgefühl es irgend zuließ –, es sei in gewisser Weise nur ein Bluff. Er hatte gedacht, wenn die Krankheit sie einholte – wenn sie über den Nordpol hinwegfegte, über die Aleuten Himmel-und-Hölle spielte, in einem ratternden alten Zug quer durch den Kaukasus fuhr oder auch Erster Klasse über die blinkenden Hauptstädte der Ersten Welt hinwegflog – wenn die Krankheit sie holen kam, dass Irina ihr zurück nach Hause folgen würde. Alles andere wäre Wahnsinn. Und er ertappte sich bei dem Gedanken, dass es außerdem in gewisser Weise egoistisch wäre: Warum sollte er Zeuge einer Tragödie werden, um die er nie gebeten hatte? Warum sollte er dafür verantwortlich sein, sich darum zu kümmern?

»Irina«, sagte er ärgerlich. »Sei doch vernünftig.«

Irina schwieg. Sie stand auf und trat ans Fenster: Draußen fuhr ein frischer Wind durch die Baumkronen. Alexander hörte das pfeifende Geräusch, mit dem sie sich bogen.

»Warum hast du mir vertraut?«, fragte sie mit dem Gesicht zum Fenster.

»Dir vertraut?«

»Ganz am Anfang. Als ich hier aufgetaucht bin. Hast du nicht gedacht, ich könnte eine Doppelagentin sein oder so? Hast du nicht gedacht, ich könnte versuchen, dich auszuhorchen?«

»Jedenfalls nicht für die Amerikaner. Wenn sie etwas von mir wissen wollen, brauchen sie nur zu fragen.«

Sie drehte sich um. »Nein, für Putin. Oder für ... ich weiß nicht; für irgendwen eben. Oder ich hätte eine Attentäterin sein können oder eine Verrückte, eine Stalkerin vielleicht, die sich eine Tonne Fotos von dir aus dem Internet ausgedruckt hat.«

»Das wäre ganz schön eingebildet von mir.«

»Ich meine – du bist immer so vorsichtig. So zurückhaltend. Du isst kein Gebäck von Straßenhändlern. Du gehst nie aus.«

Er lehnte sich zurück. »Manchmal gehe ich schon aus.«

»Du weißt, was ich meine. Du passt eben auf. Das ... das ist richtig so. Das solltest du auch. Warum hast du mich dann hier arbeiten lassen? Woher hast du gewusst, dass ich nicht vorhatte, dich zu erledigen?«

»Ich weiß es nicht.« Er massierte sich die Schläfen. »Vielleicht habe ich gehofft, du würdest es tun.«

»Was meinst du bloß damit?«

»Ich weiß nicht«, sagte er. »Vielleicht wäre es eine Erleichterung gewesen.«

Irina lächelte schief. »Das glaubst du vielleicht, aber es stimmt nicht. Das wäre es nicht gewesen.«

Alexander zog sie zu sich heran. Ihr knochiger Rücken fühlte sich zerbrechlich an, und er dachte an die Tochter, die sie einmal einem Vater gewesen war, und er dachte an die Tochter, die er selbst hätte haben können, wenn sein Leben anders verlaufen wäre. Er glaubte ihr, doch er brachte es nicht über sich, das zu sagen. Also beschloss er, lieber ganz zu schweigen.

In jener Nacht lag Alexander wach, dachte an Irina und lauschte auf Ninas flache Atemzüge. Nina schien nie ganz bewusstlos zu sein – ihr Atem klang immer ein klein wenig wach, als täusche sie den Schlaf nur vor oder stelle sich tot. Sie lag oben auf der Bettdecke, und er betrachtete die strenge Rundung ihres Beckens, die unnachgiebige Kontur ihrer Rippenbögen. Ein nacktes Bein war über das andere geschlagen; sie sahen wie pirouettierende Knochen aus. Das Mondlicht ließ Nina beinahe durchsichtig erscheinen – sie erinnerte ihn abschreckenderweise an eine Tiefseekreatur, die sich unter dem Einfluss der Tiefe, des Drucks und der Evolution in einen skelettierten, phosphoreszierenden Alien verwandelt hatte.

»Nina«, sagte er. »Die Amerikanerin stirbt.«

Das war nicht sein einziges Problem. Mischas Wutausbruch in der *Nowaja Gaseta* machte ihm zu schaffen; er hatte Alexander schachmatt gesetzt, wie es schien, und jetzt wäre jeder weitere Zug selbstmörderisch – wobei eine der Optionen körperlicher und die andere politischer Selbstmord wäre. Mischa hatte einen ziemlich klugen Zug zuwege gebracht, wobei Alexander immer gewusst hatte, dass er ein kluger Kopf war. Er wusste auch, warum Mischas Kapriolen ihn so empfindlich getroffen hatten. Wann immer er Mischa vor sich sah, hörte er die wütend gezischte Anschuldigung, damals sei der bessere Mann gestorben, und das sei Russlands großes Unglück. Die Toten oder Sterbenden waren immer so viel tugendhafter als die Lebenden – selbst wenn sie zu Lebzeiten kleinlich oder hartherzig, engstirnig oder eitel gewesen waren, übermütig oder verängstigt. Mischa schien zu glauben, und Alexander war geneigt, ihm darin recht zu geben, dass es mit Iwan alles anders verlaufen wäre. Iwan wäre auf die Straße gegangen und hätte die Truppen motiviert, ob mit Sicherheitsapparat oder ohne. Iwan wäre nach Perm gefahren. Iwan hätte vielleicht inzwischen gewonnen. Was hatte Alexander schließlich vorzuweisen? Was hatte er mit seiner Kampagne erreicht? Er hatte an einer Handvoll Nachmittage eine Handvoll öffentlicher Plätze gefüllt. Er hatte einer Todkranken auf unerklärliche Weise ein wenig Befriedigung verschafft. Und er hatte ein paar Stunden Unterhaltung für international interessierte Fernsehzuschauer geboten, die das Ganze so kurzweilig fanden wie eine Schachpartie. Er konnte von Glück sagen, wenn Putin seinetwegen eine einzige schlaflose Nacht oder eine Verdauungsstörung erlitten hatte.

Er musste nach Perm. Morgen früh würde er sich in den ersten Flieger setzen. Er musste es tun. Es führte kein Weg daran vorbei. »Nina«, flüsterte er. »Ich gehe morgen weg.« Sie antwortete nicht. Vielleicht schlief sie wirklich. Oder vielleicht hörte sie ihm einfach nicht mehr zu.

Er erwachte von einem Rumpeln im zweiten Schlafzimmer. Als er nachsehen ging, sortierte Nina gerade ihre Kleider – ein polychromer textiler Fächer breitete sich über die Tagesdecke: glänzende Blusen und Röcke mit Rüschen und mysteriösen Elementen, für die Alexander keinen Namen wusste; Tops in allen erdenklichen Farbgradationen; Kleider in komplizierten und unaussprechlich scheußlichen Mustern. Das tat sie öfter: Stundenlang sortierte und inspizierte sie, hielt einzelne Teile ins Licht und runzelte die Stirn, als seien diese Kleidungsstücke – wie alles andere auch – nicht halb so schön, wie sie sie in Erinnerung gehabt hatte.

»Du bist ja wach«, sagte Nina. »Würdest du mir wohl den Koffer da geben?«

»Was machst du da?« Er hievte den Koffer aus den Tiefen des Kleiderschranks hervor. »Den brauche ich für Perm, weißt du.«

»Sie sind ohne dich gefahren«, sagte sie. »Viktor und die Amerikanerin. Wenn ich das richtig sehe, haben sie umgebucht. Sie sind mitten in der Nacht los. Sie hat einen Zettel dagelassen. Keine Ahnung, warum.«

»Was?«

Sie zuckte mit den Achseln. »Sieht so aus, als hättest du ihnen keine Wahl gelassen.«

»Was?« Ein panisches Ekelgefühl regte sich hinter seinem Herzen – die dämmernde Erkenntnis, dass ein schrecklicher Fehler geschehen war; das Übelkeit erregende Gefühl, ein ganzes Leben verschlafen zu haben.

Nina fing an, ihre Kleider in den Koffer zu werfen. »Sie wollten natürlich nicht, dass du fährst. Sie wollten dich natürlich beschützen. Davon hängt schließlich alles ab, oder? Das ist doch der Sinn der ganzen Operation?« Sie rieb sich gewaltsam mit den Fingerknöcheln die Augen, die rotgerändert waren von Salz und Reue. »Früher hättest du wohl gesagt, es war ein forcierter Zug, nehme ich an.«

»Ich muss da hin.«

»Du musst da hin? Deine Frau verlässt dich gerade, ist dir das schon aufgefallen? Das bedeutet das alles hier.« Sie zeigte auf ihre Reisetaschen. Sie standen neben der Tür aufgereiht und sahen aus wie die Krokodile, aus denen sie entstanden waren. »Wenn du so was siehst, solltest du eigentlich versuchen, mich aufzuhalten.«

Nina wurde von dem Licht, das durch die Tür hereindrang, von hinten beleuchtet. Ihr rotes Haar sah schöner aus als je zuvor, und er erinnerte sich daran, wie sie ausgesehen hatte, als er sie zum ersten Mal traf – unerträglich schön, unerträglich zart, eine Frau, bei der man sein Leben mit dem Versuch zubringen konnte, sie zu verstehen und zufriedenzustellen. Er fragte sich, was er damals an diesem Vorhaben so reizvoll gefunden hatte. Vielleicht war es ein Bedürfnis, das aus der Zeit mit Elisabeta zurückgeblieben war. So heftig und aus so großer Distanz zu lieben; zu erleben, wie die Luft ständig blau schillernd statisch geladen ist; den Umriss des Raums, der zwischen zwei Menschen liegt, als die spürbarste Kontur seines Lebens kennenzulernen – nach all diesen Erfahrungen war ihm eine feste Bindung als einzig lebbare Alternative erschienen, wie klein und trivial, wie alltäglich und anstrengend diese Bindung auch war.

»Eigentlich«, sagte Nina, »solltest du mich jetzt anflehen und fragen, ob es nicht irgendwas, irgendetwas gibt, das du tun kannst, damit ich bleibe.«

»Nina«, sagte er. »Können wir nicht später darüber reden?«

Oder vielleicht war es etwas anderes. Vielleicht war der lebenslange Anspruch, Russland zu reformieren, so abstrakt und unmöglich zu erfüllen, dass ihm das kleinere Ziel – eine schwierige Frau glücklich zu machen – erreichbarer erschienen war. Aber es war nicht erreichbarer. Die Demokratie würde durch die Straßen fegen, eine freie Presse den Chor scharfzüngiger Unzufriedenheit anstimmen, ein transparentes, funktionierendes Gesetzeswerk würde die Macht der Regierung einhegen, ehe jemand Nina glücklich machte. Das war einfach etwas, was Alexander nicht mehr miterleben würde.

»Ich fahre zum Flughafen, Nina«, sagte er.

»Schön«, sagte sie. »Wenn du wiederkommst, bin ich weg.«

»Ich weiß.«

Er trat auf sie zu und strich ihr über die Wange, und zum ersten Mal seit Langem ließ sie es zu. In gewisser Weise bewunderte er sie für das, was sie tat. Er war unglücklich, aber Nina war in seinem abgeschotteten Leben die einzige Konstante. Sie konnte gehen, und er wurde dadurch nicht unabhängiger; sie konnte gehen, und er würde niemanden Neues finden; sie konnte gehen, und er konnte noch lange nicht tun, was er wollte. Das einzige persönliche Glück, das er kannte, bestand in den kleinen Freuden eines wohlgeordneten häuslichen Lebens; er hatte sich immer eingeredet, dass die größere, bedeutendere Befriedigung ihm noch bevorstand. Was Nina anging, so hatte er gewusst, dass sie genauso unglücklich war, aber er hatte geglaubt, dass sie die Wohnung viel zu sehr mochte, um sie je zu verlassen. Dass er sich darin geirrt hatte, flößte ihm – ein wenig zumindest, im Nachhinein – Respekt vor ihr ein.

»Ich kann so nicht leben«, sagte sie. »Und es ist kein Ende abzusehen. Es kann nur damit enden, dass ich Witwe werde. Das ist der einzige Ausweg, der mir bleibt.«

Er verstand, und wie alles, was man endlich begreift, konnte er gar nicht fassen, dass er es so lange nicht begriffen hatte. Er verstand, wie sie sich auf ihre Weise danach gesehnt hatte: nach der leeren Wohnung, ohne die vielen Fremden, die Debatten und das unaufhörliche Tastaturgeklapper; nach der glitzernden Stadt draußen vor den Fenstern, deren ganzes Potential mit Geld oder Schönheit zu kaufen war. »Hast du deshalb nie Angst um mich gehabt?«, fragte er.

»Vielleicht. Vielleicht deshalb, wenn wir wirklich ehrlich miteinander sind.«

»Na ja«, sagte Alexander behutsam. »Das erklärt einiges.«

Sie weinte jetzt, lautlos, die Hände zu zornigen Fäusten geballt, und das Haar strömte ihren Rücken herab. »Ich habe einfach gedacht, du wärst ganz anders. Ich habe gedacht …« – und sie wies hilflos mit dem Arm auf den Anblick, den die Wohnung bot, auf die Papierstapel, die den orientalischen Teppich verschandelten, auf die Schreibmaschinen und Laptops und die Kabel und Leitungen, die unter den Teakholztischen hervorkrochen und sich um die Türflügel wanden – »Ich habe mir das alles einfach anders vorgestellt.«

»Ich weiß«, sagte Alexander. »Das habe ich bestimmt auch einmal getan.«

Er zog sie zu sich heran und fühlte durch die dünne Schicht Kaschmir die schroffen Felsvorsprünge ihrer Schulterblätter. Er wusste nicht mehr, wann er sie zuletzt umarmt hatte, ohne dass sich ihr Rücken versteifte, ohne das Gefühl, eine scharf bewachte Grenze zu überschreiten.

»Es tut mir leid«, sagte sie. »Aber es bedeutet mir eben nicht so viel wie dir. Ich kann damit nichts anfangen. Ich glaube, die Demokratie wird unser Land zerstören, falls du es wissen willst. Wenn du mich je gefragt hättest, wüsstest du es schon.«

Er nickte in ihr Haar hinein und atmete den Geruch ihres fremdartigen, teuren Shampoos – Weide oder Aloe Vera oder Jojoba-Perlen von Gott-weiß-woher.

»Vielleicht hast du recht«, sagte er. »Du bist nicht die Einzige, die so denkt.«

Sie sah ihn traurig an, und er konnte zusehen, wie sie begriff, dass er ein noch merkwürdigerer und lachhafterer Mensch war, als sie befürchtet hatte. Er konnte zusehen, wie sie sein Gesicht betrachtete und sich darauf vorbereitete, den Anblick in ihrem Gedächtnis abzuspeichern. Dann wurde ihr Ausdruck weicher, verschwommener – es sah aus wie der Moment, wo jemand eine Kante loslässt, an die er sich so lange geklammert hat, dass es eine Erleichterung ist aufzugeben und man den Absturz akzeptiert.

»Der Flughafen, Nina«, sagte er. »Ich muss los.«

»Okay, Grib«, sagte sie. »Ich fahre dich hin.«

Also fuhr sie ihn – trockenen Auges – quer durch St. Petersburg. Er ließ sich tief in den Beifahrersitz sinken und trug eine Sonnenbrille, und sie hatte ihr Haar unter einem Tuch verborgen, und so glitten sie durch die Straßen. Vlad saß auf der Rückbank, starrte und murmelte finster vor sich hin und flehte Alexander an, einen seiner Fahrer zu rufen.

Die Stadt war zu dieser Jahreszeit voller grüner Bäume, und ihre Schatten zogen sich wie Spinnennetze über den Boden. Uralte Luft stieg von der Newa auf und verdichtete sich zu kleinen Wirbeln aus Blütenblättern, Zeitungsseiten und leuchtend buntem Einwickelpapier. Seine Frau hatte ihn gerade verlassen, seine Mitarbeiter hatten gemeutert, und dennoch war Alexander seltsam euphorisch. Er legte eine Hand an die Fensterscheibe, die seine Angestellten immer kristallklar putzten. Die Straßen waren von legalen und illegalen Taxis überfüllt und von Luxusautos in Panzergröße. In dem Wagen neben ihm tippte eine Frau ihrem Ehemann an die Schulter und zeigte auf Alexander.

»Hören Sie«, sagte Vlad. »Was Sie da tun, ist sehr, sehr unüberlegt.«

»Es ist helllichter Tag«, sagte Alexander. »Wir sind mitten auf der Straße.«

»Sie sind unvernünftig. Ich weiß nicht, was mit Ihnen los ist, aber Sie sind wirklich sehr unvernünftig.«

»Ich werde gleich noch viel unvernünftiger.«

Nina beschleunigte. Überall um sie herum brummte das Großstadtleben – die Straßenhändler, der stockende Verkehr, die wild im Wind tanzenden Bäume. Fehlzündungen knallten wie Pistolenschüsse, und die Kanäle zitterten, als hätten sie Angst. Alexander und Nina rasten über die graue Ausfallstraße dahin, ließen Petersburgs altvertraute Silhouette hinter sich, und dann bogen sie in die Pilotow Uliza ein, die zum Flughafen Pulkowo führte. Am Abflugterminal bremste Nina ab, ohne ganz anzuhalten. »Viel Glück, Grib«, sagte sie. Ihre Stimme schwankte ein wenig und fing sich wieder.

Damit fuhr sie in dem Auto davon – das jetzt ihr Auto war, dachte Alexander, obwohl es keine große Rolle spielte – und verschwand in der hupenden Menge von Taxis und Limousinen. Alexander drehte sich zu Vlad um und bat ihn, zum Ticketschalter zu laufen. Sie rannten los, erschreckten eine Dame mit einem langen mottenzerfressenen Pelzmantel und einem Hund in Meerschweingröße und umrundeten einen strengen älteren Herrn, der empört mit dem Gehstock fuchtelte.

Irgendwo mitten in diesem Spurt fand Alexander einen Augenblick Zeit, es zu genießen – das beglückende Gefühl, ohne Wegbeschreibung, ohne Fahrplan, ohne Strategien für jedes denkbare Sicherheitsrisiko in der Öffentlichkeit zu sein, ohne eine Armee von Helfern und Aufpassern. Es lag ein kleines Hochgefühl darin – nicht so stark wie bei der Aufhebung der Leibeigenschaft oder dem Abzug der Armee aus Moskau oder bei freien Wahlen in einer unvorstellbar fernen Zukunft, aber doch nicht zu verachten: Das kleine Glück, sich den eigenen Weg durch eine unübersichtliche Welt zu bahnen, zu stolpern, ohne dass es jemand sah, und sich dem Risiko auszusetzen, selber Fehler zu begehen.

KAPITEL 20

Irina
Perm, Juni 2007

Viktor und ich hatten uns darauf geeinigt, zu fahren. Ich hatte ihn spätabends angerufen – nachdem er stundenlang mit Boris getrunken, seinen Schimpftiraden gelauscht und unglücklich dazu mit dem Kopf genickt hatte – und gesagt: »Wir fahren doch noch?« Am anderen Ende der Leitung hatte Schweigen geherrscht, aber ich hatte von vornherein gewusst, womit es enden würde. Er sagte: »Wie wäre es mit morgen?«

Wir hatten uns frühmorgens in die Wohnung geschlichen, noch bevor Vlad seinen Dienst angetreten hatte. Viktor hatte einen eigenen Schlüssel bekommen, als Alexander ihn gut genug kannte, um ihn für loyal zu halten, und nicht gut genug, um zu ahnen, wozu diese Loyalität ihn treiben würde. Ein Netz aus Tau hatte sich über die Fensterscheiben gebreitet, und ein übereifriges, gebrochenes Licht schien herein. Es war die Sorte Licht, die sich dir vor die Füße wirft und um Gnade winselt. Oder die Sorte, die sich im Namen der Ehre in ein Messer stürzt.

Nina war an jenem letzten Morgen in St. Petersburg seltsam gütig zu mir. Wir hatten uns gegenseitig bei verstohlenen Handlungen erwischt – sie räumte gerade die teuren Seifen aus dem Badezimmerschrank, und ich schmuggelte einen Zettel in Alexanders Jackentasche.

»Also fahrt ihr doch?«, hatte sie gefragt, und während ihr Mund zu einem vage missbilligenden Ausdruck verzogen war, lag in ihrer Stimme etwas Ruppiges, das mir Vertrauen einflößte. Es rief flüchtig ein Bild von der Person wach, die sie vielleicht einmal gewesen war: jünger und raubeiniger, ein Mensch, der sich regen musste, um genug zu essen und zu tun zu haben. Ich verstand plötzlich, wie es dazu kommen konnte, dass jemand die meiste Zeit damit zubrachte, sich in einem riesigen seidenen Bett herumzuwälzen oder die zarten Knospen überteuerter Ohrgehänge zu betasten. Nichts lässt einen Menschen so materialistisch werden wie harte Entbehrungen.

(Jetzt, im Flugzeug, löst diese kleine Beobachtung ganze Gedankenkaskaden in mir aus; ich entwirre die vielen Einzelfäden meines eigenen Verlusts, koste jede Nuance dieser speziellen Katastrophe aus. Wie werde ich meine eigene Form des Materialismus vermissen, die kostbaren sinnlichen Freuden des Daseins. Nicht nur die jenseitigen, entrückenden Ausblicke oder Symphonien, Epen oder Orgasmen, so wichtig sie waren. Da waren auch – und nicht weniger wichtig – die bescheidenen Genüsse, auszuschlafen oder ein richtig gutes Sandwich zu essen. Und da war die Möglichkeit, solche Beobachtungen zu machen wie bei der Begegnung mit Nina: die Möglichkeit, dass die Welt sich ganz leicht zur Seite neigte, wenn man gerade glaubte, man hätte alle ihre potentiellen Positionen kennengelernt. Außerdem war da das Glück, die Schicksale und Hintergründe fremder Menschen und Länder zu erkunden, die immer so viel merkwürdiger und zwingender waren als jedes erfundene Schicksal auf dem Papier. Wie ich das alles vermissen werde. Aber dann erinnere ich mich wieder an die offensichtliche Tatsache – die ich wieder und wieder verstanden und doch nie ganz geglaubt habe, nicht einmal jetzt, im Flugzeug, wo die stille Landschaft unter uns dahinzieht –, dass nichts von alledem, ob kostbar oder nicht, je von irgendwem vermisst werden wird.)

Nina jedenfalls wurde an jenem Morgen zu unserer Komplizin, schlich in das Schlafzimmer, das sie nicht länger mit Alexander teilen würde, und drehte die Klimaanlage auf, damit er nicht hörte, wie wir die Unterlagen durchblätterten, in Notizbüchern herumschnüffelten, die Kameraausrüstung einpackten und die Kreditkarte einsteckten, von der Alexander alle Filmkosten abbuchen ließ. Was auch immer der Film letztendlich bewirken wird – und da ich es nie sicher wissen werde, spekuliere ich umso eifriger darüber –, Russland wird sein Zustandekommen unter anderem auch Nina zu verdanken haben.

Dann rasten wir durch die frühmorgendliche Stadt. In der Ferne hielten sich noch dunkle Flecken am Himmel, und die Sterne erblassten wie das Gesicht eines Menschen, der Angst hat und beschließt, sich nichts anmerken zu lassen. Ich lächelte Viktor im Halbdunkel zu, obwohl er es wahrscheinlich nicht erkennen konnte.

Hier, im Flugzeug, füge ich auch das meinem Katalog der Dankbarkeit hinzu, irgendwo zwischen dem Sandwich und der Symphonie: das Gefühl, sehr früh aufzustehen, um etwas sehr Wichtiges zu tun.

Die Triebwerke surrten schon, als wir Alexander auf das Rollfeld laufen sahen. Er war mit ungeahnter Geschwindigkeit unterwegs; aus der Entfernung wirkte er gesetzter, älter als von nahem, wenn er ungeduldig gestikulierte oder sprachgymnastische Höchstleistungen vollführte. Ein neon-orange gekleideter Flughafenangestellter hielt ihn an und schickte ihn unerbittlich wieder zurück. Wir konnten gerade noch die wütende Kurve seines Nackens erkennen und erschauderten bei der Vorstellung, was für Worte er wohl gerade von sich gab. Aber das Flugzeug setzte sich in Bewegung, und Alexander blieb kleiner und kleiner hinter uns zurück. Und wir wussten, was zu tun war.

Er konnte am nächsten Tag, mit dem nächsten Flugzeug nachkommen. Natürlich konnte er das, und das wussten wir auch. Aber ich hatte seine Kiste voller Morddrohungen gesehen und hatte erlebt, wie er sie anstarrte. Ich wusste, dass wir ihm mit dem, was wir vorhatten, die Möglichkeit ließen, uns nicht zu folgen.

Viktor und ich sahen einander im Flugzeug schweigend an. Ich vermute, dass Viktor sich fragte, worauf er sich da eingelassen hatte – ob er seinen Job verlieren würde; ob er eines Tages, in einem weiseren, enthaltsameren Alter auf diesen Augenblick als diejenige Fehlentscheidung zurückblicken würde, von der ab alles katastrophal schiefgegangen war. Ich hatte solche Sorgen nicht mehr. Ich wusste nicht, wie diese Reise verlaufen würde, was dabei herauskäme oder ob sie ein Fehler war. Aber ich wusste, dass ich von keinem entlegenen Standpunkt aus je mit irgendwelchen Gefühlen – Stolz oder Reue oder Trauer oder Schuld oder triefäugiger Nostalgie – auf sie zurückblicken würde. Die Person, die ich jetzt war, würde ich immer bleiben. Und was ich tat, mussten andere einst bewundern, verachten oder korrigieren.

Die Landschaft unter uns wurde allmählich ländlicher: matte beigefarbene und eierschalenfarbene Flächen; die Ballungen kleiner Dörfer; langgestreckte Felder voller Phlox oder Silbergras, von vereinzelten Bächen wie von Adern durchzogen. Ich habe es schon immer geliebt, zu fliegen und zuzusehen, wie sich die Welt in ihre einfachsten Bestandteile auflöst: reine, gedämpfte Farben; klare geometrische Muster. Wenn man vom Flugzeug aus auf alles herabsieht, fällt es schwer, irgendetwas allzu ernst oder zu schwer zu nehmen. Von oben sehen die Welt als Ganzes und ihre vielen wimmelnden Zivilisationen nicht komplexer als eine Serie von Höhlenmalereien aus.

Ich dachte an meinen Flug nach Moskau vor so vielen Monaten zurück. Die Person, die ich vor meiner Ankunft in Russland gewesen war, die durch Cambridge spaziert war, sich verliebt hatte und zum Zeitvertreib mit einem seltsamen Schweden Schach spielte – diese Person kam mir so weit entfernt vor, als sei sie eine Erinnerung an ein früheres Leben oder eine Zwillingsschwester, mit der ich eine störanfällige und doch beständige parapsychologische Verbindung unterhielt. Ich blickte auf diese Person – auf dieses Leben – mit einem Gefühl zurück, das an Gleichgültigkeit grenzte. Ich erkannte durchaus an, dass da etwas Wichtiges gewesen war und dass es Erinnerungen gegeben hatte, an die die andere Frau sich geklammert hatte, wie wir alle an unseren geliebten kleinen Souvenirs festhalten. Aber diese Frau war nicht länger ich. Oder wenn doch, würde sie es nicht mehr lange sein.

Nach den ersten paar Flugminuten drehte Viktor sich zu mir um und starrte mich lange und beunruhigend an.

»Ja?«, sagte ich. »Was ist? Hast du Bedenken? Dafür ist es jetzt zu spät.«

Er starrte immer noch, so lange, dass ich mich zu fragen begann, was Alexander ihm über mich verraten hatte.

»Also, jetzt, wo wir zusammen in dieser Sache drinhängen, gibt es ein paar Dinge, die ich wissen muss«, sagte er.

»Okay«, sagte ich zögernd. Ich dachte daran, dass es auch für mich Dinge gab, die ich wissen musste, und dass das noch lange nicht hieß, dass ich sie auch erfahren würde.

»Wer bist du? Ich meine, wer bist du wirklich?« Ich sah ihn an. Vieleicht hatte er mich das schon immer fragen wollen. Vielleicht hatte er gedacht, es könnte Alexander verärgern oder Boris gegen ihn aufbringen, wenn er es tat. Oder vielleicht ist es einfach eine von diesen Fragen, die man immer erst dann stellt, wenn es für eine richtige Antwort zu spät ist.

»Wie meinst du das überhaupt?«

»Ich meine –« Er seufzte und schloss die Augen. Ich konnte sehen, wie er sich abmühte, eine diplomatische Formulierung zu finden. »Ich meine, warum bist du hergekommen? Was ist das hier, außer einer Flucht? Weglaufen kann jeder. Weglaufen kann jeder, und zwar egal wovor. Man muss nicht im Sterben liegen, um so was wie das hier tun zu wollen. Ich meine – warum hier? Und warum ausgerechnet das hier?«

Ehe ich mich versah, erzählte ich es ihm – erzählte ihm Dinge, die ich noch nie irgendjemandem erzählt hatte, Dinge, von denen ich selbst nicht gewusst hatte, dass ich sie wusste, bis ich sie erzählte, und dann wurden sie im Nachhinein unbezweifelbar wahr. Ich erzählte von der letzten Schachpartie mit meinem Vater, wie sie zugleich eine Segnung und ein Moment der Fassungslosigkeit gewesen war: Sie hatte den Beginn meines Erwachsenseins markiert und den Abschied meines Vaters in die Bedeutungslosigkeit angekündigt. Nachdem mein Vater aus unserem Leben verschwunden war, hatte ich begonnen, zurückzublicken und nach Hinweisen darauf zu suchen, wer er gewesen war, was ihm etwas bedeutet hatte, wie er der Welt einen Sinn abgewann und wie er sich seinem nahenden Ende stellte. Die Masse der Informationen aus-

zufiltern, die er hinterließ, war so, als würde man in einem Fluss-
bett wühlen und zwischen den Kieseln nach Fossilien suchen. Aber
irgendwann hatte ich ein Bruchstück namens Alexander aus dem
Morast gezogen, hatte seinen matten Glanz begutachtet und beschlossen, das hier – genau das – sei ein entscheidender Hinweis
oder ein fehlendes Bindeglied oder ein Holzspan, den mir ein gött-
licher Scherzbold untergejubelt hatte, um mein Schicksal aufzu-
mischen. ·

Und dann erzählte ich von dem unerträglichen Druck, den es
bedeutete, vor den Augen meiner Bekannten würdevoll sterben zu
wollen. Dann war da die kindische Vorstellung, jenes Ding, das
mich hetzte, könnte sich irgendwie abschütteln lassen – die nur zu
drei Vierteln ironisch gemeinte Hoffnung, Chorea Huntington
werde kein Visum bekommen. Noch kindlicher und beschämen-
der war die flüchtige Frage, ob mein Vater überhaupt gestorben
war. Ich hatte den ganzen Verfallsprozess vom Über-Ich zum Zell-
haufen miterlebt, aber ich hatte schon als Kind die Klugheit besessen, den Dingen auf den Grund zu gehen, statt ihrem äußeren Anschein zu vertrauen. Wie konnte denn der Mann, den ich vor mir
sah – der Mann, der mit den Armen ruderte und schrie, der Gegenstände quer durchs Zimmer warf und auf den Konzertflügel
schiss –, wie konnte das derselbe sein, der Chorarrangements für
Werke von Bach geschaffen hatte, der einfache Gespräche in unvorstellbar vielen Sprachen führen konnte, der Geopolitik mitver-
folgte wie andere ihre Lieblingssportart? Selbst als junges Mädchen
hatte ich den Verdacht, das alles sei ein Täuschungsmanöver. Das
zerfurchte Gesicht dieses Mannes war nicht das Gesicht meines Vaters; dies abgehackte Gefuchtel waren nicht seine Gesten. Wenn
dieser Mann nicht mein Vater war, war mein Vater nicht hier. Und
wenn mein Vater nicht hier war, war er anderswo – vielleicht hatte
er alle überlistet, so wie er mich auf dem Schachbrett immer über-
listete, damals, bis er es nicht mehr konnte.

All das erzählte ich Viktor. Und dann sagte ich noch etwas viel
Einfacheres, ebenso Wahres: Manchmal gibt es Dinge, die wir über

uns selbst nicht wissen. Manchmal fehlt uns die Zeit, um sie zu entwirren, und wir müssen uns mit einem Schulterzucken zufriedengeben. Aber ich glaube, es gibt auch Dinge, die wir selbst dann nicht verstehen würden, wenn wir unendlich viel Zeit hätten, darüber nachzugrübeln. Dinge, die wir niemals wissen werden, noch nach vielen langen Lebzeiten nicht.

Der Flug nach Perm dauerte nur vier Stunden, und ich schlief die meiste Zeit. Wir landeten, schlurften von Bord und mieteten verdrossen ein Auto, wie verkaterte Teenager, die ahnen, dass sie in einem Augenblick hochprozentiger Inspiration ihren Zukunftsaussichten irreparablen Schaden zugefügt haben. Ich ließ Viktor ans Steuer.

Wir schwiegen auf dem Weg am Ufer der Kama entlang. Ich fuhr das Fenster herunter und sah aufs Wasser hinaus – blau wie eine Oberschenkelvene floss sie fünf verschiedenen Seen entgegen. Irgendwo hinter den Bäumen lagen die Ruinen von Perm-36, aber wir hatten nicht die Zeit, danach zu suchen. Selbst wenn wir sie gehabt hätten, wäre wohl nicht viel zu sehen gewesen: Eine geisterhafte steinerne Inselkette, die Spreu eines Stacheldrahtzauns, ein paar verdorrte Bäume. Durch das Wagenfenster wehte moosige, satte Luft herein und der komplexe metallene Geruch der Schwerindustrie. Die Silhouette der Stadt war so seltsam gezahnt, dass es aussah, als hätte sich der Horizont verschoben: Gebäude sprangen, als wir näher kamen, in bizarren Winkeln auf uns zu, und in der Ferne spürten wir die imposanten Massen des Urals, die gekrümmten Bergrücken, die wie versteinerte Oger den Zugang nach Asien bewachten. Und zwischen ihnen, wer weiß, matte Flecken interkontinentalen Lichts, die ihre Konturen ausleuchteten und die Vorgebirge in Lampiongirlanden verwandelten. Und noch dahinter: sieben weitere Zeitzonen. Fast konnte man sie sehen, wenn man die Augen zusammenkniff: Zehntausende Weizenfelder, überwucherte Agrarkollektive, wo die Natur die Industrie zurückgedrängt hatte. Die unbeugsame Taiga, von einzelnen Spuren des sonderbaren Universums leicht gesprenkelt: ein verfallenes Raketensilo hier, da ein Kometenkrater. Und jenseits davon: eine Ansammlung von Inseln aus Vulkangestein, und dann Amerika. Wenn ich die Augen schloss und daran dachte, wurde mir beinahe schwindelig. Ich bin nicht bereit zu sterben. Noch lange nicht. Mir ist noch nicht einmal die Tatsache langweilig geworden, dass die Erde eine Kugel ist.

Draußen vor den Fenstern leuchtete eine brutale Sonne, grell und abschreckend wie ein bloßgelegtes Organ.

Wir checkten in einem Hostel ein, das meinem alten Hostel ähnlich war. Ich dachte an meine Sachen in jener Unterkunft, die so etwas wie ein Zuhause gewesen war – meinen Stapel aus Myriaden von Büchern und Anziehsachen, aus lauter Dingen, die ich bald würde unerbittlich prüfen und verstauen müssen wie ein Pathologe bei der Autopsie. Besser, ich ließ gar nichts zurück als so wenig – gerade genug, dass die Leute erkennen konnten, dass ich *Krieg und Frieden* nur zu zwei Dritteln gelesen hatte und eine Vorliebe für Hemden mit Krägen besaß.

Wir fanden wortlos unser Zimmer und ließen die Koffer auf die Krankenhausbetten plumpsen. Viktor drehte sich in seiner Ecke zur Wand und zog sich um. Ich musterte ihn mit einem Gefühl, das ich als eine Art Begehren erkannte, obwohl es ein wenig ausgebleicht, ein bisschen blutleer war. Es hatte nichts mit ihm persönlich zu tun, glaube ich – obwohl er durchaus schöne Augen hatte. Sondern er war ein Mann, wir waren in einer Art Hotel, und ich lag im Sterben. Und Sex steht in dem Ruf, einen mit der Ewigkeit oder der Unendlichkeit in Kontakt zu bringen oder so ähnlich – auch wenn ich befürchtete, er könnte in diesem Kontext genau das Gegenteil tun. Vielleicht würde das Aufklatschen von Haut auf Haut mich gerade umgekehrt an unsere sture Körperlichkeit erinnern. Vielleicht müsste ich an die Evolution denken, an Genetik und Kontinuität, an die Zukunft, und vielleicht müsste ich daran denken, dass Sex seinem Wesen nach ein Akt der Hoffnung war, und dann ginge es mir danach schlechter, als wenn wir gar nicht erst damit angefangen hätten. Außerdem war Jonathan nicht hier – das Leben mit ihm war unwiederbringlich, ob ich nun umkehrte und am nächsten Tag nach Hause flog oder ob ich mich eine Nacht lang an die Knochen eines anderen klammerte.

Ich hatte es mir gerade so gut wie ausgeredet, als Viktor mich bei der Hüfte packte und mir fest in die Augen sah. Er beugte sich vor. Und dann zerrten wir an Kleidern und Haut und Haar, und ich gewann die Oberhand, und wir rangen miteinander, als kämpften wir mit unserer eigenen Sterblichkeit: Es war Alles-oder-nichts-Sex, es war Todestrakt-Sex. Wir klammerten uns aneinander fest – fremd, weil wir einander so noch nie begegnet waren, und vertraut, weil wir beide Menschen waren und beide gerade noch am Leben. Er roch nach Basilikum. Wir schrien an der Schulter des anderen, und es war aus Angst, glaube ich, ebenso wie vor Lust. Es war, als schrien wir in den Weltuntergang.

Danach berührte er mich an der Schulter. »Noch eine Frage«, sagte er.

»Ja.«

»Die ganze Sache mit den Niederlagen und wie man ihnen begegnen soll –«, sagte er, »glaubst du, du hast darüber was von Alexander gelernt?«

»Ich bin schließlich hier, oder? Wir sind beide hier.«

»Und das ist alles?«

»Ich glaube, alles, was man angesichts des Untergangs tun kann, ist, pünktlich da zu sein.«

Draußen malten Fledermäuse Schattengespinste an den Himmel. Ich vergrub den Kopf an Viktors Schulter und wickelte mich in die kratzige Decke. Für eine bestimmte Bevölkerungsgruppe war es noch früh. Unten auf der Straße kam die Stadt in die Gänge wie ein rostiger Automotor, und die ganze Nacht drang ausgelassenes Gelächter zu mir herein.

Für das Interview mit Simonow hatten wir ein Hotelzimmer im Stadtzentrum von Perm gebucht. Am Tag nach unserer Ankunft fuhren Viktor und ich schweigend dorthin. Die Stadt um uns herum ging an ihren Enden in weiße Felder und in den weiten weißen Himmel über. Die Sonne ging auf und begann ein vorläufiges Licht auszuschwitzen. Ich fuhr mein Fenster herunter und atmete den Geruch von kaltem Matsch und die blutigen Ausdünstungen rostiger Autos.

Im Hotel bestellten wir mit Hilfe von Alexanders Kreditkarte alles, was der Zimmerservice zu bieten hatte. Nach einer halben Stunde kam Simonow. Er klopfte an die Tür. »Ihr seid also die Filmstudenten?«, fragte er.

Wir ließen ihn ein. Er hatte ein wettergegerbtes, zerklüftetes, mit einer bescheidenen Auswahl zinkfarbener Zähne bestücktes Gesicht. Von seiner Hand baumelte eine Kalaschnikow herab, schlaff wie ein ausgekugelter Unterarm. Es war eine ungewöhnliche Art, eine Waffe zu tragen.

»Danke, dass Sie sich mit uns treffen«, sagten wir, und dann sahen wir Simonow eine Weile beim Essen, Trinken und Rauchen zu. Er stocherte in seinem Schweinefleisch herum und schlürfte seine Drinks. Wir bauten die Kamera auf und stellten sie mit gespreizten Beinen in eine Ecke. Simonow musterte sie und begann repetitiv wie ein autistisches Kind mit dem Knie zu wippen. Vielleicht, wurde mir klar, litt er an Lampenfieber.

Nachdem wir alle ein paar Gläser getrunken hatten, stellten wir Simonow unsere ersten Fragen. Wir befragten ihn nach seiner Kindheit, seiner Karriere, seiner Meinung über die überlegene Größe der russischen Armee. Er trank. Wir tranken. Wir schalteten die Kamera ab, und Viktor machte anzügliche Witze. Simonow lachte. Wir schalteten die Kamera wieder an und fragten ihn nach seiner Meinung zu den Spannungen in Georgien. Irgendwann hieb er mit der Faust auf den Tisch und brüllte, Russland sei der größte Waffenexporteur der Welt. Wir schalteten die Kamera ab. Er erzählte rührselig von seinen Kindern, seiner Frau. »Sie sieht aus wie eine Kartoffel«, sagte er. »Aber bei Gott, ich liebe sie.« Ich schielte zu Viktor hinüber. Wir schalteten die Kamera wieder an.

»Sie arbeiten schon lange hier in Perm«, flocht Viktor ein.

»Ja«, sagte Simonow. Er lehnte sich zurück. »Seit zehn Jahren.«

»Dann waren Sie auch 1999 hier«, sagte ich.

»Sonst wären es ja nicht zehn Jahre.«

»Dann waren Sie auch am 30. August 1999 hier«, sagte ich.

Er verspannte sich. »Ja«, sagte er gedehnt. In dem anschließenden Schweigen klang es, als machte die Kamera selbst ein leises Geräusch – das kaum hörbare Atmen fiebriger Erde oder von etwas, das auf etwas lauert. »Vermutlich.«

»Haben Sie bemerkt, dass in der Nacht erhebliche Mengen RDX verschwunden sind?«, fragte Viktor.

Simonow lachte, aber es klang wie eine Warnung. »Das ist ziemlich lange her«, sagte er.

»Vielleicht wissen Sie es ja noch«, sagte Viktor, »weil es die Nacht vor dem ersten Sprengstoffanschlag war.«

Simonows Stimme wurde sehr leise. »Schaltet die Kamera ab«, sagte er, und Viktor gehorchte. Simonow sah uns mit einem völlig veränderten Ausdruck an – der Mund stand ihm offen, aber seine Augen verengten sich zu einem harten und überraschend nüchternen Blick. Dann lächelte er. »Eine komische Frage für zwei Filmstudenten.«

Ich sah Viktor an. Er wandte den Kopf ein wenig zur Seite.

»Ich weiß, wer ihr seid«, sagte Simonow. »Ich weiß, für wen ihr arbeitet.«

Ich wollte etwas sagen, aber Simonow winkte ab. »Er wird nicht gewinnen«, sagte er.

»Nein«, sagte Viktor.

»Dann sind wir uns ja einig«, sagte Simonow. »Und er dreht diesen Film. Habt ihr wirklich gedacht, ich hätte nicht davon gehört? Habt ihr wirklich gedacht, ich hätte keine Ahnung?«

Er lehnte sich zurück und betrachtete uns. Sein Blick wirkte betroffen und unentschlossen, als hätte er sein Leben lang auf diesen Moment gewartet, und jetzt, da er gekommen war, wüsste er nichts damit anzufangen. Lange saß er nur da, sah uns an und spitzte die

Lippen. »Ihr könnt von Glück sagen«, sagte er dann, »dass meine Tochter in Buinaksk gestorben ist.«

Ich lehnte mich zurück. »Wirklich?«

»Wirklich.«

»Das tut mir leid.«

Er sah zu Boden. Ich schielte zu Viktor hinüber. Ihm war anzusehen, wie gern er die Kamera wieder anschalten wollte, aber er ließ es bleiben. »Sie haben zwei Tage zu früh davon berichtet«, sagte Simonow. »Gennadi Selesnjow hat im Parlament verkündet, dass es in Buinaksk eine Explosion gegeben hatte, und ich hatte solche Angst um sie. Aber dann hat sie angerufen und gesagt ›Alles in Ordnung, Papa. Es war in Moskau. Es war ein Irrtum.‹ Zwei Tage später lebte sie nicht mehr. Sie müssen ihre Termine durcheinandergebracht haben.« Er biss sich auf die Fingerknöchel. Ich versuchte es mir vorzustellen. Es war schwer vorstellbar, was so ein Ereignis einem Menschen nahm.

Ich beugte mich vor. »Können Sie mit uns reden?«, fragte ich.

Simonow starrte vor sich hin. »Ich habe meine Tochter geliebt.«

»Natürlich«, sagte Viktor.

Simonow schüttelte den Kopf. »Ich habe sie geliebt«, sagte er noch einmal. »Aber ich habe auch andere Töchter. Ich habe eine Frau. Und ich genieße mein Leben, auch wenn das vielleicht pietätlos klingt. Ich kann nicht mit euch reden. Tut mir leid.«

Viktor sah mich hilfesuchend an. »Reden Sie mit uns«, sagte er. »Tun Sie es für Ihre Tochter.«

»Ich wusste nicht, was sie mit dem Zeug vorhatten«, sagte Simonow kläglich. »Ich dachte, es hätte mit dem Aufstand in Dagestan zu tun. Mit irgendwas im Ausland. Ich schwöre.«

»Wir glauben Ihnen«, sagte Viktor. »Wir glauben Ihnen.« Er lehnte sich vor. »Wie hieß Ihre Tochter?« Das war ein bisschen kaltschnäuzig, fand ich – aber auch ziemlich klug.

Simonow sah zu Boden. »Walentina«, sagte er schließlich.

»Das ist ein schöner Name«, sagte ich. Viktor sah mich an, wie um zu sagen, dass ich zu weit ging. Ein langes Schweigen folgte.

»Ich kann nicht mit euch reden«, sagte Simonow. »Aber ich kann euch nicht daran hindern, da einzubrechen.«

Viktor zog eine Augenbraue hoch und sah mich an.

»Ich kann euch nicht daran hindern«, sagte Simonow wieder. »Aber wenn ihr es tut, müsst ihr auch wirklich die Scheiben einschlagen.«

Wir taten es nachts, als Simonow wie versprochen die Wachmänner betrunken gemacht hatte. Wir konnten die Zecher hören, wie sie in einer Ecke des Geländes muntere Soldatenlieder schmetterten und beherzt ihre Flaschen auf die Tische knallten. Neben dem Verwaltungsgebäude standen halb im Matsch versunkene Geländewagen aufgereiht. Unter großen blauen Abdeckplanen staken verbogene Ausrüstungsteile hervor. Wir schlugen wirklich das Fenster ein, und dann kletterten wir hindurch – erst ich und dann Viktor. Ich blutete ein wenig oberhalb des Bauchnabels. Das Büro war klein und aufgeräumt, mit niedrigen Aktenschränken, die dunkel an den Wänden kauerten. Wir machten kein Licht, aber das war auch nicht nötig. Simonow hatte es uns leichtgemacht. Er hatte auf dem Schreibtisch Dokumente ausgebreitet, auf denen sachlich die Bestellung des FSB über eine Tonne des Sprengstoffs RDX verzeichnet war. Unterzeichnet war das Formular von Simonow selbst und datiert auf den 30. August 1999.

Wir schnappten uns das Dokument. Ein paar andere Papiere fegten wir vom Tisch, warfen einen Stuhl um und schmissen Simonows Mantel auf den Boden. Wir hinterließen Unordnung, richteten aber nicht viel Schaden an. Dann schoben wir uns wieder durch das Fenster – erst ich, dann Viktor. Ich spürte, wie einer der Splitter auf meinem Rücken einen Striemen hinterließ. Das Trinkgelage im Freizeitraum schien immer ausschweifender zu werden. Zitternd und triumphierend erreichten wir das Auto und fuhren ohne Licht langsam, langsam vom Gelände.

Selbst dann, selbst mitten in der Nacht wollte ich unbedingt wissen, wie es ausgehen würde. Selbst dann, als ich besser die Hacken in den Boden gestemmt hätte, um endlich innezuhalten, um jeden einzelnen Moment als unschätzbar wertvolle Verkörperung des geliebten Lebens auszukosten. Die Neugier hört nicht auf, auch wenn die Antwort bereits näher rückt – selbst wenn diese Antwort die Vernichtung der Frage durch die Vernichtung der Fragenden ist. Also war ich selbst dort im Auto, als jede Neugier auf die Zukunft beinahe ein selbstmörderischer Impuls war, gespannt, was als Nächstes geschehen würde.

Draußen vor den Fenstern leuchtete ein anämischer Mond. Ich lehnte mich in den Sitz zurück und spürte, wie mir das Blut heiß und flüchtig durch das Rückenmark pulsierte.

Um zwanzig nach sechs am Morgen geht unser Rückflug. Als wir zum Flughafen fahren, beginnt der Himmel gerade erst sein Licht zu verströmen, das mit glühenden, ausgestreckten Armen durch kleine Nadelstiche in der Wolkendecke bricht. Die Welt ist seltsamer und schöner, als es sich je jemand im Vorhinein vorstellen könnte. Mich überkommt eine unermessliche Dankbarkeit dafür, dass ich einen Teil davon zu Gesicht bekommen habe.

Letzte Nacht hat Viktor in unserem Zimmer im Hostel das Dokument abgefilmt. Er hat es beinahe ehrfürchtig in der Hand gehalten, als sei es ein Liebesbrief oder eine Schriftrolle vom Toten Meer, und hat jede inkriminierende Stelle einzeln angezoomt. Dann hat er das Video zusammen mit den wenigen Aufnahmen von Leutnant Andrei Simonow per Mail an Alexander verschickt. Zu guter Letzt hat er noch das gesamte Dokument eingescannt und mit angehängt. »Und wer weiß?«, hat er gesagt, als er den Computer heruntergefahren hat. »Vielleicht bringen wir ihm auch noch das Original.«

Auf dem halben Weg zum Flughafen sieht es aus, als verfolgte uns jemand. Ein weißes Auto, imposant wie ein gestrandeter Wal, wechselt hinter uns die Spuren und scheint einen Kontrapunkt auf unsere Bewegungen zu spielen – es bremst und beschleunigt genauso wie wir. Ich sehe mit hochgezogenen Augenbrauen zu Viktor hinüber, aber er ist mir weit voraus. Er beschleunigt, bremst, überholt und wechselt die Spur. Zehn Meter hinter uns macht das große weiße Auto jede unserer Bewegungen nach.

»Sie verfolgen uns«, sage ich.

Er hält seinen Blick auf die Straße gerichtet. »Das könnten sie sich auch sparen. Wir fahren doch offensichtlich zum Flughafen. Wo sollten wir sonst hin?«

Und so ist es, wenn man von einem großen weißen Auto verfolgt wird: Es bleibt einem nichts übrig, als weiterzufahren, selbst wenn man weiß, dass es hinter einem her ist.

Wir stehen am Check-in. Das Licht bricht sich in den riesigen Panoramafenstern und rutscht angeknackst und splitternd über die Bodenfliesen. Wir warten, aber inzwischen scheinen wir allein zu sein. Auf einem Fernsehbildschirm spricht Putin über Alexander; er sagt, seine Kandidatur sei rechtswidrig, lächerlich und kaum der Rede wert – nächste Frage, bitte.

Wir steigen ins Flugzeug, und Viktor überlässt mir den Fensterplatz. Der Flieger ist fast leer, stelle ich dankbar fest. Die Motoren ziehen an, und wir sind unterwegs – wir heben ab, und ich sehe unter mir das heillose Blau der Kama, die sich um die Stadt herumwindet. Ich sehe auf diesen rätselhaften, in Teilen vertrauten Ort herab und denke an die vielen anderen, die sich halbkonturiert in den Nischen meines Bewusstseins verstecken: die blendenden Wirbel aus Licht über den Anden; die geschlängelten, skulpturalen Dünen in Namibia; die uralten Städte, in denen Überreste aus Tausenden Jahren liegen geblieben sind – als der Vulkan ausbrach, als die Stadt geplündert wurde oder als die Pest durch die Straßen fegte und binnen einer Woche die halbe Stadt entvölkerte. Es gibt so vieles, das ich nicht gesehen habe. Aber es gibt auch Dinge, die habe ich gesehen. Vielleicht ist es genug, eine Zeitlang auf der Welt zu sein, selbst wenn man nie alles erlebt. Vielleicht ist es genug. Mir jedenfalls wird es reichen müssen.

Ich freue mich auf meine Rückkehr nach Petersburg, stelle ich fest, in die Stadt, die sich nie ganz fremd angefühlt hat, obwohl ich in ihr, wie überall sonst, eine Fremde war. Es ist keine originelle Beobachtung, aber sie überkommt mich mit einem Mal – wie bitterschön es ist, sich auf etwas so Einfaches zu freuen wie ein paar Schlucke von einer anderen Sorte Luft. Und irgendwo hinter meinem Herzen erklingt die Fermate eines Gefühls – eine leichte Hebung, dann ein Fallen, das sich nicht wie eine Auflösung anfühlt. Ich kneife die Augen zu, und dann öffne ich sie wieder und sehe zur Erde hinunter – mit jedem Blinzeln ist sie exponentiell weiter und weiter entfernt, mit jedem Herzschlag und Atemzug. So habe ich mich immer an Geburtstagen gefühlt, als ich jünger war, aber den Preis eines vergangenen Jahres schon kannte. Wie konnte ich das geschehen lassen?, dachte ich dann. Wie konnte ich das Leben so an mir vorbeiziehen lassen?

Ich lasse mich in meinen Sitz zurücksinken, und ich fühle, wie das Flugzeug sich aufschwingt, spüre seine Widerstandskraft gegen die sirrende Kälte, das unerbittliche Blau. Der Pilot lässt die Maschine sich in die Kurve legen, und wir werfen einen unglaublich detaillierten Schatten auf die Landschaft; wir sehen wie die Ankunft eines mythischen Vogels oder eines rachsüchtigen Gottes aus. Unter uns muss irgendwo zerwühltes Gras die Erde streifen, brodeln aufgebrachte, blass geränderte Blätter im Wind. Aber wir sehen diese Dinge nicht mehr.

Ich glaube, auch wenn ich mir nicht sicher bin, dass meine Hände stärker zittern als normal, dass sie sich immer ungenierter in Eigenregie fortbewegen. Ich sehe zu. Ich lege meine Hände auf den Falttisch, und sie beben und zucken.

Aber wer weiß, vielleicht ist es gar nicht pathologisch. Es könnte einfach ein Zeichen der Ehrfurcht sein. Vielleicht ist es einfach die Schönheit des Himmels und der Wolken – das Wunder eines frühen Morgens, die Häresie der Luftfahrt.

KAPITEL 21

Alexander
St. Petersburg, Sommer 2007 bis Frühjahr 2008

Letztendlich konnte er es sich nur vorstellen. Wissen würde er es nie, nicht genau jedenfalls, was geschehen war, oder wie es geschah, oder wie Irina und Viktor und die anderen es erlebten, einundzwanzig insgesamt, deren Namen und Nationalitäten Wochen später in winzigen Lettern in der Zeitung standen, als man die Suche eingestellt, das Gepäck zugeordnet und die Passagierliste bestätigt hatte. Er weiß es nicht, also wird er es sich vorstellen müssen.

Es war eine Bombe – eine kleine nur, von den effizienten Leuten des FSB ausgetüftelt, ein zischendes Knäuel aus Fasern und Feuer, das man leicht für einen technischen Defekt halten konnte. Er weiß es nicht, also muss er raten, dass sie kurz vor Helsinki waren – gleich hinter der Küste vielleicht, über der gischtenden, trüben Finnischen Bucht. Sie wollten gerade wenden, um den Flughafen anzusteuern. (Das, stellt er sich vor, war ein Fehler. Wäre die Bombe nur ein paar Augenblicke zu spät detoniert – oder wäre das Flugzeug außerplanmäßig früh angekommen –, dann hätte es leicht zu einem Absturz über der Stadt kommen können, was sehr viel mehr Schwierigkeiten gemacht und wahrscheinlich mehr Fragen aufgeworfen hätte.)

Sie dachten, Alexander sei an Bord, weil Mischa suggeriert hatte, es könnte so sein; vielleicht hatten sie Irina und Viktor in Perm verfolgt, und möglicherweise war ihnen aufgefallen, dass Alexander nicht dabei zu sein schien, aber sie glaubten vielleicht, er sei untergetaucht oder inkognito unterwegs oder läge im Kofferraum. Es gab hinreichend Grund zu glauben, er sei an Bord, also glaubten sie es, obwohl er aus genau diesen Gründen nie, niemals mit russischen Fluglinien flog, und obwohl sein Name nicht auf der Passagierliste stand. Vielleicht dachten sie, er hätte ein Pseudonym benutzt. Vielleicht hatten sie beschlossen, es darauf ankommen zu lassen. Und einen Monat danach, als Alexander seine Kreditkartenabrechnung bekam – mit den Hotelbuchungen, dem Zimmerservice und dem Alkohol, lauter Zahlungen in Perm, die alle seine Anwesenheit dort belegten –, starrte er sie lange nur an, bevor er anrief, um die Karte sperren zu lassen.

Letztendlich war es ein kalkulierbares Risiko. Ein Fehlschlag, mussten sie beschlossen haben, wäre wenig wert. Und ein Erfolg ziemlich viel.

Im Flugzeug, stellt Alexander sich vor, stürzten sie dreihundert Meter pro Sekunde, und es war das übliche Szenario: Herabbaumelnde Sauerstoffmasken und Flugbegleiter, die Kopf runter, *runter!* schrien. Menschen, die sich an Wildfremde klammerten, weil die soziale Etikette plötzlich, gewaltsam außer Kraft gesetzt war. Sie beteten in sechs Muttersprachen. Sie zitterten, weinten, übergaben sich. Hatte Irina Angst? Natürlich hatte sie Angst. Aber das Besondere war (denkt er, hofft er): Sie war es gewohnt.

Sie schossen auf das Wasser zu, und im Cockpit herrschte ein grauenvolles Schweigen, und dann fiel das Flugzeug auseinander – ein großes Auflösen in die Bestandteile, das auch Teile von Menschenleben mit sich riss. Die Fenster barsten, und Magazine und Kaugummipapiere, Teddybären und Zahnbürsten, Lidschattendöschen und Rosenkränze und Politikzeitschriften wurden hinaus und ins Wasser gefegt. Die Koffer versanken, und was später wieder zutage kam, war absurd und banal – Tennisschuhe, Ratgeberbücher, Büstenhalter. Nichts so Poetisches und Tragisches wie ein winziger Kinderschuh oder ein noch im Schmuckkästchen aufbewahrter Verlobungsring oder ein unveröffentlichter Roman. Die Menschen starben aus einem intakten Leben heraus, mitten in der Bewegung, und waren nicht bereit, auf ein einzelnes Symbol, eine Grabrede reduziert zu werden.

Und Irina? Betete sie, als sie starb, oder fluchte sie, oder verfluchte sie sich dafür, dass sie betete? Hielt sie die zarte Hand der alten Dame im Nebensitz, streichelte sie einer Gleichaltrigen den Arm? Flirtete sie im freien Fall mit einem schönen Fremden?

Weinte sie? Schrie sie? Erfuhr sie endlich, plötzlich, was sie unbedingt hatte wissen wollen?

Wir wissen es nicht, und Alexander zieht es vor, sich diesen Teil nicht vorzustellen.

Wir wissen nur, dass ein ozeanisches Licht in Böen anbrandete. Es war reinweiß, als sie auf das Wasser prallten. Letztendlich, stellt er sich gern vor, war es – wie viele traurige Ereignisse, wenn auch nicht alle – in gewisser Hinsicht wunderschön.

Die Botschaft wurde verständigt. Der amerikanischen Presse gefiel die Geschichte einer jungen Amerikanerin, die für ein Abenteuer und ein Schicksal alles hinter sich gelassen hatte. Viktor wurde in keiner Fernsehsendung erwähnt, weder in Amerika noch anderswo, nur die *Nowaja Gaseta* widmete ihm einen schönen Nachruf. Alexander weinte, als er ihn las – teils deshalb, weil dieser arme junge Mann gestorben war, und teilweise, weil die Zeitung so viele Dinge über ihn schrieb, nach denen Alexander nie gefragt und von denen er deshalb nichts geahnt hatte.

Das Interesse an Irina schwoll innerhalb einer Woche an und verebbte wieder. Dann erschien der letzte Harry-Potter-Band, und die Welt wurde von einem universalen Gefühl der Menschenliebe erfasst, wie es sonst nur die Olympiade oder der internationale Terrorismus hervorbringt. Einen Monat nach ihrem Tod war ihr Name ins Vergessen zurückgesunken, und wer sich doch noch an sie erinnerte, konnte sich nur den groben Umriss einer Geschichte ins Gedächtnis rufen – irgendetwas mit einer Amerikanerin, die nach Russland weggelaufen und dort aus Gründen gestorben war, an die man sich nicht erinnern konnte, wenn man sie überhaupt je gekannt hatte.

Für Alexander hatte das flüchtige posthume Interesse an Irina einige Nachteile. Es warf in gewissen Kreisen gewisse Fragen auf, Zweifel, die nie ganz ausgeräumt wurden. Aber im Großen und Ganzen stiegen seine Aktien nach dem Absturz ein wenig, in der Heimat wie im Ausland. Jeder wusste, wer das eigentliche Ziel des

Anschlags gewesen war, und selbst Menschen, die Alexander nicht ausstehen konnten, mussten zugeben, dass er Glück hatte, noch am Leben zu sein. (Mischa, der inzwischen ein gefragter politischer Kommentator war, sagte auf BBC, Alexander habe »fast verdächtig viel Glück«.) Jeder mochte die Vorstellung, dass die Regierung daran gescheitert war, jemanden aus dem Weg zu räumen, und einige betrachteten das ganze Geschehen sogar mit einer Art verblüffter Erheiterung. Später verglich ein alternder Talkmaster auf BBC Alexander einmal mit einem Zeichentrickvogel, der immer wieder einen bösartigen Kojoten überlistet – und Alexander war zum ersten Mal während einer Livesendung vollkommen vor den Kopf gestoßen und wusste nicht mehr, was er sagen sollte.

Wochenlang dachte Alexander unaufhörlich, ununterbrochen an Irina und Viktor. Ihre Namen dröhnten in seinen Ohren, in seinem Schädel. Sie strömten durch jede Synapse seiner Schaltkreise. Er wurde sie nicht los, egal, was er tat. Und Viktor und Irina waren nicht die Einzigen, denen Alexander seine vorläufig fortgesetzte Existenz verdankte: Sie nahmen ihre Plätze neben Iwan ein, und alle drei sahen ihn unentwegt enttäuscht und tadelnd an. Es war einfach zu viel: Ein ganzer vergrämter Volksstamm nistete in seinem Kopf.

Gott-weiß-wie-viele Abende brachte er nur damit zu, aus dem Fenster zu starren. Wieder und wieder sah er zu, wie sich ein Vorgebirge der Dunkelheit über die Stadt senkte.

Fast sofort danach kehrte Boris zu ihm zurück. Eines sonnigen Nachmittags stand er in der Tür und fand Alexander im Schlafanzug vor, wie er kalten Kaffee in die Stapel alter Zeitungen sickern ließ, die überall in der Wohnung herumlagen. Boris musterte ihn von oben bis unten und sagte: »Das sieht alles nicht besonders staatsmännisch aus.« Alexander sah Boris aus rotgeränderten Augen an und stellte sich das lange Leben vor, das vor ihm lag – das lange Leben eines Überlebenden. Es war seine Strafe dafür, recht gehabt zu haben, oder die Belohnung für seine Angst, je nachdem, wie man es betrachtete.

Dann sahen sie schweigend Kanal eins an und zählten die Lügen, bis die Sonne unterging und das einzige Licht das Leuchten des Fernsehers war.

Mehrere Tage nach dem Absturz – vielleicht sieben, vielleicht zehn, Alexander würde es nie genau wissen, weil sein Gehirn eine Zeitlang aufhörte, neue Erinnerungen zu formen – klopfte es an der Tür. Obwohl es töricht war, hatte er Vlad bezahlten Urlaub gegeben; er wohnte allein, gab für die wenigen freien Presseorgane Erklärungen ab, wenn sie sich bei ihm meldeten, schrieb Leserbriefe an westliche Zeitungsredaktionen und lernte mit den Geistern der vielen Menschen zu leben, die ihn verlassen hatten. Vlad hatte ihm gesagt, wie unvernünftig es war, und Alexander wusste, wie recht er hatte. Aber er konnte die Vorstellung nicht ertragen, nur mit seinem Leibwächter zusammenzuwohnen – er stellte sich vor, wie Vlad mit seiner Maschinenpistole die Küche bemannte, während er in Pantoffeln Nudeln kochte. Er ertrug es nicht. Nicht jetzt; jetzt ganz besonders nicht.

Es war Abend, als es klopfte. Alexander hatte die E-Mail-Korrespondenz und die Konferenzschaltungen des Tages hinter sich gebracht und hatte mit seiner neuen abendlichen Routine begonnen, bei einer Viertelflasche Wodka seine Morddrohungen zu lesen und gelegentlich in Online-Schachforen mitzumischen, obwohl es keine Herausforderung und letztlich nicht besonders unterhaltsam war. Bestimmt war es Boris, dachte er, als es noch einmal klopfte – wahrscheinlich hatte er etwas liegenlassen oder brachte Neuigkeiten, die man besser nicht am Telefon besprach. Vielleicht gab es etwas Deprimierendes im Fernsehen, das er nicht allein ansehen wollte. Oder vielleicht war er einfach nur einsam, nur ziellos, nur verloren und war auf seinen Irrwegen durch die Stadt wie von selbst wieder bei Alexander gelandet – denn wo sonst sollte er zu so später Stunde hin? Alexander hatte Mitleid mit Boris, aber er wollte ihn jetzt nicht sehen. Er hatte schon eine nicht unerhebliche Menge Zeit mit seinem Wodka zugebracht und hatte einen Zustand angenehmer Indifferenz erreicht: Ihn beschlich der Verdacht, dass die pulsierenden Lichter Petersburgs vor seinem Fenster das Wichtigste auf der Welt waren und alles andere nur sekundär. Ihm gefiel dieser Verdacht, obwohl er nicht vollständig daran glaubte, und er wollte ihn so lange hegen wie möglich. Als er die Tür öffnete, sah er daher wahrscheinlich verärgert aus, und dieses verärgerte Gesicht war wahrscheinlich das Erste, was Elisabeta sah, als sie zum ersten Mal seit siebenundzwanzig Jahren zu ihm aufblickte.

Sein Mund füllte sich mit Asche; seine Knochen wurden brüchig, vogelgleich. Einen Moment lang, vielleicht auch länger, fragte er sich, ob er den Verstand verloren hatte – ob Einsamkeit und Trauer und die ständigen Gedanken an eben diesen Augenblick am Ende seinen Draht zur Realität durchgescheuert hatten. Allerdings war es inzwischen lange her, dass er dieses Ereignis herbeiphantasiert hatte. Es war ihm zu viel Trauer dazwischengekommen, und in letzter Zeit war nicht einmal sein Unterbewusstsein nachsichtig genug, sich mit dieser speziellen Wunschvorstellung zu befassen – es gab genug andere, gefährlichere, dringendere.

»Alexander«, sagte sie. »Wie geht es dir?«

Sie klang, als sei gar nichts weiter dabei, ihn das zu fragen, als wären nur ein paar Tage mehr als gewöhnlich vergangen, ohne dass sie sich gesehen hatten, und als sei sie jetzt neugierig darauf, was er in der Zwischenzeit gemacht hatte. Sein Arm schnellte instinktiv Richtung Türrahmen. Es war nicht auszuschließen, dass er Hilfe brauchte, um nicht umzufallen.

»Was ist mit dem Dinosaurier?«, fragte er. Wäre er nicht ein klein wenig betrunken gewesen, dann hätte er es nicht gefragt, oder zumindest nicht in diesen Worten, oder er hätte es nicht als Allererstes wissen wollen.

»Dem Dinosaurier?«

Ein Tsunami ozeanischer Geräusche dröhnte in seinen Ohren, und er musste sie beinahe bitten, lauter zu sprechen. »Dem Funktionär«, sagte er.

Sie trat einen kleinen Schritt zurück. Sie musste gewusst haben, dass er danach fragen würde, aber vermutlich hatte sie gedacht, er würde sie erst hereinbitten. »Ah. Mitja. Er ist tot.«

»Sind das nicht alle?«, sagte Alexander. Dann sagte er: »Tut mir leid.«

»Tut es nicht. Mir auch nicht besonders, dabei war er kein so schlechter Mensch, wie du wahrscheinlich glaubst.«

Er sah sie an und schwieg. Seine Körpertemperatur normalisierte sich, und er begann zu glauben, dass das, was er sich gerade einbildete, wirklich geschah.

»Darf ich reinkommen?«, fragte sie.

Es war merkwürdig, dass er am liebsten nein sagen wollte. Er wollte die Tür schließen und vor Erschöpfung zusammenbrechen; seine Wohnung wurde so schon genug von Geistern heimgesucht, und wenn er Elisabeta hereinließ, und sei es nur für eine Stunde, wusste er nicht, ob er es überhaupt noch dort aushalten würde.

»Das mit deinen Mitarbeitern tut mir leid«, sagte sie.

»Ja.«

»Ich habe es in den Nachrichten gesehen.«

»Ja, du darfst reinkommen.«

Er trat zur Seite und hielt ihr die Tür auf, und als sie an ihm vorüberging, wurde ihm schlagartig bewusst, wie absonderlich es war, in ihrer Nähe zu sein. Hier war sein Körper, und da war ihrer, und er konnte die Arme ausstrecken und sie zu sich heranziehen, wenn er wollte – und das hatte er immer gewollt. Aber er hätte nicht sagen können, ob das hier nun besser war oder schlechter oder deprimierenderweise ganz egal. Er bot ihr mit einer leeren Geste einen der Stühle im Arbeitszimmer an. Dann bemerkte er, dass sie alle mit Papieren vollgestapelt waren, und fegte die Dokumente zu Boden.

»Magst du etwas trinken? Tee oder …« – er sah, wie sie die Wodkaflasche bemerkte, deren Kondenswasser auf die Morddrohungen troff, und konnte sich vorstellen, auf was für ein abstruses Abendprogramm diese Zusammenstellung schließen ließ – »oder irgendwas?«

»Tee«, sagte sie. »Bitte.«

Er starrte sie hilflos an, dann ging er Tee kochen. Nina hatte ihr gesamtes Arsenal dagelassen, und er suchte etwas aus, von dem er hoffte, dass es möglichst bitter und unnachgiebig war – dass es schmeckte, wie wenn man eine Chance verpasst und es viel, viel zu spät bereut. Wusste sie denn nicht, wie unerbittlich sie ihn jahrzehntelang gequält hatte? War es der Grausamkeiten noch nicht genug? Flüchtig wurde ihm bewusst, dass sie gekommen sein könnte, um ihn zu töten – sie wäre nicht die Erste, die es versuchte, und sie war schließlich lange mit einem Parteibeamten verheiratet gewesen, der vermutlich mit der gegenwärtigen Regierung enge Bande unterhalten hatte. Einmal Tschekist, immer Tschekist, wie Putin selbst gern sagte. Dazu kam noch, dass Alexander diese Frau nicht richtig kannte – nicht wirklich, eigentlich überhaupt nicht. Es wäre naiv gewesen, sich über irgendetwas zu wundern, das sie tat. Außerdem wäre es peinlich, ziemlich peinlich sogar, sich vor einem teuren und technisch anspruchsvollen Flugzeugattentat zu retten, bloß um eine Woche danach in seiner Wohnung umgebracht zu werden, in Pantoffeln, mit dem Teekessel in der Hand.

Er blieb in der Küche, bis der Kessel kreischte, dann brachte er ihr eine Tasse auf dem Tablett.

»Danke«, sagte sie.

Er wollte einsilbig und zurückhaltend sein wie sie. Er wollte sie unbedingt quälend lange auf die Anschuldigungen warten lassen, mit denen sie sicher rechnete. Aber er konnte es nicht. Die Worte sprudelten aus ihm heraus, ohne auch nur die erste Sichtkontrolle abzuwarten. »Ich hätte niemanden sonst hier reingelassen, weißt du«, sagte er. »Ohne Begleitung und ohne Termin. Vielleicht meinen Leibwächter. Vielleicht einige meiner Mitarbeiter. Sonst gibt es im Moment niemanden, glaube ich.«

Sie trank einen Schluck Tee. Falls er ihr Schmerzen bereitete, wusste sie es zu verbergen. »Dann vertraust du mir?«

»Ich vertraue dir nicht. Dass ich dich reingelassen habe, hat nichts mit Vertrauen zu tun.«

Sie sah aus dem Fenster. »Du vertraust mir nicht. Das ist merkwürdig.«

Er schnaubte verächtlich. Es war ein Skandal, dass sie überhaupt herkam – nach all den Jahren und nach allem, was er ihretwegen durchgemacht hatte, auch wenn er einsah, dass sie nicht alles davon wissen konnte. Aber ganz davon abgesehen war er jetzt eine bedeutende Persönlichkeit, und er war bedeutende Risiken eingegangen, und er hatte keinerlei Grund, sich unangekündigte Besuche gefallen zu lassen, schon gar nicht von ihr. Sie hatte in einem anderen Leben einen anderen Mann gekannt, und auch den nur sehr flüchtig.

»Du hast einen Funktionär geheiratet.« Er bemühte sich, gleichgültig zu klingen, als sei das eine neutrale Tatsache, an die er sie hilfreicherweise erinnern wollte. Er hoffte, das sei grausam von ihm. Er wollte grausam sein.

»Das habe ich.«

»Du hast ihn nicht geliebt«, sagte er. Das war geraten. Vielleicht hatte sie ihn geliebt. Manchmal hatte er im Laufe der Jahre, in seinen großzügigeren Momenten, gehofft, dass es so war.

»Nein.«

»Aber du hast ihn geheiratet.« Es überraschte ihn selbst, dass er es immer wieder betonen musste.

Ihr Gesicht umwölkte sich, und er bekam schreckliche Angst, dass sie weinen würde. Es wäre ein unerhörtes Erlebnis, eine Frau wie Elisabeta weinen zu sehen – wie ein plötzlicher Meteoritenschauer oder die Entdeckung eines Meereslebewesens, das man schon lange für ausgestorben gehalten hat. So spektakulär es auch gewesen wäre – Alexander wollte es nicht sehen, weil er nicht wollte, dass sie weinte, nie, selbst jetzt nicht, selbst wenn er fand, sie hätte es verdient.

All das war bedeutungslos, denn sie weinte nicht. Sie hustete. Es war ein hoffnungsloser, jämmerlicher, grauenvoller Husten, und er wünschte sich sofort, sie hätte stattdessen geweint.

»Ist schon gut«, sagte sie, als sie wieder zu sich kam und sah, wie er sie anstarrte. »Das wäre auch passiert, wenn du nicht von dem armen Mitja angefangen hättest.«

»Was ist los mit dir?«

Sie sah ihn vernichtend an. »Generell, meinst du?«

»Mit deinem Husten.«

Sie zuckte mit den Schultern. »Zigaretten. Fang gar nicht damit an, Alexander. Es ist eine grässliche Angewohnheit.«

Er konnte sich nicht erinnern, dass sie in der Kommunalka geraucht hätte, und beschloss zu glauben, dass auch daran der Dinosaurier schuld war.

»Einen schönen Ausblick hast du hier oben«, sagte sie. Sie wollte von dem Husten ablenken, von den schauderhaften Dingen, die er anzudeuten schien.

»Das sagen alle.«

»Und du nicht?«

»Doch, er ist wirklich nett. Es ist ein bisschen anders, wenn es das Einzige ist, was man hat, aber – doch, der Ausblick ist schön.«

Sie sah aus dem Fenster, und er wünschte, er könnte nachempfinden, wie der Ausblick auf sie wirkte.

»Also«, sagte sie, »du vertraust mir nicht, weil ich den armen Mitja geheiratet habe.«

»So ungefähr.«

»Was denkst du, warum ich es getan habe?« Sie stand auf und kam näher.

»Weil es einfach war.« Er stand ebenfalls auf, nur für den Fall, dass es zu einem Handgemenge kommen würde. Er wollte nicht im Sitzen sterben.

»Unter anderem«, sagte sie.

»Weil du deinen Beruf satthattest.« Sie war jetzt ziemlich nah, und ihm blieb nichts anderes übrig, als ihr ins Gesicht zu sehen. Es war schon komisch, dieses Älterwerden. Es äußerte sich als Nachlassen um die Augen herum und als Härte in der Kinnpartie. Aber der jüngere Mensch – der echte – blieb so präsent, so unzweifelhaft lebendig. Es war, als sei der Rest – die Fältchen in den

Augenwinkeln, der gespitzte Mund – nur eine schäbige Verkleidung, die niemand ernst nehmen konnte.

»Teilweise auch deshalb«, sagte sie.

»Weil du Angst hattest.«

»Nein«, sagte sie bedächtig. »Nein, das war es nicht.« Sie roch nach Haferbrei und Flieder – und, ja, nach Zigaretten, aber nach den Zigaretten der zwanziger Jahre in Paris, denen von Ingrid Bergmann, nicht nach denen der Seki in den Gulags oder der einfachen Leute überall sonst.

»Warum sonst?«

Sie bedachte ihn mit einem Blick, der komplizierter war als ein ganzes Herz, ein ganzes Leben. In dem Blick lag teils Verbitterung und teils Zärtlichkeit und teils unaussprechliche Wut. Dahinter lag vielleicht noch etwas anderes – etwas, von dem er nicht mehr sicher war, ob er es noch erkennen, beurteilen oder glauben konnte.

»Alexander«, sagte sie. »Bist du je auf die Idee gekommen, dich zu fragen, warum du damals nicht mit deinem Freund zusammen getötet worden bist?«

Sie bat ihn nicht, bleiben zu dürfen, und er lud sie nicht dazu ein, aber irgendwie war sie eine Woche später immer noch da und machte keine Anstalten zu gehen. Sie unternahmen manchmal gemeinsame Spaziergänge an den Ufern der Newa – Vlad lief sicherheitshalber in gebührendem Abstand hinter ihnen her –, und sie erzählten einander ihr ganzes Leben: was vor der Kommunalka gewesen war und in der Zeit danach und was im Verborgenen geschehen war, als sie zusammen wohnten. Er erzählte, wie er sich nach ihrer ersten Begegnung ins Bett gelegt hatte und von diesem neuen, unwahrscheinlichen, verblüffenden Etwas ganz außer sich gewesen war. Sie erzählte, wie sie nach ihrem Gespräch im Flur den ganzen Nachmittag lang die Verwalterin mit Fragen über ihn gelöchert hatte, bis sie Elisabeta wegschickte und die Maden im Wasserhahn vergaß. Und sie erzählte – nicht direkt, aber in schwer zu glaubenden Andeutungen – dass sie vielleicht geheiratet hatte, um ihn zu beschützen. Nicht ganz, nicht nur, aber teilweise vielleicht. Nachdem die Flugschrift entdeckt worden war, hatte sie den Dinosauriermann um Hilfe gebeten (der schwerfällig und nicht bösartig gewesen war und hoffnungslos in Elisabeta verliebt), und er hatte sich bereit erklärt, Alexander nach Möglichkeit zu beschützen, wenn Elisabeta ihn heiratete. Also – weil sie nicht ewig eine Prostituierte bleiben wollte und weil sie arm war und weil damals jeder, absolut jeder irgendetwas tat, für das er sich später schämte – hatte sie ja gesagt.

Außerdem sprachen sie endlich über Irina – den eigentlichen, vorgeschobenen Grund, aus dem Elisabeta zu ihm gekommen war. Sie erzählte, wie das Mädchen sie besucht hatte – merkwürdig, dass Elisabeta Irina ein Mädchen nannte, wo doch Irina einunddreißig gewesen war und Elisabeta selbst jetzt, selbst wenn er genau hinsah, unmöglich viel älter sein konnte als neunzehn. Alexander begriff, dass Elisabeta sich ebenfalls schuldig fühlte: Sie hatte Irina auf Nikolai angesetzt, und das hatte ihr ihre Stelle bei Alexander eingebracht, und die hatte sie das Leben gekostet. Er begriff, dass Elisabeta ihn vielleicht nicht für geeignet hielt, sich um die junge Frau zu kümmern, die sie auf Umwegen zu ihm geschickt hatte. Und er begriff, dass sie darin noch etwas gemeinsam hatten.

Am Ende war es so: Er liebte sie, er hatte sie immer geliebt, und er konnte ihr nicht ganz verzeihen; er würde ihr nie ganz verzeihen können. Sie wusste das, und beide konnten damit leben – konnten damit leben, dass die besten Jahre verloren waren, unwiederbringlich, für immer außer Sicht. Andererseits hatten sie jene Jahre vielleicht für diese hergegeben – vielleicht hatte Elisabetas Schutz ihm sein ganzes Leben erkauft und alles, was – wenn überhaupt – einmal daraus werden würde. Er wusste wirklich nicht, ob es ein Tausch war, auf den er sich noch einmal einlassen würde – aber die Entscheidung lag ja nicht bei ihm. Und als sie blieb, als sie immer wieder blieb und er immer wieder morgens neben ihr aufwachte, gab es Augenblicke, in denen er einfach nur dankbar war. Es gab Augenblicke, in denen er beinahe glauben konnte, sie sei immer da gewesen.

Ein paar Tage nach Elisabetas Rückkehr brachte es Alexander eines Abends endlich über sich, das Material aus Perm anzusehen. Viktors E-Mail hatte in seinem Posteingang gewartet, bedrohlich zusammengekauert wie ein vom Hausgeist dort deponierter Scherzartikel, und Alexander hatte Angst gehabt, sie zu öffnen – er fürchtete, sein Mausklick könnte ein Duo aufbrausender, selbstgerechter Geister entfesseln, die mit untoten Fingern auf ihn zeigten und ihn fragten, warum er nicht dies oder das (oder alles) anders gemacht hatte. Aber als er sie dann doch öffnete, war die Mail genau das, was sie vorgab zu sein. Die Aufnahmen waren eindeutiger, als Alexander es sich hätte träumen lassen; das Einzige, was noch besser hätte wirken können, wäre eine Tonaufnahme von Putin persönlich gewesen, wie er sich nach den Anschlägen kichernd die Hände rieb. Es war der Beweis. Es war das Schlussplädoyer. Außer dem Filmmaterial war da noch die E-Mail-Nachricht von Viktor, drei Wochen nach seinem Tod:

Tut mir leid, dass wir es so machen mussten. Aber ich weiß, dass du es verstehst.

Alexander löschte diese Nachricht nie. Im Laufe der Jahre rutschte sie immer weiter in die Tiefen seines Posteingangs, aber er trennte sich nie davon. Sie war ein Signal, ein Semaphor. Sie war ein Leuchtfeuer über den Abgrund des Unwissens hinweg, und solange sie da war, hatte Alexander immer das Gefühl, dass noch jemand die Laterne schwenkte.

Mitten im Sommer wurde der Dokumentarfilm veröffentlicht. Er lief in Programmkinos in Amerika und Westeuropa. In Russland verbreiteten sich Raubkopien auf DVD, die allerdings hauptsächlich von den üblichen Verdächtigen angesehen wurden – den Intellektuellen mit ihren Nickelbrillen, die das Video ihren Dinnergästen zeigten und über all die Dinge schwatzten, über die sie auch sonst geschwatzt hätten. Er war in neun Abschnitten auf YouTube abrufbar und wurde fast hunderttausend Mal angeklickt. Alexander reichte den Film beim Moskauer Filmfestival ein, nur um Putins persönlichen Freund zu ärgern, der die Veranstaltung organisierte. Die *Nowaja Gaseta* berichtete über die Dokumentation und brachte eine Rezension, in der besonders von dem Fund in Perm die Rede war. Im Fernsehen wurde der Film nie erwähnt. Ende August fiel der Redakteur, der für die Rezension verantwortlich gewesen war, einem tragischen Sturz auf einer defekten Treppe zum Opfer. Im Oktober zog sich der Leitartikler, der aus den Untersuchungen vernichtende Schlussfolgerungen gezogen hatte, eine seltene, unheilbare Krankheit zu und starb in einem staatlichen Krankenhaus, wo seine sterblichen Überreste von den zuständigen Stellen beschlagnahmt wurden.

Alexander sollte nie herausfinden (woher sollte man es auch wissen?), ob es das alles wert gewesen war – den Tod dieser zwei Journalisten und eines ganzen Flugzeugs voller Menschen, die nicht alle an tödlichen Krankheiten gelitten hatten. Aber manchmal, wenn er am Fluss spazieren ging, wusste er ganz genau, dass es das nicht gewesen war. Dreiundzwanzig Menschen waren an Bord gewesen – zweiundzwanzig, wenn man Irina außen vor ließ, die schon im Begriff gewesen war, sich zu verabschieden – und dazu die zwei Journalisten, und als Alexander sich wieder unter die Lebenden mischte, verbrachte er seine ersten Ausflüge damit, von jeder Menschenmenge vierundzwanzig Leute abzuzählen: Eine gummigesichtige Frau, deren Nase wie ein großer Zeh aussah, eine glutäugige Schönheit, zwei gutgekleidete junge Männer, die gebührenden Abstand voneinander hielten, eine Mutter mit einer ganzen Horde androgyner Kinder, die wie Welpen um sie herumtollten, eine Grundschulklasse auf einem Schulausflug. Es war es nicht wert. In dieser Welt voller schmerzhafter Zugeständnisse, diesem Leben voller kalkulierter Risiken war es kein lohnendes

Opfer; es war ein Turm für einen Bauern, ein Läufer für einen Turm, eine Dame für einen entlegenen, denkbar unwahrscheinlichen Sieg.

Alexander stürzte sich in die Arbeit, und Boris tat es ihm nach. Den Rest des stickigen Sommers über bis in den rotbäckigen Herbst hinein arbeiteten sie: Sie sammelten Unterschriften, sie gaben Interviews, und sie kamen bei jeder passenden oder unpassenden Gelegenheit auf die Sprengstoffanschläge zu sprechen. Alexander schrieb Artikel für das *Wall Street Journal*, die nur von Menschen gelesen wurden, die ohnehin seiner Meinung waren. Er hielt Ansprachen für ein Publikum, das nicht kleiner, aber auch nicht wesentlich größer geworden war. Putin präsentierte seinen Nachfolger, Medwedew – einen nervös wirkenden Mann ohne erkennbare Qualifikationen –, der gleich ankündigte, Putin im Falle seiner Wahl zu seinem Ministerpräsidenten zu ernennen. Eine Woche nach seiner Kandidatenkür standen seine Umfragewerte auf 79 Prozent.

Bei den Kundgebungen bot Alexander den Zuschauern bessere Formulierungen als je zuvor: Hier in Putins Russland hat die Regierung Kollektivstrafen für Akte des Widerstands wiedereingeführt. Hier in Putins Russlands werden Menschen im Gerichtssaal in Käfige gesperrt. Hier in Putins Russland stürzen zivile Flugzeuge für politische Zwecke ab. Wollen wir wirklich noch mindestens vier Jahre in Putins Russland leben? Denn genau das ist es, was wir mit Medwedew bekommen. Und die Menge rief, nein, das wolle sie nicht.

Ende November wurde es bei einer der Kundgebungen ungemütlich, und Alexander wurde von einer kleinen Gruppe Menschen zusammengeschlagen. Der Kreml berichtete schadenfroh, er habe mit den dort anwesenden Journalisten Englisch gesprochen. »Russisch habe ich auch gesprochen«, knurrte er auf Radio Free Europe, obwohl seine Lippe noch schmerzte, wenn er zu schnell redete. »Ich kann sogar ziemlich gut Russisch, und ich wäre mehr als bereit, im Staatsfernsehen mit Wladimir Wladimirowitsch zu debattieren, um zu sehen, wer von uns beiden es besser beherrscht.«

Im Dezember, als neue, halbwegs erfolgversprechende Umfragewerte veröffentlicht wurden, wurde er festgenommen und eine Woche lang inhaftiert. Er starrte aus dem Fenster seiner Zelle in ein bleiches Himmelsquadrat. Die Woche war nicht gerade angenehm, aber auch nicht repräsentativ, wie er wusste: Er ging wohlgenährt und unverletzt aus der Sache hervor, und sie war letztlich ein PR-Coup für seine Seite (CNN brachte Wiederholungen alter Interviews, die Blogosphäre summte, und es gab Textkästen in der *Newsweek* und der *Time*). In der Woche darauf war seine Anhängerschar größer als je zuvor, und er wusste, dass die anderen wussten, dass seine Festnahme eine Fehlkalkulation gewesen war, ein Patzer mit unerwünschten Nebenwirkungen.

Es spielte keine Rolle. Im Januar wurde er nicht zur Wahl zugelassen – von 2 067 211 Unterschriften, die seine Kandidatur befürworteten, wurden 80 000 von den Behörden für ungültig erklärt. Saalbuchungen wurden storniert, Genehmigungen zurückgezogen. Alexander beging seinen Rücktritt ziemlich feierlich mit einer schonungslosen Ansprache im schonungslosen Wind. Und im März gewann Medwedew die Wahl mit beeindruckend robusten 70 Prozent der Stimmen, während Alexander sich die Hochrechnungen in einem gecharterten Restaurant voller unglücklicher Menschen ansah, die irgendwann anfingen, Dinge nach dem Bildschirm zu werfen, und dann einer nach dem anderen betrunken und deprimiert in die schwarze, verschneite Nacht hinaustaumelten.

Alexander blieb in dem Restaurant, und Elisabeta malte Fingerschnörkel auf seine Schultern, bis das Personal mit dem Aufräumen fertig war.

Selbst Mischa, den er ein paar Tage danach auf BBC hohnlächeln sah, schien unglücklich zu sein. »Ich bin kein Fan von Besetow«, sagte er. »Aber die Wahlen sind manipuliert worden. Sie wurden ganz offensichtlich manipuliert. Es haben überhaupt keine

Wahlen stattgefunden, also können Sie aufhören, die Ergebnisse zu verkünden.«

Nikolai wurde aus dem FSB abgezogen und zum Innenminister ernannt und bekam eine riesige Datscha bei Moskau im Wald. Manchmal entdeckte Alexander ihn, wenn im Fernsehen aus der Duma berichtet wurde – irgendwo im Hintergrund tauchte kurz sein rohes Gesicht mit den stattlichen Hängebacken auf. Er hatte dem Regime treu gedient. Er hätte es bis zum Ministerpräsidenten schaffen können, wäre er nicht so unverzeihlich hässlich gewesen.

Zu Hause hatte er zumindest Elisabeta – und immer wenn er den Glauben daran verlor, dass unwahrscheinliche Ereignisse irgendwann doch noch eintreten konnten, war sie da und erinnerte ihn daran. Er trug sie in der Wohnung umher, und er belebte jede halbgeformte Geste wieder, jedes Gefühl, das er jahrzehntelang hatte hinunterschlucken müssen. Das hier wollte ich schon immer mal tun, sagte er dann. Und *das* hier. Und das. Sie liebten einander, und das war ihnen genug, nur der Husten war schrecklich, und es gab Nächte, in denen sie, ohne einander zu berühren, alte Filme ansahen, während Elisabeta Sauerstoff aus Schläuchen atmete. Und es gab Nächte, in denen Alexander – der kein alter Mann war, aber schon wusste, dass er das nicht mehr lange von sich würde behaupten können – sich fragte, wie es gewesen wäre, die Liebe in jungen Jahren zu erleben oder ein Jahrzehnt oder ein ganzes Leben lang.

Seine erste Kundgebung nach den Wahlen fand in Moskau statt, und er hatte das Gefühl – obwohl Nina nicht da war, um für ihn nachzuzählen –, es seien mehr Zuschauer da als je zuvor. Neuntausend, dachte er, vielleicht zehn. Vielleicht waren sie wütender als sonst, vielleicht verbittert, und vielleicht meinten sie es diesmal wirklich ernst. Sie schrien Parolen. Sie schwenkten Fahnen und hielten Plakate hoch, und auf einigen davon war Alexanders eigenes zweidimensionales, zerknittertes Gesicht. Er räusperte sich, um sie zur Ruhe zu bringen. Er ließ seinen Blick über sie schweifen, über diese Menschen, sein Volk, Russen unter Zwang, Bürger unter Vorbehalt. Es würde ihm immer schwerfallen, an die Umfragewerte zu glauben und an die Wahlergebnisse, wenn immer wieder so viele Leute kamen und schrien.

Er zog das Mikrophon zu sich heran. Sie wurden leiser, Freunde mahnten Freunde zur Ruhe, damit sie hören konnten, was er zu sagen hatte. Er wollte etwas Unvergessliches sagen. Er wollte etwas sagen, das alles rechtfertigen würde, was der Rechtfertigung bedurfte – eine unendlich lange Liste von Dingen. Er wollte etwas sagen, das perfekt die Balance zwischen erbittertem Zynismus und stiller, unbeugsamer Hoffnung hielt. Er wollte sagen, dass ihnen nichts anderes blieb als die Verzweiflung – und dass ihnen dann nichts blieb, als der Verzweiflung ein Ende zu setzen. Er wollte sagen, sie würden es vielleicht nicht mehr miterleben, aber irgendjemand würde es erleben, irgendwann. Er wollte sagen, dass die historische Perspektive ein Trost war, dass sie ein Trost sein musste, dass sie so tun mussten, als sei sie ein Trost, bis sie wirklich einer war. Er wollte sagen, dass es ehrenhaft war, ein kleiner Zug in einem gewaltigen Spiel zu sein, selbst wenn man nie erfahren würde, wie es ausging. All das wollte er sagen, aber es gab keine Worte dafür; was es gab, war sein Manuskript. Er sah hinein. Sie warteten. Er sah wieder hoch.

»Diese Runde haben wir verloren, Freunde«, sagte er. »Wir haben die Partie verloren, um eine grauenhafte Schach-Metapher zu gebrauchen. Es hat Zeiten gegeben, als ich ein junger Mann war, da habe ich einen Favoriten nur dadurch geschlagen, dass ich mir vorgestellt habe, ich könnte es.«

Es war ein schwacher Vergleich, das wusste er. Es gehörte mehr dazu als Vorstellungskraft.

»Vielleicht erinnern sich einige von Ihnen noch daran«, sagte er, »obwohl ich vermute, dass die meisten hier viel zu jung dafür sind. Das war, als Schach noch eine beliebte Freizeitbeschäftigung war. Das war vor dem Internet.«

Es wurde leise gekichert, obwohl er den Witz nicht zum ersten Mal machte.

»Das ist alles, was ich von Ihnen will – eine bescheidene Bitte von einem alten Mann, der eine Menge durchgemacht hat. Ich will nicht, dass Sie glauben, dass wir gewinnen werden. Ich will nur, dass Sie sich vorstellen, dass wir es könnten.«

Und das taten sie. Er wusste es genau. Er spürte, wie sie ihre Phantasie anstrengten – beinahe konnte er das kollektive Knistern ihrer persönlichsten Wunschträume hören, und einige davon waren genau, was man erwarten würde: Ein Mädchen wünscht sich, dass ihr Bruder an Leib und Seele unverletzt aus Tschetschenien zurückkehrt; ein junger Mann will seine Stimme bei Wahlen abgeben, bei denen es ihm anschließend nicht den Magen umdreht; eine alte Frau möchte wissen, was zur Zeit des Großen Terrors mit ihrem Vater geschehen ist, und wünscht sich eine Regierung, die es ihr offen sagt. Vielleicht haben manche bescheidenere Wünsche. Vielleicht wollen manche erleben, wie Putin eine feindlich gesinnte Pressekonferenz überstehen muss. Vielleicht wollen manche ins Ausland fahren, ohne gefragt zu werden, was ihre Landsleute im letzten Jahrhundert oder so beschäftigt hat. Vielleicht wollen manche eine Satiresendung, die Tag für Tag jeden einzelnen Politiker aufspießt und sich begeistert über jede ihrer Institutionen lustig macht.

»Stellt euch vor, wir könnten es«, sagte er.

Einen kurzen Moment lang schloss er die Augen, während die Menge andächtig schwieg. Ihre Fahnen knatterten im Wind, und ihre Plakate wehten davon, und sie hielten sie nicht auf. In dem Moment, als sie es sich alle gemeinsam vorstellten, konnte er es beinahe sehen. Und wer wollte sagen, dass sie es nicht genauso sahen wie er?

Er verbrachte Stunden, ganze Tage damit, nach Spuren seiner Korrespondenz mit Irinas Vater zu forschen. Er wollte sie unbedingt finden, jetzt mehr denn je. Er wollte sich selbst beweisen, dass er dem letzten Wunsch einer jungen Frau gegenüber nicht gleichgültig war – dass er nicht zu sehr mit seiner Ehe und seiner Demokratiebewegung beschäftigt war, um zu finden, was wirklich zählte. Er wollte wissen, ob das, was zählte, wirklich nicht da war. Er ging unzählige Stapel alter Flugschriften durch, deren Kohlepapierschrift sich zu unleserlichen blauen Rinnsalen verflüchtigt hatte. Er blätterte in seinen strategischen Notizen. Er las seine alten Zustelllisten durch und staunte, dass er je so dumm gewesen war, sie aufzuschreiben. Er fand einen Tagebucheintrag zu Elisabeta, aber er konnte ihn ihr nicht zeigen – nicht, weil es ihm peinlich war (das war es allerdings), sondern weil ihm beim Anblick seiner zittrigen Handschrift und der Überschwänglichkeit seiner Liebe fast die Tränen kamen.

Er fand nichts von Irinas Vater. Drei Tage am Stück verbrachte er damit, Papiere, die so gelb und brüchig waren wie die Haut eines alten Mannes, in der Wohnung zu verteilen. Dann, endlich, sagte er sich, dass er es aufgeben konnte. Er sagte sich, dass Irina schon gefunden hatte, wofür sie hergekommen war.

Erst Jahre danach, als er Elisabetas Sachen sortierte, sollte Alexander den Brief von Irinas Vater finden. Da erinnerte er sich an Elisabetas vergeblichen Zustellversuch ein paar Wochen vor ihrer Heirat mit Mitja, und er erinnerte sich, wie er den Brief abgelehnt hatte, während sie in der Tür stand, so jung und lebendig, und im Begriff war, ihn zum ersten Mal zu verlassen. Er erinnerte sich an den klauenbewehrten Schmerz in seiner Brust zu jener Zeit. Er wusste noch, wie er geglaubt hatte, das sei das Schlimmste überhaupt, und was für ein oberflächlicher, geringfügiger Schmerz es im Vergleich gewesen war. Und dann setzte er sich zwischen Elisabetas Kisten und Bücher auf den Boden und weinte ein wenig und lachte ein wenig und starrte ein wenig verwirrt die Zimmerdecke an. Und dann las er zum allerersten Mal den Brief.

In der Zeit nach den Wahlen zeigt die Welt sich vorübergehend interessiert. Alexander wird in die USA eingeflogen, damit er alles den Fernsehzuschauern erklärt. (Das geschah immer wieder einmal – immer wenn es in Russland ein Ereignis gab, das man von einem englisch sprechenden Kapitalisten erklärt haben wollte, der in der Lage war, enorm komplizierte politische Umwälzungen so zu beschreiben, dass es jeder Highschool-Sozialkundeschüler verstand.) Er fährt in einer Limousine durch die aufgewühlte Stadt; er sieht am Times Square den schwindelerregenden Lichtern zu. Die Taxifahrer fragen ihn alle, woher er kommt, und er fragt sie, woher sie kommen. Ganze Tage lang hat er in New York das Gefühl, es gäbe überhaupt keine Einheimischen – die Stadt ist ein Raumschiff, und jeder Bewohner ist ein Flüchtling von einem sterbenden Planeten (aus der Zweiten Welt, der Dritten Welt, aus Mittelamerika). Die psychotischen Lichter, das ungenierte Geld, die schrille Musik – da ist ein Lebensgefühl, das ihn beinahe an Moskau erinnert. Auf MSNBC wird Alexander gefragt, was er über die Zukunft Russlands denkt. »Wir hoffen nicht darauf, Wahlen zu gewinnen«, sagt er. »Wir hoffen, Wahlen abhalten zu können.« Für einen außenpolitischen Blog fragt man ihn, ob Russland überhaupt bereit sei für die Demokratie. Könnten jahrelange Repressionen, könnte seine gewaltige Größe, könnten ganze Zeitalter der systematischen Untergrabung der bürgerlichen Gesellschaft nicht bewirkt haben, dass das Land auf die demokratische Wende nicht vorbereitet ist? Alexander antwortet immer wieder mit Nein. Er verweist auf Nordkorea und Südkorea, auf Ostdeutschland und Westdeutschland. Menschen ist keine bestimmte Regierungsform in die Wiege gelegt, in ihrer DNA ist keine angeborene Demokratie-Untauglichkeit kodiert, und es gibt keine naturwüchsige Liebe zum autoritären Unrecht in der Seelenlandschaft einer Nation. Es gibt nur die einzelnen Individuen und die Regierungen, die ihnen gute oder schlechte Dienste leisten. Demokratie ist die am wenigsten schlechte Herrschaftsform, sagt er. Sie maximiert die Freiheit des Individuums, und ist das nicht auf dieser Welt – dieser unsicheren, klaustrophobischen, schrumpfenden, aber eigentlich auch in jeder beliebigen Welt – das höchste Gut? Gibt es Wichtigeres, als schreiben zu können, was man denkt, und sagen zu können, was man denkt, und spät abends unbewacht an einem Fluss entlangzugehen? Vielleicht lässt er diesen letzten Teil auch aus. Und eines Tages, sagt er. Eines Tages auch in Russland.

Aber dann wieder, dann – wenn er ehrlich zu sich ist, und daran arbeitet er, denn von wem sonst kann er erwarten, ehrlich zu ihm zu sein? – ist er sich nicht so sicher. Er ist sich einfach nicht sicher.

Er wird vom politikwissenschaftlichen Institut der Kennedy School of Government an der Harvard-Universität zu einer Podiumsdiskussion eingeladen, und er übernachtet in einem grünen, dreieckigen Hotel mit Blick auf den Fluss (der matter ist, denkt er, und weniger theatralisch als seine Newa). Den Tag verbringt er in dem bunten Durcheinander von Cambridge. Auf dem Harvard Square sieht er den Schachmännern bei ihren amateurhaften, holprigen Spielen zu und erinnert sich daran, dass Irina oft gegen einen von ihnen spielte. Er hat sie nicht gut gekannt, und er hat sie nicht lange gekannt, und es ist nicht ihr Land, für das er immer weitermacht. Aber wenn er an ihr kurzes Leben zurückdenkt und an ihre Weigerung, es nur als Zuschauer zuzubringen, weiß er, dass er daraus etwas lernen kann, wenn er nur genug Geduld aufbringt.

Er geht dem Charles River entgegen und spürt das simple Glück, draußen in der Welt unterwegs zu sein, wo ihn vermutlich niemand finden wird, der ihn sucht. Manchmal glaubt er fast, dass es dieses Glück war, das Irina in Russland finden wollte. Manchmal glaubt er, das sei ein lohnenswertes Ziel.

Auf seinem Weg am Fluss entlang überrascht es ihn wieder, wie nah die Zukunft ist. Er kann sie gerade eben nicht sehen, aber sie ist nicht weit. Er weiß es. Sie folgt ihm überallhin – am grünen Charles River entlang, durch Bostons enttäuschende Flughafengebäude, in den sternengesprenkelten Himmel hinauf und über das Meer. Er fliegt über den ölschwarzen Atlantik, über die glitzernden Leuchtfeuer Europas hinweg. Die Zukunft ist ihm nah, denkt er – mindestens so nah wie die Vergangenheit und ihre Bewohner. Er kann sie spüren wie die verschwommene Andeutung eines unentdeckten Landes, das aus dem Nebel auftaucht, oder wie den Verlauf eines Endspiels, der irgendwo tief in seinem Unterbewusstsein Gestalt annimmt. Die Lichter St. Petersburgs leuchten ihm wie diese Zukunft entgegen – kalt und entlegen und hell wie eine Galaxie, aber mit jedem Augenblick des Sinkflugs ein bisschen weniger weit entfernt.

Vielleicht wird er sie eines Tages sehen. Vielleicht nicht. Es ist ein großes Land. Aber mit etwas Glück ist es auch ein großes Leben.

DANKSAGUNGEN

Dieses Buch verdankt sich der großzügigen Unterstützung der Stanford University und des Iowa Writer's Workshop. Mein Dank geht an meine großartigen Kollegen, besonders an die unerschrockenen ersten Leser Adam Krause, Chris Leslie-Hynan und Keija Kaarina Parssinen. Ich danke all meinen wunderbaren Lehrern, besonders Sandy Warren von der Smith College Campus School, Lisa Levchuk und Peter Gunn von der Williston Northhampton School, Alan Lebowitz und Michael Downing von der Tufts University, Ethan Canin, Sam Chang, Charlie D'Ambrosio, Elizabeth McCracken, Jim McPherson und Marilynne Robinson vom Iowa Writer's Workshop sowie Elizabeth Tallent, Adam Johnson, Tobias Wolff und John L'Heureux von der Stanford University. Vielen Dank an Connie Brothers, Deb West, Jan Zenisek, Christina Ablaza und Mary Popek, die im Laufe der Jahre eine überwältigende Anzahl wirrer Mails von mir ertragen haben.

Ganz besonders dankbar bin ich meinem großartigen Lektor David Ebershoff und meinem heldenhaften Agenten Henry Dunow, die mir mit ihrer Klugheit, Großmut und Geduld zur Seite gestanden haben. Außerdem gilt mein Dank den Mitarbeitern von Random House, besonders Evan Camfield, Susan Kamil, Jynne Martin, Maria Braeckel, Avideh Bashirrad, Erika Greber, Tom Nevins, Annette Trial-O'Neil, Richard Callison und Clare Swanson.

Ich danke Lauren Albertini, Kimberly Bastin, Prerna Bhardwaj, Dave Byron, Jennifer Cantelmi, Katie Chase, Kate Egelhofer, Bev und Emily Fletcher, Morgan Gliedman, Cassie Jeremie, Keetje Kuipers, Matt Lavin, Aislinn O'Keefe, Ilana Panich-Linsman, Justin Race, Kate Sachs, Maggie Shipstead, Luke Snyder, Becca Sripada, Patrice Taddonio, Brian Tuttle, Jeff Van Dreason und Kirstin Valdez Quade. Ich bin jeden Tag wieder dankbar dafür, euch zu kennen.

Danke an meine unglaubliche Familie, die stursten und unverwüstlichsten Menschen, die ich kenne. Danke an meine wunderbaren Freunde, die mir ein steter Quell der Albernheiten und Freuden sind. Und danke an Justin Perry, das wesentliche Wunder meines Lebens.

ZUSATZMATERIAL

Schachzüge. Ein Interview mit der Autorin

Frage: In der zweiten Hälfte Ihres Romans spielen Wladimir Putin und sein politischer Apparat eine wichtige Rolle. Wie sind Sie vorgegangen, um eine lebende, polarisierende Persönlichkeit in die fiktive Logik Ihres Textes zu integrieren? Welche potentiellen Nachteile hat dieses Verfahren Ihrer Meinung nach?

Antwort: In dem ersten Entwurf meines Romans habe ich Putins Namen nicht verwendet, obwohl offensichtlich nur er gemeint sein konnte, und es gab Leser, die meinten, dass ich damit die Integrität meiner fiktionalen Welt aufs Spiel setze – die Geschichte ist fest in der realen russischen Geschichte und Politik verankert, daher fanden sie es verstörend, plötzlich in einem Paralleluniversum zu landen, in dem eine fiktionale Figur Jelzins Amtsnachfolger wird.

Schwierig an der Verwendung seines realen Namens war, dass Irina und Alexander Beweise für eine gegen ihn gerichtete Verschwörungstheorie finden – eine Theorie, die viele Anhänger hat, aber alles andere als bewiesen ist. Dieser gesamte Handlungsstrang ist also eine merkwürdige Mischung aus sorgfältig recherchierten und genau wiedergegebenen Informationen über einen realen Verdacht gegen Putin einerseits und andererseits der frei erfundenen Episode, in der meine Figuren diesen Verdacht bestätigt finden. Ich habe mir weniger Sorgen darum gemacht, Putin zu verleumden – es ist schließlich ein fiktionales Werk, und er ist eine Persönlichkeit des öffentlichen Lebens. Aber ich habe befürchtet, dass manche Leser den Eindruck gewinnen, Putins Verwicklung in die Sprengstoff-anschläge sei viel besser belegt, als sie es in Wirklichkeit ist.

Andererseits denke ich, dass die meisten Leser irgendwie intuitiv unterscheiden können zwischen der politischen und historischen Kulisse, die in der Realität verankert ist, und den fiktiven Handlungen, die vor diesem Hintergrund von fiktiven Figuren, manchmal sogar von realen Figuren ausgeführt werden – ich selbst lese zum Beispiel gerade Don DeLillos *Libra*, einen Roman, der teilweise aus der Perspektive von Lee Harvey Oswald geschrieben ist, und da ist der Unterschied deutlich zu spüren.

F: Passend zu den Interessen Ihrer Figuren kommt das Thema Schach in Ihrem Text auf unterschiedliche Art und Weise immer wieder zum Tragen. Ich zitiere eine Passage, die sehr schön mehrere Ihrer Themen zusammenfasst: »Auf seinem Weg am Fluss entlang überrascht es ihn wieder, wie nah die Zukunft ist. Er kann sie gerade eben nicht sehen, aber sie ist nicht weit. (…) Er kann sie spüren, wie die verschwommene Andeutung eines unentdeckten Landes, das aus dem Nebel auftaucht, oder wie den Verlauf eines Endspiels, der irgendwo tief in seinem Unterbewusstsein Gestalt annimmt.«

Obwohl Schach also eine wichtige Rolle spielt, nehmen konkrete Turniersituationen oder Spielpassagen im Text eher wenig Raum ein. Haben Sie im Verlauf des Schreibprozesses einmal darüber nachgedacht, mehr Schachspielhandlung in den Text einfließen zu lassen?

A: Ich wollte unbedingt so über Schach schreiben, dass es für ernsthafte Spieler überzeugend klingt, aber auch für Laien interessant bleibt, deshalb habe ich nur die Partien detailliert beschrieben, die bei meinen Figuren einen starken emotionalen Nachhall erzeugen. So nimmt zum Beispiel das Spiel, mit dem Alexander Weltmeister wird, breiten Raum ein, genauso wie seine Niederlage gegen den Computer Deep Blue. In diesen beiden Partien werden die Züge genau beschrieben, aber man muss sie nicht nachvollziehen können, um zu begreifen, wie viel für Alexander dabei auf dem Spiel steht. Dazu habe ich hier und da ein paar Details und Insider-Gags versteckt, mit denen nur echte Enthusiasten etwas werden anfangen können – indem ich zum Beispiel die realen Züge Kasparows gegen Deep Blue und gegen Karpow in den Text aufgenommen und Passagen aus anderen berühmten Partien ebenfalls im Text untergebracht habe (zum Beispiel in Alexanders Spiel gegen seinen Lehrer an der Schachakademie). So habe ich versucht, den Text für manche Leser mit einer zweiten Ebene anzureichern, ohne dass andere schreiend davonrennen.

F: Auf Ihrer Website werden Leser dazu angeregt, zu untersuchen, inwieweit Ihr Roman wie eine Schachpartie strukturiert ist. Nabokov wiederum macht seine Leser in dem Vorwort zu seinem Roman »Lushins Verteidigung« selbst auf bestimmte erzählerische Schachzüge aufmerksam. Haben Sie als Autorin das Gefühl, sich mit Ihren Lesern auf eine Art Schachpartie einzulassen? Und inwiefern gilt das für diesen Roman?

A: Ich habe nicht das Gefühl, mit meinen Lesern Schach zu spielen, aber ich denke schon, dass Schach die Struktur meines Romans prägt. Zum Beispiel ist natürlich Alexanders und Irinas Verhältnis zu Putins Regime antagonistisch, und sie vollführen Schachzüge – und lassen sich am Ende auf Opfer ein –, die durchaus etwas von der Logik des Schachspiels an sich haben. Außerdem wechselt die Perspektive mit jedem Kapitel zwischen Alexander und Irina hin und her, was auch an eine Schachpartie erinnert; beim Schreiben ist mir aufgefallen, dass die Figuren in dem, was sie tun, oft auf etwas reagieren oder an etwas anknüpfen, was der jeweils andere im Kapitel davor getan hat, selbst bevor sie einander begegnet sind.

Ich hoffe, dass die Art, wie der Plot abläuft, insofern an Schach erinnert, dass jedes neue Ereignis sowohl unvorhersehbar ist als auch logisch auf dem aufbaut, was vorher passiert ist. Flannery O'Connor hat einmal gesagt, das Ende einer Geschichte sollte am besten sowohl überraschend als auch unausweichlich sein, und ich denke, so ist es wahrscheinlich auch mit guten Zügen beim Schach.

F: Was hat es mit Schach oder überhaupt mit Aktivitäten, die viel Konzentration und Phantasie erfordern, auf sich, das Sie als Autorin dazu bewegt, für die Dauer eines ganzen Buchprojekts ihre Zeit mit Schach spielenden Protagonisten verbringen zu wollen?

A: Zwischen dem Schreiben und dem Schachspiel scheint es durchaus Ähnlichkeiten zu geben – beides sind einsame Beschäftigungen, bei denen man nur dasitzt und sich mit etwas Unwirklichem beschäftigt, so dass einen alle anderen für verrückt oder faul halten –, und das könnte etwas sein, das mich zu Alexander hingezogen hat oder das ich an ihm verstehe, obwohl ich selbst keine besonders gute Schachspielerin bin. Außerdem fasziniert es mich besonders – und vermutlich nicht nur mich –, wenn jemand in dem, was er tut, wirklich brillant ist. Brillante Schachspieler sind besonders faszinierend, weil sie oft auf diese ganz rätselhafte Art und Weise auserwählt zu sein scheinen – sie fangen oft schon als Kinder damit an und richten dann ihr ganzes Leben darauf aus. Garri Kasparow zum Beispiel hat mit vier ein Schachproblem in der Zeitung gesehen und es gelöst – und das war es dann: Von da an war Schach sein ganzes Leben. Das kommt mir so viel merkwürdiger vor als irgendein sportliches, sprachliches oder mathematisches Können, das man auf verschiedenen Wegen erwerben kann. Große Schachspieler scheinen sich nicht in das Spiel zu verlieben, sondern es sieht eher so aus, als ob sie es schon wiedererkennen, wenn sie ihm zum ersten Mal begegnen. Das finde ich total faszinierend, unter anderem deshalb, weil es gar keinen Sinn ergibt.

F: Die andere Protagonistin Ihres Romans, die junge Amerikanerin Irina, ist ebenfalls Teil einer Art Randgruppe, nämlich der Gruppe von Menschen, die nach der Diagnose einer unheilbaren degenerativen Krankheit wissen, wie und ungefähr wann sie sterben werden. Dieses Wissen hat es ihr scheinbar unmöglich gemacht, sich in Amerika auf tiefe Freundschaften oder Liebe einzulassen, obwohl sie sich darum bemüht, ihrem Leben einen Sinn zu geben.

Am Ende geht sie doch noch Verpflichtungen ein, indem sie sich als kleine Figur im großen politischen Spiel positioniert. Das erlaubt es ihr, ihre emotionale Distanz im Wesentlichen zu wahren. Es gibt da diese sehr eindrucksvolle Textpassage, nachdem sie ihren großen Beitrag zu Alexanders Kampagne geleistet hat und nachdem die ersten unmissverständlichen Symptome ihrer Krankheit aufgetaucht sind:

»Ich glaube, auch wenn ich mir nicht sicher bin, dass meine Hände stärker zittern als normal, dass sie sich immer ungenierter in Eigenregie fortbewegen. Ich sehe zu. Ich lege meine Hände auf den Falttisch, und sie beben und zucken.

Aber wer weiß, vielleicht ist es gar nicht pathologisch. Es könnte einfach ein Zeichen der Ehrfurcht sein. Vielleicht ist es einfach die Schönheit des Himmels und der Wolken – das Wunder eines frühen Morgens, die Häresie der Luftfahrt.«

Diese Passage wird umso ergreifender dadurch, dass wir als Leser schon ahnen, was mit dem Flugzeug geschehen wird. Irina hat sich selbst zu einer Spielfigur im Endspiel gemacht, zu etwas Abstraktem, und das scheint für sie der einzige Weg zu sein, etwas Bedeutsames für den Rest der Welt zu tun. Andererseits lässt sie sich gegen Ende doch noch mit einer der anderen Figuren ein. Sie scheinen als Autorin im Verlauf des Romans immer wieder zwischen dem Realen, Direkten und dem Abstrakten hin und her zu wechseln. Würden Sie diese Bewegung als eins der wesentlichen Elemente des Romans ansehen?

A: Irina ist, als wir sie kennenlernen, außerstande, ihrem Leben einen Sinn abzugewinnen, weil sie positiv auf Chorea Huntington getestet worden ist, und diese Spannung zwischen dem Abstrakten und dem Konkreten, von der Sie sprechen, ist eine sehr gute Möglichkeit, dieses Problem in Worte zu fassen. Der Tod ist für uns alle unausweichlich, aber zugleich ist er auch etwas ganz Abstraktes, das niemand sich wirklich vorstellen kann – wir wissen eigentlich nur vom Hörensagen, dass er irgendwann eintreten wird. Für Irina ist dieses bedrohliche Abstraktum viel realer als die konkreten Umstände ihres wirklichen Lebens. Es fällt ihr furchtbar schwer, sich auf etwas Vergängliches einzulassen – oder sagen wir, sie ist zu verängstigt und zu stur, um es zu versuchen –, und weil alles vergänglich ist, übrigens nicht nur für Irina, sondern für uns alle, hat sie ein echtes Problem. Aber Irinas Ende sehe ich eigentlich als Ablehnung oder Abkehr von diesem Denken; ich würde nicht sagen, dass sie sich da in den Bereich des Abstrakten oder Theoretischen hineinbegibt. Im Gegenteil sehe ich ihr Verhalten am Ende so, dass sie sich endlich ganz und gar einer sehr realen Angelegenheit verschreibt, sich ganz hineinbegibt, obwohl sie fast sicher ist, dass ihr Versuch, etwas zu ändern, erfolglos bleiben wird – und ganz sicher weiß, dass sie das Resultat nicht miterleben wird. Ich denke, Irina hört am Ende auf, immer in diesen abstrakten Kategorien zu denken; in der Passage, die Sie zitieren, ist sie endlich ganz in der Welt und in ihrem Leben angekommen.

LEKTÜREANREGUNGEN

1. Verhält sich Irina letztlich eher mutig oder feige? Würden Sie sagen, dass die Geschichte für sie gut ausgeht?

2. Irinas und Alexanders Lebenssituationen sind einander ähnlich, unterscheiden sich aber auch in vielerlei Hinsicht. Was denken Sie, was sie einander näher bringt? Was lernen sie voneinander?

3. Die Figur Mischa stellt immer wieder Alexanders Vorstellung einer demokratischen Zukunft in Frage. Wie bewerten Sie sein Eintreten für eine pragmatische, langsamere Entwicklung? Was bedeuten die jüngeren Ereignisse in der Arabischen Welt für seine Position?

4. Irina legt großen Wert auf ihre geistigen Fähigkeiten und hat Angst, nicht mehr sie selbst zu sein, wenn sie diese Fähigkeiten verliert. Was denken Sie, was Ihr eigenes Selbst ausmacht? Gibt es eine wesentliche Eigenschaft, die Sie zu dem macht, was Sie sind, und die Sie nicht einbüßen könnten, ohne Ihre Persönlichkeit zu verlieren?

5. Warum sind Alexanders Kapitel in der dritten Person verfasst und Irinas in der ersten? Wie beeinflussen diese unterschiedlichen Erzählperspektiven Ihre Reaktionen auf das Geschehen? Haben Sie sich mit einer der beiden Hauptfiguren stärker identifiziert als mit der anderen?

6. Was denken Sie, was aus Iwan geworden wäre, wenn er überlebt hätte?

7. Irina wirkt häufig sarkastisch und fatalistisch. Gibt es Situationen, in denen ihr Verhalten im Widerspruch zu ihrer zynischen Haltung steht?

8. Sind Ihnen außer Irinas Krankheitsgeschichte und Alexanders Kandidatur noch andere »aussichtslose Fälle« in dem Text aufgefallen? Sind Sie selbst schon einmal mit solchen Fällen konfrontiert gewesen, und wie haben Sie darauf reagiert?

9. Wie wird das Schachspiel metaphorisch eingesetzt? Finden Sie, dass sich in der Struktur des Textes die Struktur des Spiels widerspiegelt?

10. Hat Alexanders herausragendes Schachtalent Ihrer Meinung nach einen besseren oder schlechteren Menschen aus ihm gemacht?